D1732945

My Oil Of Joy
For Your Mourning

Traci Wooden-Carlisle

MY OIL OF JOY FOR YOUR MOURNING
(Promises to Zion Series)

Editor: A.I.R.R.E. Firm

This is a work of fiction. Names characters, places, and incidents are either the product of the author's imagination or are used fictitiously, and any resemblance to actual persons, living or dead, business establishments, events or locales is entirely coincidental.

DEDICATION

To you Lord

I am only the vessel. You, Lord, are the true author.

I pray you continue to use me.

ACKNOWLEDGMENTS

This book is for all of my friends. Each and every one of you played an integral part in me getting to that last word in this book.

Kerri…we went from being like night and day to finding our own time. I absolutely love and adore you.

Nicole thank you for being the sister of my heart and spirit. Just your voice can bring me back to earth.

Sylvia thank you for forcing me to take some time just for me.

Brianna for inviting me to write in the Living Room

Aziza you are amazing. Everyone deserves a friend that can open a window so you can catch glimpses of God's future for you.

Jackie your smiles feel like hugs and your hugs warm my soul

Patsy this only gets better, just like you.

Clementine, you have shown me beauty in strength

Cheryl C. thank you for the liberating truth you speak.

Valerie my love… sing with the angels

Cynthia N… dance with them

Cheryl L. I'm glad you're still here

As always to my husband: There is no way this book would have been finished without your support or love.

Daddy, your love paved the way.

Mimi, thank you for being my personal PR firm

Daisy…shine.

FOREWORD

I suppose that most forewords are written after the fact. The author presents a finished manuscript for one to read, to become acquainted with, and finally to introduce to you the reader.

This foreword is different for I have had the honor to see its message unfold.

When a person is blessed with special gifts they should use what God has given them so that they may share the gifts with others and bless them.

After reading her first book "My Beauty For Your Ashes," I knew that another book was on the way. Even though the book was a work of fiction, many who read it could relate or knew someone who had similar situations.

I am so privileged to say without a doubt, this book "My Oil Of Joy For Your Mourning" is well written and a Must read. A healing of love, forgiveness and togetherness will unfold.

This book embodies and instructs that in a world filled with hate, we must still dare to hope, in a world filled with anger, we must still dare to comfort. In a world filled with despair, we must still dare to dream. And in a world filled with distrust, we must still dare to believe.

Patericiea Andrea Glaster
Counselor/Consultant

MY OIL OF JOY FOR YOUR MOURNING

PREFACE

Through the muck and mire that weighed me down clinging to my limbs trying to keep me where I lay.

I speak against the fear and reach for the peace I once remember seeing in me. Deeper still I delve hoping to grasp a tentative hold that will grow stronger the longer I hold onto it.

Ah there, I feel its warmth. Hold me still so that I will not be recognized by my enemy in this state for surely he will want to finish me off.

Raise your head child and let me shine my rays of hope for tomorrow upon your upturned face. I will see you through. My light will guide you in the dark where others have lost their way and I will use you to set a pathway that will lead them to me.

Don't let go, I am close. Don't let go for I am with you always until the end of time.

CHAPTER 1

One month, Paige kept thinking, *One month... less than that; three weeks, two days, six hours, and a measly twenty-two minutes.* That was how much time she'd had to be blissfully happy – happier than she could ever remember being with a person. With no expectations of consequences for her bad decisions, she hadn't seen it coming. She pondered back and forth as her eyes danced from one end of the carpet to the other, mimicking the racing thoughts in her head.

"Where did I go wrong? I know I heard You. It was just as clear as the blossoming love I feel for him. Augh! Why? Why am I continually denied? What is it about my life that thwarts, even repels, happiness? Why can't I have it? There are so many who never even experienced a moment of physical pain or illness. Why can't that be him?"

In the cool of the dark room, she waited; waited for an overwhelming feeling of peace; that feeling of calm and unexplainable rightness that would tell her that everything was going to work in her favor.

She waited for the feeling and a word telling her that there was nothing to be concerned about. She waited...and waited...until she could no longer hold back the feelings of anxiousness and dread. She stopped waiting and gave into the dimming feeling of fear, letting the pain of another dream lost wash over her.

A sob reverberated off the walls causing her to start at the unfamiliar sound. She held her breath listening for the sound again, before realizing it had come from her. She then wrapped her arms around her body, hugging herself tightly. She girded herself with a shadow of strength, making one last effort to stave off the gut-wrenching heartache she feared would swallow her whole.

Not even making an attempt to crawl into her bedroom, she leaned over, laid her head on the sofa cushion and pulled her knees up to her chest. She rocked herself back and forth until she fell into a restless sleep.

*   *   *

"I dreamed about you," he said, maneuvering into the right lane. In that fleeting moment, his somber expression caused a knot to form in her stomach.

"What? When? Was it good or bad?" Paige turned towards him from where she sat in the passenger's seat. She could sense a restlessness within him like he was struggling with a decision.

"The night after we met... well actually, the whole week after we first met." He glanced away from the tree-lined street he was driving them down.

She didn't know how to digest this new information, so she tried wit. "Wow. I must have made some impression on you."

She watched as a hesitant smile passed over his lips. It made her uneasy. "What were they about?" she asked, not quite sure she wanted to know.

They pulled up to a stop sign as he began relaying the series of dreams that had progressed a little further each night – the first being the one revealing him as a statue. The dream started at the beginning each night, only to advance just a little bit further than the evening before, until the last night when he was fully brought to life by her surrendering her heart over to him.

She found herself enthralled by the turn of events, wondering what it meant. She asked him if they'd spoken in his dream. He quickly glanced her way then back to the road, taking a deep breath. She was curious as to why he was having such a hard time telling her about a dream that he'd brought up in the first place.

"It fits."

She blinked after a moment, realizing that there was no more coming forth. "I don't understand."

"You laid your hand on the place where my heart should have been and gave me yours. It fit." He pulled into a parking space near her apartment building, turning off the ignition. He turned so that he could fully face her. "'It fits' is what you said before you turned to stone."

She sat there, trying to calm her heart that had just taken off at a gallop. Was he saying they were meant to be together? Had he taken the dreams as a sign that she was his? *...But then there was the turning to stone thing.* Were they not destined to be together? She shook her head, working to stay in the present.

"What do you think it meant?"

She watched him shrug as he looked down at the gear shift between them. "At first I thought it was just my subconscious trying to get my attention. I was very focused on what I came to Los Angeles to do: advance in my job and take on a position at Skylight Temple. Getting involved with anyone was nowhere in my plans."

"And after?" she asked, trying to wrangle a reason from him.

"By the time the week was over I was…curious."

"Just curious?"

He smiled sheepishly. "Yes, and that was almost against my better judgment."

"I guess I really did make a bad first impression." She didn't know what to think about this revelation that sounded like he liked her against his will, but she did know what she felt and it was causing tears to burn in the back of her eyes.

"Neither one of us thought it was love at first sight. As I recall, you thought I was self-righteous and a bit low on manners."

"Yes, and you thought I was arrogant and disobedient. Was it only the dreams that changed your mind?"

He shook his head in the negative. "The dreams only got my attention and caused me to see if my first assessment of you was due to the situation or a true part of you. I wanted to know if you were as beautiful as you were in my dreams." His hand came up to cup her chin, raising her head so she would look him in the eye before he finished. "And you were. You are."

She swallowed, her mouth suddenly going dry.

"Soooo…it got your attention. Is that all you think it was meant to do?" She was searching and she knew it, but she couldn't help it. She wanted to know if he felt what she had this past month.

He removed his hand and she watched as a hooded expression hid his thoughts from her. She felt the distance instantly.

"It could mean so many things."

"Yes, but what do you think it means? It's okay...I'm ready for the answer."

He pinned her with an intense gaze, his eyes boring through her.

"A lot of my life I have been regarded as Brandon Tatum, Reverend, or Dean Elias Tatum's son. Instead of people getting to know me, they instantly placed me up on a pedestal beside him. It was a daunting task trying to fill the shoes of a man like my father, especially when they were never made to fit in the first place." He said the latter mostly to himself.

She didn't know if she should interrupt him and try to console him, or let him continue this extremely revealing diatribe.

She took a breath to speak when he continued, "I have thought of that dream many nights and I have come up with many interpretations, but the one that seems to encompass all of the things I was feeling is that I was a statue sitting on a shelf almost out of reach, until you came along and brought me to life."

He took a deep breath. She held hers, not wanting to do anything to disturb what she felt was the beginning of a declaration.

"I see things differently than most people. I feel things deeper than most people and, though I work hard to stay in a place where I am constantly used by God for his people, it has occurred to me lately that I have lived a lot of my life on the sidelines."

"Lately?"

"I watched people fall in love and, except for my friend, Dominy, and my parents, the relationships were messy, painful and confusing, with

3

happiness mixed in here and there. At my former church, I would sometimes help minister to the youth and young adults. I would try and encourage them to get to know themselves and God better before entering into a relationship then urged them to keep God in the middle of all their relationships, allowing Him to be their mediator. Sometimes they took my advice, sometimes they didn't. All I could think of at the time was though I might be lonely sometimes, I considered myself better off. I had a great relationship with God, a wonderful family, and a best friend that kept life interesting. It seemed more than enough...until you, Paige."

He pinned her again with his gaze, his eyes warming to her new favorite color of coffee.

"You, Paige, who lives every breath as if it were borrowed, make me feel more alive than I ever have. I know I have laughed more in the last month than I have in the past ten years. You go after everything with so much passion I have to admit I find it a little intimidating...but then you smile that special smile just for me or you laugh at something I have said and I feel incredibly blessed and crazy favored just to be me. I don't ask 'why me' because just as easily I could ask 'why not me', and I would rather just concentrate on how I feel when I am with you. I simply thank God every moment I can that He saw fit to bring you into my life so that I could have the overwhelming joy of feeling my heart beat for you."

Paige sat there, unable to do little more than breathe in and out. Everything that he felt for her, she felt for him. She battled within, trying to find a word to describe her elation. Happy didn't come close; ecstatic was only a hair better. She wanted to fly, she felt so far above the earth.

She didn't even try to contain her smile at his words and breathed in to fill what little space there was left behind the influx of emotion filling her from her core, outward. It left no room for any of the doubts or concerns she'd experienced only moments before.

She placed her hand over his, silently communicating her mutual affection. She so desperately wanted to express herself at that moment but struggled with what to say first. Her inner turmoil blinded her to the fact that Brandon wasn't smiling and that he had begun to rub the back of his neck – what she recently discovered was a nervous gesture.

"I need to tell you something and I have to apologize for not telling you sooner. I know what I just shared with you may make it seem like I was stacking the deck in my favor, but I wanted you to know with no uncertain terms how I feel about you."

A fission of ice ran along her spine and the nape of her neck, raising the hairs. When she moved to pull her hand away, he grasped it in his and held fast to it.

She watched as he stared at her, holding her within his gaze. At that moment, she wanted to run...run from whatever it was that was threatening to infringe upon her high.

She watched his Adam's apple bob up and down right before he opened his mouth. "I have cancer, Paige."

She continued to watch him, but when his expression changed to one of expectancy, she had to go back to the second before and force what he said to register. She listened to the words again as they whispered through her mind, crashing into her senses. The cloud she had been riding on a few seconds before disappeared from under her and she came hurtling down to earth. Her heart dropped and the sensation shook her very being, jarring her awake.

*   *   *

Paige blinked slowly, feeling the dream wash over her, knowing that she didn't have to wait to see if this one came true. She had already lived it.

CHAPTER 2

Brandon sat on the edge of his couch, which had been his bed for the last few days. He was actually grateful for the full house. He didn't know how he would have been able to get through the last ten hours if he were by himself. He definitely would have lost the fight he was having just to keep from going back to Paige's and begging her not to leave him.

He'd thought over the last few words they'd shared and found himself more frustrated with each replay. Part of him wished he hadn't offered to have her call him by twelve o'clock if she decided to back out of spending Christmas with him and his relatives.

The other part knew he had done the right thing in giving her a choice. He'd waited too long and this was his punishment for not being completely upfront to begin with.

Not that he had been looking forward to his 'I-told-you-so' attitude, but after two hours of sitting in the dark once his family had gone to sleep, he called Dominy. Brandon needed his help in fixing this.

"I was hoping you would call after you got in, but I didn't mean for you to call me in the middle of the night."

"Sorry. I needed to talk."

He heard a heavy sigh on the other end then silence.

"Dom? You still there?"

"Yeah. I'm going into the living room so that I don't disturb Robin," he began with a whisper, "She is exhausted. We are hosting Christmas dinner and she wanted to cook most of the dishes. She just about wiped herself out. Okay Bran, what's going on?"

"I told her."

"And I guess since you are calling me now, it wasn't the early Christmas present of an answer you were hoping for?"

"No," Brandon said in a slow exhale.

"Did she break it off?"

"No, but it was eerie. She seemed to just shut down. When I first told her, she looked at me as if she didn't hear me. After a few seconds, I thought she actually didn't hear me so I was about to repeat myself when I saw her eyes go wide." He took a deep breath, reliving what he'd come to know as the worst five minutes of his life.

"What did she say?" Dominy asked.

"That was it. She didn't say anything for a whole two to three minutes. It felt like a lifetime." His voice was just above a whisper. He rubbed his eyes with his forefinger and thumb, trying to temper his emotions with the single movement. "I don't think I've felt that type of dread since I sat waiting in the doctor's office the first time I was diagnosed."

"What happened when she did talk?" Dominy hedged.

"Her voice was quiet and distant, but it sounded like she was talking to someone she would have been visiting on the sick list than me."

"How is that? I thought you said when you visited people with her a couple of months ago, you found her to be compassionate and warm?"

"Yes, she was. I still think she is amazing and gifted in that ministry, but we have a relationship. We are closer than that..."

"Maybe that was her way of digesting the information. We all have coping mechanisms. You can't blame her for being shocked."

"No, but I expected more...more emotion...something. She was almost like stone."

"Did she ask you any questions?"

"Yes, but they were leading like she was trying to catch me in a lie."

"What do you mean? What were some of her questions?"

Brandon huffed in frustration. "She asked me how long I'd known and if Pastor Lawrence knew about my diagnosis when I arrived."

"I think that might have more to do with her relationship with Pastor Lawrence than you, but go on."

"She asked me a few more about myself, but then asked if the reason why I told her now was because I invited her to meet my family?"

"Paige is an intelligent woman and, though I believe you took entirely too long to tell her, I wonder why she would be so quick to jump to such conclusions. From what you have shared with me about the time you've spent with her, I don't believe you have led her on or crossed any lines, unless..." Dominy grew quiet.

Brandon could almost hear the ticking in his mind leading him along a path that he was reluctant to venture.

"Uh, was there anything special that happened today?"

His answer was met with silence. Brandon knew he was going to share what happened with Dominy. He was just wondering how much he could keep to himself.

"Maybe you should start from the beginning, and remember I am losing sleep here so you might as well just give it all to me up front. That way I can tell you where you went wrong and how to fix it so that I can be of some use to my wife later on today."

So much for self-preservation. Brandon took a breath and began.

"So... you think you can read me well..."

If he'd been watching the storm come over her eyes instead of being distracted by her lower lip caught between her teeth, he would have already had his answer.

Instead, he was taken by surprise as those lips came closer. His eyes flew up to hers with fleeting hope.

He was transfixed by the darkness swirling in them, mesmerized by the color – now close to caramel – that seemed to reach out and hold him hostage.

He felt her palm cup his jaw. Her hand was incredibly small and soft, her fingertips fanning along the side of his face, just short of his ear. He felt each one like a hot poker emblazoning itself upon his skin, branding him to her. He was utterly lost in the sensations of her.

Her face blurred as she came closer and he had to close his eyes to keep the overwhelming feelings from swallowing him whole.

He wasn't aware of how many seconds passed by as they shared breaths, but belatedly, he realized she wasn't continuing to close the space between them.

He raised his lashes slowly, daring not to move, lest he break the spell, but as she came back into focus, he saw her smiling and the world turned on its axis, catching him beneath it.

The shudder that went through him threatened to jar his teeth. He wanted to reach out for her and pull her to him, to finish what this stupid bet began. He wanted it so much he could feel his body vibrate towards her, even as he used every ounce of willpower to stay rooted.

"I win." He heard her say with that smile in her voice, and it struck him like a bullet.

Dominy interrupted him laughing. "I was wondering who was going to win that bet. Well I'll be…finally, a woman who has more discipline than you do. I love it. Brandon unseated; I told you there would come a time when that shield of reserve would be penetrated."

"Are you done?"

"Not by a long shot. I am going to milk this baby for all it is worth."

Brandon huffed into the phone loudly, gaining back Dominy's attention.

"Okay go on."

"Are you sure?" Brandon responded flippantly.

"Christmas…wife…early. Will…hang…up…"

Brandon continued.

He had taken his coat off and held it out for her to slip into. Just so he could have an excuse to remain close to her and because he wanted to make sure she felt taken care of, he pulled the oversized coat around her and rolled back the sleeves at her wrists.

"Is that better?" he asked, wondering at the forlorn expression that crossed her face, but she looked down at the smoothed over cement slabs and nodded again.

He reached out and placed his forefinger under her chin in order to raise her face. She wouldn't raise her eyes at first.

"Paige, please look at me." His voice was slightly raspy with emotion, but when she looked up at him with an expression he couldn't discern, he felt the need to defend himself. "Did I do something?"

She shook her head. "No."

It sounded more like an accusation.

"May I?" he asked, hoping his assumption was correct.

His finger, still under her chin, he accompanied with his thumb which held her in place. The small pulse point on the side of her neck alerted him to the acceleration of her heartbeat. He watched as her eyes widened in surprise. He had been right, he thought as his mouth took on an easy smile. He stepped closer and it felt like time was moving very slowly, and he was thankful because he wanted to be able to recall every moment of this.

He brought his other hand up to trace his fingertips along the edge of her brow to the hollow underneath her jaw, his eyes following them. He turned his hand over allowing the back of it to run along the side of her neck.

At first, he didn't know if the shiver came from him or her, but as he watched the heat swim up to the tips of her ears, he was pleasantly relieved.

"I like this thing your ears do. It is quite charming." He smiled. The one she returned seemed a bit abashed.

His gaze locked with hers, asking silently if he could continue forward. He watched as her eyes traveled to his lips then back to his eyes right before he brushed his lips against hers. He closed his eyes trying to regain some control over his senses.

The kiss started out slowly, softly...

"You kissed her, Bran? Before you told her?" Dominy's voice was incredulous.

"It wasn't like I planned it."

"But it wasn't an accident either. It's not like you aren't attracted to her. If you spent enough time with her it was bound to happen, but I told you about crossing that friendship line before you told her. I told you..."

"Yes Dom. I know, I know, but I wanted to know... I needed to know what it was like to have her look at me...treat me like a healthy, grown man she had feelings for. The last month has been amazing. I have never felt this way for anyone and to know that it was possible that she felt the same was...well ..."

"Tempting?"

Brandon quenched the denial that immediately came to his lips. He was quiet for a moment. He would have used a word like 'alluring'; something less blatantly wrong. He didn't want to admit it, but it had been just that, and he gave into it time and time again.

"Yes."

"Very well. Go on."

Brandon continued, uninterrupted until he shared the conversation he'd had with Paige in his car parked in front of her house. He paused briefly to take a breath before going forward, but Dominy cut him off.

"You blindsided her, man." He spoke with a heavy sigh.

Brandon felt his friend's fatigue through the phone and began to feel discouraged.

"I told her the truth," he stated in desperation.

"You were manipulative," Dominy stated softly.

There was silence for a moment then Dominy spoke up. "You tell the woman that you have been spending every free hour with for a month that you have cancer, but you wait not only until after you kiss her, but also after a declaration of some intimate feelings for her as well, and you don't find that just a bit deceptive?"

Brandon thought for a moment about the predicament he found himself in again. He didn't have an answer that would sound complementary to his character, so he remained silent.

Dominy, mistaking Brandon's silence for stubbornness, began again. "How would you feel if the tables were turned? You have this wonderful connection with someone you have developed deep feelings for and discover that those feelings are mutual only a few moments before you are told that there is a possibility of losing them. I don't know about you, but I would be hard-pressed not to feel betrayed."

"So are you telling me it's a lost cause?"

"Noooo," Dominy responded, dragging out the word. "Thankfully for you, Paige seems a great deal more forgiving than me. With all she went through over the last few months with her family, she's still not bitter and angry about the time she lost with Vivian. I am almost half in love with her myself. She is a courageous woman with a strength you don't see many in possession of.

Give her some time; she should come around, but don't force the issue. She probably just needs a moment to get it all straight and come to grips with her emotions so that she doesn't go off on you. Not that you don't deserve it..."

"Yeah, yeah, yeah…but she was supposed to meet my family today and I am afraid she won't come."

"Good, maybe next time you will try communicating with her rather than manipulating her. You will just have to be patient with her and, if she decides not to spend Christmas with you and your family, you can't get upset with her."

"I thought you were going to help me with this, Dominy. You can't talk to her, maybe put in a good word for me; tell her that I am really sorry and suffering over here?"

"Nope."

"Dom…" Brandon implored.

"Naww. Now you are just being a wuss."

Instead of voicing his opinion of Dominy, Brandon chose to remain quiet for a moment and try to think of any way he could convince his friend to talk to Paige. Even though he'd admitted to her some of his deeper feelings, he was still holding a few closer to the vest. After almost four weeks, he'd come to care for Paige much more than he thought was possible. He'd never felt this way. Not even for Myra, whom he'd thought himself in love with in college.

*   *   *

Brandon noticed Myra the first day of statistics class in his senior year. She was one of the most beautiful women he'd ever seen. At 5 foot 6, her auburn curls came to his shoulders and he could look down at her clear brown eyes and see his reflection. She was extremely intelligent and not shy about voicing her opinion or asking the professor any range of questions. Her hunger for knowledge seemed insatiable and after three weeks of watching her from three chairs and two rows back, he finally got up the courage to speak to her.

He caught her after class one day, asking if she was part of a study group or knew of one he could join. She studied him for a moment, her eyes slightly narrowing as if she were trying to figure out what he was really asking, then let him know that she studied with a group that met in the university lounge on Tuesdays at 7 p.m. She invited him to join since it was a small group and could use a fresh eye.

He'd practically jumped at the offer, thanking her and promising to be on time the next evening. He remembered being so nervous about making a good impression that he studied ahead two chapters, but when he arrived, he spied two other guys from statistics class who seemed to have the same ulterior motive. This was easy to figure, since both were hanging on her every word and both were, at least until that time, acing all of their tests since the start of class.

His only encouragement was the devastating smile she laid on him when he arrived at the table, and her acceptance of his offer to walk her and her roommate to their apartment across the street from campus.

Not being a fast mover, it was another whole month before he asked her out on a date. When she accepted, he felt like the king of the world because she'd picked him.

He shared his feelings for her with Dominy, but was frustrated when after a few peculiar questions Dominy told him to proceed with caution.

What did Dominy know? He hadn't even met her and what could he glean by knowing how long and how often they saw each other. It wasn't every day or more than three times a week for that matter, but when they were together she was attentive, giving him her undivided attention. They could discuss a number of different topics from politics and business, to the cultural differences that caused the lack of cooperation between the military and citizens in the Persian Gulf after the war. They liked a lot of the same genre of movies, action and adventure, and her penchant for basketball sweetened the deal for him.

It didn't take him long to profess to being a believer and avid church goer, but when he asked her, she seemed to shy away from the subject, stating that though she believed in God, she wasn't ready to wholly dedicate herself to Him. She wasn't ready for that type of commitment, but she liked him and for the moment that was good enough for him. *After all,* he convinced himself, *not everyone had grown up with a bible toting, sermon scribing, and exegeses such as his father.* He told himself that with a little witnessing and short Bible studies, she would come around.

By their third month together, he'd begun missing church every so often so he could spend more time with her on Sundays – the fourth day of the week they could see each other – and on the anniversary of their sixth month, assured that they would spend the rest of their life together, he surrendered his virginity.

Two months later, he woke up in the middle of the night with intense back pain. He had been growing more and more fatigued but couldn't come up with a reason for it. His class load was no greater and the occasional sleepover at Myra's was anything but stressful.

It was Myra that encouraged him to go to the campus health center when he couldn't keep anything down for two days straight. He didn't have any other symptoms or signs of a cold or flu, so he reluctantly walked in hoping that whatever bug he had could be easily killed with a pill.

After being referred to the nearest practitioner and then sent through a myriad of tests and referred to a gastroenterologist, he was then diagnosed with colon cancer. In a matter of one month, he went from an idealistic and healthy 22-year-old to facing his own mortality.

One month later, Myra shared the news that she was moving abroad and going to work for a cousin who owned a shipping business in London. She said she wasn't cut out for caregiving, that was why she was a Business Major and though she loved him, she wasn't ready to settle down.

He let her go with that feeble excuse because he didn't want her to regret any of their time together. He wanted to be remembered as he would remember her: full of life.

At the end of May, instead of looking forward to graduate school and a future with Myra, Brandon went through surgery to remove the cancerous lesions from his colon, chemo and radiation, and then a second surgery to remove six inches of his lower intestines.

Surprisingly, the heartache healed quicker than his body. By that time, his relationship with his family and God grew stronger by the day.

The thought of losing Paige as he did Myra didn't enter his thoughts until he'd made up his mind that he would not allow the sun to set on another day before sharing the news of his latest challenge with the 'beast' that made his mother weep openly and his father go strangely quiet at his diagnosis.

*   *   *

He wiped the thought away quickly; Paige was different. She had a quiet strength that he'd witnessed on many occasions in their brief time together. She was nothing like he'd first surmised and was ever grateful, especially when the dreams started and he found himself drawn to her like a moth to a flame. She was resilient, as he'd discovered when he'd met Mason and her daughter Vivian, and learned of her tumultuous past. She was bold in her belief in the Holy Spirit's authority in her, but humbled every time God's love was manifested through her.

He may have noticed and been attracted to her love and passion for life first, but that was superseded by her open, unabashed love for God. The glow that lit her from within didn't only draw attention to her beauty, it came with an undeniable need to reveal itself tangibly, thus her willingness to donate an organ to a child she had never met just so that their parents would not have to experience life without them.

In the end, it had almost cost her life and he was finally forced to come to the realization that his feelings for Paige were not going to fade by him merely watching her from the sidelines.

If he was going to be painfully honest, he would admit that he was in trouble the moment she'd turned around in the hallway of their pastor's office.

Her hazel eyes had been lit with defiance and her chin was raised slightly, letting him know that she'd not considered backing down. He had first thought her arrogant and willful, but she was independent and used to fending for herself, even with the pastor and first lady taking her under their wing.

Then, after five days with relatively sleepless nights and one continuous dream, he couldn't help but somehow feel connected to her. He felt both excitement and trepidation at seeing her again and could barely wait to see her on Sunday to ascertain whether the dreams were prophetic, or the culmination of his overactive imagination.

Four months later, along with hours upon hours of prayer and dutiful, if not what could be deemed unnecessary, avoidance and separation, he'd received his answer. He was soulfully enamored by Paige and knowing that he would come upon that smile that widened just for him within hours of waking up in the morning had him walking a few inches above the ground.

"Brandon." Dominy's insistent voice broke through his reverie.

"Huh?"

"Man, I am tired. Daydream on your own time. Meanwhile just relax. Do that 'trusting God' thing you do so well with on other occasions."

Brandon almost laughed at Dom's attempt at brevity. He would have to talk to him again soon about persistence in keeping God at arm's length.

"Goodnight Dom. Kiss Robin for me and wish her a Merry Christmas on behalf of myself and the Tatum family."

"Merry Christmas, Brandon. Get some rest. It will all work itself out." Dominy tried one last time to ease the agitation he could still recognize in Brandon's voice.

"Yeah. Understood. Goodnight Dom, Merry Christmas."

They finally signed off, Brandon hearing the distinct disconnection of the line, hit his end button. He sat on the couch replaying the day over and over in his mind, until he turned to prayer for refuge. He succumbed to sleep with Paige's name on his lips as the last few minutes of night trickled into dawn.

CHAPTER 3

Mason swore his head was trying to pound out of his skull with each beat of his heart. He held his hands to his head as if he could keep it together with his palms and fingers. The pounding got louder.

"Daddy, are you awake yet?" came the loud voice with an even louder knock. "Daddy, it's already 8:00 a.m. and you said we could go out to see the trees this morning after I opened my presents. Daddy?!"

"Augh! All right, okay!" He paused to lower his voice which vibrated through his head like a jack-hammer. How much had he had to drink last night? He didn't even remember how he got home...

A thought swam through his mind, and he looked down to see himself dressed in his t-shirt and boxers.

"Can I come in now?" came Vivian's soft voice from the other side of the door. Lately, she had taken to asking instead of just barging in. He initially took it as a sign of maturity, but a nagging thought in the back of his head told him it may have been from too many mornings of coming in to find him still passed out in a drunken stupor. It seemed to be the only way to blot out the ever-present thought of her mother, Rachael, and now, Paige.

"Just a minute, hun," Mason finally answered as he slid back the covers and rolled himself over until his legs hung off the side of the bed. He sat with his head in his hands in a vain attempt to stop the room from tilting. After a couple of seconds, he squinted as he looked around the room for a pair of pajama bottoms. The maid, or Vivian, had cleaned because there wasn't a piece of clothing on the floor or chair, except the pants and pullover he'd worn the day before.

He rose up on his feet, staggering to the chest-of-drawers across the room. He reached it just as he stumbled over a shoe, his hands going out to steady himself, an explicative escaping from his lips.

"Are you alright, Daddy?"

"Fine, hon. I will be there in just a second. Why don't you go and fix us some hot chocolate to drink while we open our presents? I'm going to wash my face and brush my teeth like I am sure you have already done. Right?"

"Uh, right. I will meet you in the living room." He heard her scramble from the door and it brought a painful smile to his lips. How much had he drunk?

He slowly made his way into the bathroom. He turned on the water and allowed it to get warm while he set up his toothbrush. He began brushing his teeth, avoiding the mirror in front of him. He was not in the mood for the self-deprecation that would come with glancing at his reflection. He

15

had awakened too many times this way in the past few weeks not to know that his skin would hold the sickly pallor of a night of inebriation and show traces of a new diet which lacked nutritional substance. The eyes would be blood-shot and he would have to wear soft colors to keep from looking sallow. It wasn't where he wanted to be, but it kept the nightmares away and the memories didn't punch him in the gut like they used to.

What a way to bring in Christmas Day. He would try to get through it without a drink for Vivian's sake. He didn't want to ruin the holiday for her as he had done so many other days lately. He kept trying to think back to where it all started going wrong, but by the time he made it back that far in his memory, he was headed towards the mini-bar, trying to rid himself of all the other memories that spilled, unguarded.

He was back in the cycle. He knew it would be even harder to escape this time, but he had done it before and managed to stay away from it for both Rachael and Vivian. He was sure he could do it again if only he could forget the warmth in those hazel eyes or the lightning that pulsed through him when speared with one of her smiles.

He knew he was walking a fine line when he went to New York to tell Paige that they shared a daughter. The vulnerability he saw in her eyes made him want to become her knight in shining armor and slay each and every dragon, or at least person that would wish to cause her pain.

He'd distanced himself, focusing more on Vivian than ever, but it was hard fighting the attraction and the allure of Paige's compassion and inner beauty. Her desire and ability to see the beauty in people, especially him, made him long to see it as well, so much so that he fancied himself in love with her. He snorted. That was the deciding factor every night he lost to temptation. He was in love with Paige Morganson and she, from what his daughter said, was in love with someone else.

He forgot his resolution to avoid the mirror when his eyes met his reflection above the warm washcloth. He stopped in mid-sweep, disgusted. What was he doing to himself? To his daughter?

No more... No more would he torture himself over a woman who wouldn't even call him back.

He ran cool water into the basin and, taking a deep breath, held it as he dunked his head in the cool liquid to help stimulate the blood cells in his cheeks and eyelids to reduce some of the swelling.

By the time he walked from the bedroom, he looked halfway decent even if his head still felt like a busted stereo speaker, turned up too high. He would take it as punishment for his heart's weakness – it would remind him to build that fortress around it stronger next time.

Sitting on the sofa, watching as Vivian tore through yet another present, Mason had to remind himself again to remain in the moment. He watched the play of emotions flit across her face as she ripped through the wrapping of a dual karaoke and radio system he'd picked up while in New York. He had to admit after the fourth electronic device she'd opened, he may have overdone it a little. Vivian now sat on the floor stunned, her mouth gaping wide open as she stared at the third generation iPad in her hands. When she finally looked up at him, her eyes shown brightly with moisture.

"I had one sent to Gladys after talking with Mel. This way, you two can video chat, but still no Facebook, Instagram, MySpace or any of those other social networks for at least another few years." He tried to exact his most serious look to emphasize his no tolerance rule on her staying away from social media networks.

"Mandy and Sarah can't go on those sites either, so I have no need to be on them. Psh, Dad, this is so awesome! Now I can see Gladys anytime I want!" She turned the tablet around in her hands for a few moments before skimming over the front screen. Without turning it on, she set it aside and joined him on the couch to envelop him in a tight hug.

"Thank you, Daddy. It's the best present ever! Now I can see the rest of my family every day. That's the greatest part." She leaned away from him, her thin arms still hanging around his neck. "Did you know that we all started praying together in the morning? Gladys calls me and we call Mati every morning now. It's so…so…beautiful." Her smile was dazzling.

A year ago, it would have gut-punched him for a completely different reason. Her smiles seemed to waver between the sweetness of his dear Rachael's and the boldness of Paige's. How long was he doomed to continue to want things he couldn't have?

He forced himself to smile in return and concentrate on her happiness. This was what he had right now, in his arms, in his life, and he was determined to make it more than enough. He had almost lost her once. He didn't even want to consider a different outcome to the healthy glow he saw on her skin now.

He hugged her to him again to hide the overwhelming emotion that threatened to spill from his eyes as well.

She quickly sprung from his embrace, excitement dancing in her eyes. "I almost forgot. I have another present for you," she said, back-tracking a little to step around some of the wrapping left on the living room floor. Just after she exited the room into the hall, she peeked back around the corner. "Hey Dad, do you think we can go out to dinner tonight?"

"Aww, Hun. I thought I would try to cook us a little something. Make it a really special Christmas." He worked to keep the amusement out of his voice.

She stared at him in horror for a moment then narrowed her eyes, looking at him intently. She came back into the room slowly. She rubbed her hands together as if she were approaching a very delicate issue. Now, this was Rachael all the way.

"Uh…Dad…um." She took a deep breath. "I know it is Christmas and all, and you have been trying new recipes..." She raised her hands in mock surrender. "Most of them have been pretty good, but I thought maybe you could have a break tonight and we could go out." Her face held such hope and expectancy that he couldn't hold on to his laughter anymore.

He threw his head back and barked out riotous, uninhibited laughter. Her appeal to what she thought was his culinary insecurities was too adorable and very misplaced. He tried to sober up just in case he was hurting her feelings, but one glance at her twist of emotions from placation to aggravation sent him back over the edge, and he laughed even harder.

"Ugh! Dad. You can be such a… a…boy sometimes." Her emphasis on the word 'boy' made it sound like anything but a compliment, but it didn't do anything to help him get himself under control. In fact, it had just the opposite effect; his stomach began to spasm even harder, stealing the breath from him while wetness formed at the corners of his eyes.

He hadn't realized she'd left the room until she returned holding out a gift for him. He wiped his eyes as the laughter faded. He chanced a look at his daughter again, fighting to contain himself.

Vivian pushed the present further under his nose and he frowned as he looked at the delicately wrapped package. It wasn't decorated by Vivian. The lines were too sharp, the bow too neat.

Before he could voice the question, Vivian offered the information. "It's from Mati…I mean Paige, for you. She said she thought you would like it." From behind her back, came an ivory colored envelope.

He stared at both as if waiting for them to strike. He slowly reached for the card first and opened it as if in a trance. How did he not know she sent him something?

The front of the card was beautiful with an embossed painting of red poinsettias outlined in gold. He ran his hand across the vibrant leaves, feeling the ridges. "Tis the Season" was scripted across the bottom. He opened the card.

He read the inscription that came with the card.

"The true reason for the season is to celebrate the birth of Christ. Share His gift of life with someone you love."

At the bottom were three lines penned in Paige's handwriting.

Thank you, Mason, for sharing His gift of life with me by bringing my daughter back in mine. I am indebted to you. I thank God for you. Merry Christmas!

He read it three times before closing the card and reaching for the gift still being held out to him. He pulled on the gold bow carefully, both anxious and afraid to find out what she'd sent him. *Was she giving me an answer to her lengthy silence? Was she just keeping the lines of communication open?* He continued to unwrap the present, noting that his deliberate ministrations were causing Vivian to fidget. He moved a little quicker, but once he uncovered one side of the gilded-edged frame, he froze.

"Aren't you going to finish opening it up?" Vivian's question and excited eyes pulled him out of his musing. He pulled the wrap over, uncovered the framed picture of himself, Paige, Vivian, Gladys, Melanie and Mark, taken during their visit to California.

Was that really only a month ago? He stared at the smiles on each of their faces, reminiscing about those few days. He itched to glide his hand across Paige's face and lifted it just before Vivian spoke again.

"Do you like it?"

He looked up at her expectant face and forced himself to smile even as his heart worked overtime to purge the fresh surge of emotion. He wanted to cuss but refrained from speaking the words screaming in his mind. A copy...not even a copy. An image; an immovable, unlovable, untouchable, taunting image of something he could not have.

"Do you like it? She hoped you would. She said it represented God's ability to bring redemption where she failed."

He took a deep breath and heaved a heavy sigh.

"Is she really happy?" He hadn't meant to voice the question, but he didn't try to retract it once it was out.

"I think so. Well, I think she is...I mean when we spoke yesterday she was very happy..." Her voice faded as a look of consternation took over her features.

"Your answer was very confusing, Vivian. It seemed cryptic."

"What's cryptic?"

"Unclear. There seems to be something you aren't telling me, you know like there is a piece of the puzzle missing."

Vivian seemed deep in thought. If he had to guess it looked like she was weighing whether or not to share something with him, and he found himself hurt that she would purposely keep something from him.

Her relationship with Paige seemed to be growing closer by the day and it was hard not to feel left out sometimes, but in no way would he begrudge his daughter a relationship with her birth mother. They had both already lost precious time with one another.

"I've been having some weird dreams and Mati...I mean Paige is in them, but she isn't."

"Okay...I am even more confused."

"It's like her spirit is there, but it's someone else's face and body."

19

Mason nodded, now understanding what she was talking about.

"Well..." She started slowly, then stopped for a moment and he waited quietly for her to continue, now completely absorbed in what she was trying to relay.

"When they start off she is very happy like she was yesterday when we talked, but then it gets dark – I mean she gets dark, you know like…umm like you were when mommy died." She looked up at him apologetic.

"It's all right, go on."

"Well she gets really sad and there are all of these dark images around her. They aren't people, but they speak to her and she starts fighting them, but there are so many. I want to help her and I can see a door she can go through, so I try to tell her to go out the door because they can't go through the door, but she can't hear me and she keeps fighting and I feel like something terrible is going to happen, so I wake up."

"So you wake up before the thing you think is terrible happens to her?" Vivian nodded her head to the affirmative as she bit her lower lip.

"And you have had this dream before?" Vivian nodded her head once again. "How many times?"

"Maybe four or five?"

"Are you going to tell her?"

"That's just it. I don't know if I am supposed to. I don't even know if I was supposed to tell you..."

"Why? Do you think it will come true if you tell her?"

Vivian thought for a moment then raised her head. "I don't think me telling her will make it come true. I think it is already happening. I woke up in the middle of the night and I was already praying for her."

"You mean you were praying in your sleep?" He was having trouble following Vivian. He remembered Rachael mumbling in her sleep and sometimes when she had fallen asleep praying in her chair, he would pick her up and bring her to bed. Even in sleep, sometimes, she didn't seem to be completely at rest and would even turn over in her sleep saying "Hallelujah," as if she were thanking someone for agreeing on something. He'd always wondered what that meant but didn't have the nerve to find out what was really going on.

"Well yes and no. It was like my spirit started praying for her before I woke up, and it was praying so hard that it woke me up to help pray for her. I don't want to scare her though."

"Paige doesn't seem like a person easily afraid, Vivian. I am sure if you tell her she will be thankful and you may even feel better that you did. You never know; she might be able to help you figure out your dream and then you may find that you don't need to worry so much."

Vivian looked to be in deep thought, considering what he said. Finally, she raised sad eyes to him and got up to give him a tight hug. "She was fighting like you were fighting when mommy died, Daddy," she whispered, her voice full of tears, "I don't want her to be sad, Daddy. I don't want you to be sad anymore either."

She pulled back and he could see the tears threatening to fall. She placed her small hand against his jaw and looked at him beseechingly. "If you figure out how to be happy again, maybe you can show her how to be happy when she gets sad."

A small tremor of apprehension ran through his heart. "Hun, why do you think she is going to be sad? Is something going to happen?" He watched her intently but was only given a shrug.

"I don't know Daddy, that's why I don't think it's good to tell her because then she will start looking for something to happen."

"But Viv, if she is made aware that something may happen to cause her sadness, maybe she can avoid it or pray it doesn't happen?"

The control she seemed to be using to keep her tears at bay broke and she began to sob, moving back into his arms for comfort. He rubbed her back while shushing her and speaking words of comfort that everything would be okay. The only words she would speak in return were, "It's already started."

As he sat at the edge of the couch with Vivian's shaking body on his lap, a heaviness engulfed him and all he could do was hope these were just recurring nightmares as a delayed reaction to some of the trauma her body had gone through recently. It was practical, though only slightly probable. He hoped no one he knew would ever have to go through the dark hell he'd found himself in after Rachael died, but death had a way of finding everyone, especially the bright ones.

For the first time since Vivian's hospital stay, he found himself asking God for a favor. He half-expected to get an audible 'No,' but when he heard nothing, he thought he would take his chances and continue.

"Not that you owe me anything, but for Paige and my daughter's sake, answer her prayers. Step in and keep her from harm. Don't let her suffer."

Vivian pulled back far enough to look at him and remain on his lap. She looked as if she wanted to ask him a question, but was hesitant to do so.

"What is it, Hun?"

She took a deep breath. "Could we pray for Paige out loud?" She rushed forward when he opened his mouth. "I could do all the praying and you could just agree with me. Please?" She implored him.

He hesitated for a moment, raising a brow to himself and silently asking God to validate her prayer even though he was just going along for the ride. *Just listen to her. You don't have to mind what I think. She is the one who has the relationship with you and what you think is important to her. Just listen to her prayer.*

He finally nodded in agreement and watched the watery smile take over her features before she reached for his hands, closed her eyes, and began praying.

"Dear Heavenly Father, our Lord and Savior, the Spirit that leads and guides us to all truths. Father, I thank you for waking us up this morning. It is a beautiful day and not just because my dad gave me so many wonderful gifts, but because we get to share it together. It is an even more special Christmas Day, the celebration of your Son, Jesus Christ's birth. This year I am thankful for being gifted with more family and friends. You have extended my territory like Jabez, but without all the suffering he had to go through. Thank you, Lord."

Until then, Mason had just tried to concentrate on her words. It took a moment to draw his attention back to the prayer after wondering what exactly happened to this person named Jabez. He made a mental note to look it up.

"Lord, I come to You in agreement with my father today on behalf of Paige (Mati) Morganson. Lord, I am not sure what it is she is going through, but You do, and though You have shown me some things, I am left in the dark about others so I ask that your Holy Spirit guide me to pray what is your perfect will. Lord, I ask that You comfort her. She is my mom and I don't want her to hurt, Lord. I pray that You step in, Lord, and lift up a standard against the enemy and whatever pitfalls he has prepared for her. Lord, I ask that You intervene and keep her from all hurt, harm, and danger. Please don't let her suffer, Lord. Get her attention in the dark places. Let her hear Your voice and let it be her guide out of that waylay place. Father, touch and heal her heart, cause her to be happy and full of joy. Give her a praise that will lift her head and her shoulders, and cause her to shine for you. Give her peace, Father, and don't allow what she goes through to be for nothing. Keep her close to you, Lord, and let her know that you have not left her, but that you are holding her even closer than before.

And, Lord, I ask that you continue to comfort my father. Let him know that just because he may not like You doesn't mean that you don't love Him. I thank you for healing me so that I could continue to pray for him, and I ask that you keep trying to get his attention. I know it makes You sad to see him so sad, but he is a very good father and he loves me so much, I glow inside. I thank you for the best dad ever and I ask that You reward him. Bless my daddy, Father. Bless him, heal him, and make him whole again. In Jesus' name we pray. Amen."

Vivian let go of his hands, enveloped him in a tight hug, and squeezed his neck before she released him, giving him a kiss on his cheek. "Thank you Daddy. I feel much better. I'm going to go call Gladys now." She stopped for a moment, looking perplexed. "I don't want to ruin the surprise for her, but how will I know she has opened her gift form you?"

Mason smiled up at his daughter. "She opened hers last night. I put my cell number on the card and instructed her to text me when she opened it so you would know when the coast was clear."

"Wow Daddy, that was smart. Good going, I don't know if I would have thought of that. Ummm…" she murmured to herself as she walked back to her room to call Gladys.

Mason sat in that position for a long time going over Vivian's prayer. He had been struck dumb by hearing the same words come from her mouth during their prayer that he had silently prayed only moments before.

Was God saying that He heard his prayer? Did He have Vivian repeat the prayer so that it would be granted? He went over the prayer almost a half a dozen times before he conceded and just said, "Thank You."

With a half grin on his face, he went about cleaning up the wrappings from Vivian's gifts. He could hear the squeals coming from Vivian's room and concluded that Gladys had just been made aware that her twin was in possession of her identical gift.

Good thing Skype is free, he thought to himself as he went into the kitchen to fix them a Christmas breakfast of cereal and fruit.

CHAPTER 4

Victoria sat on the swing couch, watching the sunset from the west end of the porch. The colors, which were particularly spectacular in the cooling clean air, were all but lost to her.

She started out over the empty pasture, transfixed as if she were enrapt by a movie. A breeze moved by slowly, lingering on her cheeks and she lifted her chin, allowing it to wash over her neck.

She closed her eyes to the thoughts of the early morning, working to stave off the onslaught of emotions.

Richard was back in town. Her Richard…well for a little while longer.

*   *   *

She'd sat across from him in a corner table of the coffee shop decked out in garland, berries, holly, and mistletoe. The wreaths on the door and archway between the reception area and the dining room were decorated with gold colored cherubs playing various musical instruments. The red velvet bows at the top of each had seen better days.

Each table held a different Christmas-themed decoration. Theirs had been garnished with fake snow attached to the red tablecloth, surrounding a snow globe featuring a snowman with twigs for arms. All of a sudden, she had the urge to shake it to see just how long the white flakes would float around in the bubble before descending to the bottom. It certainly would give her something to focus on since she was still unable to speak, due to the fear that had clutched her heart at the sight of the divorce papers.

She peered out of the window, watching snow flurries whip around in the wind, bouncing off the steps of the old-fashioned style porch leading to the restaurant doors. She had been looking forward to a heavy snow before Christmas Day. There were still a few hours yet.

She didn't know what had come over her. Where she usually came out fighting tooth and nail for what she wanted and believed in, at the sight of the papers in his hand it was all she could do to stay upright and breathe in and out.

She chanced a look and caught him staring at her.

"You look tired, Vickie." She watched as he searched her face. The use of his nickname for her had her heart beating faster. She didn't know how to reply, so she lifted her shoulders slightly.

"How are the arrangements going for the banquet? Are you letting anyone help you with the preparation?" She saw a smirk lift one side of his mouth. He was teasing her. What normally would have brought a smile to her lips and have her laughing at herself now did little to lift her spirits.

How could he be so light-hearted with those papers in his possession? She asked him just as much.

Richard's mannerisms quieted and the tilt to his mouth rearranged itself into a line. It was incredible what his mouth did for his expressions. She dragged her eyes from his lips and back to his eyes. They were somber.

"Victoria," he began as he shifted in his seat, laying his menu to the side, "It wasn't my intention that you see those papers. I'd waited for you to go into the bathroom so that I could put them away, but you came out so quickly…" He allowed the sentence to fade.

"Why do you have the papers at all?"

Richard sighed and rubbed his eyes with this thumb and forefinger, a tale-tell sign that he was wrestling with some thoughts.

"Victoria, during our last conversation I gave you an ultimatum and said some pretty harsh things to you. I couldn't think of any other way to get your attention. You have been heading down this road of self-destruction for so long I needed you to see how much it was affecting me…how much it was affecting us." His words gave her back some of the fragile hope she had lost since seeing the papers in his hands.

"But that doesn't-" she began. He interrupted her by raising his hand with his palm facing.

"I know Rachael's death caused a chasm in our relationship, but instead of us growing closer and trying to help each other heal, we have only grown further apart. I don't know how to reach you anymore. This…" He rubbed his forehead with his fingertips. "need you have to avenge Rachael's death at the hands of Mason is not only out of place, it is unjustified. He is hurting just like us, maybe even more because he watches Vivian wake up each morning and go about her day without the help of a mother and he goes to bed each night without the comfort of a wife, just like I have been doing for the last 18 months. I won't do it anymore.

I miss my wife. The warm, loving, slightly neurotic defender of the under-served and voiceless. Those were causes I could get behind – efforts I will continue to support you and work with you on." He began to shake his head. "But this obsession you have with making Mason pay for something he had no control over is only a vain attempt at redirecting your hurt, anger, guilt and shame. It will not diminish the pain, it will only mask it for a while."

She opened her mouth to defend herself, but the look he gave her kept her silent.

"The man was in the hospital being treated while his daughter lay sick in her own bed in need of a kidney and you try to take his daughter away from him? You send a man who cannot hobble more than 20 feet without

25

breaking a sweat court documents, demanding that he appear at a hearing so that you can gain custody of the one person...the one being that links him to his dead wife. You went too far, Victoria."

"But I dropped the suit," Victoria interjected.

"Yes, but you shouldn't have done it in the first place. What would you have done if you'd gained custody of Vivian? With Mason surely headed to his grave, would you then have set your sights on making *her* life a living hell? When would have it been enough? When would your hatred have been assuaged? I can tell you when – never," he said answering his own rhetorical question.

"Your hate has been the driving force in your life for too long and I am partly to blame because I didn't say something sooner, but I cannot be a party to it anymore. I will not."

"What are you saying?"

He took a deep breath, letting it out slowly.

"We need help...you need help. I'm not enough anymore and, frankly, I don't want to be. I love you Victoria. God only knows why I still do, but I do. I don't want to imagine looking towards a future without you in it, but not if you are going to continue to allow the past and lack of forgiveness to eat away at the life in you. That, I will not stick around to see. I want you to commit to going to marriage counseling with me."

For a moment the thought of someone else invading their private lives made her physically ill, but it was eclipsed by the realization of what he was actually saying.

"So you're not leaving me?" She was filled with so much relief, moisture came to her eyes.

"That is up to you." He took a deep breath as if he were girding himself for a fight. "Are you willing to concede to marriage counseling? I would prefer Christian Marriage Counseling, but I am willing to compromise."

Her eyes went wide with her first reaction, which sent violent spasms jolting through her nervous system, heating her instantly and causing beads of perspiration to break out on her forehead.

She worked her mouth, but no sound came out for the first few seconds. *Was this an ultimatum? 'Christian' counseling?* Christian anything caused bile to rise just enough for her to taste. She swallowed convulsively a few times before she attempted to speak.

"So, if I don't agree to counseling, you will leave?"

Richard nodded.

"Would you consider another option?"

"I have thought about this for weeks, Victoria. This is the one I feel would be the most productive."

"How long do I have to decide?" She watched his mouth, making sure she didn't miss the answer.

"Until I finish breakfast," he said then signaled for their waitress.

A wry smile formed on Victoria's lips. Sometime in the last few months, Richard had grown a spine of steel. It excited her almost as much as it scared her. She was going to have to find a way around this counseling thing. She couldn't have people in this town in her business. She refused to let a stranger into her marriage and she sure as hell wasn't going to let any Christian counselor have a peek.

She would concede for now and try to wear him down in the meantime. Surely he wouldn't push for any sessions until after the banquet.

She raised her eyes to the waitress now standing at their table waiting for her to order. She looked over at Richard to see his eyebrows raised as if he were reading her thoughts. This was going to take some fine maneuvering.

The porch door creaked, drawing her away from her thoughts. She looked over to see Richard stepping outside with his overnight bag.

"You're leaving?" Victoria asked from the shadows in the corner. She saw Richard jump slightly and quickly became wary.

"Yes, I need to go get a change of clothes and catch up on some things. I will be back tomorrow," he glanced at his watch, "Um well, later today."

He continued to walk towards the steps and she rose from the couch to try and waylay him. She moved quickly so that she was only a step behind him. "I enjoyed our day together. Thank you for the suggestions for the banquet. I'm sure it will make things run smoother for next year as well."

He reached the ground before he turned around. "Well, I'm glad you considered them. You know you don't have to run every aspect of this event. That's why you hired the *event planner*."

Victoria shrugged as she took the last few steps that would bring her to within arm's length of him. She reached forward to lay her hand on his shoulder and could feel him stiffen under her fingers.

He had been avoiding her touch for most of the day. Except for those few moments in the morning when she'd awaken to find him taking care of her, he'd remained somewhat distant. If counseling hadn't been his idea, she may have thought that he was truly done with her.

"Aren't you even going to kiss me goodnight?" She stepped closer in a suggestive manner. "It is Christmas Eve after all, and I've missed you so very much over the last few months."

Richard didn't move away, but he didn't encourage her to move forward either. She waited patiently as he watched her intently, probably trying to decide if she were being manipulative. She forced herself to relax her features so that she could let him see what she was really feeling in the brief moment. She'd risk her feelings for a couple of moments. After all, he was her husband.

Her husband who'd just-as-soon abandoned her and thwarted her plans to gain custody of her granddaughter and rear her with all the privileges she deserved, but there would be other chances. If she knew Mason as well as she thought, he would give her another chance to gain the upper hand.

For now, her thoughts needed to be on the man in front of her and getting back in his good graces so she could convince him to drop this absurd idea he had about marriage counseling.

"Just for a moment, I thought..." Richard shook his head as if to clear his mind. He leaned back slightly then pressed a kiss upon her forehead. "I'll see you tomorrow." His brief smile didn't have time to reach his eyes before he turned and walked to his car, leaving her fuming at the edge of the porch.

CHAPTER 5

Christmas came in slowly as if it were tiptoeing around her, trying to remain hidden from her conscience. Paige gradually became aware of her surroundings and her position. Her arms and legs felt like lead from lack of movement. She made the wry assessment that she had not shifted from the fetal position for 6 hours. She would definitely pay for that. She opened her eyes, wondering why they were so tight when the revelations of the day before came upon her like a flood. She steeled herself against the tears she felt in the back of her eyes and the thud of her heart, which felt like it was trying to pump glue instead of the red-stained liquid she wouldn't care to spill at the moment if it would make her feel better or nothing at all.

She shook her head, trying to separate herself from the deep gash that sent a fission through her very soul. Her breath shuddered as the feeling caught her on the edge of full consciousness. She wanted to pull back, finally understanding what it was like to stand at the precipice of mental lucidity and consider jumping.

Though he was the very reason for her anguish, he was also the reason for her not to let go, but to fight through the pain.

Cancer. The word came in like an unwelcomed guest. *Cancer of the liver.* Not hers...not him...not the one God had meant for her. Surely He loved her too much to set her up to love someone so deeply, so quickly, only to take them away. *That must be it. I am overreacting.* The thought came upon her like the dawning day. Many people who have at one time battled cancer, lived to talk about it for many years later. Why had she allowed the fear to overtake her last night? *He had gone into remission before, why not again? This was the miracle season after all.*

For I have not given you a spirit of fear, but of power, love and a sound mind. She pulled on the scripture, forcing it to speak to her emotions and calm her.

Paige pushed herself into a seated position on the couch. Her head was heavy due to dehydration. The water that she had lost with all the crying and the inflammation in her sinuses warned her of an oncoming headache. She leaned forward, allowing gravity to help her come up off the couch into a hunched position until she was sure of her footing.

She swayed slightly before stepping forward and had to laugh at herself for staggering like a drunk. She sure could have used a drink last night, if only to numb the pain and quiet the voices, but that was no longer her life. She didn't go for the ease of temporal fixes. She would rather have His peace, no matter how hard it was to obtain sometimes.

She walked into her en-suite bath, tossing aside the thought of a leisurely soak in lieu of a cleansing shower. She needed to feel the sting of the water upon her face in order to help her realize the choice she was making to accept God's thoughts and no longer dwell on her own. Her thoughts were doing nothing to bring about a healthy solution to her circumstances. She could continue to throw herself the grandest of pity parties or receive His healing perspective.

As she stood under the power of the show head, reveling in the lukewarm water as it drenched her hair, eyelashes, and eye-brows, beat on her cheeks and collarbone, and soothed her heart, she thought back on the day before. The images of the day seemed to merge into one moment then scatter back into their appropriate order so that she could replay it slowly.

The day had started out beautifully, full of promise and anticipation of the opportunity to share a few moments alone with Brandon. These times had become almost non-existent with his family coming to visit for the holiday season. His mother arrived first, about a week and a half after their friendship had made that shift into something more.

They would talk on the phone every evening, even if it was only for a few minutes. She couldn't get over their ability to communicate so effectively in such short spurts. Brandon wasn't into small talk; he wanted to know what moved her that day, what she took the most delight in, and what God had shared with her. She had to admit that it caused her to pay even more attention to those things that brought her joy as well as the things that caused her even the smallest discomfort.

It was exactly because of that reason she was completely thrown when he'd finally shared the diagnosis of liver cancer with her.

He'd hinted at wanting to share some important information with her, but she had to confess that she had been distracted by the elation she received in her soul in spending time with him. Then there were those kisses that wiped most of the thoughts from her head allowing her to concentrate on the love she felt coming from them. His kisses that were warm and sweet, and caused her heart to first stop then beat twice as fast as if it were trying to catch up.

These precious moments were side-swiped by his confession.

"I was diagnosed with liver cancer," he spoke softly as if they were in *a crowd, but there they sat in his car, in front of her house, him confessing being diagnosed with a disease that she had seen too many people fear and lose their battle with. She'd even had him repeat it in hopes that she'd heard him wrong.*

"How long?" she whispered, hoping he wouldn't make her repeat *herself.*

"How long, what?" He replied in the same tone, looking forward.

"How long have you known?"

*He took a deep breath, closing his eyes. "Since June 24*th *of this year."*

She'd turned incredulous eyes towards him. "You knew before we met?" He nodded his head. She swallowed, not knowing if she really wanted to know the answer to her next question. "Did Pastor Lawrence know before you first came to Skylight Temple?"

He turned, looking her square in the eye. "No."

Her breathing returned to normal.

"Is that why your family is here in full force, or do you always get bombarded like this?"

"We've made it a practice these last eleven years to come together during the holidays. Whether it was going back to my parent's house in Garden City or any of the cities my siblings' reside in, we made sure we were together during the Christmas holiday."

"Eleven years. What happened eleven years ago?"

His hands gripped the steering wheel. "I'd had a bout with cancer."

She gasped, trying to absorb the information. "You've had cancer before? What happened?"

"It was detected early and treatable with chemotherapy, radiation, and surgical removal."

"Was it of the liver as well?"

"No. The cells were found in my colon."

She sat there weighing the situation. So many questions.

"Are you in any pain?"

He shook his head to the negative.

"Why didn't you tell me sooner?"

He shrugged his shoulders as he stared down at his lap.

She sat there wondering if he really didn't know or didn't want to tell her why. Was she really that wrong about him?

"You know why." She countered, placing her hand on his chin so he would meet her gaze. "I want to – no I need to hear it."

She watched as he blinked rapidly then latched onto her gaze. "I was afraid you would change your mind and leave."

She was only momentarily satisfied with the answer.

"Why are you telling me now?" Before he could answer a thought came to her. "Is it because I am to meet your family tomorrow?"

"Partly, but after what happened today, I couldn't keep from telling you. As deeply as I feel about you and want you to stay...it is your decision."

The silence in the car was deafening.

"I need to think," she said as she pulled on the door handle. It wouldn't give. She looked over at him pointedly.

His hand moved towards the button to unlock the doors, but he didn't press it.

"Could you call me by 12 noon if you don't want to come with me tomorrow? Otherwise, I will be here at 2 pm to pick you up."

Her heart bottomed out. He was giving her an out. He wasn't even going to fight to keep her.

She nodded her head in acquiescence then heard the locks release on the doors. She didn't look back before exiting the car. It was all she could do to put one foot in front of the other until she made it up the stairs and to her front door.

Paige turned off the water and stepped out of the shower. Her head felt better, but her heart felt like a tangled mess. She put on her terry cloth robe, glancing at the clock as she picked up her lotion. 6 o'clock glared at her in red. This was going to be a very long day. She thought about calling Lady Menagerie, but it was too early.

*Lady Menagerie...did she know? No...*Paige forced herself away from the thoughts of betrayal. *She wouldn't do that to me.* She thought back to the time when Lady Menagerie had told her to guard her heart concerning her decision to encourage Elder Tatum or Mason during her time in Chicago after her kidney donation to her recently reunited daughter, Vivian.

*Mel...*maybe her sister, Melanie, could give her the objectivity she needed to make the decision to either take the out, citing Brandon's lack of honesty early on as reason to end their budding relationship or continue to see him, hoping and praying that he would be victorious in this battle as well and be healed.

She laid across the bed, retrieving the cordless phone from its base on the nightstand. She dialed her sister in Atlanta, GA, knowing she would be up and already making preparations for the Christmas meal.

She took a deep breath as she dialed, trying to organize her thoughts. Melanie picked up on the second ring sounding preoccupied. "Merry Christmas, Paige! What are you doing up so early? I bet you're excited about today and meeting Brandon's family. If I were you, I wouldn't have been able to sleep either."

As Paige listened to her sister go on, barely breathing in between paragraphs, she allowed Mel's excitement to lift up her spirits a little then began to chastise herself for wallowing in self-pity for so long and being so self-absorbed that she would bring down Mel with her news.

When she could edge a word in, Paige spoke. "How are all the preparations going?"

"I am a little behind, but since Marc's parents aren't coming in until late this afternoon, I have been spared. I thought Gladys was going to be a lot more help, but since the one present she picked to open last night just happened to be from Mason, I haven't able to get her to pay more than five minutes worth of attention to anything but."

"Mason sent Gladys a present?" Paige asked more to herself than Melanie.

"You didn't know? How…"

"I've been communicating more with Vivian than I have Mason lately. It's been a little awkward, what with his confession and our last conversation. I thought I would give us a little time."

"No, you thought you would avoid him. This is your sister. I know you well, but since I don't know what I would do in your type of situation, I won't cast the first stone."

There was a pregnant silence on the line with both women full of thoughts of their own. Paige spoke up first.

"So what was the present that has Gladys so taken?"

Mel responded in a hushed tone. "Mason bought Gladys an iPad for Christmas. I could barely believe my eyes. Marc was a little taken aback by the costly gift, but after talking to Mason and learning it was his way of ensuring that the girls could communicate not only by voice but by video each day, he relented. Gladys has been online reading the manual and making sure she is registered, as well as setting aside all of the warranty information. Marc won't let her download a thing until he is satisfied that she knows the device well enough not to cause it any undue harm. She was so excited she didn't even blink twice when Marc gave her his conditions on her use of the tablet. She can't communicate with Vivian on it until Vivian calls her anyway. Mason didn't want her ruining the surprise he had for his daughter."

Paige was quiet, but her thoughts were racing around in her mind like a tornado. She was overwhelmed by Mason's thoughtfulness, but he had never done anything to cause her to think twice about his love for his daughter and his dedication to her happiness. If anything, she could learn a great deal about being a parent from him in regards to her girls. Though expensive, it was a perfect gift for the twins who lived roughly 800 miles from one another. She could just imagine Vivian's face when she opened her gift. She felt a painful twinge in her heart at not being able to spend Christmas Day with her girls. They'd grown closer and closer in the last month with daily calls and morning prayer. If it hadn't been for the unlimited long distance on her cell, she probably would have had to add more tour dates to pay for the overages.

They were so adorable and lively. She was amazed by their commonalities as well as the differences in their personalities. Whereas Gladys was very personable and outgoing with people in general, Vivian was shy and somewhat introverted, but when she began talking about some of her experiences with the Lord or praying, her demeanor would change. She prayed with such a confidence and boldness that Gladys, who was almost shy about praying out loud in the beginning, began to ask to pray at the end of their calls. Though she couldn't take any credit for the wonderful walk her two girls had up to this point, she was godly proud of both of them.

Paige at first felt guilty at not encouraging this type of communication with Gladys from the start, but just as quickly was comforted by the thought that this was all in God's timing.

"Paige?" Mel broke into her meandering thoughts.

"Yeah?"

She could hear the hesitation in her sister's voice which never bode well.

"Um...shoot, I am just going to go ahead and say it."

"Okaaaaay... Mel, you are only making me more anxious."

"I know, I was trying to avoid that. You know how I hate dramatics."

"Mmm um, sure," Paige responded sardonically.

"Mom's here."

The sly remark that had come to the edge of Paige's mouth evaporated with all other thoughts of levity.

"What?" *Please let me have heard wrong. Please let me have heard wrong.* She repeated this in her mind like a mantra.

"Mom arrived at our house yesterday. I came in from doing some shopping and Gladys let her in. I was in the kitchen putting things away when she walked in. Talk about the makings of a heartache."

"What is she doing there?" Paige's heart began beating faster with each word Mel said until all she could hear was the sound of her heartbeat in her ears.

"I asked her the same. She says she came to visit."

Paige's mind began spinning faster than before. She wanted to refuse to take in any more information, but it was computing. Her mother was back in her sister's life and if she wasn't fortunate, she was next.

"She came to visit...how long is she going to stay? Where is she going after? Did you tell her about me? Does she know about my time in the hospital?" Paige's breath caught in her throat at her next thought, but she didn't have time to voice her next concern before Mel interrupted her.

"Paige, get a hold of yourself before you start hyperventilating. Breathe, Paige, breathe." Mel paused for a moment. "I don't hear you breathing, Paige. I'm not going to say another word until I hear you take a deep breath."

Paige, now sitting up in bed, readjusted her position so that she was propped up amongst the pillows that were leaning against her headboard.

She spied the stuffed animal Vivian had given her while she was in rehab and hugged it to her.

She closed her eyes and took a deep breath. It did nothing to calm her. She took another and another until she began to feel some of her panic subside.

"Good, now maybe we can have some semblance of a coherent conversation." Mel began. "Like I said, Mom was here when I came in yesterday from the grocery store. She said she was coming to visit us for the Christmas holiday and, if it wasn't too much trouble, she would stay until the New Year."

"She invited herself to your house until the New Year?" Paige asked incredulously, then silently berated herself for her selfishness. Mel's relationship with their mother was nowhere near as strained as hers.

"She's our mom, Paige. Although we don't have the most traditional relationship with her, I still wouldn't begrudge her time with the family, especially during Christmas. Besides, she isn't staying with us. She checked into a hotel a few miles away."

"Have you been in contact with her lately?" Paige didn't know why she was asking except that something didn't add up. Although her mother wasn't the most communicative person, she wasn't one to just pop up unannounced – at least she wasn't when Paige was living with her – but that was more than a decade ago.

"No, not really. I haven't talked to her since before you came to visit in September."

"September? I didn't know you spoke to her. Did you tell her I was coming to visit? Did you tell her why I was coming?"

"Paige, you sound paranoid. After all this time you are really going to have to let some of that fear go."

"I'm not afraid of her," Paige responded too quickly, feeling righteously indignant, "What do I have to be afraid of? I just don't think she needs to know any of my business."

"Hmm," was all that came from the other side of the line.

Paige waited impatiently for Melanie to continue. She wasn't going to fall for it. She wouldn't ask. The silence dragged on, the anticipation grating against her nerves like squeaky brakes.

"Fine, fine, just tell me what she wants and we can be done with this conversation."

She heard Melanie take a deep breath. "She's getting married."

"Again?!" Paige nearly yelled into the phone, then calmed herself and repeated the question in a more subdued manner. "She is getting married again? What is this five…six?"

"Four and spitefulness does not become you, Paige."

Somewhat contrite, Paige spoke quietly. "Grace is there visiting and she is getting married again. Is there anything else?"

"Isn't that enough?"

"I guess, but you never know with Grace." Paige let her voice fade. Momentarily forgetting why she'd called in the first place, she asked to speak to Gladys so she could wish her a Merry Christmas.

"You know she is going to want to open her present from you while you are on the phone. Do you need a moment to compose yourself?"

"No. I think I'm good, but I need to ask you one more question."

"Yep."

"Did Grace ask about me?" She was almost too afraid to ask, but knew that it would be on her mind all day if she didn't.

"Yes." Mel didn't elaborate, which frustrated her. She blew out a sigh.

"What did she ask?"

"She wanted to know if I'd spoken to you recently and how you were doing."

"And you said..." She was going to pull it out of her like an orthodontist would an impacted tooth.

"I told her that I talk to you all the time and that you were doing fine."

"Does she know I came to visit and that we told Gladys I was her mother?"

"I didn't tell her, but it is only a matter of time before Gladys talks to her about it. I am not going to censor my child's conversations with her grandmother."

Paige wanted to throw a fit. She forgot about Gladys' relationship with Vivian. Grace would find out that Paige knew what happened to Vivian. She began to feel queasy.

"Mel, Gladys might tell Grace about Vivian."

Mel's voice was soft and placating. "I don't think there is any way around it. Gladys is excited about finding out Vivian's alive. It is hardly something I could keep her from sharing. It is bound to slip out, especially with the gift Mason gave her. Do you want to encourage your daughter to practice deceit?"

"Why can't it just be called practicing constraint?" Paige knew it was a long shot, but she was starting to feel desperate. She was not ready for Grace to come stomping back into her life. She squeezed the bear tighter.

"Right, like a twelve-year-old would be able to master constraint. I don't care what you call it, I am not going to teach Gladys to be evasive and deceitful. There is plenty of time for her to learn that on her own."

Paige sighed again, but this time in resignation. It was only a matter of time before Grace tried to contact her. "I don't want to talk to her."

"Now that's just childish. You don't want to talk to your daughter because she may share information with your mother? Now –"

Paige interrupted Mel. "Not Gladys... Grace. Once she finds out about Vivian, she is probably going to want to talk to me. I don't want to talk to her and I don't want you giving her my information under any circumstances, do you understand?"

"Don't go getting all demanding; I am still your big sister. You insult me if you think I will hand over any of your information, but since it is Christmas, I will forget your attitude and I will tell Gladys not to share your information either, not even your personal email address."

"Thanks Mel, can I speak to Gladys now?" Paige felt defeated. It wasn't that it hadn't crossed her mind that Grace may find out about her and Vivian, but she was definitely hoping for more time. She tried to push the panic-induced thoughts of Grace finding and confronting her out of her mind as Gladys came on the line, her voice full of elation.

"Mati, did you hear? Uncle Mason gave me an iPad for Christmas! Isn't that the coolest thing ever?!"

As much as Paige wanted to make this a short call, she knew the excitement in Gladys' voice was calling for participation.

"Yes, your mother told me." Her mind caught up with the rest of Gladys' sentence. "When did you start calling Mr. Jenson, 'Uncle Mason'?"

"This morning. I've been thinking about it for a while and I asked Vivian yesterday if she wouldn't mind, since we are practically family. Anyway, I asked him this morning if I could call him Uncle Mason and he said he would be honored. This is the best Christmas ever!" she said, jumping from one subject to another, "Too bad you couldn't be here. I think mom could use the help, what with Grand-mommy here."

Paige tried to school her voice so that the anger that leapt inside of her at Gladys' reference to Grace would calm. She worked her neck from side to side hoping to relieve some of the stress with a slight crack to the now overly-tight muscles. She was thankful they weren't video chatting, or worse yet face-to-face, because she would never have been able to pull off the nonchalant undulation in her voice.

"Oh, yeah, your mom told me she decided to visit. Will she be spending most of Christmas Day with you?"

"Um, I think so. She and her fiancé, Clifford, will be coming around one o'clock. I can't wait to meet him. It's kind of unreal. Grand-mommy, getting married so old."

"She isn't that old, Gladys," Paige replied trying to hide her amusement.

"She's like fifty-something." Paige pressed her lips together to smother the giggle that wanted to escape at Gladys' awe-filled voice.

She took a deep breath to calm herself before she interrupted. "Gladys, plenty of people get married that are fifty and over. It is never too late."

"Ummm. I guess. Grand-mommy said she's getting married on New Year's Eve. Are you going to come?"

"No. I don't think I will be able to make it."

"Is it because of Brandon and his family?"

Brandon. With all of the surprises in the conversation the main reason for her call had slipped her mind. *Talk about putting things into perspective.* Agonizing over whether or not to continue her otherwise beautiful relationship with Brandon seemed insignificant compared to what she knew lay ahead for her. This conversation alone brought up two people in her life she wanted to avoid. Mason, who she had tried hard not to hurt, was not taking her decision to court Brandon well, and she couldn't help but feel uncomfortable and just a little guilty with some of the admissions he'd worked from her a few weeks ago.

"Partly." She stated, not wanting to lie to Gladys.

"Mati?"

"Yes?"

"Is Brandon all right?"

Paige began feeling edgy.

"Why, honey?"

Gladys' voice became hesitant. "Well, I was praying by myself the other night and it came to my mind to pray for his health, and then when I prayed with Vivian a couple of days ago, she prayed for his health too, but it wasn't for like if he had a cold or something, it was like...for his heart and his mind. Does that sound funny?"

"No baby. Whatever the Lord would have you pray, it is for a reason. Just keep praying; I am sure Brandon would be happy to know that you are praying for him."

Desperately wanting to change the subject, Paige reminded Gladys of the gift she still needed to open.

"Oh yeah, let me get it!"

Paige became lost in thought as Gladys went to retrieve her present. Life was too short to spend any more of it in a pity party. Gladys's reference to him and her prayers for him not only got her attention, but almost shamed her in her neglect. She wasn't the one diagnosed with cancer, Brandon was, and he seemed to be handling it a whole lot better than she was

...but then, he did have more time to grow accustomed to the notion. Did one really get used to the idea of having cancer? Was it always somewhere lurking in their mind? With chemo and radiation, it had to be hard to maintain one's normal activities, but Brandon didn't seem to miss a beat. She'd considered trying to protect her heart and place some distance between them, but she couldn't fool herself. She was already in too deep. There was no going back. She took a deep breath, consciously taking with it the resolution to fight against the fear harder next time. She could do it. She lifted her chin slightly. She would do it. She would love him like there was no tomorrow.

"I am opening my present, Mati," Gladys spoke into the phone, breaking into Paige's thoughts.

"Oooh. They are beautiful. I love these earrings and there are so many I can wear a different one every day of the week. Thank you so much."

"Did you open your card?"

"Not yet."

"Aren't you supposed to open that first?"

"Sorry." Paige could hear her fumbling with the card in the back and knew the exact moment when she spotted the gift cards. Either that, or she was telling someone to, "SHUT THE FRONT DOOR."

"Oh my gosh. Oh my gosh. Mati, you didn't. You did, you did, YOU DID!" She screamed in excitement.

"What did she do?" She heard her sister say on the other side of the line.

"She got me a fifty-dollar gift card for iTunes and a one hundred dollar gift card to the movies. This is great! How did you know I was going to get the iPad for Christmas?"

"Uh…well…you know parents talk…um, okay. Well I'm glad you like your gifts. Tell your dad I said 'Merry Christmas.' Could you put your mom on the phone real quick like?"

"Sure and thank you. Your gifts were great. You have to call me back when you open yours. I want to hear what you think. Okay?"

"Okay. I love you. Merry Christmas!"

"I love you too. Merry Christmas!"

When her sister came on the line she began hastily. "You better get Marc up so she can open her presents before she realizes my gift card wasn't for the iPad, but the iPod you bought her."

"Party-Pooper. Why didn't you just let her open her card later?"

"Because I wanted to hear her reaction and I have to say, the words you are teaching my daughter these days. Clever. 'Shut the front door?' I swear my heart seized up for a moment when I thought she was going in another direction. I am going to have to use it in my next book."

"That expression didn't come from me and I was just as scared as you were as to what was going to come out of her mouth next. The things these kids think of. So, you don't sound too much worse for wear regarding my news. I'm sorry about laying it on you today of all days with you going to spend time with Brandon and his family. How are you feeling about that now? Are you nervous?"

Thankful for the change in subject, Paige spoke from her heart that was measurably lighter since the night before.

"I'm looking forward to meeting his family. I am a little nervous, but I'm going to concentrate on sharing a wonderful Christmas with the man I love and his family."

"Wait a minute. The man you love. Last week I couldn't even get you to admit a deep like for him. When did this happen?"

"While I was waiting for Gladys to open her presents."

"Huh?"

"It's been very interesting, Mel, but I have to make some more calls, and I still have to make the dessert to take over to Brandon's. I will call you later to tell you how it goes, okay?"

"Okay. Have a wonderful time, and Paige?"

"Yep?"

"Merry Christmas."

"Merry Christmas, Mel. Tell Marc I wished him a Merry Christmas as well."

"I will. Bye."

"Bye."

Paige ended the call and laid back against the pillows again, taking a deep cleansing breath. She was no longer in the mood to think about Grace. She would wait until she had more moral support around her. She glanced over at the clock. It read 7:08 am. Well, it was already after 9:00 am in Illinois. Maybe she would share some more Christmas cheer.

CHAPTER 6

Brandon found his thoughts veering for the umpteenth time as he turned the corner onto Paige's street. He glanced at the clock on his dashboard again. His mom wasn't the most jubilant about him going to see Paige early when he was already scheduled to pick her up in two hours, but she said nothing. She just tilted her head and studied him – the same way she did when he was nine – and seemed to know everything.

The apartment had been near full when he'd left, making the few moments between his and Paige's home both a reprieve and cause for anxiety. She hadn't given her answer over the phone and yet had asked for a few moments for them to talk privately. Whatever it takes; his talk with Dominy left him with a great deal to think about and he recommitted himself to being more open-minded where Paige's reaction was concerned. After all, he did have a great deal more time to get used to his diagnosis than she did.

He parked across the street from her complex and sat there for more than a few seconds before taking a deep breath and turning off the engine. His hands were clammy and the car, despite the coolness of the day, had grown almost unbearably hot. He couldn't stay in any longer, but he could barely force himself out of the vehicle. *Lord, please give me the strength to do this.* What would he do if she didn't want to be an intricate part of his life anymore?

He got out of the car, shutting the door behind him. Well, it wouldn't be the first time… He waited for a couple of cars to go by, then jogged across the street and up to the walkway leading into her apartment building. *Yeah, but she isn't Myra. She has a heart…yours.*

He shook his head, trying to clear any thoughts that would get in the way of him being open-minded enough to listen to her without screaming his denial if she said something he didn't want to hear.

The next thing he knew, he was standing in front of her door. *Just go ahead and knock. All of this waiting is only making it worse. You don't even know how she feels yet. And if she is standing on the other side of the door looking at you through the peephole, you are only giving her more reasons to walk away. Do it. Knock.* The self-deprecating pep talk did its job and he finally raised his fist to knock, when it opened. *Told you.*

He cleared his throat then wished he hadn't when his mouth ran dry at the image in front of him. He couldn't remember a more beautiful sight than the one before him. The light from her living room windows framed her, casting her into a silhouette, momentarily causing her to glow. He blinked a couple of times, thinking this was just another trick his eyes and mind were playing on him. *Man I have it bad.*

"Brandon?"

Her voice, warmer than he expected, pulled him from his thoughts and into the present. He stuck his hands in his pockets, hoping to warm them and dry them at the same time.

"Hi." He was pleasantly surprised to find that his voice was steadier than he felt.

Paige moved back from the doorway, allowing him to enter.

She was dressed in a red sweater dress with one oversized collar folding down, the tip resting in the middle of her chest. Even though the hem reached her knees she wore black leggings. Her feet were encased in flat black slippers.

Ordinarily he would have hugged her, but with so many big questions between them, he didn't want to overstep any invisible lines she may have drawn.

"Hi," she returned on a sigh.

Oh, that's not good. He glanced around the room as he tried working the lump back out of his throat.

"Come, sit." She motioned for him to follow her further into the living room. She turned slightly. "Would you like something to drink? I have water, juice, eggnog…" She allowed the sentence to fade when he began shaking his head in the negative.

She took a seat at the far end of the couch, clutching a throw pillow to her midsection. He followed suit, sitting on the opposite end, wondering how one conversation brought so much distance between them.

"How are you doing…feeling?" she asked, looking at him as though seeing him for the first time.

"Good…good." He took his hands out of his pockets, rubbing them along his thighs. She glanced down at the movement then back to his face. Her eyes were intense and he could do nothing but allow her to inspect him, because for the life of him he couldn't think of anything to say.

The silence stretched on for a full minute before she spoke, her words tripping over his as they both hastily tried to fill the quiet of the room.

"I want to…"

"Dominy wanted me…"

He grinned at her sheepishly, willing himself to calm down. He inclined his head, so she would continue.

"I wanted to tell you that Mel, Gladys, Marc, Vivian and Mason…the whole gang wishes you a Merry Christmas. I spoke to the girls while they opened their presents this morning." He watched her eyes light up. "They were even more excited than I thought they'd be, considering…" She trailed off, becoming engrossed in the fringes on the edge of the throw blanket lying on the back of the couch.

"Considering what?" He pulled her back into the conversation. "I thought they were great presents, especially since I helped you pick them out." They'd taken a whole day to shop for presents for their families a couple of weeks before. Brandon, who had nieces and nephews ranging from thirteen months-old to fourteen-years-old, stayed online from the beginning of November to Thanksgiving looking for the most requested gifts for the different age groups.

He was the one that gave her the idea of gift cards, because most tween girls liked the idea of shopping for themselves if they didn't do it already.

"…Considering Mason gave us iPads for Christmas."

Everything stopped like a needle being lifted off of a vinyl album with shaky fingers. An eerie silence engulfed him for a couple of seconds, then upon his next breath, his ears were accosted by the sound of his erratic heartbeat.

"He bought your whole family iPads?" he asked with stilted breath.

She hesitated a second too long for his comfort. She looked away then quickly back at him. "No, just Vivian, Gladys, and myself so that we can video chat."

He thought about her answer for a moment, trying to reason above the heat in his chest. He couldn't blame Mason for trying to use Vivian to keep her close. He didn't know that he wouldn't try anything he could to gain her affections if she had chosen differently…well unless God said otherwise – but Mason wasn't listening to God.

He hated the insecurity he'd created in their relationship by not telling her about his illness sooner. Almost as much as he hated the guilt. "When did you get yours?"

She hugged her pillow to her. "I got it this morning. My neighbor gave it to me while I was on the phone with Vivian. Seems Mel has been busy. She talked my next door neighbor into holding my gift after Mason sent it last week." She shook her head slightly. "You know, sometimes I marvel at her ability to keep a secret."

Brandon thought about it for a moment. "She doesn't really seem like the type of person that keeps secrets though. She's always so open, like at the hospital when she was sharing pictures of Gladys and talking about your lives."

"That's what I mean," Paige said slowly, "She's disarming. I love my sister dearly; I owe her a great deal. I wouldn't have the chance I have with Gladys and Vivian without her, but we were only as close as my mother allowed when we were growing up.

We didn't start getting close until after I told her I was pregnant. I don't mean to sound as though I don't trust her; I do with my life, but I spoke to her this morning for almost an hour and she never even hinted at knowing I had a present waiting from Mason."

"It was supposed to be a surprise, Paige," he said from too far away, wanting to comfort her with any touch she would allow.

She shrugged, trying to shake off the heavy thoughts then turned moist, frightened eyes towards him. This time he did move, crossing the length of the couch, erasing any space between them.

He placed his hand on her forearms wrapped around the pillow. "What is it?" Then mistaking her hesitancy, he dove in. "Look, I know I should have told you sooner, but there is no need to be afraid. My last tests came back with positive results. The best yet. I promise not to keep anything from you from now on. I just…I just…needed some time. Time to let you get to know me as me, Brandon, the healthy, confident, God-fearing man who you could see a future with. Not the one with this disease-ridden body. It's just a body, but I'm still me. I promise…"

She began to shake her head and reached out to place her palm to his cheek, her thumb resting on his lips to silence them. He was arrested.

"You are all of that, but your soul and spirit are housed in that beautiful body of yours and the whole of you means a lot to me; however, that wasn't what I was thinking about." She took a deep breath, placing pressure on his lips when he would have spoken, keeping him silent.

"Grace is in Atlanta. She showed up at Mel's house yesterday."

Brandon took her hand, removing it from his face, but keeping it in his. "Grace, your mother, is at your sister's house? Why? When did she tell you?"

"That's just the thing. Mel told me today that Grace is visiting until after the New Year's. She is staying at some hotel with her fiancé. They're supposed to be getting married on New Year's Eve. She asked Mel to be her maiden of honor. She knew it would send me into outer space, but not for the reason she was expecting."

"What do you mean?" Brandon began rubbing her knuckles with the pad of his thumb in a soothing motion. He didn't like the vulnerability he saw in her eyes.

"Mel isn't going to stop Gladys from talking about Vivian. Grace will know that I found out my other twin is alive." He couldn't place why such a thing would cause her bottom lip to tremble. He took her now cold hand in both of his, using friction to warm it.

"Victoria told me that Grace tried to blackmail her when she found out Victoria was doing family history research on Vivian. She said she threatened to take Vivian away if Victoria didn't pay her."

"What happened?" Brandon asked, struggling with the conversation on a whole. He couldn't see what Paige saw in Victoria or why she continued to stay in communication with the spiteful, vindictive woman.

She shook her head. "I'm not completely sure. She refused to finish telling me and said that I should ask Grace." She gave an unladylike snort. "That's not going to happen."

"I know your relationship with your…Grace is strained, but don't you think it is worth talking to her to find out what really happened when you delivered the twins?" He moved his body into her line of sight, leaning into her so that she would look at him, but he was not prepared for the desperate despair in her eyes when she looked up to meet his gaze.

She shook her head, a broken "no," barely audible, escaping her lips. He came forward, hugging her as close as he could, given the awkward position they were in.

He sighed in relief when she didn't pull away, but laid her head on his shoulder. He could do this for her. He could comfort her, pray for her…protect her. He could do this if she let him.

"Shhh. It'll be all right," he cooed. "We don't have to talk about it now. It's Christmas! We should fill it with thoughts of happiness."

He thought he felt her lips widen beneath his jaw, but figured he was mistaken when she pulled back, eyelashes starred with fresh tears.

"We need to talk, Brandon." Her expression was serious, but he could read no more than that.

"I have something for you." He reached into his coat pocket, retrieving a gaily wrapped rectangular package. He held it out to her and waited for her to take it from his hand. "I'm not trying to change the subject, but I would like you to open it now."

"Why?" She cocked her head to the side and peered at him expectantly.

"Because I don't know if you will let me later?"

She stared at him and, for a moment, he thought she would start crying again. But her golden eyes cleared as if the storm had passed, and the smile he thought he'd sacrificed shone brightly before him.

She took the present from him and began to unwrap it in earnest pieces of metallic-colored paper falling to the floor next to the bright blue bow. Her hands went still when she got to the royal blue, velvet jeweler's box. She looked up at him then back down at the box twice before she opened it slowly.

Once she peered at what lay inside she gasped, and he was almost afraid she didn't like it.

"I figured no matter what you decided, it was yours."

She took a deep breath, letting it out slowly. She shook her head, never taking her eyes off of the golden heart pendant on the gold chain, laying on a bed of royal blue silk.

"You don't play fair, Brandon." Her voice was a mere whisper, but it vibrated through him, chasing away that last piece of hope. He was lost.

She began speaking slowly, still staring at the pendant. "I wanted to thank you for coming early. I didn't mean to take you away from your family. We just left so many things unsaid yesterday and I...I didn't want to meet your family with so much insecurity between us. They are bound to wonder."

The heavy weight that had been attached to his heart quickly lost 50 pounds. "You're going to come?"

Paige looked up at him frowning slightly, but nodded her head in confirmation.

He couldn't help but smile.

"I just couldn't... you know...walk in there with them...with you, feeling the way I do about this. It already makes me nervous about meeting your family, but the uncertainty would make it unbearable. I didn't want to be the only one that didn't...know; didn't know what happened then...what's happening now..."

She looked up at him, pleading with her eyes for understanding. It seemed she was having just as much of a challenge expressing her feelings as he was. His relief quickly gave away to guilt for putting her through this.

He nodded his understanding meekly.

"I want to know, Brandon. I want to know about your first bout with cancer from the moment you were diagnosed through each session of chemo and radiation. The same with this time. I want you to tell me everything since you found out; each thought and feeling you can remember having. I want to know it all, Brandon." She shook her head to emphasize her next sentence. "No more secrets between us. No more holding back, because I have to be able to trust you."

He swallowed hard, realizing what she was asking and what she was saying. He nodded. "I'll tell you everything."

She gave a curt nod, handing him the box then turning her back to him so he could place the necklace around her neck. Once he clasped it, she got up and walked to the mirror by the door, staring at her reflection. She placed her hand on the heart, fingering it lightly. She turned back to him, crossing to stand in front of him. As he stood up, he was struck by the brilliance shining from her eyes.

"It fits." She smiled up at him, giving his words back to him.

"It's yours for as long as you want it." He knew he was revealing a great deal, but most of his cards were already on the table, and she did say she wanted to know everything.

Her lips came together and her eyes darkened just before she rose on her tiptoes so she could wrap her arms around his neck to pull his lips to hers.

Forever was the only word that reverberated through his mind for a few seconds before there was nothing left but to feel.

CHAPTER 7

Victoria smoothed a stray hair into place before taking an overall assessment of her features and dress in the full-length mirror. She ran an appreciative eye over the figure in the reflection. She couldn't be more than ten pounds heavier than she was when she and Richard first got married if that.

She ran her hands along the sides of her wool dress that skimmed her slender figure to the hips, then flared out slightly, the skirt hem swinging slightly as she walked. Richard had always liked her in this dress.

Richard. The thought of him left her feeling momentarily at a loss. Though he'd retreated from his original threat of divorce to marriage counseling, she couldn't help the feelings of unease at the distance in his eyes and actions towards her. He had not tried to touch her once after yesterday morning, even when she'd proposed that he stay and bring in Christmas Day with her later that evening. He had rebuffed her advance, leaving her feeling even more insecure about their relationship – and Victoria did not do insecure well.

If she hadn't had him trailed, she might have thought he was going back to his apartment to meet a woman, but there was no trace of any indiscretions. She snorted delicately. He was more saintly than many of the local preachers who had solicited for funds from her foundation in the past two years.

Maybe he doesn't love you anymore. She berated herself, shaking her head against the absurd direction of her thoughts. She lifted her chin slightly, waving her hand as if swatting at a pest. She glanced once more at herself before leaving the room to go downstairs to make sure preparations for Christmas supper were underway.

She had just walked into the kitchen when the house phone began to ring. Martha picked it up, greeting the person on the other line with familiarity then asked them to hold.

"Mr. Richard would like to speak to you." She held out the receiver to Victoria.

Her heart began to pound before she curbed the nervous reaction. Was he calling to tell her he wasn't coming? She squeezed the receiver tightly as if her hold on it could keep him close. She would not betray her feelings though.

"Merry Christmas, Richard." She congratulated herself on her dry tone.

"Merry Christmas, Victoria. I am sorry about the late notice, but I would like to invite a few people to join us for Christmas Supper. Would that be all right?"

The relief she felt caused her to sag briefly against the counter.

"Mmmm. I believe that can be arranged. How many are you thinking of?" So much for an intimate Christmas meal. She pressed her lips together to keep from expelling a frustrated sigh. He was taking her through changes, but she would concede this time.

"Is twelve too many?" His voice held that same quietness it did when he expected her to sound off. She took a deep breath and closed her eyes.

"Victoria, if it is too much I could..."

"No Richard, it's fine. You know we always have more than enough to share, but could you give us a little more time? Maybe we can serve hors d'oeuvres until the meal is ready. By the way, who are our guests?"

"Just some friends I ran into after church service this morning, along with Sam Wetherston, his wife, Kate, and Paul Ambross and his wife, Mary."

Sam and Paul had accompanied Richard to Uganda. The three were running buddies. She was somewhat less acquainted with Kate and Mary, meeting them only on a couple of occasions when Richard had events she couldn't wiggle out of. They were decent enough, but they moved in different circles.

"Okay Richard, it's not like you don't live here too. You should have a say on how we spend our Christmas. I'm sorry I didn't ask sooner. It was thoughtless of me." Translation: Don't I have a say on how we spend Christmas? I haven't seen you in months, and you want to spend it with all of these people when we should be working on our marriage. Did you not think about me?

"Um...okay...Are you sure?" He sounded hesitant and just a little suspicious.

"Yes, I am sure. Let me go so that I can start preparations. See you at two o'clock?"

"Perfect."

She hung up the phone and turned toward Martha, who was waiting expectantly.

She shrugged. "Martha it looks like we will be having guests. Richard has invited about twelve guests for dinner. Prepare for twenty-five. Instead of the duck, we can serve game hens and tell Taylor to see if Michael's on Automum Street has a roast or a ham." She paused for a moment, fighting the wave of disappointment that passed through her throat on its way to her heart.

"We will use the main dining room. Take the family stockings off of the fireplace mantel and use the ones we reserve for any last minute guests. Tell Thelma I will need her to stay however long it takes to set the table, pack the stockings, and freshen up a few of the guest bedrooms. No telling what Richard has planned. I'll be upstairs for a bit then I will be in my study."

Martha nodded in compliance then watched as Victoria walked from the kitchen. She was going to have to pray a little harder. *If the look on Mrs. Victoria's face was any indication, even though the thermostat read at a comfortable 70 degrees Fahrenheit in the house, it would be frosty by the end of the night.*

"Merry Christmas to me," she mumbled to herself as she went about making preparations for the changes in the evening's events.

After changing into a winter white, cashmere sweater and dress slacks of the same color, Victoria pulled her hair into twists at the nape of her neck and went to her study to make a couple of calls.

The first was to her granddaughter, Vivian, who was preoccupied with one of the new devices Mason had given to her. They spoke for a little bit, with Vivian thanking her for the beautiful opal necklace she'd sent her and updating her on some of her newest friends.

Victoria was surprised to hear that she was spending so many nights over her neighbor's house. Mason wasn't usually one to let her out of his sight. They hung up after promising to get together closer to the new year. Victoria called a few more relatives, wishing them a Merry Christmas just to keep the lines of communication open.

The last call she made before taking care of some much-needed business was to Paige, but it went to her voicemail. She wished her a wonderful day and thanked her again for the photo books on the most beautiful gardens in the world and a stunning pendant in the form of a cherub holding a rose. It was unique, and Victoria loved having things others couldn't find.

She glanced at the clock, knowing her husband and his guests would be there shortly. She picked up the receiver, dialing the next number by heart. She had a hunch about some things concerning Mason, and wanted some answers.

"Mike, I hope you have some good news for me because I need something to salvage this Christmas," she said by way of greeting.

"Actually, I was just about to call you. It may interest you that Mason is soaking himself again."

"Oh really? Yes I do find that very interesting. Are there any witnesses? How often does he do this?"

"Lately it seems to be more frequent. He patronizes this little bar within walking distance. At least he is being responsible enough not to try and get behind the wheel of a car.

Anyway, I have logged him at an average of once a week. In the beginning he would wait until Vivian spent the night with her school friend a few doors down, but last night must have been particularly rough because he actually hired a babysitter."

Victoria's lips lifted at the corners ever so slightly. It looked like Mason would be handing over Vivian before the school year was over and all she had to do was sit and wait for him to continue to destroy any chances he may have to fight for her. It was truly beginning to look a lot like Christmas.

"Mmmm, Merry Christmas indeed," Victoria murmured. It was the closest she would come to showing gratitude. His paycheck and small bonus could say it a great deal better.

"Is there anything else?"

"Umm, yes, but it may take some of the light out of your day."

She sighed; she knew it wouldn't last. "All right. What is it?"

"Grace Morganson-Dillard, soon to be Grace Morganson-Dillard-Ross, is in Atlanta."

"Damn." She was hoping to have a little more time before that woman found out about Vivian. "By that extra little hyphen, I am to surmise that she is in town to tie the knot again?"

"Exactly."

This definitely took some of the cheer out of her holiday. Not like there was much to begin with. She was going to have to take what she could get.

"Is that it?"

"One more thing."

"Well, get to it."

"Paige's friend, Brandon, has cancer of the liver."

Her breath caught for a moment. "What stage?"

"Stage 3. He went in rather early this time. His last test came back favorable."

Victoria dared to breathe, though hesitantly.

"That's it for now." Mike sounded almost sorry to have to report the last bit of news.

"Alright. I will talk to you Tuesday. Are you any closer to getting information on that other project regarding Grace?"

"I think I got a break with one of the administrative assistants at State General in Colorado Springs. I will have the information for you by Tuesday."

"Very good. Good night, Michael."

"Merry Christmas, Mrs. Lanning."

Victoria ended the call without responding. Each time he used the alias she had given him over the phone, she was relieved that she had the forethought not to give him her true identity.

She released the receiver and dialed another number as she glanced at the clock on the desk. It rang four times before the person picked up the line.

"Yes."

"The fates are smiling on you, or just think of it as a Christmas present. I am going to give you the chance to make things right."

There was a moment of silence then, "Tell me what I have to do."

Though she was the only one in the room, Victoria spoke in hushed tones while rendering instructions. By the time she placed the receiver back in its cradle, there was a wider smile on her face and she almost gave into the impulse to hum a festive tune. Almost.

*   *   *

Later that evening, after the guests had either left or been shown to one of the guest bedrooms, Victoria sat in her sitting room with an updated guest list for the Wing Cup Annual Gala. Even though many parts of the country were experiencing economic limitations due to the recession, it looked like her event was going to beat last year's attendance record. *Rachael would be proud.*

Her mind began to wander back to the evening's dinner guests, particularly Mary Ambross and Kate Wetherston. Both were a pleasant surprise and even though she didn't want to admit it; they reminded her of herself – a decade of hurt ago.

Mary Ambross, at 5'5 with her curly, jet black hair that brushed the middle of her back, possessed a dry humor that took Victoria more than a few minutes to understand. She was so sure the beautiful woman with the olive complexion was pious.

How could she not be? It was only natural for her to be overwhelmed by self-importance when she could show how big her heart could be by sacrificing the luxuries of home while visiting third world countries with the intent of introducing the people to a few of the more modern amenities, like clean running water and a pallet to lie on.

Kate was a little over average in beauty and height. She stood at 5'9, towering slightly over Victoria's own 5'7. Where Victoria had a warm cream complexion, Kate's coloring reminded her of a mocha latte. Her skin almost looked like velvet, and Victoria was tempted to ask what line of cosmetics she used.

Kate was quiet and almost too observant, but when she spoke it was with a confidence and demeanor that bespoke her experience and work as one of the top editors in the state.

Victoria found herself reluctantly impressed with both of them.

After Mary's first comment about her initial experience in sleeping out in the bushes of Uganda on one of her trips with her husband, Paul, Victoria thought the woman a closet complainer trying to pass as a self-righteous, sacrificing Christian. By the end of the meal, she found that she had grossly misjudged Mary and was giving more than just an idle thought of inviting her to lunch.

It was during their second course, with Victoria working hard not to show her disdain for the lack of etiquette practiced by more than a few people at the table. Mary, catching her slight frown and quite aware of the last minute increase in dinner guests, was moved to assuage the hostess' feelings.

"Victoria," her soft voice ringing through the room, passing through three dinners to Victoria's left. "You are either a woman with a huge heart, or a fortune teller." Conversation around the table ceased and Victoria witnessed a small yet quick shift in Mary's body, attesting to the fact that Paul had nudged her. This drew her curiosity.

"What has brought you to that conclusion?" Victoria wondered if Mary was going to out Richard in his last-minute attempt to spare some of their guests from a lonely Christmas night.

"Because not even two days ago I was putting together the menu for Christmas Dinner at our home, and all I could think about was roast duck. I mean it was so ingrained in my mind, I could hardly see around it. Paul has accused me often of having tunnel vision.

Well anyway, when we were flooded out, all I could think of was it might be a few more months before I would get to taste what my pallet had been craving for the last six weeks. You have truly gifted me with this culinary delight."

Victoria nodded her acceptance of the gracious show of gratitude. "You said a few more months. Was the damage to your home that extensive?"

"No, the pipe should be fixed and remediation done by the week after next, but since we are going to Kenya the day after the contractor's estimated finish date, I won't have time to have my cook prepare it – and I have a penchant for how he prepares it."

Victoria was momentarily speechless. Richard hadn't told her that he would be leaving again so soon, and not wanting to give away the fact that they had not spoken about it, she simply smiled.

After dessert, Richard invited the guests on a tour of the grounds. Mary and Kate chose to stay behind with Victoria.

"So I take it, Richard didn't tell you about going to Kenya next month?" Mary asked as she sat back in one of the over-stuffed chairs in the salon, a small room off of the larger living room. Victoria watched the sardonic expression play upon her lips and knew that she had found a comrade.

She shook her head to the negative.

"Sam knows that if he wants to keep the peace, he needs to let me know well in advance when he is leaving the country on mission trips, especially if he wants me to go with him," supplied Kate, as she lounged in the chair matching Mary's.

"Do you go with him often?" Victoria asked.

Kate shrugged delicately. "Whenever I can. Our children are grown and doing well. I have my editing firm, but lately I have been taking more of a backseat approach."

"Why?" Victoria asked.

"Why what?" Kate asked.

"Why do you go with him? I mean don't you miss your bed, real food, or air conditioning?" Victoria sat across from the women on her loveseat.

Kate looked at her in curiosity for a moment. "Have you ever gone with Richard on a trip?"

"No."

"Mmmm." Kate nodded. "I think if you accompany him on a trip you will understand."

"Understand what? Being eaten alive by flies and insects I can't even name, overcome by seasickness and food that my stomach revolts against? No thank you."

Kate and Mary exchanged looks.

"You've never talked to Richard about his trips?" Mary turned more towards Victoria.

Victoria shrugged.

"It's so much more than any type of discomfort you might experience for the length of time you are there. Have you never been curious about the regions, people, or culture?"

"I have my own region right here that I have to oversee every day," Victoria said with a blasé attitude.

Mary took a deep breath, letting it out slowly. "From seven to thirty-one days, we are slightly uncomfortable – sometimes – but these people don't get a vacation from no clean water, or walking two miles for food and semi-clean water – when they can find it. They don't get a break from fatal diseases, childhood enslavement, or being orphans."

Victoria started to become defensive. She didn't understand the need to go to the ends of the civilized earth to help people that couldn't seem to help themselves. There were homeless people on the other side of 'H' street. Why travel somewhere and put yourself through a myriad of shots that have the potential to make you sick just so you could go and help sick people when money did the job just as well?

Before she could voice this, Kate began. "The first time I went with the guys to Uganda, I was sick for a day and a half. I was miserable. On the second day, one of the caregivers of the orphanage we were doing excavating for came and placed some poultice on a compress and laid it on my chest. I don't think it was on for more than an hour before I was feeling better, and if that wasn't enough, she prayed for me and kept praying. This woman didn't know me from Eve, but she took care of me with such tender ministrations.

These people's hearts are huge, and I am not going to degrade their love and generosity by saying it's because of their lack of material things or luxuries. I was invited to a worship service with her the next day. For the first half hour I was floored at how they praised and worshipped with abandon. I had never seen anything like it and I have been going to church for over fifteen years.

I almost felt ashamed by their ability to worship without distraction, and after three hours I was standing right along with them, overcome by the sweetest essence of the Holy Spirit. All I could do was raise my hands in surrender and worship right along with the congregation. In that instant, I began to understand that there wasn't too much I could provide beyond an edifice that could be torn down or clean water that could dry up. They introduced me to something – someone – and I couldn't pay them back for it. After that experience, I have never been the same.

I went there with a big head and an even bigger ego, thinking they would be more than grateful for me to spend some of my precious time with them and share my superior talents, and I left with a newfound faith and a better understanding of what it meant to worship God.

One thing, though: I am finding it harder and harder to sit in church, singing the same hymns, and repeating the same prayers."

"For me," Kate jumped in, "above and beyond the new experiences with different cultures and meeting new people, I have a special love for the children and as tired as I am sometimes at the end of the day, I feel full of purpose.

After my first trip, when Sam and I got home, all I could do was look around our huge, empty house and wonder why the things that seemed so important before I left seemed so insignificant then. It will change your life."

Victoria sat there glancing back and forth between the two women, wondering if it was really all they were making it out to be. For the first time since Richard had started going on his trips, she was curious about what he did.

        *   *   *

Richard passed in front of her, pulling her out of her thoughts. He sat in a club chair across from her with his elbows resting on his thighs.

Victoria watched him, and her heart went out to him even as she tried to ignore it. He looked tired.

She laid her paperwork down and faced him.

He took a deep breath, looking away and then back at her.

"I want to thank you, Vickie, for today."

She shrugged, feigning nonchalance.

He watched her intently for a moment as if he were trying to look through her. "I want to apologize for the late notice. I know it wasn't what you'd planned for our Christmas together."

"It's okay." *If I am gracious about this maybe I can indebt him to me.*

"No it's not, but I want to make it up to you."

"Really?" She tried to keep her excitement from showing. She lifted an eyebrow, letting him know she was curious.

"I know things have been really rocky between us, but I want to get back to that place before we began withdrawing from each other. I'm not trying to punish you Victoria, but I won't stand being manipulated either." He reached out to enfold her hands in his.

"I was thinking we could take a small ride up to Roseland, have lunch, and do a little shopping."

She blinked a few times, certain she'd misunderstood him, but the look of expectancy didn't leave his face.

"Yes, absolutely. I would like that very much." She couldn't keep the breathlessness out of her voice. Things were looking up.

CHAPTER 8

Mason laid back in his recliner closest to the sliding glass door leading to the balcony. With his head resting on his forearms that were crossed behind him, he worked his shoulders up and down as he stared out at a robin taking a bath in the small fountain Vivian had convinced him to buy last year. A few more birds joined it to take advantage of an early morning bath.

He watched them for a long time while hoping to gain some insight or encouragement from their interaction. If not, he would at least find a few moments of peace as he finally surrendered to the thoughts he had battled against for the last two months.

He realized yesterday after speaking with Paige that the harder he tried to exorcise her from his mind, the more he struggled with unfinished thoughts and conversations he cut himself off from having about her on his brain.

The chime of the clock drew his attention and he sighed, enjoying the feeling of not being rushed or sitting underneath a list of obligations. It was just now five-thirty in the morning and Vivian, who had stayed up until 11 p.m. the night before video-chatting with Paige and then Gladys, wasn't due to make an appearance until late morning at the earliest.

He took a few deep breaths and allowed his mind to wander back a few weeks to the last conversation they'd had regarding any type of relationship outside of their communicating for Vivian's sake.

He'd intercepted a call Paige was making to Vivian on the house line because it was the only way he could legitimize their conversation, given the fact that she wouldn't answer his calls directly.

They'd gotten through the niceties and he knew she was hoping he would then hand the phone over to Vivian; instead, he moved forward and asked her something that had been laying on his heart and mind since she'd left the rehabilitation center in Chicago.

"Paige, I think I understand a little of why you believe things should be this way between us, but if I ask you a question, would you be honest with me no matter how you think it will affect me?"

He could hear her light breathing on the other line. He knew she was hesitating, but he couldn't stand this limbo. He needed to know what she would say if he tried everything he knew to say and do. He needed to know if there was anything he could do to win her, or if she held any feelings for him at all. What he wasn't prepared for was the absolute feelings of hopelessness her answers would cause him.

"Alright, Mason. I will answer your questions, but I need you to respect my answers for what they are."

"Okay," he said, only too relieved that she conceded.

"Paige, I need to know if you have at any time felt more for me than just friendship or gratitude for initiating the reunion of you and Vivian"

"Mason..." she began in a pleading tone that he quickly cut off.

"You said you would tell me, Paige."

"I just don't see why it matters."

"It matters to me."

He was met with more silence, and then she blew out a slow breath.

"Mason, I think you are the type of father many children wished they had. The love, affection, and adoration you show Vivian is to be commended. She is truly fortunate."

"Paige." He said her name as a warning to his mounting frustration and waning patience.

"Mason, I admire your strength and your ability to love as strongly as you do even with the effects Rachael's death has had upon you. I believe Vivian has more than most children do with two parents because of the time and effort you give in nurturing her and making her feel safe. I don't think us being together is essential to her wellbeing and esteem, so I don't see where my feelings or thoughts of you have any relevance."

Was she reneging on her word? What a...

"But, I told you I would answer your questions honestly. When I first met you, I admit that I felt things I have never felt towards any other man, but it was physical, and I won't let my body rule my actions."

"So you're saying that all you feel for me is some strong attraction?"

She huffed, sounding frustrated. "No good could come from you knowing these things."

"Indulge me, and I will decide."

"In the beginning, yes, but as I spent more time with you and got to know you better, I found that I really enjoyed your company and came to appreciate your friendship."

"Friendship? Is that as far as it goes? You don't want anything more from me?"

"I don't think you are capable of giving me what I would need."

There was silence on the other line that built to an uncomfortable level.

"Mason?"

"Are you talking about God?" He felt his heartbeat kick up a notch.

"He is my whole world. To try and have a relationship without Him being in the middle would only lead to heartache."

"But why couldn't we have worked up to that? You don't think you weren't being the least discriminating?"

She was quiet for a moment. "Absolutely, and that is my prerogative. No matter what I felt when you were near me, there were and still are things I need to be able to express and be given that you can't give me. I have had one-night-stands and month-long affairs and they didn't work because the most important part of me wasn't given the right attention. I left them feeling empty, hopeless, and resenting the person I was with them because they couldn't fulfill the part of me that was crying out for attention. There are too many variables to our relationship for me to consider acting in such an irresponsible manner.

In my relationship with God, I was able to find a place of solace and peace that went deeper than the physical. It filled me in a place where I was empty for far too long. I didn't even know it existed until I came to know myself; I need someone that will understand that, touching me. Paige doesn't begin with the physical, but ends with it. I have had dreams of having my soul caressed and embraced and I don't want to give that up. The physical is only one way to communicate, but I want to be with someone that I can communicate with on all levels of my being. I have been given that promise.

I love myself too much to settle for only one piece of the equation in a relationship that is supposed to embrace all of us, and I will not cheat you by allowing you to settle with me. There is so much to you that is lovable and precious, but you won't acknowledge half of it, and I will not put myself in a position where I can't show affection, encouragement, and edify that part of you openly.

I need to be able to express my love in all its facets, otherwise it will begin to kill me slowly from the inside out, and I will begin to resent you and hate me."

"You seem so sure of this. How do you know that I wouldn't change? How do you know your love wouldn't be the catalyst and bridge in the gap in my relationship with God?"

"Why can't you do that without me?"

He didn't have an answer, so she kept going.

"I can't be your main motivation for going to God. As flattering as that can be, I will not hinder the potential of your walk with Him by being some type of conduit. Your need for Him has to be your main purpose for beginning a relationship with Him. I couldn't have that on my heart if something were to happen to me or if we were to break up. I would need to know that your relationship with God eclipsed anything we could have because as beautifully as I have seen you love your daughter, I would need more. I need the assurance of your trust in Him to guide me."

"Is that the reason you picked Brandon over me? Because he has a relationship with God?"

"It is really none of your business, but I am going to tell you because I don't want you to have any misconceptions. It was never about choosing between you and Brandon. It was about me walking in God's perfect will. My main concern was making sure I stayed open and quiet enough to hear Him over what I wanted."

"What did you want? Who did you want?" He asked before he thought of whether or not he wanted to know.

Her voice was overly soft. "I won't answer that question."

"But you said…"

"I think I have already said enough. Besides, I have answered all of your other questions. I believe we should just let it rest."

"Paige…"

"Mason, don't you long for peace? Don't you need a break from some of the anger you try to survive on?"

"Yes and I thought I'd found a way to do that with you, but you are running from me – from what we could have – and I think your real reason is that I don't fit into your perfect world." He knew as soon as he said it he had gone too far, but he was frustrated by her calm demeanor and her impassionate speech that told him there was no place in her life for him beyond being Vivian's father, and he wasn't ready to let it be. He couldn't. "I'm sorry, that was unfair."

There was a moment of quiet before Paige spoke. "Is that what you really think of me?"

He heard the hurt in her voice, and berated himself for causing it. "No, but you are so much more distant now and you've placed God in between us like a shield. You leave no room for me to argue my case."

"That's just it Mason, God isn't the force that is keeping us apart. He is the one that brought us together. Just not the way you want."

He heard her inhale deeply, knowing that she was about to say something important, but once again wary of the outcome of what knowledge it would bring.

"I treasure you and our friendship, Mason. I treasure you not just because you brought my daughter back into my life, but because of you. I treasure your friendship, your loyalty, your candor, your courage, and your ability to survive. I admire the depth that you love – I just wish it was stronger than your anger."

He felt as if he'd been punched in the stomach. It took a moment for him to catch his breath, to find the words that would negate her last statement and allow her to see them as a possibility.

"You're wrong; I can prove it. I will prove it."

"Mason, no, don't do it for me. It's too late for us. I've made my choice. Augh, God, I'm so sorry," she said, in a whisper he knew she didn't mean for him to hear. "Mason, I'm sorry. I didn't answer your questions to give you hope for the two of us. I thought it would help you to see that we aren't compatible in that way. I was being honest with you and how I feel about you, but it won't change anything."

"But Paige, if you would just listen-"

She interrupted him again. "Mason, tell Vivian I will call her back after she comes in from school. Have a good day. I need to go. Goodbye, Mason."

"Good…" There was no need to finish, she'd already hung up.

Mason rubbed his eyes then refocused on the sun peaking over the horizon. She had made her choice, whether it was *God,* as she put it, or Brandon; it wasn't him, and he needed to move on.

He just didn't have the slightest idea of how he was supposed to do that without the aid of Jack. He knew his drinking had gotten a little out of hand lately, and he was determined to keep his tentative resolution to concentrate more on Vivian, and less on the unfairness of it all.

He didn't know how long he'd reclined there, going over the conversation in his head, trying to press it into the space in his mind next to all the other loss, but the next time the clock gained his attention with its chiming, there were seven bells.

He knew Vivian would be getting up soon, and he wanted to put on a serene face for her even if it couldn't be a happy one. After her video chat with her mom and sister, he would take her to breakfast and then to the Winter WonderFest at the Navy Pier Chicago for a day of fun. Maybe he would allow her to invite a couple of her friends so that he could continue to work Paige from his thoughts. He needed to do whatever would make him want her less and think about her only when her name came through his daughter's lips.

CHAPTER 9

Friday morning, Paige set the receiver down in its cradle for the fourth time in the last 30 minutes. How hard could it be? Just pick up the phone, dial, and wait for an answer.

Then what?

She leaned forward on the edge of her bed, resting her elbows on her knees, regarding the phone as if it were a threatened python ready to strike. *Maybe if I do this from another room...* Before the thought was finished, she was up and moving towards the office, but even before she passed the threshold, she knew she didn't want to have any memories regarding her upcoming call attached to anything in this room. It would make it almost impossible to work. She thought about the living room, but that was a no go. She finally decided that this call was going to have to take place outside of her sanctuary.

She knew she was making a big deal about placing this call, but except for Victoria's mention of Grace's plotting and scheming and the Christmas call four days prior with Melanie, she had not heard Grace's name, let alone talked to her, in many years. It had been just long enough for her to form a more objective opinion of the woman she used to call mother.

As she donned a pair of wool slacks, she thought of where she could make the call that wouldn't haunt her. She thought of the park, but that place was now tied to memories of Brandon and she wasn't willing to share. Her thoughts moved uninhibited to him, the source of the smile that crept unheeded to her lips.

She was propelled back to Christmas day, after they'd finished their talk and cleared some of the air between them. From her standpoint, it was magical. She didn't necessarily like that word, but she was hard-pressed to think of another description for the overwhelming feelings of warmth and welcome she was surrounded by the moment Brandon helped her from the car.

As if they'd been watching from the window, the family began to file out of the apartment, causing Paige's eyes to widen as the steady stream came forward to hug her. Just how big was Brandon's apartment?

His mother reached her first, embracing her tightly and holding her as if she were a long lost friend instead of a new acquaintance.

"Wow, you are lovely. Brandon has shared a little about you, but I am looking forward to us getting to know each other better. I'm Ava Tatum, the mother of this rambunctious group." Ava's smile was bright against her toffee colored complexion. Her eyes shown like newly-minted pennies as she leaned back, taking Paige's hand in hers.

Paige was struck dumb by emotion at being so readily accepted into what was beginning to look like a small village still trickling from Brandon's apartment. She nodded in acquiescence.

Brandon's father stepped forward. "Hello, I'm Elias Tatum, Brandon's father." He clasped her hand then pulled her into a hug as well. At that moment she knew what Brandon would look like when he turned 50. Even more handsome, distinguished, and more strongly built – if that were possible. What exactly had Brandon told his family about her to cause them to greet her with such graciousness?

Brandon caught her eye between being enveloped by his father and eldest brother, Elias Jr., sending her a silent plea for understanding. She tried to relax so that she could play her association game and have a fighting chance at remembering which names went with which faces.

What struck Paige deeply was the warmth and open acceptance from the eldest to the youngest. She knew her emotions were on display as her eyes grew blurry with tears from young Reina's hug. She'd had to kneel down to receive the embrace from Theodore and Everzie's beautiful little girl and was rewarded by a tight squeeze from the five-year-old that made her long for all the missed hugs from her own children.

She then received hugs of welcome from Sara Tatum-Connor, her husband, Samuel, and their four children; Makayla Tatum and her fiancé, Brice Westin; Marjorie Tatum-Brown, who also held her tight and longer than was customary, her husband, Paul, and their two girls.

At the end of the line, Brandon's mother reclaimed her by placing her arm around Paige's shoulders and ushering her to Brandon's apartment, with Brandon following behind.

Even before they got close to the door the different aromas reached out to her, teasing her senses, causing her mouth to water while she tried to remember the last time she'd eaten.

"Brandon, leave me with this beautiful woman. You can have her back later." Brandon hesitated for a few seconds, looking as if he were going to argue with his mother then relented by asking Paige for her coat.

The women followed Ava and Paige into the kitchen that was a great deal more spacious than her own and the men retired to the living room where Paige was sure Brandon would be headed to for his interrogation.

The kitchen was silent with expectant expressions on the faces of the women. Paige watched as Ava sat down at the breakfast nook, making herself comfortable while others also took chairs and leaned against the countertop. Paige took a deep breath and a seat, preparing herself for what she was sure would be an inquisition.

The questions started being launched by Ava, who wanted to get her side of the story of how they'd met and how she knew she had feelings for him. Paige, having been warned that Brandon's mother was straightforward and tenacious as a pit bull, latched onto an armchair to help anchor her nerves.

"Whatever you do, don't try to avoid the question. She will only question you until you give up more information than you would have by just answering her question in the first place," Brandon had said when she'd asked if she should be nervous about meeting his family.

Paige took another deep breath and began by sharing her first meeting with Brandon and their shared impressions of one another. Hers of him being arrogant, and his of her being spoiled and rebellious. The women shared what Paige took as a covert look amongst them, but when they didn't share, she went on.

She shared her version of their first lunch with the Elder's group and her resolve to give him the benefit of the doubt regarding his character after talking to him out in the parking lot.

In an answer to Ava's second question, she replayed for them the night the Elder's fellowship went bowling and he picked her – after Dominy, of course – to be on his team. She thought back to that night many times, and was convinced that it was then that her feelings shifted from friendship to the hope of something more.

She then shared her time in Chicago when she woke up to him praying and cajoling her. She recounted the moments she woke up in the hospital to hear him speaking to her in such an endearing fashion, she thought maybe she was dreaming. It was his voice that drove her to the surface, wanting to know if it was real or a figment of her imagination.

"What did he say?" Sara…or was it Everzie…well, one of the younger women asked. Paige hesitated, wondering how much she wanted to share with these women. Her memories of Brandon's impassioned prayers and pleadings for her to wake up so that he could see her beautiful eyes were treasures she was fiercely protective of.

"It wasn't so much what he said, but how he said it. It was his voice that seemed to draw me out from the dark place I was in. It didn't cause me to feel anxious in the place I was in, but it coaxed and lulled me out, guiding me to him. He continued to pray for me and hold my hand, squeezing it softly until I felt compelled to respond to him." She looked up from the counter where she'd stared unseeing, lost in the moment of the deep pull of his voice and the pressure of his hand. Everyone's breath seemed to have caught in their throats, hanging on to her words. She glanced from one face to another, trying to force her neck and face to stay cool, but it was to no avail. The tips of her ears pronounced the telltale sign of her blush.

Dreamy-eyed Sara spoke first, breaking the silence that was beginning to crowd the room. "I didn't know Brandon had it in him to be so romantic. He must like you a lot."

Paige couldn't help the smile that crept to her lips. "I accused him of the same thing when I was finally able to open my eyes and get a full sentence out."

Makayla's eyes rounded. "What did he say?

Paige, unable to stop the giggle that passed through her lips, replied, "He just shrugged his shoulders and said 'Aaaaaaa' like he couldn't care less that I'd overheard him."

Makayla placed her hand over her heart and sighed. "It's so beautiful. You in bed, recovering from a devastating mishap, on the edge of consciousness, and my brother, the knight in shining armor, pulling you out of from the depths of darkness with his prayers and pleas…"

Ava came over, placing her arm around the youngest of the Tatum brood. "Never mind all of the pain, slow recovery, and loneliness of being in a strange place alone. Honey, I am going to ask you to come down from that cloud and take the salad out of the refrigerator so that we can finish setting the table. Meanwhile, I am going to go warn Brice that he has his hands full."

The women in the kitchen laughed at Makayla's indignant expression and dispersed, going back to previous duties around the kitchen.

Paige didn't know until that moment just how much Brandon had shared with his family. She felt she was at a disadvantage. She didn't have much time to dwell on that fact, however, because Ava released her daughter and signaled for Paige to follow her to the cutting board at the edge of the countertop. "Here, help me cut up some of this fruit for another salad. Everything is just about done, but I like to give the children a few more options. Most of them like fresh fruits and with all of the sweets they have been consuming, I want to get a jump on satisfying their pallets. Reina will eat little more than anything without fruit in it."

Paige mimicked her movements, relieved by the change in topics and finding the automatic cutting motion relaxing, until Ava leaned over speaking close to her ear. "Do your ears always do that when you blush?"

Paige, caught momentarily off guard, stopped in mid-slice. She looked at the woman that she now knew didn't miss a thing with her keen eyes. "Every time," she answered.

"That must be a nuisance." Ava looked back down at the board.

"You don't know the half of it," Paige breathed.

As Paige sat next to Brandon, watching the interaction between his siblings, parents, and nieces and nephews, Paige couldn't help but feel the slightest twinge of envy. They were such a close-knit family. They razzed each other, lightheartedly. They discussed family milestones, such as the children's first days in school and pop warner wins and losses; anniversaries and pregnancies – the latter being a surprise shared by Everzie and Theodore who were expecting another little boy in the early summer of the following year.

Congratulations, hugs and kisses were exchanged with the expectant couple, while Ava pouted as if she were hurt that they had not told her sooner. Theodore explained that Everzie had been so busy with her real estate business, she didn't know until a few days prior to their visit when she had gone to the doctor to find out why she was having such a hard time shaking the 'flu'.

What touched Paige the most was their ease at including her in all the conversations, no matter how much history they had to give in order to bring her into the present part of the conversation. Not once did she feel like the outsider she considered herself to be in her own family. She could easily come to love these people.

After dinner, they settled in the living room, sitting anywhere they could find a seat. The children happily sat on the floor, content to be within arms-length of the presents. Brandon leaned in close to her and as the night went on, sat on the arm of her chair. She would look up at him from time to time, gauging his reaction to the expressions of his family as they unwrapped presents from him. "Uncle Brandon, here is one for you from Ms. Paige," said Philip, who'd appointed himself as the "present-retriever" as he handed the medium sized package wrapped in navy blue and silver.

Accepting the package, he leaned down to whisper in Paige's ear. "I thought we were going to exchange gifts afterward."

Paige nodded.

"We are. This is just one I wanted to give you now."

He gave her a look that said they would talk about it later.

"No we won't," she said out loud for everyone to hear, "Now stop being stubborn and open you present. Your family is waiting to see what I got you." That brought a round of snickers from his siblings. He ignored them, pulling at the hand-tied bow and pulling down the paper to reveal a leather-bound journal, each page stamped with a different, inspiring scripture. Along with it came a thick bookmark with a small display for digital pictures. He stared at it for a moment.

"So you can keep your family and friends even closer." She watched him intently, hoping he would like this first gift they could share with his family.

"I love it. I am deeply touched that you would put so much thought into this." He glanced at her quickly then stared back down at his gifts, his Adam's apple working furiously as he tried to contain his emotions.

Finally, he just reached out and hugged her hard. "Thank you," he whispered in her ear then just as quickly, released her and began showing his gift to the rest of his family as they'd been doing for the past hour.

In all, Paige had an amazing time with Brandon and his family. They made her feel as if she was already a part of the family, and when Ava hugged her goodbye it felt more like a welcoming home. She would have cried if it weren't for Makayla and Everzie pulling her aside and making her promise to go shopping with them before they went back to Kansas.

"I need a new pair of jeans and I was thinking we could take on the Galleria and the Beverly Center."

Paige's eyes went wide. "What do you know about the Galleria?"

Makayla sucked her teeth. "We do have internet in Kansas, you know."

Paige raised her hands in surrender, laughing at the younger woman's saucy attitude. She was rescued by Brandon who grabbed her by the wrist and began to drag her away from his sister and sister-in-law. "You can have what's left of her vacation time. I have a few places in mind myself."

Paige was slightly puzzled by Brandon's possessive display, but didn't object in front of his family. She waved goodbye, promising to see them again before they left and allowed Brandon to assist her into the car.

*   *   *

The vibration of her cell phone pulled her away from her musings, and she automatically reached over to check the incoming text.

'Staring at your gift. Wishing we were there together.'

Paige sighed, remembering Brandon's response as he opened her second gift back at her place after Christmas dinner. She watched him just as anxiously as she had as he opened the ones amongst his family. As he uncovered the painting of the park they frequented and had their first kiss, the room became eerily quiet.

She looked back and forth between the eight by eleven-inch painting and his face, but his head was bowed in such a way she was only able to make out a slight frown.

She tried to wait him out, but after a full minute of silence she couldn't hold out anymore. "Don't you like it?" She immediately wanted to take back the question revealing her insecurity, not wanting him to give her an answer he knew she wanted to hear.

He didn't look up, but nodded his head. Didn't he know he was driving her crazy?

"I don't know how to express what I'm feeling...I..." He ended in a shrug, his voice strangely hoarse.

A lump began to grow to the size of a grapefruit in her throat. The emotion she heard in his voice pulled at a place deep within her chest. She looked down at the floor, trying to collect herself and give him time to do the same, otherwise she would wrap her arms around him and she wasn't sure if that would embarrass him or not.

After taking a deep breath, he spoke, his voice a little more clear. "You are amazing, Paige. I am deeply touched by how well you read me. Not just because of this," he held up the painting briefly, "but the way you listen and show you care, and the small and large ways you express your feelings for me with no inhibitions. You don't do any of it in half measures. You do everything on such a deep level, it throws me sometimes. I am overwhelmed with gratitude that you are in my life, in this way."

She tried to smile, but was unable to force the command. He asked for so little. It was easy pleasing him because he made her feel extremely valuable just by being herself. She couldn't help but try to find the words, experience the places, or give him the things that could express how much she treasured him. If only she could have more... She shook herself before succumbing to the dark thought. They were together now.

He finally looked up, his eyes mysteriously moist. "I wish I was better at this...this expressing my feelings for you. Too many times I find myself with a lot of emotions and no way to share them with you. I think to myself that you would probably have 20 or more words and phrases for what I feel sometimes for you, and I may have two and those seem lacking or inadequate."

She laid her hand over his to make her point. "I will take it," she pleaded.

"But you shouldn't. You should hold out for more."

She slowly took her hand back, placing it on her lap. "What are you trying to say, Brandon?"

"I am trying to say, obviously in a very bad way as I am definitely no expert, that you give so freely and with such intensity that I wonder if there would be anything left...if..." He glanced away, then back at her. "If I don't live through this."

She was momentarily taken aback. He had never voiced any doubts before. Probably because he was trying to convince her that his doctor's optimistic view was also his, otherwise he would have ended his pursuit of her.

She knew she needed to address this now. She didn't think she could deal with him doubting her along with everything else they would be up against. "I only know how to express myself one way, with everything I am. I can't – I won't – hold anything back." She looked up from her hands, pinning him with a look. "I don't want to look up years from now and regret holding something back that would have otherwise brought you joy, clarity, or strength and if you are telling me you can't handle it, then this would be the best time to let me know." She clasped her hands so he wouldn't see them shaking.

He placed his elbows on his knees and brought his head to his hands, rubbing them back and forth over his short hair. "That's not what I am saying. I knew I would mess this up." He took another deep breath then turned to her, their knees almost touching. "I want you just the way you are. I appreciate who you are and how you live so fully. I am just afraid that if I am not given the time here that we are hoping for, that you will feel as though you've wasted all of this on me." His hand waved back and forth between himself and the print he was still holding. "I don't want any regrets from you where we are concerned."

She closed her eyes briefly, relieved that he hadn't changed his mind and wanted to end their short relationship. At that moment, she was very aware of how much she didn't know about Brandon. His thoughtfulness and concern for her welfare were new to her, and just a little unnerving.

"No regrets, baby. None now, none tomorrow." She said, placing a hand against his cheek. Before she could remove it, he covered it with his, clasping it lightly and turning his head so he could brush his lips against her palm. She felt the warmth of it all the way up her arm.

She watched his eyes lighten and the atmosphere seemed to change with his smile, allowing her to breathe easily again. "Good," was all he said before he released her hand and looked back at the gift in his.

"How did you get this done?"

"Actually, I saw it in the window of a small gallery down the street from our park. The trees at the end of the path are what first caught my attention."

"Any particular reason?" He asked looking at her, a sly grin lifting one side of his mouth. She couldn't help the blush that crept up her neck. She hadn't made the correlation between the picture and their kiss until that moment since she'd bought the painting a week before their first kiss. It now beheld even more sentiment to her. She shrugged and was rewarded with a laugh from him.

*   *   *

She came back to the present, reclining back on her bed.

'Thought U went 2 work,' she texted back. She only had to wait a few seconds before receiving his reply.

'At work. I found a perfect spot 4 it on my desk. Wanna go there when I get off?'

She thought about it for a moment. It may be just what she needed after speaking to Grace.

'Yes, I'll be ready by 4:00'.

'See U @ 4:15'.

Pocketing her phone, she breathed in some resolve and went to get her keys. She would think of a place as she drove.

Twenty minutes later, Paige nervously expelled two more breaths as she listened to the phone ring for the third time. 'Two more and I can just leave a voicemail.' It rang again and she began to relax when it was answered.

"Hello?"

She froze. What was she supposed to say? She panicked. She could hear her heart pounding. Her hand hovered over the end button.

"Hello?"

No annoyance in the voice, just hesitation. When was Grace ever hesitant about anything? Just that one thought calmed her down enough to respond. "Hello."

There was a pause. "Paige?"

"Um…Yes. It's Paige."

"How are you doing?"

"Alright. And you, Grace?"

Another pause. "Just fine. Well, actually more than fine, but I guess you know that. I'm getting married in a few days. Your sister said she mentioned it to you when you last spoke."

Mel could really get on her nerves sometimes, but she couldn't say she hadn't been warned.

"Oh, yeah, congratulations." She wracked her brain for some other piece of small talk they could discuss until an appropriate amount of time passed, and she could get to the reason she called.

"Thank you. Don't you want to know his name?"

Right then, she knew it was going to take more than a walk in the park with Brandon to help her get over this call. As usual, Grace saw her coming and was letting her know it.

"Oh, sorry. What's his name?"

"Cedric Eldridge."

That name sounded familiar, but she couldn't place it.

"You may remember him. He worked with your father when we lived in Los Angeles."

"Wasn't he daddy's friend? Not just a co-worker." It left her mouth before she could cage it. It wouldn't do any good to antagonize Grace before she got the information she needed.

"Actually, Paige, Cedric was both our friend. We'd all gone to high school together, but that won't change anything in your eyes so let's move on, shall we? I hear that your books are doing well. You were always such a prolific writer; even in grade school, your teachers seemed to think you had an extraordinary gift. I read some of your creative work, but after a few paragraphs I usually had to put them down. They were so dark and depressing. I sure hope your subjects are lighter now. I'd hate to think so many people want to walk around in such a morose state."

And there it was. Twelve years of silence and Grace's first words to her about her profession were little more than a put-down. What was it about this woman that, even with her value rooted deeply in the Lord, could make her second guess herself – even if it was only for few seconds?

"I suppose some may consider what I write to be deep, but no doubt by the time they reach the end of the story there is definite cause to feel uplifted, encouraged, and hopeful. No one can help how their story begins, they can only move towards a wonderful ending and work to encourage others to do the same."

"So, your sister tells me you found Jesus. Just do me a favor and don't use Him against me, okay?"

Paige waited patiently to hear any sign of lightning striking on the other side of the phone. After a moment, she shrugged, figuring He wouldn't let her off the hook that easy. Even still she indulged in the image of Grace's hair standing on end with smoke coming out of her ears.

"Don't worry. I don't wield him like a weapon against heathens, Grace. I just try to see people as He sees them."

"Hmph," was the only response she received.

Paige expelled a long, silent breath. *God, I don't know how to see past the woman I remember and the woman Victoria said she was.*

She was just about to open her mouth when Grace threw another statement at her. "I spoke to your daughter – you know – Gladys."

Paige's ire was instantly up. Twelve years, and this woman thought she would try and remind her who her daughter was? *What gall?!* Paige worked hard to sound unaffected by the verbal jab.

"Yes." Her heart was beating so fiercely she was almost thankful for the heated emotion she was feeling, otherwise she was sure she would have stammered through the one syllable.

"She is always such a well-mannered child. I think it was good that you let Melanie raise her."

Paige ran the words through her mind a few times, trying to find the compliment. Wouldn't this be something Jesus did?

"Yes. She is an amazing child." She threw caution to the wind and quickly decided to get a jump on this conversation with her next statement. "Just like her sister." She was rewarded with a thick stretch of silence.

"I'm not going to apologize for what I did, Paige. You were not in any condition to care for twins. You couldn't even look at the one you knew was alive."

Paige began to tremble. She held the phone tighter, angry that she couldn't deny the fact that some of what Grace said was right. She had worked through the shame. She wouldn't allow her to send her back there.

"And what were you thinking, telling Gladys that you're her mother? You should have left well enough alone. She was happily adjusted with Melanie and Marc. She has everything she needs. Don't you think it was just a little bit selfish? You don't have anything to offer her as a single woman whose time is spent between some fantasy world and traveling from state to state, selling that fantasy to easily influenced, idyllic readers. Not to mention this church stuff you are involved in…"

Paige interrupted her. "Grace, as her mother I have every right and both Melanie and me agreed it was time to let Gladys know the truth. I've dealt with my past and some of the decisions I've made. She understands and if she has any questions, she knows she can ask me."

"Really? Have you told her who her father is?" Rising panic formed in Paige's chest, but before she could voice any concern, Grace continued.

"What about that other one? I know she has questions. Gladys says they talk every day and now that the father bought them those gadgets for Christmas, they video chat. Oh, that's right. He sent you one too. What is really going on with you and that man?"

"We share a daughter. That causes us to have to communicate." She held her mouth as tight as possible to remind herself not to give more information than needed. It was a trick of Grace's that she knew well; she put you on the defense and, when you surrender information to explain yourself, she would hang you by it.

This was her chance and she was going to seize the opportunity. "Speaking of Vivian, my other daughter, I met her grandmother." She let the sentence hang for a moment. "I got to spend some time with her and we had some interesting conversations. She said she knew of you. Her name is Victoria Branchett. Does that ring a bell?"

"No."

Paige waited for more, but when there was nothing forthcoming, she sighed. "Are you sure? She seemed pretty certain the two of you were acquainted with one another."

"No, Paige."

"Will you tell me how you did it? How you got Vivian out of the delivery room without anyone being the wiser?"

"Why?"

"Why? Because I spent twelve years thinking my daughter was dead."

"What's the big deal? You didn't want her. I was doing what I thought was best. I was being merciful and making sure she had a family to go to that would appreciate her. As it is, it apparently took you quite a while before you could acknowledge Gladys as something more than a curse."

Unable to bear the hateful words any longer, Paige spoke up.

"Grace, I just want to know how you did it. We have been through why you feel what you did was for the best and we can agree to disagree, but I feel I have a right to know- "

"Paige, you threw away your rights when you failed to take responsibility for your actions. I stepped in and did my best to clean up your mess. Some would thank me, but not you. You always blamed me for your shortcomings, and it sounds like you still are. Didn't your God teach you to look in the mirror and face the consequences of your actions? You could take a lesson from your sister. She never made excuses, she just stepped in."

Paige had heard enough of the angry barrage. The hate-filled angry and offensive innuendos suggesting that she was in some way responsible for being raped threatened to set her back a few years.

She was so upset she was visibly shaking, and her eyes were on the verge of clouding with tears of anger. She'd lost her calm and knew she wouldn't be able to get the information she needed right now.

"Goodbye, Grace." It was all she could do not to choke on the words.

"Aren't you going to wish me luck in regards to my nuptials?"

"Why? One would think you'd had enough practice to get it perfect this time. Goodbye, Grace." She pushed the 'end' button quickly then turned her phone off.

She leaned back in the driver's seat of her car and watched as plane after plane took off in the distance. The tears that had been threatening began to pool over, and she wiped at her cheeks angrily over and over again. Grace wasn't worth the wasted emotion.

It took almost an hour to regain some of the peace she had surrendered during the call. She was more upset with herself and her behavior, than Grace's. Grace had never acted out of character for herself. She had been consistent in her regard for Paige since puberty. It hadn't fazed Paige much at first. She had her relationships with her father and sister to act as a buffer. No, Grace had always been the same. The very fact that she couldn't bring herself to call her mom should have been a sure sign as to the fate of their call.

You have to give more if you want more.

"But all I do is give. I have always given, and she has always taken."

Give more.

The answer rubbed against her flesh and she wanted to shout 'no', but knew that wouldn't get her anywhere. She was so tired, so tired, and all she wanted to do was imagine herself crawling up into her Father's lap, tears streaming down her face, and allow him to comfort her by squeezing her tight, wiping the tears, telling her it would be all right and that she was right to feel the way she did.

A trace of a smile lifted up the edges of her mouth at the last thought. Of course she wanted to be told she was right, even when she knew she was wrong but didn't want to do anything about it.

Sometimes it could feel so unfair. She took a deep breath and shifted her thoughts.

Heavenly Father, I am sorry for my thoughts, words, and actions that brought You grief instead of glory. I apologize for not leaning on Your words and allowing myself to be guided by You. I repent of those things, and ask that You forgive me. I promise to do better and work harder to listen to Your promptings next time, and less to my flesh. That alone may allow for a better work to be done.

I didn't do so well, Father. Actually I'm feeling like a failure. I didn't think she would have such an effect on me, but the resentment was still there. The burning in my gut was still there. The angry girl was still there...I thought I'd been delivered of these things. I worked so hard to make peace an integral part of me in everything, but as soon as I heard her voice, it left.

I need Your help. I am at a loss. Was I fooling myself – lying to myself? How was it that the burning in my gut came back so quick? How is it that it came back at all? How can I love You so much, and dislike her the way that I do? How could a mother have so much disdain for her daughter? What did I do wrong?

She felt her prayer veering off track. How desperately she wanted to succumb to a pity party, but it wouldn't help her find answers to the questions regarding the ugly emotions that reared their heads.

God, I know I haven't arrived, and I am all the more humbled by the fact that You could use me with all of this still within, but I thought I had forgiven her enough not to be ruled by these emotions. I was supposed to be so far removed that becoming a victim to her bitterness was not supposed to have an effect on me.

Have I not sought You out, spent time with You, loved You in and out of pain? How do You allow me to be so close to You with all of this still in here? I thought love and hate couldn't abide together...and I think I hate her. I hate the way I feel around her. I hate her ways, the way she belittles me with one word; I hate that she is incapable of showing me love.

She began crying in earnest again, trying to purge the feelings of being unwanted along with the anger in her gut.

The sound of a door slamming nearby brought her back to her surroundings. She rocked herself, trying to soothe herself enough to be able to make the drive home.

Lord, I need Your help. I need answers, and I will be open to listening to what You want me to do. I need You more than ever. Please incline Your ear. Let me know You have heard my plea. Wrap me up in the comfort of Your arms again and help me find that peace-giving haven. All of this is for Your Glory. In Jesus' name. Amen.

For the first time in a very long time, she closed out a prayer before getting even a glimpse of her answer. She would go home and continue to seek answers.

CHAPTER 10

Brandon didn't know what to do. He'd called Paige Friday morning and she seemed hopeful, albeit anxious about talking to Grace, but when he'd finally reached her later that afternoon – after numerous calls going to voicemail – she sounded lifeless. Of course, he was instantly concerned and wanted to at least come over and see if she was okay, if she wasn't going to keep their date at the park, but she told him she needed to be alone and he conceded. She said she'd call him back soon, but it was now Saturday, late afternoon, and still no call.

He spoke to his mom, explaining as much of Paige's relationship – or lack thereof – with her mother as he dared, and she advised him to give her time. They had not been together long enough to know each other's ways of dealing with hard blows, and she warned him that pressing too hard may cause her to pull away.

He called Pastor Lawrence and asked to speak to Lady Menagerie, but she'd not heard from Paige since the day after Christmas. He could hear her concern over the phone and felt guilty for provoking it. He told her what he knew even though it wasn't much, but was unable to glean anything from her responses.

"I'll make a call and see if she will speak to me. I won't tell her I spoke to you unless you want me to give her a message for you."

Brandon thought about it for a moment. "No, she knows I want to talk to her. I will either see her in church tomorrow or go by her house afterward."

"Okay. How are you doing Brandon?" Her question surprised him.

"I'm fine." The silence on the other end of the line was telling. He tried again. "Physically I am doing well, but I don't know what to do here…with Paige. She won't call me and I know she is in pain, but my hands are tied."

"I know you have found yourself in new territory with Paige, but understand that she is in good hands. When she comes up against something she is having problems with, the first one she goes to is God. I'm sure she doesn't mean to alienate you. She is just seeking help. Give her a moment. She's in the best place possible. When she is ready to talk then you can discuss maybe a compromise in how you two communicate. You're learning each other; that's what people in relationships do."

"Yeah."

"I heard your family is in town. Will they be joining us for service tomorrow?"

"Yes."

"Do they usually all come out like this for the holidays or is it because of your condition?"

He hesitated a moment, not sure where this was going. "A little of both."

"That's nice. It is wonderful to have family around, especially at times like this. How are your tests looking?"

"My doctor was optimistic regarding my last results."

"Wonderful. I and my husband are holding you up in prayer."

Without giving him a chance to respond – if he had one – she began, "You know with everything going on with you, Paige and her family, we haven't had a chance to talk." There were a couple of beats of silence where he didn't know what he should say, so he remained silent.

"My husband and I are pretty close so we share many things, but there are still things – due to confidentiality – that we don't discuss. You can imagine what type of stress that can be for a person – a marriage – but we have had quite a few years to get to know each other. We have agreed to make the effort to learn each other's ways of communicating; when we want to express ourselves and when we don't because we aren't sure how to.

Brandon, my husband and I find it more comfortable not to discuss certain things regarding you and Paige, so I don't want you to think that anything that we discuss will be talked about outside of this conversation. That includes Paige as well."

He was feeling like he'd just been sat down at the kitchen table with his mother to discuss women and he was no more looking forward to this discussion than he would that, but he respected her just as much as his mother so he acquiesced.

"Understood."

"Brandon, I am going to start off by letting you know that I was a little disappointed that you took so long to tell Paige about your bout with cancer."

Brandon was taken aback by her opening statement. He worked not to speak or be moved by his first reaction, which was a sense of invasion of privacy.

"I have known Paige for almost six years now, and I am very protective of her. I think of her as one of my own and so does everyone else in this household. She is a very caring and loving woman, but she is also still quite fragile."

He opened his mouth because he thought he should say something to show that he was in agreement, but she continued before a sound was made.

"Due to Paige's family history, she has a hard time trusting people and I'm hoping that you will understand that keeping information from her is not the way to go about gaining that trust, no matter how justified you feel in keeping it from her."

"I informed your husband a few months ago..." He was aware of his faux pas before the sentence was fully out of his mouth. The phone line held a pregnant silence.

"So you told my husband months ago and placed him in the difficult position of watching you pursue one of his Elders that he thinks of as a daughter while binding him with his confidentiality clause?"

"Ummm..."

"Don't worry Brandon, I don't intend to act as judge and juror. That last statement was just the wife coming out in me. I'm not good with him having to deal with undue stress. Okay, back to the subject at hand..."

Brandon remembered his thoughts of Lady Menagerie when he'd first met her just outside of her husband's office in August (not at all a good first impression on his part). He'd admired her strength and character, and hoped never to find himself on the receiving end of any of her tongue lashings.

He shrugged and hoped it didn't get too much worse because he wasn't about to open his mouth again.

"I like you, Brandon; I think you are a true man of God with a love for Him and his people. I think you are caring, patient, and gentle. Your passion and compassion are what draws people to you, and you seem determined to lead by example. I believe you are sensitive enough to pull Paige out of herself regarding some of her family issues, but strong and clever enough not to make her feel pressured. I think you are good for her – I will warn you though. If you leave too many things unsaid and Paige begins to feel she cannot trust you, even I won't be able to convince her otherwise.

Now please understand the only reason Paige brought up your illness to me was because she was torn. Not in having a relationship with you, but because of her hesitancy due to you withholding information. In light of all the revelations she has had over the past three months, it would behoove you to be as straightforward with her as possible. May I ask you a question?"

He paused for a moment not sure if she was just going to go ahead and ask the question, but after continued silence, he answered, "Yes, sure."

"Where do you see your relationship going with Paige?"

This was the question he had been waiting for, and he planned to be as honest as he could.

"I am courting Paige, Lady Menagerie, and it is my wish to take this relationship as far as it will go."

"Which is?"

"Til' death do us part."

He heard the gasp on the other side of the line, then quiet. It lasted so long he thought the line disconnected.

"Lady Menagerie? Are you still there?"

"Um... Yes. Sorry. I'm still here." Her voice sounded suspiciously heavy – full of emotion. "So you plan to marry her?"

"That is something I would like to see happen."

"Excuse me for playing devil's advocate, but you haven't known her for that long."

"How long is it supposed to take when the Lord has given His blessing?"

There was another lengthy silence. He didn't know how to take it. Was she happy or skeptical?

"Please forgive my surprise. I wasn't expecting you to be so candid. Honest, yes, but this was more than I expected. Have you told her?"

"She knows that I wish to court her, which usually leads to marriage."

"Have you told her that this is your intent?"

He thought about it. He hadn't come straight out and said it, but they had agreed on so many things in regards to their individual futures and what they were looking for. She'd shared with him some of her conversations with God concerning him, and he had done the same.

He was happy the relationship had progressed as far as it had, considering where they were only a week ago. It was pretty much a given for him that if God had told him that she was the one for him – if given the time - they would eventually get married. Wasn't that the normal course of things? He wasn't going to rush anything for the sake of having something to report to anyone. He had voiced those same things when he'd discussed it with his father, and they were of like mind.

He didn't feel comfortable speaking with any specified dates or in too much more detail with Lady Menagerie. Paige could do that when they got there.

"In so many words." He said it with finality. It was as close as he dared come to telling Lady Menagerie that the rest was between him and Paige.

Now, how did he stress his concern to Lady Menagerie in regards to Paige's demeanor before and after the call she made to her... Grace?

"So are you going to call her now? I really don't like the way she sounded the last time we talked. She sounded...defeated." His gut wrenched at the memory of her voice the day before.

"I'll call her right now. Brandon, I'm glad we had a chance to speak. Pastor Lawrence and I will see you tomorrow?"

"Yes I will see you tomorrow, and thank you."

*   *   *

"Hello." Brandon picked up the phone on the second ring, not even bothering to look at the caller I.D.

"Either things went so well on Christmas Day that you forgot about your best friend, or things went so bad that you are lying in your own filth because you are so depressed you can't get out of bed or call your best friend."

After peeking at the time display, Brandon was tempted to hang up the phone but knew Dominy would just call back, and he didn't want to take the chance of waking anyone up this early in the morning. He gave a half-hearted greeting. "What's up Dom?"

"You obviously aren't. Just thought I would return the favor."

Vaguely understanding Dominy's intent, Brandon tried to feign the appropriate emotion but was just too tired to care. He'd waited up for Paige's call – that did not come – and had just given up and gone to bed three hours before.

"Alright, you got me back. Goodnight Dom."

"Hey, not so fast. How did it go with Paige?"

"Great. Wonderful. I will talk to you about it later." Brandon said on a breath, trying to remain on the edge of consciousness so he could quickly drop back off. His hand was already on the button, ready to hang up the call, when Dominy quickly revealed his other reason for calling.

"Robin's pregnant!"

"Huh?"

"I couldn't hold it in anymore. Robin's pregnant. We are going to have a baby."

The excitement in Dominy's voice and the news caused Brandon to stop struggling and relinquish his hold.

"Robin's pregnant?"

"Yes, Bran. Wake up! My wife is pregnant. I am going to be a daddy, and you are going to be a godfather if you can do more than talk like a parrot."

"How…when…?" He tried sitting up, hoping his initial questions didn't sound as off as he felt. He took a deep breath trying to shake off the tremors rolling through his body that were also fighting against waking up.

"Really Brandon…don't you think that's a little personal? Do I need to have that talk with you again…?"

"Shut up, man. I didn't mean it that way. What do you expect, calling me at 3:30 a.m.?"

"I expected you to be asleep, but when has that ever stopped us? I expected you to call earlier this week to tell me how things went with you and Paige. I was hoping both of us could share good news."

"When did you find out?"

"Christmas Day. It was one of my presents. My best present. She gave me a gold link I.D. bracelet with 'DADDY' engraved on it. At first I didn't know what to think of it. It was so out of the blue. We have been hoping for so long. Then she showed me her wrist with an identical bracelet, except the word MOMMY was on it, and it hit me like a ton of bricks. I didn't know whether to laugh, cry, thank her or kiss her so after I recovered from feeling lightheaded, I did all of them."

"Wuss." Brandon ragged on his friend, happily using Dominy's own word on him.

"Whatever. Wait until your wife gets pregnant. See how you fair."

"Well, I think I have some time before I get there, so I will prepare myself – better than you."

"So you have some time… That means things went well?"

"You are like a dog with a bone. Yes. Things went well. We had a long talk and we are still together. My mom likes her. She said 'hi' by the way and was disappointed her other son was not here to celebrate with her."

"Ahhh. I told you she likes me better than you. Wait until I tell her I'm going to be a daddy. She will disown you for dragging your feet."

"A likely story. So soon-to-be-daddy, when's the big day?"

"Late June, early July."

"Congratulations man, I am really happy for you." He stifled a yawn. "Tell Robin I'm looking forward to my job as godfather. I have church in a few hours and I am on duty. I will call you later on in the day. I know this will probably mean you won't be back out here soon, but you know the family won't let me out of their sight too long."

"Okay. You better call me later. We need to discuss some things."

"Yep." They hung up and he laid back down hoping sleep would come back quickly and that Paige would be in church so he could stop missing her so much.

* * *

Brandon spotted Paige the moment she walked in the door. Greeted by an usher, he saw that her smile was overly bright and didn't reach her eyes, but if you didn't know her well you wouldn't have noticed. He thought his concern for her would ebb if he was able to see her, but now he was even more worried.

He wanted to go to her and wrap her in a comforting embrace, but he was on post as one of the Elders, serving his pastor and the people of the church.

Even though he'd been in favor of the pastor's decision to relinquish her of some of her duties until after the New Year to help aid in her recovery from the kidney donation and the 'complications' from surgery – he was having second thoughts.

She'd been lead to a seat on the pew with his family and he was relieved to see that she didn't seem hesitant. She greeted his mother and father with warm, lingering hugs and quickly spoke to everyone else before service began.

Still, there were moments in the service where she looked lost sitting in the middle of the pew with her hands in her lap. Sure, she made all of the expected responses and prayed with the person next to her when prompted. He was even able to catch and hold her gaze a couple of times thus wringing a tentative smile from her lips, but it was as if she were on autopilot and he was more concerned now than yesterday.

Immediately after the service, he made his way towards her, half afraid that she would try and slip out before really having to talk to anyone, but Lady Menagerie pulled rank and spoke over the crowd inviting Paige to join her and Pastor Lawrence in his office. The look on Lady Menagerie's face relinquished no room for denial.

He watched as Paige sighed, nodded her head and sat back down to wait for them to finish greeting everyone and make their way to the office.

Brandon sauntered over, a little hesitant as to how he would be received. He hated this feeling. It seemed as though he was here once a week: three steps forward, and five steps back. He pushed aside the thoughts as he took the vacant seat next to her.

"Hello."

"Hi, Brandon." Her voice was airy, her smile tentative, but true. It encouraged him.

"I missed you."

She looked down at her hands then around the church over his right shoulder before returning back to his face. Pain flashed briefly in her eyes, and it was all he could do to stay right where he was.

"I missed you too. I'm sorry I didn't call you back. I've been…thinking." He watched her intently, trying to figure out what she wasn't saying. He wanted to know it all, but she was wearing a mask.

He placed his hand on hers to keep her attention directly on him. "I was wondering if you would to allow me to come over later and pick you up. I would like to show you something."

"I don't know if I will be good company..." She allowed the rest of the sentence to fade.

"I promise it won't take long, and I will not press you to talk if you don't want to. I just...I just would like to show you something. I think it will be worth your while and if you want to go home right after I won't hold you, but if you do decide that you aren't ready to go home, there is this little eatery that I would love to take you to."

She took a deep breath and let it out on an, "Alright."

He looked over her shoulder and acknowledged his mother, who began to edge forward. "How about 2:30 p.m.? And I think you should dress warm."

He saw the question in her eyes, but before she could form the question, his mother drew her attention by taking her hand.

Brandon watched something pass between them as Paige turned back to look at her. He looked over at his dad, working to keep the impatience out of his eyes and got only a shrug for all of his work.

Ava leaned and whispered something quickly in Paige's ear that wrung a hefty sigh from her. When she turned back to him, her eyes were misty.

Elias Jr. placed his arm around Brandon's shoulder, startling him. Never taking his eyes of Paige, he interposed, "So, are you going to put my little brother out of his misery and come over for brunch? He has been moping around for the last couple of days looking like he's lost his favorite toy."

Brandon felt the flush rise in his neck, but his brother held him tight. He continued to watch Paige who graced E.J. with a brief apologetic smile. "No, I'm sorry. I won't be able to make it to brunch, but I may stop by later if Brandon feels like sharing..." She leaned closer as if conspiring with him. "So you behave."

He laughed, shrugging nonchalantly, "I can't promise you anything."

"Then neither can I," she replied flippantly then came forward and pushed E.J. gently, forcing him to remove his arm and hugged Brandon for a few seconds. It was the first time in two days that he had a feeling that things would be all right. Her talk with Grace hadn't taken her humor or the fight out of her.

"I have to go now, but I will see you later, okay?"

He pulled back, holding on to her forearms, looking in her eyes, wanting more than anything to take away the reason for the shadows beneath them. "Yes ma'am, two-thirty and not a moment later."

"Good." She turned and said goodbye to all of his family members except Elias Jr, but before she left turned back to him, giving him a short warning glare that wasn't missed by any of them.

Brandon could not have been more proud of her, and to know that she had his back even with his siblings, made his heart lighter.

His mom slipped her hand in the crook of his elbow as he led her out of the sanctuary. "You have a gem there, Brandon. Anyone who can give E.J. what-for with one glance is worth her weight in gold."

"More than that, Mom, much more."

"You think she is worth fighting for?" she asked, slowing her stride and forcing him to do the same.

Already knowing where she was going, he answered the only way he could. "Everything and everyone, but God."

She stopped, turning him to look at her for a moment, not caring that she held everyone else up. After what seemed like five minutes she nodded, reaching up to cup his jaw with her palm. "Okay, baby boy." Her smile wavered.

He took her hand, kissing her palm and continued to lead her out of the sanctuary. "Come on mom, I'm hungry. What did you say to Paige, by the way?"

"Umph. You know better than that. If I wanted you to know, I wouldn't have whispered it in her ear."

*   *   *

Brandon looked over at Paige again. He didn't know what to make of her serene expression as she looked out over the Los Angeles basin from the side of the mountain he'd found while playing tour guide earlier that week.

She hadn't said much on the ride up, but she did express her delight in the view and peacefulness that surrounded them. For the moment, he was content to just sit next to her.

After what seemed like half an hour of staring out over the rolling hills, roofs of closer houses, and the more distant downtown skyline, she took his hand, garnering his attention.

He watched her frown with concentration and worked harder to keep from asking the questions pressing on his heart.

"I had a very interesting talk with Lady Menagerie," she said, then grew quiet again.

The hairs on the back of his neck stood up. Had Lady Menagerie given him away? The only thing that kept him from confessing was her firm grasp.

"Really. Was it beneficial?" was all he could think of to say.

She nodded slowly, her gaze still roaming back and forth across the panoramic view.

"I got beat thoroughly with a wet noodle." She shrugged then looked him square in the eye. "But it was exactly what I needed to come back to reality." She smiled sheepishly.

He let out a breath he didn't know he was holding. He waited a couple minutes more, then pressed forward.

"Are you ready to tell me about your call with Grace?"

She shifted towards him, placing her other hand over his. "I want to ask your forgiveness for shutting you out." He began shaking his head not needing an apology, but she tightened her hold, regaining his attention.

"No, please, let me. I need to ask this of you because I was wrong." Her plea pricked his heart and quieted his words.

"I am asking for your forgiveness because instead of coming to you and accepting your comfort or even being open to any encouragement, I went back to my old ways of self-depreciation and self-pity. There was no room for you there."

He simply nodded, filing away the information to meditate on later.

She began talking softly and he leaned in for support and to hear better almost to the point where their foreheads were touching. He needed to prove to her that she wouldn't have to go through anything alone as long as he was breathing. She went over her conversation with Grace and how devastated she was to find that her reaction to Grace hadn't changed that much from before she'd given her life to Christ and had been filled with the Holy Spirit.

"Did you curse her out or hang up the phone in her face?" He asked, eliciting a reluctant smile and receiving a shake of the head from her.

"No, but I did throw her less-than-perfect marital track record in her face when she asked me to wish her luck."

"It was just your hurt talking," he said, trying to smooth over her consternation at her own reaction.

"Yes. Exactly. I thought I was better than that. I certainly know better than that. She defeated me and took me back to when I was the insecure child looking for any type of approval from her."

"Are you still looking for approval from her?"

She looked down at her shoes. "No." The one word spoken with resolve at the end of a long breath.

"Well, it sounds like there is only one thing left to do."

"What?" She looked back at him.

"Forgive her."

She heaved a sigh, her shoulders drooping a little.

"Yep. That's exactly what Lady Menagerie said right before she pulled out the wet noodle."

"What was your response to her advice about forgiving your mom?"

"That it was easier said than done. That I thought I was on the road to doing so before the call which made me doubt the authenticity of my relationship with God."

"Ooooh." He blanched at her words –he was sure it elicited a stinging tirade from Lady Menagerie.

"Yeah." The word was her only expression of agreement.

He decided she'd received enough reprimanding and looked to place a salve on her heart. "I don't know too many people who live their love for God as explicitly as you do. Why would you doubt your relationship with Him?"

"I saw so much ugliness in myself that I wasn't aware of before that call that I was hard-pressed not to second guess other parts of my walk. I felt like the lowest form of hypocrite. I mean, I am flown in to talk to women about forgiveness, learning how to see themselves as God sees them so that they can do a self-evaluation without condemning themselves and falling prey to pity parties and potholes the enemy lays up for them." She wiped at her forehead, her hand shaking slightly in agitation.

"What do I look like, not even being able to hold a decent conversation with the woman that gave me life?" Her gaze slipped back down to the earth at their feet.

He took her hand back in his and waited until her eyes came back to his. "You would look like a beautiful child of God that pursues truth and His face in every facet of her life. You would look like a woman graced with His unconditional love who may be on this earth for just a little longer – to my delight – because she hasn't reached perfection. You would look like a human being whose love and compassion for people who are hurting and stumbling around in the dark motivates her to seek out any spot or wrinkle in herself so that she can be used even more powerfully by the Father. So now that you found one or two that you didn't know you had, don't stop.

I know I don't have to tell you that you are going to find a many more before your work is done, but how can you minister and relate to those who are also striving toward the same goal of getting closer to their Father without coming upon a pebble or boulder in the midst of your path. It only leads to magnifying your sensitivity to His voice, His guidance, and His healing ways."

She began to chuckle, which pulled him back from his thoughts.

"What?"

"You did that much nicer than Lady Menagerie, even though it was very much the same."

"Really. How did she say it?"

"Oh, she said something to the effect of I should know better than to allow the enemy to talk me into a pity party. That she thought I would have handled my response to my mother with more maturity. That neither she nor Pastor Lawrence had ever taught me that once I'd been born again that I, my walk, or the world would be perfect, so she couldn't see why I boxed myself up in a corner to suck my thumb. Something like that." She shrugged her shoulder, feigning nonchalance. Then, she began to laugh and he joined her – more from the freedom and lightheartedness he heard in it than Lady Menagerie's reprimand.

"Wow. She is scary enough to cause me to get it right with God quick if I have any issues. I don't know if I can take her beatings."

His breath caught because she smiled one of those luminous, full face smiles that caused her to shine brighter than the sun, at him. "Well it worked this time, and I have been rightly chastised." She nodded emphatically. "I fell for one of the oldest tricks in the book. I confined myself to my own special type of torture, cutting myself off from any type of help or encouragement you or any of my family and friends could give me, while the enemy dealt me my conviction and sentence."

She surprised him by rushing into his arms and embracing him in a tight hug that made him feel the elation in her heart. A feeling of warmth and love enveloped him, seeping into his chest, making his heart beat heavily.

"Do you forgive me?" She asked near his ear.

"Anything," he replied because it was the only answer that would come to mind.

She pulled back slightly so that she could study his face.

"That's a dangerous answer."

"No, my sweet Paige, it is liberating. But just because I would forgive you of anything doesn't mean I could sit back and let you take advantage of that fact. At some point you would have to face the consequences of your actions."

She went back to hugging him. "I will make sure it doesn't come to that, but thank you for trusting me so implicitly."

He didn't respond out loud, but sent up a silent prayer that she too wouldn't cause him to regret opening himself up to her. But even as he prayed, he reminded himself that Paige was nothing like Myra.

His vulnerability regarding her, gave him pause. He tried to ignore the temptation to protect his heart with that shield he'd slowly lowered over the last few weeks. Maybe he should slow things down a little. They had time to get to know each other better, time to move at a slower pace into something that would last a lifetime.

Without being aware of it, he squeezed her tighter. If his muscles remembered the feel of her, he wouldn't feel so bereft if she decided she couldn't deal with the reality of his illness. This time he would be prepared.

She pulled back out of his embrace. "This place is really beautiful. Thank you for showing me." And without another breath, she continued, "Can we go eat now? I am starving."

Her admission drew a laugh from him that echoed all around them, and he couldn't help but kiss her cheeks in gratitude for lifting him out of his solemn thoughts.

He'd led her halfway down the hill before he remembered he'd not shared Dominy's news with her. As soon as the last word of his sentence left his lips, she shouted her joy but then quickly sobered.

"What did your mom say?" He turned in time to see a mischievous smile slide across her lips.

"Everyone's a comedian," he replied sardonically, continuing forward. "Speaking of my mom, what did she whisper to you in church?"

She stopped him from progressing with a tug on his hand then sidled up to him. "You know how your mom seems to see everything, even those things you think you've kept hidden?"

He nodded in agreement.

"And you know how she speaks to those things at the perfect moment to encourage you?"

"Yeah," he replied on a breath.

"Then you also know that what she tells you is special and usually meant *just for you.*" She punctuated the last three words by tapping his nose with her forefinger then walked ahead with sass in her stride.

He was stuck in confusion for a few seconds until he realized she was teasing him. "So…are you going to tell me?"

Her only response was a laugh.

CHAPTER 11

"So, is it too soon to ask if you would be my date for New Year's Eve?" Victoria watched Richard as he glanced at the rearview mirror then at the road in front of them before looking at her.

"There is nothing I would love more than to bring in the New Year with my wife." He didn't look away until he'd finished his declaration.

Victoria wasn't sure, but she could sense a double-meaning behind his statement. "I was thinking we could go down to the Four Seasons. They have a big band this year and we could dance the night away like we did on our fifth wedding anniversary. We could get a room so we wouldn't have to drive back right away; sleep in late…order room service. What do you think?"

Richard was quiet for a moment, but his face didn't give her any clue to his thoughts. She waited, feeling her annoyance rise at the level of insecurity she felt with each passing moment. Only he could do this to her, but she'd already given too much control away. She began to convince herself that if he didn't really want to spend New Year's Eve with her, it would be no big deal.

"I was thinking maybe we could go to Watch Night and bring the New Year in at His Graces Fellowship. They're putting on a concert that I think you'll enjoy, plus Mary and Kate will be there as well. You seemed to hit it off Christmas Day."

Victoria swallowed and swallowed again, but the panic that had risen to her throat wouldn't budge. She turned toward her window so as not to give away her reaction to his suggestion. She called on her anger, which was never too far from the surface, to quell the anxiety that the thought of stepping into any church brought about.

"Is it your way or no way, Richard?" She turned to look at him, pleased that her voice was firm.

He looked over at her, perplexed. "No Victoria, you made a suggestion and I made one as well. We can try and come to a compromise. That's what people do when they love each other but have different tastes – they compromise. Let's give it a try and see if we are any good at it."

Was he making fun of her? She watched his face for any signs of guile but saw nothing less than genuine hope in his clear eyes, and that bothered her even more.

"What are the hours for the big band?" he asked.

"The dance floor opens at eight p.m. and the band plays until two a.m."

"How about we go to the concert for a couple of hours then head over to the Four Seasons around eleven p.m. so we can ring in the New Year on the dance floor?"

"Why go to the concert at all? I thought the reason you really wanted to go was to bring in the New Year in prayer?"

He turned back to her, quietly assessing her mood before turning his attention back to the road. "I didn't think you remembered," he said quietly.

"I remember quite a bit." She stared at the two-lane highway stretched out in front of them.

"And yet, here we are," he said gravely.

"What is that supposed to mean?" Her defenses rose.

"We were once so close. I only needed to be near you to know your moods. Now there are so many walls and masks between us that we can barely hold a civil conversation. We couldn't fathom spending holidays, let alone New Year's Eve, apart. It didn't matter where we were as long as we were together. Now we are working to *compromise* and I can already tell that if you feel that you are giving too much you will pull out completely, but I will concede to you if that makes the difference as to whether or not I get to spend time with you because I love you.

I remember spending afternoons and nights in each other's arms, intimately sharing of ourselves. We would talk for hours, and I felt closer to you than any other being. We had everything, not because of the money, but because we could make any place our paradise. A sunrise was the most beautiful thing I'd experienced because it was done with you.

I remember you trusting me to take care of you when you would have nightmares or have an argument with your father that upset you to tears. I remember how you would turn in my arms and let me comfort you, kiss away your tears, speak words of love and encouragement to you, and make you laugh.

I remember hardly being able to wait to get home to tell you about a presentation gone right or wrong, or a new project I wanted to get your opinion on. I remember the little notes you would leave in my briefcase that would touch my soul."

"I never told you," he glanced at her to see if he had all of her attention, "but the first time I found one I was in the middle of a staff meeting, and it touched me so I had to pretend I had something in my eye and slip out. I felt sorry for some of the men I worked with because they didn't have the same type of relationship you and I had, and I thought 'what a tragedy that must be.'

I was inspired by your courage and ability to turn this failing land your grandparents left you into a success, and because you'd been ostracized from your family for choosing to follow your passion, I considered it my honor to fill in the gaps so that you wouldn't miss any of their love. I was foolish enough to think that I could love you enough for you to be full, but I was wrong. That wasn't my place because I could never love you enough for you. *You* needed to do that. You *need* to do that.

I remember as well, Vickie, and that is why I am still here, and even now I am willing to surrender some of my wants for your needs. If you don't feel that you can come to the concert I will go with you and we can dance the night away, but know that it is because I love you and wish to see you happy, and nothing to do with any form of manipulation or illusions of control. When it comes down to brass tacks, Vickie, you can only control you. So, what's it going to be Victoria?"

Victoria had turned back to stare out of her passenger window during his impassioned soliloquy, biting her lip to stay its trembling even as she blinked furiously to keep the tears at bay. She remembered as well, but how did one get back across such a large chasm?

Things had started going awry long before Rachel's illness and death, but those events seemed to shake the very foundation of their relationship like an earthquake shaking cracks and holes in cement. Now they seemed to live in two different worlds, and she had no desire to enter his except for the fact that she didn't think she could live without him.

She thought it over for a few more moments. She wasn't one to knowingly let fear keep her back. Finally, after taking a deep breath and letting it out slowly, she turned back to him. "Are you sure we can leave the church by 11 p.m.? Because I don't want to be sitting in traffic when the New Year comes in."

He glanced at her quickly, trying to assess her. "We don't have to go. I told you I would spend the night at the Four Seasons with you."

"I know." She raised her chin slightly.

"This isn't a competition." She watched his hands tighten then loosen on the steering wheel.

"I thought we were working at compromising."

"A few moments before, you were against going anywhere near the church, even for New Year's Eve."

"True, and I'm still not too keen on it."

"Then why?" He looked back and forth between her and the road quickly, wanting to catch her expression as she answered.

"You reminded me of something," she replied, looking forward again and letting the sound of the tires on the well-worn road fill the silence of the car.

*   *   *

"Are you looking for a bonus for this call? I didn't expect to hear from you until after the holiday."

"I didn't think you would be pleased if I let this information sit that long."

"Fine, make it quick; I'm pressed for time."

"Grace has been making some inquiries about a Victoria Branchett and hasn't been the least bit inconspicuous. It looks like she is looking for personal information. I have been very careful not to leave anything that can be traced back to you, Mrs. Lanning, but she seems like a piece of work. I don't know what she is looking for, but I hope this Branchett woman has huge firewalls in place."

Paige, she thought, *I am mildly surprised I didn't think she would ever want to open that door again. I will call her tomorrow and see how her New Year came in.* "Was that it?"

"Mr. Jenson is drying out. He hasn't been to the bar at all this week."

"Then shake him up a little so that he will need a drink. Send his daughter some pictures of his favorite girl with her new beau. That should do it."

"One more thing."

"Come out with it."

"I think I found some of what you were looking for at State General. Her files were sealed up tighter than Jimmy Hoffa's right-hand man's lips."

Really. She didn't have time for theatrics.

"I found Grace's employee records and some more personal files that I know you will be interested in, including where she worked up to 24 years ago, and some peculiar hospital bills for the immediate family. I made a copy and sent them to you. You should have it the day after the holiday. I was able to get a lead on Mr. Grossenberg."

Her heart started pounding hard against her breastbone.

"What?"

"It happened rather accidentally, but I found some of his records there as well. They are also in the package."

"What type of records?"

"He had a stay in the mental ward's wing."

"How long?"

"Nine months."

She couldn't keep from repeating the words that threatened her next breath. "Nine months?"

The walls of the library were closing in on her and tilting at an odd angle. She took some deep breaths, trying to right things and push the panic back down to the pit of her stomach.

Michael cleared his throat, uncomfortable with the emotion he heard in hers. She had forgotten herself.

"I will look for that package, and contact you towards the middle of the week. Happy New Year, Michael."

"Happy New Year, Mrs. Lanning."

She slowly hung up, standing in the middle of the library in a daze when she began to tremble violently. The horror at what had just been revealed was coming in like a fog off the coast at night, and she was having a hard time keeping it at bay. She didn't know. How was it that she didn't know? She should have felt something, anything. Was there anyone there? Did he have to suffer alone because she wasn't? Could she have prevented this? She stopped herself in mid-thought. There were too many questions without answers and even knowing how desperately she wanted the truth, too many years had passed for it to be anything but painful and destructive.

She held on to the mahogany desk in the middle of the room, searching for a center. She slipped off her pumps and swung her foot back and forth across the Berber carpet, concentrating on the pendulum motion. The small connection of her foot against the rug soothed her enough to allow her to calm most of the trembling.

She hadn't had an anxiety attack in a while, and she wasn't going to succumb to one just a few hours before what could be her first full night with Richard in almost two years. *Woman, you better pull it together! You still have to get through two hours of fake smiles, suffocating and perverted hugs, and empty promises.*

Hopefully the music would be worth it, and the two hours would go by quickly.

She stepped back in her pumps and cataloged the information from the call in a file in the back of her mind. This was bad, but there were plenty of dead-end roads that she had set up just in case someone was trying to play connect the dots. There was nothing she could do about it until after the holiday anyway.

She looked at her watch. That little episode cost her precious minutes. She quickened her steps up to her room, looking forward to being in her husband's arms at midnight.

*   *   *

Victoria's steps were measured as she walked into the building next to Richard. The earlier attack had been interrupted by following her therapist's directions with breathing exercises and meditation, combined with a type of aromatherapy.

She loathed drugs, but decided to take half of the low-strength valium she'd been prescribed when first dealing with Rachael's death, half an hour before she was to accompany Richard. She was still feeling fragile from the afternoon, and she hated that feeling more than taking drugs.

The feeling of Richard's hand enclosing around hers pulled her away from her thoughts.

"Are you all right? You've been very quiet."

She pasted a smile in place, and imagined them leaving. "I'm good."

He watched her intently for a moment. "You have your mask back on." He stopped in midstride. "If you really don't want to do this, we can leave before we get all the way in."

She took a deep breath. This was not going to continue to control her – in any form.

She tugged lightly on his arm, urging him forward. "Come on," she said, with more courage than she felt. "You promised me a concert with good music."

He looked like he might argue with her, but finally shrugged and stepped forward.

He found them a seat toward the middle of the large auditorium used for special events other than those held on Sundays. They'd been sitting for no more than five minutes, her hand still encased tightly in his, when Paul and Mary Ambross sat down next to them. Mary pulled Victoria into a quick hug before she was even able to fully let go of Richard's hand.

The action startled her, triggering an annoyance she tried to feed, but Mary's excitement soothed her nerves just as quickly.

"I'm sorry, I didn't ask if you were a hugger. I'm just happy to be out of the hotel and not heading to the house to see what more the plumber can find to charge us for," she expelled an exasperated breath. "I think you will like the music tonight. Our music ministry invited a few other choirs in the area. Some of them are on the younger side, so that means fast-paced gospel with beats you can really praise and stomp to."

Victoria relaxed a little once she realized she wouldn't have to hold a full conversation. Mary was handling both sides just fine.

Mid-spiel, Paul interrupted, hugging and holding his wife from behind. "Victoria, I want to apologize. Mary truly has only had me to talk to all week, and by the third day she was hard-pressed to find something new to discuss."

Mary smiled sheepishly, mumbling another apology. Victoria laughed out loud. She felt Richard jump slightly at her side. Had it been that long since he'd heard her laugh? Since she had actually laughed? She considered taking valium more often, but quickly squashed the idea.

Sam and Kate joined them soon after, and Victoria allowed herself to be hugged again then settled back to observe the large room and some of the people greeting each other eagerly, and with enough warmth to save the church on electricity for the winter.

They interacted with one another like they hadn't seen each other for years when she was sure they'd seen each other in church just a couple days before. She observed other people talking, her eyes darting back and forth across the room, looking for any expression of guile as people wearing collars welcomed the attendees.

She found herself uneasy. There was no way all these people could have a genuine affection for one another. Where were the cliques, the older ladies sitting in a circle gossiping, or the dirty old ministers leering at the teenagers and young adults? She wondered if she went to the bathroom, would she catch some of the younger generation hanging out and smoking just outside.

After a few minutes, she began to feel as if she had stepped into a sick Christian world made of Stepford wives, children, and preachers.

"What's wrong?" Richard asked, concern clearly written on his face. "And don't say 'nothing'."

She hesitated for a moment then leaned closer so no one could overhear her. "Are these people always like this?"

"Like what?"

"So..." She made a face as if she'd tasted something spoiled, "affectionate and ..." she couldn't think of another word to show her distrust and distaste for the situation she was in.

"Caring, warm, loving? They're not perfect or robots, Victoria, just happy and at peace. They are surrounded by others that feel the same way. This is not a cult, if that's what you're thinking. It's just a place where hurting people have been able to come to be healed and develop a lifelong relationship with God while using what they learned to help others who are hurting, because they love Him and are grateful not to have to continue to suffer."

This was so far outside the scope of Victoria's understanding or experience in regards to churches and its people, she didn't know how to respond, so she didn't.

The choirs were lively and most of their music had a soothing quality, even the ones with faster beats. She found herself tapping her foot discreetly to the music on a couple different occasions, and even caught herself smiling at some of the really young participants that seemed to be putting their all into each song.

The two hours went by quickly and Victoria, though she wouldn't say she was thrilled she came, wasn't sorry either.

Richard nudged her when it was time to go, and they tipped out.

By the time they reached the Four Seasons, checked in, freshened up and changed, it was 11:35 p.m. They walked into the ballroom, and Victoria was instantly transported back to happier times as Richard stepped with her onto the dance floor and led her through swinging moves to a Rob Palmer song performed big band style.

The next couple of songs were much slower, and they reacquainted themselves with the feel of the other and how they moved now compared to years ago, and Victoria was pleasantly surprised that it was very much the same – well, maybe they were just a little slower and a tiny bit thicker in some places. She smiled quietly to herself as she laid her head against his shoulder.

The countdown began with the wrestling of the cymbal, top drum, and high hat, shushing all other conversation in the room besides their count down into the next year.

"Faults, mistakes, hurts we have inflicted upon each other, words we can't take back, even the distance that still separates our souls won't keep me from loving you, but I want my Vick back." He tapped the area above her heart with his forefinger lightly.

"Will you at least try for me?"

At that moment she would have promised him anything. She simply nodded.

"Good."

He placed his palms on either side of her cheeks and raised her face to his. He whispered against her lips, "Happy New Year," then closed the distance.

Her heart soared. Had it always been like this? *Yes, you just chose to concentrate on those things you'd lost, and ignored what was in front of you.* She pushed the haunting thought aside and concentrated on the heady sensation of her husband's love.

*　　　　　*　　　　　*

Victoria stretched herself awake New Year's Day, and that's how she knew Richard was no longer in bed with her. She raised herself up, straightening her elbows. She surveyed the room and spied the door to the balcony open.

She sat up slowly, grabbing her robe off the back of a chair beside the bed. She went to the door of the balcony but was arrested by the utter sadness frozen on his features. He was leaning on the railing deep in thought so he didn't notice her for quite a few moments.

What could have put that look on his face? Did he regret spending time together yesterday? She raised her hand to her throat to stifle the cry at the thought that she was the cause for his unhappiness. He turned to her and the pain in his eyes was stark and piercing, then he blinked and it was gone.

Hmph, whose mask is on now?

"Good morning," he greeted.

"Good morning," she responded, suddenly feeling vulnerable under his direct gaze.

He watched her for a moment and she fought not to squirm, but smiled tentatively.

"Hungry?"

She nodded, not sure whether or not to address what she had seen.

He moved away from the railing and hugged her quickly before ushering her back inside.

"I was hoping we could start the counseling before I left," he began as they ate their breakfast at the small table in their room, "but there have been a few complications with some of the equipment that was held up at the border. I am going to have to make sure things are clear before I leave Thursday."

"How long will you be gone again?"

"Six weeks. Why, are you going to miss me?"

"Yes." She answered without hesitation, on a sigh.

"Maybe next time you'll come with me."

Stark fear swept through Victoria, only to be quickly replaced by repulsion at the thought of sleep out in the 'bush'.

"I can see that is not exactly something you would be thrilled about." His lopsided grin made her chuckle. She shrugged unapologetically.

"I guess it's for the best though. There are a few things that need to be established before we begin and though I'm not eager to risk this fragile truce today, I need to address it."

Her body stiffened slightly, but she forced herself to maintain at least an air of mild curiosity.

"About what?"

"Trust, security, respect; all of which we can't even begin to bridge this gap without."

"You don't trust me?"

The question was out before she could ask herself if she really wanted to know.

His lips lifted in a grim smile, his eyes soft. "No, Victoria, I don't, but I want to be able to again." He reached forward rubbing the knuckles of her hand. "And I want you to be able to trust me as well."

She wanted to tell him she could, but he would have seen right through that lie.

"Thank you," he said, pulling back.

"For what?"

"Not insulting me by lying."

She shrugged her shoulder, feeling slightly put off.

"How do we do that – bridge that gap?"

"Simple. We are straightforward with one another. No plotting, scheming or trying to manipulate each other. We ask and respect the answer we are given, even if we don't agree.

In regards to our feelings about the present and the past, I need the truth Vickie, no matter what the consequence; without fear of condemnation."

A knot began to form in the pit of her belly, taking up what space was left for her meal. Could she even consider doing what he asked? Could she risk him finding out? On the other hand, those divorce papers were real and even though she knew he loved her, he seemed pretty adamant about 'working on their marriage' and counseling. She hadn't been able to detect signs that he would be willing to relent on his condition to their reconciliation.

"What if I can't?"

"Can't or won't?"

"Either."

"Then I will walk away. I told you before, I won't continue in this marriage the way it is. We aren't even moving forward anymore. There is nothing to build on; the lies and distrust are unraveling everything I have come to cherish with you, and I won't allow them to start destroying the memories of the happiest times of our lives with their shrouds. It's all or nothing, Victoria."

She nodded, making her choice. It wasn't a choice, really. You needed air to breathe, and he was that for her.

"May I ask you a question?"

A deep heat swept over her, quickly leaving a light sheen of perspiration at the base of her spine.

She nodded again.

"Why did you petition for custody of Vivian?"

"You don't waste time do you?"

"I don't know. It depends on how you look at it. I'd say eight years is a lot of time wasted."

She looked up, startled by the mentioned time frame. Sure it coincided with Grace's blackmailing attempts, but she thought she had been careful to keep it hidden, at least until her tongue got the best of her with Paige.

"Like I said, I thought we could give her more. She has the benefits of having two people in the home and our money. There are a lot more privileges and luxuries we can afford her. She would have the opportunity to have the best education as well."

"But what about the love of her father? She lost her mother only two years ago, and you wish to separate her from her father now? I don't understand."

"You sound like we aren't family. I love her, and I have the ability to give her the attention she deserves. Mason works all of those hours. How is he going to be there for her?"

"So what was Mason to do when you obtained custody of Vivian?"

"I would have been more than happy to allow him to come with her. He is talented; I'll give him that. He could find a job here in a second."

"You know he wouldn't take anything from you after all of the history between you two, not to mention he has pride in himself and has made more than a decent living for Vivian. No. I think it is something a great deal more personal, but I was hoping you wouldn't be that blind to the needs a child has for their parent. Is your hatred so great for Mason that you would be willing to risk the happiness and well-being of a child, your grandchild, to make him suffer?"

"How can I trust him to take care of her? Look at what he did with Rachael?"

Richard blew out a calming breath. "Yes. Let's take a look. From the moment she told us about him, I have never heard her as happy as when she was born again. She loved him and felt safe with him, adopted a child with him because she trusted him to continue to take care of her and make her happy, and she wanted to share that with a child that otherwise might not get to live in a loving household. I could not have asked for more from a son-in-law. And yes, she got sick, but he didn't kill her, Victoria. She contracted a disease that her body could no longer fight off, and she died. No one was to blame."

"How can you speak of her death so callously, with so little regard?"

"Don't tell me how I feel, Victoria. I was there in that room too. I watch the life slowly leave her body those last months, and I also saw the way Mason put everything in his life, but Vivian, on hold, trying to save her."

"Yes, and still she died. I offered to help, but he wouldn't take it."

Richard snorted. "You know it wasn't so much of an offer, as a demand – which caused strife between the two of you. She made the choice, not Mason. Rachael chose her path. If you want to be angry with anyone, it should be with her or...or you can just let it go," he finished quietly.

Victoria was fighting mad by the time Richard was done speaking. She wanted to yell and scream at him, but they'd been through this all before – many, many times, and each time they'd left the argument more hurt than healed – and angrier than when they began – making them less willing to bring up the subject of their daughter at all. It was an ongoing cycle that aided in the deterioration of their marriage.

Maybe Richard was right. Maybe a marriage counselor was needed to help moderate their conversations about Rachael until they could do it on their own. That way, Richard would be able to see that she was right to want custody of Vivian.

"I guess we will agree to disagree."

Richard's eyes narrowed slightly, but he didn't comment. He just stared at her until she looked away.

"Like I said, I leave on Thursday." He got up and began stacking his plates.

"Is that the only thing you want to ask me? I'm sure there must be other things you want to discuss outside of Mason," she said, looking up at him, seeking to keep him with her for a little while longer in hopes that they would end their small holiday on a lighter note.

He stopped what he was doing, and looked at her as if he was trying to decide to take her up on her offer. He sat back down slowly.

"As a matter of fact, there has been something that I have been unable to grasp. It's in regards to Paige Morganson, the woman that donated her kidney to Vivian. Well, actually, Vivian's biological mother."

Victoria took a sip of her water to wet her suddenly dry mouth. She nodded.

"I spoke to Mason after my lawyers found some potential donors for Vivian's kidney transplant, and he told me that you were adamant about not choosing Paige because she was Vivian's birth mother and you said you couldn't risk Paige finding out."

"Yes." It took everything she had not to choke on the word. This could get really bad. If he asked her about Grace, would she tell him the truth? Could she?

"I just want to know. Did you have anything to do with what went on in the hospital the day Paige delivered Vivian?" He watched her intently.

She let go of the breath she had been holding in relief. "No. I did not have anything to do with whatever went on in that delivery room." Victoria looked him square in the eye so that he would know beyond a shadow of a doubt that she was telling the truth.

His breath expelled with a whoosh of air through his lips, and he looked visibly relieved. Then another question formed in his eyes.

"So how did you know before Paige that she was Vivian's biological mother, and why were you against her finding out?"

She had to think on this one. She picked up her half-empty glass and walked to the wet bar to refill it, all the while reworking the facts in her head. What could she give away that would satisfy his curiosity? By the time she'd sat back down, she was relatively secure in her answer.

"Um, well, I kinda did a little digging on Vivian's family health history just after Rachael had been diagnosed. I wanted to be prepared as best I could, or at least better than I was with Rachael.

There were some discrepancies with the records regarding what her mother died of, and I had an investigator do some digging. There were other women that delivered that night and we discovered that the woman who was named Vivian's mother had a child that died during childbirth. I was afraid if Paige learned the truth, she would sue for custody of Vivian." She erected a look of pain and distress before glancing back up at Richard. It wasn't all that hard to do since the thought had crossed her mind.

"Why didn't you tell me? I could have spared you the worry and angst."

"How? There was nothing you could do to change the fact." She tilted her head to the side to study him harder. What did he know?

"Not to change the past, but to relieve you of the notion that Paige was vindictive. I met her in the hospital right before she was going to be transferred to the rehabilitation center. I could have told you after talking with Paige just for a few minutes that there was no way she would try and take Vivian from Mason. It just isn't in her."

Victoria held onto the table so tight her knuckles changed color. Paige had talked to Richard, but hadn't said anything to her? She leaned back in her chair to stare at a man she no longer recognized. She didn't know how to respond.

CHAPTER 12

"Daddy?" Vivian stopped just short of handing Mason a slip of paper as he sat the drafting table in his office. He looked up from the plans he'd brought home from work to see his daughter dressed for bed with huge pink, rabbit slippers on her feet. He glanced at the clock on the wall, surprised to see it was passed 9 p.m.

"What's up, honey?" He watched her hesitate and turned to face her.

"I need you to sign my progress report for next week." He reached for the slip of paper, reading it over. Once again, pride lit in him at her excellent marks. He was so fortunate. He'd heard the stories of young girls becoming the prey of internet predators, kidnappers, gangs, and drug dealers. His child's favorite pastime was praying; praying, and now talking to her twin sister and biological mother – oh, and he couldn't forget church. He couldn't deny that things could be so much worse. He knew co-workers who would give their right arm for a daughter like his, and all he'd done was consider what he'd been missing.

He knew she still missed her mother, and since her time in the hospital he had maintained an 'open door' policy when it came to discussing Rachael, Paige, and Gladys. He would not stifle her again. It had done more damage than he ever could have imagined, and he had been on the verge of losing the most precious thing in his life.

Judging from the nights they were able to eat together and catch up on the activities of the day, she was thriving at school and church. She'd not only caught up in her classes but also put in for extra credit, and was able to maintain her high scores. She had always been exceptionally gifted and he wouldn't be surprised if she continued this way on through high school. He was hard-pressed not to take it for granted.

If he had to admit it, she was doing a lot better than he was in many ways, even if he hadn't touched a bottle in almost two weeks.

"Um, I'm getting my Certificate of Completion for my Sunday school class this Sunday, and I was…" She took a deep breath. He watched her wet her lips. Her nervousness was apparent. "I was wondering if you would come. You don't have to stay for the fellowship afterward." She rushed on quickly, pleading with her eyes. "It's just that the other parents are going to be there with their children, and I didn't…want…" she trailed off, staring down at the floor. His heart squeezed painfully in his chest. Had he done this to her? Had he made her so insecure about mentioning church?

Sure, he wasn't ready to commit himself to attending every Sunday – or even a Sunday a month for that matter – but she obviously felt his aversion to the degree that she didn't even think she could ask him to be there for an event that meant a lot to her. He would have to rectify that.

"Viv, hon…" He waited for her to meet his eyes before he continued, "You make my heart proud and I would be honored to be there to see you get your certificate."

The smile that transformed her face, lightening up her eyes until they glowed silver, stopped his breath.

She squealed. "Really?" She jumped forward, hugging his neck in a choking squeeze, but he didn't mind.

"You are the best, Daddy. Like I said, you don't have to stay after for the refreshments and all that. We can always get something after, or I could cook lunch for us here–"

He interrupted her. "We stay as long as you like."

She pulled back, seemingly shocked by his offer. She looked as if she would argue but thought better of it. She just nodded and hugged him again. "You're the best. Thank you."

He held her long, absorbing this moment to think back on. How much longer would he be the best in her life? He didn't want to admit it, but his little girl was growing up, and he'd missed a lot. He once again reaffirmed his commitment to himself that she would remain first in his thoughts and life – a perfect weapon against those demons that raided his subconscious at night, stifling his dreams.

He leaned back slightly, pulling her arms. "No setting me up though. Promise?"

She rendered over a sheepish smile and agreed. "Promise."

He signed the slip, handing it back over to her. "I'm proud of you, Hon. You are doing a fantastic job. Remember, tomorrow I pick you up early for your follow up. How are you feeling tonight? Any pain or puffiness?"

"No, but do you think if the doctor is all right with it, I could go to P.E. again?"

Even though the thought frightened him, he was not in a hurry to dispel her hope.

"We will see what the doctor says," he responded, not committing either way. He kissed her cheeks before she turned and left the room.

It was a few minutes before he could get his concentration back.

He could tell that she spent a lot of time speaking to Paige because it was reflecting in some of her speech patterns. He wondered how she was doing. It had been a few weeks since they'd spoken. She was going to be touring soon to promote her new book.

He thought of going on her site to see where she would be headed first, but just as quickly squashed that thought. She was with someone else. Besides Vivian, they didn't have anything to discuss, and he needed to keep his mind on work. He had been tossing around the offer Richard had made him a few months back regarding some developing his organization was doing in Uganda. He was in need of another project to fill in the idle hours – all four of them during the week, and many more on the weekend.

He found that staying busy helped keep him sane and sober.

Awww Rachael, I wish you could see her now. She is so beautiful, and though I should have admitted it when you were alive, I love the light that shines through her eyes from her spirit – just like you. I miss how you were always there with a positive perspective on things, and able to see the hope in every situation. I even miss the way you would pray for me when you thought I was sleep. I miss you baby, and our daughter can't help but remind me of you.

You know I accidentally found Vivian's biological mother, and I know you would have loved her; she is like you in many ways. She has the same smile that feels like a ray of sunshine when it's directed at me. I know you will forgive me when I tell you I think I love her. I fought it though. I fought it hard, but her heart is so beautiful. It kept calling to me just like her bewitching eyes, but she denies it and says she loves another.

I don't know what it is. No one but you has affected me nearly as much. I feel like some obsessed lunatic; I can't stop thinking about her, and this isn't healthy. If you still pray for me, please, please tell

Him to release me from this hold. If this is His idea of a joke, tell Him I'm not laughing.

He shook himself from his fanciful thinking and worked to concentrate on the plans that needed to be finished by the next afternoon.

       *   *   *

For the third time in as many months, Mason found himself in a sanctuary, seated amongst people who seemed to share in one huge, inside joke. They laughed lightheartedly and spoke amongst themselves with warmth and familiarity. He felt distinctly disconnected. That didn't faze him so much as the accolades, appreciative glances, and credit that he became a target of due to his daughter's latest achievement. There was no doubt that she was a shining example of what every parent would consider a warm and loving child. He just wished the true influence of her inner strength could be present. Rachael truly deserved the credit for Vivian's accomplishments in *this* world. Even after two years, her mark was deeply imprinted upon Vivian's character.

When the parents were asked to accompany their children as they received their certificate, he felt the burning of hundreds of eyes on his back. He resisted the urge to loosen his stifling tie and collar, and took his daughter's hand to assist her up the stairs to the pulpit.

Watching the pastor intently, careful to listen for any cues, Mason kept his eyes centered on his immediate surroundings. It wasn't until the presentation was over and he reached the last step that he glanced out over the congregation. In that flicker of a second, he thought he saw dark and curly, shoulder-length hair framing caramel colored skin. He scanned back over the crowd but shrugged it off as an overactive imagination when he didn't find any fire-lit eyes.

If he could think of one word to describe the rest of his experience that morning it would be 'relieved'. The conversations seemed more focused on his work and Vivian than why he didn't accompany her more often, and he felt the knots that had been there when he woke up, loosening. These people seemed to be genuinely concerned for him and his daughter, and on more than one occasion extended an invitation to a social gathering or activity without pressing him for an immediate commitment.

They were halfway home before he got up the nerve to ask about Paige. "So, Viv, how is Paige doing? Does she seem to be feeling pretty good? I know she will begin touring soon, and I was hoping that she was feeling well and recovered enough to keep her dates."

After a few seconds of silence, he glanced at her and saw the inquisitive expression puckering on her lips. "What?" he asked, immediately feeling defensive. "I can't ask about her?"

Vivian smiled, nodding her head quickly. "Just thought…" she trailed off.

"Go ahead; you just thought?" He didn't take his eyes off the road.

"I thought it made you sad when you heard her name."

"No… Hon, why would you think such a thing?"

"Because you get a sad look on your face whenever I talk about her."

Well, you couldn't really argue with that.

He tried to think of a convincing way to deny it, but Vivian was way too intuitive for any of the things that sprang to mind. She'd just proven to him that she was more sensitive than he realized.

"I'm trying to do better, my love."

He could feel her eyes on him, and glanced at her quickly.

"You are a good daddy. You're just hurting because your heart is cracked." She reached over and placed her small hand on his.

"Cracked?" He repeated, trying to ignore onslaught of emotion.

"Yeah," she nodded, glancing out the window as if that explained everything.

The silence stretched on, so he tried again. "Is your heart cracked?"

She looked over at him with a tremendous smile. "Not anymore…" Then she seemed to think about it. "Well maybe a little, but it's okay. I didn't really expect it to go all-the-way away."

"Why not?" His curiosity was peaked.

"Cause I will always miss mommy. It's just the memories don't hurt so much anymore."

He was thoroughly stunned by her thought process.

"How?"

"How what, Daddy?" She never took her eyes off of him.

"How did you get better? How is it the memories don't hurt so much?"

"God's been healing me."

The thoughts were whirling in his head. Did he even want to know how? Would it work for him? What would he have to give up?

"It's worth it," she said, as if reading his mind.

He didn't know whether or not to admit what he had been thinking. He decided to play it safe.

"Huh?"

She made a clicking noise with her tongue. *Did she just suck her teeth at me?* That wasn't going to be tolerated. He didn't care what the discussion was.

"Young lady, I would suggest you keep your tongue away from your teeth if you want to keep from getting a fat lip."

She turned to stare out of her window. "Yes, Daddy."

After a few moments of silence, she heaved a sigh.

"If you want God to take the pain away, all you have to do is believe that He sent His son to die for you, and accept Him in your heart." Her voice was so quiet, he could barely hear her over the car's heater.

He wasn't going to tell her that He'd accepted Jesus in his heart at nine-years-old in Vacation Bible School, but the feelings of betrayal caused by his father's polygamy and his mother's suffering had a long time to fester, and he didn't think there was any room left in his heart now for God or forgiveness.

"I'm not sure I have any room left for Jesus," he said, voicing some of this thoughts.

"Don't say that, Daddy. You won't get to go to heaven if you mean that..." she began to cry huge, choking sobs. "I don't want you to go to hell. You will hurt forever there..."

He chanced a glance at her. Her face was buried in her hands. "Don't honey, you'll make yourself sick. It will be all right."

"NO IT WON'T!" she screamed at him, and began wailing.

He turned the corner as quick as he dared and pulled into the driveway, throwing the car into 'Park.'

He released their seatbelts then grabbed her shoulders, and turned her towards him.

"Vivian." He shook her gently to get her attention. "Vivian, calm down." She didn't respond to his words; she just cried harder.

"Vivian, Vivian Leigh Jenson, you pull yourself together right now." He tried sounding stern, but he was starting to worry. Vivian wasn't one to give into hysterics.

"Vivian." He shook her harder. "Vivian, listen to me. I am not going to hell."

"Yes, you are. You will be tortured over and over again with no rest, and you will never get out. You will never see me or mommy again, and…"

The sound of the slap bounced off the car windows, surprising him almost as much as it surprised Vivian.

With her eyes wide and mouth opened in shock, she pressed her palm to her cheek. Her tear-stained face, flushed red from her tantrum, became void of color.

"I'm sorry, baby. I didn't mean to hurt you. I just didn't want you to scream and cry until you became ill." He reached for her, but she leaned back, her grey eyes reminding him of shards of glass, cold and accusing.

He let his hands fall between them.

Three hours later, Mason found himself staring out the same sliding glass door. Vivian had gone to her room without a word, and he hadn't heard a sound from her since.

He was filled with a riot of emotions, and there was no sorting them out. He had slapped his child to pull her back from a hysterical episode, but was any of it done in anger? He didn't think so, but he couldn't completely escape the feeling that he'd wanted to quell her tirade about his soul.

He ran his hands through his hair. Only a few hours ago, he was standing next to his daughter while she accepted a certificate mapping her spiritual maturity, and now he feared some of that knowledge. Who was telling his child he was going to hell, and why would they give a twelve-year-old such graphic details about what happened in hell?

The heat from his rising anger, combined with indignation, blanketed him. He didn't even realize he had moved until he was at Vivian's door. He took a deep breath, trying to calm himself then knocked on her door. It was just a formality since the door had no lock. He waited a few seconds then knocked again, and opened the door.

Vivian was laying on her bed, her back facing the door. He walked in quietly, just in case she was sleep, moving to the edge of the bed.

Vivian was awake staring at nothing in particular.

"Did you hear me knock?"

"Yes."

"Why didn't you answer?"

"You woke me up."

He sighed. This part of parenting he could do without.

"Sit up. I want to talk to you."

She slowly raised herself up on her palms and turned towards his voice, but wouldn't look at him.

He sat on the bed facing her, but didn't try to close the distance.

"I'm sorry I slapped you, Vivian, but I did it for your own good."

She let out a loud breath. "Yeah." She looked so forlorn, he was momentarily at a loss for words. He remained silent until he remembered his original purpose for entering her room.

"Vivian, who taught you about hell?"

She looked up at him. "It's in the bible, Daddy."

"But who showed you where to find it?"

She shook her head. "Nobody. I looked it up."

A foreboding rose up inside of him, but he smothered it.

"Why would you look it up?"

She looked as though she didn't want to answer him, but sighed with resignation and whispered. "I didn't want it to be real, so I was hoping not to find it." Her voice raised a few octaves, gaining confidence. "Mati told me that if you couldn't find something that people say like it's religious, in the bible, then it doesn't exist...but there it was, like over at least 10 times. It's really real." The last was stated in a whisper again.

"Did you discuss this with Ms. Paige?" he asked.

She shook her head in the negative.

The anger seemed to drain away from him, along with his strength.

"Are you hungry? We could go out. We still need to celebrate you getting your certificate." Hopefully a little food would make them both feel better.

"No...I just want to go back to sleep for a while, if that's okay?"

"Sure, sure Hon. I'll just make sure to wake you up in time for dinner."

She nodded and turned to lay back down.

He didn't get up right away, but stared down at her still frame for a few minutes, wondering what else he could do.

"Vivian, you do know I love you, right?"

She glanced at him then closed her eyes. "Yes, Daddy. I know."

He watched her until he thought she was asleep, then rose to leave. He was at the door when she called him. "Daddy?"

"Yes?"

"Are you still angry at mommy for leaving?"

He turned around. "Why do you ask?"

"I was angry at you...really angry at you when you hit me, but I forgive you because you thought you were helping me. And though I still don't get it, I know you love me, so I forgive you. Mommy loved you too. I know she did and she didn't mean to hurt you. I just think you will feel better if you forgive her."

He nodded, turning back around and walking out the door, closing it behind him.

It wasn't getting any easier. He didn't answer Vivian when she asked if he was still angry with her mother because he knew what her next question would be and he didn't want to look at the heartbreaking expression on her face when he told her it was God he was really angry with. He still remembered how she'd pleaded with him in the hospital to let it go, but it was all much easier said than done.

*   *   *

The call he'd begun to expect after Vivian's third day of moping came Thursday afternoon, just as he was getting ready to leave the office for lunch.

"MarsdenTech, Mason speaking."

"Hello Mason, it's Paige. How are you doing?"

"Hi Paige. Fine, thank you, and yourself?"

"Very good. I would like to talk to you. Is this a good time?"

"Sure, but let me call you from my cell. I have a good idea of what it's about, and I would rather my co-workers didn't get an ear full."

She agreed and severed the call.

He got some of his things together and headed for the elevators. Once he was in the lobby headed to his car, he dialed her number.

"Hi."

"Hi. Sorry about the delay. I wanted to get out of the building. The reception is better outside. What did you want to talk about?" *Might as well get right to it.*

"I'm a little concerned about Vivian."

"Okay."

"She seems listless. Did something happen this weekend?"

"She didn't tell you anything?"

"No. Not directly, but she asked me how long it took for God to answer a prayer she knew He wanted to happen."

For all of her maturity, the question reminded him of his daughter's child-like tendencies.

"What did you tell her?" He placed his key in the ignition, but didn't turn the car over. Lunch would have to wait.

"I told her the truth. I didn't know, and that there were a lot of deciding factors. One was whether it was the right time, or if it could be something that brought happiness now but destruction later because she wasn't prepared to take care of it. Two was if other people were involved. I told her she could not ignore that people have free will." She blew out a deep breath.

"What did she say?"

"She said she had to go to school and quickly got offline."

Mason leaned back on the headrest of his chair. He didn't know what to do, and stated as much to Paige. He then heaved a great sigh and relayed what happened on Sunday after church.

"Awww, Mason, I'm sorry."

"Why? You didn't do anything."

"Yes, but she has been asking a lot of questions about salvation and hell lately. I've been trying to temper my answers so they would be age appropriate, but I guess Google doesn't have the same points of digression. You might want to see if there is an age block regarding the search engines," she rambled on nervously.

"Meanwhile, your daughter is worried her father is going to hell and is in danger of spending eternity in torment. Do you have any suggestions on how to allay her fears?"

"I'm out of my element here. I hate to admit it, but I don't know what to do. I am hoping she will slowly forget about it, but that's as likely as forgetting that an elephant lives with you."

"I usually wouldn't even think about suggesting this, but would you consider going to church..."

"Don't you think there are enough people in church every Sunday for reasons other than for God? I won't add to that number. I won't become something I loathe more than..." He didn't finish, almost afraid to say it out loud.

"I didn't mean for you to go to church just for her, but for yourself... I mean as a way to seek out answers to some of those questions that are causing you so much angst. I am not without feeling, Mason. I remember some of the conversations we've had and though I will take the blame for some of the distance between us, I will not pretend that I don't care for you."

His heartbeat doubled, but he wasn't going to fall into that trap again. He wanted everything spelled out. "What are you saying, Paige?"

There was a long silence on the other line before she responded.

"I will never forget the time we spent getting to know each other when I was in Chicago. We became friends, close friends, and not just because we share a daughter, but because of what we shared of ourselves. I came to care about you, Mason. We both have had less than stellar childhoods and even though you didn't go into detail, I could tell that your hurt and anger go deeper and farther than what we discussed regarding Vivian, her mother, Rachael, or Victoria. Was I wrong?" He heard her release a breath.

"No," he said quickly, wanting to know where this was going.

"Not so much for Vivian's sake as for yours – I don't want to see you continue to suffer."

"You said you wouldn't pity me, Paige." It came out through a set jaw with minimal use of his lips.

"Don't mistake my concern for pity, Mason. You, more than others, should know that I don't hand out things I don't want in return. I just don't think you have to continue to hurt the way you do, and now seeing the way it also affects your daughter I'd think you might give some more thought to having an open mind towards…"

He stamped down his anger, trying hard not to allow this conversation to take an even worse turn. "Towards what, Paige?" He asked so that she would finish where her voice had faded.

"Towards whom, Mason. Towards whom."

"Paige." Her name came out with exasperation.

"Please, just hear me out, and I will not bring it up again."

"Fine."

"No one can say that you don't love your daughter. It seems that your life is centered on her and that is commendable, as I have said many times. But, it's also a hazard because no one can guarantee that she will outlive you. And what are you teaching her?

Anyone can see that she adores you and thinks the world of you. There is very little that you can do wrong in her eyes, and that is why this is particularly painful for her. As much as she loves you, she loves God. He is as much a part of her life as you are; your wife made sure of that and now that I am part of her life, I will continue to help nurture that relationship. This isn't to spite you or win over a place in your child's heart that has been set aside for you, but I don't believe God would place both your wife and myself in Vivian's life if He didn't want her to remain so close to Him.

This isn't a fad or a passing fancy. Her love for Him isn't in spite of or because of anything that has happened in her world. It is ingrained in her, and if by chance something does wiggle its way between her and her daily communication with Him, she will always come back. I just think you would want to be a part of that instead of encouraging its demise."

"I would never discourage her relationship with God."

"Aren't you doing that now? I don't think you understand your influence on Vivian – as you have every right to have as her father.

You are the first person she sees in the morning, and many times the last one she sees at night. You regulate a lot of the rules in her world. She continuously looks to you for approval on just about everything in her life. Your deep dislike for all things surrounding God will filter its way into her psyche and she will doubt, especially now that Rachael isn't there to counteract it.

I am just asking you to give it some thought. Whatever anger you have stored up against God, would you please consider that He isn't against you. That, as much as circumstances, emotions and life have distanced you from Him, He loves you and wants the chance to show you that He isn't against you being happy."

"Name one reason why you think He hasn't forsaken me or set me up as a pawn for His work," he replied snidely, because it was the only defense he had left to her entreaty.

"You could have adopted a different child, fallen in love with a different woman, and you and I could have never met. And there could have been no one in your life that cared for you enough or knew enough to pray that the hurt and pain you experienced would be cured so that you could have peace, joy, and a deeper understanding of how precious you are."

He didn't have much to say. Paige had a way of taking not only his words but the fight out of him. He went for joviality to lighten their conversation and skirt around the issue until he was able to process it all.

"Precious, huh? I didn't know men could be considered precious."

He heard a light giggle on the other side.

"No Mason, precious would not be the first word that came to mind when I thought of you. But as my friend you have many attributes, like your willingness to listen, that I do find precious, and I am sure many more that God deems so as well."

He wasn't going to touch that with a 10-foot-pole. "I have many words that come to mind when I think about you too, Paige. I will tell you mine if you tell me yours."

The line was quiet for a moment.

"Mr. Jenson, are you flirting with me?" She sounded disapproving at the turn the conversation had taken.

"It depends on the word." He said dryly.

"Frustrating." He could hear the definition come through the line with the word loud and clear.

"Funny, that's mine for you. What are the odds?"

CHAPTER 13

"Mason, can we get back to the reason why I called?"

"No. It's not nearly as entertaining as this is. I bet your ears are as red as cherries."

"And you are avoiding the subject."

"If that's what you want to call it."

"What else could it be called?" She was working hard to stay on point.

"It could be called light conversation, friendly banter, or sparring wits."

"Or a stubborn man showing his character."

"What's that Paige? I don't think God would be too pleased with you using insults as a way of recruiting." All humor had been exchanged for sarcasm on Mason's end.

"I just don't understand why you won't give it some thought?"

"And I don't know when you stopped being human. We used to be able talk and play with one another. Now you come to me like some pious woman on behalf of my daughter. This is what I wanted to avoid." His words were like darts, piercing armor that felt way too thin.

He knew just where to aim – the one place that she tried to avoid.

"I'm sorry," she said contritely, truly afraid his thoughts were justified.

"So am I, Paige. More than you know. I was hoping that our circumstances wouldn't cause you to put up your defenses. You seem to do that whenever I get too close or you feel threatened. My question is 'why'? Why do you feel threatened by a little bantering with me?"

She opened her mouth a couple of times, but she was so surprised by his accusation, nothing came out.

"I will give your sermon some consideration. For Vivian's sake," he finished, "Look, I need to head out and grab some lunch, and I don't have my Bluetooth with me so I'm going to have to go…"

"Mason?"

She heard the breath he expelled before answering her. "Yes, Paige."

"I really didn't mean to call you and make it seem as though you aren't a good father. My only intention was to help ease Vivian's fears and give you some insight as to why she is hurting."

"I know, Paige." He sounded tired. "Just once, I wish you would call, more interested in Mason, the man, than in my soul. I know it's selfish and you don't owe me anything. It's not like we have a relationship. We are just two people who share a daughter."

"But…" She wanted to somehow explain that he meant more to her.

"No, Paige. No more apologies or declarations of concern. I don't think I could take any more *concern*." He said the word as if it were some communicable disease that could be spread by speaking of it.

"Okay, Mason." Her voice was small. She just wanted off the phone now.

"Goodbye, Paige."

"Bye, Mason." The phone line was dead before she finished his name.

Why she felt like crying, she didn't know. It was as if something had been severed in that phone call that had been precariously dangling between them for a while, and she somehow knew she was going to miss it.

She wanted to growl in frustration. *Shoot. I'm by myself.* She pushed out a rough sound from her diaphragm, working for as much volume as possible.

It felt so good, she did it again. Why, why, why was it that every time she spoke to Mason about God, she ended up feeling like the one in the wrong?

She shook herself. She refused to harp on it. She was in the right this time – she knew it. She poked her lip out in a pout, not wanting to hear anything less from her conscience or the Holy Spirit.

She turned her attention back to her computer, looking over the newest revisions on her website. She knew that in order for people to continue to visit her site, she needed to have something new for them to look at. She was just happy she didn't have to do them herself.

The expected release date for her new book was now pasted on the home page along with its cover and a short summary. She recalled how Carmen had vented her frustration at the publisher's confusion at their change in genres from self-help to fiction. Carmen had spoken with a friend in the fiction department and received more than positive feedback regarding Paige's change in genre. She knew they would get some resistance, but since the fictional book was still steeped in research and had many places of instruction that the reader could lean on for support in similar situations they may be dealing with, she didn't think they had ventured too far from some of Paige's other work. It was good that they had fulfilled the original contract and were open to working with a new publishing house, otherwise they would have had nothing to negotiate with.

That was one of the wonderful things about Carmen; she was tenacious and made Paige feel safe when it came to contract negotiations. Their relationship had rented Paige with the security needed to venture out into the world of fiction – even if it were a glossed over rendition of her cousin's life with a blatantly happy ending that the character experienced longer than her cousin had the chance to.

She often wondered how different their lives would be if her cousin was still alive and moving in the knowledge and acceptance of Christ.

Would she have had the courage to tell her daughters who their father was? Would he have wished to meet them?

She dispelled a long sigh, thankful and regretful of both of her thoughts. It was indeed bittersweet, but really, how much could she expect from herself or her girls? It was best that things ended and began as they had. She didn't think she had the strength to have to deal with more of her family's dysfunctions than she was already living with.

Which brought her back to Mason.

She wanted him to get it so badly sometimes her heart ached for him, but no one could go to God in his place. No one could release his burdens of worry, fear, and anger to God but him. No one could forgive God for what he felt had been stolen from him except Mason.

Outside of the surface inquiries made to Vivian about her father, Paige didn't discuss Mason with anyone, but that didn't keep her from thinking about him and praying for him with a fervor she'd failed to do so with her cousin, Stone. She knew it kept him close to her heart, and considered it safe and reassuring to be able to pray for him as she did by not only listening to what the Spirit would have her to pray concerning him, but to receive small glimpses of what he was battling with when she was led to war for him in the spirit.

She knew this was where the comment about him being precious came from. She'd felt the urge to share with him some of what God had revealed to her in regards to His love for him. She felt compelled, actually, and didn't see the harm in it, but when he turned it around and began to flirt with her, she didn't know how to react. She had been taken totally off guard then terrified that she had in some way encouraged it.

She stood up from her desk and crossed over to the window. Placing her fingers on the pane, she welcomed the coolness but squelched the urge to press her face against it.

She fought the temptation to venture deeper into her feelings for Mason. She had closed that door the moment she decided to explore a relationship with Brandon. Mason would remain in the category she'd placed him – *very* distant relative.

She cautiously thought back on their conversation, working to remain objective. She realized they'd only touched the surface regarding Vivian's fears. There had been no definite course of action planned out, just what seemed to be acceptance of the issue and a half-hearted commitment to give their conversation some deep consideration.

Oh God, Abba, Father,

Please. I need your guidance right now. I don't know what more I can do. I have tried to be that constant representative of you; the example of what You wish people to see when they think of Your love, but I feel like such a failure when it comes to Mason.

There are so many things you have shown me regarding him and what he means to You. Why? Why do you show me these things? It is like looking through a window at all of the things I want, not only for my sake but for Yours, and then being told to wait.

I have been obedient. I pray and pray, and then I wait. I wait upon You and I feel some of your longing, and it pains me and motivates me to pray harder, but now the threat of his disobedience is at my child's feet and I'm fighting this urge of desperation.

Please continue to cover my child. Show her even more of the things you have in store for her. Continue to reveal to her how beautiful she is to you, and encourage her with dreams and visions. Keep her heart light and show her how to encourage herself when darkness creeps close. I and Rachael have dedicated her to you; please do not let her stray far from you ever. I promise to do my part. I will pray, I will war, I will fast, I will consecrate myself, and continue to praise and worship you for what you have done in my life and what is yet to come to past. But most of all, I will worship You because it is the sustainer of my life. Amen.

She moved away from the window, still in an attitude of prayer and felt a prompting to speak in her heavenly language. She walked through her apartment uttering the language she could not readily interpret, but could glean impressions from. She felt as if she were on the precipice of something huge. She could see nothing passed the tips of her feet as if she were on a ledge looking over a vast space, and though the blackness in front of her should have been frightening she sensed a presence there, just beyond her grasp.

She didn't move; just looked out into the deep, waiting for her spiritual eyes to adjust, but there was nothing she could make out. She quelled the urge to step back and just prayed for the strength to move when He said to move.

She continued walking in and out of the rooms as she had done many times before; sometimes speaking forcefully and others with pleading tones, pouring out her heart and spirit. Amidst the language she discerned the supplications for Vivian and Brandon then continued to lift up friends and loved ones, calling them by name. Melanie, Marc, Brandon's mother, Ava; his father, Elias, Makayla, Everzie, Margret; back to Brandon, Lady Menagerie – she listened intently for how to pray for each one individually, even as her spirit went forth in prayer. She prayed for her mother, Grace – which threw her into weeping in her living room – and then for Mason, where if she was aware of the volume of her voice, she may have been afraid of being overheard by her neighbor, but she was caught in the midst of warfare and only knew that she would not stop until her voice gave out or the heaviness and urgency passed.

A full hour passed before she began to feel a release and found herself spent not just physically spent, but spiritually invigorated. With a quiet and tired smile, she resumed her work on the outline and story idea of her latest work. The vision was clear and her hands moved quickly over the keys, trying to catch every word flowing through her head. What would have normally taken a couple of hours came through in 15 minutes, and as she typed the last words her stomach began to rumble. She couldn't recall her last meal, but as she shut down her workstation she glanced at the clock, noting that her last full meal had been more than 16 hours before.

Mmm, I wonder what Brandon is doing tonight? She went in search of her cell phone to see if she had any missed calls. As she scrolled through the missed calls, she pressed the button to listen to her voicemail and smiled at the sound of Brandon's voice. She knew she'd shut him out the previous week when she'd had "delusions of grandeur" as Lady Menagerie had bluntly stated, but hoped she wouldn't find him to be as stubborn as she was.

An amused smile lifted her lips as she thought about the 'wet noodle beating' she'd received from Lady Menagerie the previous Sunday. She'd sat across the desk from the First Lady, more nervous in her presence than she could remember. Her insecurity so poignant she could smell its fragrance wafting up through her very pores. She had buried herself in self-pity since her phone call with Grace, and her isolation only proved to give the enemy the foothold he needed to keep her in a place of shame.

When she began to voice what she was feeling – the failure in not being more of an example of God's love, and the hateful words they'd exchanged by the end of the phone call – Lady Menagerie's features became impassive.

"Who do you think you are?"

"Huh?" Sure she'd heard the woman wrong, Paige sat up straighter.

"I asked you, who you think you are? Don't you think you're given the same grace when you fall short? Is there some special type of deal you set with God that you can't falter? If so, you need to squash that now. I haven't heard from you in an entire week. Is this what has been going through you head – that you should have been able to talk to a woman who emotionally abused you for most of your adolescent life after a silence of over 12 years and *not* be vulnerable to any emotional outbursts?"

"I'm a child of God, a representative of Christ. One of my first prayers in the morning is to be used to show His love to someone. I can talk to strangers and appeal to them by being open to speak what God has to say to them. With Grace, it was like every word I said made her dislike Him more. By the time the conversation was over, I was so angry I didn't care what she thought." Paige bowed her head, still feeling the ebb of shame that had shrouded her over that week. "I'm ashamed of my behavior."

"Alright." Lady Menagerie leaned back in her chair and continued with nonchalance. "Now get over it."

Paige's head snapped up at the comment. Her eyes were wide with surprise at the lack of compassion she felt coming from her mentor.

"What?"

"I said, 'get over it'. Ask God for His forgiveness, seek out those things in you that caused you to respond to her the way you did, and ask Him for His help in healing you in those places. Then repent. Wallowing in shame is not going to help you grow in this situation. It is only keeps you from seeking God's face and accepting His forgiveness.

If you feel you need to be punished for your actions, I will be more than happy to do that for you. I will start by telling you that your delusions of grandeur, where your walk is concerned, will get you in hot water."

Paige opened her mouth to comment, but the look Lady Menagerie gave her had her closing her mouth as quickly as it opened, without a sound.

"So you have a conversation with a close relative that knows how to push your buttons and you react. You react badly. I think your first error was making the call, mistaking 12 years of avoidance for forgiveness and deliverance on your part. You called her, expecting her to change when you obviously haven't made the necessary changes in yourself to have a civilized conversation with her."

"I have been working on my feelings for her," Paige barked, instantly contrite. She cringed, waiting a reply in like fashion, but was only met with quiet.

When Lady Menagerie did speak it was gentle, but compelling.

"Grace couldn't have said anything more or less about God than you've heard from strangers when they became defensive. Why was it so much more galling when she did it?"

Paige swallowed. "She has always had the ability to provoke emotion in me. When I was young, all I wanted was to know that something I did pleased her, but she always found something to complain about. After the first six years I was away from her, I realized that it wasn't anything I'd done or not done. It was me. It took God, and six more years, for me to realize that it was her, but it is so hard to remember when I feel she should be more…more of a mother. I feel cheated and angry."

She watched as Lady Menagerie got up and walked around the desk to stand in front of her. She looked up at her, waiting for the proverbial shoe to drop, when Lady Menagerie squatted down unexpectedly in front of her.

"You are a beautiful child of God and even more than that, you shine with the love you have for Him. It is unmistakable, and as easily as it draws people who are looking for that missing piece of them, it will convict those who wish to remain in darkness. I venture to think that even though your relationship with God wasn't acknowledged by you until just under a decade ago, He has always kept you close. Though you have struggled with identifying yourself by your past, you missed the kindness and gentleness embedded in your character.

Some people cannot stand peace and kindness. It is so foreign to them that it almost hurts to accept it. I'm not saying that this is what she is dealing with, but you can't accept full responsibility for her reaction to you as a child.

My sweet child, you will have to find a way to release yourself from the shackles of fear of this woman. Once her approval or acknowledgments don't move you, then she won't have the power to make you second guess yourself. Whether she knows what she is doing or not, it is a weapon that the enemy has seen works on you. Take back the control and render his weapon void by taking your mom off of that pedestal you've placed her on."

Paige's brows creased. "I don't think highly of her, nor am I under any misgivings that she is a good mother."

"No, but if she were just a person in your life, not disrespecting her position as your mother, she would not hold so much power over your emotions when you interact with one another."

Paige felt defeated. Conversations about Grace usually left her feeling particularly spent, which was why she avoided it as much as possible.

"You were courageous enough to overcome being abused, raped, and ostracized. You even found the courage and strength to forgive your abuser, reveal yourself to and begin a new relationship with your daughters. You are full of God's strength, grace, and love; it emanates from you. Don't let this relationship dim that light." Lady Menagerie took the hands that were laying in Paige's lap.

"You are loved by me and Pastor Lawrence like a daughter, by your daughters as a mother, and I suspect by Brandon as a very special woman he would like to keep in his life. Don't render any of that void by being unable to release your anger and hate."

She leaned forward, gathering Paige up in a fierce hug and remained like that for a few minutes. When she released her and grabbed the edge the desk to hoist herself back up to a standing position, Paige hid her smile by biting her lip. Lady Menagerie would hardly allow Pastor Lawrence to help her up the stairs or down unless they were in public and making a statement. She prided herself on being spry enough to kneel, bend, get on the floor with the some of the children in the after-school nursery, and get back up on her own.

Paige bit her cheek to keep from making a comment about her knees not being as young as they used to be. When she looked up she saw that Lady Menagerie was watching her.

"So, in light of everything, I believe it's time for you to get back to work. As of right now you are back in rotation for the Visitation Committee and duty on Sundays, but you will not be made to stand more than an hour at a time." Paige opened her mouth to protest, but was silenced by a look from Lady Menagerie.

"It doesn't look like you can take time off without thinking yourself into trouble, my daughter, so I will see you bright and early Sunday morning." Lady Menagerie started shuffling papers on her desk, signifying that their conversation was over. When Paige didn't make a motion to move, Lady Menagerie looked up from her paperwork.

"Will that be all?" Paige asked, barely holding a straight face.

"Don't push me child, or I will put you on toilet duty. Now you better go. I'm sure that beau of yours is anxious to see that you are all right."

Paige giggled. "My beau?"

Lady Menagerie's eyebrow lifted slightly. "What would you call him?"

Paige shrugged nonchalantly. "A good friend?"

Lady Menagerie returned her attention to her work. "You better get out of my office with that 'good friend' stuff and tell Brandon I said 'hello'."

*   *   *

Paige pressed the return call button. The phone rang three times before it was picked up and she heard the voice that raised delightful goose bumps on her arms.

"Hello beautiful."

"Hi Brandon." She was amazed at how his smooth voice alone could elicit such a reaction as to have her almost breathless with anticipation to hear his next words.

"How was your day?"

"Very productive."

"Mmm. What exactly does that mean?"

"That I was so caught up in my work that I forgot to eat," she said sheepishly.

"Are you done then?" he asked with a hint of something she couldn't quite read.

"Yes. Actually, I was calling you to see if you had any plans for dinner." She stated, feeling bold enough to be direct.

"Well as it happens I do have plans." He drew it out as if he were thinking of something else while speaking. Her heart dropped slightly. She was puzzled by the strength of her disappointment.

It wasn't as though she hadn't seen him just a few days before. Maybe she was allowing her feelings for him to get too deep, too soon. They'd just recently cleared the air – again – between them, and she was able to see herself trusting a man for the first time in many years.

"Well, that's all right, maybe another day." She wasn't about to name another specific time that could be turned down.

Her doorbell rang and she sprang up from the bed to answer the door. "Brandon, someone is at my door…"

"That's all right, I'll wait," he responded before she could finish.

She looked down at her faded jeans and worn sweatshirt that she loved, and shrugged. She reached the door and looked out the peephole to see Brandon. Her breath caught momentarily, but once she found her voice she couldn't smother her surprise or her smile.

"Brandon? What are you doing here?" she cried into the phone, "I thought you said you already made plans?"

"Yes, plans to be with you. Plans to take you out and feed you if you'd like."

She looked down at her clothing again. "Um, um, um." Her mind was swirling. "Do you mind waiting there for a moment? I need to aah, um…I need to get ready. It will only take me maybe five minutes at the most." She glanced back through the peephole to see what he was wearing so she'd know how to dress.

He looked splendid in a pair of khaki shorts and a pale green long sleeve, button-down shirt. His close-cropped hair held a light wave, and the goatee he wore was so clean, she had the urge to run her finger along the edges.

"Five minutes, okay?"

"Sure. I'll wait right here."

Eight minutes later, Paige opened her door to Brandon dressed in a mustard-colored silk top and a pair of rust-colored slacks. Since she'd not taken down her hair all day, it fell in perfect ringlets that she'd pinned the night before.

He seemed to hesitate when she first opened the door, and she looked down to make sure that she hadn't skipped a button or, heaven help her, failed to finish zipping her pants. Her quick perusal assuaged her fears, and she looked back up at him quizzically.

"Is something wrong?"

He shook his head, seeming to collect himself. "You are a sight for sore eyes. I didn't know I'd miss you so much."

She felt winded by his admission. His direct gaze captured her and rendered her immobile, but freed her mind from all of her previous reservations. "I missed you too." She took a deep breath. "A lot."

She watched as a wide smile took over his features, then he blurred as he swooped her up into a tight hug. "Thank you," he whispered in her ear.

Since she couldn't breathe until he let her go, she had a moment to consider what it was he was thanking her for, and was comforted by the thought that just her admission could bring him such joy.

"For what?" She pulled herself out of his embrace just far enough to gaze into his eyes.

"For being my heart's desire." The war to breathe was compounded by the burning at the back of her eyes. She returned to his arms, successfully hiding the sheen that had come to her eyes.

"You're really going to have to warn me before you say things so beautiful. You have taken my breath away so much in the last five minutes, I am starting to feel light-headed."

He held her tighter for a couple of seconds, then loosened his hold. He didn't step back however, just spoke in her ear, sending small shivers down her neck.

"It's all right. I'll hold you up." He punctuated it with a light kiss on the curve of her ear.

Perfect answer and an even more wonderful move.

She silently sent up a prayer that felt more like a wish that she could have this extraordinary man in her life longer than...well, he had already been in her life longer than any other love interest. Would she even dare hope for a lifetime? *One day at a time.* No, one moment at a time. That way, she could always be guaranteed just what she wanted. A new understanding of a healthy relationship between a man and a woman.

She was even more resigned to live in the moment. She didn't want to skip over a look, a caress, and definitely not a kiss, though he could express himself in such a way with her that would cause her heart to beat faster.

This beautiful man was causing all of her dreams to come true. She pressed her cheek to his while she memorized what the nape of his neck felt like under her splayed fingertips. Up and down, she skimmed across the skin, from the hairline to the bulge of his T5. She could feel the shiver pass through him, and wondered at the feeling.

She wished they could stay like this, but she knew she would be asking for trouble. They couldn't remain like this and not want more. Already the smell of his cologne was making her mouth water. It was spicy with a hint of musk, and so very masculine.

"Don't you have any flaws?" she murmured into his neck, taking another whiff of his skin. She felt his body tense slightly, breaking into her mild trance.

"Plenty." He began to disengage himself from her. "Don't confuse my adoration and joy in expressing my feelings for you for perfection. I can't hold you or comfort you from a pedestal – and how I love to hold you. I also wouldn't be able to show you all of my other flaws."

"Like what?" She looked up at him, intrigued.

"How quickly they forget," he said with a dramatic sigh, moving around her to retrieve her jacket from the couch. "You couldn't have forgotten your introduction to Mr. Stubborn already?"

She smiled sheepishly, a twinkle of lightning in her hazel eyes. "No, just as I am sure you won't forget Ms. Bullheaded any time soon."

He smiled wide, and she could see how much he enjoyed their banter.

"Makes you wonder who would win an argument?"

"Oh that's easy," she said as she slipped her hands into the sleeves of the jacket he held up for her. She looked back at him slyly over one shoulder but didn't continue.

"Really?" He chuckled, turning her to face him with his hands on her shoulders.

"Yep."

"Are you going to share this with me?" He asked, holding her motionless.

She stared at him for a moment then, feeling a little daring, stepped up to him placing her hands around his neck and brought his head down, stopping when his lips were within inches of hers.

"Ask Robin or Lady Menagerie, or any of your sister-in-laws. They will let you know," she replied, gave him a quick peck and stepped back, trying to get around him. He stopped her with his hands.

"I'd rather hear it from you." She looked up and knew she'd miscalculated. He was blocking her route to the door, and though she knew he wouldn't take advantage of the fact that he eclipsed her by at least half a foot, her quick and slippery exit had been foiled.

The left hand resting on her shoulder crept up her neck to her cheek. His palm was warm to the touch, and she couldn't help swaying into it. Her breathing became shallow as nervous quivers raced back and forth across her stomach. Why was she nervous? It wasn't as if he'd not kissed her before. She gave one last ditch effort for control of the situation.

"I would win," she replied, unable to keep the lightness of play in her voice, completely unaware of the darkening of her eyes.

"Then I consider myself warned," Brandon said, as his other hand splayed between Paige's shoulder blades, adding just enough pressure to close the space between them. He bent his head slowly, his eyes roaming from her eyes to her lips. She could feel his gaze like a warm caress.

She gave up trying to fight him. He could have this one – she just wanted him to kiss her.

She stilled even more, hoping beyond hope he wouldn't change his mind and that this kiss would be all his eyes were promising.

As his head bent closer, she watched him watching her, but didn't have the desire to raise any shields. She trusted him enough to allow him to see what she was feeling. His thumb swept across her cheek to her chin in a motion that made her feel as though he was handling her like crystal. He was discovering her facets.

When his thumb caressed her bottom lip, her heart stopped and started again. Her nerve endings were sparking and he hadn't even kissed her yet.

She fisted her hands at her sides to keep from reaching for him in haste, but raised herself ever so slightly.

His lips met hers tenderly as if they were whispering to each other. Then he skimmed hers, moving back and forth, just barely touching even though the static between their mouths was growing.

She closed her eyes and just…felt. She felt the way his lips pressed into hers and released only to do it again. She felt the way he stepped into her space, wrapping himself around her and embracing her with his warmth and smell. Her world tipped.

She slid her hands under his arms and gripped his shoulders to keep herself from sliding to the floor.

He pressed his fingers to her jaw just enough to tilt her head so that he could gain better access to her mouth. He sealed her lips with his, molding them as if he were trying to reshape them to his firm ones. After a few sweeps, he released some of the pressure and began to nibble at her bottom lip with his, introducing her to yet another set of sensations.

He began to pull away and she prepared to take a fortifying breath when his tongue slipped out and licked her bottom lip.

She froze.

She had kissed men, though those thoughts were vague and yes some bordered on pornographic, but never had she been truly tasted before. It was humbling, shattering, and melding at the same time. He did it again from one corner of her mouth to the other, and her knees nearly gave out from beneath her. She clutched at him tighter, fighting to get enough air in her lungs, but the short pants weren't accomplishing their goal. When he made another pass – this one lazier than the others – she had to break away or risk passing out and embarrassing herself.

She hugged him to hide the wobble in her stance and tucked her head under his chin so that she could take deep gulps of air. She could hear his heart pumping like a jackhammer.

"I really like the taste of your lip gloss on your lips. It's fruity, but you add a little bit more…like whipped cream on strawberries." His breathless sentence clung to her mind, shrouding her in a heady envelope of warmth and feelings of being cherished.

"Are you all right?"

"Yes," was her only response for a long while. When she finally felt steady enough to stand on her own, she moved out of his arms. She felt oddly unsure of herself after that kiss. Maybe she'd shown him too much. She hugged herself momentarily avoiding his eyes.

"Paige."

She dragged her eyes away from the floor to meet his eyes.

"If I overstepped, let me know. I…"

She shook her head forcefully, cutting off his line of questioning.

"I am just feeling…" She searched for the word that felt right, then weighed it in her mind. "I am feeling a little vulnerable after that kiss. You've got me wide open and I don't know what to do with that feeling just now. I, I…" She gave up trying to explain something she didn't know how to categorize herself. She needed time to think. Her feelings were chaotic, strong, and just plain overwhelming. She touched her fingers to her bottom lip.

"Why do you have to do anything with them? Why can't you just feel?"

She shrugged.

He stepped closer, leaning in to take her hand. "I know it started out as a challenge, but I only wanted to show you how I feel for you. How you pull me into that light of you. How I wish to take you into me and absorb you so no one can ever get close enough to hurt you again. How your beauty overrides my senses, causing them to short and spark like live wires. I feel all of that to the degree that there are no words. If I could just sit and watch you go through your day, I would consider myself the most blessed of men. You are a jewel to me – a rare and precious jewel. If I could lay myself bare with words as you do, I would."

"You did a pretty good job just then," she said, a smile slowly lighting her features.

"Good. Come, let me take you to dinner before I get the overwhelming urge to show you how I feel about you in other ways."

"Elder Tatum," she teased, "I don't know what my Father would say about me going out with you."

"I can tell you," he said, as he led her to the door. "He said, 'This is my daughter. Take care of her, cherish her, protect her, keep her safe, and make her feel priceless.'"

Paige stopped and stared at him, surprised by the quick admonishment. "Really?"

He nodded. "Really." He held the door open for her. "You'll tell me how I'm doing?"

"Absolutely," she replied, trying to keep her voice level.

*   *   *

Paige sat her desk, staring at the bouquet of a half dozen pink and white roses with calla lilies and baby's breath. She leaned forward again to inhale the rich, deep scents. How was she supposed to get any work done? Her mind was consumed by Brandon, the evening they shared the night before, and the flowers and card that arrived an hour before noon.

She fingered the gold, embossed lettering on the front of card, savoring the texture as she unfolded the card, extracting the inserted letter once again. His handwriting, bold and clear, ran continuously across the page, making her heart beat a little faster. She'd read the note three times already, and it still elicited excitement. She was a goner, but she couldn't be blamed. Who handwrote letters anymore? It felt so personal, and the fact that he took the time to pen what he wanted to convey made it that much more special:

Dear Paige,

I was sitting here, once again thinking of you. I find that you invade my thoughts often. At first, I wondered if my discipline was lacking and I worked hard to keep thoughts of you relegated to times of my day that would cause me the least amount of concern. You would not remain nor be denied. The more I tried to control my thoughts of you, the worse it became. Thoughts of you came unbidden at the most inopportune times as well as in those moments of rest; so I stopped fighting and I realize that because the mere thought of you brings my soul and spirit so much joy, I would be dense to continue to fight such happiness.

Paige, for the last decade, it seems as though I have only given myself permission to live for today. I worked to finish and be used entirely for today because I, more than most, knew that tomorrow wasn't promised. I didn't dare hope for tomorrow, let alone next week, but being around you and watching how you embrace it all – this very moment as well as the hope for what is to come – I am beginning to understand what I have been

130

missing. You make me hope for tomorrow; the tomorrows filled with you. I look forward to the smiles, words, and touches of encouragement and caring you have just for me. Reminiscing about our time together is like opening my favorite present over and over again.

You make me believe that I'm enough – that my presence is enough – to make your day and it causes me to want to do more. Whatever I can do to help you understand how very blessed I feel for you being in my life, just let me know, because you deserve nothing less.

Thank you for your company last evening. It meant more than you know. If it isn't too much I would like to take you out again tomorrow. Maybe we could visit the place where we began.

Yours truly,
Brandon

Paige folded the note, knowing she wouldn't be able to go a full hour without opening up the card again, but that was one of the benefits of working for one's self: no one to watch her go gaga over a man. At least this time she was able to read it without tears coming to her eyes.

With that thought, she picked up her phone and dialed her sister's number. She was floating way too high to keep all of this joy to herself.

CHAPTER 14

The morning seemed like one, big meeting. The vendors wanted details on arrivals, departures, and orders being delivered days before the event as well as the day of. The band wanted to know if they could modify the list of songs. Roma, the new catering company referred by Mary that replaced Victoria's first choice (due to a difference in opinion between her and the owner), wanted to move up their scheduled food-tasting appointment. Eagerness sometimes had its setbacks. Victoria was tired, though she wouldn't admit it to anyone – no more than she would admit to needing an assistant. She'd put on these galas successfully for the past few years. There were bound to be a few hiccups before she hammered everything and *everyone* into place.

She was taking a break, sipping some tea and checking personal email messages when her cell phone rang.

"Victoria speaking."

"Mrs. Branchett. It's Paige."

"Hello, Paige. It's lovely to hear from you. How are you doing?" Victoria leaned back in her chair to watch some of the action around the barn. A ride later would really help release some of her tension.

"Very good, and yourself?"

"I am keeping busy."

"Oh yes, I forgot. How are the arrangements coming for the gala?"

"Everything is in place." Victoria would never allude to anything less when she was in charge. "How was your holiday?" Victoria asked, even though she had a good idea.

"It was nice and eventful," came Paige's slightly wary response. "I'm sorry for not being able to speak to you longer when you called the other day. Things have been moving quickly."

Victoria felt a momentary pang over her quiet knowledge of the young woman's recent budding relationship and encounter with her mother, but it was over almost as quickly as it stole over her.

"Tell me about it. I have had a hectic morning and I am in need of a distraction. Did you enjoy the young man, Brandon's, family?"

"Yes. I had a wonderful time with his family. It was a little overwhelming at first. There were so many of them, but they made me feel really warm and welcome like they'd been waiting to meet me for a long time. I asked Brandon what he told them about me, but he was so nonchalant I couldn't read him. I swear I must have been hugged more than 20 times throughout that day. His sisters are characters and as different as I think sisters can be, but they all love each other so openly." Paige's voice softened a little with her next sentence.

"His mom, Ava, was one of the most nurturing women I have ever met. She's small in stature, but you can tell that she has a quiet, unsuspecting strength that gathers and holds that family in place. When she embraced me, I wanted to hold on for a few seconds longer, and when I hugged her goodbye, I'm afraid I did." She finished with a self-deprecating laugh.

Victoria's heart lurched slightly, knowing the young woman was still in search of that special bond between mother and daughter, even if she wasn't fully aware of it. Victoria knew the signs all too well. If the child had better survival instincts, she would curve that desire before she became disillusioned.

"Did you talk to your family? I heard from Vivian that you were given some gadget that allowed you, her, and Gladys to communicate with each other through a video monitor?"

"Something like that," Paige responded, unable to keep the amusement out of her voice. "You don't fool me, Victoria. I know you aren't that far behind in technology. I know you don't want to hear it, but I think it was very thoughtful of Mason to give us iPads. The distance between us isn't as obvious this way."

Victoria chose to ignore this last part of the conversation, and tried again to bring Paige's family to the forefront of the conversation.

"I know you spent time with Brandon's family for Christmas. Did you miss your sister and niece too much?"

"We did spend Thanksgiving together, but yeah I did miss them a bit, especially with all of the developments and the close call in October. I seem to be even more protective now that I have been dubbed 'Mati' by the girls. We spent the better part of the morning conversing." Her voice dropped off, and there followed a heavy silence.

Victoria was willing to let it go on, suspecting that Paige was on the verge of sharing something deeper.

"I spoke to her… Grace, I mean," Paige finally said.

Victoria's only response was, "Oh?"

"I asked her about you." This was followed by more silence as if Paige were waiting for more. After a few moments, Victoria surrendered a flat "mmmm," to move the conversation forward. She glanced at her watch to gauge how to massage this discussion.

"Is that all you have to say? You aren't interested in what she said about you?" Paige sounded slightly irritated, which peaked Victoria's interest. *It must not have gone well at all.*

"Judging from our last talk regarding Grace, I assumed we both assessed that she is…difficult. Though I do hold some interest in your wellbeing, I can't imagine there would be anything she said that I would find the least bit appealing."

"That's just it. She didn't have anything to say. She acted like she'd never met nor heard of you."

"What did you expect?"

"I don't know… More than I got. But now that I think about it, I don't know why I expected anything at all. She hasn't changed, and that didn't surprise me. What did was my reaction to her." She became silent again, and Victoria could almost hear her brooding.

"Are you going to share the rest of that conversation with me, or are we going to start playing guessing games?" She heard a small sigh on the other end of the line.

"I was not as gracious…no…I wasn't even as tolerant as I thought I would be with Grace. There is no room for a decent conversation between the two of us." Victoria waited, growing more impatient by the minute.

"Why don't you just tell me what you and Grace discussed? It was so long ago; I am sure it doesn't have much precedence now."

"Then why dredge up the past?"

"Because it has to do with Vivian and me, if I read the signs correctly, or are you always so distrustful of people helping your family? Your mother said she'd never heard of me. How do you know I wasn't making it up or being paranoid?"

"Oh, give me some credit, Victoria. Even though I look for the best in people, I am still able to discern outright lies."

"Are you sure? You are awfully close to the subject. It makes it hard to be objective."

"Who are we talking about here, Victoria? You or Grace?"

"Both," Victoria stated, her voice flat.

The line was quiet for a moment. "Are you telling me you made it up?"

"Would you be able to discern whether or not I was?" Victoria mocked.

"I know I may have looked out-of-it in the hospital when you came to my room that first time. I'm not going to lie. I was working hard not to show my pain. Everything I'd heard about you told me you would use it to your advantage. So I watched and observed. You honestly thought I had something to do with Grace and whatever piece of degradation she'd formulated against you. I saw the anger and loathing in your eyes, the disgust in the way you set your mouth, and the haughty set of your shoulders – though now that I think about it, you always hold your shoulders that way.

I'm a writer; it's my job to notice and look for these things – and I am good at it – but even more than that is what God shows me about you. You aren't wicked, just incredibly wounded which causes you to lash out and do things to hurt others. I'm not looking for any acknowledgment of truth from you; I am just letting you know that I'm not as naïve as you think.

So with that said, you and Grace have history regarding my daughter, and I would like to know what it is. Please." The last word was added a second later as an obvious afterthought.

Victoria, slightly taken aback by Paige's little speech, decided it was just as good a time to make some demands of her own.

"I'm sure you do, just as I would like to know why you kept the fact that my husband visited you in the hospital a secret."

The silence seemed to grow with each breath until Paige responded almost too quiet to hear.

"You're not going to tell me, are you?" Victoria steeled herself against the hurt in Paige's voice, struggling with her own feelings of betrayal.

"You first, my dear." Victoria rolled her gold-tipped Mont Blanc pen between her fingers, watching the sunlight glint off of it again and again.

"I got the feeling he didn't want you to know. I was respecting his privacy."

Victoria let her last statement sink in for both of them then said as politely as she could muster, "Paige, we will talk later. Thank you for calling." She purposefully waited for Paige to respond.

"Goodbye, Victoria," she said quietly and hung up.

Victoria leaned back again in her chair. That should show Paige not to play her little psychic games. The child had no idea what she was asking; Victoria had no desire to share what Paige's scheming mother had been up to – not even with Richard.

If Michael turned over some of the skeletons, she thought, *he was about to trip over this.* It would be her ace and she was going to play it for all it was worth. If Paige's eyes were opened in the process – which was inevitable – then she would try to delay that as much as possible.

Meanwhile, maybe it was better if there was some distance between them. Victoria didn't like admitting the fact that Paige was getting under her skin, even to herself. It would be better in the long run. She couldn't afford to have Paige as a liability and, with every call, she was caring for her more.

Victoria walked down the hall to the ringing phone in the library.

She moved as quickly as she could without skipping, jogging, running, or jaunting because a lady did none of those things. The caller would just have to wait.

The first thing she heard was deep static. "Hello?"

"Victoria?"

"Yes. Richard?"

"Hi."

"I can barely hear you through all of that static."

"I know. I lost my cell phone and I am waiting for a replacement. I just wanted to call you and let you know we made it here safely."

"Thank you, Richard. You haven't done that in a long time."

"We all have things we could improve on. Communication is definitely mine. How are you doing? The gala keeping you busy?"

"Yes," she replied, knowing that she could have coordinated the gala in her sleep. She'd almost hoped Richard wouldn't call – that way, she wouldn't know how much she missed him. She was happy he'd arrived safely, but just hearing his voice caused her to wish he was right there beside her, and she hated wanting things she couldn't have. She worked too hard on too many levels of her life to be without.

"There was another reason I called." She heard the hesitancy in his voice.

"Okay," she pressed her ear to the phone so she could hear him more clearly.

"I would like to move some of my things back into the house."

A giddy sensation ran through Victoria, but she schooled her emotions so that her voice was steady.

"Okay. Should I make arrangements?"

"No. My secretary, Anna, will take care of that. I wanted to know if this is all right with you."

"I wasn't...Yes," she amended quickly.

"Good. I have also made arrangements for our first session of marriage counseling to be held the Friday after I return."

There were so many excuses she could make, but he was having his things moved back in. She didn't want to jeopardize this fragile truce. She could let it go for now. She realized she hadn't said anything when she heard her name.

"Victoria. Are you still there?"

"Yes, sorry, I'm here."

"Victoria?"

"Yes?"

"I am trusting and believing that you want this as much as I do. If you come up with an excuse or cause us to have to cancel this session, I am going to take that as your true answer to our reconciliation."

"That isn't fair, Richard. You know I have a busy schedule. I have been working nonstop with the gala and what if Vivian needs me? You know she isn't 100% yet, not to mention my growing relationship with Paige. I was even thinking of going out to visit her and make sure she is recovering well."

"You can do all of those things, Victoria, but if you aren't back and ready to meet with the counselor by the middle of February, I will know where you place our marriage in your list of priorities – and for once, I will not take any place but first," his voice came firmly through the line.

"You *are* first," she nearly pleaded, trying to think of something that would render her a little wiggle room.

"Then I will see you in a little less than six weeks."

"I will see you then."

The line disconnected and she slowly placed the receiver back in its cradle.

She idly tapped her finger on the desk, scaling and reorganizing a timeline through her head. If she was going to achieve her goals before Richard came back to the states, she would have to move up her plan. She couldn't risk him getting his lawyers involved in her play for custody of Vivian. She would be heartsick if they found themselves on opposite sides of court, but she would do it if it meant making sure her granddaughter was in the best environment.

She reached into the drawer, retrieving the package from Michael. She had scanned it earlier, but was concentrating on gala details. She sat behind the desk and spread the contents out before her.

There were doctor bills and insurance information for Grace Morganson-Dillard; health records and some lab paperwork dated a year before Paige's birth. It all looked routine and not too much more information than she'd already acquired some years back.

What was Michael so interested in?

She'd come to the end of the second page of Grace's employee paperwork before she saw what he'd been referring to and her heart sped up. She double-checked the year and shuffled back through the medical records, but was unable to find any paperwork with a corresponding date. It was as though the incident had never happen.

She read it over twice more before she forced herself to calm down. It didn't have to mean anything, necessarily. There were many women who'd gone through like procedures and still conceived.

It wouldn't have even fazed her except for the constant disquiet in the pit of her stomach. There was the sense that there was more to the story than what lay before her.

She read over Grace's file once more with a more discerning eye, and the disquiet escalated to apprehension. There was definitely something out of place and, though she could only guess at what it was, she hoped it could be used in her favor.

She set the file aside and with anticipation raising her heart rate even more, she reached for the next folder belonging to Brian Grossenberg. She slowly opened the folder, almost afraid of what she would find after her talk with Michael.

She read over the chart's contents written by a few different doctors. As she began reading over the notes, a rage gathered in her that kept her heart, which would otherwise have crumbled in despair, burning white hot. *How dare they put him in this place? What were Bill and Lilith thinking?* If they weren't already six feet under, she would have been tempted to put them there herself.

Almost five months. The thought was an echo whispering in her mind. He'd spent 145 days in this institution. She couldn't even begin to imagine what had gone through his mind while he was in there. Was he afraid? Did he feel abandoned, alone, forgotten? What was he really doing in there in the first place and where did he go after?

The questions swirling in her mind grew louder and louder, until the only way to assuage them was to physically release the anguish building in her. The red haze that had drifted over her eyes at the thought of her love being locked up like an animal blurred her vision, but not enough to keep her from picking up the sculpted glass paperweight and throwing it at the door.

The wave of anger, once released, continued to expand, and the urge to destroy something reverberated in her so deeply she swiped the contents from her desk in one fluid motion, causing everything to fly across the room in chaotic waves. The papers floating to the floor worked against her anger, and she barely stifled the urge to stomp them to the ground. She wanted to scream, the fury was so high in her. It was beating at her insides looking for an outlet, but when she spied his picture amongst the debris, the anger quickly receded and all she felt was loss. Heartbreaking, mind-debilitating loss, and the tears started.

How could they do this to you? She bent down to pick up the picture of the solemn-looking teen-aged boy that had been attached to the file. *My baby.* She wiped the tears from her eyes as she carried the picture back to the desk with her.

She sat back down, recovering some composure with a few deep breaths before picking up the phone and dialing Michael's number.

It rang only once before he answered. "Yes?"

"You have my attention and my gratitude. Don't waste it. I want you to find the missing pieces to this puzzle you gave me regarding Grace. I want to know the results of her surgery as well as an in-depth search of her pregnancy the following year. I want to know about every visit, sonogram, ultrasound, and prescription she was given up until the day she delivered Paige. If you see anything that looks remotely out of place, I want you to send it to me. Don't call me, just send it to me; I don't want to discuss this any further over the phone. Understood?"

"Yes."

"Where are we on that little project I gave you last week?"

"New photos were taken over the holiday. My friend got some nice shots of the couple that should get a reaction out of him. They should be delivered 'care of' to both father and daughter by tomorrow afternoon."

"It's nothing illicit? I don't need the child getting an eye-full."

"No. They are very clean, but if I was the poor sod you were sending these to, I would have to chase these pictures with a bottle of Jack for sure."

"That's exactly what I want to hear." She took a deep breath before she continued.

"Anything else on Grossenberg?"

"No, but I'm following a couple of hunches on his whereabouts after he left the facility. If I come up with something, I will send it to you."

"Very well. I will call you in a week unless you find success with that project sooner."

"Yes ma'am. Oh, and thank you for the bonus."

"You earned it. We will talk." She hung up the phone feeling measurably better. She looked around the room and heaved a sigh even as she berated herself for her behavior. She would have to clean up this mess on her own. There could be no evidence of her loss of control.

She went to the door to inspect the damage done by the paperweight. The indent was small, but noticeable. She would have to make up something. She picked up the pieces of the shattered sculpture thinking it an appropriate symbol of what she was going to do to whoever retained her son in that institution for 142 days longer than was required.

*   *   *

A week later, Victoria was at the end of her ride on Matriarch, a six-year-old, chestnut thoroughbred that had almost as much sass as she did. Victoria was there for her birth, and made sure she was in on every part of her development. This was Victoria's and Rachael's project. More than taking on the challenge of working in the world of breeding, it was something she and Rachael could do together.

The sectioning off of land and raising of the barn and stables were done while Rachael was still in high school. She had been an excellent horsewoman. She sat a horse better than Victoria, who'd learned much later in life. Her equestrian competition trophies still lined the shelves on the left side of the library.

She'd hoped it would be more of a distraction, especially after Rachael had been diagnosed.

After Rachael's death, Victoria lost interest in the business aspect of breeding, selling off four of the six horses they housed in the stables to neighboring ranches. She couldn't, however, talk herself into letting go of Caesar, a Palomino stallion that Rachael had fallen in love with, or Matriarch.

She pulled up short when she saw a golden lab running all out towards them. Matriarch shied slightly, taking a few steps to the left before Victoria tightened her grip on the reins, bringing her back in line. She turned back towards the stables, incensed at being interrupted by the wayward dog on her land, scaring her horse.

She was almost at the stable doors before she saw Mary Ambross standing there with an apologetic smile stamped across her face. She was instantly seized with anxiety. Why was Mary here? Wasn't she supposed to go with Paul and Richard? Did something happen? She looked around the area of the stables and up towards the house to see if Mary was being accompanied. She was about to pose whichever question reached her lips first when Mary began.

"I am so sorry if Breaker caused any trouble. I was on my way from the vet when I decided to stop by and see how you were doing. He got away from me as soon as I opened the door. He is used to horses, but I can understand your wariness. I do hope you aren't terribly upset. Are you all right? Is your horse all right? I will be more than happy to pay for any damage that may have been caused..."

Mary stopped when Victoria raised a hand to silence her. She was sure the woman would go on and on if she didn't interrupt her.

"Is everything all right with Richard? Paul? Didn't you go with them to Kenya?" The woman was so apologetic and distraught Victoria was almost tempted to console her, but first she wanted answers. She didn't trust her legs, so she remained on her mount looking down at the woman.

"No...Yes." Mary raised her hands as if to stop herself. "I mean, no, I didn't go to Kenya."

Victoria took a deep breath, berating herself for jumping to conclusions. She gave Matriarch a brisk pat, allowing herself some time to calm down, and slid off of the saddle in silence. She considered how to approach this subject. It would be good not to alienate herself from Mary or say anything that could get back to Richard, especially right now.

"You might want to leash your dog," she said as she handed Matriarch's reigns over to a stable hand, who stood wide-eyed for a moment before reaching for them. They knew that she preferred to brush Matriarch down herself. She figured this could be used as an opportunity to keep them on their toes. Mary took hold of Breaker with one hand, attaching the leash that had been forgotten in her other hand.

"Mary, what brings you here today?" Victoria gave Mary an ingratiating smile as she removed her gloves. She began walking back to the house, making the assumption that Mary would follow.

"Like I said, I was on my way back from the vet and thought I would stop by to see how you were doing. I know it was rude to show up without calling, but I'm hoping you will charge it to my heart more than my head. I had such a lovely time with you at Christmas and you were so gracious to open up your home and prepare dinner at the last minute.

I was hoping you might have a minute or two to talk or make an appointment to get together. Maybe we could visit the spa. There is a quaint..." She ground to a halt, leaving the sentence unfinished.

Victoria took a few more strides before acknowledging the silence then turned towards Mary with her brows raised in question. Mary wore a look of defeat, which surprised Victoria and made her wary.

"I know I'm intruding upon your day, but I was hoping to speak to you for a moment," Mary said slowly.

Victoria stopped advancing. "After my ride I usually shower and have lunch, but since it was cut short I have a little time. Would you care to join me for lunch? You can leave the dog tied to the edge of the back porch. I will have someone from the house give him water."

A tentative smile touched Mary's features, relaxing them a little. Victoria's curiosity was peaked even as she glanced at her watch, silently bemoaning her wasted afternoon. Mary didn't seem to be one to mince words. Hopefully she would be quick about whatever was distressing her and Victoria could salvage the last few hours of her afternoon.

She led Mary through the house, to the kitchen where Martha was laying out bowls of pasta salad, green salad, fruit, and lentil soup. "Martha, didn't Max and George say they would be going to town? I couldn't possibly eat all of this." Her speculative look completed her wary thoughts.

"Joseph saw Mrs. Ambross at the stables and her dog near the crest where you were riding, and let me know that you might be having company." She then turned to Mary.

"Good afternoon, Mrs. Ambross. It is a pleasure to see you again." Martha bestowed a warm and welcoming smile upon Mary and Victoria found herself slightly annoyed by Martha's attentiveness when she had been nothing short of obstinate towards her recently.

She gestured Mary to sit at the table and waited until after they were seated comfortably, their plates were filled and Mary had said her grace, before Victoria leaned back in her chair, indicating that she was waiting for Mary to begin.

She watched carefully as Mary took a deep breath, returning her spoon to her bowl without tasting her soup. "I know you aren't very familiar with the work Richard, Paul, and Sam do, but depending on what part of the government they have to deal with, it can be challenging."

Victoria stared at Mary for a moment. "Challenging or dangerous?"

Mary stared back at Victoria, her expression open. "A little more challenging than dangerous most of the time, but they are very cautious and try hard to consider all sides, especially when they are helping put up a new building." She shrugged her shoulders. "There are some that would rather see the children in that region starve and remain uneducated. It makes it easier to intimidate and rule." Mary's face twisted into an unbecoming scowl.

"Kate and I were asked to remain stateside on this trip." Mary picked up her soup spoon again before continuing. "Well...I was asked." She shrugged her shoulders. "Kate and Sam's relationship is a little less serene. Kate argued with Sam almost until he walked out of the house. She didn't want him to go without her."

Victoria absorbed the information slowly. "Is there a reason why they didn't want you to go this time?"

Mary took a deep breath. "They are almost done with the orphanage, and more than any other time there is a lot of attention drawn to the site. It attracts many types of people. There are those that would be happy to see it open and those who would be all right if there was something in it for them as well." Mary tasted her soup and Victoria waited impatiently for her to continue, her stomach closing in on itself more with each word.

"I know this sounds daunting to someone who is not familiar with the process, but I don't believe there is anything to worry about."

"Really? How do you know? Have they ever discouraged you from accompanying them?" Victoria watched for any guile in Mary's expression, but was unable to discern anything but a willingness to help.

"Yes. A few times." She nodded and took a bite of her pasta salad.

"How did you manage?" Victoria asked.

Mary finished chewing. "In the beginning, it was pretty hard. I was a wreck the first few times he went. I think I had him call me three times a day, just so I knew he was all right. I didn't know much about the areas he was going into or the people, and I had heard and seen so much tragedy, destruction, and death on television. Actually, when he first told me he was going, I forbade him." Mary ducked her head sheepishly, taking another spoonful of her soup.

"Actually, I threatened to leave him if he went." Victoria sat forward, surprised by this admission.

"What did he say? He obviously went because he is still going now."

"He said I could go, but that I would have to leave everything that belonged to him." Mary went back to eating, leaving Victoria to wait expectantly.

Annoyed at being left hanging, Victoria began eating again as well, but goaded Mary. "So how long were the two of you apart? Because you seem to be a woman of your word."

Mary looked up, a wide smile spreading across her face. "I never left."

Victoria's brows furrowed. "I thought you were a strong woman."

Mary finally placed her fork against her plate. "Paul and I said both the traditional vows, making a covenant to God, and recited special vows," she made air quotes, "because I wasn't saved at the time and I wanted to say something to him that really meant something to me." Her laugh was self-deprecating.

"Anyway, one of my promises was that I would never take what was his. It was a slight play on words, but one of the things I'd given to him early on and continued to remind him of was that he owned my heart. All of it. My vows repeated that fact. If I left, I would have taken my heart and since it was his, I was stuck. That's what he was counting on to keep me right where I was." She shrugged and went back to eating.

Victoria made a conscious effort to close her mouth and keep it shut. She watched the woman for a moment, then surreptitiously glanced around the room to see if there were any hidden cameras.

"That was it? That was all it took?"

Mary just nodded.

"Why?"

Mary looked up at her quizzically. "Because I love him. That... and he loved me enough to call me on it."

"Weren't you afraid he would always think he could win?" Victoria debated.

Mary seemed to think on her question. "Well I guess it's how you look at it." She sat there, staring into space.

Victoria nudged her, feeling slightly impatient. "Are you going to elaborate?"

"Let's just say, he left me with plenty to remember him by and just in case, he more than made up for being away." She wiggled her eyebrows. "Besides, I could tell it made him extremely happy to be used to help so many people. He always comes back with such a profound appreciation for God and everything He has given him..." She leaned forward with a conspiring whisper, "Including me."

"After his third trip, I went with him because I felt I was beginning to miss out. It changed my life. I received God's gift of salvation on that trip." The far-off look was back in her eyes.

Victoria wasn't interested in traveling down that road right now. She guided the conversation back to the men's work in Uganda.

"So you said this particular trip was going to be more challenging than the others? Will they be coming home sooner?"

Mary shook her head. "They want to get the children housed during this trip. There has been a great deal of unrest in the area and they want to make sure certain paperwork and security is in place before they go. They hope it will ensure the safety of not only the children but the people working in the orphanage. It is getting harder to get supplies into the area. There are more and more hands out and more roadblocks along the way."

Mary took a deep breath and continued, "It may sound like a lot to you right now, but it isn't anything they didn't plan for. They have been doing this for years, but you and I haven't had a chance to get to know one another, and Richard said you were incredibly busy." She allowed the sentence to end in a shrug.

Victoria didn't know how to react to this news. She wasn't sure what to expect and that didn't sit well with her at all. She worked the news around in her mind, but was unable to come up with a practical solution to the turmoil laying siege to the now tenuous grasp on her self-control. She ran through a few scenarios before she spoke again.

"What do *you* do?"

Mary looked at her, obviously judging whether or not she should share this information, but she finally began speaking.

"Paul is doing exactly what God wants him to do. I pray and trust that God will take care of him. He did before I met him. I need the peace; leaning on God gives me that."

Victoria paused, but didn't consider that a workable answer. She had been staring down at the tablecloth since Mary began speaking to avoid giving too much away, but looked up to judge Mary's expression while voicing her next question.

"What did you do before you were saved?"

Mary looked at her a moment before responding. "I cried."

"Then what?"

"Worried, lost sleep, didn't eat, and nearly lost my mind."

Victoria sighed. It was obvious Mary was not going to be any assistance in helping her cope. She would have to find her own ways. She felt a restlessness growing. She needed to end this visit so she could be alone with her thoughts. Best get as much information as possible before she sent Mary away.

"Did Richard send you here to tell me all of this?" She asked setting her fork and knife on her plate, signaling she was done.

"Yes and no." Mary said hesitantly. "He knew I intended to visit you, but I made the decision to tell you what was going on. I don't think it is right for wives to be left in the dark."

This intrigued Victoria, but she wasn't yet willing to explore her fondness for Mary. Maybe there was room for an acquaintance with her, but she hoped Mary wouldn't ruin it with any hidden agendas to try and convert her.

"He also asked me to deliver this to you," she said as she took a small envelope out of her pocket.

Victoria was skeptical. Why had it taken Mary so long to tell her about the letter? Did she even want to open it? *Did Richard change his mind even though some of his things had begun being delivered?* Did Mary mean for her to open it now in her presence? Would there be a need for a reply?

Mary answered her last question by pushing back from the table and setting her napkin down beside her empty plate.

"Well, Victoria, I want to thank you for sharing your lunch with me. I have to get going; the men are still at the house and I wanted to make sure they were on their job while I am off staying at a bed and breakfast." She scrunched her nose as though she smelled something distasteful. "They are more lenient about Breaker. I really hate having him stay in a kennel. I figure if I'm uncomfortable, why not show up unannounced and make them feel just a little uncomfortable as well? That way, they will try to finish sooner."

"I will give you a call in a day or two. Maybe we can schedule a day at the spa after all. The beds are comfortable enough, but I just don't like sleeping without Paul. I could use something to relax."

Victoria barely got a word in but managed to finally stop her by placing a hand on her shoulder.

"Why do you have this? Did Richard give it to you before he left? Because I don't see a post date on it. Why did you wait so long to give it to me?"

Mary turned back around, placing her hand on Victoria's forearm resting at her side; her expression, one of serene patience. "He gave it to me before he left, only with the request that I give it to you when I came to visit." Mary smiled as she stepped away. "I will call about that spa date."

Victoria surrendered her hold on Mary and placed a small smile on her lips in return, the envelope weighing heavy in her hand, taking over her full attention.

She went upstairs to the privacy of her room to open the envelope. She sat on the edge of the chaise lounge, and stared at the envelope with Richard's beautifully slanted scroll of her name on the front. *Victoria.* Her pulse sped up and a moment of anxiety seized her before she took herself in hand, adding a brief mental scolding for the loss of control.

She opened the letter with frustrated annoyance, yanking out the small card.

Remember how much I love you.

She turned the card around, sure there was an explanation on the back, but there was nothing. She turned it back to the front and reread the six words over and over, trying to read in between the lines, but after another half an hour of trying to decipher all imagined codes, she came back to the six beautiful words and tried to do just what they'd instructed of her.

CHAPTER 15

Brandon leaned his head into the palm of his hand. "Yes mom. Everything is ready. Matthew scheduled it with his brother last week and Roman called me yesterday to finalize all the details. It's all set."

"She will be so surprised. I'm sure she will love it. You do my heart proud, son. Any woman would be more than fortunate to have your attentions in such a way. You will tell me how it goes, won't you?"

"Sure, if she doesn't call *you* first. I have to tell you mom, I was a little surprised to learn that the two of you talked so regularly." He could almost see his mom's imperceptible shrug.

"It's not what you think, Brandon," Ava stated with practiced patience, "Paige is working on a new book and wanted to get some background material. She had some questions about…well…I'm sure she will share that with you if you ask her. Are you sure there isn't anything I can help you with?"

"I'm more than sure. You have been more helpful than you know."

"Okay." She sounded hesitant to end the call. "You will call me, right?"

"Yes mom," he said for what seemed like the 20th time during that conversation. He tried to keep the exasperation out of his voice.

"Alright, well, you have fun."

"Mom, for the last time, I am only taking her out on a Valentine's Day date. It's not like I'm asking her to marry me."

"Funny you should bring that up."

He wanted to groan. What had he been thinking? To be perfectly honest, he hadn't been. He'd been floating somewhere on cloud nine for the last few weeks with Paige. Between the scheduled events with the Men's Ministry, work – which he'd started back on full time – and Paige's local touring season underway, it had been hard to find time to spend together. They spoke on the phone every evening, had gone for ice cream or a walk in the park a few times, video chatted when she was out of town, and kept up an almost steady messaging conversation.

Even though they saw each other in church, there was no time to talk between Sunday school, church service, and the individual auxiliary meetings used for updating each other if they'd been unable to meet during the week. It was only during the late Sunday afternoons, when Paige didn't have a speaking engagement, that they could spend time together and share the things too close to their hearts to say over the phone.

Today, though, would be the first evening they would see each other in almost a week. He knew her touring would be hectic, with her wanting to keep her scheduled calls with her girls, but he had no idea she was working on a new book or that she'd come to his mother for information. She astonished and humbled him; there were few others he could say gave as much of themselves as she did.

It was just that thought that galvanized him into planning this little surprise for her. She needed an evening where all she had to do was just...receive.

"Brandon, are you still there?"

"Oh, yes." What were they talking about? *Oh yeah.*

"Have you given any thought to making her my daughter? I really like her."

"Mom, really, we've only been seeing each other for a few months. Don't you think you could be pushing things a little? There are a lot of factors to think of, not to mention we are still learning about one another. That's what this time is for. What's the hurry?"

"There is no hurry. I just wanted to know if you'd given it any thought. You're the one that got all bent out of shape. I didn't think it was too much to ask if you were at least thinking about it. You haven't shown any interest in a woman since that little hussy in college."

Brandon dragged his attention back from the computer where he was answering a last minute email from a co-worker.

"What?! Who are you talking about?" The air around him became stifling and he was met with a brief pause on the other side of the line.

"Brandon, I may have five other children, a host of grandchildren and a church family, but I am never so involved that I would not know when you are hurting. When you came home sick from school that year and decided to take the next semester off, I knew it was more than the cancer that had you so quiet. I'd seen that form of brooding before on your older brother's face and it had nothing to do with an ailment of the body."

He let her words sink in. Wondering why she hadn't approached him about this before, he sat back in his chair, shaking his head.

He had to give it to her; his mom was good. "When did Dominy tell you?" There was another moment of silence then she sighed.

"He called me a few days after you'd arrived. I think he was hoping I could not only nurse you through your chemo, but also your broken heart."

"Don't try to defend him, mom. He was supposed to keep it to himself."

"Don't be so hard on Dominy. He was worried about you."

"He's a mother hen; he worries about everyone. I actually feel sorry for Robin right now. I don't think he will allow her to see the light of day until she delivers."

"Brandon, why didn't you feel you could tell me yourself?" She sounded hurt and since he couldn't tell if it was a ruse or real, he had to treat it as authentic.

"Mom, it wasn't like that. I was...embarrassed."

"Why, because you fell for a hussy?"

He hung his head. Dominy was going to pay for this one. He didn't know how, but he would give it lots of thought. He couldn't believe he was talking to his mother about this – at work, of all places.

"How about we talk about this later, mom?"

"This is later, baby." She clucked her tongue. "Did I do or say anything that would make you feel like you couldn't tell me things like this?"

"No, mom...it's just..." Dang he was going to have to tell her. He ran his hand down his face, blowing out the frustration.

"I was jealous." He thought his mother would jump in with questions, but she was quiet so he went on. "You know I wasn't the most popular boy in school. My class picture probably read 'Most likely to be forgotten'."

"Don't speak like that. You had plenty of friends growing up."

"I'm not talking about my siblings or church family, mom. I am talking about people my age. Dominy was pretty much it."

"Why do you think that is?" she asked, her voice hinting the question was more so for the continuation of the conversation.

"I wasn't comfortable speaking to people. I didn't know how to relate to kids. I never knew what to say and it was only compounded by the fact that so many people knew dad and thought I was just like him. They assumed I thought like him and shared his characteristics because I was quiet, when the real reason I was quiet was because I was so afraid I couldn't think of anything to say."

"I know you have always been quiet and shy, but I also know that you are sensitive, compassionate, and perceptive. That's why I was a little confused as to why you would choose someone who was clearly not worthy of you. There were so many nice, pretty girls I could have introduced you to." That brought a smile to his lips. His mom was fiercely protective; another reason why he'd chosen to keep the Rowan 'fiasco' to himself.

"I wanted someone of my own – someone outside of Garden City; outside of my friendship with Dominy, or any other influence."

"Well, I guess you got her."

"Yes. I guess I did."

"Are you afraid of embarrassing yourself with Paige?"

"Paige wasn't someone I picked and then found myself changing to keep. Actually, Paige wasn't someone I chose, but God chose for me, and I have to say that I like His choices an awful lot more than my own."

"I'm happy to hear that, because I like her too. You know, I am glad to hear you say that God chose her for you. Do you think..." She hesitated, and he saw the question coming from a mile away.

"Do you think since He chose her for you that it might be a sign that you should concentrate on having a future?"

"Mom, no one wants me to be healed more than me – for my sake and hers. It's only been a few months, but I can't imagine what it would feel like to have to live without her and I wouldn't want to do that to her, even knowing that God would comfort her because she would let him. I would sooner break it off."

"That's pretty absolute, Brandon. It doesn't leave room for much."

"What is there?" he stated, more than asked.

"There is life, love, memories…memories that help to solidify the truth in one's mind. The truth that life isn't about the quantity of days you get, but what you fill them with; the truth that those days without love are less valuable; the truth that loving and being loved is not just a momentary or fleeting thing. It lasts forever, so invest as much as you can into it while you can because the memories are just one of the beautiful gifts love provides."

Brandon tried to take in everything she said, but knew he was going to miss some of it. "How did you get to be so wise and profound?" He made an attempt to lighten the conversation.

"I sit at my Father's feet and ask Him questions. This one He answered over time." Her voice was soft and just a little rough.

As realization of who she was referring to dawned on Brandon, his heart jerked. The wave of sadness that washed over him was almost palpable. He was able to get one word out before his throat closed up. "Peyton?" he asked, referring to his sister who'd drowned just a few months shy of her seventh birthday.

Peyton, 18 months his senior, had been his favorite sister. He followed her everywhere, which is why it was fortunate he was visiting with his godparents that weekend, otherwise the Tatum family may have had a double loss that day.

For many years, he'd wondered if he had been there could he have saved her, gone for help, or notified everyone that she was missing sooner. Her absence in his life was like a missing limb, and Brandon had been reluctant to let anyone get as close. Dominy had been the exception.

"Honey, burying a child goes against the natural order of things. You are filled with questions, doubts, fear, shame and more questions, but there is still hope."

"Hope for what?" Brandon was perplexed. His mother seemed to have begun talking in riddles.

"Hope for a word of comfort. Hope for an answer that brings enlightenment and peace, which dispels a lot of the doubt and fears that cause you to hold tight to people and things you have to let go of in order to receive His healing.

If I had not sought out answers to why my Peyton was taken so young and been open to receiving those answers, there would have been no room to nurture the love I had for the rest of my children. If I didn't trust God to help bring me to a place of peace, I would have suffocated each and every one of you because I wouldn't have allowed you out of my sight."

"Peyton's death was hard on all of us, mom," he stated, not knowing how else to show his empathy without becoming too emotional at work.

"Yes, baby. Some of us more than others," Ava said with sadness roughening her voice a little more. Then she did an about-face, catching him off guard. "Listen to me going on like a sad song on repeat. You have a date to get ready for and probably some work yet to finish. I will be looking forward to your call," she said almost faster than he could comprehend.

"I will call you tomorrow. I love you."

"I love you too, baby. Have fun."

Pushing the conversation to the back of his mind, Brandon worked at giving over all of his attention to his work. There would be plenty of time to go over the pieces of knowledge his mother had been trying to give him.

*　　　　　*　　　　　*

Brandon waited outside Paige's door, shuffling his feet from side to side, balancing a box neatly under his arm, and trying to contain his excitement so he wouldn't give away any of the evening he had planned for Paige. It had been a challenge giving her enough information so she could dress warmly enough without spoiling anything for her.

She opened the door. Every thought fled and every sense shut down except his ability to see. She was beautiful. His eyes took in every bit of her 5'3" frame encased in a rust-colored sweater that ended at the thigh with an oversized turndown collar. The sleeves were so long, only her fingers were visible. Her deep-blue jeans were slim and straight cut, stopping at the edge of what looked to be chocolate brown boots.

The color of her top brought out the gold in her eyes that shined brighter than he'd remembered. Her hair rested in wavy layers around her shoulders, softening her look.

He wanted to stay right here in this moment and just look at her – no he wanted to hold her and watch her eyes light up even more with one of those smiles just for him. Yes, that would be worth it all.

She shifted in the doorway allowing the sun behind her to cast her in a shadow, pulling him from his stupor.

He blinked a few times to regain his equilibrium, working hard to bring the past, present, and future back into perspective.

"Hi." Her greeting was breathy, as though she'd been running. It was edged with excitement, which caused him a moment of anxiety, but he refused to give into any doubts that she would have the time of her life.

"Paige." His breath stuttered. "Paige, you are beautiful." He tried again to jumpstart his brain – to find the words to better describe what she was to him – but when the edges of her mouth began the smile that lit her eyes, he conceded defeat in his endeavor to be suave or charismatic. He would consider it a gift from God if he could remain coherent for the evening.

"Do you want to come in or are you ready to go now?" She asked after a few seconds of them standing in the doorway.

"I can just get my coat. You did say it was going to be a little cool right?"

He willed his head to work and nodded, thus drawing a baffled look from her. "Which is it: do you want to come in, or should I just go and get my things?"

He blinked and the lights finally went back on, sound resumed, and though it was drier than the Sahara, he regained feeling in his mouth.

"Are you alright?" Paige asked, stepping closer.

"Yes," *Oh, thank you Lord, that could definitely pass as an answer.* "Yes, sure, fine." He let what he hoped was a smile stand as his exclamation mark.

She quirked an eyebrow at him, but instead of commenting, she just asked. "Sooo…out or in?" She gestured using her forefinger to point behind him then her thumb behind her.

"I'll step in while you get your coat."

She stepped back, allowing him to finally step over the threshold, closing the door behind him. She was about to turn when he caught her arm and pulled her to him in a tight hug.

One moment he'd been flying high, anticipating an evening of sharing new things with her and the next he was falling, struck dumb by love. He was wholly and inconsolably in love with Paige. A wonderful warmth spread through him with panic riding hot on its heels. He released her just enough to see her smile at him and tried to breathe through the raw emotion coursing through him. He was in love with Paige.

"Go get your things. I'll wait right here." He turned her towards her bedroom and pushed her gently. He plastered a smile on his face, just in case she looked back. He was in love with Paige. It shouldn't have been such a shock. They had been heading this way, hadn't they? Hadn't he let Lady Menagerie in on some of his intentions? Then what was it about this moment that proved it to him without a shadow of a doubt?

He placed his hands in his pockets to keep them still. He wanted to shout to the hills one second and rant and rave the next. His moods were swinging to and fro, hitting every emotion in the kaleidoscope in between. He would have been on top of the world if these feelings didn't scare the mess out of him. They were so intense, he didn't know which one to study first. He took a deep breath using the action to stuff his feelings under a rug, lest Paige come out and see it all on his face.

What was he going to do? This wasn't the same warm, comfortable pull with the overlay of attraction he felt he could step away from if needed without being scared. This had taken a hold of something essential to him. This was bone deep. There was no way of stepping away for either one of their sakes without surrendering a part of himself.

Maybe he was being too fanciful. Maybe the conversation with his mother was affecting his judgment and ridged stability where his emotions were concerned.

He looked up when he heard her enter the room and knew that this was no illusion or play on his emotions. He was sunk.

If he could just get through the rest of the evening, maybe he could then get to the sanctuary of his apartment and work out – or just smother – some of these feelings.

"Are you sure you're alright? You're not feeling ill? It's been rather cool. We could maybe do this another time."

He looked at her, and with simple determination pulled himself up by his proverbial bootstraps. He wouldn't disappoint her no matter how much his practical side screamed at him.

"I'm feeling fine," he lied. "I'm just anxious to show you your surprise." He watched her assess him. He thought she might call him on it, but she shrugged her shoulders and let it go.

"Well then." She looked at him pointedly. Puzzled, he looked back at her. He watched her eyes glance down to his arm and back up to his face.

"Is that for me?" she asked, pointing to the forgotten box under his arm. He groaned inwardly, mortified to have forgotten about it.

He handed it to her, careful not to allow their hands to touch. "Yes. It's a part of your surprise."

She opened the oblong box and withdrew a multicolored, satin scarf in the earth tones he saw her wear most often.

He watched her blink in surprise. "It's really lovely, Brandon. The colors are beautiful."

He felt the warmth emanating from her smile and unabashed delight at the gift. He watched as she wrapped it around her shoulders, tying it in a simple knot in front. If he wasn't already a goner, that smile would have tagged him.

"I'm ready for my surprise, Mr. Tatum. Open the door." Appreciative of her effort in lightening his mood, he opened the door wide then bowed as she walked through with exaggerated grace.

*   *   *

"The view is absolutely amazing from here. I have seen the sunset from a plane before, but this is surreal. I never imagined I would be part of the sky at this time of day!" Paige exclaimed with reverence.

He watched the expression of awe on her face, her eyes moist from air and emotion, and knew he'd chosen correctly. The scarf was now wrapped around her head, securing her hair close to her scalp.

"I know exactly what you mean. The first time I came up here was with a cousin of mine."

The landscape so far below made him feel like they were the only two people for miles. *Well, us and the pilot.* Paige was like a child experiencing Disneyland for the first time. There was so much to see, she was all over the basket. It was a gift to him to watch the unabashed animation of her reactions to different landmarks the pilot pointed out.

During most of the drive to the balloon's take-off point, Brandon was quietly working out his emotions. He tried responding in more than mono-syllable answers so that Paige would stop sending concerned looks his way.

He finally decided to set the thoughts aside when he'd made his third wrong turn and began to jeopardize their on-time arrival to the takeoff site.

Once they landed, he was grateful there were so many points of conversation he didn't have a chance to retreat into his thoughts.

He drove them to a small restaurant on the edge of Santa Monica where they could watch the ocean and the lights of the pier. It was a little crowded, which was to be expected on Valentine's Day, but not stifling.

They were seated in an outside corner that afforded them at least a modicum of privacy. He watched her to gauge her reaction to the place he'd found only a few days before via the internet.

After looking around her, and after staring at the ocean for a moment, her eyes came back to him.

"I'm impressed. I never would have found this place. It is a little treasure." His breathing eased as he placed his napkin on his lap.

He looked back up to find her watching him. "Yes?" he prompted.

"I'm glad you've rejoined our date. I was feeling a little lonely." Her smile softened the statement.

He shifted uneasily. "I'm really sorry, I –"

"I know," she interrupted. "You had a lot on your mind. Do you want to share?"

No way.

"Naaa, it isn't all that interesting."

"Let me be the judge. Besides, if it could take your mind away from this beautiful evening you've planned, it must be weighing heavily on you. Maybe I could give you another perspective."

Oh, that isn't going to happen.

If he could have laughed and not drawn more attention to himself, he would have. What irony.

"It's deeply personal, and I know the person would be uncomfortable with me sharing this information. It was just dropped on me today and it took a moment to set it aside, but now you have my undivided attention." *There, that should hold her off for a while.* Either way, it was as close to the truth as he was going to get.

"Pick up your menu. I was told they have great crab cakes here."

Her reluctance to let the subject go was obvious in her slow and deliberate opening of the menu in front of her. He began to chuckle, knowing this wouldn't be her last attempt to find out what he'd been struggling with.

The rest of dinner went just as he'd hoped: light conversation, great food, and easy banter. He was still marveling at his fortune in finding a woman he felt so easy with (when he wasn't tripping over his emotions) when they arrived at her apartment.

Placing the car in park, he reached in the back seat for her second gift of the evening. He placed the rectangular box on her lap and waited patiently for her to open it.

She looked at him, surprise then hesitation racing across her features. "But you already gave me a gift," she said, fingering the sapphire-colored bow.

"Psh. That was preparation," he said, amusement in his voice.

When she continued to hesitate, a hint of trepidation skimmed across his shoulders. He quietly said her name when she continued to stare at the box, and she looked up, her eyes over bright with moisture. He was instantly on alert. He hadn't expected tears.

"Um...well. I can take it back if it makes you upset..." He let the sentence fade, knowing he sounded like an idiot. When did presents make women upset?

"Sorry. I tried to hold them back, but..." Her voice broke and she cleared her throat, trying again. "It's just that this day was already so perfect. I have never had anyone put so much thought into a date with me. It's a little overwhelming."

He leaned closer, catching her gaze. "You are worth this, and more."

"Oh, I know that," she responded, with a watery laugh then sobered. "It's just nice to be treated like I should be by someone I want the attention from."

Touched, he moved to cover her hand, but she shifted away from him.

"Do you mind if I open this inside? I want to give you your gift."

He stopped, surprised. "You got me a gift?"

"Sure. It's not my birthday or anything. I can give you a gift too."

"Well, yes, technically..." he started, bemused by it all.

"If I can't give you a present, then you can take this one back." She handed over the gift box. He pushed her hand back in her lap.

"Come on," he said getting out of the car to walk around and open her door. Why couldn't the woman just let him spoil her for one night? For one night, couldn't it be all about her?

When they walked in, he helped her out of her coat and while she went to retrieve his present, he went over to the couch. This, the exact place he was hoping to avoid since being hit with the revelation earlier that evening. Thankfully, there wasn't time to get bombarded with thoughts because she was right back in the room with him.

She sat facing him with one leg tucked underneath her. She placed a wide, flat square box in his hand with a shy smile on her lips.

"You first," he said with anticipation.

"But."

"You first. Please." He drawled out the word enlisting a pleading expression known to work on his mother on occasion.

She sucked her teeth. "Does that actually work?" He shrugged his shoulders.

"I don't know, does it?"

She shook her head as she began to unwrap her gift.

I guess so. He smiled to himself.

She gasped as soon as she lifted the box cover away to reveal an airline ticket. She picked it up to find another one underneath it then began to shake her head slowly.

"It's too much. It's too much," he took her hands to draw her attention to him.

"There is only so much you can say on Skype. I know you are missing your girls. This way you can give them a hug for me as well."

She looked at him, tears brimming one second; the next, she was hurtling herself at him, nearly knocking him back with the force of her hug.

"Thank you." The emotion in her voice threatened to be his undoing. He didn't dare speak, not that he had a chance before she pulled back and kissed him breathless, caressing the nape of his neck to secure him to her.

When she pulled back shortly after, he was disoriented by the swift change and reluctantly let his hands drift from her waist back to his lap, where he found his discarded present.

"Open it! Open it!" Paige chanted, reminding him of his nieces and nephews at Christmas.

He took his time, working to settle his hormones. He saw her squirm out of the corner of his eye, but figured this was better than dragging her back across the length of the couch and sprawling her on top him.

Two measured breaths later his hand uncovered what looked to be a customized phone cover in emerald green, edged in gold. "Wow." It was all he could utter as he turned the item over, only to discover engraving on the inside back.

Brandon, was as far as he got before she placed her hand over it, obstructing his view. He looked up in question.

"Read the card first," she pointed to the heavy stock, gold velum lying in the box.

My Dearest Brandon,

I figured it was about time I was completely honest with you. You see I have been wrestling with how to tell you this for some time, but what I call caution and others may call pride or fear, has kept my mouth closed.

The time I have spent with you these last few months has given me the very thing I feared would remain elusive. With you I feel safe, cherished, and exactly where I am supposed to be: next to you, wrapped in God's perfect will.

All of this gives me the courage to tell you that I not only love you, but I am in love with you and no matter what comes, I will always treasure this place in my life.

He read the last sentence three times before he could comprehend the full meaning of what she was saying. She didn't only say that she loved him and believed that it was part of God's will, but she was also in love with him, which was her acceptance, willingness, and her moving in the same direction. She loved him of her own accord as well, and was courageous enough to tell him.

He felt slightly ashamed of his earlier reaction to his own emotions, but bolstered by her unabashed declaration. He continued reading.

I've spent so much of my life on the outside looking in. I'm thankful that when I had the courage to step back into life, you were there.

I love you Brandon Tatum,

Paige.

The words began to blur, and he blinked back the tears.

Not yet ready to look up, he reverently set aside the letter and read the engraving on the inside of the phone cover.

Brandon
This moment, this hour;
Tomorrow and the next.
You have my love.
Paige

Overcome with emotion, he reached for her, hugging her tightly to him. He worked at the lump in his throat, but couldn't stop the tears from falling. She was in love with him. As ironic as it all seemed, he was ever so grateful. He reveled in the feeling of euphoria that accompanied her declaration, and continued to hold on for dear life as he made a confession of his own.

"I love you too, Paige. I mean I really, truly love you. You are what I've been waiting for." He whispered in her ear, "You have my heart."

"I know," she whispered back.

He pulled back, staring at her as he wiped the wetness from his cheeks. "How?"

Her brows furrowed. "You showed me. In everything you say and how you say it. It's in how you treat me, how you touch me…" She cupped his cheek, "With respect, tenderness, protectiveness, and just enough passion to curl my toes. Plus," she reached around her neck pulling the gold heart he'd given her from her blouse, "you trusted me with this. How do you think I felt comfortable enough to tell you how I felt?"

He fingered the pendant, clasping it. He carefully pulled her forward so he could kiss her until the dazed feeling subsided. Then, he would see if he could do more than curl her toes.

*   *   *

Brandon, sat on the edge of his bed, staring off into space. He played all of his favorite parts of the evening over and over as if repeatedly pressing a rewind button. The feeling of euphoria caused him to put off calling Dominy back for the last half hour. He wanted a little more time to keep these feelings to himself. She loved him. Not only loved him – she was in love with him. He had everything and more.

He reached out, fingering his newly covered phone, his fingertips gliding across the engraving along the back. It took a few moments for him to realize he was smiling. Thankfully neither his mother nor Dominy were in the vicinity, otherwise he would have been razzed the entire evening.

He lay back on the bed with one hand behind his head, the other remaining on the phone that had not been out of his reach since he'd swapped cases. He didn't even want to entertain thoughts of this not lasting for the rest of their lives – hers in particular. He could have kicked himself for even allowing the thought to intrude in this space of perfection.

An hour later, he figured he was home-free. It was much too late now to call Dominy or his mother. *They would under.-*

He picked up his now vibrating phone, and quickly opened the line.

"Are you still awake?"

"Very much so, but I thought you would sleep the rest of the evening. You looked so peaceful when I left."

"For the record, it was the fire, not your company. I don't make it a habit of falling asleep on people who gift me with priceless pleasures."

"Listen to the writer. 'Priceless pleasures'. Sounds like a romance novel."

"No. It was just a perfect storm. My very comfortable couch, a warm fire, a full stomach, and my man giving me plenty of wonderful kisses to dream about."

"Your 'man'?" he asked, liking the sound and wanting to hear her say it again.

"Yes, my man."

"So, tonight wasn't too much?"

"That is like asking a lottery winner if receiving $130 million is too much."

"Arc you comparing me to winning the lottery?"

"Are you still fishing for compliments?"

"It's not fishing if you're handing them out."

"True. Let's just say I had an absolutely wonderful time, and I will not forget it anytime soon. It was one of the most perfect evenings of my life."

"I feel the same, and I got to end it with you too. You know you are the first person to call me on my newly stylized phone?"

"What? I was sure Dominy would have been first. He's like a high school cheerleader on crack."

"Oh, don't get it wrong. He called; I just didn't feel like sharing yet. I kinda want to hold this new feeling close to the chest for a while. No pun intended."

"I know exactly how you feel. I'm actually looking forward to going to sleep so I can dream about you."

He was speechless.

"Is that too much?" she asked quietly.

"No, but next time you might want to wait until I leave. You never know what other things I may say or do that could give you even better dreams."

"I'm in no hurry. I'd rather not pack everything in one day. What would I look forward to for tomorrow?"

He was silent for a moment thinking of all of the things he still wanted to do and say with her in a matter of seconds.

"You can look forward to more 'I love you's, more kisses, more couches we could share, more walks, more hugs...long hugs."

"I'm sold. I think I will take the 'more' please."

"It is my endeavor to give it to you by God's grace." He listened to her light breathing on the other line. After 30 seconds, he'd hoped he hadn't lost her.

"Did you fall asleep on me again?"

"No. I was just taking it in and forcing myself not to waste time asking myself 'why me'? When the real question should be 'what can I do or say to give God thanks for you'?"

Brandon was floored. He never thought he would be someone's reason for seeking sufficient ways to thank God. He was deeply humbled by her. It was more than he could have imagined. He wished he was in front of her right now so she could see his expression. She read him better than most, and right now he couldn't think of a thing to say.

*　　　　　*　　　　　*

Brandon rolled towards the sound of his cell scraping across his bedside table. "Yes," he mumbled into the phone after connecting the call. It felt too early to be anyone but...

"Why didn't you return my call last night, Bran? You know I was waiting to hear how it went. You know your mom taught you better."

Dom.

Brandon stretched and returned to a comfortable position that would enable him to hold the phone next to his ear. After a jaw-popping yawn, he managed to murmur a barely comprehensible 'morning'.

"Don't give me that 'I'm-too-sleepy-to-give-you-the-details' greeting. Sit up. This is the price you pay for not answering or calling me back last night."

Brandon took a deep breath, not bothering to shift his position. "You do know I can hang up on you."

"You wouldn't dare. If you hang up on me, I won't name my son after you," Dom threatened.

"You weren't going to name him after me anyway."

"Good. I was just checking to see how awake you are. Now tell me how it went."

Brandon groaned, knowing his fragile hold on the memory of his last dream was slipping quickly through his grasp.

"She loves me, Dom," he said quietly. He heard nothing on the other end but light breathing for a few seconds.

"Did she say this or was it implied?" Dominy responded just as quietly.

"She said."

"And did you tell her how you feel?"

"Which is?"

He heard Dominy suck his teeth. "Don't make me put Robin on the line. She isn't nearly as compassionate."

"Nor is she as nosey," Brandon bit back.

"True. True." Dominy sighed. "Did you tell her you loved her too?"

"How do you know I do?"

"Wow. Did you really ask me that? What did I do to make you treat me like Bobby, the new guy at work?"

"What…what are you talking about? It's way too early for you to be drinking…"

"Brandon, I've known you were in love with Paige since the moment you got back from Chicago. You were so devastated and shaken by everything. I'm used to your compassionate heart, but this was far and away from you vehemently praying for a person in your church, or immediate family. The way you talk about her, not to mention the way you've come alive in the past few months…" His sentence died off.

"Brandon?"

Brandon hesitated in answering, almost afraid of where Dominy's train of thought was headed.

"Yep."

"When did you realize you loved her?"

"Um, a while ago," Brandon hedged.

Hearing the finality in Brandon's voice, Dominy pressed just a little further. "Okay, just tell me who said it first and I will drop the interrogation."

"No. I don't think it is any of your business."

"Alright so…you're saying that she said it first."

"I didn't say anything, Dom."

"Did you at least tell her?"

"Yes."

He heard Dominy expel a breath. "Good."

He knew he would regret asking, but curiosity won out. "Why 'good' Dom?"

"You, Brandon, have a habit of ignoring your more challenging feelings. Not necessarily the deep ones, just the ones that may make life a little more complicated and anyway you spin this, you loving Paige is going to make your life more complicated. It's a fact."

Brandon sat up slowly in bed, propping up his pillows. "Why 'complicated' Dom?"

"I'm not saying complicated has a negative connotation in this instance. I'm just saying that it may bring about some decisions you normally would not have had to consider."

"Dom, stop beating around the bush. What decision?"

"Man, Brandon, has it really not occurred to you how your lives will change in church with her travels, her newly reunited family...your sickness?"

"We are already dealing with most of those things together. I told you about the tickets I bought her?"

"Brandon, where do you see this relationship going?"

Brandon swallowed his caustic answer filled with sarcasm. His friend was obviously trying to lead him somewhere.

"I love her and she loves me. Isn't it obvious?"

"I want to hear you say it, Brandon."

"Why?"

"Because I want you to hear yourself."

"I want her. I want her to be mine. I want to marry her."

"You want to or you are going to?"

"What's the difference, Dom?"

"You know more than most that what we want isn't always what we move towards. Is this a 'no matter what decision'?"

"That isn't a fair question. God ultimately makes that decision."

"But if God has given you His blessing in regards to Paige... If you felt free to explore your feelings towards her to this degree, why would you not continue?"

"I mean to, but there are extenuating circumstances."

"No Brandon, that's what I'm saying. There are no extenuating circumstances that should stop God's will for your life. Even I know that there are no circumstances outside of God's grasp."

Brandon could feel the heat rise up the back of his neck, and tried to tamp down the temper rising in him.

"I'm not going to hurt her if it can be avoided," he spoke through clenched teeth.

"What are you saying?"

"You know full well what I am saying. I'm not going to make her a widow if I can help it. I would sooner walk away."

"Are you living in a different world than everyone else? Do you have a crystal ball under your bed? There is no way to know for sure how things will turn out, and, meanwhile, the two of you have professed your love for one another. If you meant to save her from any hurt, you should have stayed away from her in the beginning.

Don't fool yourself into thinking that you are acting as some kind of knight in shining armor where she is concerned. Those days of sacrificing to save her feelings have passed. No, it's either step forward or admit to being a coward, and let her go. As soon as you told her you loved her, it was all in. To treat her with any less of a commitment would be doing both her and yourself a disservice."

"Is it time to pass the offering plate?"

"Brandon, you may be able to make light of this, but I know you. I know how you think."

"No, you don't. You have no idea of what I'm thinking. You've never seen me in love. You don't know the feelings that I'm assaulted by. You don't know how I will react to some of these emotions or to her. You don't know because I've never been in love before. So before you continue to lecture and preach at me assuming I'm going to turn coward and run, give me the benefit of the doubt as a friend.

Better yet. I'll just call you later. I want to thank you for wrecking my high. One day. You couldn't even give me 24 hours of bliss with the knowledge and dreams."

He knew what he sounded like and didn't care that it was suspiciously close to one of his sisters when they were younger, whining about how they weren't to blame for any particular mishap. He just wanted to get back to last night when everything in life seemed possible.

He hung up without saying "goodbye," then slid back under the covers, hoping to regain a semblance of the peace he'd had before picking up the phone.

CHAPTER 16

Mason woke with a blinding headache. He loathed trying to work his way through the foggy veil of unconsciousness, but it was inevitable. He forced himself to let go of the dreams of having Paige in his arms during the night, the fragrance of her taking over all of his senses, and the feeling of well-being and warmth as he woke up surrounding her.

He groaned as his eyes and skin began to react to the sun that had already risen above the horizon. He regretted, yet again, his pick of a room that got the eastern sun.

He allowed his senses to slowly take in the warmth of the sheets, trying desperately to use the feel to minister to him medicinally. He breathed in slowly and deeply a few times before he could hear anything beyond the pounding in his head.

Since the light in the room warned him that he had slept beyond dawn, he already regretted his binge with the alcohol the night before. He just couldn't take another night of reminiscing and recalling what could have been. The pain of her rejection was just as painful as the day she served it. The phone call replayed in his head at the most inopportune times, catching him off-guard and distracting him. Most of the time he was able to stop the scene mid-stream along with the humiliation and anger, pressing it towards the back of his mind, but Wednesday…Wednesday had been too much. He was faced with irrefutable proof that there was no chance for him and Paige. It was all he could do to make it through Friday, drop Vivian off for her school friend, Camille's, slumber party before making his way to the bar four blocks away.

The pictures he'd found on the dresser in Vivian's room of Paige and Brandon on what looked like Christmas Day shook him to the core. They were holding hands, her looking up at Brandon the way he'd wished…It didn't even enter his mind to wonder why the pictures had been mailed instead of emailed.

His next deep breath was arrested when his nose caught a foreign scent. His muscles froze and his other senses heightened, causing him to forget the vice-like headache. He lifted his head slowly. He was terrified of what he might find as his squinted gaze wandered the room.

He raised himself on his forearms and turned his head to look over to the other side of the bed. It was empty, but the scent was stronger. As he leaned into the pillow, he drew in the perfume, triggering a memory from last night. A trickle of apprehension ran along the back of his neck. His ears strained to hear any sounds coming from his bathroom or beyond his bedroom. His heart stopped at the thought of Vivian coming face to face with the owner of that perfume.

After what seemed like minutes, he allowed his body to relax and breathed a deep sigh. Vivian wasn't home. She'd slept over at one of her friends' house, but it still didn't condone his lack of judgment.

He drew himself up and sat on the side of the bed, taking a slower look around the room. The tail-tell signs were evident in his strewn clothes cluttering the floor. Snatches of scenes from the night before ran up on him, only to elude him when he tried to grasp the whole of the situation. He couldn't come up with a face, but the picture of a jaw, a neckline leading from behind the ear to the shoulder, and an elbow would come at him like a game of Peek-A-Boo.

He didn't know what caused the queasiness first: the thought that he had brought someone home, or the memory of his fifth double of scotch. He raised himself on unsteady limbs and tried to reach the bathroom before purging some of last night's 'balm'.

He turned on the faucet, palming water to his face and breathing in as the cool liquid helped quell some of the inner turmoil of his body and emotions. He reached for a towel and wiped his face before eyeing a note taped to his bathroom mirror.

'If you find my card, don't call me. I hope you get over her.'
Signed, *S.*

He groaned into the towel feeling even worse than when he first woke up.

*   *   *

When after two hours, including a stomach-clenching workout and a prune-inducing shower, he was still feeling most of the effects of his hangover and couldn't conjure up more than a scent or an image of a scant slip of skin, he gave up and went back to bed with a jug of water on his nightstand.

This was exactly how Vivian found him when she came home that afternoon. Not used to him taking naps, she became concerned when he didn't respond to her immediately when she tried to wake him.

"Daddy, are you sick? Do you need me to call the doctor?" He heard the words through a haze and it took a few more minutes before he could respond.

He opened his eyes, peering up at his daughter. "Vivian? What time is it?"

He lifted his head to peer at the clock across the room.

"One of the girls woke up sick, so Camille's mom dropped us all off early. I decided to go with them and come home last." She shrugged her shoulders. "You seemed so sad. I hoped you would be doing something fun."

Mason rolled over, thankful he'd thrown on a T-shirt and shorts, despite the heat of his body. "Sometimes sleep is fun."

She quirked a brow at him while twisting her lips to the side. *When had she learned that look?*

"You don't look as though you believe me."

She stared at him for a moment and he could see the wheels turning. "I believe sleep may feel good, but fun is taking it a little far, don't ya think?"

He watched his pre-teen daughter, who to him, only yesterday would hop on his lap asking for another sip of hot chocolate so she could steal his marshmallows, place her hands on her nonexistent hips, and scowl at him.

When had this happened? Where had he been? A wave of guilt washed over him. As much as he saw his daughter and took care of her immediate needs, he was missing in his daughter's life.

"Would you believe I was just waiting for you to come home so we could have some fun?" He sat up, slipping his feet into his slippers then glanced up at her.

"No." The one word rang in his ears, but the hurt in her eyes stopped him in his tracks.

"Are you calling your dad, the best man in your life, a liar?" he asked with a small smile, trying to pull a smile from her petulant expression.

She shrugged her shoulders, instantly transforming back into the venerable little girl he was more familiar with. With a moment of regret for the ping of gratefulness for being relieved by the familiarity, he patted the bed beside him.

She obediently sat, but kept her head low. "Okay, Hon, what's going on and if you say 'nothing', I just may have to spank you."

She looked up, an indignant expression warring with surprise on her face. If he wasn't afraid of her avoiding the question, he would have laughed.

When after a few moments she still hadn't answered him, he shook her lightly. "Is it that hard to talk to me now? Do you dislike me so much now that you can't share?" He knew it wasn't playing fair, but he needed her to talk to him again, to open up to him so he could make everything alright. "I've never known you to hold a grudge. Would the God you serve approve?"

She turned to him, eyes turned liquid and stormy with anger and he lifted a brow, daring her to speak her mind, but she took a deep breath and hunched her shoulders.

"Do you promise you won't get mad?"

He watched her for a moment, all different types of scenarios running through his head. "No, but I promise to listen. Will that work?"

He watched her take a deep breath, letting it out slowly.

"I think I should go live with Gran or Mati."

He was stunned. She wanted to leave him? *No.* He wouldn't allow it. It never would have occurred to him that she would want to leave him. Before he knew it, he'd voiced his fear.

"No. I don't want to leave. I just…" She clasped her hands in her lap. "You don't seem to want to be around me. I know you and God aren't doing so well right now, but there are a lot of things I want to do at church and I don't feel like you want me to be a part of them. Most times, I get Camille's mom to take me to youth group bible studies and other functions because you are so bothered by being near the church, but …"

"I'm not bothered by being near the church or in it for that matter," Mason said, working on not getting defensive or allowing the hurt in his heart to cloud his mind.

"Have you talked to Mati about staying with her?" It took more strength than he was used to just to deliver the sentence with composure.

Vivian shook her head to the negative.

He swallowed hard before asking the next question. "Have you asked your Gran?"

"No. It was just something I've been thinking of."

Mason took his first full breath since her admission. He was walking on a thin line after last night. If Victoria caught wind of what he'd done… he couldn't even finish the thought, it scared him so much.

He ran his trembling hands down his face slowly, trying to collect his thoughts and calm the emotions threatening to blind him. He wanted to yell and bully her one minute, then hold and beg her the next. This wasn't natural; this couldn't be right. He felt as though he was losing his grip on his control and Victoria and Paige were pulling the strings in the background. He just wanted to be free of them.

He took a deep, quiet breath, and then another and another until he was no longer seeing red.

"Vivian. You are my daughter. I am your father. I am the one you are to come to when you have problems. I'm the one you come to when you have questions, even if it's regarding me."

He didn't know what else he could say without shouting. He looked over at her and she looked ready to cry, and if she did, for once, he didn't know if he would be able to hold back his own.

"Sorry." Vivian's lip quivered and her chin stuck out in rebellion, showing her fragile hold on her anger.

He suddenly wanted to laugh all of a sudden. His twelve-year-old daughter had a better hold on her emotions than he did.

"Is it still okay to talk to Mati when you are moping or working late, or too angry at God to talk?"

He took back his last thought. *This child wielded her tongue like a sword when she was angry.* He sighed. He hated to discipline his child. Their relationship was already so fragile and most of that fell on him.

"I know you are angry, Viv, but it does not give you cause to be disrespectful. You are the most important person in my life. The decisions I made to go back to work and stay in Chicago were with you in mind. The decision I made to make it easier for you to communicate with your biological mother and sister were made with your happiness in mind.

But I will not allow you to dictate how I handle my relationship with God. It is not for you to decide if or when I give my life to God and I will not make that decision just to make you happy. If you can't understand that, then I don't know what to tell you, but it's you and me. I am here to provide for and take care of you."

The tears began to hit her hands resting in her lap.

He got off the bed, kneeling in front of her. He took her hands. "Vivian, honey, I know it's been hard and I haven't exactly made it a walk in the park. I have just been…" How much did he actually tell his twelve-year-old daughter about his broken heart?

"I've been hurting, but I didn't mean for you to think I didn't want to be around you. You are the reason I get up in the morning. You are my reason for smiling. I can't imagine my life without you. I love you very much and I need you, maybe even more than you think you need me."

"Are you hurting because Mati's with Mr. Brandon and not you?"

His first instinct was to deny it, but one look at her and he knew it was futile. He just shrugged. "Can you blame your old man for liking such a woman? She has a lot of qualities I like. She gave me you. She looks a little like you. She has your laugh and a heart very much like yours."

Finally, the smile he was aiming for came.

"You are all wrong. I got those from her."

"Ha, but I knew you first." He smiled up at her, pinching her nose.

"So what are you going to do?"

"I will take it one day at a time, and be ever grateful that I still have you in my life." He was surprised and not just a little embarrassed when she took his head between her small hands and hugged his head against her bony chest. She rocked him slowly and he was mortified to feel a lump form in the back of his throat.

"Shh," she crooned, "It's alright. I will stay. I will pray that God makes your heart feel better."

He took a deep breath, taking in the fresh and familiar scent of fabric softener, and his Vivian. The peace that flowed through him made him want to give in to the tears, but there was only so much he would allow his daughter to see. Already their relationship was sorely unbalanced with her rocking him like she was his mother.

He wrapped his arms around her waist and stood up, bringing her with him. She squealed when her feet left the floor.

"Daddy put me down. I'm too big." She pulled slightly at his hair.

He pulled away, seeing light dance in her gray eyes. He swore right then that he would make more of an effort to live in the moment.

"Only if you promise me something." He jostled her a few times to show her that her weight had no bearing on him. She laughed out loud.

"Don't drop me!" She yelled. "What? What do you want me to promise?"

"I want you to promise to go out with me tonight. We can go to dinner and the movies. Will you go? Will you go?" He continued to jostle, raising her up just enough to create space between them before he tightened his hold. She squealed again.

"Okay. Okay, I promise. Could I have a promise too?" He began to turn around with her. "Stop! I can't think. You're making me dizzy." He stopped abruptly and watched her sway slightly side to side until she got her equilibrium back.

"If I promise not to ask you to go up front in church, will you start taking me to church again and..." she paused slightly, "and maybe stay a couple of times a month. I promise, promise, promise that is all I ask." She placed the palms of her hands together, pleading.

He set her down, still holding onto her shoulders to make sure her legs would support her.

"It means that much to you? That I go?" She just nodded.

"No more talk about leaving me?" She nodded again.

He stuck out his hand to shake on it, but she ignored the hand, moving back in his arms, hugging him tight around the waist.

"I missed you, daddy. I've felt so alone."

His heart broke again. Would he never stop failing her? This was the last time he fell this short. He laid his chin on her head, fighting hard to keep the burning at the back of his eyes from forming tears. His daughter had thought to leave him. Never. He would never allow it.

"I won't leave you alone again. I will work harder." He would do anything in his power to make her happy from now on. No more wallowing, no more drinking, and definitely no more women.

Now, if only he could remember the woman that shared his bed last night. He was still slightly sickened by the fact that he couldn't recall her name and she knew where he lived. He hoped she would remain resolved not to try and contact him.

He'd looked high and low for that elusive card she may have left, but found nothing. He tried to console himself with the thought that many people had one-night stands and never contacted each other again. He hoped for his sake this was one of those times, but his gut churned nonetheless with reservations.

CHAPTER 17

Victoria set the card down next to the other ten she'd received over the last month and a half. Each card had one line scrawled across it in her husband's handwriting. She fingered the gold leaf edges with reverence.

Late at night, when the house was quiet and she was too wired to sleep, she would spread out the cards on her bed in the order she'd received them, and reread them. No doubt it was exactly what he'd wanted her to do.

Remember I love you. Remember the day we met. Remember when you agreed to go out with me. Remember our first date. Remember the first time we held hands. Remember the first gift I gave you. Remember our glen. Remember our first kiss. Remember the day I asked you to marry me. Remember, my Vicki.

She was ashamed to find that some of the instructions were easier than the others. Some memories came quickly to mind, while it took several minutes of backtracking to bring to mind other particular instances.

She picked up the second card and let her mind take her back to the day she noticed a young man with eyes the color of warm chocolate watching her from a few booths away. She was celebrating her first birthday in a new city. A few of her friends were visiting just for the occasion, and she was desperately homesick, but too stubborn to go back home.

Recently inheriting her grandparent's farm, she'd moved to Oklahoma against her parent's wishes to help restore it to its former glory. The past six months were nothing but one challenge after another. There were hands on the land to help with bigger projects, but there was so much to do. One job was hardly finished with a crisis narrowly averted when another problem would arise. This was the first day in three months she'd taken off and it was forced on her with a surprise visit from her friends, Catherine, Tonie, and Claudette.

They couldn't understand her wanting to move 200 miles away to a place out in the middle of nowhere, and voiced that opinion often. In fact, they were voicing it once again when 'Mr. Chocolate Eyes', as she was beginning to refer to him, got up from his booth and sauntered over, never taking his eyes off of her.

She remembered thinking that he walked like a panther: slow, direct, predatory. A chill raced down her spine, causing her to sit straighter in her seat. Her change in demeanor didn't escape her friends' attention, and they turned to follow her gaze.

"Oh Lordee," Catherine whispered on a breath that seemed to pass between each of them. Even though Victoria had watched him surreptitiously under her lashes, she found now she couldn't take her eyes away from his. When he finally arrived at her table, it was all she could do to keep breathing. Her heart pounded so hard in her chest she thought she would pass out and embarrass herself.

"Good evening, ladies," he said, releasing her gaze long enough to acknowledge all of her friends. "My name is Richard Branchett."

"Hello Richard, I'm Tonie Channing," her friend said, seeming to have found her tongue first. She offered her hand and he shook it gently. This began a round of introductions until his eyes came back to rest on her. *Speak idiot.*

She cleared her throat, but before she could speak Catherine gave her name. "This is Victoria Langston."

"Victoria, it's a pleasure to meet you," he said. She wiped her clammy hand on the napkin in her lap then reached forward to take the proffered hand, but to her surprise, instead of shaking it he brought it to his lips, skimming her knuckles and leaving a path of heat in their wake. She retrieved her hand, trying to rub away the sensation with her other hand under the table.

"I don't mean to interrupt your celebration," he motioned towards the special birthday cake Claudette had made and brought with her for Victoria. "I couldn't leave without offering you my wish for a very happy birthday. I was also wondering if I could be so bold as to request that you might consider adding me to your wish before you blew out your candles."

The small gasp from Catherine told her that she wasn't alone in her reaction. She could have sworn the candles on the cake in front of her had been lit. She looked down quickly. No such luck. It was her face that was flaming and thanks to her mother's alabaster complexion, she was pale enough to light up like Rudolph.

"I may consider it," she answered, trying to employ an air of nonchalance.

"Might you also consider allowing me to see you again?" She watched him. Nothing in his eyes told her he was being anything less than sincere, and oh how she wanted to see him again. So much so it terrified her.

"Mr. Branchett, I can no sooner keep you from seeing me again than I can keep the sun from shining, but I'm afraid it will have to be more by chance than with any provocation from me."

Tonie's groan of regret from her left mirrored her feelings, but she pinched her to shut her up.

Richard's face fell slightly, but the determination in his eyes didn't dim. "Would you give a gentleman even the slightest hint of where the sun might shine on any given Saturday at 12:30 p.m.?"

Victoria shrugged, glancing at Claudette for help. "I guess where one might find books," Claudette said before Victoria could reply.

What was she thinking? She wasn't. None of them were. All of their sense had been zapped by his darn handshake. Claudette knew the library was her only sanctuary.

She looked up to watch his smile spread across his features so that a dimple winked in his left cheek. *Oh Lord. You have got to be kidding. Is this some cruel joke? I won't ever be able to go to the library again. Not if I want to keep my vow.*

"Would this be the place where one borrows books or buys them?" He bent forward, speaking in a conspiratorial tone meant to draw in their confidence.

Tonie opened her mouth, but Victoria pinched her again. "Ouch! Stop pinching me," Tonie cried, rubbing her thigh.

Victoria's face took on a whole new level of heat. She couldn't imagine what she must look like. She watched him watching her, and the disappointment in his eyes stung her. She felt like a heel, but darn it, this was self-preservation.

"Look," she began, hoping some great line would come to her that would assuage his feelings and make him understand that she was just the wrong girl to waste his attention on.

When his face went stony, she panicked and blurted out the thought. "You seem wonderful, but you would be wasting your time on me." When the smile returned full force, she thought back to what she'd said and wished the cake was 10 times bigger so she could hide in it. Did she actually say the man was wonderful? That was it. She was not going to speak anymore. She couldn't trust that her mouth wouldn't betray her.

"Catherine," Claudette began, "What's the name of that library on 10th street? You know the one. We usually pass it while heading to the…"

"So Mr. Branchett," Victoria interrupted Claudette before she could give out any more information about her. "What brings you here this evening?"

Richard placed one hand in his pants pocket and leaned to the left. *Was there no end to the madness? Come on. Wait, was Tonie drooling?* Disgusted with her friends, she looked back at Richard. She just wanted him to leave, but her last sentence had invited him to stay.

"I just got a promotion on my job today and I thought I would celebrate."

Victoria looked around him at the now empty booth he'd been occupying. "Alone?" she asked skeptically.

"Well, it wasn't meant to be that way, but I kinda got stood up by a couple of friends. It seems they couldn't get away." He smiled sheepishly.

Victoria's heart went out to him. She knew what it was like to celebrate alone.

"Here, have a piece of cake," Claudette said, picking up a knife so she could cut Victoria's cake. *What the heck?* Victoria opened her mouth, but Tonie beat her to the punch.

"You can't cut Victoria's cake," she said. *At least someone has my back,* Victoria thought, smiling.

"The candles are already on. We might as well light them so she can blow them out before we cut it," Tonie continued.

Victoria looked at Tonie to make sure she was still the same girl she'd been friends with for over fifteen years. *Was this one of those Candid Camera moments?* She'd heard about that show and its pranks. Victoria began to look around for people hiding out with cameras in the restaurant.

"Do you mind, Victoria? It is your birthday after all," Richard implored, pulling her away from her thoughts.

Well at least someone remembered.

"No, I don't mind. Do you like marble cake? The frosting is chocolate, but the inside is chocolate and vanilla swirled together with caramel."

"It sounds decadent," he said, his eyes flickering to her lips briefly before returning to her eyes, but she felt it just the same.

"Where's the lighter, Claudette?" She asked almost urgently.

Claudette retrieved the lighter, but it was absconded before she could pass it. "Please, let me. It's the least I can do since you will be sharing your cake with me."

She wanted to take the lighter from him so he wouldn't feel entitled to a piece of her cake or a piece of anything else of hers… ever. Knowing she would look like a lunatic if she yanked it from him, she sighed and nodded.

He began to light the candles. All thirty-five of them, but started frowning slightly as he passed number thirty. He obviously had been counting to see how old she was. He looked back at her and finished lighting them, and handed the lighter back to Claudette.

"You look surprisingly young for your age, Victoria," he said.

Tonie burst out laughing. *Maybe he wasn't into older women and she could get rid of him that way.* Victoria moved to pinch her again, but Tonie moved out of reach and slapped her hand. Hard. She pulled it back, her eyes beginning to water.

She looked back up and saw their little duel didn't go unnoticed by the other three. *Could this get any more embarrassing?*

"It's a running joke between us. We all give the birthday girl 10 to grow on." Tonie said. "Victoria is the baby of the bunch though you wouldn't know it with her old soul. She acts older than the three of us put together sometimes." Tonie looked over at Victoria. "Come on Vic, the candles will burn out. Go ahead and blow."

Yep, Victoria thought. *It definitely could get more embarrassing.*

Fortunately, the blowing out of the candles and cutting of the cake were less noteworthy. Victoria was able to get the attention of their waitress and get a to-go box for Richard.

He tried one last time.

"Are you sure I can't convince you to have coffee or a meal with me?"

Victoria shook her head, looking away momentarily.

He nodded, conceding defeat. "Ladies, it was more than a pleasure; it was an honor," he said, looking at all three of them then pierced her with his gaze one last time.

" Happy Birthday, Victoria," he said almost too softly to hear, "I hope all of your wishes come true." *She definitely hoped not or she was in big trouble.* She just smiled in gratitude and watched him turn to leave. It was a whole month before she went back to the library and, even then, she made sure it wasn't on a Saturday. Though she hadn't forgotten him, she figured he must surely have forgotten her or lost any desire to see her. Two months later, on an uncomfortably hot Saturday afternoon, she took refuge in the building, always cooler due to the overabundance of trees surrounding it and the ceiling fans inside.

She had only been there 15 minutes, perusing the classics for a romance she'd not read when she heard his memorable timbre.

"Just when I thought I was doomed to nothing but gray skies. How are you sunshine?" She turned around to see Richard leaning against the shelf at the end of the row.

She took a deep breath and sighed.

"Dang."

*   *   *

Victoria placed the card back down on the bed, shaking her head, a slight smile on her face. His relentless pursuit of her exhausted her excuses and then her reservations until her curiosity and long fought desire won out.

It would have been so much easier for her to continue to reject his advances if he came at her with the same insistence and languid charm as he used at the restaurant, but he didn't ask her out again right away, nor did he treat her to those heated looks that made her feel like a foregone conclusion.

What he did was so much more devastating to her newly acquired freedom. He became her friend and made her feel like she finally belonged in the time she lived in.

She reached for the next card, unable to resist taking one more trip.

*   *   *

After two and a half months of walking into her favorite town grocery store, the post office, or the library and finding Richard in the next aisle, in front of her in line, or sitting at her favorite table in the back corner, Victoria wasn't surprised when he accompanied an order of feed that was delivered to the farm the last Saturday in August.

She walked out of the shed on the east side of the barn, adjusting her gloves when the truck drove up. Discouraged from doing any of the heavier lifting, Victoria would wait until after the delivery to come over to the far side of the barn, but this day she'd been feeling restless; a restlessness that neither the painting of the newly raised fence or working in her herb garden could feed. She needed to push, strain, lift, and pull until her muscles were so tired she didn't have the energy to do anything but place a few morsels in her mouth before she dragged herself to bed.

She came up short when it wasn't just Harlen and Steve, the store owner's sons, but Richard jumping from the truck.

"Miss Victoria," Steve and Harlen greeted simultaneously, smiling brightly.

Victoria regained her composure and continued walking towards the identical twins. "Thank you for making this run for me. I know you are getting ready to go back to school. I really appreciate it."

"Are you kidding? Not only did this run get us out of that hot store, but I get to gaze upon you one last time before I'm shipped off to Temple. I have this last chance to take the memory of you with me to keep me warm on those cold, lonely nights," Steve said as he stepped towards her. The sincerity in his voice rang clear and his eyes never strayed from her face.

She smiled warmly, catching the strange stillness that came over Richard from the corner of her eye. She focused all her attention back on Steve, then began clapping her hands. "Very good. Great line, and you delivered it perfectly." She continued to applaud him until she was close enough to embrace him with a brotherly hug.

"The girls of Pennsylvania won't know what hit them. Just go easy on them okay?" She leaned back, smiling up at the normally, painfully shy but handsome young man. With one last pat on the arms, she released him and stepped back.

She looked over at his brother. "Harlen, you make sure your brother doesn't get into more trouble than he can handle."

Harlen grinned. "And how do you suppose I do that, Miss Victoria? You've created a monster. April at Merclane's Cleaners can hardly keep our order straight when he comes in now. Last week she did a heavy starch on my whole order."

Victoria looked between Steve, now shuffling uncomfortably in the dirt, and Harlen's disdainful expression. "Why is that bad?"

"I had a couple of undershirts in the order because I wanted to just pack everything." He ended his explanation with a chuckle.

Victoria pressed her lips together as she looked back at Steve, gauging his reaction. She burst out laughing at his shrug then shook her finger at him in bemusement. "What did I tell you, Steve?"

"I didn't do it on purpose. Honest. All I did was say 'Hi' and ask her how her day was going."

"That is true, Miss Victoria, but since he never said much to her before you started coaching him, what little he does say now seems to go a long way." Harlen slapped Steve between the shoulder blades and laughed.

"Oh boy." Victoria sighed deeply. "Well Steve, it looks like you may need to say goodbye to one last person on your way out of town."

Steve looked pained. "Do you really think that's necessary?"

"I warned you before we began that there could be good and bad consequences to what I was showing you and I told you that you were responsible for making sure there was no confusion. This may be a little different, but at least make an effort to clear the air."

Steve nodded then Victoria turned to Richard, who'd slowly walked up to join them.

"Oh, sorry Richard. Miss Victoria, this is our cousin, Richard Branchett. He lives in Durby, but comes over on the weekends when he can."

"Hello, Ms. Langston. It's nice to see you again." He shook her hand.

Oh boy, there went those goosebumps again. What was it about this man? She should be upset at the least that he would assume he was welcome on her land. She was a very private person, and the last thing she needed was for her workers or heaven forbid her parents get wind of him and his intentions. Though try as she might, she couldn't summon the emotions that would discourage his attentions because when she got down to it, each time she looked up and saw him coming her way she was reluctantly grateful.

She couldn't have chosen better if she'd been asked to design her dream man. Richard was breathtakingly handsome with his smooth, hazelnut colored skin, chocolate eyes, tall lean physique and southern charm. Their 'chance' encounters all over town were wearing at her resolve to stay clear of any entanglements. She didn't leave her family, friends, and everything she was familiar with to come out here to the middle of nowhere to find herself in the same situation she'd left.

"Mr. Branchett, how convenient this all is."

"Really? I see it more as serendipitous. Not only do I get to spend one last weekend with my cousins, but I get to help one of the most beautiful women in Oklahoma."

"I thought I told you those charming words don't work on me?"

"I know, but I was feeling left out." His lips tipped up on one side, and she had to turn to hide her amusement.

"Miss Victoria, Richard isn't a bad guy." Steve said, mistaking the situation. "He recently got promoted at this high-end brokerage firm in Oklahoma City, but he still comes over to help us on the weekends."

"Really? How nice of him." Victoria turned back to look at Richard who had the decency to look embarrassed.

She thought of the half-hour talks they'd sometimes share after he conveniently ran into her around town.

"I wonder how your dad stays in business what with all the generous breaks he gives those who work for him." The twins looked at her with confusion for a few seconds before the light changed in Harlen's eyes and he looked over at Richard, who began heading back to the truck.

She knew she was close to stepping on his feelings and wondered if she should continue forward, full-gallop or stay where she was. She could embarrass him enough that he would leave her alone.

She mentally shook herself for her cowardice then retreated.

"Alright. Barker is waiting in the shed. Let's get this truck emptied," Victoria said, heading back towards the shed doors.

As was the custom, Victoria invited the Merclane twins in for iced tea and sandwiches after filling and organizing the shed. She'd tried to help out more, but three against one were daunting odds when it came to her helping to lift anything around the men.

She finally gave up and resigned herself to straightening the bags and delegating. She worked hard to avoid doing anything that would cause her to be in or out of the shed alone with Richard.

She wasn't interested in sharing any more of her personal life with the twins than was necessary and from the looks that Harlen kept giving her, he already suspected too much. Everyone in town knew their father could keep a secret as well as a sifter could keep water.

Not that she had anything to hide really. She'd run into Richard maybe a dozen times over the last two months. Sure they'd talked, but it was mostly about the weather, what was in her basket, or what she was reading at that time. They would even talk about his job when she got up the nerve to ask, but when he asked about anything she thought was too personal, she would bring an end to the conversation. He caught on quick and usually waited for her to introduce a subject. She knew it was selfish and just short of rude, but it was safe – and him showing up at her farm today was anything but safe.

How was she supposed to keep him at arm's length when he was constantly in her space? How was she going to keep him from wheedling his way into her heart?

"Oh, by the way, Miss Victoria. My dad is throwing Steve and me a little going away thing tomorrow afternoon. Nothing fancy, just some family and friends, and Aunt Rose's peach cobbler."

She'd had Aunt Rose's peach cobbler. It was almost worth a couple of hours of uncomfortable questions.

"I know it's short notice," Harlen went on, "but it would mean a lot if you came by. You wouldn't have to stay the whole time," he said in a rush, "and Richard would be there to keep you company."

"I'm not too sure that would be an argument for the plus side," Richard said, sipping his tea.

Victoria glanced at him, but his eyes were guarded.

She looked back at the twins, pressing her lips together to contain a laugh when Steve pressed his hands together, widened his eyes, and poked out his lip in a pleading gesture.

"Oh man, I really have created a monster. You do know that won't always work on women," she said balefully.

"It doesn't have to work on women. It only needs to work on you," he replied, to which she burst out laughing.

"Okay. I will come. What time does it start?"

"It'll go from 2, until."

She wanted to groan. Well, she'd already committed herself, and Harlen did say she didn't have to stay the whole time…

"How about I arrive around 3:30. Do you think there will still be some peach cobbler left?"

"I will hide some for you if it looks like it's going fast."

"How sweet of you Harlen, but I was only kidding. I wouldn't ask you to babysit cobbler for me at your party."

Harlen shrugged. "It's the least I could do with you agreeing to come. Speaking of the party, we need to be heading back to town soon. Steve and I have a few more details we need to take care of."

"I thought you said your dad was putting it together for you?" Victoria said, starting to get an uneasy feeling.

"He is, but you know dad. He may remember the cups and the plates, but he will forget the forks, spoons and knives, and I don't think you will want to eat cobbler with your fingers."

Victoria shrugged and got up to collect the dishes. She walked them through the back door to the kitchen and was going to turn back for the rest when she bumped into Richard hard enough to displace a glass from his overflowing hands. It shattered as it made contact with the floor.

She reached down to pick up the larger pieces when Richard startled her with a yell. "Don't touch it! You could cut yourself and you are way too far for us to try to get you to the hospital in my uncle's truck."

Victoria looked up at him from where she squatted ready to yell back, but she noticed the deep concern on his face and decided to try and alleviate it by lightening the mood.

"Pshaw, we could use my car. It's much faster." To her dismay, he didn't even crack a smile, but he did bend down to join her.

"Not much scares you, does it?"

"Why would you say that? It's only glass—"

He cut her off. "It's not about the glass." He took a deep breath. "You are doing it. You are making this place work. I have to admit I was a little more than curious about you running this place by yourself."

"I'm not by myself. I have plenty of help. Besides, it's not like I'm starting from scratch. This farm has been in my family for a few decades. I just wanted to do my part." She unthinkingly reached for a piece of glass again, but he stayed her hand with his.

She looked up to see if he felt the same tingle of awareness she was experiencing, and was arrested by the warmth she saw enter his eyes. She couldn't move or gather a coherent thought. She could only watch as the milk chocolate of his eyes turned to coffee with the widening of his pupils. She was fascinated by his reaction to her, and hers to him.

He blinked and she was released from her trance, her first clear thought, *Oh Dang, I'm in trouble...*

He began to straighten, pulling her up with him. When she finally had the presence of mind to pull away, he tightened his hands around hers for the briefest of seconds then let her go.

She was speechless, but he placed his hands in his pockets and seemed to pick up where he left off.

"I don't know any young women your age who would take on even half the amount of responsibility you have with this farm. From the moment I saw you I knew you were like no one else I'd ever met, but you continue to amaze me with your strength. You don't seem to need too much help. You're strong, courageous, independent; from what your friends say, wise beyond your years and from what I've heard from my cousins and can see here, you have achieved more in six months than most people do in a couple of years.

Please tell me something you don't do well because I am feeling just a little intimidated right now."

"You're wrong. I am afraid," she said just above a whisper. She watched him open his mouth, but kept going.

"I'm afraid of failing."

She watched the surprise and then compassion wash across his handsome features.

"I'm sure your family would understand and pitch..."

She interrupted him by shaking her head. "No, they won't come. When I told them I was going to take over the farm, they made me choose. Choose what they wanted for me or choose to be on my own." She looked past his shoulder for a few seconds, garnering any courage she had left then looked back at his face. "I can't ever go back."

He reached up to touch her cheek with his fingertips and she made the barest of movements seeking more of that light caress, before she stepped back out of his reach.

"I need to get a broom since you won't let me pick up this glass with my hands. I will be right back." She all but ran from the room.

They had just finished cleaning up the last of the glass when Steve came through the door. He watched the two of them warily. "Um, Richard, we are going to need to make a move soon. Harlen's getting a little antsy. He wanted to get back to town before some of the other stores closed." He turned towards Victoria. "Do you need me to help with the dishes? We can get them done quicker with six hands."

"Have I ever had you do dishes? Get going and thank your dad again for me. I really appreciate the delivery."

"Will do." He began walking towards the door, but turned when he didn't see Richard move.

Richard laid the dustpan against the wall. "Give me one second and I will be right out."

Steve hesitated, looking between Victoria and Richard, then with what seemed to be a bit of reluctance he turned back to the door. "Okay. See you tomorrow, Victoria."

Victoria waved and watched him saunter out of the door before she returned her attention to Richard.

He came to stand in front of her. "I know I will see you tomorrow at the party, but you seem to be very protective of your privacy so I won't stay too close, but I was wondering if you might go out with me next week. You know... we could schedule to meet somewhere instead of it being happenstance, or I could pick you up."

She stared at him. Oh how she wanted to say 'yes,' but then what? Things would only progress, and she wasn't ready. She could barely think of the last year and a half without crying, let alone find a way to share it with someone she was close to.

She looked down at the floor. "I, ah...I..." She couldn't think of a way to tell him she wasn't ready, wasn't sure she ever would be, but when she was he would be the one she would pick. She took a deep breath.

"It would have to be no right now." She looked up trying to relay what she couldn't in words. *Please don't give up. Please wait for me.*

It was hard to miss the disappointment that clouded his eyes. *Such beautifully expressive eyes,* she thought.

He watched her for a moment, and she had the odd sensation he was looking for something. He opened his mouth then closed it only to open it again, but still nothing came out.

"What?" She asked before she was aware of forming the word.

"Would it be alright if I asked you again, maybe sometime later?"

She wanted to ask him why, but was just too relieved that he'd offered to wait.

She nodded and saw him visibly relax. A grin had just begun forming when Harlen called from the door.

"Richard, come on! We need to go. Whatever you need to say to Miss Victoria can wait until tomorrow."

"That's my cue," he said impishly, "I'll see you tomorrow?"

"Yep, Aunt Rose's peach cobbler! I'd be upset if I missed it." She smiled, feeling a heavy weight slide off her shoulders. She followed him through the door and waved at them as they pulled off.

As optimistic as she felt at that moment that she would one day say 'yes' to him, it still took another four months and just as many invitations before she had the courage to do so.

When she did finally accept, she asked him what caused him to continue to ask her. Till this day she remembered the answer.

"Sometimes when you first spot me in a place you're not expecting to see me, your eyes get this light in them that tells me you are happy to see me before you catch yourself. It reminds me of the first time I saw you and the way your eyes got all big and gorgeous when you saw me staring at you. Not too many people get to relive that over and over. It's worth it just to know you hold that special look just for me."

She was speechless and well on her way to being in love with him.

*　　　　　　　　*　　　　　　　　*

It seemed like lifetimes ago. Sometimes it felt like it had happened to two other people. *Where did it all begin to unravel?* Maybe if she'd shared... Well, it was too late for that. They could go around and around for hours discussing the things they didn't say or do over the last 33 years. A humorless laugh escaped her lips before she could stop it.

She knew what he was doing. She knew he hoped that the memories and his absence would wear her down. Why wouldn't she yearn for what they had? It was a fairytale. Her greatest desires couldn't even come close to what he gave her. He gave her the love and the family she never thought she'd have. He encouraged her and gave her the confidence she needed to keep pushing when things didn't go smoothly on the farm. He made her feel as though she belonged.

The only thing he couldn't give her was a way to assuage her guilt over giving up her son, or a way to combat the nightmares she had of her son not having the wonderful, whole life she'd hoped for him when she'd given him over to the Grossenbergs.

For more than forty years, the peace she thought was a mere breath away still eluded her and it would continue to do so until she found her son.

She was so close. Michael had gotten further than any other investigator since the family had moved out-of-state when Brian was five.

Victoria shook her head. Not today. Today she would begin with happy thoughts and thanks to her husband, she knew exactly what she would daydream about.

She picked up the fourth card, taking it with her to the window so she could watch the moon finish its decent.

Remember our first date?

She looked out over the darkened land trying to imagine what Richard was doing in that moment.

Two weeks, four days, and twelve hours was how long she still had before she could see him again. Fear raced across her psyche. She was almost right back to where she'd begun.

Everything else near and dear to her had been taken from her. If anything ever happened to Richard, she wouldn't survive it if she couldn't find a way to protect herself against this onslaught of emotion.

Sure it was fine when they'd started out. Life hadn't used her love for her family as a bat to pulverize her. There was no excuse now though. She knew better. She knew how weak her love for him made her, and here he was trying to awaken these feelings and succeeding.

Oh how she'd tried to bottle them up. Oh how she'd worked to care for only the very essential things in her relationship with her family, but she was no more prepared for Rachael's death than she was for Brian's disappearance. Now Richard was thousands of miles away in some unfamiliar country with even more unfamiliar laws and he was tempting her to feel; tempting her to give up her control for a love that was, at its best, fragile, and at its worst, devastatingly painful.

Didn't he know that he was torturing her with the memories of their love and her naïve thoughts and dreams for a family she could call hers?

She would continue to do what he asked. She would remember and play this little game, but she would not wish for any more than what they had. She would not desire or hope for more than what she could hold in her hand.

When Richard came back, she would hold him close.

Meanwhile, she would work to keep her granddaughter safe until she could also hold her close.

She glanced at the clock once again. It read 3:35 a.m., the digital numbers throwing their green illumination across the left edge of her bedroom.

She absently rubbed the card between her thumb and forefinger again. Pictures had arrived in her email two mornings before of an extremely inebriated Mason in a bar with a pretty, curly-haired brunette with skin the color of caramel.

Normally, these pictures may have made her smile in anticipation of organizing and witnessing his demise, but instead she felt nothing but anger and resentment that he was making it so damn easy.

He was throwing away the second best thing that had ever happened to him, all because he couldn't see beyond what he couldn't have.

Pathetic. She sneered to herself, her expression freezing when she looked up, catching her reflection in the darkened window.

CHAPTER 18

"Haha. Think long, think wrong!" The petite woman yelled. Her exclamation rang out in the small room awash with light from the naked window.

The sound of cards hitting the small table, used intermittently for everything from dining to shelving books, was as loud as a bullet ricocheting off of the walls of an alley.

Paige sat back in the hard plastic chair shaking her head at the older woman. "Such modesty. It's almost overwhelming," she said, working to keep her lips firm. The woman was incorrigible as it was. She would not give her any more fuel.

"Mrs. Marr, Elena, you might want to keep it down. The last time I came and played Bid-wiz with you, I nearly got my head yelled off by James."

The older woman shrugged her shoulders as she began stacking cards. "James wouldn't hurt a fly. You just have to know how to talk to him. Actually..." She let the word slowly roll off her tongue while looking at Paige slyly. "I think he has a bit of a crush on you."

Paige laughed. "Mrs. Marr, I think you are finally in need of glasses, which is a good thing because I was thinking you seemed just a little too young and healthy to be in here."

"Don't get me started. That son of mine is the only true reason why I'm in here. He doesn't use the sense God gave him when it comes to that monster he's married to."

Paige regretted her comment almost as soon as it left her lips. She knew to steer clear of the subject of her son or any of her immediate family, but lately Paige felt like she was tiptoeing around eggshells. The woman was growing bitterer by the day.

It was hard coming up with things to talk about that didn't trigger her anger. Paige's heart went out to the woman who until a year ago lived with her husband in an upper middle-class neighborhood in Los Angeles.

The massive heart attack that claimed his life was only the beginning of what seemed to be a landslide from a life of independence to confinement. Two months later, Elena was diagnosed with breast cancer. Distraught and grieving, Elena handed over executive right to her eldest son, Mitchell, who for all intents and purposes seemed to love his mother, but from what his mother said, was seduced by his fiancé into believing Elena would be better off in nursing home.

The stroke she had during her first week in the facility did nothing to dissuade him or keep her down for that matter. Though her use of her left leg was slightly hindered, it had no effect on her sharper-than-steel wit, and her anger for being 'caged' gave her the energy she needed to fight the disease.

"I'm not going out like a puff of wind. It would serve him right if he had to pay for me to stay here for another 20 years," she said during one of her rants that were growing more frequent.

Paige visited Elena for a few hours every other week. It had been hard not going to see her after she'd gotten home from the hospital, but a nursing home was high on the list of places Paige could not go due to the germ factor. It pained her to see the anger that had taken root in that time.

"So, I have some news that I think you might enjoy, but I'm going to need you to do something for me," Paige said as she moved the table back near the window so they could share some tea while sitting on the window seat. This was their usual routine towards the end of Paige's visit.

"Alright, chick-a-dee. Spill," Elena said when she was seated comfortably. Paige couldn't help but shake her head and smile. The woman must have placed two or three dozen endearments upon her since she'd known her. At first she thought it was because Elena couldn't remember her name, but after one particularly awkward moment when Paige tried to remind her, she went off like a rocket.

"I know what your name is, child. I'm just not particularly fond of it. Don't you have a middle name that sounds more like a flower or a season? You know… something that sounds less like a piece of wood. Shoot, it's a wonder she didn't just name you 'Table' or 'Pencil'. Yes, this is my daughter, Chair. Isn't she beautiful? She looks just like her father, Tree." The woman kept on as if she were holding a conversation with a quilting group.

Paige wanted to be mad, but the conversation was so ridiculous she couldn't hold back the smile.

"It's Rosen." The woman stalled in her antics, and stared at her.

"What is?"

"My middle name," Paige explained.

The woman blinked a couple of times then went on like they'd never had the conversation. "Will you be joining me for tea, honey?"

Paige wanted to howl in laughter, but used every thread of discipline and a hefty bite to her tongue to keep her expression sober. "Sure," she answered and they'd become fast friends.

"Okay, but before I tell you, I want to ask you a question."

Elena just looked at her expectantly. Paige took a deep breath.

"I know I was gone for a little while, but lately you seem more…" Paige stuck her tongue in her cheek for a second hoping she was doing the right thing. "…Disappointed in your son and daughter-in-law than before. Did anything happen?"

"Call a sucker a sucker, Paige. Disgusted is the word." Elena heaved a weary sigh. "Nothing more than usual, except his blatant disregard for his father's memory. That heffa talked him into selling my house. The house Ben and I bought with our hard-earned money. The house Mitchell, John, and Candice grew up in. The house Mitchell and John came back to after they graduated and stayed until they were forever old," she said the last with a careless wave of her hand. Paige's heartfelt bruised.

"It's not the house, but what it stood for. My grandchildren and great-grandchildren could have grown up in that house. There was so much love in that house." Her voice faded out and Paige knew she'd traveled to another time.

Just as quickly as she'd gone, she came back with a fine sheen covering her eyes. "Well, what's done is done and there is no going back, but there is one thing they can't take away from me." Elena pointed her small chin in defiance with the last part of the sentence. Paige was always floored by this woman's tenacious hold on life.

"What's that?"

"They can't take the memories or the love I have in my heart for Ben." Her chin trembled slightly. "Nope. That, they can't have." Elena turned to look out the window, obviously trying to compose herself. She turned back and patted Paige on the hand resting near her forgotten cup.

"So is there a reason why you had me take us on this trip through the town of 'Crazy' and the men who fall for her?"

Paige shook her head because she couldn't think of anything else to do at the moment.

"Well, I have a rather interesting piece of news to share with you and I was looking to get your opinion."

Elena sat up straighter in her seat and clapped her hands a few times.

"Oooh. Don't do it, girl. You'll regret it. Besides, you are more than capable of getting your own man."

Taken aback, Paige moved back from Elena, pressing herself against the window. "What are you talking about?"

"Aren't you going to tell me that you are in love with your pastor or some other married man in your church and you are pregnant with his child?" She blinked at Paige innocently.

Paige gasped, "No! What? No!" She sputtered. "H-E-Double-Hockey-Sticks, no. Where do you come up with these things?" Paige said, offended to her core. Was this what Elena thought of her?

"Why, television, dear. It's not like I get out much." Then she placed her hands demurely in her lap and fluttered her lashes, and that's when Paige finally tuned into the fact that Elena was teasing her. *Maybe her daughter-in-law was on to something.*

She quickly banished the thought, but it did make her think again about what she was preparing to share.

"Awww, go ahead and spill it. I was just having a little bit of fun with you. You know I think the world of you," she said, catching Paige's gaze. Then she patted her hand. "Even if you have a messed up name."

A chuckle escaped from Paige's lips unbidden. She was at war with herself. This tiny, feisty and absolutely inappropriate woman kept her guessing, but was dear to her and though she was rough around the edges, Elena had answers to questions Paige didn't have the courage to ask anyone else.

"Don't you have a counselor or a spiritual mother you can ask this?" Elena replied a short time later when Paige had shared some of the particulars of her relationship with Brandon, what he was battling, and what she wanted.

"Yes, but you've experienced both. I need to know if you thought it was worth it."

"Why? My story is different than yours. My walk didn't begin until after."

Paige didn't ask again, but she didn't move either. Elena rolled her eyes, mumbling to herself. "Stubborn child, reminds me of myself sometimes."

"Sometimes an answer that works for someone else doesn't work for you. You really need to stay close to the Lord on this. You need to leave no room for doubt. It will take you down if you aren't prepared."

Paige sat there quiet for a good long while searching for peace in the answers she'd gained. Finally she shifted, looking at Elena with a small smile.

"Is there anything you would like me to pray for you before I go?"

Paige saw the little gleam come into Elena's eyes. "And no I will not pray that your daughter-in-law gets cast down, cast away, cast aside, or gets put in a casket. I would just be wasting my breath."

Elena harrumphed. "Well then I guess you can just go on and pray whatever the Lords leads you to pray."

The woman wouldn't give an inch. Paige shook her head, gave the woman a kiss on the cheek and began to pray.

*   *   *

Paige shuffled through the throng of cheerful fans whose attention wavered from one exhibit to another. She'd been sitting so long her legs felt like wooden pegs, which did nothing to help her plight in getting to the restroom that continued to loom too far for comfort.

This Christian Writer's Conference was the third event on her book signing tour. As excited as she was to be on this new circuit with her novel, she was missing home. She missed her church, she missed her bed, her fuzzy slippers (she'd have to remember to pack them next time) and oh how she missed Brandon. She didn't give herself many chances to daydream about him because it pierced her heart. She didn't know how people in the military dealt with deployment. She'd only been gone two weeks, and she was ready to drop everything and catch the first flight back to warm and sunny Southern California.

She wondered from hour to hour, when not bombarded with books and questions about her characters, what he was doing, which was an improvement from the moment by moment waxing and waning of emotion she was ravaged by when she first got on the plane to Colorado Springs.

A year ago, she was at a similar event in Florida, but for non-fiction writers, with no hint of Brandon in sight. It was amazing that he could come to mean so much to her in so little time.

She was so in love with him. It amazed and satisfied her, created a need and filled it. She couldn't help but pray for him because she adored talking to her Father about him, and it made her feel closer to him.

The first few days of her trip they would talk often. He would call her when he woke up since she was an hour ahead, and they would pray their day in. Either he or she would call the other a couple of times throughout the day, or she would call him as she got ready for bed. It was what she needed to get through the day even with being constantly busy. God bless Carmen because she made sure there was no downtime on this tour, otherwise Paige would have found a way to fly home for the day.

This week Brandon had tapered off a little. He still called her in the morning, but the midday calls were lightening. She knew he was probably busy trying to catch up on a lot of the time he'd missed while undergoing chemo and radiation, but the less rational side of her didn't care. She wanted to tell him they could live on love. She would sip from his lips when she was thirsty and he could fortify himself with the feel of her embrace. She wanted to be with him so bad it hurt sometimes. She wanted to be free to watch her fill, sit close enough to touch him anytime she wanted; to share an embrace and seek the peace she'd not found in any other man's arms.

She remembered their last evening together. They'd come back to her place to share the chocolate cheesecake she'd made as a surprise for him. After they'd run out of things to discuss regarding her trip, they had just sat there on the couch watching the flames dance in her fireplace. She snuggled into him, catching the scent of his cologne, which made her mouth water. She wanted to taste him, but tamped down on the urge.

189

They'd done so good respecting each other's boundaries, she didn't want to chance upsetting their commitment not push one another's buttons.

Early on in their relationship they'd discussed, over the safe distance of a telephone line, what things were more of a temptation than others. Paige found out that Brandon was a kisser. He loved kissing and felt relatively safe with kissing of any type as long as it remained on the face. His neck was strictly off limits, as were the insides of his elbows; he was extremely ticklish.

Paige was hesitant at first in telling him some of her erogenous zones, but had to concede with the fact that if he trusted her enough not to press his buttons, she should do the same.

What started as a reasonably safe conversation became smoldering by the time they were finished naming all the places that were absolutely off limits.

They weren't perfect. There was a time or two that she accidentally grazed a no-touch zone and he firmly but swiftly set her away from him, and vice versa. Those were the evenings that she almost said goodbye on the other side of the doorway in her rush to bring enough distance between them to clear her thoughts.

Brandon, with God, was her safe haven and she would fight herself to keep it that way.

She couldn't remember how they'd gotten on the subject of a wedding. It could have been one of the few wedding magazines she had around the house because she loved the fashions and flowers. It was her form of a boost when she was feeling a little low on creativity and didn't have the time or energy to go outside.

He was playing with her fingers, intertwining them with his long, tapered ones when he'd asked her what type of rings she liked. It was as nonchalant as if he asked her what types of candy she liked. They discussed yellow gold vs. white gold, platinum or titanium, beget vs. princess cut, and if she had ever given thought to designing her own settings. 'It was all part of getting to know each other,' she told herself. There was no need to read anything into it. ...Was there? She couldn't keep her mind from going there. A man should know that if he were to even entertain the thought of speaking to a woman he professed to love about rings, she was bound to do more than her fair share of daydreaming.

She had been laying in yet another unfamiliar hotel room bed watching the light play across the ceiling, waiting for sleep to take her when her cell phone rang. She turned to look at the clock on the nightstand before she answered.

"Hi Lady Menagerie."

"Hi sweetie, how are you? I'm not interrupting one of your nights out on the town with your author friends, am I?"

"No. Actually, I was about to make another pass at finding the perfect slumber position. Otherwise, I'm doing good, missing all of you."

"Really? I thought you might be schmoozing with Angela Benson, Victoria Christopher Murray, or Robin Lee Hatcher right about now."

"Christian authors don't schmooze, Lady Menagerie. We do what other mothers, teachers, speakers, pastors or pastor's wives do. We find a relaxing restaurant, huge hotel suite, or comfortable corner in a ballroom and encourage each other by talking about how hard we have it."

"I better not get any more calls or letters saying that people are praying for me about my anger management issues, or that God is saddened by my physical abuse towards to my husband," Lady Menagerie said in mock outrage.

"I told you that wasn't me that started that rumor. I was nowhere near Cleveland that year." Paige responded in a sing-songy whine, referring to the barrage of letters Lady Menagerie received two years prior, postmarked and stamped by a post office in Cleveland, OH that accused her of an explosive temper and abusive behavior towards her husband. By the tenth letter, Lady Menagerie was asking for prayer, but it was to curb her husband's anger towards the mislead author.

Whereas she was able to take it in stride and shrug her shoulders, Pastor Lawrence was not so ready to forgive and forget. He even went as far as to make mention of it in the pulpit, albeit in a more indirect manner. By the time he was done, most of the congregation were on their feet cheering at what they thought was an impulsive public expression of his love and devotion for his wife.

"Yeah, yeah... well, I thought I would check on you and make sure you weren't getting into any trouble."

Paige smiled. "Lady Menagerie, you know I could get into much more trouble at home than I ever could here. Carmen would have my hide if I even thought of stepping out of line."

"When you speak of trouble, I assume you are talking about Elder Tatum. How are the two of you doing by the way?"

"Very well. He is more than I could have known to ask for."

"Mmmmm. That's a strong sentiment," Lady Menagerie said quietly.

"They are some strong feelings," Paige replied in turn.

"Is it time for us to have the talk?"

"Um...I'm thinking we might be a little too late for that talk."

"What are you saying, Paige?" Her voice became stern.

Paige smiled to herself. "I am saying that I learned how the birds and bees thing worked about 12 years ago first hand."

Lady Menagerie's voice softened. "Yes, well... I guess I opened the door on that one, but since we are on the subject, do you need a refresher?"

"Nope." She pretended to think. "I think we're all good over here."

"Good." Lady Menagerie paused. "So, how are the conferences going? Were there any interesting questions regarding the new book, 'I'll Take Heaven'? Have you gotten finger cramps from signing and selling all your books?"

Paige giggled. "Nope. I'm big time. I have someone that massages my fingers after every 50th book I sign. It's in my contract."

Paige's response turned completive. "I did have a few questions regarding a couple of the characters. Marilyn and Keith to be more specific. Either I didn't bury the emotions enough in the story or the readers were extremely perceptive.

Even though I wrote Keith's character in line with my cousin, I wrote more from his perspective and didn't reveal what act caused him to reach the breaking point that brought him face to face with his morality. Even when he began having conversations with God, I didn't enlighten the reader as to what vial acts he committed but his remorse and inability to continue to live the way he was doing so.

I had one woman ask if I wrote the book as a form of self-healing for the things the main character may have done to me. She said he was almost too real to be a fictional character."

There was a small gasp on the other line. "What did you say?"

"I thanked her for the compliment in regards to the development of my character and I told her that there were many men and women struggling with Keith's same issues, and if my book could be viewed as an unobtrusive instruction on how to obtain peace even when you didn't think you deserved it, I had achieved my goal."

"Did she believe you?"

"I hope so. It was the truth."

"Yes, but you didn't answer her question. Was it a form of self-healing?"

Paige only paused for a moment. "Yes, because I was able to give him a life after his new beginning with Christ on this earth in my book that he didn't get in real life."

"Is it enough?" Lady Menagerie asked quietly.

"With God's help, it is. Besides, I'm a sucker for a happy ending and what more could you ask for than to experience God's grace, mercy, and peace in life here and then get to have eternity with Him?"

"I might have to say more time. More time with my husband, more time with my little girl, and more time with you."

Paige laughed. "Your little girl is 22 and almost ready to graduate from college."

"Paige, you will soon find out that no matter how old your children get, they will always be your babies."

Paige staunched the pain of longing in her heart. She wished for what could have been the thousandth time that she had been there when they were younger, but just as quickly thanked God that she hadn't. She could have done some irreparable damage to her two precious jewels.

"Speaking of more... Any more updates on my newest favorite couple?"

Paige had been waiting for this conversation with Lady Menagerie, but so much was happening, it seemed like they'd had little to no time to talk recently. She was surprised she hadn't already burst at the seams.

"I'm in love with Brandon, and he loves me," she stated.

There was a slight pause. "And..."

"And what?"

"You two have been dancing around that for a while; have you gotten any further? What are you planning on doing with that?"

Paige frowned to herself. "We are taking our time. I only met him in August and there have been a few variables thrown into the mix since. Even though I have incredibly strong feelings for him, I don't see any reason to rush things.

In less than a year he has made a big transition. He has moved to a new state, changed his job position, and acquired a new role in ministry, not to mention the bout with cancer he is just getting over.

I want our time to be just about us, for as long as it can be anyway. I know I'm coming into this relationship with the twins, and they each bring with them the potential for many nights of lost sleep. I just want to take the time to be wooed more. I like this place we are in. I love that even as fast as I think we are moving sometimes, I can keep up. I don't feel like I'm moving to someone else's timetable or deadline.

I'm excited about the discovery of Brandon. He may seem to be moving slowly to some, but I was there when he would call me up nervously, hoping we had a good conversation. I was living in those moments when we would share some of our love and passions for God. I was there when he told me his feelings for me went beyond friendship. I was there when we first held hands, and I was there when he first told me he loved me even though I knew it months before.

I'm not living for tomorrow; I am living for today. I am living for each kiss, each hug, and each word. I feel like that kid that is on his way to Disneyland and considers himself the most fortunate person in the world at that time, but I feel like that every day.

I am in love with a man of God who I have received permission to call mine. I'm not in a rush because he will be the same person I get to spend time with when this relationship moves to the next stage, and I will be right there living that moment." Paige took a breath, knowing she'd gone on a rant, but it felt good to express her true happiness to someone that would get it.

"Paige." The one word brought her out of her reverie with a jar.

"Yes?"

"This is your spiritual mother you're talking to. I know you have been looking forward to finding your husband, getting married and having a family, and now you play like you would be willing to wait forever."

"Not forever," Paige stated haltingly. "I'm just not in a rush."

"Why not?"

Paige was taken aback. Did she seem anxious? Was that what she'd been portraying?

"Um, I told you," she began with a timid voice.

"I know what you told me, but I don't think that you are being completely honest with me. Let me restate my point. How long would you be willing to wait to move forward with your relationship?"

"That's just it. I don't feel like I'm waiting. We are constantly moving forward, I am discovering new things…"

"I know, I know, you are living in the moment," Lady Menagerie said with exasperation. "Okay, how long would you be willing to live in the moment of being single, in love with the man of your dreams, going out on dates, holding hands and sharing light kisses, then leaving each other at the door for the night?" There was a brief pause. "You *are* leaving each other at the door for the night, aren't you?"

Paige nodded then remembered they were on the phone. "Yes ma'am."

"Don't 'ma'am' me. What's really going on? You aren't curious?"

"Curious about what?" Paige asked, hoping they weren't talking about what she thought they were talking about.

"About how Ronald McDonald walks in those huge red shoes," Lady Menagerie said sarcastically, "About how Brandon looks with his shirt off, whether he is a boxers or briefs man, if he is hairy or slick as a Native American. You can't tell me you haven't wondered or been tempted to see what he feels like…"

"I thought you were supposed to help me stay away from temptation, not lead me to it," Paige interrupted, feeling her ears heat up. A flash of Brandon's lips raced across her mind.

"I'm just asking you some simple questions. When Pastor Lawrence was courting me, we stayed mostly in public places because I knew there was no way I could behave myself if he had a mind to test my resolve."

"But you were saved," Paige blurted.

Lady Menagerie guffawed. "And? As fine as my husband is now, can you imagine him 24 years ago?"

"I'd really rather not." Paige began working hard to keep the thought of her pastor being a fine man out of her mind. She shivered.

"I'm just saying that the chemistry was off the chart. We couldn't be within five feet of each other and not feel the currents racing between us. To tell you the truth, we can still give each other a bit of a shock here and there."

"Augh. Lady Menagerie, please..." Paige pleaded. "I mean no disrespect because I think of you like parents, and it's because I consider you like my mom and dad that I would rather not be privy to any of this."

"It's all a part of life, sweetie. Young people aren't the only ones who can set fire to sheets."

Paige blanched and quickly looked for anything she could stare at for a while to keep at bay the mental images that would ruin her for life or at least cause her to change membership because if she went there, she would never be able to look at her pastor again.

"Lady Menagerie, please stop," she tried again.

Lady Menagerie conceded with a giggle. "Alright, I'm just making a point."

"Point's not only taken, the shot met its mark and has taken down its prey, who is now writhing blindly on the ground – or she wishes she was," she ended almost under her breath.

"So, are you saying you've had no challenges with keeping your hands off of each other?"

"No." The one word was drawn out until it disappeared altogether.

"'No', what?"

"No. It hasn't been without its challenges. I mean, I am attracted to him. He's really handsome and he has the most beautiful lips."

"Now we're getting somewhere." Lady Menagerie's response would have come out as a squeak, if Lady Menagerie ever squeaked, but she didn't. "So what do you do? Stay in public places, say goodbye at the door? How do you keep from being overwhelmed?"

Paige was a little reluctant to share these more intimate details with Menagerie, but took a deep breath and dove in.

"We, uh, talked about the things, or uh, places that, um make it more difficult to um." She faltered. "We don't press each other's buttons – on purpose – that is."

The other line was silent for so long Paige wondered if they'd been disconnected.

"Lady Menagerie?"

"Yes?"

"Did you hear me?"

"Yes."

Paige bit her bottom lip. She wasn't going to ask her what she thought. She would just wait her out. Lady Menagerie never had a problem speaking her mind. If she had an opinion about what Paige had just shared, she would share it. Besides, this was between her and Brandon. She thought they'd handled it very maturely. True, it didn't always work, but in the times they'd gotten a little too hot and heavy they'd quickly said goodnight. She didn't even know why she had been moved to share that information in the first place. She regretted it now.

"So…you discussed each other's, um – how did you put it –buttons? How did that talk go?"

"Well. It was a lot easier than it sounds."

"Oh, I hope so. And where exactly did you have this discussion?"

"Over the phone." She heard Lady Menagerie's sigh.

"Mmmm."

"'Mmmm' what?" As soon as it was out of her mouth she placed her hand on her head. She just did what she said she wouldn't do.

"I was just wondering if knowing where some of his 'buttons' are makes it easier to avoid them or harder not to see what happens when you press them."

Paige opened her mouth to reply, only to shut it. She couldn't deny that it had crossed her mind a few times, but the information was shared trusting that each other would respect the other's boundaries.

"I admit I've wondered, but he trusts that I won't use it against him just like I trust that he wouldn't use what I told him against me."

"What do you do when you discover buttons neither one of you knew were there?"

Paige's ears and face were on fire. "We call it a night."

"Just like that?"

"Yes."

"Wow. I have to say you two are handling this in a very mature manner." She became quiet.

Paige, knowing there was more, was no longer willing to sit back and wait for Lady Menagerie.

"What are you trying to get at, Lady Menagerie?"

"Hey, I'm not trying to offend you. No need for the tone. I'm just curious and more than a little impressed by your restraint."

Paige held her breath. It couldn't be *this* easy.

"Only," Menagerie began.

Paige let out the breath slowly and silently.

"I'm wondering why you aren't more eager or enthusiastic about taking that next step."

"Should I be? I mean, I'm enjoying where we are. It's nice here. I know what to expect and so does he. I thought you would be proud of the fact that we aren't jumping into marriage because we are so ardent for each other. We are taking our time and getting to know each other."

"With almost anyone else I would be more elated than concerned, but you, my daughter, have a habit of pressing just enough to say you have done something then you sit. You stick your foot in the water just enough to say that you have touched it, and you can even state the temperature, but you haven't truly experienced it."

"You want me to take him to bed?"

"Where did you get that from? No, you know better than that. I am telling you that though you have 'living for the moment' down better than most people I know, there is a balance. Live for today and plan for tomorrow, because tomorrow is going to happen.

Though you knew it was inevitable, you acted like your sister wanting you to tell Gladys you were her mother was a surprise. You and I both know it wasn't because you were actually surprised, but because you'd been avoiding it for so long you almost talked yourself out of it.

I want to make sure you're not doing the same thing with Brandon."

"I don't get it."

"I just want to make sure you aren't using the living in the moment as an excuse to delay dealing with things that come with marriage."

Paige began to feel uneasy. As confused as she was, she was beginning to berate herself for not seeing this coming.

"I want to make sure I'm hearing you correctly. Just come out and say it."

Paige heard the huff on the other end of the line.

"I want to make sure that you aren't prolonging this part of your relationship because you wish to delay the sexual part of your relationship."

And there it was. Paige had to hand it to Lady Menagerie, once given permission, wasted no time leaving the gate.

She glanced at the clock and made herself more comfortable.

As much as she'd missed their talk tonight when she'd tried to reach him, she was almost grateful Brandon hadn't tried to call her. She knew she would only be good for sleep once Lady Menagerie got through with her.

Now that she was sure of the direction of their conversation, she knew she would be hard-pressed to get off the phone without revealing the one fear she held so close, but this was Lady Menagerie and if no one else could give Paige some of the answers she needed, she could.

*   *   *

Paige dragged her suitcase over the threshold of her apartment, weary to the bone. Her last flight had been delayed so badly she told Brandon, who she'd originally planned to meet at the airport, that Carmen would just drop her home.

The sight of her living room went a long way to calm her. The familiar surroundings enveloped her with a peace she'd been missing over the last week and a half. There was nothing she could readily put her hand on, but the last few times she'd spoken to Brandon there seemed to be a distance growing between them. When she'd voiced her concerns, he would blame it on his workload or questioned if maybe she was just missing her home.

She tried to shrug it off, but as their calls got shorter and less frequent, she became more anxious. The last 24 hours were the longest she remembered trying to get through in a long while. If it hadn't been for the constant calls from her daughters, she would've tried to find alternate transportation. True she would not have gotten back any sooner, but she would have had more to preoccupy her time than watching people come and go.

She flopped on the couch, biting her bottom lip in indecision. Brandon had told her to call him when she walked into her apartment, but it was just after 11:30 p.m. She pressed the speed dial button associated with him.

It rang a couple of times before she was gifted with a sleepy, "Hello?"

"Hi, honey, I'm sorry for calling you so late. I just wanted to let you know I'm in the house all safe and sound."

"Thank you." She could hear the rustling of the sheets as he turned. There was a heavy sigh as if he were trying to pull himself up.

"How are you feeling? How was the flight?"

"Happy to be home and close to you, and any flight I can walk away from is a good one."

"I don't want to keep you. I just wanted to let you know I got in safe." She felt awkward because she didn't know what she would say if the call went on any longer.

"Paige."

"Yes?" Her heart started pounding harder.

"I'm happy you're home."

Her stomach did a little flutter. Everything was going to be alright. "So am I, Brandon. I…"

"I will call you tomorrow, okay?" Brandon said interrupting her declaration. Not knowing if it was accidental or not, she waited a beat and was going to try to repeat herself when he spoke again.

"Oh, and don't try to unpack everything tonight. You sound worn out. Get some sleep."

"Okay."

"Goodnight Paige. Thank you for calling."

What did she say to that? 'You're welcome?' What was that? They were a long way from this type of closing. What was wrong?

"Brandon?" She said his name in a desperate plea for an answer.

"Tomorrow Paige, please. I'm wiped. We will talk tomorrow. Meanwhile, you get some sleep. Goodnight."

It took a few seconds for her to realize the line had been disconnected. Sleep would come very hard this night.

CHAPTER 19

Brandon sat in the cushioned chair wondering at the odd things that go through the mind at such times. Why were the chairs padded? Did a person really care if the chair was padded or not at a time like this? Who was the decorator and did they take a survey of what would be considered sufficient padding when receiving news in an oncology office? Did they swap out chairs for different diagnoses? If so, he would tell them that there was no amount of padding that could bring him any type of comfort right now.

He wanted to just get up and walk out. Actually, there was no reason why he couldn't. It wasn't like he could get any direction or instruction from this doctor that would change his outcome.

He thought he was ready for this. Hadn't he prepared himself for this side of the story? No, not really. If he were to be honest, by the behest of his family, best friend and girlfriend, he had laid this option to rest. He'd retired it to the land of "Those Things We No Longer Give Breath To". He'd turned a deaf ear to anything other than living. Living for his family and Dominy; marrying Paige, living with Paige, sharing a home with her, discovering exactly how aroused he could make her by touching that place behind her knee she called 'off limits', watching her belly swell with his child and seeing himself in their eyes.

He closed his eyes against the dream purposefully stemming the tide of tears he felt behind them. When he opened them, all he saw was the man sitting before him with concern on his face.

What was he so concerned about? It wasn't as if he hadn't delivered this type of information to people before. True, with the results of the last test from two months ago still ringing in his ears, Brandon found himself asking the doctor to repeat himself.

Though the initial results from the rounds of chemo and radiation showed shrinkage of the lesion on his liver, the cancer itself had metastasize, attacking the lymph nodes.

Dr. Connor suggested a more aggressive cycle of chemo and radiation, but Brandon was wary of the effects it would have on his already waning energy. The more intense nausea wouldn't help the 15 pounds he was already trying to gain back either. At the end of it all, they still couldn't guarantee that he would be healed. Only God could, but that wasn't the question roaming back and forth in his head like a ping-pong ball.

"Brandon, would you like me to call someone. You shouldn't be alone at this time. What about your friend, uh, Dominy? I was surprised he didn't come with you."

"He is home with his wife right now. She is pregnant, so he has been staying close to home," Brandon replied, all the life leeched from his voice by the realization that he would never get to say that about Paige. He would have to come to terms with that fact soon. He couldn't afford to fight to hold onto something he wasn't meant to have.

"What about your pastor?"

Brandon looked up, having lost track of the conversation. "What about my pastor?"

"Do you think he could be with you at this time? It is important that you not be alone."

"Why? I was alone when you talked to me the last few times. I was alone the first time I was diagnosed. What is it you are more concerned about? My emotional or physical state? 'Cause I have to tell you, doc, I don't feel in any way as sick as you are claiming.

Whatever areas the cancer has metastasized to don't know it yet, so I should be good to at least make it home on my own. Unless you think that just hearing about it will cause my body to begin to shut down."

"That's not what I meant. I am just concerned. I want to make sure you aren't going to go through this alone." The doctor looked on helplessly.

Brandon knew in the back of his mind that this was an opportunity to tell the doctor he would be well taken care of. He had God and no one could do better, but all he said was, "I won't be alone."

The doctor handed him the paperwork, going over a list of medicines he'd prescribed. Brandon wanted to laugh. He didn't know how many times he had to tell the doctor he wasn't in any pain and if the medicine couldn't cure what was going on in his body, he didn't want them.

Twenty minutes later he found himself standing out on the sidewalk in front of the medical center, watching the cars go by. The sun was still shining, people were going about their day as if nothing had changed. The world was still spinning on its axis. The buildings behind and in front of him were still standing. He looked up and watched a couple of birds flit around each other in play. Everything around him continued to move forward and go on. He felt as if he were being left behind. He was silently screaming for life to come back and pick him up and carry him along with the rest of the world, but all he could do was watch the life he'd surrounded himself with over the last eight months slowly move out of reach.

He shook himself hard, knowing he was headed in dangerous territory. He'd been here before and he had eight full years to show for it. This didn't have to be a death sentence. He held on to that thought as he walked the rest of the way to the parking area and unlocked his car, but another thought took precedence once he was seated behind the wheel.

How was he going to tell her; but once he did, would she stay? Did he want her to stay?

He needed to get to a quiet place before he was blinded by the tears threatening him.

*   *   *

Later that evening, Brandon woke to the insistent drone of his cell phone. He reached over, looking briefly at the read-out. He'd forgotten to turn it off when he took it out of his pocket earlier as he walked in the house. Dominy knew about the trip to get his results so he called him as soon as he got home, knowing Dominy would take any silence from him as an excuse to visit.

Brandon had to give it to him though. Dominy bounced back faster than he had, encouraging him to take the doctor up on his suggestion for the additional sessions of chemo. Outside of asking if Paige knew, he hadn't urged him to call her – for which Brandon was relieved.

After promising to call him the next day, Brandon hung up and turned the ringer off, walked into his bedroom and climbed under the covers. He needed just a few hours to avoid making any kind of decision, and if he was awake that was exactly what he would do.

He texted Paige to let her know that he was going to make it an early night and that he had a very hard day, none of which was a lie. He promised to call her the next day. Hopefully Paige would be too busy or tired to be too disappointed.

He almost laughed at the thought. He'd just found out that he may not live to see another birthday, but he didn't want to disappoint Paige. Was this a sign of insanity?

*   *   *

The hardest part of the mornings would be his calls to her. He had carried the thought into his sleep and held it to him even as he was swimming towards the surface of consciousness. How was he going to tell Paige? Telling her over the phone was out of the question, so he was going to have to wait until she came back home from her tour.

This was her first tour since her operation, and he wasn't going to cheat her of the experience by sharing this with her. A part of him yelled its denial and rebelled against the thought of keeping something so life-altering from her, but he clamped down on it, smothering its voice. Until he knew which way he was going to move in regards to Paige, he would say nothing. He would act as if everything was normal. He would employ every gift and talent he had to convince her that everything was the same as it was before she left.

He sat at the edge of the bed and picked up the receiver, staring at the holes in the mouthpiece, feeling a weight come upon him that brought him to his knees. Facing away from his bed all he could do was fall forward with his head in one hand and the phone in the other.

"God, I need your peace. Right now, I need your peace, Father. I don't know how I am going to take another breath with this darkness pressing upon me. God, my Father, my Lord. I can't move another inch without Your help. I need Your direction. I need to know which way to go. I can't get my bearings. Each time I make a move towards the surface, I feel as if I am only going deeper. I don't want to die, God. I love You, but I'm not ready to go. I love her...I love her...I love her..." It became a chant that he couldn't stop. It came on the heel of every breath, even as his mind changed the mantra to 'I want to stay. I want to live. I want my life...with her...with her'.

"OH GOD, PLEASE!" He yelled a few minutes later, his voice rough with the sobs that were taking over. Then more quietly he said, as if this may reach God's ear quicker because he could hear the sincerity in his heart. "Please God, let me live. You have given me so much to look forward to.

Please Lord, I won't second guess You. I will strive to be more like You, just please let me stay." He allowed his body to lean forward until he was lying prostrate with his nose ground into the carpet.

"I know what it means now. I know what it is to have everything to live for. If I need to fight, I will fight. I will fight with the best of them if that's what You want me to do. I will show people how precious life is. I will be a representative of how beautiful each moment is. Just please, please." His next sob stole the words from his mouth.

"Please heal me." He lay there, tears pooling around him, the weight from the day before resting squarely between his shoulder blades. It felt as though he were being pressed through the ground. He couldn't catch a breath, but he couldn't move his head either. Panic raced through his mind and he fought to find purchase with his feet and hands, but they were useless. His head started to spin and light began to dance around his eyelids, and just as he was about to black out his body's survival mechanism kicked in, and he opened his mouth taking in a lung-full of air.

Once his heart had eased, he remained there, quiet, brought low and unwilling to try God's hand at the moment. He lay there for minutes longer, listening so intently he didn't realize how loud his mind was until he stopped. He stopped listening, looking for a sign, hoping the wait wouldn't be too long so he could still call Paige; all the while, asking for patience to endure the wait, even if it meant he couldn't call Paige until he heard his answer. He stopped and that's when he heard it; the faint stirring in his spirit, the light flutter that called him to let go.

No fear, son. His mind jolted as did his body and he stilled himself, wanting to hear it again…wanting to make sure he heard what he thought he did, but even as the unction ebbed, the essence stayed and he found it to be the still, small light that had been there from the moment he'd first been diagnosed. *No fear, son.* Not the plank of encouragement and uplifting that he'd been crying out for, but it edified, it calmed, and it brought peace because he knew he was not alone.

*   *   *

"Baby, I am on my way. I should be on the first flight tomorrow morning."

Brandon groaned, knowing before he tried he would not be successful in talking his mother out of coming. "Mom, I'm alright. Really I am."

"Well, I'm not. I need to see you, touch you. It's a mother's prerogative. Just humor me, please. I will only stay a couple of days past your first session of chemo and radiation. This way I can cook for you and make sure that you get through it as easy as possible."

He thought of trying to talk her out of it again, but deep down he knew he wanted her there. Well, at least the whole clan wouldn't be on his doorstep in the morning. That would take too much pretending, and he knew he wouldn't have the energy after his next round of chemotherapy.

Dominy hadn't wasted any time sharing the news from his latest tests with his mom. If he hadn't been hundreds of miles away, Brandon would have driven to his house and punched him, only to get back in the car and drive home.

He ended up on the phone for hours trying to explain the reasons why he failed to share the news of this bout of cancer with each of his siblings and parents. None of them were appeased to hear that he was trying to save them unnecessary worry or grief. Not that he thought they would be, but he couldn't feel remorse for sparing them the few months he was able to.

"Are you sure you won't consider coming back home for a while. It would do my heart a lot of good if I could look after you for a longer length of time. I just don't like the thought of you being in that place all alone."

"Mom, I'm not alone. I have Pastor Lawrence, Lady Menagerie and the congregation, not to mention Paige and Dominy, who will take over guard duty after you leave."

His mother's only response was a lengthy sigh.

"Mom, I will be fine. Paige will be back from her tour at the end of next week, and I would rather she didn't know until she came back so I could tell her in person."

"You haven't told her? What are you doing, Brandon? She will be hurt that you kept this from her. She may want to be there to comfort and encourage you."

"I don't believe this is something that should be shared over the phone. She will have a lot of questions, and what if she decides to end her tour early because of me? I couldn't let her do that. She has finally gotten her footing since her surgery in October. She deserves to enjoy this time and celebrate her achievements."

"Brandon." The quietness of his mother's voice snatched his attention away from his meandering thoughts as if she'd shouted.

"Yes?"

"She isn't Myra."

A hot flash raced up his spine, causing perspiration to break out on his upper lip.

"Huh?" He didn't even hope this wasn't going where he thought it was. This was Ava Tatum. She went where most grown men wouldn't dare to roam.

"Paige isn't like Myra."

"I know that, Mom." He didn't even think she knew Myra's name; she always called her 'heffa'.

"You aren't listening to me."

"I am, I just don't understand the correlation?"

"Paige loves you."

"Yes, I know this." He agreed readily in hopes she would be appeased and move on to a new subject.

"Baby, I am saying Paige won't leave you. She will stay by your side. You don't have to worry about telling her because she is a strong, faithful, praying woman of God."

"That's what I'm afraid of," he mumbled to himself.

"What's that, baby?"

"Nothing. I know she is different Mom. She is very special, but I'm still exercising my right to tell her in my own time, my own way, so no calling her and telling her that there is something she and I need to talk about, okay?"

"But Brandon..."

"Mom, please. I need to do this my way."

He was subjected to another long sigh before she conceded.

"Alright. I'll be there early tomorrow morning. I will have Elias Jr. send my flight itinerary to your inbox."

"My email, Mom," he said, shaking his head.

"But it goes into your inbox once it gets to your email, right?"

"Well, yeah, but..."

"So there you go," she said, interrupting him.

He could continue along this line of conversation with her, but he had a former best friend to tell off.

"Mom, I have to go. I have been on the phone for hours now and my ear is hot, and my phone battery is low. I will wait for the email from E., and I will pick you up from the airport in the morning."

"Yes. Well, do you want me to bring anything from the house?"

"No, I'm good. I will see you in the morning. Bye, Mom."

"Bye, Baby."

He sat on his couch going over the last of the conversation in his mind. Paige wouldn't leave him. He knew this, but if the next cycle of chemo and radiation didn't yield the results they were hoping for, he didn't know if he was willing to trade in a girlfriend for a nurse.

The last couple of days had been tougher than he thought it would be, keeping up the charade with Paige. She was so excited about how well her new book had been received and her new fan base, he couldn't help but smile into the phone. She became so animated at one point he imagined her movements taking on an unrealistic speed. He was so proud and happy for her his heart ached. *This is what her world should be full of; this, and her daughters.* She'd been through so much over the last year and now her ministry, writing career, and family were all prospering.

He longed to see the laughter and smile he heard in her voice right now. His desires and wishes regarding her were bittersweet. He wanted to be close enough to hold her, but that same closeness would bring sadness to her eyes when she found out that his fight was not over as he'd led her to believe when she left.

He had run through the different scenarios over the last few days regarding his and Paige's relationship over and over, and he still couldn't come to a satisfying conclusion on any of them.

He ran his hand over his hair, knowing all too soon he would be sporting a new haircut. He sat back on the couch and picked up his cell phone to dial Dominy. It rang until the voicemail came on.

"Coward," he said into the phone after the beep then he hung up.

A second later his phone rang. He read the Caller I.D. and groaned loudly. It read Pastor Lawrence.

Was it possible that Dominy had gotten a hold of Pastor Lawrence as well? He shook his head at his paranoid thoughts and pressed the button to accept the call.

"Hello, Pastor Lawrence." He schooled his voice to sound light.

"Good afternoon, Elder Tatum. How are you doing? I didn't interrupt you, did I? I know it's the middle of the day, but I had a pressing issue that I thought you might be able to help me with."

"No, you're good." He gave a sigh of relief. "As it turns out, I was out of the office today and am tomorrow as well. I would be happy to help you out. What do you need?"

"Well, I was wondering when you were going to call me and let me know about your latest diagnosis?"

A few thoughts went through Brandon's mind, but he couldn't fully commit to one before the next began. Most of them involved him finding a way to convince Dominy to stand, sit, or lie still while he choked the life out of him. How dare he cross this line? Heat stole up his neck and he worked his hands into fists. His silence must have been telling because he could hear the haste in Pastor Lawrence's next words.

"Now before you start getting angry, I want to tell you that Elias and I have been friends for a long time and we both care for you as fathers. I was hoping we'd reached a point in our relationship where we were no longer keeping things from each other."

He listened to his pastor's scolding tone with only half an ear. His father had called him. He didn't know if he was relieved that it wasn't Dominy or if he wanted to throw a tantrum because he couldn't reprimand his father for his concern. Both thoughts left in the wake of his next.

"Does Lady Menagerie know?" His voice quivered.

"Not yet, but this isn't something you keep to yourself, son. You need to be wrapped in prayer and surrounded by the comfort of those who love you."

"Could I ask you to reconsider that for a few days?"

"I take this to mean you haven't shared this news with Paige."

"I have every intention of doing so, but I would rather it be face to face. I would rather her not cut her trip short because she feels I need her close right now."

"Don't you?" Pastor Lawrence questioned sharply.

Brandon's response was a bit more hesitant. "Yes, but I feel it would be selfish to pull her from her first conference in almost a year, and divide her attention from this new venue. I want her to enjoy it fully and she won't be able to if she knows that I'm here going through another round of chemo, let alone one so aggressive. My mom will be here so I should be back on my feet by the time she gets back in town. It's for the best."

"For you."

"For both of us," Brandon corrected quietly.

"Mmmm. You say you have the day off tomorrow?"

"Yes, but I have to pick up my mom in the morning."

"Excellent, I think you and I also need a face-to-face. Bring your mother along. Lady Menagerie and Lady Ava love getting together, but didn't really get a chance during the holidays while that brood you call brothers and sisters were in town."

"Well, I…"

"Are you going to tell me 'no'? Because if you are thinking about it, stop it right now. I am pulling rank as your pastor. Call Pamela after we get off and have her schedule you to meet with me tomorrow afternoon."

Brandon, seeing no way out of the meeting, said what he knew Pastor Lawrence was waiting to hear. "Yes, sir." He hoped his acquiescence would buy him some time.

"Good. I will see you tomorrow. Oh, and Brandon?"

"Yes, sir?"

"Don't think your seemingly humble acceptance will have any bearing on my decision on when I tell my wife."

"Yes, Pastor," Brandon said once again, an intense feeling of defeat washing over him. He needed more time.

*   *   *

"You sound a little tired. You're not overdoing it, are you? Do I need to talk to Carmen?" He exclaimed late one evening after hearing Paige's groggy voice greet him on the other line.

"No." He heard her try to stifle a yawn. "It's just been a long day. I attended a Writer's Breakfast with V.I.P. fans. It was an honor to be asked. New authors don't usually get to sit on the panel."

"But you're not a new author. You are just new to the genre. Either way, I am really proud of you. I know you questioned your approach to some of the more sensitive subjects in your book, but I believe God is showing you that you heard Him correctly. You don't know how many people who've read your book needed another perspective so they could receive His healing."

"You know what?" Her voice sounded warm and dreamy.

"What?" He asked, drawn in by her timbre.

"You helped heal me."

His breath caught. "You think so?"

"I know so." She yawned full out this time.

"It sounds like it is someone's bedtime."

"I don't want to get off the phone yet. I miss you and want to hear your voice a while longer."

"It doesn't sound like you're going to hear anything for too much longer."

"Please. You've been quieter than usual lately. I know you are interested in what's going on over here and that's sweet, but you also seem preoccupied. You may not want to talk about it now, but I just wanted to let you know I noticed." The last of her statement lost its firmness on another yawn.

Obviously, he needed to work on his acting skills just a little bit more. "Alright, how about I read something," he said, placing more excitement in his voice than he felt. "That way you can snuggle down in bed and not worry about responding. When I hear you snoring, I will hang up."

Paige gasped. "I don't snore," she said, sounding affronted.

"You think not? Remember, you've fallen asleep on me before. In fact, it was one of the most romantic nights I have ever planned, and we ended it with me tip-toeing around your living room like I stole something to keep from waking you up."

"I don't snore." He almost laughed at the pout he heard in her voice.

"Just lay back and relax, and let me read to you so you can stop struggling. You're tired and I want you to regain some of your energy."

"I can't go to sleep now."

"Baby, I was just playing with you. Now cut out the light and let me read you to sleep."

"What are you going to read?"

"My mom sent me this book. Let it be a surprise. I will show it to you when you get back here, and I will continue to read it to you then." He found a comfortable position on his bed and picked up the book laying on the nightstand.

"Before I begin though, I need to let you know that I'm going to be really busy tomorrow so I might not be able to talk to you tomorrow night, but I will call you in the morning, okay?"

He heard her sleepy 'okay' then began to read, using a soothing cadence to lull her further into sleep. He had been reading no more than 10 minutes before he heard her soft, even breathing.

"Paige?" He said softly but got no reply. He listened to her breath for a few minutes, reveling in the peace he gained from this quiet moment with her. He missed her something fierce.

"Sweet dreams, baby," he said just as quietly before he ended the call.

He just needed to get through one more week.

*   *   *

He leaned over the bedpan, coughing to interrupt the dry heaving. The shivers and icy fingers were replaced by a blasting heat that zapped the rest of his strength. He was so weak, his limbs felt like gelatin until he tried to lift one, then they may as well have been thousand-pound weights.

A cool damp cloth came to his forehead, and he laid back down on the bed trying to catch his breath and stay in the present. He reveled in the moment of reprieve. No cramping pain, nausea, reeling head or deep dull pain in his joints. Just a few moments in between the culmination of one cycle of pain and the beginning of another. He sighed in relief and smiled up wanly at his mother who was working to keep her tears at bay like a champ.

That was their deal though. She couldn't care for him unless she could do it without crying all over him. She could slobber and tear up in any other room except his because he didn't have the strength to comfort her, and he would want to. He would take the humiliation of having Dominy take care of him before he subjected himself to that type of torture.

The last three days were filled with restless nights, slightly better early mornings which he thanked God for because he could summon just enough strength to play off a call to Paige. She wasn't dumb; she knew something was wrong and tried to bring it up a few times, but after the second day following his chemo session, he was considering using it in his favor. Maybe this way it wouldn't be as traumatic or out of the blue when he ended it.

There was no way he was going to subject her to this. The side effects were like night and day in comparison to his earlier sessions of chemo. He wasn't 100 percent before, but he could function and even work if he had to. This was so debilitating; he couldn't even get out of the bed and he had five more sessions before this cycle was over. No, he couldn't do this to her.

He didn't know if his extreme lack of energy was due to the changes his body was going through or the thought of letting go of the only woman he'd ever loved.

When he had hinted at his intentions to his mom, she told him it was the drugs talking and that one of the side-effects was depression. She asked him to think of it again after the first waves of pain and nausea subsided and most of his energy had returned. He said nothing but turned his head signaling that the conversation was over.

He was brought out of his reverie by another bout of nausea. Surely this would have to end soon. He didn't have anything else in his stomach. The taste of bile swamped his senses and the chills began again, racking his body, making him feel like a rag doll being thrown to and fro. He used the shaking sensation to propel him back to the edge of the bed so he could lean over the newly cleaned bedpan.

His mother's arms came around him, careful not to rub against his sensitive body. She just brought herself close enough to him to share her warmth and ease some of the cold stealing away in his bones.

The knock on the door summoned a soft groan from both of them.

"You stay there, I'll get it," his mom said, in an attempt at levity as she moved away from him and replaced her warmth with a blanket. "That's probably the nurse. You will be feeling better in no time."

He tried to breathe through the stomach cramps and gain strength in knowing that the nurse came relief from the pain.

"So Mr. Tatum, how are we doing today?" He didn't have the strength to shake his head, let alone answer her. Her melodic voice smoothed some of the edges of his overwrought nerves.

"What's your pain number? Are you ready to take something?"

He bobbed his head slowly, the movement sending shards of pain through his spine. He took a deep breath and let out "nine" on a low growl.

"Not to worry. I've got something to make it all better." Her voice became a little muffled, and he could tell she had turned to talk to his mom.

"I will give him something to ease the pain and nausea. We will work on replacing more of the nutrients as well. Has he kept anything down in the last eight hours?"

She continued to ask his mother questions, but a warmth began to spread through him, easing some of the cramping in his stomach and his calves. When had that started? He was such a mess.

This won't last. It was only this bad because it was more aggressive. This will be over soon. He had to think of the positives otherwise he would begin to wallow. It was already getting better. The drugs were working and he was already getting warm again. He wondered if Paige would take him back after he got a clean bill of health. The next thought was too fuzzy to hold onto, then a pain-free darkness enveloped him.

*   *   *

Friday afternoon found Brandon standing outside of Paige's apartment, staring at an intricately carved cherry wood box the size of a jewelry box. He had placed a couple of articles he'd found about Paige, a women's conference she'd spoken for, and a few reviews of her latest book. He placed a few copies of pictures they'd taken that he adored, a movie stub of the first movie they saw together, and one of the rocks he kept from the first day they'd kissed in the park.

He wrote a lengthy note thanking her for giving him the best months of his life and what knowing her had meant to him. It was the hardest letter he'd ever written. One sheet he'd had to write over because of the tear stains that gave him away. He would have to be steely resolved and immovable. He expected tears and confusion, but he knew Paige was not one to plead, so he considered himself somewhat prepared for the worst few hours of his life.

He'd spoken to Paige briefly the night before but was so tired it was all he could do to answer the phone when she called to tell him she was home. He was finally going to get to see her after what felt like months, and he would be sure to take in every breath. He inhaled deeply then knocked, and let it out slowly.

*   *   *

Paige stood up from the couch with the box forgotten in her hand. "How dare you cheat me? How could you be so selfish?"

"I'm trying to spare you more pain. I don't want to be another cause for heartache." He followed her with his eyes, growing more anxious by the moment.

"Don't you understand? It's too late. You already have my heart. Whether you leave me now or later, it will hurt just as much. More even, because you are rejecting me and what we could still have."

"What can we have, Paige? Days of staring at one another over the toilet I am too tired of retching over to move, or nights full of long moments to think about all of the things we won't be able to do together?"

"We will be together. We can comfort one another, hold one another. We can still make good memories."

"Well, I would have never taken you for a morbid person because that is what you would have to be to watch me waste away. I don't need another nurse, Paige," he said, standing up just in time to stop her from making another pass in front of the couch.

"Well, I'm sorry that's all you see me as because I thought we needed each other to be there in whatever capacity was most important at the moment. That's what couples do. Besides, it's not as if I haven't seen it before. I visit sick people in hospitals and their home as a part of my ministry, remember?"

"Yes." He paused for a moment to collect himself. "But this is me."

"Is that what this is about? Me seeing you outside of your perfection? Me watching you go through what other humans do who fight to live?"

He looked down, no longer meeting her gaze.

"Oh. I have this all wrong." He looked up in time to see her step closer and peer into his eyes.

"It isn't the struggling you don't want to share. You don't want me to see you give up. You're giving up.

Wow, I was so wrong about you. You are even more selfish than I thought. You would trade the possibility of us having a future and a life together for the yearnings of death. You would taint and trade in every memory we have for hours of waiting on defeat. Shame on you and this man you are subjecting me to. Shame on you and your love that caused me to believe in the promise of forever in your eyes."

"That's what I've been trying to tell you. We don't have forever. If this next round doesn't work, we barely have months. I can't leave you broken with a whole life of dreams and desires you would want to bury with me. I need you to love again and go on with life. I can only be immortalized through you, but not if you try to stop living when I do. You can't follow me into the grave, so we need to part now." It sounded right, even if he were grasping at straws now. He was so ready to give in. He didn't think anything would hurt this much. If his nurse asked him right now where he was on the pain scale, he would have to say 25 out of 10.

"I see. I have to pay more attention to those first impressions. I really thought you were full of yourself and now I see I was right. Just because you are my first love doesn't mean I will go find a dark place and let life pass me by until I can be with you again. I will rejoice in what we had all the way up until the last moment. I will wait expectantly for another miracle with you and enjoy getting to know everything about the keeper of my heart because whether you leave me now or months or even years from now, you will have my heart."

Uh oh. That obviously was the wrong thing to say.

"But I also promise you," she continued, "that if you leave me now, I will do everything short of taking my own life to forget you ever existed. I will pack up everything I own and the life I have here and I will leave without a word, and no one will ever see me back in Los Angeles again. I will not do another book signing or conference for fear of running into someone who will remind me of you.

I will take each and every beautiful sunset, phone call, intimate conversation, gift and prayer we have ever shared, and I will find a way to desecrate it to the point that I won't be able to tolerate thinking of you. I will finish destroying what you began today. If you give up today, you don't deserve any type of immortality through me."

Brandon felt sick, but this was to his very soul. "You don't mean that. You wouldn't do that to us."

"Oh wouldn't I," she quipped. "You would only get the ball rolling. Do you think yourself so in control of this situation that you could tell me what I am and am not capable of? You want to see how strong I am. Watch me walk away from the ashes you are trying to leave me in."

"I don't see it that way. I am trying to do this for you." He held his hands up in a placating gesture.

"Well, I don't see it any other way." Her features had gone stony. He couldn't read anything on her face.

"I will give you 72 hours to reconsider, otherwise you will never see me again. I don't think I will have to tell you not to try and contact my family, otherwise, you will force me to let go of them too."

"Damn Paige, why are you being so stubborn about this." He'd tried calm and cool, but she had shaken him to the core with her last words.

"I am just making it clear that I have no life without you. If God takes you then I know He will take care of me. But if you do it, you will be moving outside of His will and in complete selfishness. My reaction is only to protect and shelter myself the best way I know how.

Good night, Brandon." She handed him back the box. The slight shaking of her hand was the only thing belying her calm demeanor.

"If you decide to come back to me you can bring this with you, otherwise you can keep it. I will only burn it."

Brandon took the box back, stunned speechless. She led him to the door, opened it, gently pressed his speechless form to the other side of the door jam, and raised up on tiptoe to plant a whisper-soft kiss upon his lips.

Brandon stood outside the door for a few minutes dazed and truly confused. Wasn't he just here a few hours ago, box in hand, rehearsing what he would say? What had happened? Nothing went as he planned. She hadn't cried, gotten angry, fought, screamed or tried to beat him senseless so he could take her in his arms one last time and comfort her while he convinced her this was for the best.

No. Instead, she had faced him with icy calm and told him if he went through with his plans to end them that she would pack up her life and every memory of them together and leave. She wouldn't think of them, and to her, it would be as if he never existed.

Those words had ripped the very breath from his lungs. That she could be so sure and render such a statement with such unrelenting resolve. It was as if he were dealing with someone he'd never seen before.

It could be a bluff...but what if it wasn't? Could he live out the rest of his days knowing he'd been the cause for her throwing the life and friends she had in L.A. away?

He shook himself, forcing his legs to move away from the door. He looked towards the stairs, but only saw the same void he'd felt forming in him since he'd made up his mind to come to her. If she felt even a tenth of what he was experiencing, he was sure the calm had dissipated the moment the door was closed. He was tempted to go back and urge her to open the door, but then what? He couldn't be that cruel even if it called her bluff.

No, she wouldn't destroy the proof of their relationship and if she did it would ultimately be her decision to leave everything behind, but even as he thought it, he couldn't help feel bereft in knowing she would no longer think of him.

He had three days to come up with something they could both live with, because the destruction of the memory of them was not an option.

CHAPTER 20

Victoria stood in front of the French doors leading out to the lawn. Her mouth was quirked in a way that caused anyone watching her to puzzle at what was going through her mind. Though it was fitting for her warring emotions, it didn't help at this moment that half of her guests' attention was equally divided between her and the helicopter touching down in their backyard.

Once the makeshift heliport had been discovered during one of their events a few years ago due to a guest having to be medevac'd after suffering a major heart attack, she'd received requests from guests to arrive by helicopter, but she flat out denied them. She didn't want anyone sponsor to portray a sense of favoritism that wasn't there.

Those that knew Victoria or had the honor of attending more than one of her functions knew that the only guest of honor in the room was the cause she was raising money for, which was why the guests watched with rapt fascination as her husband, Richard, exited the helicopter in the middle of the Gala. If it had been any other time, Victoria would have excused herself and made her way to the library to wait for him where he was sure to get a dressing down… But today…today she was just happy to see him.

He'd promised to make it back before the Gala, but when he hadn't arrived by 4 o'clock that afternoon, she was resolved to host this particular event for the first time by herself.

He was just reaching the veranda when the propellers stopped and she opened one of the French doors for him. "You've just made it almost impossible to say 'no' to those who believe themselves V.I.Ps when they ask to ride up to the backyard," she said, greeting him with a huge smile.

She watched him watch her warily for a few seconds then heave a huge sigh and laughingly embrace her in a hug she seemed to have waited a lifetime for. "Oh how I missed you, Vickie." He punctuated the heartfelt statement with a quick firm kiss then loosened his hold. "Maybe I should arrive by helicopter more often. I really like the reception."

"You better not," she scolded. "You nearly blew away my begonias."

"I'll buy you new ones," he responded, before giving her a little squeeze then releasing her altogether.

That's when Victoria realized they had an audience, and she had to think quickly to dispel the crowd. "Well, now that my wealthier half has arrived, I can afford the open bars on all four edges of the ballroom. Champagne for everyone! I feel like making a toast." A small cheer went up and as if on cue, she could hear the music in the next room increase in volume.

She walked hand-in-hand with Richard, signaling the servant carrying his luggage to take it into the library until later.

After a few minutes of greetings and handshakes, she escorted Richard to one of the private guestrooms downstairs. "I was hoping you would make it. I put a few of your toiletries in the en suite bath just in case you needed to clean up." She looked down at his sports coat and tsked. Shaking her head, she smiled back up at him. "Sir, I don't think you got the memo. This party is 'black-tie'."

Richard watched her, seemingly struck dumb by her teasing manner. "Victoria?" He caught her hands as she began to undo his jacket buttons. "You alright?" She looked up from her task, arrested by the concern she saw in his eyes.

"Yes. Are you? I know you were worried you weren't going to make it, what with that storm coming in off the Atlantic Ocean, but it wouldn't have been the end of the world." She was telling the truth. It wouldn't have been the end of the world, but she hated having to host this Gala, named in honor of their daughter, by herself.

Her last statement seemed to really confuse him. He continued to stand there looking at her like he'd never seen her before. She sucked her teeth and huffed at him. "Okay, tell me what I can do to get you to stop looking at me as if I'd grown another head."

He replied quickly, neither abashed nor apologetic by his response to her greeting. "You can go get my wife. I'm sure she isn't too far, what with such a big event going on at the other end of the house."

Victoria decided to push the feelings of impatience aside. How could Richard know how his notes had affected her? She was more determined than ever to show him that she was indeed remembering as he had suggested in his messages. Hopefully, if he truly believed she'd changed, he would forget about scheduling their appointment with the marriage counselor. Surely, what he'd been able achieve over the last two months in regards to reminding and causing her to desire the life they'd once had together was more than enough to appease him for a while.

She raised up and leaned into him, planting a kiss on his lips. She watched his lips recede as she rocked back on her heels before allowing her gaze to meet his. "I am your wife. Do you doubt your persuasiveness?"

He shrugged his shoulders. "Maybe. But I am also aware of your talent for resisting my…" He seemed to give his next words great consideration. "Suggestions."

She broke into laughter. "Suggestions, huh. They sounded more like ultimatums."

His grin died on his lips. "I'd like to think of them more as recommendations towards a cure to what was ailing us."

"I'm sure you would, but let's just call a spade, a spade. That way, we will have no misunderstanding to what we are both striving for."

Richard bent down ever so slightly so that he was eye to eye with Victoria. "What are we striving for, Vickie?"

She placed a palm against his cheek. "A place out of the storm," she said quietly, referring to the memories evoked by his note for her to remember their first kiss which took place in her barn after they'd gotten caught out in a flash storm.

He kissed her then just as sweetly as he had that day 33 years ago, and she melted against him. It had been worth it, just for this. She had missed this; the way he held her as if she were fragile and the most valuable thing to him. He used to hold her like this before…before… She shook the thoughts away and concentrated on his hands roaming across her back through the rhinestone encrusted bodice of her gown as he deepened the kiss. When breathing became impossible, she pulled her mouth away and was satisfied to hear his labored breathing as he sprinkled kisses at the edge of her jaw.

"Richard…we have guests…and they are bound…to think…"

"That I am (kiss) one extremely (kiss) fortunate husband (kiss) to receive (kiss) such a thorough (kiss) reception from my wife."

The last kiss elicited a ticklish giggle from her and she pushed him away. He looked at her quizzically then raised his eyebrows. "That's new."

Spotting the glint in his eyes, she backed away from him further, not willing to continue with hundreds of guests down the hall. "Your tux is in the closet," she said, just managing to avoid his grasp as he reached for her.

"Vickie, I just want to hold you. We've been apart for so long." He stepped closer, reaching out with both hands. "You don't know how much I've missed you."

The look of longing on his face was nearly her undoing. She took a deep breath as she walked backwards in the direction of the door. "Then four more hours will be a piece of cake. That way, we won't have to worry about being interrupted or missed."

She watched his full lips turn into a pout and felt her resolve giving away. "I see I'm not the only one who has perfected some of my talents."

He watched her for a few seconds more then shrugged and relaxed his expression. "It was worth a try."

She laughed and turned to walk out the door when she heard him call to her.

"Vickie." She eyed him over her shoulder.

"I love you."

She couldn't help the warmth that stole over her at his words, and it took her back to a place she never thought to see again.

"And I love that you're you," she repeated the response she used to give him.

His eyes clouded momentarily and she wondered what he was thinking, then he blinked and she thought she'd imagined it.

"I'll meet you in the ballroom," she said when she was halfway through the door.

"I'll be the one wearing the black tuxedo."

"Corn, pure corn," she said, laughing as she closed the door behind her.

Richard was home and she was, for the first time in a long time, happy.

She took a detour through the kitchen in an attempt to delay her arrival in the ballroom. She knew she wasn't the one that people had the best rapport with, but she did get people to give.

She heard Martha barking out orders like a sergeant and smiled to herself. Martha was in her element anytime she could boss people around. Though the caterer was new, the detail that was given made it almost impossible for them to mess up, but Martha watched everything and everyone going in and out of her kitchen like a hawk.

Victoria stepped out on the side veranda, sifting through the last two and a half weeks. She had hoped that Richard could have made it home a couple of days before the Gala so she could share some of the inspirations his notes had given her. She hadn't felt this excited since she'd accepted his invitation to go out with him.

She leaned against a column staying well hidden from roaming guests and looked out at the barn where the old shed used to stand, and let her memory take her back one more time.

*   *   *

"Ms. Victoria?" She spun around at the sound of the deep velvety voice, her hand to her throat. She had been absorbed in sorting through the different colors of ribbon in the clearance bin of the material store.

She looked around to see if he'd garnered anyone else's attention, but there were very few people in the store at this time of morning, which caused her to wonder why he was.

"Hello, Mr. Branchett," she said, self-consciously winding the blue, satin fabric around her forefinger.

The smile he gave her made her catch her breath. He was one, truly gorgeous man. Why had she kept putting him off? Oh yeah – she didn't trust men. Especially tall, good-looking men.

When his smile dimmed, she continued to stare at him with a curious expression. "What's the matter?" She asked before she could stop herself.

"I was wondering the same thing. Did I do something to cause that veil to come down over your eyes?"

She was momentarily taken aback. He read her too well. She looked away so that he couldn't continue to gauge her response. She shrugged.

He was quiet for a moment. "Well, at least you didn't insult me by denying it. Have I hurt you or given you any reason to distrust me?"

She looked up startled, but was only able to shake her head.

"Did you hear something about me you didn't like?"

"No." She didn't like where this was going. He was either pushing her into a corner or about to chastise her.

"Do you think I'm too good for you?" He asked, leaning down so that he could look her square in the eyes. She backed up slightly, feeling overwhelmed by his presence.

"Do you have any idea how intimidating you can be?"

She was utterly surprised by his admission.

"I'm not." She just barely got it out.

"Oh, yes you are. You are aloof, confident, and seemingly fearless," he said, straightening his posture while raising his palms up.

"I like you, Victoria, and I truly believe you are worth each painful attempt I make towards earning your trust. You are well worth the violent kick to my ego every time you reject my invites. You are even worth the dreams that leave me longing for the mere sight of you and the gas I have used to double my chances of doing just that. And it is because I think you are worth all of this that I wonder what I may have done to cause you to think that I would do anything less than admire you."

She glanced around and saw a couple of women unabashedly listening in on their conversation. She ducked her head and placed her items back in the clearance basket. Her skin turned a brilliant shade of red and it was all she could do to keep her footsteps slow and deliberate as she walked out the door. Richard walked out behind her.

"I'm sorry. I didn't mean to embarrass you," he began, but she raised her hand, looking for someplace more private. She motioned for him to follow her across the street and she kept walking in silence until they reached the diner on the corner.

She walked in with him close on her heels. "Faye, we are going to take the booth in the back," she said to the waitress walking towards them – or towards Richard. After a couple of seconds, Faye gave her just enough attention to nod and followed them to the booth with the menus. She handed one to Victoria and then to Richard with a wicked smile. Richard all but ignored her as he sat across from Victoria.

Victoria waited until Faye left with their drink order before she began. She watched her hands which she rung in her lap, getting her thoughts in order. "Richard, I don't think I can live up to the image of the woman you described back in that store. I'm afraid you will be greatly disappointed if I were ever to accept your offer to get to know each other better."

"Prove me wrong; though, I don't see how you could. Let me get to know you better, and you get to know me better, so you won't doubt that what I see in you is real."

"I'm not her." She locked gazes with him. "I'm not that fearless, confident woman that you see. I am afraid and gripped with insecurity daily. What you call aloof I call a need to protect myself."

"From who?"

"Not so much who as what." She stopped as Faye set down their drinks. "Are you ready to order?"

Victoria looked at Richard in question. "Could we have a few more minutes?" he asked Faye with a sheepish smile, "We may take a while, but I promise if you give us more privacy than service there will be a big tip in it for you."

Victoria worked to keep from rolling her eyes at the mooning expression Faye threw him before she nodded and slowly walked away.

"Alright, what are you afraid of?" he said, never missing a beat in the conversation.

Victoria took a deep breath. This was where the rubber met the road.

"I am afraid of making another mistake. I don't have anywhere else to go from here. If I give you a chance and things don't work out, I don't know how I will face the people of this town. I've worked so hard to become invisible, but you stand out like a bright light in the middle of a desert at midnight."

"First of all," he interrupted her, "you couldn't be invisible if you tried. You walk into a room and your beauty stuns and holds men captive. And that light you're talking about is the reflection I throw off by being near you."

She couldn't take it. He needed to know the truth and she needed to know if he would still feel the same about her after he found out she wasn't all that she seemed.

"I have a son, Richard," she blurted. She stared at the table in front of his hands and didn't miss how still they went. She looked up into his wide brown eyes.

She took a deep breath. "I was entering my last year of college when I met and fell in love with Antonio Sable. He was a few years older, attending grad school. He was so refined and charismatic, and I was a very shy and late-blooming debutante." She paused for a moment to let out a small, self-deprecating chuckle.

"I was flattered that he would want to spend time with me out of all of the women in the graduate program, but he did, and I fell hard and fast.

I graduated that spring, top of my class, a shoe-in for law school, and six weeks pregnant." She finally dredged up the courage to look at him, expecting at the worst, disgust, and at the best, pity. Instead, she found him listening intently, his eyes ablaze with an indescribable expression.

"I approached Antonio with the news and he seemed to take it well, at first. He was very patient, even a little happy. We talked about getting married and I thought, 'Well, this isn't how I wanted to enter marriage', but I loved him and I could continue school later. I wasn't averse to working while Antonio finished school, and then he could do the same for me. I thought we could make it work." She grew quiet for a moment, lost in thought.

The return of Faye jarred her from the past. "Have you two decided?"

Victoria, feeling even less like eating than before, ordered a chicken salad sandwich so she could take what she didn't eat home. Richard repeated her order, adding a slice of apple pie to it.

"A month into summer break, we were to go to his home and I was to meet his parents. I had told my parents the week before and they were so angry I couldn't get a word in, but after a few days they called me back and begged me to come home. I told them that I would at the end of the month. Antonio said his parents weren't necessarily ecstatic about the news. He was the first generation in his family to go to college and their dream was for him to go all the way.

The morning we were to leave, I woke up to a letter on the pillow next to mine." She heard a grinding noise and looked up to see Richard's jaw clenched tight. She recognized the emotion on his face this time though. It was anger. *That was something.*

"In a nutshell, Antonio said that he wasn't ready to become a father and he wasn't sure his parents would help support us if they found out he was having a child with a woman of mixed race. Like I was ready to become a single mother of a child who would wonder why they didn't have a father," she bit out.

"I didn't just go away. I tracked him down and showed up on his doorstep. I was going to demand that he was at least going to be in our child's life." She saw a quirking of Richard's lips as if he were going to smirk, but it didn't develop past a twitch of his lips.

"When I arrived, they were in the middle of what looked like a huge party. I thought it might have been a homecoming bash for him, and oh how I was going to crash it. The joke was on me." She was so glad she was passed crying for the sad excuse of a man.

"It was his party alright. His *engagement* party. He hadn't told them anything about me. It wasn't his parents that couldn't stomach having a child by a fair-skinned, 'not-quite-white' Negro."

Faye returned with their meal and, sensing the intensely dark mood at the table, served them and made a hasty retreat.

Victoria stared at Richard as he watched her, saying nothing. She didn't know what else to do but continue.

"I went home, shamed and wholly humiliated. I was so sick those first few weeks that I was hospitalized due to dehydration, and I am ashamed to admit that I'd hoped I would lose the baby so that I could forget everything." She shrugged. "But seven and a half months later, I gave birth to a beautiful baby boy. He had the softest jet black hair and skin the color of gold in the sunshine. He was Antonio's son physically, but he was more mine." She began playing with her fries.

"I was home with Brian for two weeks when our pastor came to visit. I thought he was coming over to bless or dedicate my child, but instead he came to tell me that I was being selfish and cruel to my child. That there were countless, childless parents out there that could give my son a better home – a chance at a more well-rounded life. So, my parents and I had discussed it," she gave a wry smile, "in loud angry tones, many times, and I was completely against it. I wouldn't budge. I loved my son and I wasn't running from my obligation. His father had already done that.

I was in church with my parents a few weeks later when a couple came up to me at the end of service and began cooing over Brian. I thought nothing of it. Brian was a gorgeous, well-mannered baby, but when the woman asked when I wanted to start the paperwork, I was puzzled and not just a little wary. I moved away from them as people began moving towards the door of the church, when the pastor calls me out. He berates me for my blatant disregard and lack of reverence towards God and my overt sexual behavior that I was flaunting by bringing my child to church."

"What the hell kind of conclusion is that?" Richard barked out, startling her out of her storytelling trance. "Why didn't your parents back you up?"

She shrugged. "They were on his side. They were kind of all in cahoots with one another. By the end of the summer, they gave me an ultimatum. Either I give up the child or they would throw me out. I buckled." One tear escaped, falling onto the table beside her forgotten plate. "I gave Brian up for adoption on a rainy January morning. It was fitting that it would rain that day. It was right that the skies would open up and let loose their grief just as I was. I went through an adoption agency where I had a modicum of control on who was picked." She used her napkin to wipe her tears and sniffed hard. She blew out a breath.

"I went back to school in the fall, enrolling in a completely new university. I couldn't go back to that campus. I graduated with a degree in family law, took my bar, and received a job offer from one of my father's friends. When I got home, I told my parents that I was going to take over the farm. It was the inheritance my grandparents left me. They were so angry, they threatened me with everything but bodily harm, but there was nothing left that I valued that they could hold over me.

"I've been at the farm since." She stirred her straw in her now watered-down glass of Root Beer, watching the condensation pool into heavy droplets.

"Brian will turn five on December 2nd and though I haven't looked upon those huge hazel eyes since he was a little more than two months old, I think about him every day."

She saw something move in her periphery and felt Richards warm hand envelop hers.

"Victoria." He said her name with such warmth she couldn't help but look up at him. "Did you tell me that to see if I would go or see if I would stay?"

Confused by the question, she shook her head. "I don't understand. What's the difference?"

"One was to prove yourself right. I just want to know which one it is."

She swallowed hard. "To see if you'd stay."

The hard lines that had taken shape around his mouth during her story softened, transforming into a lazy grin.

"Victoria, I have a question to ask you." Her heart picked up its pace at the expression on his face. She licked her suddenly dry lips. "Okay."

"Will you go out with me?" He still held her hand across the table, but the comfort it brought before was replaced by small pulses of excitement.

She nodded. He didn't say anything else. He pulled her hand towards his mouth and kissed her knuckles.

CHAPTER 21

Richard finished taking off his coat and sat on the bed. *Thank you Father for what You have done.* He knew they still had a long way to go, but the fact that Victoria had been receptive to his overtures went a long way to instill hope in the rebuilding of their marriage.

He was sure she would make him pay in some way for arriving as he had, but it couldn't be helped if he was going to make it to the house before midnight. He'd been watching her reaction closely as he ran from the helicopter. His relief almost overwhelmed him when she closed the door to the guest bedroom and instead of giving him the reaming he expected, she ignored their guests and teased him as she would have so many years ago.

He was almost paralyzed with fear at losing what he'd just so fleetingly won. He'd grabbed her hands, not to still her, but to reinforce in his mind that he wasn't dreaming and that she wasn't an illusion created by lack of sleep. He watched for any signs of guile or calculation in her eyes, but was only able to detect the playful teasing he'd come to love about her when they were first dating.

As he untied his shoes he thanked God once again for the idea of implementing steps to reclaim what he'd once considered broken. For months after giving his life to Christ that fateful evening, he'd prayed, asked, pleaded, begged and tried to bargain with God to save his marriage and to both heal Victoria and draw her close. However, he'd failed to ask God to help him change until one church service aided in changing his perspective of his marriage

*   *   *

He'd been in the audience during one particularly heart-wrenching sermon that a guest preacher had delivered regarding his life and how it had spiraled beyond his control after serving 15 years as a pastor. The preacher had lost his church, was separated from his wife and family, and was on the verge of giving into the temptation of driving his car off of the road in hopes his death would be ruled an accident for his family's sake because he felt his insurance was worth more than he was at the time.

The preacher went on to tell how a man who he'd ministered to years before came upon him sitting in a 24-hour diner off the beaten path, eating what he'd thought of as his last meal. To his annoyance, the man sat at his table. He thanked him for taking the time to speak to him and giving him the strength he needed to step away from a life of drugs. By the time he finished talking about everything that had happened in his life since that day it was morning and way past the preacher's time to be on the road.

The man finally looked at his watch and asked him what he was doing so far away from his church.

Not wanting to hinder the man's walk, he gave him a watered down version of what he'd been through over the past year. He told him that he was no longer pastoring that church and was on a road trip to someplace unknown.

The man sat there and stared at him for what seemed like minutes. In fact, the man was quiet for so long that the preacher began to feel distinctly uncomfortable in sharing. Yet, when the man began to cry, the preacher said he began to feel like a heel. As it turned out, the man had been praying for the preacher and had been led to seek him out months earlier, but put it off thinking it was more of him wanting to share his thanks than, God wanting to use him to get a message to the preacher.

The man asked for the preacher's forgiveness for sitting on the assignment for so long. Humbled by the man's show of remorse, the preacher quickly accepted his apology, trying to convince him that it was alright and that he wasn't too late to deliver the message.

Once the man got himself under control he told him, and he quoted, "God didn't allow you to be brought low because you were lost to him, but you were lost to yourself. He wants to reintroduce you to the wonderful man He made you to be. He wants to redeem you for His Glory and make you whole again."

The preacher told the audience of how he broke down and confessed his true intentions for the day to come. That he'd felt as if he'd out-lived God's grace. He had defiled God's house, the edifice he ruled as pastor, His altar and God's temple in his heart. He was a pastor gone too long without a mentor, and didn't know which way to turn.

He told the man that if he'd come to him sooner that he may not have been in a place to receive what he'd said because he was so angry and felt as though God had given up on him. The crying continued between for so long the waitress came by to ask if there was anything she could do.

Long story, made short: they prayed for her and she rededicated her life to Christ. The waitress' daughter had been inviting her to church, but past hurts had caused her to never want to set foot in another church.

Before they left the diner later that afternoon, two more waitresses gave their life to Christ and a cook rededicated himself after hearing the two men's testimony.

By the time the preacher had come to Richard's church, it had been two and a half years since his rededication at the dinner and though he still was not pastoring a church, he'd reunited with his family and shared his testimony with churches throughout the Midwest. He ended his message with one profound statement: "Sometimes you have to get to the edge of hell before you understand that without God there is nothing to keep you from going over, but even in that moment, He considers you redeemable and has already made the arrangements to pull you back."

During altar call, the preacher asked all those who felt as though they were at 'the end of their road' to come forward and receive a new assignment. Half of the church came forward and he prayed with each person individually. When he reached Richard, he looked at him for a moment then asked him if he could give him a hug. When Richard nodded he gave him a long hug then began praying for him. The anointing of the Lord overtook Richard and for the first time in his life, he was slain in the spirit.

Once he came back to himself, which was the only way he could describe it, he heard it. The unexplainable yet audible words that engraved themselves upon his mind and heart. *Love Me, love yourself, love your wife, and I will take care of the rest.*

He woke up confounded, but as the days and weeks went on, the fuzzy edges became more clear and the places he thought there were gaps came together seamlessly until he fully understood the phrases. It seemed simplistic after he realized that God wasn't talking in riddles. God wanted Richard to love Him first, himself second, and his wife third. In practicing and experiencing his love for God, he learned how to begin to truly loving himself and was finally able to love his wife as God loved him.

He battled with the latter for a while, not because he didn't think he already loved his wife, but because he was sure he did. It was hard coming to the conclusion that as much as he loved his wife, it failed and fell short because it wasn't unconditional. His judgment towards his wife had been condemning rather than critiquing, and it caused him to pity her instead of encourage her.

He'd asked God, who pulled out all the stops to get his attention and show him how much He loved him, how he could do the same for his wife. The answer came to him through his pastor's sermon the next week. "You have to learn to love yourself in order to truly love someone else."

If he were to regain his wife's love, he needed to show her how to love herself again and what better way than to show her how beautiful she was through his and God's eyes.

*   *   *

He had to admit, God's idea for him to share some of his favorite memories with her scared him at first because it made him feel extremely vulnerable. She could easily discount every beautiful, intimate detail that had so profoundly touched his heart, but she didn't. She instead followed his suggestions, giving him hope that she was indeed willing to work for their marriage and not just offer him lip service.

Now, everything he'd worked so hard to reclaim, even from thousands of miles away was being jeopardized by her relentless need to find out what happened to her child. Well, not so much finding her child, but her need to do it without telling him. It was going to make sharing his findings with her that much harder. He could wait until her man, Michael, found the information his people had found – only 24 hours before – but he wasn't willing to keep her in the dark for much long just to make things more convenient for himself.

She wasn't aware of it, but he had done everything but move mountains to get to her side this evening; one, because he promised, but more importantly, he wanted to make sure she didn't get the news about Brian without him being there.

After a quick shower and donning his tuxedo, he took a deep breath and exited the bedroom. *Lord, I'm reminding you that I'm going to need your strength to get through the rest of this evening. Please prepare her heart, comfort her, and show her that I'm on her side.*

*   *   *

If Victoria had to kiss one more cheek, shake one more hand or deliver one more smile, she knew she would be drunk by midnight. She'd underestimated Richard's ability to schmooze, coddle, indulge, and compliment. He was a gifted host with enough patience for everyone, and she needed him desperately.

She looked through the crowd once again and let out a low sigh when she spotted him across the room. *Thank you, thank you, thank you.* Maybe he could appease the few people she'd snubbed on her way to the bathroom. As wonderful of a cause as this gala was, she couldn't wait for it to be over.

When he came fully into view, her breath caught. Wow, the man could fill out a tux, and at 62, he looked incredible. She became even more anxious for the night to be over. Spying the looks a few women were giving him, she excused herself from the conversation she was only half listening to, and began to make her way towards her husband.

She couldn't remember the last time she felt so possessive of him and didn't know if she cared too much for the feeling, but it was there so she would go with it.

She placed her hand in the crook of his arm, hugging it close to her bosom. He gazed down at her as if he expected no one but her, and it made her feel valued. A few minutes later, after speaking to a few guests, he guided her to the bar and cupped her chin as he studied her face. He ordered her a cranberry juice cocktail then whispered, "Sorry for leaving you on your own so long, love. I can take it for a while if you want to get some fresh air." When he leaned back to gaze upon her again, she had to reassess her feelings and what she came up with was *cherished*. She felt cherished.

She gave him her most dazzling smile. "No honey, I'm sorry, because I underestimated the stir you would cause in that tux. I'm afraid you might be absconded if I move from your side. The vultures are already hovering."

He frowned down at her before allowing his gaze to roam from his immediate left to right then he let out a deep chuckle that she could feel rumble through her in the most delightful way. *Nope, she wasn't budging from his side tonight.*

"Come on," she tipped her head to the side. "Let me buy you dinner." He began to follow her towards the dining room.

"And what did I do to deserve that?"

"You came."

*   *   *

Four hours, two layers of cold cream, and she could swear one huge blister later, Victoria sat in front of her vanity going over the evening's events. She could have patted herself on the back for another successful gala, but she was just too relieved it was over and that Richard was back home.

She looked over her shoulder as he walked through the door to their bedroom, but turned, warm towel in hand, at the serious expression on his face.

"What's wrong, Richard?"

He came through the bedroom to lean against the dressing room door jam. "I wanted to wait until after the gala to talk to you about something. I don't know how you are going to take it, but I'm hoping you can remember that I did what I did because I love you, and I didn't want you to feel like you had to handle this on your own. Can you remember that for me? I can handle any reaction you have as long as I know you realize I did this for you."

"Richard, you're scaring me," Victoria's heart began to race with trepidation as different scenarios raced through her head.

"Will you remember that for me?"

The lump in her throat was the size of a grapefruit. *Oh crap. Remember he loves me. What did he do? What did he do?* She nodded her head.

He took a deep breath and walked over to kneel down in front of her.

Oh, this so isn't good. If he had an affair, I will kill him… But he wouldn't have an affair because he loves me, would he?

"First, I want to tell you how much it meant to me all those years ago when you told me about the child you had that you put up for adoption. You didn't have to tell me about it because it was before us, but you were completely and totally honest with me and it was one of the things that drew me to you so irrevocably."

Her heart rate went into overdrive. *Brian? Why is he bringing up Brian after all of this time? Did he have a child from the past that he hadn't shared with me?* She could deal with that. It was before they met…

Richard continued. "For all that you went through with your parents and the forced adoption, I wanted to put your mind at ease in regards to your son. I wanted to give you a sense of peace and so when I'd made enough money, I hired a private investigator."

"You what?" Why did she not know this? How was he able to hide this so well?

"I wanted to give you some of the answers you seemed to be looking for. You didn't say anything, but I would watch you sometimes when you would be around children – before Rachael was born. You seemed as though there was a tiny piece of you missing. I'm not saying you were unhappy, because I knew it was the complete opposite, especially after Rachael was born, but still there were those times when the light would go out of your eyes and you would take on a far-away look."

"Why are you telling me all of this now?"

Richard took her hands. "I thought if I could find any information on your son, I could help take that look out of your eyes."

She squeezed his hands, hope starting to spark in her chest.

He studied her for a moment. "Could we take this to the bed? My knees aren't as young as they used to be." He took the washcloth out of her hand and wiped the few spots of cream she'd missed by her ears.

Once they made it to the bed, he continued. "It was slow going at first because the people who adopted your son left the state, and since the father was in the military, finding them was almost impossible." He took her hands and rubbed them in between his. He always marveled at how soft her skin felt; no one would ever guess she ran a farm.

He watched for the emotions in her new-penny colored eyes, and prayed for the strength to endure whatever came next.

"At the end of last year, one of my men got a tip from a friend in Colorado. His girlfriend does odd jobs, and one of them is the cleanup before estate sales. She procures paperwork and things of that nature. I'm not going to bore you with all of the details, but the paperwork gave my man the information he needed to fill in the gaps." He wished he could save her from this and he would have had a significant fight on his hands on whether or not to tell her if Michael wasn't already close to finding the same information.

He let out his breath slowly. "Mrs. Grossenberg passed away at the end of October last year. Her husband died from injuries sustained in a car

229

accident three years ago. The house and its belongings went to the state."
He watched Victoria's eyes narrow as her mind quickly worked through
what he was saying. When they widened, he went on.

"No family came forward to claim the estate because their adopted son,
Brian, was already deceased."

He watched her fair skin grow pale and squeezed her hands as if that
one action could assuage the emotional storm she would have to endure.

"Though I found this out during my trip in Uganda, I wanted to have
as much of the story as possible before coming to you with this
information. That, and I wanted to be the one to tell you. Not Michael."

Her mouth dropped open and she snatched her hands away from him.
He felt her separation as though it were a physical blow.

"You knew about Michael? How long?"

"From the beginning." He didn't look away.

"Why didn't you tell me?"

"I figured if you wanted me to know, you would have told me." He
shrugged to show her he wasn't upset by her secrecy.

"Did..." Her voice squeaked and she began again.

"Did you try to hinder his progress?"

"No," he said gravely. He took a deep breath to keep that question from
hurting. Did she really think he would want to keep her from finding out
what happened to her son? Well, wasn't that what he'd been considering?
It took a great deal of discipline to keep from placing his head in his hands
and giving in to the despair he felt trying to overtake the situation.

"Go on," she reminded him quietly.

He didn't know if he could. The last thing he wanted to do was hurt his
wife or see her hurting, which was exactly what he was about to do.

"The details are still a little sketchy, but I believe you already know
that Brian was placed in the psychiatric ward of State General.

He was released and seemed to be doing okay his first week out, but
some paperwork found in the home revealed that he'd began having severe
issues in school. Two months later, when his mother came home from
work, she found him in his room dead by his own hand. There was a letter
found in the family's safe."

Victoria gasped and covered her mouth with the back of her hand. Her
eyes began to fill, but when he leaned forward to hug her she'd become as
stiff as a statue. "Please....I can't...don't...I won't be able to. My son.
My..." She shifted her hand to cup her mouth and ran towards the
bathroom, where she became violently ill.

He followed her into the bathroom, wrapping an arm around her lower
belly as she bent over the commode. He could feel the tightening of her
stomach as she heaved and it tore at him, but he refused to let her go. She

needed his strength whether she was willing to admit it or not. He whispered anything he could think of that would help, but couldn't shake the feeling of helplessness that stabbed him with each groan she made.

He rubbed her back in long, soothing strokes as she continued to heave even after emptying the full contents of her stomach. He felt a shudder run through her back then heard the wrenching sobs begin, and he began to panic.

"Honey...oh Vickie." He picked her up off the floor and cradled her between himself and the sink so he could clean her face. All the while she cried with body racking sobs until he felt, more than heard something snap in her and she began screaming out her pain. It was a soul-piercing sound that had him momentarily immobilized with fear, but he turned her around and wrapped her in his arms.

She fought his hold for a second then clutched him to her as she continued to scream. "Shush honey. You'll make yourself sick again."

"MY SON'S DEAD!" She began yelling and he could feel the wetness from her tears and spit on his shoulder, and he died a little with each word she chanted. Out of the corner of his eye he caught the horrified look on Martha's face as she stood in the bedroom doorway.

He mouthed for her to call Dr. Starling, who had attended the party and was one of the last to leave. If he'd been thinking ahead, he would have asked him to stay just in case.

Victoria's legs gave away and he picked up her slight frame, and carried her back to the bed. He sat her on his lap still holding her as tight as he dared, rocking her back and forth, and then he was caught up in another time when Victoria came to him crying hysterically and clutched at him as if he were her lifeline, even as she slipped into a dead faint. He cursed himself at that moment for not being more prepared.

It was ten minutes later before he heard the doctor's voice as he bounded up the stairs, and Richard was so relieved he was near tears. Victoria's wails had subsided into aching moans, but she'd continued to repeat, "They were supposed to take care of him. They were supposed to protect and love and nurture him. They promised, they promised..." He continued to rock her as he spoke to the doctor.

"I had to give her some extremely bad news, and she isn't taking it very well. I think she's going to need a sedative." She shuddered again and it went through him. He swallowed convulsively, working even harder to hold back his own tears. "Please."

"Richard, I'm going to need to take a look at her first. Can you lay her down on the bed?"

He didn't want to let her go. He didn't know at this point if it were more for her or him, but he was afraid one of them would splinter into a thousand pieces if he let go right now.

"Couldn't you examine her like this?" He pleaded.

"Richard, it really would be best if you let her get more comfortable." Richard could hear the soothing tone in his friend's voice, and knew he must have looked like he was on the edge as well.

He slowly stood up with Victoria still in his arms. He turned towards the bed and bent to set her down, but her hold tightened around his neck and her moans began to increase in volume.

"Honey, Vickie, the doctor needs to take a look at you." The tears started unheeded, rolling down his cheeks. "He's going to make you feel better." She became agitated, pulling at his shirt.

"Baby..." his urging was cut off by her scream.

"No." It hurt his ear it was so loud and she held onto the word so long it broke the last of his resolve. He began pleading for the doctor to sedate her between his sobs, and felt only a modicum of relief when the doctor conceded.

It wasn't until her hold began to slacken that he was able to take a deep breath. He sat on the bed next to her unconscious form, knowing he wouldn't move until she woke up.

"Richard." He heard as if it were coming from a long ways away. It came back again and again, each time getting closer until it reached him, and he was pulled from his daze.

Dr. Starling cupped his chin and shined a penlight in his eyes. "Richard, I need you to respond." He reached up to move the man's hand away.

"I'll be alright," he murmured.

"Can you tell me what happened?" The doctor asked.

Richard looked back down at his wife. "I hurt her."

"You hurt her?" The doctor repeated. Richard nodded his head.

"How Richard?" The doctor asked, but when Richard failed to respond he shook him slightly.

"How did you hurt her Richard?" he asked him in a softer tone.

"I told her, her son was dead." There, he said it. He'd done it. He'd hurt her and hurt her badly.

"Come on. She's going to sleep for a while. Let me take a look at you in the other room." The doctor tugged at his shoulder.

"I'm not leaving her. She thinks I'm all she has. I'm not leaving her." He shrugged away from his friend and stood up only to go to the other side of the bed and lay next to his wife, not taking his eyes off of her face.

"Richard, this isn't healthy. If you don't come into the next room with me I may have to sedate you."

Richard shifted his eyes from his wife to the Dr. Starling. "Touch me, and you'll need a doctor."

Dr. Starling's eyes widened slightly then he sighed heavily. After taking Victoria's pulse, blood pressure and checking her pupils, he began to gather his things.

"I'll have Martha keep me informed of both of your behaviors." Richard stared at his wife and took so long to respond, Dr. Starling was nearly to the door when he said, "Make sure you send me the bill, Daniel."

"Oh don't worry. I know where you live." Then Dr. Starling closed the door behind him.

Richard watched Victoria through the night. It wasn't until the dim light of dawn was peeking through the blinds that he surrendered to exhaustion.

*   *   *

Victoria woke up slowly as if she were sifting her way through a heavy fog. She rolled to her left, encountering something warm and immovable. She peered out of painfully heavy eyelids and blinked only to groan slightly at the grainy feel. She focused on the man breathing heavily beside her. The lines around his eyes stood out even in sleep and she wondered for a moment what he must be dreaming, when the night before came back upon her like a flood.

She smothered a whimper, but couldn't help the sob which caused Richard to frown deeper and stir. He opened his eyes and she saw the haze of sleep fall away only to be replaced with sorrow and pain. He reached out for her and she made the conscious decision to move towards him instead of away this time. She just couldn't get through this one by herself.

CHAPTER 22

Mason watched Dr. Mitchell Seagret's booted sole bob up and down in a lazy fashion from the man's crossed legs. He'd asked himself for no less than the fifth time why he had been compelled to seek out this man's card and schedule an appointment. He didn't really feel like sharing with a grief counselor, but he'd run out of options and run out of people in his circle of family and friends to talk to.

He knew the man was waiting for him to begin, but he wasn't sure how. It had been so long since he'd voiced the thoughts that had placed him on this road. The boot stilled and he looked up at the man who still held a patient, thoughtful expression.

It put Mason on edge. "You seem to have a lot of time on your hands," he quipped.

The doctor shrugged. "Not necessarily, but for the time being we are in this office and you have my undivided attention."

Mason watched him for a moment, expecting him to continue, maybe with a question, but he went silent again. Mason looked towards the window in the corner of the respectable sized office. Suddenly he felt like a trapped bird and his heart began to beat just as quickly as one of the small feathered creatures. This was a mistake. He would have to find some other way to wrestle this demon.

He pressed his palms to his thighs and looked back to face the doctor. "I think I've made a mistake. I'm sorry to have wasted your time."

"May I ask you a question?" The doctor said, not changing his posture.

If you'd asked questions from jump we may have gotten somewhere today instead of staring at each other for the last 15 minutes, Mason thought but simply nodded.

"Why would you wait two and a half years to call me, then give up after 15 minutes?"

"How would you know how long I've had your number?" He asked, feeling defensive. Exactly how much did this man know about him?

"How did you come by my information?" The man asked quietly.

Mason hated when people answered a question with a question, but it was no hardship to remember the colleague that handed him the card. It was three days after Rachael's funeral and the house was blissfully quiet. No one was looking at him with pity in their eyes, trying to feed him, send him to bed or asking him if he needed anything to eat. Vivian was staying with her "Auntie Michelle", one of Rachael's friends who had girls around Vivian's age.

His doorbell rang during his mid-afternoon nap and he was sorely tempted to ignore it. He sat up on the couch and tried to make out the person by peeking through the side stain glass window panel to the left of the door. Taking a deep breath he stood, wavering a little on his feet before he made his way to the door. He considered trying to right his appearance by straightening his shirt or running fingers over his hair, but unless this was Publisher's Clearing House, he didn't give a fig what they thought and even then he would be hard-pressed to care. He almost smiled at the thought of opening the door gruffly, taking the huge check and closing it back on their shocked and bewildered faces.

He called out, "Who is it?" Not necessarily caring, but habit prevailed. "It's Chuck Stance."

Darn. He didn't feel like talking and no doubt Chuck, whose wife had died three years prior, would want to give him some advice or sympathize with him. If he wanted to be a help, he should have remembered how much he wanted to be alone right after Sara died.

Mason opened the door standing at an angle that made it clear that he was not inviting the man in. Chuck looked up at him from a couple of steps off the landing to the doorstep.

"Mason," he said by way of greeting, his hands in his pockets.

"Chuck," Mason mimicked, wanting to do the same, but had no pockets in his shorts so therefore kept his hands on either side of the door jam.

"I uh, well, I wasn't just in the neighborhood. I didn't just happen to be driving by and you didn't just happen to come into my mind. I've been thinking about you a lot since Rachael passed."

Well this was a different approach. Mason's interest was mildly peaked.

"I remembered how I felt right after Sara died."

Yep, here it comes.

"And I didn't want to have anything to do with anyone. I wished everyone would just go away so that I could get enough time to think."

Well if he knew him so well, what was Chuck doing on his front steps interrupting the first real sleep he'd had in weeks.

"So I'm just going to hand you this card. This is someone that may be able to help you when you are ready. He's a grief counselor and he is really good." Chuck stepped forward to hand Mason the ivory colored card. Mason looked at it for a moment trying to decide just how much of a waste it would be if he took it.

"You probably aren't ready to call him now. Shoot, if my instincts are right, you won't be calling him in the next few months, but one day you may need to talk to someone so I want you to put this in a place you can remember when you need it."

Mason took the card, looking very much like he was going to do just that.

Chuck started to turn, but caught himself. "It gets easier you know; the breathing and coping thing. Being around people may be a little easier too because you have Vivian. Sara and I never had the chance to have kids." He took a deep breath.

"You'll be okay eventually, Mason." He turned and began heading down the steps to the sidewalk then turned back one last time, "but I will still look in on you from time to time." He gave a small wave to match his ghost of a smile then walked to his car.

Mason watched Chuck until he drove off then he looked down at the card. Not wanting to give any more thought to it than needed, he placed the card on top of the table in the entry hall and thanked his lucky stars that Chuck did indeed understand what he was going through.

Mason was pulled out of the past by the re-crossing of Dr. Seagret's leg. "Did you and Chuck talk about me often?" Mason plied.

Dr. Seagret continued to look at Mason, his only answer being a barely perceptible shrug.

"So, how is this supposed to go? I tell you about my wife and you make me feel better?"

"There is no set structure. It's what you want it to be. You are here so on some level you feel the need to talk. Most people have the notion that that is what I am here for."

"And?" Mason asked dispassionately. He was not in the mood for mind play.

"And in most cases they would be right. I am here to listen, but I am also here to ask the questions others won't because they are afraid of causing you any more pain."

"So you hurt people?"

"The pain is inevitable. Most people who come to me are already in some kind of pain whether they have found a way to mask it or not. I just help them sort through the rough spots."

"How?"

"I listen then I ask the hard questions. The ones they don't think of or want to ask themselves."

"Like what?" Mason leaned back in his chair, taking on an air of nonchalance when he was feeling anything but.

"Like why it took you two and a half years to visit me then wish to leave inside of 20 minutes." Dr. Seagret uncrossed his legs and leaned his elbows on his knees.

Mason instantly wanted the man to go back to leaning back and crossing his legs. His eyes were too sharp, his mouth too thin, and that widow's peak made him look barely out of college, though from the research Mason had done, the man had owned his own practice for over 15 years.

"I finally felt like talking," Mason hedged.

Dr. Seagret sat up straight. "I don't believe you."

Mason raised his eyebrows. *The gall of this man.* "You don't believe I felt like talking?"

"I don't believe that is what brought you here after all of this time. I believe you have something to talk about and we can start with your wife's death, but that isn't what caused you to finally dial my number."

Mason opened his mouth, but was interrupted.

"Let's get some things straight from the beginning so you don't waste your time or mine. I am here to help you face the things you haven't had the inclination or courage to face on your own. I am not here to judge you, cajole you, lie to you or give you false hope. So if you want someone to take the bull you want to sling we can part here, but if you want to get that anvil off of your chest and get back enough of yourself not only to survive, but to prosper, then I have plenty of time to listen."

Well, Dr. Seagret had a dark side. *Maybe Chuck did know what he was doing after all.*

"Alright then. I will begin with the day I met my wife because getting to know her will allow you to understand what drove me to your doorstep."

Dr. Seagret leaned back and folded his hands in his lap like he was getting ready to read a book. "I'm ready when you are."

Two hours later Mason finished with a wan smile, the image of Paige fading with the sound of his voice in the room.

"You aren't nearly as far gone as I first thought."

His interest peaked, Mason leaned forward. "How so?"

"Well I have to admit, and I know I shouldn't, but usually when someone waits as long as you do before seeking help, they are well past what they believe they can tolerate in themselves. Your control and restraint is to be commended, but I believe a lot of the credit goes to your daughter who seems to adore you in spite of your faults.

"I would like you to tell me a little more about this Paige. You say she's an Elder?"

Did the man hear nothing I just told him? She is the very person I am trying to forget and Dr. Strangelove wants me to elaborate?

"Yes. What would you like to know?"

"You seem pretty impassioned when speaking of her. What is it about her that causes you to feel so?"

Mason shrugged, trying to use the motion to release some of the tension the thought of her caused. "I don't know. From the moment I ran into her, literally, I was arrested by her. I have never felt such an immediate, intense physical and emotional reaction to someone like I did with her. Even with my wife, who I was almost instantly smitten with, I felt like I was making the choice to pursue her. Paige pulled me in, even seemingly against my will and now that she has chosen to be with someone else, I feel as though I am left in some type of limbo unable to catch hold of any stabilizing agent. The closest I can come to it is the love I have for my daughter. She is the reason I get up in the morning, otherwise I am afraid I would waste away to nothing." He shifted slightly in his seat.

"You say some of the people who come to you have passed the point of being able to live with themselves in their condition." He leaned forward in his agitation. "I can't continue to pine after a woman I can't have. I am now mourning the loss of two women and the latter is killing me swifter than the former."

"Besides the obvious pull and connection you feel to this woman who is the biological mother to your child, what is it about her that causes you to hang on?"

"She is real. I mean almost transparent and she is unapologetic about it. It's as if she never learned how to wrap herself in the guile that people use to cloak themselves when they have been hurt and betrayed. She trusts people. You see in her eyes that she is willing to believe and hope in you. It is as alluring as any expensive perfume."

"You are in love with her." It was said as a statement.

Mason was slightly startled by the revelation, but thought quickly back to the different interactions he'd had with Paige and came to the painful conclusion that the doctor was right.

This wasn't some sickly obsession built on a foundation of infatuation and a misguided attempt to give Vivian back the family he felt guilty about her missing out on. He was in love with Paige Morganson. A more tragic turn of events he couldn't have imagined for himself. Even if she was free to love him back, she belonged in his world just as much as he belonged in someone's pulpit. How could you love someone and hate what they stood for?

"Mason," Dr. Seagret called.

Mason refocused on him. "Yes. It's a freakin' Shakespearean tragedy."

"So what are you looking to accomplish with these sessions?"

"Well it should be obvious after your last revelation."

Dr. Seagret's only response was a slight lifting of the eyebrows.

Mason gave an exasperated sigh. "I want to fall out of love."

*　　　　　*　　　　　*

Mason sat on the couch watching his daughter go through some of her geometrical equations. He didn't fail to notice that if Vivian had more English homework than anything else, she would remain in her room, probably to go over some of her studies with Paige if needed. If she had more science or math she would study in the living room, close to him. If he passed through the living room to the kitchen for some water – which he did every evening – he would check to see if her books were spread out on the coffee table. If they were, he would relegate himself to watching television in the living room instead of his bedroom. It had become an unspoken routine that brought him comfort. His child still needed him.

He rocked slightly in his easy chair, itching to tell her to recount her last solution. She wouldn't be able to finish the equation with the key she wanted to use. He watched her move through it slowly then backtrack, but before she tried again, this time using the right key, she looked up at him, knowing he was watching. He smiled and returned his attention to the CNN program. It was all the approval she needed to continue on her present course.

"Daddy?"

"Yes?" he answered automatically before turning towards her.

"Do you think you will get married again?"

Stunned by her question, he chose to concentrate more on the reason behind it.

"Why do you ask?"

She shrugged and he saw himself in her at that moment. He knew this was something bigger than she was letting on. "I was just thinking about it recently. I'm not saying you need to get married tomorrow or anything. I was just wondering if you were open to one day getting married again."

He watched her until she began to squirm, then he got his answer. This conversation was heading somewhere he didn't want to go. He would head this one off at the pass.

"Is this your, not-so-subtle way of telling me you would like to have 'The Talk'? I can go and get the video your mom made for you and we could watch it together."

The look of puzzlement that transformed into one of shock and embarrassment was worth the tiny twinge of guilt.

"No, eh, uh, eww Daddy no," she sputtered. "I wouldn't watch that with you. That's gross."

It was all he could do to keep a straight face, but he couldn't help goading her. "Why not? You don't even know what it's about."

"We covered it in health a few months ago. Besides, I went through some of the videos she left a little over a year ago." Her face reddened even more in abashment. He stilled.

"You watched the videos?"

"Not all of them. Just the ones from 10 to 14." She began to doodle in her notebook.

"Why?" He schooled his expression to remain open.

She looked at him, her wide gray eyes squeezing his heart. "I missed her...miss her. When it gets unbearable, I go in and take one. I think that is the real reason why she made them. Not necessarily to tell me about the birds and bees or how to shave my legs, but to comfort me with her voice or her face. I could have learned all that stuff from the internet." Her voice became very quiet.

"You know sometimes I think I can smell her?"

Mason leaned forward in his chair. He remembered Rachael's smell the best early in the morning. She smelled like sweet-scented dew. It was probably because of her shampoo, but that mixed with her skin made him miss her all the more when it rained.

"What do you smell?" He asked.

Her eyebrows came together for a moment then lengthened again, and a smile came into her eyes.

"Clean sunshine!" she said, sounding happy that she'd come up with a description.

"Clean sunshine," he repeated, mulling it over. His daughter was clever with her words. He thought of what he might be able to smell on a sunny day right after a heavy rain. He nodded his head in agreement and smiled at her.

"Would you do it?"

"What?"

"Would you get married again?" He watched her, but this time he gave the question the consideration she seemed to be asking for.

"It would take an extraordinary woman to make me want to get married again. She would have to be someone I couldn't imagine living my life without. I would snatch her up so no one else would have a chance at claiming her. Just like when I saw you. You were the perfect bundle of sweet and I fell in love with you the moment I saw you."

She laughed at his wording. "It's not the same. I was brought to you special like."

"Well honey, she would have to be as well, otherwise no go."

She seemed to ponder that for a moment then nodded in agreement. She looked down at her paperwork and he watched her find her place and resume her studying.

"Is that all?" he asked

She looked up, giving him only half of her attention. "For now," she said, appeased.

He was happy he'd gotten off so easy. He looked back at the television seeing nothing in front of him. He concentrated on the smell of sweet dew and when the murmur of longing whispered in his heart this time he found that the pain was bearable. He took a deep breath and relaxed into the sigh. He had finally listened long enough to notice that he was actually getting better.

Dr. Seagret had said it was all one breath away. He'd just stunted the process of his healing by holding his breath for two and a half years because he was afraid of feeling. Though it had not made much sense at the time, it was beginning to ring true.

He took another breath and could almost catch that sweet scent.

Four days later, he was sifting through the mail, idly considering what to burn for dinner when a bulky gold envelope caught his attention. He looked for a return address on either side. A feeling of apprehension rolled across his shoulders when he failed to find one. He checked Vivian's bedroom door to see if it was closed then proceeded to open the package.

He turned the opened side down so that the contents would fall into his hand. His blood ran cold at the sight of the first photo. It was one of him and a woman with curly ebony hair looking way too familiar with each other. He looked up again to make sure Vivian wasn't sneaking up on him. He sifted through the pictures becoming more distressed with each progressing photo. By the time he reached the end a light sheen of perspiration coated his upper lip and his stomach roiled. This was the woman. The one he'd smelled on his pillow almost a month ago.

A feeling of dread came over him when he spied the letter in the envelope. No good would come from this.

CHAPTER 23

Paige sat on the couch with her face in her hands. Her breath came fast, her eyes and nose filling her hands with moisture.

"Paige?" Lady Menagerie said, her voice imploring.

She shook her head, not ready to speak. She knew right now it would all come out in an incoherent mess.

"Paige, honey…"

She raised one hand in a gesture for a moment more.

Lady Menagerie went silent.

Paige knew it wasn't fair to have burst into Lady Menagerie's home as she done earlier that afternoon and basically held the woman hostage with her hysterics, but she couldn't seem to control her emotions.

She'd held it in for a day and a half hoping that Brandon would change his mind and they could move forward as though their last discussion was a mere hiccup in their relationship. She had convinced herself that all couples had misunderstandings. Even as she thought the words she caught herself and wondered when she'd become delusional. This was so much more than a misunderstanding. After what seemed to be the most beautiful six months of her life, Brandon had broken up with her.

She suddenly wished she could go back a few hours. She needed to go back and assess what she had done to keep herself shrouded in numbness. She wanted that back because this pain was near unbearable. She slowly began to rock herself back and forth in a soothing gesture. All the stories of lost love where the owner of the unrequited love crawled into themselves, a bed, or a hole in the ground made sense to her now. How did one function with such a massive hole in their center?

She was so wounded she couldn't even imagine herself climbing into her Father's lap. She could only lay before Him and hope that He would pick up her inert body and breathe life into her again.

She finally found the courage to look up and saw Lady Menagerie staring at her with concern from where she'd perched herself on the coffee table in front of Paige.

"Are you ready to talk yet? I only ask because if this is going to be an overnighter I will need to change the sheets in your room. Dana came home with a guest last weekend and I haven't had time."

Paige waived her hand dismissively. "I'm sorry to be such a bother…" Lady Menagerie took her hand firmly to get her attention.

"You are never a bother. You may annoy me a little having chosen my couch to have a pity party, but a bother you are not." Lady Menagerie offered a small smile to cut at the edge of her remark.

"He broke up with me," Paige said in a quiet voice.

"What?" Lady Menagerie said leaning closer.

"Brandon broke up with me," she repeated choppily.

"I don't understand," Lady Menagerie began.

Through her tears she watched the woman open and close her mouth a couple more times before she decided on, "Did he tell you why?"

Paige nodded, struggling to keep the fragile hold on her emotions.

Lady Menagerie squeezed her hands as if she could transfer her strength to her.

"The cancer has metastasized. He doesn't want me to see him..." she broke off to take a breath. Her heart stuttered. "He doesn't want me to see him sick."

"What did you tell him?"

Paige shrugged slightly and gave Lady Menagerie a brief account of her response, to which Lady Menagerie gave a spontaneous, unladylike snort.

After a moment, she looked closer at Paige. "Did you really mean it? Would you actually leave?"

The tears began to fall again as Paige nodded.

Lady Menagerie sat back for a moment then got up to head towards the kitchen.

"What –" she began, but Lady Menagerie's raised hand stopped her.

"We are going to need reinforcements."

A few minutes later she came back with a serving bowl of vanilla ice cream covered in hot fudge, caramel, and maraschino cherries.

She sat next to Paige and handed her a spoon. They both took a scoop. Paige allowed the cold texture to rest at the back of her throat for a couple of agonizing seconds before swallowing. She took a deep breath, turning to look at Lady Menagerie who just watched her with an expectant look on her face.

"I provided the numbing agent. You talk. I want to know what happened from the time you noticed a difference in him."

Paige took another deep breath, scooped up some more ice cream and stuck the spoon back in her mouth. She hoped Lady Menagerie had a lot more ice cream in her freezer.

*   *   *

Paige lay on her side in the guest bed of her pastor's home, staring at the closed window shade. This had always been a place of serenity for her. She's always felt as though nothing could reach her in this place. This night was no different except she wondered how many more opportunities she would have to do so. She wasn't surprised at Lady Menagerie's refusal to accept her decision to leave, but she wasn't ready to consider altering that decision.

Her thoughts roamed back and forth between a smiling Brandon holding her hand at the park to the thoughtful Brandon that asked her how many children she wanted as they sat on her couch the night before she left for her book tour. It was hard reconciling those images with the one of him standing in the middle of her living room trying to give her a parting gift filled with memories of their relationship. Even Lady Menagerie had shaken her head in disbelief at what she called a piece of sentimental foolishness.

"What was that supposed to accomplish? Did he think you were unable to form memories on your own? It's not like you could hug a box and it fill in the gap that he was making. Men." She ended the small tirade with a huff. It had drawn the first real, albeit small, smile since Brandon had walked in her door.

She shifted in the bed hoping the different position would help in redirecting her thoughts. *How did I not see this coming?* She asked herself what must have been the 10th time.

She had been busy with the tour but the small hints in the change of his behavior didn't do much to prepare her.

Paige had laid on her bed in her overly warm hotel room waiting for another call from Brandon that didn't come. She loathed calling him, but she missed him and needed to hear his voice. She picked up her cell phone from where it was resting on her stomach and dialed his number. She stared at the display of his number through all six rings. Her heartbeat picked up with a trickle of anxiety. It had been a day and a half since they'd talked.

"Hi Baby. I was calling to pray with you and wish you a good night. I'm missing you something awful. Give me a call. It doesn't matter how late it is. I want to know how your day went." Not feeling the most comfortable in leaving messages and unable to think of anything else to say, she hung up and decided to text.

Brandon, I miss you and love you. I hope everything is well. Will you please call me so that I can hear your voice?

She fell asleep with the phone laying on the pillow next to hers. He'd neither called or text.

The next morning when he didn't call, she called him and was a little more than relieved when he answered the phone on the third ring.

"Hi Paige." His voice sounded groggy.

"Sorry, did I wake you? I tried to wait as long as I could before I had to leave for the conference." She heard him moving.

"I had a very late night and I'm not feeling 100%. I'm sorry I didn't get to talk to you."

"Are you alright? Do you need to go to the doctor?" Concern spiked her heart.

"No. It's nothing like that. Just feeling a little low on energy. How are you doing? Are you getting a little more sleep than the last time we talked?"

"Yes, but after today I'll be going to Philadelphia so my time zone will change."

"Yes, but by only one hour."

She expected him to continue but as the silence spread over the line the restless feelings came back.

"Brandon, may I ask you something?"

"Sure."

"Has something happened? You seem..." she searched for the least threatening word, "a little distant or distracted. Is your family alright?"

"Yes. My family is fine. I have just had a lot on my mind lately. I'd rather not talk about it over the phone though. Do you mind if we wait until you get back?"

She knew it was going to bother her if she let it. She just needed to know one thing. "Have your feelings changed? I know my touring can be..."

"My feelings towards you haven't changed, Paige. I love you. I don't want you to worry about me not being able to handle you touring because I can."

He still loved her. He wasn't having second thoughts about his feelings. She could wait.

"I love you too, Brandon."

*   *   *

The shutters came back into view and Paige blinked rapidly, trying to stave off the tears. She'd known as soon as the ultimatum was out of her mouth that she would pay for it, but she couldn't think of any other way to shock him off of his determined path. If he didn't come around in the next couple of days she would use his gift to her and visit her daughters. It had been too long since she'd seen both of her girls anyways. Maybe she would go and see them even if he did come around.

Feeling a little lighter with something more to look forward to, she turned off the lamp hoping that sleep would finally come. Two minutes later, she turned it back on.

She turned on her back, sketching the pattern the lampshade made on the ceiling until it blurred into another sweep of pictures as her mind took her back to Friday morning.

She felt curiously refreshed for a person who'd spent most of the day before moving from one airport to another, only to be dropped off in front of her doorstep during its last few moments.

She could vaguely remember dreaming, but the semiconscious thoughts of seeing Brandon lifted the haze of sleep faster than any type of ingestible caffeine. She glanced at the clock and carried her phone to the bathroom so she could hear any call or text come in while she was in the shower. She knew she didn't have to wait until he called her but the last week had left her with feelings of uncertainty that caused her to defer to him. How could three weeks dismantle the bond she was so sure of before they'd parted?

She was dressed and almost finished unpacking before his call came. "Hi," she answered almost breathlessly.

"Hi. Are you busy?"

"No, just finishing up on my unpacking. I took your advice and waited until this morning."

"Good. How did you sleep? Are you still tired from all the travel?"

"Actually, I am feeling pretty good. Nothing compares to one's own bed." She felt horrible. This was worse than when they'd first started dating.

"Could I come over?"

Not 'Can I come and see you?', 'Would you like company?', or 'I need to see you'. *Something was definitely wrong,* she thought.

"Absolutely. That's why I got done with all of my chores early."

"Um, alright, I'll be over in say about a half an hour," he said quietly.

"Sure. Are you hungry? I could fix something."

"No, Paige. Seeing you will be all I need."

Now that sounded more like Brandon except he sounded more anxious than excited.

"Brandon?" She let the question hang.

"I'll see you in a few minutes, Paige."

"Okay." She took a few deep breaths after the phone disconnected and forced herself to concentrate on the rest of her unpacking so that she didn't overthink Brandon's upcoming visit.

When she opened the door to him 30 minutes later, Brandon's noticeably forced smile from across the threshold brought about such unease that she had to school her features.

His eyes were slightly vacant and the lines around his mouth seemed strained. All she wanted to do was hug him and tell him that whatever it was, they would get through it together. So she did. She pulled him through the door and embraced him in a hug meant to communicate her love, need for him, and strength she wanted to share. He held her so tight at first she couldn't breathe, but she didn't mind. This was her Brandon. Then almost as abruptly, he released her and moved out of her embrace. She had no choice but to let him go.

She caught the distressed look on his face and panic washed over her in waves. *This couldn't be happening...*

She walked over to the couch, snatching up a throw pillow and hugging it to her middle as she sat down. She didn't know what else to do but sit and wait for him to explain his behavior. She certainly wasn't going to give him any ideas or make what she suspected any easier for him. Her world tilted at his next words.

He sat down facing her on the couch. He was clutching a beautifully carved wooden box in his left hand. "I'm sorry, Paige because I have racked my brain on how to say this better, but nothing has come to mind so I am going to be pretty frank." He paused slightly.

"I got my test results back that measured my progress from my last cycle of chemo and radiation. They weren't good. Well actually, that's an understatement." She noticed that he didn't once look her in the eye.

"I wanted to be the one that told you."

"Who, my carpet? Why won't you look at me, Brandon?" she said, fear starting to taint the edges of her thinking. He finally looked up and she saw it. The devastation clearly etched across his features before he schooled them. He was giving up.

"Told me what?" She needed the words. She would make him spell it all out for her.

"The cancer has metastasized. Though there was shrinkage of cells on the original site, there were cancer cells found in my lymph nodes."

She nodded. *Wow, alright.* They could work through this. "What did your doctor say?"

Brandon looked like he'd been waiting for a different type of reaction from her. He blinked a few times. "The doctor said I should consider a more aggressive type of treatment. I began it earlier on in the week."

That accounted for the lines so stressed around his mouth. *He must be exhausted.* She reached out towards his face, but he caught her hands before they made contact. He looked up at her, his eyes beseeching.

"I don't think we should continue this aspect of our relationship."

"Which aspect is that, Brandon?" She asked after a few moments of silence. She was going to make him say it.

He sighed heavily. "I don't think there should be anything more than friendship between us." His eyes slid away somewhere in the middle of the sentence.

"And how do you propose we do this?" There was a fission of heat melting the cold that had come over her at his admission of the doctor's diagnosis.

He looked back up at her face, watching her eyes for a moment. "We stick to socializing at church and in groups. I'm not saying it will be easy, but we will need to stop talking for a little while. You know, until..." He trailed off for a moment and looked at her expectantly. She looked back at him as if she had no clue what he was going to say.

"Until our feelings aren't so strong for one another," he continued.

"And how long do you think that will be?" she asked unable to keep the sarcasm out of her voice. She was angry now and it was a welcomed feeling compared to the fear that had been pricking her heart before.

"Paige, look, I don't have all the answers. It's not like this is what I want, but I don't see another way."

"And what happens if the more aggressive treatment works? Will you come back here and tell me we are a 'go' for a relationship outside of friendship?" She finished the last word with air quotes.

Brandon just looked at her with sorrow in his eyes. She couldn't give in to him. He was wrong. They belonged together. She looked around for something to help her win the case she was about to bring up when she spied the box again.

"What's that?" She pointed her chin at the wooden box in his hand.

He looked down at it as if he'd forgotten it was there. He reached forward as if to hand it to her, but she made no move to take it. "It is a box of memories I carry with me from time to time. You know, like the first movie we saw together, one of the rocks from our lake, a button you left in my car one Sunday." His voice faded when it was evident that she was not going to take the box from him.

She was glad they ended up in a relationship together because this was pure stalker material. *A button?* But then how much better was she? There were copies of his notes to her all over her bedroom and office which only told her that he loved her just as much as she loved him and his actions stemmed more from fear than love.

He set it down next to her hand on the couch.

"So you are taking the more aggressive route with the chemo and radiation," she said, repeating his earlier words. He only nodded.

"Was this your decision or did Dominy talk you into it? Does Dominy know?"

His eyes became guarded. "Dominy knows. We talked about it, yes, but it isn't as though I am suicidal."

"Does your family know? The last time we talked you said you wanted to get the results back first before you said anything."

He nodded. "My family knows. In fact, my mom is here visiting for a while."

Paige took this in slowly, trying to let it calm her. "Do they know you are breaking up with me?"

"This part of my life is none of their business," Brandon said with a coolness entering his voice she was not used to. It made her spine stiffen.

"I was enough of their business for you to introduce me to them as more than your friend," she quipped, but regretted her pettiness immediately. This wasn't going to get her anywhere.

"Alright Brandon." She breathed out heavily.

The look of surprise on his face was priceless. She might have smiled if her heart wasn't hammering to its end.

"Alright, what?" He responded, seeming lost in the direction of the conversation.

"Alright, I've heard you." She slid towards him on the couch, keeping a hand on the box to make sure it stayed close.

She watched as panic quickly registered on his face. "Paige, what are you doing?"

"Brandon, I heard what you said." She slid her hand along his jaw, her thumb rubbing under his bottom lip. "Just give this moment to me, please." She looked at his lips then back at his eyes and waited for his permission. The moment she saw it she pounced.

Her lips met his in a hungry kiss that communicated her longing and pent-up desire. She memorized the feel of his lips as she tugged at the bottom one then nibbled at the top. If she overwhelmed him then so be it.

Her hand crept to the back of his neck to hold him to her when she slanted her mouth on his and licked the seam of his lips in a quest for entrance. He acquiesced on a sigh and she finally got the taste of him she'd been longing for. She poured all of her feelings into the kiss determined not to think on the present or future.

Her other hand skimmed his neck and collarbone, causing him to shiver right before his hands came up and wrapped around her upper back and waist. He held her as if he could absorb her and she reveled in this edginess in him she'd unleashed.

He took over the kiss, rubbing his tongue against hers trying to reach each and every spot in her mouth. He repositioned their faces so he could reach her with another angle and hoisted her closer. The action thrilled and scared her. She could let this move to a place that neither of them wanted to control, or she could stop it now.

With regret she pressed at his chest and snatched her mouth away from his, heaving for breath. She could feel his runaway heartbeat before she put distance between them.

She picked up the box, at a loss for what else to say or do. She opened it and after spying the airline ticket stub for Chicago O'Hare Airport, she stared unseeingly at the rest of the contents. She couldn't let him run.

She slowly closed the box and placed her hand over the engraving on top. She waited until she'd gotten her breathing under control before she looked up at him. She reigned in her emotions and silently prayed that what she was about to do wouldn't backfire on her.

"So, is this your final decision? You want to break up with me?" She watched as the haze of desire left his eyes slowly. He licked his lips as if he could still taste her. She watched the movement and clenched her hands to keep herself rooted in place.

He finally nodded, looking like someone had just kicked his puppy. Her heart went out to him. She couldn't imagine the loss and hurt he was feeling in his confusion right now, but she was not giving up without a fight. There was no way he could kiss her the way he did and sincerely want to break up with her.

She stood up from the couch and laid into him as cool and concise as possible. They went back and forth until she led him to the door where she handed him back the box and kissed him goodbye.

She'd hoped it would remind him of what she'd said. Their time together would be like a whisper forgotten even before it reached its target.

She stepped back and closed the door, resting her back against it, trying to muster up enough courage to breathe. She knew the next breath would bring unbelievable pain or numbing calm. She whispered a silent prayer that it would be the latter then breathed in slowly.

She slid down, only slightly aware of the tears that were trying to race her there. Three days and her life could change forever.

*   *   *

Paige left her pastor's house early Monday morning. Today was the day, but whether it reaped success or destruction, she would be going back out of town soon. She needed to regroup.

She dialed Melanie soon after she walked in the house. First, she made sure that the few calls on her home answering machine weren't Brandon. With a resigned sigh she carried her cell into the bedroom where she took down the recently stored luggage.

"Hey Mel," she greeted.

"Paige? Are you home from your tour or are you still skipping across the globe?" Paige could hear the pride in her voice. Mel had always been her biggest fan. She didn't realize how much she'd missed her until this moment.

"I'm home, but hopefully not for long."

"Why? I imagine there's a gentleman over that way that would do just about anything to keep you rooted to the West Coast. Where are you going now?"

"Well, I was hoping you wouldn't mind a little company. I'm missing you and Gladys, and I have time to do something about it."

"But if my calendar is correct, you just got home a few days ago. What does Brandon think about this?"

"What Brandon thinks about me coming to see my sister and daughter has no bearing on this."

The silence on the other line stretched to an uncomfortable length.

"Paige?"

"So how 'bout it? Can I come, or are your planning some huge soiree?"

"You know you are always welcome. Gladys will be happy to see you. She will think it's 'the Bomb' or 'Dope' or some other oxymoronic word for 'great to see you'."

Paige laughed. Mel was forever trying to win the fight for properly used English in her household while Paige secretly asked Gladys for all of the new words of her generation. It wasn't necessarily fair, but even after Gladys was told of her real birth mother the roles didn't change. Mel continued to be Gladys' mom and therefore got to continue along the line of discipline she'd set forth in the beginning. Paige continued to relate to Gladys along the perimeters of aunt and friend.

"When were you thinking about coming?"

"Tomorrow if it wouldn't be too much of a bother." The other line went quiet once more.

"Paige?" Mel's tone was telling.

"How about when I get there, huh Mel?" Paige held her breath.

"Sure, Hon, sure. If you time it right, we may have a few minutes to ourselves before your charge comes home from school."

"Thank you, Mel." Paige breathed a sigh of relief.

"Paige, is there anything I can do?"

"You're doing it Mel."

"Okay. Just call or text me your travel arrangements and I will be there to get you."

"I really do miss you. It will be good seeing you."

"Same here, Hon."

Paige removed the phone from her ear, but heard Mel call from the other end.

"Yes?" she called back.

"I'm praying for you." The statement nearly brought Paige to tears.

"Thank you Mel."

Paige hung up and debated calling Mason to see if she could visit with Vivian for a few days after seeing Gladys. Spring Break would be starting soon. Maybe she would take both girls away for a couple of days.

She was searching through her phone for Mason's number when it began to ring. Her heart skipped a beat but relaxed back into its regular rhythm when she noticed that it was a private number. She decided to answer it anyway.

"Hello?"

"Paige?"

"Yes?"

"Oh, thank God. I was afraid I'd lost your number. This is Dominy."

Paige was momentarily frozen.

"Paige?"

"Uh, yeah. Dominy, how are you?"

"Good. Well good for a man who had the unfortunate luck to be best friends with a moron."

Paige giggled more out of relief that this wasn't an emergency call on Brandon's behalf than the actual reply.

"How are you and the mother-to-be?"

"We are well. You are the first person to ask me how I am doing in weeks. Most people just ask how Robin is doing, like I'm not going through anything."

"Awww, poor guy," Paige crooned.

"I mean it. The foot rubs, late night craving assignments, and don't get me started on the morning sickness."

Paige was intrigued. "Are you having sympathy pains and nausea?"

"Ew, no. I'm talking about holding Robin's hair while she's ill. That 'morning' sickness is no joke. I was kissing her the other evening and she shot up and ran into the bathroom. I'm starting to wonder if she is just using it as an excuse."

Paige rolled her eyes and stifled the laugh at his antics. "Maybe it's just you that makes her sick."

"You wound me, Paige." She could imagine him with his hand on his heart.

"You'll survive," she chuckled.

"Yes. Alas I will."

"How are you doing?"

All humor evaporated.

"Fine."

"Burr, it suddenly got chilly on this line."

"Dominy."

"Look Paige," he cut in, "I am just calling as a friend, not a messenger or an instigator – at least not yet."

That's what she liked about Dominy. He was straightforward. You never had to wonder what he was thinking.

"Okay, Dominy. I'm doing okay."

"May I say one thing, then I will leave it alone."

"I think you will find a way regardless. Go ahead, Dominy," she said with no reservations.

"Thank you for being you. Thank you for being the woman of God that you are. Thank you for praying and being led to do what you did on Friday. I thank you for seeing his visit for what it was and not allowing your emotions to get the best of you. You rocked his world and got his attention like his mom and I weren't able to do. I am only telling you this to encourage you to stand your ground. He needed this shake up so he could remember."

"Remember what?" She could barely get the words out she was so surprised and moved by his statement.

"Remember what he's fighting for. Those results really took him for a spin, but he told me how you reacted to him trying to break up with you, not to mention the few words I had to say to that ridiculous move..."

"Dominy." Paige tried to interrupt feeling as though she were betraying Brandon by listening to Dominy's less than stellar rave.

"Sorry, my mouth got away from me. I just want to say thank you for sending him back to the only person he can really listen to at this time."

"Who do you mean?"

"God." She sighed feeling the weight of a boulder lift from her chest.

"He listened to the doctor that tried to take credit for him still being here. He listened to me who tried to talk him into wanting to stay no matter what. He listened to his mom who really doesn't want to lose another child, not to mention himself, and only God knows what's going on up there right now, literally. I'm glad you tipped him in the right direction."

"Dominy, I didn't know if I should have stayed on the phone with you after finding out who you were, but I'm glad I did. Thank you for the encouragement."

"Why do you think I called from my private line?"

Paige shook her head. Dominy's value had just been raised 10-fold in her heart. "He's blessed to have you, Dominy."

"You're darned skippy."

Paige laughed. "And oh so humble." Dominy went quiet, but Paige could hear a muffled female voice over the line.

"It sounds like my master is calling me. We will talk later?"

"Sure. Okay."

"Keep your head up, Paige."

"And you keep yours down."

Dominy laughed out loud. "Bye."

"Bye."

She hung up feeling much brighter. She would go to Atlanta and from there if Mason was open to it, she would go to Chicago. It was time to pour more attention out on her girls and let them heal some of these pieces. She would deal with the decision to move when she got back.

CHAPTER 24

Brandon knew if he weren't so sick his mother would have spanked him as if he were seven-years-old again. He could see it in her eyes, but that was nothing compared to the disappointment in them when he told her he'd broken up with Paige. He tried to explain it the best way he could, but she just raised her hands after a moment, got up from the kitchen table where they were eating, and walked out of the room.

Dominy was no better. Instead of sympathizing with him over Paige's response, he said 'good' then hung up in his face. His own *friend* hung up on him.

Brandon was feeling low. It was as though the universe was now moving against him.

He knew it would be hard to walk away from her, but he hadn't been prepared for this constant feeling of loss. Not just from her, but from everything. He'd made sure his mind was made up the day before she arrived because he needed at least that much time to reinforce his will upon the rest of him. As it was, there had to have been four times he could clearly remember placing the box in the back of his closet because he'd changed his mind.

When she opened the door and pulled him inside to hug him, he reveled in the embrace as if it had been months instead of weeks since he'd seen her. She was even more beautiful than he remembered and he had changed his phone's wallpaper to her picture, so it wasn't as if he couldn't look upon her whenever he wanted. It was the one he had the pilot take of her with the sunset as the background on Valentine's Day.

He wanted to keep her. That was the only thought running through his head until the box digging into his hand reminded him of his ulterior motive. He let her go, working hard to step away.

He needed to stay focused, say what he came to say, and give her the box.

He'd joined her on the couch because he didn't want to seem too harsh. If she loved him even half as much as he loved her, this was going to wreck her. He hinted at his intentions and even kept his patience when she made it clear that she wanted him to spell it out. She wasn't going to give him an inch. He even saw fire come into her eyes and he prepared himself for her temper, but what he got instead nearly destroyed all his resistance.

She'd kissed him, and not one of the chaste or even semi-chaste kisses they'd been playing with. She kissed him with all of her. He'd never felt a kiss all the way to his soul before, but in that moment he knew she was branding him and he couldn't do anything to stop her. She'd tasted so good and knowing that she was holding him to her so she could have her way with him pushed his self-control to its very limit. After a few moments of her teasing him with her tongue, he only wanted to stop the torment and took over. If she was going to brand him it was only fair that he leave his mark in return. He could take this one piece of her. Surely they could have these last few moments and come back to the world later. Then she pulled away, and he wanted to cry out at the unfairness of it all. He was so close to changing his mind at that moment. He was ready to concede defeat and call himself a coward, but she opened the box and the world came rushing up to meet him.

After trying to plead his case, she'd laid down the gauntlet and he found himself adrift. He couldn't find any true anchor in his thoughts. She'd closed the door on him and every memory they'd made. It was a wonder he made it home without causing an accident. To let his mother tell it, he was a walking zombie for the first few hours he was back at the apartment.

He'd walked in and sat in the first chair he come to, unmoving. It was only when the fear in her voice reached him that he began to come back to himself. He told her what he'd gone to Paige's to do, starting and stopping when a part became particularly painful to voice and when he was done he looked to her for any type of comfort. The look of disappointment in her eyes broke him, but he was able to hold the tears back just long enough for her to leave the room.

Often times he'd heard of men in the bible doing things that took more strength of character than he thought even he could summon. Well, none of them had been in love with Paige Morganson and had to let her go knowing soon he would be less than a distant and infrequent thought. Chemo had nothing on this.

Brandon moved to sit near the sliding glass door in the living room. He slept on the couch because every time he got in bed he became wide awake. He ate only when prompted by his mother, but since everything tasted like cardboard it was hard getting most foods past his throat. He didn't go to church because he knew seeing Paige would be too painful. He didn't answer his phone anymore because the one person he would have taken a call from wasn't speaking to him anymore, but he was going to stand his ground. He was doing the right thing. If his next tests came back more favorable he would track her down, get on his knees if he had to and beg her to take him back.

On the third day, he watched the clock over the kitchen stove. She had given him 72 hours and he was now down to six. It would get better once her time limit was over. The hope would be over and so would this struggle with his body and heart. He was happy she hadn't given him a week to change his mind. He probably wouldn't have made it.

A sound to his left caused him to glance away from the window. His mother sat down on the couch facing him. He watched her, feeling wary. She reached forward and took his hand gently, knowing how raw his nerves were.

"I know you were young when your sister, Peyton, passed, but I also know you were very close to her so I'm not going to insult you by stating that losing her was any harder on me than you. What I don't think you remember was your father and I separating for a time soon after that.

She smiled wanly at his perplexed expression. "Nature is not designed for a parent to outlive their child," she said as though this one statement would explain everything.

He thought back to the time she was referring to, but didn't notice his father's lack of presence.

As if she'd read his thoughts, she said, "He would come to the house after he got off work and have dinner with us, and go to a hotel nearby after most of you were in bed."

Rocked by this information, Brandon opened his mouth to speak, but didn't know what to say. The family image his parents had portrayed for so long was a pretense? He wasn't in the right mind to accept this. He started shaking his head to keep her from sharing anymore, but she came and sat next to him so that even if he didn't look at her, he couldn't avoid her or what she was saying.

"It was a very hard time for all of us. Peyton was one of those children that instead of waking up with the sunshine, the sunshine seemed to come up when she woke just to keep from missing a moment with her. Don't get me wrong. All of you are special to me. You hold a separate piece of my heart and my life would be that much dimmer without you." She took a deep breath and his mother seemed to age right before his eyes.

"I didn't handle Peyton's death well." She paused for a moment. "That was an understatement. I didn't handle her death at all. I shut down. I couldn't understand how a child so full of life could die. I didn't know what I had done for God to punish me the way he was doing."

Brandon was having a hard time reconciling the woman in her story to the mom he knew all of his life. She always seemed so strong and sure. She adored his dad which, if he were honest, confounded him sometimes.

"Why did you put dad out? What did he do?"

His mom gave him a small sad smile. It kind of favored a grimace. "It was me, Brandon. Your dad left me." He knew the look on his face mirrored his thoughts and right now she was seeing what thunderstruck looked like.

She began to chuckle. "Yeah, I knew that would throw you."

An unwelcome thought crept into his mind and he blanched even as he tried to dismiss it. Ashamed to voice his thoughts but compelled to know, he turned towards her. "Did you...were you?" How did you ask your mother if she'd been with someone else?

"No. I didn't have an affair. Your father is the only man I've ever loved, but with that said he is also one of the most stubborn men I know and after this week, he is second only to you."

Brandon scoffed, a little more than hurt by her observation.

"And third to me," she said with the throaty laugh that had lifted his heart for so many years. This only gave a small amount of appeasement.

"How long were you apart?"

"Six months and four days." He racked his brain trying to remember a time he looked for his dad and he wasn't there, but he couldn't. There was a time when his mother was ill, but it was only a vague memory now.

"Were you sick around that time?"

She shrugged her shoulders. "In a way. I wasn't well."

"I'm not sure now. It could have been three or four days after Peyton's funeral I went looking for your dad. He was so late coming to dinner I was starting to get worried. I worried about everything and everyone at that time. I came upon him lying prostrate in front of the altar in the chapel." Her voice went soft as though she were in the back of the chapel watching and he knew she was seeing it all over again.

"He wasn't just crying or weeping, he was wailing and screaming. Two words, over and over: 'My child, my child'."

Tears started running down her cheeks, but she seemed unaware of it.

"I'd never seen him or any man make such a sound. It was soul deep and caused goose bumps to form on my skin, and even as it frightened me it gave me a sense of camaraderie. How could a man mourn so deeply but still love God? I didn't think he could, and I was secretly but unabashedly elated."

If Brandon thought his mother's earlier admission shocked him it was nothing compared to what he was feeling now. He didn't know whether to sit and listen in hopes she'd redeemed herself, or run from the room for fear that she had something worse to confess.

"When he came home to bed that night I expected him to agree with me when I told him I was angry with God for allowing Peyton to die, but instead we fought like cats and dogs I told him I saw him in the chapel and called him a liar. I told him there was no way he could cry like that and expect to be comforted by the same being that caused his grief in the first place. I told him it was insane and something to the effect of him not being the man I thought he was. I told him I couldn't stand to look at him. Needless to say, that night he ended up sleeping on the couch and the next morning he packed some clothes and told me he would be staying at the hotel in town for a while. He would come home to be with your children to help with homework and sit through dinner, then he would leave."

"What happened? How did you get back together?"

"I wish I could say that I came to my senses on my own or that I listened close enough to any of the Sunday sermons, but nope. I was too ornery and stubborn for that, but then God knows just how to speak to even us stubborn folks. I know that Elias was praying because I wasn't."

Brandon still tried to give his mother the benefit of the doubt. "Well, it is hard listening to God through someone you are angry with."

His mother looked at him blankly for a moment then a light went on in her eyes. "Your dad sat himself down during the time we were apart. He called in a favor from a pastor from a sister church and utilized some of their elders.

Brandon was struck dumb. As long as he could remember, his father seemed to live to preach. Teaching and preaching were what he did.

"What did he do?"

"He sat on the front row with you children between us."

Brandon gave his head a small shake hoping the movement would help him absorb everything. Things were so different from what they'd seemed.

"What happened? How did you two get back together?"

She seemed lost in thought for a moment then spoke. "Remember Miranda Staton?"

"Yeah, she lived across the street when I was young. We all used to play with her cause she was an only child."

"Yes, well her father had a stroke that year. Elias was the one that found him slumped over the wheel of his car. He called 911 and took Carol and Miranda to the hospital. He called me when he got there so I wouldn't look for him for dinner. I called Ms. Crocher from across the street to watch your children, then I went to the hospital to see if Carol needed anything. I overheard him talking to Carol in the hall. He was trying to console her. She asked him how he did it. How did he continue to trust God even when he'd lost a child? I still remember what he said to her.

"I'd have less without Him than I would if I lost everything I hold most precious. Each child and the love of my life, Ava, are the greatest gifts He's given me, but who am I to curse the same being who gifted me with my jewels when one is taken out of my hands? Does it hurt? More than I can express. Do I wonder why? Of course. Do I trust that He can heal this hole my Peyton filled? Yes, because no one else can. Each morning that I wake up I am guaranteed a little more healing because I have His love and the love of my family to add a little more balm. If I were to reject His love I would be throwing away the very miracle that is my healing."

His mom's eyes came back to focus on him intently. "In a way that is exactly what my husband did for me. He gave me the opportunity to *allow* him to comfort me without bombarding me." Her eyes drifted to the carpet. "I still can't imagine what he went through those six months. He would only shrug his shoulders or say it was in the past whenever I would ask him about it."

Brandon saw her wipe at an escaping tear and moved closer to her. She put up a hand. "I need to finish." He opened his mouth to argue, but the look on her face stopped him.

"After regaining my composure, I let myself be known and asked Carol if she wanted me to take Miranda home so she could sleep in a bed. She said she would be grateful, but wondered if I could stay a little longer with her. Elias and I switched places and I told him I would meet him at home. He seemed surprised by the comment, but took the sleepy Miranda with him.

Carol sat back down in one of the waiting room chairs and was quiet. She looked like she had a lot on her mind, but then so did I. She started by asking me not to get offended by her prying into my business, but you know how it goes, as soon as someone tells you not to be offended your walls come up." She smiled sheepishly.

"Well, since we were pretty close friends and her husband was in recovery, I gave her a pass."

His mother's attempt to make light of the situation didn't go unnoticed. It was one of the traits he loved most about her. This latest revelation floored him, but he didn't know if he would have been able to believe it coming from anyone's mouth but hers.

"Carol came straight out and asked me why I was wasting moments of happiness. Of course, I gave her the 'I beg your pardon' stall because I wasn't sure what she was saying nor was I sure I wanted to hear it.

She said to me, "You have a wonderful husband who adores you and his children. You have children that love you and would do anything for you, and they do. Why are you giving up moments with them so you can keep your anger for what you've lost?"'

His mother shook her head. "I tell you Brandon, it was all I could do to remember I had given her a pass. Indignation, or rather, pride and hurt rose up in me so steep I could barely see around them, so I sat there silent.

"I told her she didn't know what she was talking about. I told her she didn't know what it was like losing a child. That Elias was right, it was like a hole in your soul that couldn't be filled. Carol just looked at me for a moment. I thought she would try and empathize because her husband was in the hospital or try and tell me, as others had, that God could help fill that void and I was all prepared with my comeback, but instead she asked me the question that finally got my attention. "What would you do if you outlived any of your other children or your husband? What would happen to that hole then?" I couldn't believe what she asked. I thought she was being insensitive and I was more than ready to revoke her friendship pass, but she interrupted me and kept going.

"I know you have heard it time and again that no man knows the hour Jesus is coming or when he will take his last breath. Children and husbands are not excluded, so why don't you fill yourself to overflowing now with their love and memories you can cherish rather than wait until it's too late to ask for more? You don't have to forget Peyton to continue to build memories with the rest of your family and participate fully in their lives again."

His mother sighed. "Of course, stubborn me asked how she knew I wasn't fully participating in my children's lives and who had made her an expert. Well, my good friend shut me down by telling me that over the last few hours she'd gotten her Ph.D. in regret and was hoping she didn't have to live with it for the rest of her life."

His mom placed her hands on either side of his face in a soothing but firm gesture. "You and I are very much alike, and so are you and your father. Stubborn, sensitive, and willing to give everything for the people they love." Brandon knew exactly where she was going with this.

"Mom," he began, but she cut him off by shushing him.

"Everyone dies, Baby. I'm sure if given a choice we would pick it to be late in life while we were sleeping, but we don't get that choice. What is not guaranteed is the type of love you have with Paige." He moved to extract himself from her hands, feeling suddenly claustrophobic.

"I need you to hear me because I believe you are making a mistake. Life is precious and valuable, and some of that value comes from the fact that we aren't in control of when it begins and ends. Don't waste it playing the martyr when you haven't been asked to do so."

"But mom," he said placing his hands over hers, but making no move to take them away, "wouldn't you chose to have a lifetime of love and grow old with someone like you are doing with dad rather than love someone and have them leave you after a few months or years?"

"Awww, Brandon," his mom said, sadness tingeing her voice. "To love a lifetime isn't measured by time, but how you love in that time. When Elias and I were apart, I would have taken six days of loving him with all I knew how rather than waste the six months we did. We were fortunate that that was all the time we lost. I had a chance to make it right with your dad. Take your chance with Paige."

"Mom, I love her so much. I don't want her to regret the time she spent with me."

"Then don't waste it. Whether you live for two more years or 62, you will always want more time with each other. This disease isn't signing your death certificate, only God can. God forbid, Paige could die before you. Would you regret knowing or loving her?"

Brandon shook his head to the negative. "So what are you going to do?" Brandon looked down at his watch. He still had four hours.

He stood up on wobbly legs, full of nervous energy. "I'm going to go tell her I was wrong and beg her to take me back."

His mom's elated smile turned quizzical. "What?"

"Are you going empty-handed?"

He stared at her, trying to discern her thoughts. "Do you mean flowers?"

His mom watched him, seemingly waiting for more. After a few minutes, she shook her head. "How long have I been here with you Brandon?"

His mother's tone made him feel 15 again. "Uh, two and a half weeks?"

"Two and a half weeks. That's 17 to 18 days of cleaning, feeding, taking care of you, doing your laundry, and picking up your mail."

Did she want to leave? What was she getting at? "And I'm thankful for every moment. I –"

"Shush," she said, interrupting him.

She shook her head again; slowly this time. "You know as a mother it isn't always easy to stay out of your children's lives when they are moving slowly or heaven forbid, going the wrong way, but I think you understand that sometimes interventions are important."

The doorbell rang and the confusion that Brandon felt at someone showing up unannounced was not mirrored on his mother's face.

"Mom, what did you do?"

She shrugged. "Reinforcements." Since she didn't make a move to answer the door, he got up and looked through the peephole.

He opened the door to Pastor Lawrence. "Hi Pastor." He didn't ask him what he was doing there but instead ushered him in.

"Pastor Lawrence, you remember my mother, Ava Tatum," he said only because the manners were deeply ingrained.

"Would you like to sit down or may I get you something to drink?" Brandon said headed towards the kitchen.

Pastor Lawrence, dressed in a pair of khaki slacks and a light sweater, looked very stylish and relaxed. "Actually, I was wondering if you could accompany me on an outing. I need to pick up a few things and I wanted to get your opinion."

Brandon was at a loss for words. Normally he would jump at the chance to get some one-on-one time with his pastor, especially if they were going outside of the church, but he needed to clear his mind so that he could ask Paige to take him back before she gave up on them. The thought of her fulfilling her threat to destroy the memory of them made him ill.

"I would really like to Pastor, but I need to take care of some personal business and I'm afraid it can't wait. Could I take a rain check?"

"Actually, no. I really need your help and I don't trust anyone else."

Brandon looked between Pastor Lawrence and his mother, and gave up all pretense of doing anything but trying to get to Paige.

"Look Pastor Lawrence, I really would like to go with you, but if you haven't heard yet, Paige and I had a pretty big...misunderstanding when she came back from her tour and I really need to clear things up with her."

"Mmmm." Pastor began stroking his chin. "As I hear it, you broke up with Paige because you didn't want to hurt her, which by the way is the dumbest thing I have heard in a while, and I hear some off the wall things."

Brandon was speechless. There was no arguing with that point, but even though there was more to it, he knew enough about Pastor Lawrence that he said things like he saw them and even if you didn't see it that way in the beginning, by the time you finished trying to state your case you found yourself seeing things his way. Brandon chose to save some precious time and just nodded.

"Yes, Pastor, and that is why I can't go with you. I need to make things right with her as soon as possible." He checked his watch. He still had to shower, shave, and from what his mom was hinting at, go to the flower shop and maybe the candy store.

Pastor Lawrence looked at his watch as well, stating they had plenty of time. It was still early in the day. "If you are going to try to get back a woman like my Paige, you have to come with more than what you left her with."

Were his mother and Pastor Lawrence in cahoots together?

"What do you suggest I do?"

"I suggest you come with me," Pastor Lawrence said without a hint of a smile.

Brandon let out a breath slowly. He was beginning to see that he wasn't going to be able to talk himself out of this.

"May I shower and change first?"

"By all means. I will just sit here and keep you mother company, but Brandon I don't have all day and neither do you by the way you started shuffling a moment ago."

Brandon nodded as he made his way to his room. He was happy he'd left his phone in his room to keep away from the temptation of calling Paige. He raced to his phone and started dialing as he turned on his tap. If he couldn't get there soon he could at least call her and let her know he was coming. The call went straight to voicemail and he worked to keep the panic from rising. He hung up and tried again hoping she might have been making a call of her own, but it went to voicemail again so he left a message.

"Paige, it's Brandon. Please don't delete this message. I want to tell you I'm sorry. I was wrong. I want to come and see you but I have some errand to run with Pastor Lawrence. I will be there as soon as I can, but I want to make sure you don't give up on us. I'm so sorry for what I said and what I put you through. I hope to see you soon and tell you all of this in person. Okay…I love you and I want us to stay together…okay…I love you…okay bye."

He hated leaving voice messages, if he wasn't being clocked by Pastor Lawrence he would have recorded it again. He decided to leave a text message as well.

Paige, I'm sorry. I was wrong. I want to be with you. I will be by later. He hit 'send' then threw the phone on the bed as he headed towards the shower.

*   *   *

Brandon looked at his watch for what he was sure was the 50th time as Pastor Lawrence looked between a navy blue, pinstriped, three button suit jacket and a slate gray, long style suit jacket.

His anxiety had ratcheted up about six notches between visiting the home of a widow in the first hour of their outing, Pastor Lawrence picking up Lady Menagerie's dry cleaning, purchasing a cake from a bakery that seemed to be on the other side of Los Angeles, and two ferns from a home improvement store. The dry cleaning was stored neatly in the back of the car, the cake was delivered to one of the Mothers of the church for a surprise baby shower she was giving for a young woman who'd joined the church six months prior. Her family consisted of a mother who was also pregnant, a father who was nonexistent, and a boyfriend who was slowly coming to the realization that in order to keep her they would have to get married. Pastor Lawrence and a few of the Elders had thrown him a 'Big Brother is Listening' party the weekend before. It was a type of intervention, but mostly an overabundance of love and advice for the man of the hour.

The ferns went on two separate gravesites, and now they were in a men's store while Pastor Lawrence picked out a new suit jacket for one of his Elder's birthday. The man loved his members. The man was a machine. The man was getting on his nerves.

He looked at his watch again. They were down by almost three hours now and he'd thought of leaving Pastor Lawrence to the rest of his outing and taking a taxi to Paige's house, but he had no clue how far he was from her home. He had never been on this side of Long Beach, *or was it San Pedro*, before.

He checked his phone again, but there was no answering text or phone call from Paige. He had no way of knowing if she'd gotten his call. He'd tried calling her again while Pastor Lawrence was in the cleaners and when they'd gone to the bakery, and even when they'd dropped off the cake, but it went to voicemail each time.

He took a few steadying breaths and willed Pastor Lawrence to hurry up. "I like the gray one," he called out, hoping his input might help Pastor make up his mind.

Pastor Lawrence looked up from the suits, eyeing him suspiciously then he looked back at the suits. Brandon wanted to sigh, but knew that would only draw unwanted attention. Finally, Pastor Lawrence placed the navy blue back on the rack and began moving towards the front.

Brandon stared at him with the hope that they would soon be on their way back taking up residence in his chest.

Pastor Lawrence looked back. "Are you ready? I have one more stop to make and I wanted to make sure we got there before it closed." Someone shot hope. Hope was laid out bleeding on its couch.

"Pastor Lawrence, I really appreciate this time with you, but I was hoping we might be done soon. I really need to speak to Paige."

"Did you call her?" Pastor Lawrence said as he maneuvered his way onto yet another freeway.

"Yes, but it keeps going to her voicemail." Brandon clenched his jaw to keep the comment from coming out like a whine.

"Keeps going to voicemail," he repeated.

"How many times have you called her?"

Brandon shrugged, not wanting to admit the true number. "A few." Pastor Lawrence stared at him for a very uncomfortable amount of time, given he was the one driving. Brandon looked at him a couple of times before he returned his attention to the road.

"Four times," Brandon said, just so Pastor Lawrence would keep most of his attention on the freeway.

"Hmm, and it went to voicemail each time? Maybe she's turned it off?"

The retort that came to Brandon's mind stuck to the roof of his mouth. He pressed his lips together to guarantee he didn't bite his pastor's head off. He looked out the passenger's side window and tried not to think of her screening her calls, purposefully not taking his. He had really messed up and if it wasn't for his mother, he'd still be sitting in the house, devastated. He was going to have to get her something really special for Mother's Day. Maybe he would call his dad tomorrow after he was breathing easier about Paige.

They exited the freeway long before he saw any familiar signs leading towards their part of town, and he wanted to growl in frustration. They made a couple of turns, all of which he'd paid little attention to, but as they pulled into a parking space in front of what looked like a row of boutiques, his mouth fell open.

"How did you know?" he said, turning to Pastor Lawrence as he put the car in park and unlocked the doors.

"Know what?" Pastor Lawrence asked, his eyes just a bit too wide and innocent looking.

Brandon tipped his head to the side barely refraining from sucking his teeth.

Pastor Lawrence chuckled. "Your mom picks up your mail, boy. If you want to keep a secret this big, you will have to do a lot better."

He put the car in park and rolled down the windows. "I think it's time we talked."

Brandon wanted to pout like he'd seen his niece do. He didn't have time talk. A small drop of perspiration rolled down his back. He didn't answer his pastor because he didn't want to give him any encouragement to talk.

"You don't want to know what we need to talk about?" Pastor asked.

Brandon bit his lip working hard not to cut his eyes.

The small quirk of Pastor Lawrence's lips told him he wasn't successful in hiding anything.

"Let me begin with this," Pastor unfolded a piece of chewing gum from its wrapper.

"Your actions this weekend told me you aren't worthy of my Paige. I think you take her love for you for granted, and you assume too much by her."

The pain to Brandon's heart was quick and sharp like being stabbed with a knife. This man that he looked up to had just dealt him a blow. He couldn't do anything but blink at him.

"I don't understand how, after we spoke the day you got your last report, that you could do such a thing to her."

Brandon felt shame wash over him, but the heat of anger wasn't too far behind.

"I have a mind to ask you if the cancer has spread to your brain, but that would be crass and insensitive."

Brandon gritted his teeth so hard the sound of his teeth grinding against each other almost drowned out what his pastor was saying.

"Imagine my supreme discontent when I walked in my house to find my spiritual daughter, who I love just as much as my flesh and blood, sitting knee-deep in tissue, threatening to leave her church family and the

266

town that she loves because you. You, who is confused and stuck in your own pit of woe, thought it would be best that the two of you parted." Pastor Lawrence started shaking his head.

"I pegged you for a much smarter man, Brandon."

"And I pegged you for a more compassionate man." The words were out of his mouth before he even finished the sentence in his head.

Pastor Lawrence turned towards him, staring at him so long Brandon squirmed inwardly.

"You're walking a fine line with me, Brandon. Sick or not, if you disrespect me again, I will leave you right here in this shopping center."

Brandon knew his retort would serve him up some trouble and he knew all he would be able to do was take his lashing because he was wrong, but it irked him to no end that his pastor would come at him this way, at this time, in this place in the middle of nowhere.

His future was on the line. Not his mortality, but his world that held Paige. He hadn't thought of his illness once since deciding to keep Paige in his life. He'd been too busy worrying over whether he was too late, and here was their pastor telling him he was disappointed in him. Well, he needed to get in line.

"I'm sorry," he mumbled.

His pastor watched him for a moment longer then touched a button that sent his seat back away from his steering wheel, slowly. He held it for so long the sound began to grate at Brandon's nerves. By the time he lifted his finger Brandon wanted to heave a sigh of relief, but he kept it inside, not wanting to let his pastor know how such a small thing could affect him.

"What was going through your head, Brandon?"

Brandon stared at the dashboard in front of him. He warred with the voice in his head stating that he didn't owe his pastor any answer. That this was between him and Paige, but he was clear-headed enough to know that he may need Pastor Lawrence to speak on his behalf, which wasn't going to happen without some cooperation.

Without looking away, he began to speak. He explained the helplessness he was feeling at having to call his mother to come and take care of him, the raw ache in his heart at not feeling like the same man Paige had fallen in love with. He shared his concern and reluctance to continue a relationship with Paige that may end with her just taking care of a body he was trapped in. He voiced his opinion on how unfair he thought it would be to subject her to such heartache.

"Well, if you think it is inevitable then why try to get back with her? If you think all she has to look forward to with you is pain, why go back on your decision?"

Brandon tried to think of everything his mother had told him, but his mind was in such a state of flux, all he could come up with was what kept reverberating in his heart.

"I love her too much."

"I would think that your love would cause you to sacrifice what you have together so that she can be happy with someone else. Perhaps with her other child's father in Chicago. They seemed to hit it off well."

Brandon turned so quickly he felt his neck protest. He felt the deep scowl bring his brows together. What was this man getting at? One moment he considered him less than a man because he'd sacrificed his relationship with Paige for her wellbeing, and the next moment he was throwing Mason in his face. There was only so much he could take.

"I just bared my soul to you, and you come back with some mess like that?" He said incredulously. "Mason is the one that isn't good enough for Paige. He wouldn't think twice at letting Paige take care of him until his dying breath. She would grow old quickly as his caregiver and nurse, and before he left he would probably try to get her to promise that she would never love anyone else."

"Well, at least he would give her enough respect to make her own decision. Did you ever think that she could make her own decision on whether or not to stay by your side if, and we will get back to that word later, if you succumbed to this disease? I don't think you did. Instead, you made all the decisions for her including the decision to give up on the two of you, and that is what takes you out of the running in my book. Paige deserves someone who won't give up on her."

"You keep saying I'm giving up like I'm choosing to walk away. I may die and leave her. I don't have a choice in that. It's God's choice, and I have to be able to accept it without a fight if that is to be His will."

Pastor Lawrence looked down at his folded hands for a while. Brandon could tell that he was deep in thought, but he wasn't sure he wanted to know what it was.

"I don't think that is the real issue here, Brandon. I think your pride is the issue." Brandon would have sputtered if he hadn't been rendered speechless.

"You said you felt helpless because your mother had to take care of you and you don't feel like the same man Paige fell in love with. Where did he go? Where did the praying, warring man of God go? If cancer has already taken him out, you might as well lay your sword down because you have already lost. Your character, faith, personality and emotional ties to Paige haven't been compromised by the cancer – you are destroying that all on your own.

So what if you feel sick to your stomach for a while and are low in energy because your body is fighting hard to stay alive? So what if you lose a little weight and are too weak to get to the toilet on your own? Your body houses your soul and spirit, and those won't change unless you cause them to," Pastor Lawrence stated with conviction.

"Are you telling me that your psyche wouldn't go through changes if you were faced with your mortality?"

"Of course they would, but I would hope I would make the decision to allow God to guide me through those changes so I would come out stronger in my faith and wiser in how I love my family. I have a hard time imagining what you are going through, but this is your test. We all go through them and each one has been specifically designed for us.

You know, Brandon, the one thing that struck me about you when we met in August was your confidence in hearing God's voice. It allowed me to feel comfortable in placing some of the men's needs before you, but with that confidence comes continued testing grounds and this is one of them. My concern is your lack of willingness to engage."

"I don't understand. I thought my pride was on the stand here. Now you say my confidence is an issue?"

"I'm going to need you to put down that wall for a while, Brandon. I'm trying to help you here."

"Stop talking to me like I'm a child," Brandon nearly growled.

"Son, you are a child. You are my child and I need you to listen to me otherwise there will be no future for you and Paige whether you live to see the ripe, old age of 80 or not." Pastor Lawrence's face brooked no argument.

Brandon, somewhat pacified by the 'son' comment, tried to calm down. He nodded his head, but kept his eyes trained on the doors of the store in front of their parking lot.

"Your pride is the very thing that is keeping you on the fence. You wear it like a preening peacock. You aren't afraid of Paige playing 'caregiver' to your 'waning invalid'. You are afraid of what you will look like to Paige and others if your body isn't healed. So much so, you are willing to play the martyr so that you can be the hero. It's time to stop playing roles and just be you. If God has told you that your body will not survive this, work through it then consider yourself blessed that He got your attention well before the last hour, and you have people who care for you and will surround you with their love and prayers.

If God hasn't told you that this is your last fight in this body, then you fight and you allow others to fight with you. You choose this day and you see it through to the end. I won't have you using my Paige like a yo-yo. She deserves more than that.

If you aren't sure either way, then you come clean and you allow people help you. It doesn't matter what people think about you. This is your life and your battle, and you need to make sure that your eyes and ears are open to the Lord's will because His goal is to receive glory from your life. He could care less what people see when they look upon your body, just as long as you fully represent Him in every other way. There is no room for fear of any kind here – fear of man not being an exception. If you're going to fight to live a long and healthy life in this body, do so. If you are going to fight to represent Him by taking hold of each moment you have left to praise Him during this transition, do so.

Now what I'm about to tell you may make you angry, but I think you need time to truly get yourself together. Paige is leaving tomorrow.

Brandon's blood pressure spiked. "She can't go. I changed my mind. She said I had 72 hours to change my mind, and I have. She can't go without knowing that I want us back together."

Pastor looked at him with something akin to an amused expression on his face. "She gave you 72 hours?"

"Yes, and I called before that deadline; today I called. I texted her and I left messages. She can't leave. I can't lose her now that I understand that the memories we make are gifts." He knew he was rambling, but the desperation that ran thick in his blood wouldn't allow him to think straight. He could only think about getting to her before she left.

"We have to go. You have to take me to her so I can tell her that I was wrong. She can't go. She said if she went, she wouldn't come back." Panic suffused his voice so that it came out as a hoarse whisper.

"Calm down, Brandon," Pastor Lawrence put a firm hand on his shoulder to still his movements.

"Paige needed some time away. She has some decisions to make as well. If you love her and want the best for her as you proclaim, then you will give her this time. You can't be selfish in this."

"But she wouldn't have had anything to think about if I hadn't broken up with her."

"Maybe not, but you can't stop this train once you put it in motion. You will have to see it through and give her the time to consider if you're worth it now."

Brandon thought of begging or bribing his pastor, but one look told him it wasn't going to happen. "How long is she going to be gone?"

"I don't know and neither does Lady Menagerie, so don't pester her."

"If she leaves tomorrow it means she's still in town. Can't I see her before she leaves?"

Pastor Lawrence gave him a look that said 'nice try'. What they were considering was pure torture. He didn't know if he could survive it.

"I suggest you get your house in order while she's gone, Brandon. You come to some decisions on your own because this is going to be a tough road and I need you to pull your own weight. If she decides to take you back, you better be willing to see it through."

Brandon nodded, feeling like a kid who was brought to a candy store, but was told he couldn't go in. He was pulled from his despair by the sound of the opening of the car door.

Pastor Lawrence pulled his long form from the car and after a few moments Brandon followed suit, pausing just before they reached the door of the jewelry store.

"Why are we here?"

Pastor Lawrence looked back at him. "I wanted to check your taste and you, my son, are in need of some serious reinforcements."

CHAPTER 25

Richard woke slowly to the sound of birds. He lifted a brow as he lazily opened an eye to assess the earliness of the morning. The cool breeze moving through the curtains wasn't always a clear indication of the time. One of the curtains moved just enough to allow him a glimpse at the blue hues painting the horizon. He always loved this time of morning. It was so peaceful, as if all the world was watching the day begin. When he was young, he could imagine all of nature holding its breath as the sun broke past the horizon; just those few seconds where everything was still.

The heaviness of the comforter and sheets fed his languid feelings. From what he could recall, he had no place to be at this moment. For a few more minutes, he could just be and breathe it all in.

Heavenly Father, I adore Your work. No one can paint peace like You can. No one can place joy anywhere but You. You are amazing. Thank You for my life. Thank You for my wife. Thank You for Your love. I am ever so grateful. I am standing on Your Word and promise that my wife's soul is in Your hands. Thank You for the small step and encouragement You have given me. I know it won't be an easy road, but I will remember it to encourage myself when things don't look like they are getting better.

He considered letting sleep claim him again but wanted to be awake when Victoria stirred. He was desperately hoping her desire to reach out to him wasn't a fleeting action interpreted by her as a momentary sign of weakness.

The stirring of the covers at his back alerted him to her gradual rise to consciousness. Victoria slept like a corpse. She rarely moved in her sleep and only began to shift or stretch when she was close to waking up in the morning. He was constantly reminded of it when they first got married. The scare she gave him almost sent him into shock. The last night of their honeymoon, he woke up wishing they had more time to themselves so he decided to take advantage of the moment but when his slow ministrations failed to rouse her or even cause her to shift, he tried tickling then shaking her but she was so deep into sleep, he became concerned.

He made sure she was breathing but watched her otherwise paralyzed state until she began to stir in the morning. Only then did his breathing even out.

When he asked her why she didn't tell him she slept so deep, she said her whole family was like that and since she'd never spent the night with anyone, she didn't know it was rare to sleep without moving.

Though he felt a little better after her explanation, he still found it uncomfortable to watch her sleep.

He slowly turned over to catch her first moments of recognition. It still had the impact of a punch to his gut. The small tilt to her lips as if she'd been caught stealing. Those light brown eyes still pulled him in so deep he didn't know which way was up.

"Morning," he greeted.

"Morning," she replied, barely opening her mouth. He shook his head, amazed that even after all this time she could feel shy about morning breath.

He lifted his hand to trace her cheek with his fingertips. The small creases at the edges of her eyes did nothing to take away from her beauty. She was still a stunningly beautiful woman that made him proud to have been the one she chose to spend her life with because he never deluded himself into thinking that his charm alone had won her heart. This was a woman who, even at 29, was self-reliant. She'd had money, land, an education and a family in the people that worked the ranch. There was little he could offer her that she didn't already have except his love, support, companionship, the ability to make her laugh, and teach her to absorb life instead of analyze it. He would have conquered any fear for her if he could have. Even now he had to smother the instinct to champion every challenge that came her way. If he'd had his way she would go to her grave believing Brian had lived a full and healthy life, but there were too many pieces to this puzzle that could find their way into her hands. He had to comfort himself in the thought that this was the way it had to be even as he watched her eyes grow cloudy with pain.

"Why did he do it?" Her quiet voice was full of emotion.

"I don't know." He shook his head slightly, silently vowing to continue until he found the answer for her.

He watched the vulnerable expression come to rest upon her features and knew her next words would break him wide open.

"My heart hurts." She looked away, her gaze landing somewhere around his collarbone. She avoided his eye as if she were embarrassed by her admission.

"It physically hurts," she continued after a deep sigh.

"I think I'm bleeding out somewhere," she glanced up at him briefly, her eyes overly bright.

"I used to think people were weak when they talked about dying from a broken heart. I was wrong... I could die from this pain." She shifted slightly and he felt her begin to retreat. He stretched his leg filling the space between them and wrapped his foot around her calf. His hand had found the crevice between her neck and shoulder, and began to stroke it gently. He wasn't giving up any ground.

"Rachael's death was hard. She was so full of life and love. The sun dimmed the day she died and it hasn't regained its glow for me since. I was so angry about the time we lost, about being so helpless. She bound my hands. She and Mason cut off my ability to help her get well."

He felt his body stiffen. "Do you really still believe that?"

"In a lot of ways, yes." She stared into his eyes, seeming to will him into understanding.

Richard, happy she wasn't as absolute in her answer as before, felt he could venture into this particular mind field with a hope of coming out unscathed.

"What if you'd gotten your way and had her under every microscope, probed, stuck, fed pills and herbal medicines, and flown from one specialist to another only to find there was nothing that could be done?"

"I would have known I'd done everything I could do."

He slid his hand to the nape of her neck to gain her attention.

"But you did. You did everything she was willing to let you do. Don't you see that she had everything she wanted? She was at home surrounded by the love and peace of the people that adored her. She was happy." He prayed the conviction in his voice would ring in her soul.

"Are you saying that she wouldn't have been happy with me in her life?" The tears she'd been valiantly holding back began to spill over.

He pulled her head closer, never releasing her nape and kissed her forehead, temple, and cheek.

"No. I am saying she wouldn't have been happy with the type of love you wanted her to accept. Your only concern was in saving her and as commendable as that is, it wasn't her main focus. I'm not saying she didn't struggle with it initially, but once she conquered the fear, embraced the peace she needed and had the understanding that she might only be healed in her transition, she decided to make each moment count, and she wasn't going to be able to do that on some cold metal table or in yet another MRI scanner. Instead, she took that time to make tapes and videos while Vivian was asleep so the child could have a piece of her to aid in the most important decisions of her life. And even though it crushed him when she left, she tried to fill Mason up with enough love to hold him until he could accept God's."

He tried to pull back to see if his words penetrated, but she wrapped herself around him, holding on tight. He accommodated her by pulling her in until there wasn't an inch of space between them. It was some time before he let his body go lax and just reveled in the feel of her allowing him to hold her.

"I've wanted to do this for so long, love."

"What?" she responded, not moving.

"Comfort you. Be let in. Listen while you trust me with your pain, anger, regret…all the emotions Rachael's death evoked."

"Why?"

"Because I need the same thing from you."

"I thought you had God for that…"

He listened, but didn't hear any derision behind the statement.

"My acceptance of God in my life was never meant to replace you. Just as God in Rachael's life wasn't meant to serve as a substitute for you."

Victoria's silence was telling.

He finally forced space between them so he could look her in the eye. "I love you, Victoria. I have loved you almost from the moment I met you."

"Almost?" Her eyes began to sparkle.

"Well it isn't as if you made it easy," he quipped. "But I love you more today than I did the day I married you, and that's a lot considering I wouldn't have believed I could love you more than I did at that moment. You supported my dreams, bore my child, we went into business together, and your beauty is only surpassed by your intellect. You are strong, formidably clever and your perseverance is daunting, but all of this was just icing.

For me, your ability to forgive was one of the things that drew me deeper into love with you. When you shared your past with me that first day in the diner, all I could think about was the fortitude and inner strength it must have taken not to crawl up in a corner and wait for life to end, but your love and continued desire for their acceptance is what caused me to want to champion you. That you could forgive them and love them enough to accept them back into your life at any time made me ashamed for the slights in my family that I struggled to forgive. You looked at them, but didn't condemn them. You assessed the situation and vowed to yourself that you would never do that to your children and for the most part, you haven't." Did he have the courage to tell her the rest?

"Most part?" She began to disengage her legs, but he clamped down on her because he needed her to stay long enough to hear him out.

"Yes. Rachael may be gone, but your granddaughter and son-in-law are still very much alive. If you think about it carefully and as objectively as you can, you will see that what you are doing to Mason is similar to what your parents did to you."

"It's not the same," she said indignantly, on her way to angry. He tried to head her off.

"I said 'similar', but the outcome would be the same. A parent that adores their child would be forced to give them up," he said tip-toeing around her emotions.

"But I only want what's best for her."

"And they only wanted what was best for you."

Victoria was silent for so long he was almost afraid he'd gone too far until her next question.

"Do you see me that way? Like them?"

"Aww, Baby, no. Not like them, but hurting." He held his breath, hoping she would at least receive that.

She was quiet again, just long enough for him to have to resume breathing.

"That'll teach you," she said flippantly.

He chuckled. "Touché."

She shrugged. "To be tabled?"

He wanted to press. He didn't know when they would be this open with each other again and it made him want to take advantage of this to show her how much she needed God, but he'd made that mistake before and she'd closed right up. He quelled the anxiousness and tried to listen.

"To be tabled," he repeated.

Her tremulous smile grew bright enough to reach her eyes, and he felt rewarded for his pause. When it dropped, he felt bereft.

"Will you find out what happened to my boy?"

He nodded. "Yes."

"Thank you," she replied, before laying her head on his chest.

*   *   *

"Did you research every part of that file?" Richard rubbed his hand over his short hair to the back of his neck where he squeezed, trying to release some of the tension from the call.

"Yes, sir," came the quick response on the other side of the line.

Richard let out a frustrated breath. He had his investigative team cover every part of the last house that the Gossenberg family lived in, but they were coming to dead ends.

The initial information was encouraging and removed any doubt that Brian was Victoria's son, but the military records and the continuous movement of the family was making it almost impossible to follow the boy's life in an uninterrupted pattern.

They already had information from Victoria regarding Brian's birth and adoption, but the trail went hazy after the family was transferred due to the father's promotion in the Air Force. From that point on, there were big gaps in the timeline.

He laid his palms flat on the desk. "So go over what you've discovered since the last time we spoke, Sam."

"Okay, we all know that Staff Sergeant William Gossenberg was stationed at Tinker Air Force Base near Oklahoma City when they adopted Brian. Four months later, he received orders to Arizona and we assumed they moved because our paper trail dried up for a moment. We didn't think he was special ops or anything, but it was almost like an eraser was scrubbed over their lives until they were transferred.

Five years after being stationed in Arizona, the family moved to South Carolina when he was promoted to Technical Sergeant but what we found after following Michael, Victoria's man, had us scratching our heads.

Michael was looking up records for a Grace Morganson which baffled us. Even in knowing your wife's penchant for controlling a situation, we couldn't understand why she was so interested in Paige's mother.

"From what Paige told me when I visited her in the hospital, Grace tried to blackmail Victoria. Paige believes it has something to do with Vivian's adoption arrangements, but she wasn't able to get more than that. I put Barry on it a few months ago, but you know how secretive Victoria can be. If she doesn't want something found, there is a good chance that it won't ever see the light of day."

"Oh, I guess that explains why she was focused on her, but we also found out that this Grace Morganson seemed to pop up from nowhere. There is very little information on her besides what Victoria came upon last year. I tried to follow some of those leads, but they came to dead ends. It's almost as if the file on her work history, marriages, and places she lived over the last few years were surface information used to lead people with the wrong information. Our first good break was on the records Michael stumbled upon in Colorado. It isn't unheard of with both of them being at that hospital, but it seems like one heck of a coincidence."

Richard's thoughts were heading in the same direction, but he couldn't even imagine the ramifications if this woman had anything to do with Brian's admittance in the psyche wing at State General.

"The few documents we found in the house lead us to Brian's stay in the mental wing of State General in Colorado Springs 26 years ago. It filled in more of the timeline."

"What about Brian's doctor and caseworker? Were you able to track them down?"

"Brian was admitted under 72-hour watch care and unfortunately since he was a minor, his files were sealed. The fact that Michael was able to find any paperwork on him was fortuitous. Either there was a breach from the inside or someone was very careless, but I'm not complaining."

Richard walked to the window, hoping the view from his study would calm him. "So where are we now?"

"Well, Michael is on to something. I don't think I should hinder his search. With Brian he may have hit a snag, but I don't foresee him allowing that to keep him from finding out what really happened. Something just doesn't smell right," Sam said more to himself.

"I don't understand how a boy with no history of mental instability could go from suicide watch to being institutionalized. From some of the paperwork we found, he was an 'A' student with a passion for biological science. The teachers' reports were stellar and he was even due to begin advanced courses the next year when he entered high school." Richard placed his hands in his pockets, needing to do something with them. He was torn between tampering with some of the information they'd found from the house, and telling Victoria everything.

"In regards to this Grace Morganson," Sam went on, "either she and her family are being protected, or she leads more than one life."

"What about her husband, Paige, or Paige's sister, um, Melanie? What about getting information on her through them?"

"That's what's so weird. It's like she has one name and life with them but outside of the house, she's another person. Truly, the only ones that may know anything about her is her family."

"You have information proving she worked outside of the home?"

"Yes. I thought Victoria told you?"

Richard's body went ridged. "Told me what?"

"The paperwork Michael found in regards to her being at the hospital. Grace wasn't just a patient at the time Brian was admitted. She worked there," Sam finished quietly.

Richard felt all the air leave his lungs. "What? Why wasn't I told?"

"We thought you knew. It was in the report Michael gave Victoria. We sent you a copy at the beginning of the year, plus a couple of pages Mya found when she was double-checking his findings."

Richard went back to his desk. He unlocked a drawer to his left and retrieved the file on Victoria's son. He scanned the papers until he came to the one with Grace Morganson's employee information. How had he missed that? A cold shiver crawled down his spine causing him to shudder. He turned to the next page and frowned. There was an area highlighted on the third page referring to her diagnosis. The file showed that a previous prognosis over a span of five years lead up to the need for the surgery scheduled in the documents.

"Richard?"

"Yeah, I see it, but ..." He turned to the previous page, narrowing his eyes to make sure he was reading the date correctly.

"You say Mya added some pages. Which ones were they?"

"Pages five through eight."

Richard read the noted pages and didn't know whether to sigh in relief that Victoria was not yet privy to this information or in regret that he may have to keep it from her.

Richard ran his hand down his face, weary with the thought of giving Victoria any more ammunition against Grace. He knew Paige would be caught in the crossfire.

"What's the matter Richard? You sound vexed," Sam asked, wariness in his voice.

That was an understatement. "If these dates are correct, Sam, Grace cannot be Paige's mother. If her fallopian tubes and ovaries were degenerating as it states in this report, not only would she be in excruciating pain, there would be no way for her to conceive."

The silence on the other line was deafening, but Richard was too caught up in his own thoughts for the woman who was already going through so much.

"Are you going to tell her?" The wariness in Sam's voice was now coated.

"Her who?" Richard worked his jaw convulsively.

"Victoria."

"No. I won't tell her unless I have absolutely no way of keeping it from her."

He sat back in the chair, rubbing his eyes. He was tempted to ask what could happen next but was too afraid of the answer.

"Meanwhile, this information can't get to Victoria."

"But Mya..." Sam began but didn't finish.

"Mya what?"

"On your orders, I told Mya to put the paperwork in a place Michael would happen upon. It could be hours or days."

"Well then, it sounds like you have a call to make. Tell Mya to extract that information before Michael gets a hold of it." The rock forming at the pit of his stomach took that moment to make itself known by squeezing his insides with an onslaught of cramps. He gritted his teeth and continued quickly.

"I know I told her I wasn't hindering her search but this can only cause pain. Do me a favor. Send Michael on a wild goose chase until I can think of how to deal with this. Give it a week."

"Are you sure?"

"No, but the alternative is unthinkable right now. If Victoria found out Paige wasn't Grace's daughter, she would use that information to exact revenge for Grace's attempt to bribe her. She won't care that Paige will be hurt in the process."

"I'll give Mya a call, but would you do me a favor?" He continued before Richard could answer. "Would you please give thought to handling this another way. You never know, this past week and a half may prove to have a life-changing effect on Victoria. Besides, as you said this effects Paige as well. The information may be better tolerated if it is presented with love and compassion. That way she can't be used as a pawn in this feud between Victoria and Grace."

Richard considered Sam's words briefly, but was too tired to delve into the different scenarios. "Just give Mya her instructions and I will be back in touch with you tomorrow to make sure Michael hasn't retrieved the information." He hung up before Sam could find another way to talk him into telling Victoria.

Richard sat in his chair, pressing his palms to the upholstered arms, struggling to stay seated when all he wanted to do was get up and walk over to the decanter of scotch and lift it to his mouth.

He closed his eyes against the temptation to look to that side of the room and when he couldn't take anymore, he began praying. *God help me. The right decision seems so wrong in this instance. I need Your help to see this through without making more of a mess of my marriage than it already is. I need Your strength God. I need Your wisdom.*

He sat there for a few more minutes beseeching God for any type of intervention that would take the decision out of his hands. Then he pulled out the Bible he kept in his desk and opened it to Romans 15:4-5. *For whatsoever things were written aforetime were written for our learning, that we through patience and comfort of the scriptures might have hope. Now the God of patience and consolation grant you to be likeminded one toward another according to Christ Jesus...*

He read the scripture over and over again, taking the peace he need from it, but two questions still remained. Would he ever be able to trust his wife with the information he found out today? If he didn't, would she forgive him for keeping it from her?

He'd just stood up when his cell phone rang. He pressed the call button. "Hello?"

"Hello, Richard?" said a familiar voice.

"Yes?"

"This is Mason."

"Oh, Mason, how are you doing? It's been a moment. How's my beautiful granddaughter?" He was happy to have something else to think about.

"Vivian is doing well. She is recovering wonderfully. She says the pain is almost gone in her back, but every now and then she does get an itching sensation and it 'drives her crazy'." He stated the last with his best 'Vivian' impression.

"She asked me yesterday if that was where the term 'Seven Year Itch' came from. It nearly cost me my tongue I bit it so hard trying not to laugh. When she gets older I am going to love reminding her about it."

The smile that came to Richard's face was the first of the day and he was grateful to Mason for the reprieve. "Well, you tell my gorgeous granddaughter that her itch is much less painful than the seven-year variety."

"Uh, yeah, I'll let you tell her that about ten years from now. Once you bring it up, she's going to hound you like a dog going after a bone to get its true meaning and I don't want you turning her against marriage at such an impressionable age."

"Consider me warned. So how's work? Have you given any more thought to joining my project?"

"Not as of yet and after what I have to tell you, you might change your mind."

"Oh. What's up, Mason?"

"I think I'm being blackmailed."

Richard got up from his chair and headed out of the study door.

"Richard? Are you still there?"

"Yes. I just needed a change of scenery," he said as he walked downstairs heading towards the back porch.

"Alright Mason, start talking."

He walked down the back steps and out to the barn to ensure he wouldn't be overheard. He listened to Mason's story with disappointment and regret, but by the time he was done the uncomfortable pressure in Richard's head had graduated into a full-fledged headache.

This had Victoria's name all over it. "I'm not sure what you want me to do? You've only just received the pictures. How do you know there will be more communication?" he asked, playing devil's advocate. "Maybe they were just taken to scare your idiot-self straight."

"Do you really believe that, Richard?"

Richard breathed heavily. "No, but you can't do anything about it until there's a demand. You've already slept in that bed, excuse the pun, and you can't undo it. If I were you I would hope it's the girl whose name you got wrong during the most inopportune time. Do you have any way to reach her, maybe go back to the bar you met her in?"

"That might be hard," Mason responded, his voice just above a whisper.

"Why?"

"I don't exactly remember what she looks like."

Richard was incredulous. "How do you do that?"

There was a slight pause on the line. "I was drunk, Richard."

"What about the pictures? Wasn't her face in the pictures?"

"Well, that's what made me think your wife might be involved. Though the pictures seemed professionally done, the only face in them was mine. The rest of the pictures were filled with, um, body parts, but they were taken in a way that I could recognize myself."

Richard didn't know how to respond to this, so he didn't. He gave a conciliatory grunt hoping it was enough to appease Mason.

Mason was quiet for a moment then as if it were being pulled from him, asked, "But what if it's more? What if it's your wife?"

Richard kicked at a small pile of discarded hay. "Well, like I said, there isn't much you can do until she, whoever she is, makes a move. We'll cross that road only if it becomes apparent that we have no other move. I'm going to give it to you straight, Mason. You messed up. You have a daughter to look after and with Victoria already on you about wanting custody of Vivian, this wasn't one of your smartest moves."

"I just want to know if I can count on you to take my side in this."

Richard huffed out his irritation. "I can't get in the middle of you two anymore. I'll try to feel Victoria out, and if those pictures are from her I'll try to get her to reconsider, but she's been through a lot lately and Victoria is like a wild animal when she's hurt: she lashes out. You may not want to be in arms reach when she decides to take a swing at you. Do yourself a favor, Mason, and be on your very best behavior. It may be the only thing that keeps Vivian with you for the foreseeable future."

"Mmm." Mason's reply was non-committal and Richard was ready to hang up with him when he spoke again.

"Paige is coming to town."

At first he thought he heard wrong, what with the previous conversation he'd had, she seemed emblazoned in his thoughts.

"What?"

"Paige is coming to Chicago. I spoke to her a couple of days ago. It sounds like she's making the rounds. She's going to spend a few days in Chicago. Vivian doesn't know yet. We'd thought it would be a great surprise."

Richard frowned to himself at the familiar way Mason spoke of Paige, as though they were a couple. He hoped he was reading more into it than was there.

"Mason, have you come to terms with the fact that Paige is with Brandon?"

There was a slight pause. "It's alright, Richard. I have come to terms with that. This is about Paige and Vivian."

Richard didn't believe it was that simple, but he would let it go.

"One other thing."

"Yep." Richard's growing impatience was starting to wear on him.

"She told me she was considering giving Victoria a call as well. She might be headed your way after seeing us…Vivian."

Richard stilled. "Victoria didn't say anything."

"Huh, maybe she changed her mind. After all, it would be a considerable amount of time spent away from her Brandon. One might start to think there's trouble in paradise."

Richard shook his head. "Mason, you need help. I suggest you get it before Paige gets there. I need to go. I'll call you back in a day or so and see how things are going, but if you receive any more special mail, call me."

"Okay, thanks Richard."

"Thank me by staying away from the bottle and giving more thought to following Vivian into church instead of just dropping her off."

"Did you two rehearse this?"

"Why? Is that what your daughter has been asking you to do?"

"I'll call you if anything comes up."

"Yeah, I thought so. Talk to you later, Mason."

Richard hung up the phone and sat in a chair near the tackle room. It seemed whether or not he asked, he was going to find out what else could happen. He just hoped he would be given a little time to digest it. Now more than before, he was determined to keep the information on Grace's past out of Victoria's reach.

Two hours later, he got the news he'd been desperately hoping to avoid. Michael had retrieved the paperwork. The question now was whether he would try and beat him in delivering the news, or let Michael tell her and play dumb.

CHAPTER 26

"Have these been authenticated?" Victoria asked, her heart beating a staccato in her chest.

"You wound me, Ms. Langston."

Victoria rolled her eyes. "Arrogant much? If I wanted a demonstration in prideful preening I would brced peacocks. Just answer the question."

There was some throat clearing on the other end. "Yes ma'am. The documents have been authenticated."

The thrill that Victoria felt upon reading the medical files on Grace were tempered by what this may mean to Paige. She'd grown fond of the child whose mannerisms gave her a vague sense of familiarity.

This would no doubt be another blow to her already shaken up world, but she would have her God to comfort her. Victoria drummed her fingertips along the polished desktop. Maybe if Paige pulled out of this with her faith in tack, Victoria might consider giving some thought to God's authenticity.

She'd been through the papers two and half times already and she still couldn't believe their good fortune. She finally had something to play with. A thought came to her, wrestling with her moment of bliss.

"Mike, have you heard any more on Paige's young man? Has there been a change in his condition?"

"No. My source said that he is now undergoing a more aggressive form of treatment in hopes that it will slow then stop the spread of the cancerous cells."

"Very well," she said, feeling a moment of compassion for the woman but shook it off almost violently. Whether Paige was Grace's biological child or not, she was still raised and by that fiend and there was a measure of influence Grace had as a mother.

Victoria would find a way to use it against her. She could taste her victory. The sound of papers shuffling on the other line brought her back to the conversation.

"What?"

"The package was delivered a couple of weeks ago as you asked. Would you like to proceed with the next step?"

It took her mind a moment to shift from Paige to Mason. There were so many variables involved now. Maybe she should come up with some type of code so they could talk about the different people she'd hired Mike to watch without saying their names over the line.

"No, give it a little more time. I'd rather keep him guessing for a while. I want to see him squirm. You just concentrate on finding more information on the woman and her family."

Now that she knew Grace wasn't Paige's mother, she wanted to know who was.

"I'm already on it."

"Did you notice anyone following you or around the area while you were going through the files?" Victoria asked, finally voicing a concern she'd had since Richard told her about his people.

"No. I was alone."

"Have you noticed anything out of the ordinary?"

The thoughtful silence suffused the line.

"No, Ms. Langston. Is there something I don't know about? Should I be concerned about being followed?"

"No, this information is extremely sensitive. I just wanted to make sure you take precautions with your health. You have become a useful tool that I wish to keep. Take care of yourself. Where are you headed next?"

"With the information I found I am more confident than ever that her secrets lie with the rest of the family. How one woman can have so little history is questionable at best. I'm going to see where the father was during a nine-month span up to Paige's birth and it might be a long shot, but I will see if her sister's schooling was disrupted as well."

"It sounds reasonable," Victoria said, already miles away.

"I'm sorry I haven't been able to find out any more about Mr. Gossenberg. I just knew that file would lead to more, but getting around some of that red tape with him being a juvenile is proving difficult."

"That's fine. I know you won't let it go until you have successfully uncovered every stone. You did good work. Call me if you find out more."

"Ms. Langston? Forgive me, but I'm getting the feeling…"

"I don't pay you to feel. Until next time," Victoria hung up.

She leaned back in her chair staring at the rays of sun casting themselves across the Berber carpet, dividing the room into triangles.

She was uncomfortable with Richard's people not being detectable by Mike. Her biggest worry was that they would discover who Mike was really investigating. She thought it over for a little bit longer and came to the conclusion that the information they found on Brian was from a completely different source, and there was nothing to prove that their investigation crossed Mike's during his initial research. It was possible they had no clue Grace was in the same hospital as Brian, but she didn't want to take the chance of Richard finding out.

Of course he knew how she felt about Grace. The reason for the search in the first place was to find damning information on Grace and bring irreparable damage to her life. This was definitely that, but people would be hurt in the process and she held that power in her hand. She breathed in its heady scent for a moment. Control over a family worth of lives were in her hand. She looked down at her own hand lying supine in her lap and thought of how empty it looked. No daughter, no son, no life from her womb moving forward in the gene pool. It would all end with her. With that sobering thought, she walked over to the windows overlooking the back garden and spied Richard walking back from the barn. When had he started looking so old? If she were a betting woman she would have bet her new Jimmy Chews that he was carrying the world on his shoulders. What was riding him so heavy? Had he found out more information about Brian? Did he know about Grace? He would tell her if he knew, wouldn't he? Didn't his God have rules against keeping secrets from spouses?

If only she could be sure Richard didn't know. She turned her bracelets, deep in thought. The last thing she needed was Richard's conscience getting in the way of her revenge.

She wondered how far he would go, for Paige's sake, to keep her from destroying Grace and decided she didn't want to take the chance of him trying to dissuade her, let alone give any more credence to their need for marital counseling.

She put the paperwork away in her desk safe, walked out of the library and out onto the veranda. She knew Richard would be livid if he found out what she was planning, but she would need to keep this information to herself until she formed a strategy. It was time to go feel out her husband and see just how "Christian-like" he was.

*   *   *

"Vickie."

Victoria turned in her chair on the veranda towards the sound of Richard's voice to her left.

"Mmmm?"

She saw the concern he was trying to hide and chose instead to look out on the east field and watch the rest of the sunrise. She had a fleeting thought that it was almost a shame she couldn't seem to wake up in time for this picture every morning. The day was so new and full of possibilities. This moment in time of each day gave the day the opportunity to be the very best or worst she'd ever have. At this hour in the morning, she knew the day had the potential to be the best or the worst she'd ever have.

"Vickie?"

"Yes, Richard," she responded without taking her eyes off of the horizon. The feel of Richard's hand on her arm finally drew her gaze to his.

"Talk to me, Victoria. You've been extremely quiet since yesterday afternoon, but when I ask you if there's anything bothering you, you look at me as if I were the one acting peculiar." His eyes were beseeching and soft. She nearly gave in, but she was way too close to figuring out if Richard was hiding something from her.

"Honey, I know this has been incredibly hard for you. I just don't want you to think you have to go through any of this alone. If there's anything I can do to give you comfort or help get your mind off of things for a little while, I will."

"This isn't some bad news relegated to my mind, Richard. This was one of my children, a part of me that I will never get back."

Richard moved to kneel in front of her, rubbing his hands up and down her calves. "Then let's talk about it. I lost a child as well and I need to talk about it. I need to talk with you. I need us to be able to comfort one another. I need you."

"You want to talk, Richard? Let's talk about the people you have working for you to find out more information on what happened to my son." She watched the shield come down over his eyes and she knew.

"What do you want to know other than what I told you? My people are working every angle to see if they can unearth a lead. As soon as I hear something regarding Brian I will tell you and if you don't get it from me, you'll get if from Mike. I told you I wasn't hindering his investigation."

Victoria gave him a sidelong glance. Was he placing the ball in her court, watching to see what decision she made? Was this his game? She covered her smirk with a quick kiss to his cheek.

"Yes, I remember you telling me. It's just so frustrating. We have so much at our disposal and this is the best we can come up with?"

She watched him watch her from her periphery. He was too busy trying to solve the puzzle before him to mask his expression. Pain, remorse, worry; it was all there.

"I've been putting this off for the last few days, but I am low on time now." That got her full attention. Her eyes zeroed in on his eyes and lips.

"I have to go out of town. Some things came up that I have to deal with now so it doesn't become a problem later. I would put it off, but you know better than most that a deal can go south with only a seconds notice. I think this will be a start of a new venture for my project in Kenya and if I can procure a viable aspect of this project now, I will avoid a lot of red tape in the future."

"When do you have to go?"

"The end of the week, the beginning of next at the latest."

Victoria hugged herself, her heavy cable-knit sweater suddenly unable to keep out even the softer breeze of the morning. As much as she wanted

287

him to stay, him leaving might work in her favor. She wondered if she could put her plan together that quickly. No, this couldn't be rushed. She had to think this through thoroughly. She needed to make sure that each scenario she plotted ended with her the victor.

She closed her eyes briefly.

"Don't do that."

She opened her eyes quickly, wondering what he thought she'd done.

"Don't shut me out. I need to know what you're thinking. No airs, no false bravado, no more lies. Show that mask to others if you must, but not to me." He slid his hand down her arm to take her fingers. "I need to know how you feel."

She thought about it carefully and decided to be as honest as she could. "Can't someone else go?"

It was Richard's turn to avert his eyes. When he began shaking his head, she wanted to push him away. What good was telling him and doing what he asked if she couldn't get what she needed in return?

"I need you to stay." She wasn't ready to deal with the thought of him being thousands of miles away just yet. While he was close, the dreams of Brian were bearable. She could concentrate on exacting her revenge on Grace. Life could move forward, but if he left so soon, she didn't have him as a safety net to keep the darkness at bay.

"Are you sure you can't put it off for a while longer?"

She realized she also needed him near her so she could make sure he was safe.

"How long will you be gone?" She avoided his eyes.

"Just one week. I was able to schedule the few meetings close enough to allow me to be back on a plane to you at the end of next week. Maybe you can come with me on my next trip to Kenya?"

She snorted in derision. "After all this time you still ask?" she said, hiding the small sigh of relief. *One week,* she could get through a week. *Many people could hold off sleep for a week.* Couldn't they? She tried encouraging herself.

Richard shrugged. "I keep hoping you will change your mind. You know me, I'm not one to give up easily."

"Why?" The word came from her in a rush.

Richard looked at her as if he were trying to look through her.

"Why do I hope you will one day go to Uganda or Kenya with me, or why don't I give up on you?"

Victoria took a deep breath and removed her fingers from his grasp. There was no way she could enter this territory while touching any part of him.

"Yes," she answered flippantly, daring him to correct her instead of answer her straight on.

"I want you to go with me because I think you will find the land and cultures extraordinarily beautiful, and it would be my honor to show it to you for the first time. I also admit that it would be nice to show you what I do." The last was delivered with a sheepish grin.

"I won't give up on you because God didn't give up on me."

Victoria sucked her teeth. "Really Richard, you expect me to believe that the reason you haven't divorced me is because of some mountaintop experience?"

Richard had shared the story of the traveling pastor with her a couple of days after he'd gotten home. It was one of many stories and thoughts he'd shared with her over the last two weeks. Once she'd showed the slightest bit of interest in his relationship with God he was like a faucet on full blast. If she were being honest, it wasn't all that bad and she was happy he'd come to some type of resolution where Rachael was concerned, even if it didn't make a great deal of sense to her. She just liked hearing his voice and with the timbre of excitement in which he spoke of God, it was soothing.

"I love you, Victoria, but my loving you was not nearly enough to keep us together. Just like keeping me close will not erase the fear you have of losing me to death as well." Since Victoria didn't want to focus on the latter part of the sentence, she chose to address his opinion of his love.

"Am I so abhorrent that it took a deity to help you love me again?"

"No, it took God to show me how to love myself so I could love you the right way." She thought about his words for a moment before she spoke.

"No one stays in the honeymoon stage for their whole marriage. People grow, they mature and experience things that change them. With everything we went through, you seemed to be doing a pretty good job before." She gave a ghost of a shrug then looked up to see the incredulous look stamped on his features.

"Don't delude yourself, Victoria. We were heading from separation to divorce. The growth and experience wasn't to blame. It was us and how we chose to deal with or avoid those experiences that brought us to that point."

She'd heard it all before. She chose to board up her feelings instead of leaking them all over the place like a sieve, and for this she was being judged. She couldn't turn to the bottle like he had; there would have been no one to run the ranch – and he called her 'selfish'. She had sacrificed, grieved, cried quietly in the night and had forgone the comfort she so desperately needed because he'd become more fragile than some of her

Frobisher eggs, but because he'd had stumbled drunk into a bible study one night and 'found God', he was now in a position to hand out advice on how to deal with grief? She was tempted to tell him he could take his God and his secrets and play psychologist elsewhere, but after all was said and done she was mortified to find that the thought of him leaving her evoked a paralyzing fear deep within her. She hated being so weak, but had yet to find a cure for him.

"You've made up your mind, Richard. Go take care of your orphans." She heard him expel a loud breath. She smiled on the inside. *Good,* neither one of them would leave this conversation satisfied.

Richard slowly rose to his full height. She could feel his eyes on her head, but she stubbornly refused to meet them. "Victoria, I know that there is a lot about me and my walk that you find perplexing and I'm willing to share and answer any questions you have, but don't take my love for God as a weakness. I am no one's puppet. I chose to love you and I pray the Lord continue to give me strength in that choice because woman, sometimes you make me wonder at my own sanity. Maybe I should leave tomorrow," he mumbled almost inaudibly.

She looked up into eyes the color of melted chocolate, wincing slightly at the flaring nostrils and hard set mouth. She instantly regretted goading him. She reached out, grasping his hand. "I'm sorry. I…" she rubbed her forehead with her other hand. "I just don't know if I'm coming or going lately. Please don't rush your departure. I will work harder to be more patient with you traveling, but you have to understand. Everyone I love and hold dear is slipping through my fingers and I'm feeling…" Should she admit it? Would he use it against her? No, this was Richard, her husband, "lost and vulnerable, and you can just imagine how fun that is for me." She looked up at him with a sheepish smile. "Please, I'm just asking for a little bit more patience and I give my word that I will not purposely provoke you."

She watched his eyes soften and he ran the back of the hand she held along her jawbone, but he didn't say anything when he disengaged their hands and left the veranda from the side door.

She let out a long deep breath. She was treading on thin ice, she could feel it, but she would not pass up the chance to show Grace who she'd messed with. She would just have to be extra careful to hide it from Richard because if her guess was right, he knew about Grace's surgery and the need for it.

She got up, deciding she would help Martha make a big breakfast for her husband and the hands on the land. For the next few days she would be the best wife any man could want. It would serve a few purposes. It would give him something to think about while he was away, make him want to come home as quickly as possible and soothe some of the feathers she'd ruffled today. She wondered if he still loved mandarin marmalade. That, plus the lilac chiffon negligée she'd been holding would be a start.

After four days of attentive pampering, long walks and talks, and plenty of reminders as to why Richard was the only man she would love, she kissed him goodbye at the door, her heart aching.

Why hadn't she done that sooner? Why hadn't he let her? She sat in her library drawing invisible hearts on her desk, working up the motivation to continue her plans where Grace was concerned. Richard always had a way of drawing all of her attention. He'd now been gone two days and she was still mooning over him like a lovesick teenager. She'd even lain in bed talking to him until almost 11 that evening. She was more confident than ever that their relationship was not only on more stable ground, but well on the mend. If she had ever learned to whistle and it wasn't a serious breach in etiquette, she would play herself a little tune.

She turned on her computer, planning on doing a little work before she planned out another strategy. Her phone rang and upon checking the time she knew it wasn't Richard. "Good Morning."

"Good Morning, Ms. Langston." She was instantly alert. Why was Michael calling her?

"I didn't expect to hear from you so soon?"

"I know. This is just routine, but I thought you might want to know if you already didn't."

"What is it?" She hated suspense of any kind.

"Paige Morganson is in Chicago."

She sat forward. "What? Are you sure it was her?"

"Yes. It looks like she came to visit the child."

Victoria took a deep breath. *Well, it was inevitable.* It wasn't like she could keep the two apart. If she had a daughter she just found out about, nothing short of death could keep her away.

"Well, thank you for the update. I'm sure they will have a lovely visit."

"There's one more thing." He paused. She sucked her teeth.

"Get on with it."

"Richard is here too."

Her mind stopped as did her heart then started up again in a flurry to catch up. The room tilted, but she took in a few deep breaths and it righted itself.

"Richard…"

"Mr. Langston. He arrived a couple of days ago."

That lying, scheming, sorry excuse for a… Michael broke into her silent tirade. "Mrs. Langston, did you hear me?"

"Yes, I did. Thank you for the information. I will speak to you later."

"Yes."

She hung up the phone before any more could be said. She was too stunned to know how she felt.

All this time she thought he was in Kenya, Richard was in Chicago. She thought back to their conversations regarding his trip and not once did he actually say he was going to Kenya, but she knew he'd hoped she'd just assume he was, and she had. She felt a moment of reluctant admiration for his plan. Her husband was no fool, but evidently she was. The rage built slowly and she was going to put it to good use.

It was obvious what he was there for. Now she had to find a way to get around it and get to Grace before Paige did.

She would deal with Richard later.

CHAPTER 27

He was rocked by the news he was hearing, and it wasn't even about himself. It took him back to those days after his father's death, and he hurt for the woman sitting ramrod straight in the oversized chair in front of him.

He'd been curious as to Richard's request to come and see him while Paige was in town. At first, he thought Richard was trying to play *bodyguard* but after hearing the bomb he just dropped on Paige, he almost wished it were so.

How he wanted to go to her, to pull her into his arms and be the one she held onto. He would do everything in his power to soothe the pain she was feeling.

He watched her features move from bewilderment to shock. "Are you sure? I mean…I know you think you're sure. No one would tell someone this without believing they were positive, but is it possible that you could be mistaken? Miracles do happen. I've witnessed them for myself –" She stopped herself.

Her eyes were unusually large in her face and her skin was slowly losing its glow. "Sick." She covered her mouth and ran from the room. He was on her heels. There had to be something he could do. He followed her into the bathroom where she'd barely made it to the commode before she was violently ill. He knew this part; he'd been here many times. He knew how to help. He opened one of Vivian's drawers full of ponytail holders, retrieved one along with a face cloth from the shelf. He placed it in the sink and turned on the cold water then gathered Paige's hair at her crown, making sure to avoid her face and secured it with the holder.

He then crouched down next to her and rubbed her back in slow circles, feeling the shivers race down her spine. When her body began to tremble, he rubbed harder and leaning back took the washcloth from the water, ringing the excess water out. Perspiration was just beading on her forehead when he placed the cool cloth against it.

Yes. This he knew how to do. This he could and would do well.

It was a full half hour before Paige slowly walked back into the living room on her own. Mason had left her after the first 15 minutes. He stayed long enough to make sure she didn't have anything left in her stomach and had recovered enough not to pass out and hit her head on anything.

He'd come back into the living room after pouring glasses of water and apple juice and putting some bread in the toaster, hoping Vivian had set the dial back to the right spot otherwise Paige would have really dark toast when she was through.

He sat in a chair located between the couch where Richard sat and the chair Paige had occupied. He watched Richard with his elbows resting on his thighs, head in hands. He couldn't imagine having to be the bearer of such awful news. Richard didn't seem to be fairing much better than Paige.

"My room has an en-suite bath if you need it."

Richard raised his head as if he'd forgotten Mason was there. After a moment, he just shook his head and placed it back in his hands. Mason leaned against the back of his chair trying hard to think of something comforting to say, but he was at a loss. Rachael was always better at these things. *'You did what you thought was right'* could blow up in his face, as could, *'It was either you or Victoria',* or *'You did the right thing', 'It was for the best', 'She has a right to know',* or the big daddy of them all: *'I would want to know'.* ...Because he wasn't sure he would. He knew he would have wanted to know that his father had another family way before he died and left them with nothing, but if he could have chosen never to have found out, he wasn't too sure he wouldn't have done just that. It was hell knowing you were second best, and it was miles away from first.

He shook himself away from his thoughts and brought his focus back to Richard. He stared at the broken man in front of him and opened his mouth as he tried to think of what Vivian would say when Richard spoke. "I didn't think it would be easy, but I didn't think it would be this hard."

He looked at Mason, his eyes sorrowful. "Did you see her face? She was pleading with me to take it back, to make it as though I'd never said anything. I was wrong. I should have let this play out naturally. Victoria may have decided not to do anything at all, and I just smashed a woman's life to pieces."

The man looked as though he would cry and Mason couldn't have that.

"What if you're wrong? What if Victoria planned to use Paige as the pawn to get Grace back for trying to blackmail her all of those years? You couldn't risk that happening, not with you knowing the truth."

"But I'm the reason why she found out. It was my investigative team that found the information."

"Then why did you give her the information?" Mason asked, puzzled and uneasy.

"I didn't, but I gave strict instructions for my team to leave things as they found them so as not to hinder Victoria's man or give him reason to think he was being followed. I've been at this a long time. I only recently shared my team's existence with Victoria because I needed to give her some devastating news as well. God, for once I wish I could find some news that was more helpful than harmful." He said the last as if he were praying.

Mason stewed on this for a moment. "Why would you want to leave this information for Victoria to find?"

"I didn't, but I was originally given the information when I was heading out of town. I only scanned the information but I didn't know what I was looking for. When I spoke to my people last week I told them to pull the evidence, but it was too late. Victoria's man had already come upon it."

"How do you know?"

"I've been tailing him since he was brought on her payroll and before you ask, I watched Victoria this past week. She knows; there is a destructive gleam in her eye when she thinks I'm not looking."

"And you love this woman?" Mason asked, a bit incredulous but more so in disgust and pity.

Richard sent him a look that told him he was trespassing. He raised his hands in surrender.

"Uh, was Victoria's man the one who took the pictures?"

"I'm not sure, but I have a hunch."

"If so, she may already know you're here."

Richard nodded his head in agreement. "It was a chance I had to take. If me trying to spare a woman like Paige from being used as a pawn in those women's games ends my marriage, then it isn't worth the paper the certificate is written on."

Mason's head was spinning. "Wow."

"Was she really going to use me to get back at Grace?"

They both looked up to see Paige disengage herself from the archway to the kitchen and walk slowly to her chair. Each step looked painful and Mason got up, bringing the glass of water with him to encourage her to take a few sips. She obediently complied after smiling her thanks.

He returned to his seat and watched her collect herself. Brandon better know how fortunate he was.

"I feel like I'm trapped in one of my own stories. Drama, intrigue, lies and betrayal, but I'm not seeing my happy ending." She looked up from the glass she'd been staring into.

"I think that was her ultimate plan. It still may be. Grace isn't aware we have this information."

"I'm really sorry, Paige. I thought I was doing the right thing by racing over here, but…"

Mason watched Paige stare at Richard as the sentence drifted into silence.

"What else do you know?"

"Not much. We only stumbled upon the information of your mother because she worked in the same hospital we were lead to by another case."

Paige's eyes narrowed in confusion. "My mom worked in a hospital? As what?"

Richard began to look extremely uncomfortable. "As a nurse, a L.V.N.," he added in a perfunctory manner.

Paige turned her head to the side, as if she were trying to see Richard clearly or work out a puzzle. "I think you have the wrong person. My mother was never a nurse. She didn't even like picking up after me when I was sick and that was just tissue." The room was deathly silent.

Mason looked back and forth between Richard and Paige feeling as though he were held hostage by a bizarre dream.

"Where was this hospital?" she asked.

"Colorado Springs."

She stared at Richard then blinked. "I was just there for a Christian Writer's Conference. There were thousands of people there." She got lost in her thoughts for a moment then abruptly shifted back. "Wouldn't I know if my family used to live in Colorado Springs?"

"Not if they didn't want you to."

Paige brought the glass back up to her lips with shaky hands.

Mason was compelled to know what brought back the trembling. "What are you thinking?"

Paige shook her head. "It's my writer's mind trying to take me places I'd rather not go."

"Where?" he asked.

"You know like, was I taken at birth? Was I a black market baby? If I'm not hers, why do I look like her? If they took me, why does she act like she never wanted me? Who are my real parents and do they know each other? Do I want to know the answers to any of these questions?" One moment she was rabbling on as if she were unable to stop herself, and the next she went statue still.

"Paige?" Mason inquired with quiet concern.

Paige responded in like fashion as if she were afraid to hear herself speak the next question. "If I'm not Grace's daughter, why didn't Melanie tell me?" For the first time since she'd received the information, tears sprang into her eyes. "Why would she keep something like this from me?" She looked at Richard again. "You have to be wrong. My sister loves me. She wouldn't keep this from me. She protects me and loves me. She's my best friend. She would never betray me like this. You have to be wrong...you have to..." She stopped because she was crying so hard the words became garbled.

Mason watched in abstract horror while he inwardly screamed to be released from this day-mare. This woman – no, the woman he loved – was being tortured and he didn't have the freedom to comfort her as he wanted. After her second heave, he stole a glance at Richard who looked as pale as a ghost.

He was torn for an instant, but got up and walked over to Paige. He pulled her to a standing position and hugged her to him. He watched Richard struggle to his feet and walk to the bathroom. The man had aged years inside of a few minutes.

Paige's body shook against his and he had to grit his teeth to resist the temptation to rub his hands along her back, nape and shoulders. She needed comforting, but this was as far as he could take it. He couldn't risk the fragile truce he'd won with himself in regards to her. He wanted no memory of how she felt or smelled to keep with him when she left. He would have to start all over. Instead, he resigned himself to patting her back every now and then. When he felt her regain a modicum of control, he stepped away and drew her back to the chair.

"I'm going to check on Richard. He isn't looking too well."

The slightest of nods told him Paige heard him. "Drink the rest of that water," he ordered over his should as he left the room.

He walked to the bathroom, but the door was ajar with no Richard in sight. He moved on to Vivian's room. He backtracked through the kitchen to the hallway leading to his room. He stopped short at the door listening to sounds of weeping. He pushed the door open slightly to reveal Richard sitting on the bench at the edge of his bed, shoulders shaking and head bowed. He stepped back, not wanting to be noticed.

Walking back down the hallway, Mason glanced at his watch. They had three more hours before Vivian came home. Hopefully most of these waterworks would be over before then. He walked back in the living room to find Paige gathering her things.

"What are you doing?"

"I need to go. I need to get my head together. I can't let Vivian see me like this. It'll scare her and I don't want her affected by this on any level."

"Do you forget that this is Vivian you're talking about? She is as intuitive and sensitive as Mother Theresa. It doesn't matter how much covering up you do; she sees through it. Believe me I know," he finished, shaking his head. "Besides, I don't think it would be good for you to go out by yourself just yet and I'm not sure what to do with Richard in my bedroom balling like a baby." He watched her straighten to her full height, purse and jacket forgotten.

"Where's your bedroom?" He looked at her and blinked a couple of times. How many times had he dreamed of her saying those very words? "Mason?" He shook himself at her voice.

"Uh, I don't know if he would welcome you going in there. He obviously wanted to be left alone to…" She pushed past him, walking towards the more private part of the house.

He followed at a distance, not sure what either of them would find when they reached his room, so he was surprised when he arrived and found Paige sitting next to Richard with her arms around him, comforting him. She was unbelievable. *Who did such a thing?* He wondered as she shushed Richard, telling him that everything was going to be alright. Then it came to him. She sounded like his daughter.

Mason sat at the kitchen table with Richard an hour and a half later after having finished a light lunch of soup and sandwiches, compliments of Richard. Silence had taken over his home the moment Paige had left to go freshen up at her hotel. She'd promised him at the door that she would be back in time for them to take Vivian to dinner. "I just need to go and put my game face on," she had said, shifting her things around much as she had done the day they'd met in the hospital. "Thank you for today."

He was totally confused and didn't mind voicing it. "The part where I invited Vivian's grandfather to come in and wreck your vacation time with your daughter, or when I sat there watching you crumble to pieces?"

Her smile was little more than a lopsided grimace. She reached out and laid a hand on his shoulder. "The part where you held my hair back and nursed me while I emptied the contents of my stomach, then kept me from sliding into a puddle on your living room floor."

He shrugged off her gratitude. "It's nothing a ponytail holder and a pair of strong arms couldn't handle. Besides, how would I get you out of the carpet? Sop you up with a biscuit?"

She laughed and it seemed to startle her. She sobered and her eyes softened. "You never fail to make me laugh. Even now when I feel like my world has been upended and I am holding on by my pinkies, you surprise a laugh out of me. Thank you Mason, truly."

"Yeah, yeah, yeah." He needed to change the subject or he would tell her she could thank him by moving to Chicago and staying with him and Vivian. "Are you going to talk to your sister when you get back to the hotel?"

She shook her head. "No, it's too raw. I wouldn't know what to say which means I would probably say the wrong thing and make the situation worse than it already is."

Mason couldn't imagine it getting much worse than what he'd witnessed but he nodded.

"Besides, this is something we will have to discuss in person. I'll see if I'm up to paying her a visit on the way back home."

"That's a lot of traveling," he stated, noting the fatigue circling her puffy eyes.

"You should see me when I'm on tour. Five states in two weeks, and don't get me started on any of the European circuits. We're talking countries then."

"You don't have to do that, you know...act flippant about any of this. It's alright if you show your vulnerability in front of me. Hell, it was almost all over my living room rug."

The smile left her face and he instantly regretted his words, but he wouldn't take them back.

"It's either laugh or cry right now, Mason, and I have a little girl to see tonight. I will cry later," he gave her a swift hug, more in apology than comfort then turned her around towards her waiting cab.

"See you later." He called out.

She lifted a hand high over her head in acknowledgment, but didn't turn around as she made her way to her ride.

Mason turned around and breathed in so deeply his shoulder's lifted as he reluctantly went in search of Richard.

"I wanted to hate her so much in that moment." Richard's voice brought him back to the present.

"I couldn't believe how low I'd sunk. To watch someone go through that kind of devastation and know you're the cause of it." He shook his head. "I did that. I hurt that poor woman because my wife is a heartless, unforgiving, revenge-driven machine.

She could have gone her whole life without knowing, but I took it upon myself to take her off of the chess board so she couldn't be used."

"Used by whom?"

"My wife. Oh how I wish I hated her." He placed his head in his hands which were propped on the table by his elbow.

Mason sat there listening, wondering why this man struggled with hating his wife. He had no problem at all hating the woman. She was evil. If Rachael had started showing signs of going to the 'dark side' he would have divorced her rather than put up with this.

He couldn't imagine the type of torture someone went through when they were married to someone so heinous.

"What are you going to do?"

Richard shrugged and Mason respected his silent wish to end the subject.

"Do you think Paige will come back for dinner with Vivian?" Mason asked after a few minutes went by.

"Yes. I think Vivian is the closest thing to Paige any of us will get for a while. I know I need it," Richard finished on a sigh.

"What do you think she'll do? Paige, I mean," Mason asked, wanting to get a believer's perspective on things. He knew what he would do, but Paige didn't seem the type to hire an assassin to take out her family. He hoped she would come back. No one who suffered the type of grievousness she had that day should be by themselves for too long.

"I don't know. She has a lot of decisions to make. I would have to do a great deal of praying before I could confront any of my family. There's no way to get around the emotions, and if they refuse to answer her questions, it could cause a rift to form between them."

"You don't think there already is?"

Richard lifted his head and stared at Mason. "Were you in this house the last couple of hours? Mason, I wrecked that woman's world with my news, but she didn't start to shatter until she realized that her sister kept the news from her. Melanie is ten years older than Paige; she had to know that Grace wasn't Paige's mother. To hear her tell it, Melanie was more of a mother to her than Grace ever was and I can't say I'm surprised, especially after finding out what Grace tried to go to Victoria." Richard was lost in conversation with himself. Mason was still back at Mel, reveling at the incredulity of it all.

When he'd met Melanie at the hospital, she'd hovered over Paige like a grizzly bear. He would be hard-pressed to find two sisters that loved and looked out for each more. To discover that one was keeping such life-altering secrets from the other shook what little belief he had in the institution of families. It dredged up memories better left buried with his mom and dad.

"I think Paige would find it hard not to forgive Mel. They've been through so much together and Mel still has full custody of Gladys. That bond is not so easily broken."

Mason didn't want to give the man anymore cause for concern, so he kept his mouth shut. Those family bonds weren't as strong as Richard would have liked to think.

*   *   *

Vivian talked a mile a minute, first to Paige then to Richard, then to anyone at the table that looked her way. Mason didn't remembered the last time she had so much to say and thought she was just happy to have someone besides him to converse with, but as the evening meal wore on he noticed that whenever the table got quiet she nervously looked around for something else to ease the silence.

Paige did her best by nodding and asking the appropriate questions. She even indulged Vivian in one of her newest loves: the creation of book covers. She pulled out her cell phone and quickly glanced at her dad to see if he would say something, but he was as grateful as Paige was for the distraction so he nodded his head in approval. She showed Paige what looked to be her portfolio, her finger swiping over the phone screen every few minutes as she explained the inspiration for the colors, font and its sizes, as well as backgrounds and superimposed pictures. When she moved into special effects, he glanced over at Richard who was watching them with amused affection.

Dinner along with dessert at Vivian's favorite ice cream store lasted about three hours. The most excruciating three hours he'd ever spent over dinner. The lasagna he'd barely finished sat like a ten-pound weight in his stomach. Thank goodness Paige was picking Vivian up early from school tomorrow for a spa day while he caught up on some work.

Richard had decided that instead of going back to the ranch he would go to his apartment in the city and catch up on some much-needed work at his office. Maybe he would hold some of those meetings he told Victoria about. He would spend one more night, and they would say their goodbyes in the morning.

Mason was wiped. The emotional strain had taken its toll on his body and mind. He just wanted to slip into oblivion and forget everything for a while.

A knock on his bedroom door had him groaning quietly. He was hoping she would wait until Paige left for some answers, but like him, her curiosity always got the better of her.

"Come in," he called out.

"Daddy?" Vivian poked her head in the door. He motioned for her to enter and she crossed the room and climbed up on the bed at his head.

He turned his face towards her watching as her stormy gray eyes misted over. "What baby?" He sat up so their faces were level.

"Mati...Ms. Paige is very sad, isn't she." This was more of a statement than a question so he just nodded his confirmation."

"Is it Mr. Brandon?"

He shook his head. "I don't believe so."

"It's on her heavy. I know she tried to hide it, but the light wasn't in her eyes."

"I know, Baby. Granddad Richard had some very hard news to give her and she is dealing with it the best way she can. One thing I do know is she's looking forward to spending time with you tomorrow, and tonight you made her feel heaps better."

"She said she would let me design her next book cover. She said I have a beautiful eye for detail. Isn't that great?" Her excitement was only slightly tempered by her worry.

"Yes, I think that's a wonderful opportunity. You should be proud of yourself. You do really good work. I was impressed that you've done so many."

"It's fun," she shrugged. "Daddy, remember when we prayed for Mati at Christmas time?"

He thought back to Vivian's agitation regarding some type of darkness she believed Paige would be going through. "Yes."

"I think we need to pray harder." He looked at his child, moved by this slightly eerie gift she had.

"Okay."

She took his hands and bowed her head. He watched her, still caught up in thought. She opened one eye, then the other.

"Aren't you going to pray with me?" she asked. He shook himself free of his immediate concern and bowed his head, closing his eyes. He listened to her praise God for the beautiful day they had and the knowledge He gave them to be able to come to Him in thanks for everything He gave them. She thanked God for him, her Granddad and her Mati, and then the prayer shifted over into a form of... *warring* was the only way he could describe it. When had she learned this? His wife would only pray like this when Vivian was ill or another person was dealing with heavy emotional issues. She started casting down demonic forces that he wasn't able to keep up with, but they sounded more like emotions. She prayed protection, strength, peace and joy over her Mati, and Mason sat there quietly agreeing. She prayed for a long time, sounding angry one moment and pleading the next. He even opened an eye once when her voice raised with such authority he had to make sure it was still her.

She prayed and he listened like that for minutes until she referred to him, and he began to focus more specifically on what she was saying. She was praying for grace and mercy for him and that *a crooked path be made straight?* He would have to ask her what that meant. She prayed that his heart would be lighter and that he would understand that he didn't have to do everything himself but that God wanted to do some things for him. She spoke of his generous heart and asked God to heal all of the broken pieces. Then she stopped abruptly. He opened his eyes to see her watching him with an odd expression. "What is it, Hun?"

"God said He's proud of how you took care of his own today. He said, 'You did well, My beloved.'" *Beloved?* He hadn't heard that term since he was a child. *Beloved.* He would hear it when he prayed, before...

Vivian placed her small palms on both sides of his face, forcing him to focus on her silver lit eyes. "He loves you, Daddy, very much. God loves you, Daddy, and I have to keep on saying it until you remember."

He nodded, swallowing against the tears. He *was* starting to remember, and it scared him.

CHAPTER 28

"Why would you do that? You love her." Paige stared at Richard from across their table in the small café they'd chosen to meet for breakfast before Richard headed out of town.

"Has all the pain you've been dealt gone to your head? She's not the same woman I married. I don't think I will ever see that woman again," he said, slowly stirring his second cup of coffee, staring into its depths hoping he would find the answers he was seeking.

"I can safely bet that you will never see that woman again," Paige replied, pushing her half-eaten breakfast croissant aside. "That is life; it changes people. How we change is up to us, but we change nonetheless."

"How can you expect me to want to go back to her after what I've told you?" He finally looked up with remorseful eyes.

She felt so bad for this man who had invested so much in his marriage to a woman who seemed hell bound. Anger stirred in her again when she remembered walking in on him the day before as he sobbed out his shame and regret at hurting her, when all he wanted to do was save her from his wife. If she had the time she would shake some sense into Victoria. The woman had a wonderfully compassionate man who adored her, and she was literally and figuratively killing their marriage.

She shrugged. "It isn't too far removed from what she said to me while I was in the hospital. She's hurting, Richard, and I mean in a layer-upon-layer kind of hurt. True, with you two being married for so long there have been disappointments and tragedies that you share. The difference is you learned how to deal with the pain, forgive yourself and others, and let it go. She never dealt with the pain. She just wrapped it in anger because it was a familiar emotion that at some point she found served her well. That first hurt is still there, lying under layers of disappointments, pain, and anger. It isn't easily erased or melted; it is a moment by moment decision by her to either hold onto her hate or trade it for love. I think if you give up now, you will only instill her fear that love will disappoint her."

"But I'm still there and she doesn't see me, she's so blinded by her drive to get your mom back. Even if I give her an ultimatum of picking me or continuing to go after Grace, I think she will pick Grace and I don't understand why."

"Well for one, an ultimatum is not a choice – it's a trap. When people find themselves trapped they either fight their way out or burrow into themselves for protection.

Two, if I've learned anything about Victoria it's that she is fiercely protective of her family –"

"Yeah, yeah, like a bulldog," Richard interrupted. If she didn't know better she would say he was close to sulking.

Paige smiled in spite of herself. "Yes, maybe, but that's because of life. There is something that happened to her early on that caused her to grasp and hold onto those she loves with such tenacity that when one slips through her fingers, she's unable to cope with what she sees as her own failure to protect them." She took a sip of her own coffee, blanching slightly at its cool temperature. She looked up for their server but was interrupted by his next question.

"How do you know?" He stared at her intently.

"Because people who have lost greatly and haven't come to terms with it hold on to what they have with a death grip. Unfortunately, she has failed to realize that God is the only one who can hold life and death in the palm of His hand."

Richard breathed a heavy sigh. "I honestly don't know what to do."

"What have you been doing?" She got the waitress's attention and signaled for another cup then returned her focus to Richard. He was still such a handsome man with his toffee-colored skin and brown eyes. She bet those eyes broke a few hearts in his younger days. She still had a hard time believing he was Victoria's husband. Their personalities seemed as opposite as their coloring. Where Victoria's light-as-cream complexion fit her delicate features, Richard was bronze, tall, and broad-shouldered. Paige wondered if Victoria ever tried to pass as white in her younger years. She could have succeeded, but the fact that she married a man so confident and proud of his heritage spoke volumes. There was truly more to Victoria that met the eye. It was a relief to see that in spite of the animosity she had for Mason and Grace, color played no part of it. She was a non-discriminating elitist. Paige chuckled to herself, but it quickly evaporated when she spied upon the look of desolation on Richard's face. She had almost forgotten his question she was so wrapped up in her own thoughts.

"What did you do to show her that your love was worth her putting her sword down?"

Richard looked uneasy and totally reluctant to share what seemed to be a very personal answer, but Paige reached across the table and placed her hand on his.

Richard opened his mouth and out flowed his plan to get Victoria to remember where they had begun as well as who she was. Paige was a little in love with him herself after he told about the cards he had one of their mutual friends deliver to her while he was out of town. "It seemed to be working, but I had to deliver some bad news when I came back for the gala."

"Oh, that's right. She told me about the gala. Was it extremely successful?"

Richard nodded. "Do you talk to my wife often?"

"No, maybe once a month."

"I had no clue." He shook his head seeming to pondering something. "Should you have?"

"No, I don't mean it that way. I'm just surprised she kept in touch with you what with you being Grace's daughter."

"Oh, that, well, I believe I convinced her in the hospital that I didn't have anything to do with Grace's attempt to blackmail her and because I don't see her as a threat, she doesn't see me as one."

Richard gave her a baffled look, but she was not in the mood to go into her history with him. "You were telling me how romantic and dreamy you were being towards your wife," she prompted.

He gave her a reluctant smile. "Well, so much for that project. The moment she got information on Grace, thoughts of reconciliation went out of the window and it all became covert operations surrounding the demise of Grace Morganson."

"Grace Morganson-Dillard. She got married New Year's Eve." "Speaking of names, did your mother have another one when she and your dad were married?"

"No, not that I recall." She tried to think back through Grace's family and didn't notice anything odd by their standards. "But I know Melanie wishes she had another name." She snorted distastefully then took a sip of her newly warmed coffee.

"Why?" Richard said, taking a sip of his own.

"Because they share the same name. Mel's middle name is Melanie. Her first name is Grace. I understand a man naming his first son after himself to continue the line, but it always struck me as odd that she would name her first daughter after herself."

Paige speaking more to herself than Richard, didn't realize the stillness on the other side of the table until the silence ran for a few seconds. She looked up to catch the remnants of shock on Richard's features.

"Are you alright?" She looked behind her then around the restaurant wondering if he'd seen something or someone. When her eyes returned to his, he seemed a little more composed.

"Yeah. I think I burned my tongue. It startled me that's all." He smiled sheepishly and averted his eyes.

She was sure there was something more, but if he didn't want to share she wouldn't push it. Anyway, she wanted to hear more about his plan to win back 'his' Victoria. It reminded her of Brandon. She missed him so much and was tempted to call him yesterday after getting the news about

Grace, but after more consideration she knew it wouldn't be fair to have their first conversation in a week and a half surround the newest devastation in her life, and she also knew he would get on the first plane to be by her side. She was going to have to make another trip to Atlanta before she went back to Los Angeles, and it was one better made on her own.

She took a deep breath and turned her undivided attention towards Richard, thinking that if she couldn't solve her own problems, why not help him solve his?

"You know, after we went through marriage counseling I was going to ask her to marry me?"

"You still can. If she is going to marriage counseling it means she's willing to fight for your marriage," Paige said, thinking the situation might be better than she originally thought.

"She agreed to go to counseling if it wasn't led by a Christian organization, but we haven't started yet. I had the trip to Uganda, and when I got back it just wasn't the right time."

"I think you should continue with your plan. It's a wonderful plan, a God-given plan."

"I agree," Richard said reluctantly. "But it seems like an uphill battle now. I don't know if I have it in me to continue to fight like this anymore. I'm just tired."

Paige nodded. "I know exactly what you mean. Brandon and I are going through something similar; so much so I had to get away for a while and clear my head so that I didn't throttle him the next time I saw him."

Richard looked puzzled. "I thought things were going pretty smoothly. By what Vivian tells me, you get all moony-eyed whenever she and Gladys brings him up so they do it regularly just to see your face," he chuckled.

Paige could feel her ears perk and tingle in embarrassment. Her daughters were way too observant.

"No need to feel embarrassed. It's nice to see two young people so in love." She looked up, opening her mouth to deny it but he spoke before her.

"And don't try to deny it. Rachael's ears used to do the same thing when she was young and got caught doing something she wasn't supposed to be doing."

Paige shrugged, trying to act nonchalant about the whole thing.

"Brandon decided to play the hero. He had good intentions, even if they were somewhat misguided and when I couldn't get him to change his mind, I called in some reinforcements and left town."

"What?" Richard looked befuddled.

"Let's just say my pastor and First Lady are sticking closer to him than ever before this week, and sharing plenty of wisdom."

"Wow...you're scary clever," Richard said with deep admiration.

Paige shrugged her shoulders. "See why you need to take my advice? Don't give up just yet. I don't think you're at the lost-cause stage. Besides, if Jesus decided that the amount of people that would acknowledge Him as Lord and Savior wasn't worth dying for, we wouldn't be here.

Richard leveled a stare on her. "I'm not Jesus."

"No you're not, but you were once just as lost as Victoria. She just needs a little more time."

"Why are you so concerned for a woman who has made it her goal to destroy your family?"

"Because I used to be just as hurt as you and just as angry as she is...and I am a sucker for happy endings. I really need a happy ending. I guess you could say I'm self-serving."

Richard continued to watch her without saying a word. She moved her now cold croissant back in front of her and continued with her meal. She was looking forward to spending the rest of the day with her daughter, getting all dolled up. Maybe after the spa they could go to the mall and buy new outfits so Vivian could model for her dad. Mason would make some woman a good husband one day, especially if he loved her like he loved their daughter. He put his heart and soul into it.

"So, Mason said you're planning on going to the city after this. How long do you think you're going to stay?"

Richard shook his head. "I'm not sure. I have a lot of things to think about and I'm pretty sure Victoria has been told that I'm here. It won't take much for her to put two and two together. I think I will give her about a week to cool off."

"What about you? Have you decided what you're going to do about Mel?"

"Not yet," she replied, thinking it would be nice if she could put it off.

"Well, I'm just a call away if you need anything," Richard offered, and Paige smiled at his generosity. She watched him grab the check the waitress had laid down during her last pass and pull out his wallet without a word.

"Would you like anything else?" he asked before placing the cash in the leather folder.

She shook her head to the negative. *Boy, they didn't make them like that anymore. Victoria had herself a jewel and if she didn't come to her senses soon she would lose him.* A thought sparked in her mind and she hid a mischievous grin behind her cup.

Maybe she would put her procrastination to some good use and take a slight detour before confronting her sister.

*   *   *

"Victoria," Paige greeted, standing in the doorway of the most beautiful home she'd ever seen.

"Paige," Victoria followed suit with the one-word greeting and opened the door wider to allow Paige entrance. She led Paige through the grand foyer, passed the curving staircase that seemed to go on forever, and down the marble floor hallway to what looked to be a library. She looked around the room and thought she could easily live in this one room.

"Have a seat, Paige." Victoria motioned to a pair of loveseats facing each other in the middle of the room.

Paige purposefully made her strides long and leisure, giving Victoria the hint that she had all the time in the world and she planned on taking it.

Paige sat down, still looking around trying to make out the titles on some of the spines on the shelves. When she turned her attention back to Victoria, the woman was watching her with a smug grin on her face.

"What brings you here, Paige?"

That was Victoria. Niceties be darned.

"You told me whenever I was in this part of the country I could come see you. I thought I would take you up on that offer."

Victoria's gaze grew assessing while her lips thinned into a line. "Is that all?"

"No," Paige said.

Victoria was silent for a moment, obviously waiting for her to continue, but she didn't.

"Are you going to share this information with me?"

Paige wanted to roll her eyes at Victoria's dramatics. "Of course I am going to share it with you, but first...how are you doing?"

Victoria's eyes narrowed slightly and her body tensed, but after a couple of seconds she relaxed herself from the neck down.

Paige filed it away in her mental Rolodex. She would ask her later how she did that.

"A little tired after the gala, but I'm recuperating nicely and yourself?"

"Not too well, but I heard your gala was the best yet and extremely successful."

"From whom did you hear this?" Victoria asked, smiling sweetly. *Saccharin has nothing on her,* Paige thought sardonically. This woman always brought out her rough edges. She'd have to be careful if she wanted to remain open to be used by God. It would be a shame to come all this way for nothing.

"Richard, but then you probably already know that. I ran into him while I was visiting Vivian a few days ago."

"And how would I know you saw my husband?"

"Oh, I'm sorry, I thought he would have mentioned it to you when the two of you spoke over the phone. My pastor calls my First Lady a couple times a day when they are apart, but you've been married much longer than they have. I guess it's different with everyone."

"Speaking of couples," Victoria interrupted Paige's rambling. "How are you and your young man doing? Do I hear wedding bells in your future?"

The blood ran cold in Paige's veins just before it went to scalding. She could see it in the woman's eyes if the smirk didn't give it away. She knew how they were doing. *How does she know?* She didn't want to play anymore.

She shrugged but didn't answer.

Victoria sighed. "Paige, what do you want?"

"I spoke to Richard –"

"I think we've established that," Victoria interrupted.

Paige relaxed her features into a blank stare, no longer willing to indulge her.

Victoria rolled her eyes. "Sorry. Go on."

"He told me he found information proving Grace wasn't my mother."

"Really?" She seemed momentarily surprised. "What does that have to do with me?" Victoria asked, blinking her eyes.

"He told me, because he believed you knew as well and would try to use me as some type of pawn to get back at Grace for trying to blackmail you."

Victoria nodded. "He said that, did he?" Though her eyes were downcast, Paige could make out the hurt.

"Is it true? Were you going to try and use me to get to Grace?"

Victoria raised her eyes, defiance and haughtiness glowing through them. "Yes."

"Even after I told you of our estrangement. Why? You thought she would care if I found out she wasn't my mother?"

"She must have had some reason for keeping it secret."

Paige pursed her lips together in thought. If nothing else, the woman was honest.

"Is that why you came? Because you wanted me to know you knew?"

Paige shook her head. "Psh. I could have called and asked you to desist for the rest of my family's sake, but I'm not holding out too much hope for that. Believe it or not, I really came here for you."

"Forgive me if I don't believe you, Paige. I have only been lied to, betrayed and cheated a handful of times in my life, but they were attention grabbers and I took notes. Why are you really here?"

Paige's shoulders slumped. She was actually hoping she wouldn't have to go this route.

"After Mason kept me from falling to pieces all over his living room from the realization that the person I loved and cherished most in the world was keeping secrets from me, he told me that Richard was in his room barely holding it together after witnessing my reaction. He was so shaken up by the pain he had caused me, I ended up trying to console him while he cried."

The stricken look that came upon Victoria's face let Paige know she was at least on the right road.

"What I came here to say is that you have a wonderful and caring husband. He is a man who puts other's need before himself. So much so he knew he was risking his marriage by coming to warn me yet he still did it."

Victoria opened her mouth to speak, but Paige interrupted her. "And before you say that he put another person before you, I need to make you aware of the fact that he blamed himself for finding the information in the first place. He thought that if he hadn't stumbled onto it then none of this would have happened, and you wouldn't be given the opportunity to make a choice that would cause you to hate what you saw in the mirror so much you couldn't forgive yourself. And he needs you to be able to forgive yourself."

Paige could tell the woman was struggling against asking, but she did it all the same. "Why?"

"Because he thinks that if you can't find your way back to loving yourself, the two of you won't have a chance at a truly happy marriage."

Paige noticed Victoria's hands tremble before she clasped them together. "He told you this?" She looked angry. Paige moved quickly to assuage it.

"No. He wouldn't talk about the intimacies of your marriage. He's too much of a gentleman for that. Not that I didn't ask. He mostly talked about himself, basically trying to prove me wrong in my assessment of him being such a rare jewel. It was then that I decided to come here to talk to you.

Your husband is hurting, but not as much as you, and you can't deny it because I saw it when you came to finish me off in the hospital with that whip of a tongue you have. I was barely coming out of a coma and you barged in with fire in your eyes and poison at your lips."

Paige was relieved to see the steel leave Victoria's eyes. It gave her the strength to continue. "There are quite a few things I admire about you Victoria. You are honest, extremely intelligent, loyal to the people you love –"

"If I needed a pep talk I would have called –"

"But that," Paige said, interrupting her as she pointed at Victoria's mouth, "that is dangerous, and before you use it on me this time I need to get a couple of things from my heart to your ears. If you want me to go afterward, I will go."

Victoria gave no inclination that she even heard Paige, but she didn't continue to try to talk over her, so Paige took that as her 'go' sign.

"I think you're an amazing woman with incredible strength and most of that probably comes from things you have gone through since you have such an air of confidence surrounding that strength. So, I don't need to talk you about those things. I want to talk about the things that surpass your strength and intelligence, the things you don't have a solution for."

"Why? What can you tell me about myself and what I'm missing when from where I stand, I have more than you?"

Paige nodded her head slightly, expecting some type of barb. After all, this was Victoria and she was on the defensive since Paige began the conversation about her husband.

"It may look like you have more than me. You have definitely accomplished a lot in your lifetime. I googled you," she added hastily, seeing the challenge come into Victoria's eyes.

"But I think I'd win this hands down."

"Really? What do you make in a year? Eighty, maybe a hundred thousand a year, and until recently you spent so much time at church you looked like a spinster in training. So you happened upon the daughter you gave away by being a generous giver or trying to get over that guilt trip, but don't make your life seem any more glorious than it is. Up until a few years ago, you were well on your way to following in Grace's footsteps."

"All of that is true. Thank you for that recap, by the way. It saved me some time in coming to my point." Paige took a deep breath to tamp down on some of her anger, trying to stay on course.

"I spent the first 14 years of my life so full of anger with self-destructive tendencies that the one person I picked to befriend was a predator. I spent the next five years using every man that even looked my way for the two to 20 minutes of fleshly heaven I could find. I didn't join my church or the eldership to achieve any type of title or life-long goal. I did it because I couldn't survive without Him and that was His perfect will for my life. Who was I to say 'no' to the only being known to me at the time to love me unconditionally and truly only want my happiness? I have peace, I know what it means to love myself, and I know that I will spend eternity with the very One whom I've fallen in love with after He saved me from myself. I can look in the mirror and love what I see, and for that I would trade everything I have.

I will hand it to you. You have some precious and invaluable jewels yourself. You have the love of a man who would do anything to see you happy to the point that he could admit that it was outside of his power and thus went to the One who could make it happen. That is a love I want for myself; a love that survives." Paige looked at Victoria beseechingly.

"I know preaching at you will get both of us frustrated so I am really hoping you just take this as some well-meaning advice."

"There was a time to fight and you did it well, but it's time to put away the sword and pick up your needle and thread because your husband has been bleeding for you. Each time you chose anger and revenge over healing, he paid the price either directly or indirectly. I even bet that when you were separated from your daughter those last few months that Mason told me about, Richard chose you. He stayed here with you.

You can't remain angry and hateful, and be open to all the possibilities of love. It is physically, emotionally, and spiritually impossible. Each time you chose to use anger as a shield, you were also locking him out. You just can't have it both ways. Something has to give and from what I saw in Chicago, if you don't let go of the anger, it will be your marriage."

"You can't really know what you're talking about. You barely know me or my husband."

Paige felt sorry for the woman, but she swallowed her pity. Actually, she was surprised she let her talk for that long without interruption.

"It only took a few moments in your presence to recognize the anger. I lived with it too long not to know all of the signs. I know it well. I grew up with it sitting on my shoulder, whispering in my ear, heating me when my heart grew cold. I fooled myself into thinking that I could hold on to it for those moments when people would try to hurt me, but truthfully it was like cancer eating away at all the other emotions. It ate at the happiness, satisfaction, peace, kindness, patience and love, leaving me bitter, resentful and judgmental, but I was quick to defend myself and quicker to protect my territory.

True, I barely know your husband, but I do know a hurting man when I see one, and your beautiful and compassionate husband is just that. It's time to put down the anger and mend your husband."

Paige was through. She didn't know what else to say, so she sat there and let it all sink in.

Victoria got up after a few moments and walked over to the floor-to-ceiling windows. Paige kept her eyes on her. After what seemed like 20 minutes, Victoria spoke.

"I've lived with it for so long. I don't know how to let it go."

Paige strained her ears. She wasn't sure she'd heard correctly so she remained quiet.

"Did Richard tell you I had a son before we got married?"

Paige shook her head, surprised Victoria was opening up; she realized Victoria couldn't see her so answered audibly, "No."

Victoria breathed in deeply and let it out slowly. "I fell in love with the wrong boy in college. I thought we had a future together, but he already had one planned out for him by his parents – girl and all.

By the time I caught on, I was pregnant. I had the baby and was determined to keep it, but my parents threatened to cut me off without a cent, which was fine for me, but I didn't know how I was going to give my child everything I thought he deserved. I let them and their pastor coerce me into giving up my child. My precious baby boy.

For many years I blamed God for taking my child away from me. The only thing that kept me standing upright was my anger. I wanted to show my parents that they were wrong – that I could take care of myself – and I did. I turned this place into a small town.

Two weeks ago, the night of the gala, I found out that my son was dead. He never made it to his 15th birthday." She stopped, seeming to breathe in the strength she needed to continue.

"I was nearly forced to give up my son by my parents…and a man of the cloth." The last was said with an ugly sneer. "He embarrassed me and told me I wasn't welcome because I chose to keep my child. He said I was flaunting my shameful ways and I was too selfish to give my child to a loving mother and father who could do better by him."

Paige couldn't contain the gasp that tore through her. No wonder Victoria hated all symbolisms of God.

Paige got up and walked over to her. "That man wasn't a true representative of God or Christ. He represented himself and used his pulpit to further his views. God doesn't embarrass or shame."

Victoria turned around with a sad smile on her lips. "You sound like Rachael." She touched Paige's shoulder. "I know he was abusing his authority and he wasn't a true man of God. I just can't seem to get over the fact that God didn't intervene on my behalf. He didn't touch my parent's hearts so they would change their minds and let me keep my child. That old pastor died in his sleep of a heart attack while my baby girl suffered for years and died a painful death, and she loved Him with her whole heart." Victoria's eyes began to shimmer. "He let my little boy die alone, thinking he had no other option but to take his own life. You talk of love and your God in the same sentence, but I don't see it."

"I do," Paige said in a whisper. Searching the woman's eyes, she continued. "I saw it in your husband's eyes when he would say your name." Paige wiped her eyes and rubbed her hands together. "You did a background check on me I'm sure so you know all the facts about the conception of my twins, but what you don't know is that I wasn't too much older than your son when I was ready to call it quits. I accepted a friend's invitation to Bible Study and ran smack dab into Jesus, only He was in the form of a little church mother." She reached out and touched Victoria's hand, needing the assurance that she had her attention.

"I'm going to tell you what she told me because it applies to you as well. God does love you and He is going to prove to you, you're worth it." Victoria went still and Paige knew denial was warring with the hope in her mind and heart. She waited.

"Worth what?" Victoria finally asked, and Paige smiled.

"Worth His Son's death on the cross. Jesus died on the cross so you don't have to. He took upon Himself every sin of mankind and sacrificed Himself so you wouldn't have to spend your life fighting battle after battle, nor spend your afterlife away from Him. Aren't you tired?" The dam broke and Victoria crumpled into Paige's arms.

"I am…" she spoke between racking sobs. "I'm so tired." She repeated it over and over again while Paige rocked her back and forth, praying silently.

When Paige felt Victoria getting heavy she walked her back over to the couch and retrieved some tissue from a side stand. "What do you think?" Paige asked after a few curt blows from Victoria.

"I think I want to sleep for a week."

"And when you wake up?"

"I want my husband," Victoria said fervently.

"Why?" Paige asked.

"Because I love him and I want to see what you saw when he talked about me."

"Why wait? I can show it to you now," Paige leaned over and pulled her compact Bible from her purse. She knew exactly where to go. Jeremiah 29:11, "For I know the plans I have for you, thus declares the Lord, plans to prosper you and not to harm you, plans to give you hope and a future."

"But how do I trust that He will do that when what I've experienced is so different?"

"Not that I am anything special, but I'm part of His intervention for you. From what I understand, you weren't going to step in anyone's church and the very appearance of a clergy made you squirm. Neither your daughter nor your granddaughter could convince you, even just in example. God has been trying to get your attention for a long time, Victoria. All it takes is one step and He'll do the rest."

Victoria took a deep breath that was still shaky with unshed tears. Paige watched and waited as Victoria slowly smoothed her hands along her slacks. Her attention was zeroed in on the Persian rug coming from underneath the couch they were sitting on. After what seemed like half an hour, she looked up at Paige with sorrowful eyes. "I'm not ready."

Paige swallowed her disappointment before Victoria could see it. This was Victoria's decision and it meant nothing if it was coerced or forced. Paige smiled warmly, wanting to convey her acceptance of the woman's decision.

"You know that I am here if you ever need to talk."

She nodded her head. Paige stayed and talked with Victoria into the early hours of the morning, then was put up in a guest bedroom. Every now and then she would see the woman Richard had talked about. She hoped he wouldn't give up on them, and even if Victoria wasn't ready to give her life to Christ, she would take into consideration all of the things they talked about. Victoria would have to lay aside her need for vengeance if she wanted to save her marriage.

When she awoke later that morning, she met Victoria downstairs for breakfast. Victoria took her on a tour of her grounds which were more extensive than Paige realized. It hurt her heart to see a woman with so much, be so unhappy.

Before she got in the car to head for the airport late that afternoon, she said one more thing she felt was terribly important to Victoria. "God is not just your husband's God. He is your God. He does love you."

Victoria only nodded.

They hugged goodbye and Paige felt like she was leaving a long lost sister. She had to wipe the tears away in order to see several times before she made it to the airport.

*   *   *

Paige called Mel from the airport. She hadn't truly decided to talk to her until she was booking her flight. Puzzled but pleasantly surprised, Mel told her she would be at the airport to pick her up. Paige knew that by the time she got in Gladys would be home, so she wouldn't be able to say anything until the next day.

She asked if Mel could take a sick day because there was something extremely important she needed to talk to her about, and Mel obliged her.

Throughout dinner, Mark threw her concerned glances. He'd commented on her color and the fatigue in her eyes, but she told him she was just doing too much. The lack of sleep was well worth seeing her girls though. He let it go after that and they fell into a comfortable and warm night mixed with board games and family-style selfies on Gladys' iPad.

Paige was sitting at the kitchen table when Mark walked through the kitchen on his way to take Gladys to school. He pulled her up and hugged her hard. "Whatever it is you're going through, take refuge in God. You look like you need some time to recuperate. Take that time and rest in Him."

She hugged him back. "Thank you, buddy."

He pulled on her hair as he backed out of the room, calling for Gladys to come down.

She wasn't too far behind with a messenger slung over one shoulder. "I wish you could stay longer."

"I know, I'm just popping through. I'll be back soon." She hugged Gladys to her tightly then let her go.

Thirty minutes passed before Mel came into the kitchen. She stopped short when she spotted Paige. "Oh, I thought you were still sleep."

"I wanted to say goodbye to Gladys before she went to school."

"Are you sure you don't want to stay one more night? We could all go to the movies," Mel began pulling out fixings for a large breakfast. Remembering her reaction when Richard told her, Paige opted for fruit and cottage cheese.

"Are you sure?"

"I'm sure."

Mel poured herself some coffee from the pot Paige had made earlier that morning. "What's this all about Paige? What's on your mind?"

No time like the present, Paige thought.

"While I was in Chicago visiting with Vivian and Mason, Richard, Victoria's husband, dropped by."

"Oh really? I bet that was a nice surprise. He seemed like a pleasant man from what you were telling me. I still can't believe you were able to share Christ with Victoria. Miracles still happen."

Before Melanie could go on, Paige interrupted her. "Richard came to Mason's to tell me that he'd found some records at a hospital in Colorado Springs disproving that fact that Grace is my mother."

Paige watched as Mel stilled at the mention of Colorado Springs.

Melanie swallowed hard. "Why would he come to you with that?"

Paige watched Mel closely. "I don't know, you tell me."

"I've never met the man. I don't know why he would say such things." Mel got up and went to the cabinet to retrieve some non-dairy creamer.

317

When she sat back down, she glanced at Paige briefly before concentrating on stirring her coffee.

"Mel, please, I didn't come here to confirm the truth. I just want to know why you kept it from me."

"Kept what from you?" She could see the restless energy thrumming through Mel.

"Kept the fact that Grace is not my mother from me. You were ten years old…you must have known. We're close Mel – too close for these types of secrets."

"I don't know what you're talking about," Mel said, but her hands were trembling when she brought the cup up to her lips.

"You're going to deny it?"

"There is nothing to deny. Have you seen the paperwork with this proof you're talking about?"

"Not initially, but Victoria showed it to me yesterday."

"Well, see there?" Mel got up. "It could be some elaborate hoax."

"Why would they go through all of that trouble, Mel? Come on, I thought we were close?"

"We are close. I love you and you love me. We've always had each other's backs. Why would you allow someone from the outside come between us with something this sensational?"

"Because you're lying, Mel," Paige said softly.

Mel went still as she stared across the room at a very calm and resigned Paige.

"You're so sure?"

"Sure enough to call you out on it."

"So, if you're so sure I kept this secret from you all of this time, what makes you think I'm going to tell you the truth about why I kept it from you? Right now I'm just a liar to you."

"Don't make this about you, Mel. I just want to know why. It's not a big secret that Grace can't stand me, and now I have one of the pieces. I just want to know why you didn't share it with me even after I left the house."

Mel was silent.

"Well, if you can't tell me why, do you know who my real mother is?"

Mel didn't move nor did her expression change.

Paige got up from the table. "Alright, if you aren't going to tell me I will have to find my own answers."

Mel moved forward. "How are you going to do that?"

Paige gave her a mock salute. "I'm a writer, Mel. I do a lot of research. It shouldn't be too hard to come up with some answers. I can also go back to Richard and see if he has anything more to tell me," she tried to pass Mel on her way out of the kitchen.

"Where are you going?" Mel reached out and grasped her forearm.

"I'm catching a cab to the airport. I can wait there for my flight."

"Don't do that, Paige. It doesn't have to be like this. Why do you really need to know anyway? You've done well thus far." Paige could hear the pleading in Mel's voice.

"How can you say that, Ms. 'It-would-be-better-if-I-take-Gladys-so-she-will-still-be-in-the-family'? You know what family means to me, and you're going to stand there and tell me it doesn't matter?"

"No, it doesn't because I'm your family."

Paige scowled but said nothing. She yanked her arm from Mel's grasp and went upstairs to collect her things.

As she was coming down, she heard Mel on the phone with someone. She caught the end of the conversation and anger flooded her at her sister's betrayal.

"Did you call her?"

Mel nodded. "I thought she needed to know."

"Oh you thought she needed to know? You are a piece of work, Mel. You thought that woman needed to know." She pulled her bag through the hall. "What about me, Mel? You didn't think I needed to know? I had to learn about it from someone completely outside of our family.

Get out of my way!" She growled when Mel stepped in front of her.

"Now Paige, don't be like this. I don't want you leaving here angry."

"It's way too late for that, Mel. I am way past angry and well on my way to incensed." She burrowed her way past Mel, luggage in tow, to the front door.

She turned back before she opened the door. "You know who my mother is. Why don't you tell me so I don't have to find it out from another source?"

Mel shook her head.

"So help me Mel, if I have to find another way, we will never be the same." Mel's chin began to quiver.

"Just tell me who my mother is!" Paige half-pleaded, half-yelled.

Mel's chin rose slightly but she kept her lips close. "I can't tell you." Her chin trembled slightly, but she held her resolve.

"You can't or you won't?"

"Does it matter?"

"Yes."

"Both."

Paige stared at her for a long moment then turned on her heal and walked out the door.

"Paige please, don't go like this. We can talk."

Paige whipped around, her vision going red. "What are we going to talk about, Mel? The one thing I want answers to, you aren't willing to give me. I don't see where we have any place to go with this." She turned back around.

"I promised. I promised I wouldn't tell. Please Paige, I love you."

Paige's grip on her purse was the only thing grounding her. "You promised who?" Mel quickly shook her head. "Who did you promise, Mel? Grace? Did you promise Grace you wouldn't tell me who my mother was? Grace, who never treated me like a part of this family. Grace, who never gave two cents for me. What does she have on you? Why does she keep you so close?" Paige saw the stark fear in Mel's eyes even as she shook her head to deny it. "What Mel? Why is what she says so much more important than our relationship?"

"It's not." Tears began streaming unnoticed down Mel's eyes.

"Then prove it. Who is my mother?"

Mel bowed her head, growing silent.

Paige took a deep breath. "Alright Mel," she said in a cool voice. Mel's head snapped up, her eyes warily assessing Paige.

"You want to pick sides? I don't want my daughter being influenced by her. If I can't trust you to keep her out of that woman's grasp, I will have to take measures of my own."

She began walking down the side path to the sidewalk.

"What do you mean 'measures'? What are you going to do?"

"I'm going to sue you for custody of Gladys. Whatever Grace has over you is too strong for me to trust you to make the right decision by my child. The lines are so clear now I wonder why I never saw them before."

"You can't do that."

"Just watch me."

"Paige, I'm begging you. Don't do this!"

"Begging me? I begged you! I begged you to love me enough to give me the answers you have been holding back from me for 26 years. Twenty-six years, I thought I belonged...well at least to you, but darned if my eyes aren't open now. Goodbye, Melanie. Look to hear from my lawyer."

"You can't do that. Think of Gladys. You'll risk her, your family, and our relationship over this?" Mel said, coming closer. Paige stepped back as she saw the taxi come into view.

"Your choice, Mel. It's your choice."

Mel reached out and grabbed her arm. "Paige, you don't know what you're asking. I can't tell you."

"Then we have nothing more to say to each other."

She pushed Mel away as hard as she could and ran for the back of the cab then locked herself in. She watched as Mel tried for the handle, but the cab driver told her if she damaged the car in any way he would call the police. She ran around the car screaming for Paige to get out, but Paige could only watch her in shock.

When she couldn't watch anymore she closed her eyes. She felt the driver get in and pull away, and the sounds of Mel's crying grew further and further until they faded completely.

Six o'clock that evening she let herself into her apartment, dragging her suitcase behind her. All she wanted was a bath and the bed, but she had to make one call first.

She hit speed dial on her landline. When a woman's voice come over the line, she spoke quickly. "Hi Lady Menagerie, I'm home. I am exhausted so I am going to take a bath and go to sleep for the rest of the evening. I just wanted to call and let you know I made it in safe, but I'm going to disconnect my phone for the night, okay?"

"Paige, this isn't like you."

"In the morning please. I just called so you wouldn't worry."

"Okay. I love you."

"I love you too." She set the handset down. She wasn't in her bedroom before the first tear fell. She'd almost made it.

CHAPTER 29

Brandon ran up the steps to Paige's apartment, flowers in hand and heart in his throat. He smoothed his shirt with his hand as he took a deep breath before he knocked. He looked down at his shoes as he listened intently for her footsteps on the other side of the door. After a few moments, he knocked louder and brought his head even closer to the door. He stepped back slightly to see if he could make out any shadows moving across her peephole.

Paige had been gone a week and a half, and he was shredded. Half the time he didn't know if he was coming or going. His mother had extended her stay, more out of her concern for his sanity, he guessed, than anything else.

So here he was after a brief call from Paige that morning asking him to come by. It was the only call he'd gotten in the time she was gone and that had nearly sent him over the edge. If it weren't for Dominy's continual encouragement and his semi-weekly meetings with Pastor Lawrence, he would have tracked her down and forced her to take him back.

His nervousness was replaced with a deep shiver of doubt. What if she'd asked him to come over because she wanted to end it? No, Pastor Lawrence wouldn't have continued to minister to him in the ways a healthy relationship would go, and he definitely wouldn't have taken him to his jewelers.

He still remembered his reluctance at showing Pastor Lawrence his choice of ring, but how did you tell your pastor 'no' when he was trying to help you? By the next Wednesday when he'd not heard from Paige, he was climbing the walls. He and Pastor Lawrence had returned to the shop so he could pick up the newly engraved ring.

"I'm not sure of this, Pastor Lawrence. I can't even get her to call me back. Do I really want to set myself up for a rejection of that magnitude?"

"You set yourself up the moment you uttered the words 'we are through'. She doesn't have to take you back, you know. There is no guarantee that she hasn't been sitting there rethinking her relationship with you. You never give a woman that much time to mull over things."

"Way to boost my confidence level, Pastor."

"I'm here whenever you need me."

The sound of movement on the other side of the door brought him out of reverie. His heart picked up even more. At this rate, if he didn't calm himself down, he would surely give himself a heart attack.

He heard the deadbolt disengage and held his breath until the door opened enough for him to see her.

He nearly gasped at what he saw. Paige's eyes were red and puffy with purple hued circles underneath. Her hair was caught in a messy bun at the crown of her head and she wore a pair of faded jeans and a zip-up cardigan. He also noticed she'd lost weight. How did you lose noticeable weight in two weeks? With all of that though, she was beautiful to him.

"Hi Brandon." She breathed the greeting, sounding tired. He had to fight to keep from assuming more than he already was. Had he done this to her or had her trip to visit her children not gone as well as she'd planned?

"Hi Paige. You look beautiful."

She snorted in disbelief, but stepped back to let him enter her apartment.

Instead of going straight to the couch, he turned and watched her slowly close the door and lock it. Everything she did seemed so purposeful as if she were putting all of her concentration into each movement.

This had to be more than what was going on between them. The last time he had seen her she was full of so much fire and life, it was disconcerting to see her so stoic.

She turned and seemed surprised to see him still standing there. He handed her the bouquet of flowers and watched her place her nose to them as if she were on automatic pilot. She offered him a whisper of a smile and motioned for him to have a seat on the couch while she saw to the flowers. When she reentered the living room, she sat across from him in her chair. With her feet underneath her and her face scrubbed free of make-up she could have passed for 18, but it was the lost look in her eyes that shook him. What had happened while they were apart?

"Paige?" All he could get out was the one word. It blanketed a lot of the questions roaming his mind at that moment, but he didn't want to overwhelm her.

He watched as she rung her hands together and he had to control his desire to cross over the coffee table and take her in his arms. He just didn't know if she would let him since he'd given up that right.

She took a deep shuddering breath and began speaking in a disassociated fashion. "I got your messages, both email and voicemails. I see you got in under my deadline."

"Then why didn't you return my calls?" he asked before he knew he was speaking.

Her gaze was piercing. "Because there shouldn't have been a reason for the deadline in the first place."

He knew what she said was the truth. He'd heard it from Pastor Lawrence more times than he could count the last few days, as well as from his own heart. He nodded, not speaking. This seemed to placate her because her features softened the slightest bit.

"I know you love me and want the best for me. I know you never want to be the cause of pain for me, but you were. You hurt me so much, Brandon." Her eyes became misty and he saw her swallow convulsively. It was at that moment that he understood the true magnitude of his actions. How did he think he could just waltz back in and try to pick up where they'd left off?

"I'm so sorry, I was wrong." He let the sincerity in his voice show in his eyes. He didn't know what he would do if she didn't believe him. In the short time they had been together, she'd become an integral part of his life. He could barely remember life without her and the part he did seemed dim. He could live without her if he must, but he didn't want to. He was sure God would be there to comfort him but he had to admit, for the first time since he'd begun working on a personal relationship with God, He chose the woman. The only consoling factor was that he already knew God meant for them to be together.

It was her turn to nod. "I know, you said it about three dozen times in your voicemails. I know you're sorry, but what I don't know is what will keep you from doing this again. What if you get worse before you get better? Are you going to place our relationship on the sidelines until you feel all is clear with your health? Are you still going to try to hide your physical vulnerability from me?"

He wanted to adamantly deny it all. He knew his mind and heart now. He was sure that no matter what happened, he wanted her with him every minute – every second – of his life if she would take him back, but he also knew it would be just words until he could prove it to her and for that, he needed time.

"I could say anything to you right now, but the only thing that will prove it to you will be the time we spend together. I know two things, Paige. I know that I love you more than any weapon of the enemy or my flesh can compete with. I also know that you are the woman God has meant for me. Part of the reason I am apologizing to you is because I failed to be the man you could trust to lead you when I began listening to myself more than God. Give me the chance to prove to you that I have thought this through properly and am of a mind to be the man both you and God would be proud of.

I'm not saying that I will always get it right, but this is definitely one battle I chose to win with God's help." He watched her from across the coffee table wishing they were closer. Maybe if he could touch her he could convey some of the determination he felt.

The small smile that slowly spread to her eyes brought with it a song of hope he'd been missing. He got up and crossed over to kneel in front of her. He drew her hands from her lap. "Please give me one more chance. Please let me show you how much a man can cherish and love a woman."

She leaned forward slightly, placing her palm on the side of his face. "I already know, Brandon. You did that every day we were together until a few weeks ago. That's why it was so devastating. I went from every one of my dreams coming to life, to being faced with a life full of memories of what I had just only tasted."

He swallowed back the emotion she was evoking in him. "Never again, sweetie…not by my hand if I can help it."

She nodded over and over then placing her other palm on the other side of his face, she brought his face to hers for the sweetest, softest kiss he'd ever received.

"I missed you," she whispered against his lips. His heart beat heavy in his chest, full of joy.

"I missed you too."

She stood up, half pulling him with her, and they hugged tightly. "I needed you so much last week. I needed your strength and encouragement so badly, but I couldn't tell you what was going on because I could barely believe it myself," she said against his shoulder, but when he made a move to pull back, she tightened her hold. "No, just a little bit longer," she whispered.

"Paige, what happened while you were gone?" He began rubbing her back, trying to soothe the trembles he felt running through her.

She shook herself and pulled away slightly, but he scooped her up and sat down in the chair with her half on and half off his lap. She was facing sideways cuddled against him in the side of the oversized chair. He wiped a new tear away from her cheek. "You have me now and everything that comes with it. Let's see if talking about it makes it any better."

She gave him a dubious look. He squeezed her and ran the back of his hand along her cheek. "Try," he said.

"I went to visit my girls. I needed some time to clear my head and make sure I wasn't forcing you to do something you really didn't want to do. Plus," she raced on when he opened his mouth, "I needed to get perspective." She looked at him to make sure he understood what she was saying. It was clear. She was telling him that she ran after him once, but she may not do it again.

"While I was visiting Vivian and Mason, I received some disturbing…no disturbing isn't the word." While she pondered this, Brandon's respiration spiked. If Mason did something to her, he would… "Crazy news." She finished more to herself than him.

"Did Mason hurt you?" She blinked at him, looking confused.

"No, why?"

Brandon shook his head. "Sorry, I was jumping to conclusions."

He leaned back, perturbed with himself. If it weren't for him she may not have gone there in the first place. "What happened?"

She licked her lips nervously. "While I was there, Richard, Victoria's husband, came to visit."

"From what you've told me, I thought he was pretty decent."

"He is."

Brandon was honestly and thoroughly puzzled.

"Let me get it out while I can."

He nodded and she went on to explain everything she learned from the moment Richard arrived, to leaving her sister's house the day before.

It was the last thing Brandon would have imagined and now he understood Paige's fragile appearance. He wanted so much to share some of his strength with her. He sat there with her in his arms absorbing everything she'd said and felt sick to his stomach. She'd gone through it all alone.

She raised her tear-streaked face towards him. "I went through half the day and all of last night wondering who I am."

"You are still the extremely resilient and beautiful woman of God that I fell in love with. Your earthly mother and father's identity may have changed, but your Heavenly Father is the same and so are you.

I can't imagine what type of shock that was for you. I'm so sorry it happened to you. Have you talked to Melanie since you got home?"

She looked at him as if he'd grown two heads. "I wouldn't begin to know what to say to her. She betrayed me."

"She was ten, if your calculations were right."

"She hasn't been ten for a long time."

He nodded his agreement. "There are obviously other factors."

"Whose side are you on?"

"Always yours, but right now your emotions are clouding your ability to think objectively. I saw her in the hospital before you woke from your coma. She guarded over you and made sure the nurses were doing everything possible to precipitate your healing. She was quite intimidating." She stared at him blankly.

"I'm just saying, there has to be more to the story."

"Yes and her name is Grace, but knowing that makes it so much worse. Melanie always covered for me or took my side against Grace when she was going off on some tangent." She stopped, thinking of what she'd said. Her face seemed to crumble before him and he shushed her as he hugged her to him again.

"It's okay. We don't have to talk about this anymore right now. We can stay like this and you can absorb all the strength you need from me. It'll be alright. You'll see."

"You don't know how much I needed to hear that." She snuggled closer into him and let the tears fall freely. As they wet his neck and shirt he wished he could slay this dragon for her, but besides holding her and letting her know that he wouldn't consider leaving her, he didn't know what to do. She was a rare gift and he would do good to remember that, especially if she agreed to be his wife.

After a while, she lifted her head and covered her mouth and nose. He reached over and pulled a few tissues from a box on her side table and gave them to her. She turned away to blow her nose since he'd tightened his grip when she made to get up. Losing her had become too real. He couldn't let her go just yet. His phone vibrated in his pocket alerting him to a call, but he still wouldn't move. He finally shifted Paige slightly and reached into his pocket when it rang for the third time. Unfortunately Paige saw the number, recognizing it before he did.

She snatched it up quickly opening the connection. "Why are you calling Brandon's phone?" She asked by way of answer.

Brandon could barely make out the response on the other side of the line. "I've been worried."

"Well you can stop. I made it back," she stated quietly.

"Can we talk? I need to tell you…" Melanie pleaded.

"Not now." Paige ended the call and handed him back the phone.

"Do what you want, but I won't talk to her right now." She moved to get up and this time he released her.

She walked over to the window, her shoulders sagging.

His phone rang again and he answered it speaking quietly. "Hello?"

"Brandon? Oh, Brandon. I am so sorry for this, but Paige's phones are going straight to voicemail. I really need to speak to her."

He looked at Paige. She hadn't turned around. "I don't think she wants to speak to you right now, Mel."

"I just need you to tell her something for me."

"Mel, I don't…"

"Please." The hurt and desperation in her voice was his undoing.

"Just this once," he said, never taking his eyes off of Paige. He saw her body stiffen and felt caught between a rock and a hard place.

"Ask her how she would have felt if Gladys had responded this way to her when she finally confessed to being her mother."

"I don't think you want to do that right now. She…"

"Brandon, please, just this one question. She'll understand."

He took a deep breath, letting it out slowly.

"Paige, Melanie wanted to convey one question to you." Paige gave no indication that she'd heard him, but he went on anyway relaying the question.

Paige turned around and he saw sparks light up their depths. His only hope was not to be caught in the crossfire.

"You tell her the difference between her and myself is that I intended to tell my daughter the truth. She only said something when her back was up against the wall and still she's hiding secrets."

"Did you get that?"

"Yes," he heard the defeat in her voice.

"I think you need to give her the time she's asking for otherwise you will only make it worse."

"Okay. Can I call you?"

"I don't think that would be a good idea. Just be patient with her." He waited for her reply then hung up.

He got up, walked to her and without a word encircled her in his arms.

*   *   *

"Did you ask her?" Dominy asked.

"No. I was more concerned with her taking me back."

"Did she?"

Brandon finished pulling his shirt over his head. "Yes."

"Then when are you going to ask her? Inquiring minds want to know."

"Sounds more like nosey minds. I don't remember asking you when you were going to ask Robin when you were going to pop the question."

"That's because I asked her before you could think about it, and I didn't jeopardize our relationship by trying to play knight in shining armor when the damsel didn't need saving."

"Wow. Are you ever going to let me live that down?"

"Mmmm, maybe, let me think about it for a while."

Brandon chuckled, bending down to tie his shoes. "By the way, how is Robin?"

"Alright. Her mood swings are off the chart though. One moment she's all over me and the next she's colder than Alaska. I think she's having a girl."

"Oh, I'm telling."

"Tattle-tale."

"You really have to do better if you want to threaten me into keeping my mouth closed."

"I don't know. Maybe I could try telling Mama Ava one of the many misadventures with her son, Brandon."

Brandon thought about it for a moment. "You would do it too, huh?"

"In a heartbeat."

"You are one cold piece of work. What did I do to deserve you as a friend?"

"You must have been really, really good in your last life," Dominy replied easily.

"BS." Brandon half-attempted to cover with a cough.

"What are you doing? You sound like you're moving around."

"I'm getting dressed, if you must know."

"Why so early?"

"Because I have a question to ask a young lady and I just couldn't wait until tonight. I'll tell you how it goes later. Bye Dominy." He thought he heard a 'wait', but other than that he didn't let Dominy get in a word before he hung up.

He pulled on his sweater and picked up a jacket as he left his room. He'd asked Paige to join him in viewing the sunrise in the spot they'd talked in the hills. He'd been there a few times since and watched the sun come up over the mountain, washing the Los Angeles basin with light.

He'd text Paige as he walked to his car. *Are you up?*

Not even a minute passed before the reply came. *Yes and waiting.*

On my way, he texted one last time before starting up his car and pulling out onto the street.

The last few days had been bittersweet. Brandon had spent every possible hour with Paige. The pain in her eyes receded a little more each day and he finally felt reasonably sure she wouldn't think he had ulterior motives for asking her to marry him.

He felt like he'd been waiting forever. Either that or it was all the people in his immediate circle that constantly asked him that kept it forefront in his mind. His mother had gone back home the day before Paige returned, but she called him every day to check up on his health and her Paige. He was already sharing and he hadn't even been able to claim her yet. He shook his head as he maneuvered the car through the streets of L.A. in the early morning darkness.

They'd spent last evening with Pastor Lawrence and Lady Menagerie going over some of Paige's visit with her relatives, but mostly just in quiet companionship showing their support and love. After dessert, Lady Menagerie suggested they play a card and board game. Paige's initial stiffening told Brandon that she was remembering or associating the game with her – Mel – and he was about to decline for them, but Paige pasted a smile on her face and set for a challenge to the men. They spent the next couple of hours ribbing each other, joking and laughing. Paige looked the most relaxed he'd seen her since she'd come back to Los Angeles. He was happy she had such loving parental figures. In fact, she didn't lack for love in any of her Skylight Temple family. They all adored her almost as much as he did.

He pulled up to the all-night diner located a few miles from his house. He'd called in his order of hot drinks, breakfast sandwiches and muffins only a few minutes before Dominy called him. He ran in, retrieved his order and jogged back to the car. The breakfast was part of the surprise for Paige so he didn't want to keep her waiting.

Ten minutes later, he was knocking softly on Paige's door. She opened a few seconds later. Dressed in black jeans and boots with an emerald green sweater she looked incredible and ready for her 'hike'. "You are gorgeous," he whispered more out of awe than respect for her neighbors.

The smile she gave him in return warmed his heart. "How're you feeling this morning?" He asked as he moved in for a hug.

He felt her sigh against him and tightened his hold before releasing her.

He looked into her eyes, rubbing the soft skin at the underside of her jaw with his thumb. He wasn't surprised to see the pain still lingering. He hoped this morning would give her happy things to think about. If she said 'yes'. He shook himself.

"Pretty good. This is a great idea. I really love those hills and being there to watch the sun come up will make it that much better."

He smiled to himself. "Are you ready?"

She stepped back to retrieve her coat from the rack next to the door and rejoined him in the doorway. He moved away while she locked up and led her down the stairs and out the door to his car.

He had just slipped behind the wheel when he heard her sniffing. Well the first of his surprises was about to be revealed.

"What's that smell?" she asked, looking at him then towards the backseat.

"I thought it would be fun to eat while we watched the sunrise."

"Boy aren't you full of surprises." She giggled but sobered a few moments later. She placed her hand on his forearm drawing his attention to her face.

"Thank you. It would be so much harder without you to help me through this." He saw her heart in her eyes and knew he couldn't make light of it like he'd wanted to. He just nodded then turned on the car, putting it in gear.

They rode in silence until they reached the site. He parked and got out so he could let her out. He transferred the drinks into two thermoses and placed everything in his backpack. "Ready?" He asked as he reached for Paige's hand.

"Yep."

He turned on his flashlight even though there was enough light to find their way until they reached the summit. The last thing he needed was for either one of them to turn, twist, or break anything.

They arrived at the area he'd selected a few minutes before the sun peaked the hill. The sky was already streaked with hues of burgundy, purple, and deep gold. He took the blanket out of his backpack spreading it on the ground then proceeded to unpack the rest of the items.

He knew Paige was watching him, but he waited until everything was finished before he looked up to see what she was thinking.

"Wow Brandon, you really planned this down to the 'T'."

He shrugged off the compliment, noting her slight unease.

"I didn't bring anything but myself. I would have done more if you'd told me what you were planning."

"That's why I didn't tell you." He took her hands and led her to the blanket facing him. "I wanted to pamper you for a change. This way all you have to do is eat, drink, and watch God put on a show."

They'd just finished their breakfast when Brandon looked up and saw the sun coming up over the ridge behind Paige. She was a mere outline, but she turned to see what he was watching and her breath caught. At that moment while she marveled at the beauty of God's hand, he knew he wanted to share this moment with her forever. He slipped his hand in his pocket quickly just in case she looked back. He took out the white, leather box that had been burning a hole in his pocket and situated himself so that he sat to her side.

"It's so beautiful," she whispered as if they were in a theater watching a play.

"I think some of His most valuable creations are inherently beautiful."

She turned to him briefly with a smile of pure joy on her face. She turned back to the scene in front of them as if she were afraid she'd miss something then stiffened a couple of seconds before she turned to face him again. She looked down at what was in his hand and gasped. Her wide-eyed gaze moved back to his face, a small question lingering in their depths. If he wasn't so nervous he would have laughed.

"I love you, Paige, and I know some of my recent actions, though they were done with good intentions, spoke more out of fear than faith but if you would allow me, I would like to go back to the day before I started seeing things only with my natural eyes."

"What's the difference?"

"The difference is, the day before, I could see through my spiritual eyes as well and I saw us together. I saw the joy in sharing my life with you. I saw the peace you allow to reign in your life and how it surrounds us when we are together. I saw the way you love me, and with God, it's more than I could have ever hoped for. I had a moment and lost sight of one of the most precious gifts God has given to me, but not anymore."

He opened the white velvet box, presenting her with the two-carat emerald cut diamond surrounded by a cluster of smaller princess cut diamonds in a platinum setting.

Paige placed her hand on over her mouth. He watched her eyes mist up, but no sound came out of her mouth. He continued as he stood up, bringing her with him then kneeling.

"We've got this, Paige." His hand spanned the area scene before them. "We have this moment and whatever else God deems to give us. It's enough as long as I have you in my life." He continued, never taking his eyes off of her. "Paige Rosen Morganson, would you make the rest of my dreams come true by agreeing to be my wife?"

He was almost afraid to breathe as he watched the various emotions roam across her face as she looked down at him. "My family–" she began, but he cut her off.

"Paige, no family is without drama. Even mine." He thought back to what this mother had shared with him and thought with time he may share it with Paige. "But you have a wonderful family. You have two wonderful daughters, Pastor Lawrence and Lady Menagerie, not to mention the whole of Skylight Temple Church, but most of all me and my family. If God would allow it I would take you away from it all, but you have your daughters who are the middle of all of this, so I will stay right here to cover, undergird, protect and pray for you unless you tell me to go.

I know I will be marrying into that group you call 'family', but first I will be your husband." He watched her close her eyes and held his breath knowing he would see his answer when they opened.

She began nodding almost before her eyes opened and to him her smile eclipsed the scene playing out around them.

"Yes."

The elation he felt made him want to jump up with her in his arms but he tempered it. "Really, yes?"

"Really, yes," she responded. He stood, placed his hands on either side of her face and stared into her eyes, and there he saw it. The love that fortunately, he'd failed to smother with his idiotic tendency to play her knight in shining armor.

He retrieved the ring box, taking out the delicate ring, lifting it so she could see the engraving. *Just another place for you to carry my heart.*

She was laughing as he picked up her left hand and slid the ring onto her fourth finger. It looked as though it had been made especially for her.

He brought her hands up to his cheek then lips to seal their agreement. His heart was so full. He wanted to shout that she was his. God had done what He'd promised in spite of Brandon's help. He felt incredibly blessed and he couldn't help but smile. He pulled her to him and as she wrapped her arms around his neck and his lips sought out hers, he could feel her tears wet his face. He was just thankful that this time he brought her tears of joy.

CHAPTER 30

Richard roamed back and forth wearing a small line across the expanse of his office. He had been over the many different scenarios in his head at least half a dozen times, but nothing made sense.

He ran his hand over his hair, grimacing when his hand came across the stubble on his jaw. How long had he been at it? The clock on his desk read two in the morning. He let his hands fall to his sides. He knew he couldn't continue like this, but work was the only thing that kept him from losing what dignity he had left by sitting in the corner of his office and crying for the unfairness of it all. He knew he was just feeling sorry for himself, and he was disgusted with himself even as he gave in to it. He just hurt so much.

With the contracts finally signed regarding the development of land usage in Uganda and all parties coming to a satisfactory agreement, there wasn't much to do except think about Victoria or go over the gaps in her son, Brian's, case. The case was easier to figure out even if it was riddled with holes big enough to store ships.

He had long before divested himself of his coat and tie. Nancy had peeked her head in to wish him a goodnight what seemed only ten minutes before, but she was probably well into REM by now.

He was back near the couch now so he let himself fall onto it. He was so tired. So very tired. He'd avoided asking about Victoria during his prayers to God. He wasn't ready to hear what He had to say. If it was for reconciliation, he knew he was still too angry with her and himself to hear it, but if it was to let her go, he didn't know how he would be able to do that either. He was stuck right here in the in-between until he could at least reconcile his feelings if nothing else.

All the same, he bowed his head and asked God for the strength to endure and the courage to ask.

The next morning he was startled awake by Nancy. "Mr. Branchett. I'm sorry to wake you, but you fell asleep on the couch and you have a 9:30 a.m. conference call with Malin and Hinch in Chicago."

He sat up, rubbing his face. "What time is it now?"

"Eight o'clock. I thought you would have enough time to go back to your apartment and get in a quick shower."

Just, he thought to himself, wondering when he had finally fallen asleep.

"Thank you Nancy. I will do just that." He picked himself up off the couch and was halfway to his desk when he noticed Nancy had not moved. He glanced at her briefly before taking his jacket from the back of the chair. "Yes, Nancy?"

"Sir, I've been trying to stay out of your personal business and keep my opinions to myself."

"And you have done an exceptional job of it. Why go and ruin your stellar record now?"

In his periphery he saw her flinch and tried to take the edge out of his tone. "Nancy, I'm fine." He finally looked her squarely in the eye and saw that she didn't believe him. "I will be fine," he modified.

"I'm just concerned." She rang her hands together. He walked over and placed his hands on her shoulders.

"I just have a few things to work out. It will be alright."

She nodded. "You know it's been a long time since you've come to dinner. I know Gary would love to see someone besides me across the table." She let the sentence fade.

"Can I think on it?" She stared at him. It was obvious she thought he would decline the invitation straight out. It made him feel like a heel that he had taken such pore care of their friendship.

She nodded. "Alright then. I should go so I can be back in time for the call."

Richard looked around the now sparse apartment trying to remember where he placed his keys. There weren't too many places they could hide since he'd had most of his possessions sent back to the house when he had hopes of winning back the woman he used to know.

As he was going through the pockets of his old coat, his cell phone rang. He turned in a full circle until he was able to get his bearings. He was losing it. He followed the sound to the bathroom and picked up the phone off the vanity. He sighed, trying to focus as he read the number and connected the call.

"Sam, please tell me you have some good news for me."

"Well, it's your lucky day but I'm not completely sure it is good news." Richard stopped moving and looked at his watch. He had a few moments, but he needed to find his keys.

"You there?"

"Yeah, I misplaced my keys…"

"Ah, okay. For a moment I thought you were losing it."

"You're not too far from that mark," he mumbled to himself.

"Hey, try what I do."

"Huh, what's that?"

"I walk back out my door and walk back in like I just came in, and try to retrace my steps."

"I am ready to try almost anything at this point. Meanwhile, go ahead and give me the news," he said, walking to the front door.

"Okay, Grace is Melanie's first name, but the records were about Grace the mother. I'm going to need you to sit down for this next part, Richard."

Richard opened the door and was startled and relieved to find his keys jangling in his outside lock. He really needed to get it together. He turned his mind back to the conversation. "Alright. I'm walking to the couch." He followed his words and sat on the living room couch, and proceeded to tie his shoes.

"Mya has a friend who has been feeding her some information. She won't tell us who he is or what he does, but she said he is a trustworthy source. She said she was able to confirm the information about Grace the mother with him. It seems she has to be very close to getting the information herself or have it already, and he will just confirm it.

Anyway, Mya was stumped, as I said before, because a few things didn't add up, so she took a chance and made a couple of assumptions. She went to the guy with them and he confirmed them."

Richard slowly took in what Sam was saying. "What did the man confirm?"

"Grace Melanie Morganson gave birth to a baby girl two days before her eleventh birthday. Paige is Melanie's biological daughter. There are no records. Mya asked for them, but the man wouldn't give over anything that would put his work in jeopardy."

Richard's thoughts went reeling and his day took a decided left turn.

"Who's the father?"

"We were able to eliminate Mel's father."

Richard breathed a sigh of relief. He'd heard too many horror stories of children conceived in incest being handed off as the legitimate son or daughter of the wife, instead of the grandchild.

Sam went on. "He was deployed at the time Melanie conceived and though he came back for a few weeks leave early on in her pregnancy, he didn't come back until two months after Paige was born, and at that time she was presented as his daughter and not his granddaughter."

"So this woman covered it up from her own husband? I guess it could have been worse. So, any clues on the father?"

"Not a one, and if Melanie doesn't speak, we will be hard-pressed to find out. She must have had Paige at home because there is no sign at all that she was in anyone's hospital, let alone General."

"Would her mother really do that?"

"She would if she didn't want anyone to know."

"But why? I mean I know the girl was very young, but we were far past the days when she would have been burned at the stake or considered untouchable for life. Why all the secrecy?"

"I'm not sure, but Mya has a few theories she's checking out. Do you think Paige might be able to get it out of her?"

"I'm not sure. She wouldn't even tell Paige she was her mother when Paige confronted her, but I guess she figured the admission would wedge a wider gap between them." Richard stood up from the couch and walked once again to the front door.

"Yeah, I guess not. That mother must be some piece of work to have orchestrated this farce and kept the daughter from saying anything for so long."

"That, and she's holding something pretty huge over her daughter's head."

"I don't know about you, Richard, but I got that feeling deep in my gut."

Richard slowed his walk towards the elevator not wanting to miss any of the conversation. He knew when Sam started talking about his gut instincts, you'd best listen.

"About?" He pressed the down button.

"About the fact that we are only at the beginning of this puzzle. I think this rabbit hole goes deep," Sam said.

"Unfortunately, I'm getting that same feeling. To find such life-altering news about a woman who is as easy to find as a ghost, is feeling less like finding the winning piece of a treasure hunt and more like we're being bated."

"I'm glad we're on the same page. No pun intended."

Richard groaned. "Yeah, I bet." He stepped into the elevator. "Give me a moment and I'll call you back on my headset once I get in the car."

"Okay."

The elevator let out into the garage, and as he walked to his car his steps slowed as he spied a piece of paper tucked under the windshield wiper. He looked around the garage, but saw and heard no one. He quickened his steps and snatched the folded piece of paper from the windshield, straightening it as he unlocked and opened his door. He froze when the words penetrated his preoccupied mind. *Remember our first kiss?*

Richard let out a breath, knowing full well that if it had been a few years before, there would have been a colorful explicative on it.

She was using his own game against him, but what was her motive? He threw the card on the passenger seat and engaged his Bluetooth. He used his voice to have his phone dial Sam then started his car and drove out of the garage.

"So where were we?"

"We were pretty much done with the girls until Mya comes up with something or Melanie says something. I was doing some thinking about Victoria's boy though."

"Okay." Richard prompted as he turned a corner. He had about seven minutes before he arrived at his office and wanted to conclude this call before then.

"There was something that seemed off about the house the mother lived in. It took a moment, but finally it dawned on me. There were no pictures."

The news surprised Richard so much he found himself arrested at a newly green light. He didn't even notice until the car behind him honked to get his attention. He let off the brake wondering why he hadn't thought of that himself. His group had found school records, small drawings of the mother doing various chores obviously created by a child; toys, books, collectible planes, even a few pieces of boy's clothing, but no pictures. This was getting more bizarre by the moment.

"What are you thinking, Sam?"

"That we weren't the only ones that had been in her home."

Richard nodded, not realizing Sam couldn't see him. "What are you going to do?"

"We're going to go back to the beginning and see if we missed anything. I will keep you posted."

"Okay, good job by the way. I'm going to have to think about if or how I will approach Paige on this. I can't go through a repeat of two weeks ago. She will have to make the decision on how she will handle... Wow, I'm confused on what to call her, and I don't even know the woman."

He drove into the parking lot of his office building. "I know the whole situation is like something out of a suspense novel," Sam said.

"Well, keep me posted and tell Mya she has my go ahead."

Sam snorted. 'Yeah, like she was waiting for it. You know Mya lives for a good mystery."

Richard cut his engine and looked at the clock on his dash. 9:20. "Look Sam, I have to run. Thank you for the information. I'll call you later in the week."

"Sure, take care."

"You too."

Richard let himself out of the car, thinking of how many situations Grace could have manipulated by using her daughter's identity. The list was staggering. He honestly didn't know what the woman had been up to and he wanted to know, not only for his and Victoria's sakes, but Paige's as well.

He shook his head at the bizarre way he continued to be the bearer of mind-shaking news for her. He knew he would tell her because if he were her and faced with the question of his parentage, he would want to know. He just didn't know whether it should be sooner or later. He would pray on it and hopefully get the direction he needed to share it with her in the least hurtful way. He would also pray that God would comfort her and give her the strength to handle the information, without it causing irreparable damage to Paige and Melanie's relationship.

He couldn't imagine what Paige was going through even now, but he was happy for her and Brandon. When she called him two weeks ago to tell him about the blowout she had with Mel, she'd also shared the news that Brandon had proposed on top of a mountain or hill, something high – he knew – and she had accepted. He just hoped they could be happy with each other for a lifetime. With God in the middle of their marriage, they were bound to jump over many hurdles that felled many other marriages.

His thoughts came back to the note on his passenger side. He chided himself even as he walked to the other side of the car and retrieved it. Who was he fooling? He was still in love with his wife, but he didn't always like her.

He looked up as he walked into the elevator and pressed the button to his floor.

"I guess if Mohammad won't go to the mountain, You will bring the mountain to Mohammad?" he said to God. His mouth curled into a wry grin as he shook his head at himself.

*   *   *

Later that evening he lay in bed, note in hand, and let himself remember the balmy, overcast day they spent in Oklahoma City.

He'd wanted to take her away from the small town where everyone knew what you were going to do before you did it. He talked to a few of her hands and arranged for them to be away from the farm for half a day.

When she protested, he was ready for her. She looked as though she didn't know if she wanted to be angry or flattered so instead of letting her sit there and make up her mind, he took her by the hand and led her to his car.

The first of the drive into town was quiet. He looked over at her every now and then, watching her take in the scenery. The planes seemed to be shrouded in mist that day and he wondered if they were in for some showers, though the newscaster had stated otherwise.

He was anxious to show her a few of Oklahoma tourism spots because he wanted her to fall in love with it as he had. He wanted her to have plenty of reasons to stay because he was already falling for her.

As he took her from the State Capitol Building to the National Cowboy and Western Heritage Museum, the influx of people had him protectively clasping her hand but he didn't release it. They walked hand-in-hand through the halls at a leisurely pace. His heart leapt at the fact that she hadn't retreated like she did in the beginning of their relationship. She had grown comfortable with him and it made his world right. When she saw a sculpture she was particularly fond of, the light in her eyes stole his breath. This day was worth all of the patient breaths, rejections to his initial invitations, and the snail's pace at which she allowed him to get to know her.

He originally thought they would move forward at a comfortable pace when she'd finally told him why she kept him at arm's length. He couldn't blame her for being cautious, even overly so, but he needed to make sure she didn't see him the way she saw the guy who abandoned her. He could be paying for that guy's mistakes for…he didn't know how long.

He knew she was attracted to him. He saw it in her eyes when the awareness between the two of them was elicited by something either one of them said, or when they brushed skin. She would watch to see if he felt it too and that would cause his pulse to race. So many moments had passed with him wanting to kiss her he felt like it would never happen, but he was made hopeful by every agreement she made to see him.

She always seemed so confident, like she knew where she wanted to be and went there. Like the farm. Who in their right mind would separate themselves from the city life in their twenties and choose to plow, shovel, lift, and tend to animals almost all day long? Victoria seemed a natural at it and she seemed happiest when she was doing all of the labor right alongside the hired hands, but she could hold her own in a conversation on business law and taxes when she would accompany him to business socials…when she felt like it. She was a conundrum, and he wanted to solve her. He was privileged to have the opportunity because he knew not many people saw beyond the calm, cool exterior that she used to keep others at a distance, but the glimpses he caught kept him coming back for more.

If he told his parents, they may have thought he was a glutton for punishment. They might have pegged her for another 'Brenda Lattimore', but where Victoria was deeper than the brown pools he fell into each time he looked into her eyes, Brenda had been shallow and easily manipulated by her mother.

He forced himself back to Victoria and what she was saying. "I am having a really great time. Thank you for kidnapping me today." Her mischievous smile pulled at him.

"I didn't kidnap you. I asked you politely and when you tried to come up with a reason why you couldn't, I wouldn't let you because I know what's best for you better than you know yourself."

"Really?" she said, and he could see the witty comeback forming. "Well then, I was mistaken. There is a whole other term for you. Would you like to hear it?"

He paused for the briefest of moments as if he were contemplating her question, then shrugged.

"So I kidnapped you. You needed it."

She laughed at his quick retreat then acquiesced. "Yes I did, and I thank you very kindly, sir, for the selfless gesture."

"Oh, there is nothing selfless about it. I get to walk around this huge museum for hours holding hands with the most beautiful woman in the place. I would say it was more self-serving than anything else." He shrugged again.

The blush that stole across her cheeks to the tips of her ears told him his compliment had been well-received.

"Good then, I guess I can stop trying to come up with some way to thank you." She sashayed ahead a couple of steps but was impeded by his grasp on her hand.

"Well, there was the drive into town where you said so little it made me feel like I was in the car alone."

"Mmm hmm," she gave as a reply while looking up at pictures of Midwestern and West Coast Rodeos in the 1950s, then led him on by the hand.

"I think my ego took a hit too." He started looking around himself for said ego but looked up at her laugh.

"What?" he said, acting disgruntled.

"Your ego isn't down there," she said through chuckles.

"And where, pray tell, would it be?"

She let go of his hand and unzipped her purse, retrieving a compact case. She opened it up and brought the mirror up to show him his reflection.

"Aww see, there it is looking quite big and unruffled from what I can make out," she said with a smirk.

He pushed her hand away with a small frown. "I don't have a big ego."

"Says the man who doesn't take 'no' for an answer."

He stopped walking, wondering if they were still kidding around. "I can take 'no' for an answer. I just don't like to. Besides, I've taken 'no' from you almost 50% of the time."

She looked as though she were deeply contemplating his last words then met his eyes. "True, but I say 'yes' to the things that really count."

He was having so much fun bantering with her, he didn't want it to end. "Well, I think I have a really important question for later."

She raised an eyebrow. "If it's so important, why don't you ask it now so I can think about it?"

He resumed walking and took her hand. He ran his thumb back and forth over her knuckles lightly. "No. I think I will ask it at a more propitious moment."

"*Propitious* for who?" she inquired, placing an emphasis on the first word while walking forward so she could see his expression.

"More propitious for both of us."

She turned around, walking backward so she could watch. He was only too happy to guide her as she walked. "Are you thinking you might get lucky, Mr. Branchett?"

He nearly tripped over his feet at the question, but quickly regained a comfortable, confident gait.

He watched her watching him and decided to see what she would do if he gave her a glimpse of his true feelings.

"I am lucky. I'm spending the day with you."

She stared at him blankly for a couple of seconds then warmth registered in her eyes and a smile grew on her lips. She nodded slowly then moved to walk next to him, facing forward. "Nice answer, Moneyman."

He looked over at her. "Moneyman? What's that supposed to mean?" He tried not to jump to conclusions.

She seemed to pick up on his change in mood. "Well," she started haltingly, "you work on Black Wall Street. Moneyman." She said the last words as though it made all the sense in the world.

Being from a wealthy family, he had been made fun of for most of his childhood since his father wanted him to get a well-rounded education and enrolled him in public school at the beginning of middle school. He tried to hide it by dressing down or trading book bags with friends, but once he was seen getting out of his father's limousine on a day he was running late, he had been pegged as the rich kid and the torment had begun. He didn't even realize it still bothered him until she teased him.

"Could you pick another name?" he said solemnly.

"You really don't care for it?"

"About as much as you would like me calling you 'Counselor'."

Her brows drew together and her lips pursed. "Point taken."

They walked for a little while, then Victoria turned to him. "I'm sorry. If I'd known it would be a sore subject for you, I wouldn't have said anything."

"You have no reason to apologize. You wouldn't have known and to tell you the truth I didn't know it still stung, but you live and you learn right?"

"Right," she said almost hesitantly.

He was disappointed that his reaction had dampened the lightheartedness of the last few minutes.

They continued their tour of the museum and he took her to dinner at a cozy mom and pop Italian restaurant he'd frequented over the years.

It wasn't until they were close to her place that his continued attempts at lightening her mood broke her resolve.

"Well, if you just want to continue to beat yourself up you can, but I'm going to need a smile before you get out of this car." She looked over at him and shifted her lips upward, but it didn't reach her eyes.

"Wow, that was sad. I mean really pathetic." He guided the car over to an indent in the road leading to the main house. He thought this was as good a place as any to ask her his question. "So, I would like to ask you that question now." He saw her look out her passenger side window, then in front and in back of her. Instead of the unease he thought he would see at her perusal of the area, there was a twinkle of amusement in her eyes.

"Is this what you'd consider a propitious moment?"

"Absolutely."

She looked at him, waiting patiently. It actually made him more nervous. This was the effect she had on him.

He unlocked the doors and exited the car. He breathed in great gulps of air as he walked around to her side. He opened the door and pulled her out by her hands. "So Victoria," he said as he ran his hands up and down her arms.

"Yes?" she said, her eyes dancing.

He smiled. "Victoria," he moved his hand up the back of her neck and stroked the nape with his thumb. "May I kiss you?"

She bit her lip in false consternation, which drew his gaze to her lips. When he looked back into her eyes, they were overly warm. She nodded and he pulled her towards his mouth.

The moment their lips touched he felt it to his toes. This woman was like lightning to his system. One moment he felt confident he could control the situation and the next he was scorched. He brought her closer, essentially hugging her to him and slid his lips against hers.

He wanted to sip at her and take it slow, but her taste and smell were so intoxicating he felt his control slipping. He deepened the kiss, slightly moving his lips so that his bottom lip slipped between hers and rubbed, absorbing the texture of her. After one more squeeze, he released her and slowly ended the kiss.

He could hear her heavy breathing and was happy to know he wasn't the only one affected so strongly.

He laid his forehead against hers, trying to catch his breath. If he didn't do it soon, he was going down.

Once he felt his heart resume a decent tempo, he chanced speaking. "You are amazing, Victoria." He loosened his hold of her nape and ran his hand up and down her upper back.

"So, that was the important question?"

"Yep."

"Good question," she breathed out heavily.

"Great answer." He smiled

"I told you I say 'yes' to the things that really count."

"So kissing me really counts?"

She shrugged. "Let's just say my curiosity was peaked."

"And?"

"And what?"

She looked at him with a too-wide-eyed innocence that spoke of her mischievous act.

He chuckled at the embarrassment he felt at just kissing her. "What did you think of the kiss, woman?"

She feigned concentration on this question. "I think I will need another one to give you an intelligent answer."

He could feel the warmth spread through his heart. "By all means, allow me to give you another demonstration."

*   *   *

Richard took a deep breath. He focused back on the ceiling he'd been staring at and wiped the wet from his face. He loved his wife and the thought made him almost as sad as it made him happy. He had placed so much on her ability to remember the Victoria of 33 years ago that he missed the beauty and resilience of the Victoria today. He thought back to the two young and hopeful people who just wanted to love each other for life, and they were no longer there. In their place were two life-weary, older adults who had experienced great joy and crippling pain, who were trying to clear away the debris around them enough to find the love they'd set on the shelf years before for safe keeping. He pondered those bittersweet feelings, then turned his head to pray.

Dear Father, I'm ready. Your answer can't be any worse than what I'm going through now. I will be obedient and do what You say. I trust that whichever way You have me go, You will keep me and continue to guide me. You will be my comfort and my rock. I ask that You give me peace in this decision and get my attention if I try to build a fortress around my heart. I wish to be open to seeing things as You do so that I can escape this cycle. You are my Lord. You are my life and You are the reason I am still here. I'm sorry it took me so long to acknowledge that at this time in my life. Lord, I love her, but if we aren't to be together please take it away, but continue to place people in Victoria's life that will lead her to You. Remind her of the beautiful soul that is under all the anger and give me the strength to see it even now.

He continued praying in earnest until the early hours of the morning and when he laid his head on his pillow, he had the peace he sought.

CHAPTER 31

Victoria dug deeper with her spade, almost willing the hard clay earth and rocks to give under her ministrations. She thought a new flowerbed would help her expend the energy that kept her awake at night. She was determined to get some rest tonight. She was so tired, and something else she hadn't felt in a long time: lost. For the first time since moving to the ranch and leaving her family, she felt lost. She was at the edge of a precipice and had been there since Paige had left her with a small ache in her soul that was spreading.

She could use her former tactics for numbing the pain, but recent history had proven it to be faulty. She had grown cynical, bitter, and insensitive to anyone's plight except hers. She used to see it as being direct; knowing her mind and having the strength of character to proceed with her plan no matter the cost.

She put her arms and shoulders into the motion, feeling perspiration break out on her brow. This was exactly what she needed to take her mind away from the constant bombardment of guilt she was feeling. It didn't even make sense. It wasn't as though she told Richard to inform Paige of the truth about her lineage, but she couldn't shake the feeling of responsibility.

"Ms. Victoria?"

Not hearing anyone come up behind her, Victoria glanced up quickly to find Martha accompanied by Mary Ambross.

She leaned back, surprised by the visit. She hadn't seen Mary since the gala and before that, a handful of times while Richard was in Uganda. Even more surprising was her happiness to see her.

She dropped the guarded expression, allowing her warm smile to greet Mary, and slowly climbed to her feet while taking off her clay covered gloves and wiping her hands on her gardening apron.

"Mary, I can't tell you how nice it is to see you again." She turned slightly. "Martha, we'll have refreshments on the south side veranda." Martha inclined her head in acknowledgment and walked back towards the side of the house.

Victoria gestured for Mary to join in step with her. "I know how rude it is just to pop by, really I do, though I seem to do it quite often with you," Mary smiled sheepishly.

Victoria made a shooing motion with her hand. "No bother, I needed the rest. I've been going at that hole in the ground for some time now, trying to make something of that eyesore. It's just taking a little more energy than I thought."

Mary looked around at the surrounding area. "Why don't you ask one of the hands to take care of it?"

"The gardens are my pride and joy. No one touches them except me and George, our landscaper. He's taught me everything I know."

Victoria sat down at a small table for two in the corner of the veranda overlooking the south pasture. She placed her hands in her lap and regarded Mary.

"Is there any particular reason why you came today? Not that you can't any time you wish."

Mary looked a tad bit uncomfortable, which absorbed some of the ease Victoria had been feeling.

"No, no reason in particular. I was just out and I was wondering what you were up to. I called a few weeks ago to thank you for inviting me to the gala, but Richard said you weren't feeling well. I called again but when I didn't get a callback, I thought I would come by."

Victoria breathed a little easier. "Oh, yes, the gala took a little more out of me than I thought it would, and I received some disturbing news shortly after so I've been dealing with that."

Mary's brows knitted in concern. "Are you alright?"

Victoria nodded. "I will be." She smiled wanly.

"Good to know," Mary said, then went quiet for a few moments while she looked out at the land in front of them.

Martha placed a tray with two small carafes, glasses, and plates of various pastries on the table. Victoria continued to watch her, waiting for Mary to divest her real reasons for coming by. She knew Mary well enough from their few visits to suspect that the woman couldn't hold her true reasons for stopping by too much longer.

Finally, Mary swallowed hard and looked her squarely in the eye. "Paul spoke to Richard last week." Victoria stiffened. One of the things Victoria liked best about Mary was her predictability and as sweet and mild tempered as Mary was, Victoria still didn't want her in their business.

"Oh? And how is Paul doing?"

"He's well, thank you," Mary said, looking back out over the land.

"Um, Victoria, Paul said Richard looks, um, not like himself and though he wouldn't tell Paul exactly what happened, Paul could tell that Richard was feeling guilty about something." Victoria watched as she took a deep breath, and she felt a moment of unease. Where was Mary going with this line of questioning?

"I have never known Richard to be anything but adoring towards you, but you never know what goes on behind closed doors." She sighed heavily as though she were about to do something she'd rather not do.

"Did you throw Richard out? Is that why he's been staying in town?"

Victoria almost laughed at the absurdity of the question, and would have if Mary didn't seem so distraught. She couldn't help the incredulous look she knew played across her features.

"No, Mary," she said, in a soft reassuring voice.

"But..." Mary's puzzled look transitioned into one of chagrin. "I'm sorry. It really is none of my business. I was just so confused to hear that he was still in the states, but staying away from you and this beautiful land." The last of the sentence faded into a whisper.

Victoria watched Mary, a little puzzled herself. Why was she so concerned about their marriage?

"What do you mean, Mary?"

Mary looked really uncomfortable now. Victoria couldn't gauge where the tension was centered though. Was it due to the fact that she knew Richard had been staying in the city or the possible reasons why?

Mary rubbed the palms of her hands together. "Richard and Paul have known each other for a while. I only met Richard after their first trip to Kenya, but once he joined our church I got to know him better." Mary glanced away from Victoria briefly and Victoria knew she was still struggling with whether to tell her the following information.

"Like I said, Richard and Paul have known each other for some time and they have gotten close. Did you know they go away for the weekend every other month?"

Victoria was ashamed to admit that she hadn't paid close attention to Richard's comings and goings over the last five... no, six years. She had been consumed with their daughter's life, illness and death, not to mention the energy she'd expended trying to exact revenge upon Grace.

Victoria shook her head to the negative to Mary's question.

"But in all of those years, the first time we were invited to Richard's house was this past Christmas. We knew Richard had a wife because he definitely didn't give us cause to think he was hiding you. When the topic of discussion would turn to wives, Paul said he would get this adoring look in his eye when he would speak of you. It was what came after that always brought Paul up short."

Victoria was more curious than wary at this point. "How did he look?"

"Paul said he looked like he missed you. Like you had been gone a while, but it didn't make sense with Richard referring to you in the present tense. I believe he asked Richard once in the beginning if you were still together and when Richard answered in the affirmative, he let it go."

Victoria thought about what to say. How could she reply to all of this without giving too much away? She sipped slowly at her lemonade.

"I have been somewhat preoccupied over the last few years," Victoria finally offered.

"I can't imagine what it would feel like to lose a child," Mary stated solemnly with a warmth that did little to heat the chill running through Victoria's blood. Mary went on quickly.

"Richard would also bring up Rachael often. It was as though he needed to talk about her to sort through his feelings or share her memory...later...when." Victoria felt gut-punched. Richard had talked to these people about Rachael. What else had he shared with them about their family?

Her look of hurt and confusion must have been pronounced because Mary quickly took her hand from across the small table.

"Please don't feel betrayed because I learned how generous and kind you could be from your husband before I met you. It only made me want to meet you more and now I am sorry I just didn't take it upon myself to come and visit you sooner. I didn't know if you would think I was a loon because I already felt I knew you so well and you didn't know a thing about me."

Victoria blinked. She was at a total loss for words until one thought came to the forefront. "Why...I mean, why did it take you so long to say these things?"

Mary looked sheepish. "I don't know about you, but I would be a little more than uncomfortable meeting someone for the first time who seemed to know all about me. It would be disconcerting to me and I might have to keep my distance until I felt we were on even ground."

Victoria agreed. Mary knew exactly what she would have felt and it would have kept her on the defense, thus destroying any chances of them developing a friendship. It caused her to feel a kinship with Mary she'd not found in a long time with any woman. She figured she could be blunt with Mary as well.

"So why are you telling me all of this now?"

Mary let go of Victoria's hand. "Because at the gala I saw the way the two of you were with one another. It reminded me of the earlier days of my marriage with Paul when we couldn't keep our hands off of each other. All it took was one look and we would be at each other. It didn't matter where we were. If Paul looked at me a certain way, rubbed up against me or whispered in my ear, I would feel it all the way to my toes." Mary had the nerve to blush.

"What's the difference now?" Victoria asked before she could stop herself.

Mary shrugged. "Not too much except we went through almost seven years of allowing work and other priorities to get in the way. The feelings were still there, but I'd learned how to stifle them or quiet them because I started falling for the lies society, friends, and the media served up about growing older with your spouse. I brought my work home then it came to bed with me, and I pushed our sex life into a corner of the bedroom. When Paul finally got my attention, we were miles in our relationship and he told me to make a decision on whether I wanted to end us or put forth the effort of reclaiming every aspect of our marriage.

At the time I was very defensive because I didn't think things were that bad. We still were able to go out to dinner and talk to one another with quite a bit to share. I considered those times as special moments, but I began to buy into the excuses I would hear from others at work or advice I would find online and was willing to make just enough extra effort to feel comfortable with the rare moments of quality. My husband, on the other hand, was not willing to settle for comfortable. He wanted the exceptional bond we had in the beginning. The, 'I couldn't wait to get home' kisses and the 'I need to just be up under you or in your space because I was feeling a little off today', and 'I need the reassurance that all is well'. He wanted the long talks into the night and the spontaneity that I thought we should have outgrown. He wanted the 'I don't care if we're late' morning cuddles and the 'I can kiss my wife whenever and where ever I want to' moments to be more frequent.

I thought he was just going through some type of mid-life crisis, but it was me who was going through the crisis of allowing my work and outside influences to slowly kill my marriage and relationship with my husband."

Intrigued by Mary's transparency and the subject matter, Victoria sat up. "What did you do?"

Mary sat back in her chair, idly playing with her spoon.

"I started giving him more attention – after all, we were spectacular once – but it took more effort than it had when we first got together. It was like I was stroking a fire that never needed stroking before and I was putting forth so much more energy than I'd had to before but was getting less in return. After a few months, I was afraid my marriage really was in trouble. I began to wonder what came first: my distraction from my marriage which caused the loss of intimacy, or was it the loss of the feelings of intimacy that made me seek out distractions instead of investigating what was lacking."

Victoria watched her for a moment, waiting for her to continue instead of asking another question that would give Mary a deeper look at her own marriage. She couldn't take the criticism at this moment.

Mary huffed. "Well after six months, Paul suggested we go to this marriage support group, but I balked at the idea of sharing our private lives with complete strangers. He said we didn't have to say anything, but I thought our very attendance would speak volumes and I was too caught up in what others would think or if there would be anyone there that I knew." Mary shared a self-deprecating smile with Victoria.

"God Bless him, he tried. He suggested we go to private marital counseling sessions and I told him I would consider it if he found one outside of our community. He was so patient with me and when I think back to those days, I'm even more assured of his love for me." She glanced at Victoria then away as if embarrassed by the admission.

"Well anyway, I finally caved and started going to these sessions with him. I was ready to be whipped with a wet noodle or blamed for the failings in my marriage, but the counselor was very objective and just asked questions for the first few sessions. I was wondering if he was ever going to give us advice." She took a sip of her cold tea before she continued.

"It wasn't until we'd been going for a couple of months that I realized what he was doing. We would answer the questions during the sessions and more often than not, on the long ride home we would ask each other why we answered the way we did. I learned a lot more on those rides home than I ever did during the sessions, but they were the catalyst. By the sixth month, I could confidently ask Paul questions that would have scared me too much to ask in the beginning. We even had a few heated fights that I normally would have shied away from in the beginning, but once I was secure enough to know that he wasn't going to walk out if I touched on those sensitive areas of his psyche or our relationship, you couldn't stop me." She paused, giving Victoria a small, less than innocent smile.

"It was only then that I found that the more I delved into those places I'd once considered forbidden, the more intimately tied I felt o him. I also realized that at some point in our marriage we stopped growing together and became two people learning new things about ourselves and hiding the things we didn't necessarily find flattering. We built walls around those things and ultimately created fortresses to keep each other from finding out our dirty little secrets. It caused a level of insecurity within us that didn't fit with our marriage, especially if we wanted to regain the intimacy from before."

Victoria could relate to most of what Mary said, but even with being transparent, it seemed Mary and Paul had an easier go of it than she and Richard would. Not to mention she was mostly to blame for their separation. She just couldn't seem to find the confident, self-made woman she once was and after Paige's visit, she barely knew what she would find from one thought to the next. If it weren't for her occasional visits with her therapist she would bet if she went to a marriage counselor, as soon as she opened her mouth she would be escorted to her next destination in a comfortably padded paddy wagon.

"What made you cave?" Victoria dared to ask.

"My husband wasn't happy, and my mother always told me that an unhappy husband doesn't stay long. I wasn't only afraid of my marriage failing – I was afraid of losing my best friend. Even if I'd started taking him for granted."

Victoria ran some of the information she'd just gleaned from Mary around in her mind. Could she do it? Could she save her marriage or resuscitate what was left of it? Richard had suggested, well more like demanded they start marriage counseling, but she'd not heard anything in that regard since he'd been back. At first, she thought he was just relaxing on his threat, but maybe he was just giving up.

"May I ask you a question that you would be perfectly justified in denying to answer?"

Victoria looked at her, studying her long enough to see her squirm. "Go ahead, you can ask."

"I can tell Richard loves you greatly and I believe you love him as well, but some of the things you've gone through are too heavy to deal with without help."

Victoria felt the mention of their tragedies like salt in a fresh wound. "Is there a question coming soon?"

Mary looked visibly uncomfortable now and Victoria inwardly cringed at making her feel as such, but she couldn't seem to help herself. It was still too raw.

"After Paul and I were in marital counseling for about nine months, one of Paul's co-workers invited us to a marriage retreat. I wouldn't have been for it when we first began because I couldn't stand the idea of anyone in our business, but by then I was a little more secure in us. It was better than I thought, and the games and small workshops we entered encouraged but didn't demand participation. The first year we went we mostly watched, but the next year we participated much more. This year we get to head one of the workshops and I wanted to know if you might consider coming out for the long weekend and hanging with us. Kate and Sam will be there as well."

She looked so hopeful, Victoria couldn't reject her invitation outright. "I'll consider it," she said and saw Mary's face droop in disappointment before she tried to hide it by taking a sip of her drink. She knew; she had been right where Victoria was.

"Honestly," she said as a way to placate the woman, but she was pretty sure Mary wasn't buying it. Just like she wasn't buying that the only reason Mary came to visit was because she wanted to invite her to a couple's weekend.

Mary didn't press the issue and their conversation turned toward lighter subjects, allowing Victoria to take her first relaxing breaths since Richard's trip to Chicago.

That evening she gave great consideration to what Paige had shared with her and what Mary said what Paul found when he'd seen Richard. Richard had been able to forgive her many things, but she didn't know if he would be able to forgive himself enough to continue to fight for them as a couple. His lack of communication and refusal to take her calls over the last two weeks caused her to consider that she had used up all of his patience – Christian or not.

As she went through her nightly ritual, her contemplation deepened enough that she finally placed herself in her husband's shoes and what she saw as she turned toward herself wasn't pretty. She doubted she would have been so forgiving or patient if the tables were turned.

She had the love of a good man, there was no doubt about it, and though she wasn't ready to trust nor concede to the thought that God was a loving being instead of the wrath wielder her parents and pastor represented, what Paige had shared did penetrate her thoughts daily. She just couldn't stop blaming Him for not intervening for her son.

She turned her thoughts back to Richard and their marriage. This was something she could do something about. She watched her reflection in the mirror while she brushed her hair. Her eyes followed the movement of the brush until she spied the note cards on the bedside table.

She walked over to the small stack, picking up the bottom two in the pile. A plan formed in her mind causing her to smile wistfully. It was time she went after her husband.

After two hours of writing out her plan and making lists of things that needed to be done in her absence, packing then the three and a half hour drive to Oklahoma City, Victoria should have been exhausted. Instead, she felt vibrantly alive and full of nervous energy. She headed straight to his apartment, arriving just before sunrise to find his car missing from the garage. Her heart skipped a beat when her mind went immediately to the possibility that he might be with someone else. She tamped down on the rising fear and drove to his office building's garage and the overwhelming relief she felt in spotting his car almost brought her to tears. He was either worked extremely late and didn't feel like going back to the apartment, or he'd come in very early. Neither of which bode well for his health. Paul's assessment was probably spot on. Her husband wasn't taking care of himself and it was her fault.

She went to a nearby all-night coffee shop and waited until she thought Nancy was headed into the office then dialed the woman's number, prepared to eat crow.

The phone rang several times before Nancy answered. "Hello?" "Hello Nancy, this is Victoria Branchett."

There was a decidedly long pause followed by what she could only describe as a dry reply which she chose to ignore. "Mrs. Branchett."

"Nancy, are you heading into the office today?"

"I'm entering the building right now."

"I was wondering if my husband was in his office. I've not been able to reach him. Could you call me back and let me know when you get in?"

"Yes, Mrs. Branchett."

"Thank you, Nancy." She hung up and took one last sip of her coffee while she waited. Seven minutes later, Nancy called her back to confirm that Richard had indeed spent the night in his office and would be on his way to the apartment to freshen up for a meeting he had at 10 o'clock.

"Nancy, I don't know what you must think, but I'm going to need a favor from you today."

"Mrs. Branchett, I'd rather not get in the middle of anything –" Victoria cut her off.

"You already are, simply due to your position. I know what I am about to ask you is slightly out of line with your job description, but you're the only one that can help me."

The silence was finally broken by a sigh of resignation on the other line. "What do you need me to do?"

Victoria released the breath she'd been holding then shared her plan with Nancy to get her husband back. Nancy was decidedly more civil by the time they were ready to hang up, and it brought home the fact to Victoria that she had really been caught up in her own world for a long time. She just hoped she hadn't waited too long to finally come out of her single-minded rage.

She arrived at the apartment after Richard and placed the first note on his windshield, then waited for him to come out and discover the card. His response showed her that though she'd never considered begging, this might be a good time for her to start considering it.

She followed him back to his work, but lost her nerve when she saw the disgusted scowl on his face when he picked the card up off the passenger's seat. She would have to woo him back from afar.

She checked-in to her hotel and got some much-needed sleep. Late that afternoon the long, soothing bath and room service went a long way in reviving her spirits. She made another call to Nancy to double check that things were set for the next evening. Nancy confirmed the arrangements she'd made for them the next evening, causing Victoria to consider giving Nancy a secret bonus at the end of the quarter. Victoria had a bout of regret as she sat in on the sofa of her suite. She'd turned a farm into a ranch and small town. She'd made money in every venture or investment she'd put her hands on.

The gala had raised a record-breaking amount this year, but she had no children, her parents were gone, and her marriage was teetering on the edge of oblivion. At that moment, she would have happily traded her failed relationships for all of her money. Okay…most of her money. She wasn't into martyrdom, just in case God was honing in on her thoughts at the moment.

She walked to the window that overlooked the city skyline and began rehearsing what she would say to Richard to convince him she was ready to do what it took to save their marriage.

The next morning she woke up to the incessant ringing of her cell phone. She peered at the alarm clock trying to get her mind to register the hour. The red LED display read 7:30 a.m. She spied Nancy's number on the display. "Hello?" She cleared her throat as she sat up.

"Mrs. Branchett, sorry to wake you," Nancy began as a way of greeting.

"That's alright. What is it?" Victoria responded reaching for her bottle of water.

"Mr. Branchett asked me to make arrangements for his travel to the ranch."

Victoria sat straight up in bed. "What did you say?"

"I told him I would take care of it."

Victoria was not appeased. "When did he say he wanted to travel?"

"He has a few meetings today so it won't be until after 4:30 p.m. I can try and stall him."

"Don't try, Nancy, do. I have a lot riding on this evening and it won't work with us in different towns." Victoria felt a small nagging at the base of her skull.

"I'm aware of that, Mrs. Branchett. I will do what it takes to make sure that Mr. Branchett is where you need him to be this evening. I just thought it would be prudent to inform you of his intent since I will be going against his wishes. It will make him a little frayed at the edges."

Victoria swallowed back the prideful retort. Nancy had been Richard's secretary long enough to be able to read him. If Victoria had been paying more attention over the last five years maybe she would too. "I appreciate all that you're doing, really. Thank you."

Her response was a muffled 'humph', but she took it. She realized she needed the woman's full cooperation and was grateful for the heads up.

After a few more words, they hung up and Victoria began what would either be a happy reunion or the end of her marriage. She didn't take Richard's return to the ranch to mean that reconciliation was imminent. It could just as easily mean that he was giving her the respect of ending it in person.

She chewed on her lip in consternation until she realized what she was doing. It had been a long time since she'd shown such outward signs of angst. She needed to pull herself together otherwise she wouldn't even make it to the evening.

She glanced at the clock again and decided to get a few miles of walking in before breakfast and her appointment at the spa. This way if Nancy couldn't stall him past 5:00 p.m., she would be ready for him.

Victoria let herself in Richard's apartment at 4:00 p.m. Housekeeping had already come by, packed up and delivered to his office what few pieces of clothing he'd brought with him. She set the packages down on the counter and hung up the suit she'd bought him the day before. She hung up her dress next to his and smiled at the thought of sharing space with him again.

She went about putting the finishing touches on the decorated apartment. The light and flowers were just as she had instructed. She attached her iPod to the surround sound stereo, happy it was similar to the one they had at home. She opened the drapes, went back to the counter and began taking out the items that would lead him through the apartment to her once he opened the door.

One hour later, Victoria was dressed, primped, and waiting for the sound of Richard's key in the door. Her phone was on vibrate, but she'd gotten Nancy's message that a slightly disgruntled Richard was on his way back to the apartment by way of taxi. He'd come to the garage to find that the car he was going to drive home had two flat tires and wouldn't be ready until the next afternoon, and since Paul was using the corporate jet, Richard had no choice but to stay in the city. Victoria would have giggled if she weren't so relieved.

Her heart sped up when she heard the latch on the door. She listened intently as the door opened and his footsteps paused. Everything was silent and she noticed she was holding her breath, so she let it out slowly. "Victoria?" She stilled herself, further begging him quietly to read the card on the entry table.

He began to move again and she heard him set his suitcase down as he set his keys on the table. When she heard the swipe of the card against the table top, she began breathing again. She knew that card would send him over to the kitchen counter where he would find a glass of champagne. He would be ordered to at least take a sip before he was sent to the bathroom to freshen up and put on the suit she'd hung in there for him.

When she heard the bathroom door close, she waited a few seconds before she tiptoed passed to the living room so she would be waiting for him when he followed the next directions.

So far he had followed every card, but Victoria wasn't completely sure he would be willing to continue once he got a look at what she had prepared for him. Maybe he didn't want to continue down memory lane.

Victoria was startled from her thoughts when the bathroom door opened. It took all of her discipline not to fidget. When Richard walked around the corner she knew he would see her bathed in candlelight, her cranberry colored shift dress embroidered with small flowers of a slightly darker hue was much like the one she'd worn 33 years before.

He stopped short upon seeing her and she folded her hands to keep from ringing them. Instead of biting her lip, she chose to speak. "Hello, Richard."

She watched Richard swallow before he spoke. "Good evening, Victoria."

"Won't you come have a seat?" She motioned towards the table that had been made up with a white tablecloth and black napkins folded to look like fans.

He walked towards her instead and opened his mouth. She lifted a finger, her eyes imploring him to do as she asked. He continued to watch her for a moment, an unreadable expression etched on his face. Finally, he inclined his head and took a seat at the far side of the table.

Victoria continued to stand. "Would you like an appetizer or more champagne?" she asked, thankful her voice belied her nervousness.

"Both, thank you." He must have been as nervous as she was. She walked over to the sidebar, placing selections of food on a plate and picking up another filled glass of champagne. She set both in front of him and began to move away when he caught her hand. The puzzlement on his features made her want to kiss the furrow between his brows. She patted his hand and moved to her seat.

She looked at him over the candlelight and took a huge breath before she began.

"I want to begin by telling you I'm sorry," she said quietly, looking him square in the eye. The only sign he'd heard her, came from a slight tilt of his head.

"It seems I have been very selfish," she nearly choked on the lump in her throat. She took a sip from her glass of champagne to moisten her now extremely dry mouth.

"I got stuck for a while between grief and anger, bouncing back and forth between the two. I couldn't seem to find my way around the rage at losing yet another relationship I cherished and the pity sessions I wrapped myself in because the one thing I wanted most eluded me.

I sat in that house and cursed God for all that he had taken away from me in the name of what was sovereign, and all it did was cost me more time with the people I cherish more than anything.

Unfortunately, it took the betterment of three years for me to develop close enough relationships with people I would listen to, who would tell me in no uncertain terms that I was the one destroying the very thing I treasured. All I can do is take care of what is in front of me." She took a shaky breath. Her heart was beating a mile-a-minute and she couldn't keep her hands from trembling, but she would finish even if her heart seized afterward.

"Do you know what's in front of me?" she asked, knowing every loving feeling towards him was in her eyes.

She watched as Richard shook his head, seeming at a loss for words. Matter of fact, he looked a little stunned.

"You are what's in front of me, and in you is everything I value. I'm sorry I haven't treated you with the care you deserve, but if you can forgive me or at least see your way to giving me another chance..." Her throat closed up with the tears she was perilously close to shedding. She swallowed one, two, three times before she felt capable of continuing. "If you could give me another chance, I promise to treat you how you deserve."

"How?" Came his whisper and she raised her eyes to meet his.

"What?"

"How are you going to do that? How are you going to treat me like a wonderful man deserves?"

Victoria's blood pressure jumped. His tone was distant and business-like, as though he were making a deal.

She was momentarily at a loss but rallied quickly. Pride was a cold bedfellow. She smoothed the invisible wrinkles in the tablecloth in front of her before looking Richard squarely in the eye. "I will share my victories and my fears with you. I will listen to your concerns and they will become mine just as your accomplishments become something to celebrate as my own. I'm saying I won't shut you out, but I will work to include myself more in your pursuits. I will no longer try to manipulate your 'no' into a 'yes', and I will try to remember that we are a team and that what I do represents you. I will work to find that forgiving, generous, and loving young girl you fell in love with."

Richard shook his head and Victoria's heart dropped into her stomach. She didn't know what else to offer. If he wanted her to go to church, she didn't know if she was ready and couldn't promise him that. *Marital counseling.* She would go to marital counseling with him. She would offer to schedule it for the next week if he wanted. She opened her mouth to say so when he held up his hand.

She forced down the sob. He didn't want to hear any more. She watched as he got up, and she did the same. He came to stand in front of her, took her hands then guided her back to her chair kneeling in front of her.

"I don't want the girl I met back then. I want the woman who has weathered the storm and yelled back at it saying she would not be moved. I want the woman I've grown with who knows my idiosyncrasies, likes, dislikes, and flare for last minute parties." He lifted his lips in a sheepish smile she felt all the way to her heart. She promptly and unceremoniously burst into tears. He wanted her.

He continued, "I was wrong in trying to make you relive our early days because they are gone. I was just hoping that you would find that beautiful heart somewhere in all of that anger you've used to keep it safe. I want to make new memories with you. I want to celebrate every day we have left together with kisses, hugs, or by making love to you when you aren't so busy saving the world." She laughed through her tears at the reminder of what she'd told him on their first date when he'd asked her what would cause her regret if she didn't do it every day. She had responded by telling him she wanted to do at least one thing a day that would help save the world in some way. From recycling to funding a life-saving cause, she wanted to be a part of it.

"I want that woman who has experienced life-altering devastation and still gets up every morning, screaming, 'World do your worst!'"

She shook her head. "That wasn't me. I just didn't know how to stop breathing."

She watched the smile fall from his lips. "I'm glad you didn't figure it out, baby. I would have missed you a great deal."

She leaned forward, wrapping her arms around his neck. "I love you, Richard. I'm so sorry for…"

Richard pulled out of her arms and placed a finger on her lips. "You've already apologized and I have forgiven you so let's seal it with a kiss." Before she could reply, he kissed her sweetly and she melted against him. Her body may have aged and her mind may have recorded the experiences of 59 years, but when he looked at her a certain way, touched or kissed her, she was transported back to that twenty-six-year-old woman who found herself dazzled by the confident, considerate, and drop dead gorgeous man that helped her feel again.

Richard pulled away from her for the second time and she wanted to whimper in frustration. He pulled himself up and moved her out of the chair so he could sit her on his lap. "All of this is fortuitous." He began. "I was on my way back tonight."

A lesser man would have kept that to himself, she thought.

"But none of my rides worked out."

"I know." He glanced up to stare at her.

"You slashed my tires?"

She shook her head. "No. I just told Nancy to do whatever needed to be done to keep you in the city one more night. I didn't know she would go to such drastic measures. I was actually planning on giving her a raise myself," she giggled.

She watched him shake his head in disbelief. "How long have you been in town?"

"Since yesterday morning."

"Really? What have you been doing? Why didn't you come to the office or the apartment sooner?"

She shrugged. "I lost my nerve."

Richard's eyes went wide. "Why?"

"You are too important to come at any old way. I needed a plan. You know how much more comfortable I feel with a plan."

He looked around them while he chuckled. "And your plan was?" She waited for him to meet her eyes. "To remind you of our first date and how wonderful we have been together since."

"And you couldn't do this when I got home?"

She shook her head. "Why?" He asked.

"Because I needed you to know that I would come for you instead of just wait for you to come back. I wanted you to know that I would put forth the effort, that I value you and our relationship enough to do the chasing."

His eyes misted slightly and he kissed her softly before his lips quirked. "Well, now that you've caught me. What ever will you do with me?"

"I'm going to love you, Richard, and I won't ever let you go."

"You promise?"

She smiled then replied with her lips against his. "Yes."

"I don't know if I believe you," he said, the twinkle in his eyes belying his gruff tone.

She took in a sharp breath. "But..." He cut her off. "But I believe there is one way you can convince me."

"How?" She said quietly.

"Marry me. Again."

She stared at him for a moment, not believing what she'd heard, but as she continued to stare into his earnest face, the anxiety of the day melted away and hope took flight in her heart.

"Yes," she whispered, as tears began to course down her cheeks again. "Yes," she said louder so he was assured of her answer. She found herself scooped up and held tightly to his chest.

He kissed her again and she had a sense of floating. She thought it was the euphoria of it all until her head touched the pillow. He pulled back briefly. "What about dinner?"

He looked back and forth between her eyes they were so close. "Did you want to reenact our whole first date?"

She shrugged. "I ordered your favorite dish."

She watched his smile transform into wicked grin. "You're my favorite dish," he said before joining her on the bed.

CHAPTER 32

Mason sat across from Dr. Seagret not sure where to begin. Since Paige had left his thoughts were full of her. He'd picked up the phone at least a thousand times to see how she was, to see how she faired after her talk with her sister. The little pieces of information that she'd gotten from Vivian through Gladys only told him how Mel was doing which was too good by the report Vivian had gotten from Gladys.

At first he chalked up the constant thoughts of her to being concerned for her well-being, but it was now a full month later and he could still feel her back pressed against his chest. He could smell the fruity scent of her shampoo and conditioner and he still heard her voice in the wind. Yesterday Vivian finally told him that Paige and Brandon were engaged and she wanted his permission to be a junior bride in the wedding. Instead of going out and getting drunk he called and made an appointment with Dr. Seagret. He still wanted that drink though.

"It's been a moment Mason? How are you doing?" Dr. Seagret asked he ushered Mason into the office.

"I think it's safe to say that I will be one of those clients that only come to you when things get so bad it becomes a toss-up between you and drinking. Mason responded as he sat down in the club chair."

Dr. Seagret seemed to think about this for some time before he spoke and this time instead of becoming frustrated with the wait Mason relaxed back in his chair comfortable in his choice.

"I'm not sure that's the healthiest way to handle our appointments, but I have to applaud you on your choice to pick me instead of the bottle."

Mason shrugged one shoulder. "I picked you first. If talking to you doesn't get me what I need then I will go to the bottle."

Dr. Seagret quirked a brow. "What did you come here looking for today?"

Mason considered the question briefly. "Something like an exorcism. Do you offer that service and if you do, how much more will that cost me?"

A small smile tipped Dr. Seagret's lips at the edges, but it didn't touch his cheeks let alone his eyes. "I'm sensing some latent hostility coming off you in waves. Did you make this appointment because you needed a punching bag or because you wanted to work through some disturbing thoughts you couldn't wade through on your own?"

Mason chuckled mirthlessly, rubbing his chin with his thumb and forefinger as he surveyed the room looking for something he could concentrate on while he opened up this wound.

"Paige is getting married." Mason decided to rip the Band-Aid off first.

Dr. Seagret stared at him with the blank expression that made most of his more dramatic announcements anti-climactic. He hated when he did that. After a few moments, it became obvious Dr. Seagret wasn't going to respond.

"I was nearly resolved to the fact that Paige and Brandon would be together. From what I could gather the few times my daughter spoke of them Brandon made her happy... until almost six weeks ago." He paused slightly more out of self-preservation than for effect. "Paige came to visit Vivian and me a month ago. She was taking a little holiday, visiting her girls, sister and whomever else she could think of to keep her from going home for a while. Brandon broke up with her because his last health report came back less than favorable. Instead of holding her closer and making the most of their time together he pushes her away."

"He must have changed his mind because you began with the fact that Paige is engaged to him."

"He doesn't deserve her." Mason groundout.

"According to what standard?" Dr. Seagret asked just above a whisper.

"He hurt her. I would have cherished her and kept her first."

"What changed Mason? The last time you were here you seemed almost resolved in the fact that Brandon and Paige were going to be together. You know that relationships can be rocky sometimes, emotions rule out common sense, but the underlying factor is the same." The words, though true, did little to appease Mason.

"I watched her sit across from me and receive news that would have fell a grown man and I couldn't comfort her."

"How do you know?"

"I couldn't touch her or hold her."

"But you were there. How do you know that wasn't enough?"

Mason looked away for a moment, feeling uncomfortable sharing the next piece of information. They were moments he could hold just for himself, but they also haunted him.

"She didn't handle the news well and ended up in the bathroom. I helped her."

Dr. Seagret's eyes narrowed slightly before he spoke. "What did that mean to you?"

Mason looked at him, unable to hide his emotions. "Too much obviously. I think I'm right back where I started."

"Maybe not." Dr. Seagret replied and Mason hoped he'd just been thrown a lifeline.

"You were there for Paige, Vivian's biological mother. You helped her through some rough spots when there was no one else. Now, unless you took advantage of the situation and used it to gain a foothold in your relationship with her or widen the gap between her and Brandon, you were the person she needed to lean on at that moment and you should be proud of that fact."

"Like I said before. You aren't as far gone as you think. Your knack for self-preservation is stronger than you give yourself credit for. When you stop underestimating yourself you find someone you believe deserves to be happy."

"Wow Doc. That was profound." Mason replied sardonically.

"And it is obviously lost on you at this time." He shrugged. "Even I'm wrong sometimes."

Mason stared at him, not knowing whether to be encouraged or insulted by the remarks. He finally set it aside promising himself he would study it later.

"So what do I do now?"

"The healthiest thing would be to get to know yourself again. Find out what you like and what you don't like in everything. Define yourself by your priorities, not your obligations. This is the best time to get to know Mason, the good and the bad then tweak the things you don't like until you do?"

"How do I do that?"

"Spend time getting to know yourself. Take the focus off of the 'what ifs' and place it on what is right in front of you – you and your daughter."

Mason was about to tell him he'd been trying to do just that, but he knew it would make him sound like a whiner.

"I'm going to do suggest something outside of the box here, but bear with me because we will be on swinging pendulum." He waited for Mason's nod. Let's pretend for a moment that we can see into the future and there is no scenario that can be worked to bring you and Paige together." Mason felt the words like a punch to the gut. He had to work not to show any visible signs of his reaction.

"What would you do with your life? " He waited long enough for Mason to realize he was looking for an answer, an answer Mason hadn't considered in the month since Paige's visit.

"Okay." Dr. Seagret wrote something down on his pad then continued. "If you haven't considered yourself have you at least considered your daughter? What does she think?"

Mason didn't want to bring Vivian into this, but she was his life. The part of his life that he had once again put on a shelf while he sorted through his feelings for Paige. "I'm pretty sure she wishes I would get over Paige. She loves her as if they weren't apart the first 12 years of her life. They Skype with each other for prayer time almost every morning with Vivian's sister."

"And what do they pray about during the mornings?" Dr. Seagret asked as if Mason should know then Mason wondered why he hadn't considered asking Paige straight out.

"Mostly for their families, I guess, I've heard them pray for Brandon's health, Vivian's grandmother Victoria as well as for their individual churches' and the pastors. It seems innocent enough and from what I can tell Paige shares the same beliefs as Vivian and Rachael. I trust her."

"Now let's work with what we can see." Dr. Seagret went on. "You are the father of Paige's biological daughter who you felt a certain connection with at first sight, but she chose not to move on it because she was looking for a connection on each level. How am I doing so far?"

Mason's teeth clenched, but he nodded his agreement.

"Paige, in turn, chose a man who shares in her beliefs and lives on the same side of the country as she does. She not only keeps the lines of communication open between her daughters she nurtures and helps cultivate their relationship with the same God your wife loved while serving as a mother figure. She seems to know who she is Mason. Don't you think it's time you did the same?"

We have very different lives. Our struggles and challenges are miles apart."

"Yes, except for one thing."

"What?" Mason asked before he knew what he was saying. He didn't really want yet another difference between him and Paige spelled out.

"She has made peace with or comes to terms with her challenges. I think in her religious culture it would be called forgiveness. Now you have to do that for yourself otherwise you may find yourself right here after every encounter with her and that is no life to live"

"But I thought you missed me, or at least my money,"

Dr. Seagret leaned back in his chair a small smile playing on his lips. "You couldn't resist could you?"

Mason shrugged.

"Say what you'd like Mason, just give my advice some consideration. You deserve to be happy. I hope the next time you come through my door you're ready to work on what's behind door number two so we can begin putting your life back together."

"What's behind door number two?" Mason asked and once again he regretted his lack of discipline.

"Where all great challenges begin. Your childhood."

The fear that struck Mason sent chills down his spine. He was sure Dr. Seagret saw it.

"Until then," The doctor said rising from his seat to signal the end of the session. "Write a true list of your likes and dislikes. Get to know yourself again Mason otherwise, no one else will be able to." Mason shook hands with the doctor because he didn't know what else to do and exited the office. Breathing heavy and feeling as though he'd just escaped by the skin of his teeth, Mason took the stairs leading outside as quickly as possible. He was nearly to the bottom before he looked up into a startling pair of green eyes right before he ran into their owner.

He caught the woman by the arms trying to steady her even as he worked to regain his balance. He began to mumble his apologies but was overtaken by a sense of familiarity as he took in her features. She was either biracial or of Latin descent, her coloring reminding him of a deeply tanned olive complexion. She had high cheekbones and almost wildly curly medium brown hair that seemed to absorb the sunlight turning it the color of cinnamon on top. He found all of these features interesting in an analytical sort of way with his mind pondering how it all worked together, but it was her eyes that arrested him. He was sure he would have remembered meeting her because he had a knack for cataloging colors, but try as he might he couldn't shake the feeling of familiarity.

"I'm sorry." He said, letting go of her arms. "Are you alright? I didn't hurt you, did I?" He continued as he looked for any damage he may have caused. He took a cursory glance at her chocolate suede boots and tan slacks that didn't seem the worse for wear. He took in the zip up sweater that matched her eyes and surmised that he hadn't mussed her up too badly. It wasn't until she stepped away that he registered her surprise and the fact that she had not spoken.

"Are you okay?" He repeated, slower this time.

She seemed to snap out of her stupor and began nodding. "Yes. Fine. Thank you." She smiled briefly. He took in her features again but came up blank. "This isn't a line because you are way too pretty for it, but I get the feeling that we've seen each other before. Have we met?"

He watched her for any sign of recognition, but she shook her head. "No." She looked at the steps he'd just descended and he knew she wanted to go, but she was like a puzzle he needed to solve.

"Maybe we work in the same building, MarsdenTech, we might have ridden the same elevator once or twice?"

She shook her head again. "Actually I just moved here."

"Oh, from where, if you don't mind me asking." He delved, hoping her next answer would give him a clue.

"Miami, Florida." She said hesitantly and he could tell that his interrogative approach was making her wary.

He took a step back making sure he was out of her personal space. "I'm sorry if I'm coming off a bit forward. I am just usually very good with faces and yours seems familiar, but I can't seem to place you. It's a little disconcerting that's all."

She seemed to relax after his last statement and the space he'd put between them. "I know it's going to haunt me for a while, but we learn to live with the little disappointments right?"

Her smile fell and she nodded solemnly. He wanted to apologize for whatever he'd said to cause the change, but he could trace back the words.

He knew Dr. Seagret would shake his head in disapproval at his next move, but he didn't particularly care at the moment.

He reached into his back pocket pulling out his wallet. He retrieved one of his cards holding it out to her. "Since you are new to the area you might want to take a tour sometime or get to know the neighborhood. I would be willing to offer my services."

Her eyes widened then narrowed suspiciously. "You do tours?" She asked peering at the card but not reaching out to take the card.

He chuckled sheepishly. "No, I'm an architect, but I've lived here for years and sometimes it isn't so easy finding the best places to shop and the best attractions a city affords." He lifted his card bringing it closer to her. "It's alright. You can check me out if you wish and if you're interested we could start with a walking tour." *Where was all of this coming from? He'd never been this forward. Was he coming off desperate? He wasn't sure.* He was about to retract his hand when she reached up and took the card, bringing it closer to her face. "Mason Jenson." She read from the card.

"I'm not all alone. I came to live with my sister." She looked up and he noticed that her eyes were lighter now that the surprise affecting her pupils had abated. "Alright Mason, I'll think about your offer. If I'm interested I'll get back to you." She said fanning his card and hitting it against her palm.

"You know my name now." He said inclining his head towards the card. "May I have yours?"

She seemed to think about that for a moment. "If I call you I'll give it to you, how's that?"

He shrugged. "I'm not particularly fond of that option." He said trying to keep the playfulness in his voice.

"Would you like me to give you a fake name?" she said quirking a brow.

"No. Are you into playing games?"

She frowned slightly. "No. I'm just being cautious. I did just bump into you on the street."

He conceded. "Very well. Woman with the beautiful green eyes, I hope you give me a call so I can show you around the most beautiful city in the

United States." *And so I can figure out why you seem so darned familiar.* He thought to himself.

She lifted the card and walked around him so she could ascend the stairs. "Thank you, Mason Jenson, for the compliments. You have brightened my day."

He wanted to say something that would keep her there talking to him. He was enjoying the confidence he seemed to find around her.

He bowed slightly. "The feeling is mutual and all I had to do was nearly run you down."

She giggled as she continued up the steps.

"I hope to hear from you soon." He called after her.

She lifted the card up one more time in answer to his spoken hope then opened the door disappearing behind it.

Mason watched until she was completely out of sight and just a little bit longer, sealing the moment in his memory. He rolled his shoulders looking up and down the street for nothing in particular.

He moved towards his car, but light reflecting off of an object near the edge of the sidewalk and a squared-off planted tree caught his eye. He picked it up flipping it between his fingers until he came upon two letters engraved on what had to the front. T. A. it read. He finally recognized the narrow rectangular metal object as a card case. He found the fastening and opened it to reveal elegantly scripted cards with an initial and last name of Anderson. He peered into its corner and saw the picture of the women he'd nearly knocked down. He closed the case and raced back up the stairs and through the door hoping she walked slowly, but he saw no one in the wide hallway which housed four doors on each side. He hesitated before the first door before deciding to abandon the search. This was a brownstone that held therapist offices. She might not take his intrusion into her session well, even if it did mean she could have back the expensive looking case. He waited a moment, hoping she might realize she dropped it and retrace her steps, but as one minute rolled into the next it became obvious that she hadn't and that he was standing in the middle of a hallway that held no lobby. Growing more and more uncomfortable by the moment and suddenly paranoid that someone other than her would exit one of the rooms and see him loitering he walked back to the door leading to the outside and walked back down the steps to his car on the street.

He slowed his steps as he approached his car hoping beyond hope that she would come out, but to his disappointment, she did not. He unlocked his car and got in but didn't start the car right away. He opened the card case and retrieved a card once more, reading it more thoroughly. T. Anderson, Marketing and Design Consultant. No address or phone number, but there was an email address. He would email her and let her know that she dropped the case. That would assure him at least one more chance to convince her to take him up on his offer to show her Chicago. He placed the card back in the holder and placed it on the passenger seat. A small smile crossed his lips as he started his car and check his side view mirror for traffic.

That evening he took Vivian to her favorite pasta restaurant and listened with slight distraction at her replay her school day.

"Daddy?" He looked up at her, his features set in thoughtfulness. "Yes?"

"What are you thinking about?"

"You, Hun. I've been listening to you talk about your day. You were telling me that next year you might take chemistry because Amanda is taking it." He was happy he'd zoomed back in on the conversation just before she'd asked him. It wouldn't do to get caught daydreaming. Not with Ms. Observant watching.

She stared at him for a moment. "What? I'm listening." He reiterated trying not to sound defensive.

"Something's different about you." She said slowly and he instantly felt like a bug under a microscope.

"Really, how?" he asked as he took a bite of his linguini.

She cocked her head to the side as she continued to study him. "You seem…happy."

He frowned. "Am I not allowed to be happy?"

She seemed to realize what she said and became a little flustered. "Yes…yes, I want to see you happy. I'm just wondering why."

He took another bite and chewed slowly trying to absorb her comment and come up with an answer that would assuage her curiosity.

"I'm sorry I've been such an Eeyore." He said referring to one of the characters in her favorite Saturday morning cartoon.

"You haven't been an Eeyore, Daddy. Not exactly a Tigger, but not an Eeyore." She stopped to ponder the thought more, placing her forefinger to her lips. "You are Rabbit."

He scrunched up his nose getting into the swing of the conversation. "Rabbit, naah, he's too staunch. I think of myself more like Owl." He sat up ramrod straight, raising his head so that he could look down his nose at her. She giggled.

"Daddy you aren't like Owl, he's too old. Besides Rabbit is very important and he's concerned about everyone. Just like you."

"You think I'm concerned about everyone. Well yeah. You are concerned about me. You were concerned about mom and that's why it hurt you so much when you couldn't save her. You're are concerned about Ms. Paige."

"Really, Ms. Paige isn't ill." He interrupted wanting to know where his child was going with her thought process.

"No, she isn't, but someone she loves is and that hurts her. You, daddy, like to be the hero. You save people and when you can't it bothers you."

He was slightly disturbed by her assessment, but even more so by the disapproval in her tone. "Is that so bad?"

She stopped rolling her spaghetti around on her fork and looked at him as though she were looking through him. "Daddy you can't save everyone. Only Jesus can do that." Then she went back to getting enough noodles on her fork for a decent bite.

He leaned back in his chair staring at his child his food forgotten. This child was something else. Would he never get used to what came out of her mouth? He shook his head to himself. No, he wouldn't and he wouldn't have her any other way.

He checked his watch. If they skipped desert he could get her home and into bed in time to do some web searching on his green-eyed woman. "Hey Hun, how about we save dessert for home. We have ice cream and chocolate fudge." She smiled her little girl smile at him full and he felt their roles line back up properly.

"Extra fudge?"

"Don't press your luck." He said with a smile.

She shrugged and turned her attention back to her meal. He sighed in contentment and returned to his linguini as well wondering how long it would take for Ms. T. Anderson to return his email.

CHAPTER 33

"Jesus, Jesus, Jesus, Jesus"…His name became her mantra because she could not clearly think of another word or name to consider at the moment. How she needed His help in this. She grasped at the small measure of peace that allowed her to get a rein on her emotions.

She moved restlessly about her apartment, carrying the phone with her.

"Paige?"

"I need…I need. She handed the phone to Brandon who'd watched her like a hawk since taking the call. Richard had called her the day before and asked that Brandon be present for their conversation. Since he was coming over today anyway she asked if it could wait that long. Richard's tone didn't give her any reason to believe the conversation was dyer. She thought, maybe he wanted to congratulate them both on their upcoming wedding?

This was not a congratulatory call. It wasn't even a pleasant call.

It may have just killed any chances for reconciliation between Melanie and herself. Mel was her mother?

She didn't know what to do first. She rubbed her hands along her arms to warm the cold that had taken over. Her body and mind were a mass of confusion. Why wouldn't she tell her? What more was she hiding?

"And this person who gave you this information. You trust them?" Brandon asked Richard.

"Absolutely." Came the disembodied voice from the phone's speaker.

Paige slowed her breathing. After the last time, it didn't occur to her to ask Richard if he'd double checked the information. She knew Richard considered her well-being, but why and how was he coming by information that no one else had for over 26 years, 27 if he'd waited two more days, but she figured he knew that as well.

"Did you tell Victoria?" She asked as loud as she dared.

"No," Richard responded just as quietly.

"She won't like you keeping secrets from her." Paige turned back towards Brandon and the phone.

"I know, but things are already too complicated between us right now. But you know that since you paid her a small visit before you saw your sister."

Paige's voice went quiet. "How do you know?" Was he watching her as well?

"Martha told me." He said quietly.

"She loves you very much. Richard." She said by way of apology for jumping to conclusions.

"Yes, but for once I'd like that love to come without conditions." Paige nodded. "Give her some time to think on things. I believe she will come around.

"I hope so. Paige, for what it's worth, I'm really sorry to be the bearer of this news, but I figured you would want to know. Was I right?"

Paige moved to sit next to Brandon. He offered her the phone, but she waved it away.

"You were right Richard and I thank you for making sure I would be alright."

She looked into Brandon's eyes taking note of the concern in their depths.

"I know we haven't known each other long but I think you are an incredible woman. I see a lot of my daughter in you."

That almost brought tears to her eyes.

"She was blessed to have a father like you."

There was a brief pause on the other line. When Richard's voice came back on it was deeper. "Thank you. You'll tell me if you need anything."

"Yes. Oh, Richard. Any word on my biological father?"

"I don't know. If you'd like I can see what I can do. You never know, maybe Mel will tell you."

"Don't hold your breath and neither will I," Paige said with more heat in her voice than she'd intended.

"Yes, well, Paige either way, don't let this change who you are. Who you were conceived by is not who you are today. They are just the vessels God used to get you here." Richard said with loving firmness.

"I will try to remember that Richard. Thank you. Goodbye."

"Goodbye Paige. Goodbye Brandon."

"Goodbye, Richard. Thank you." Brandon replied before he ended the call laying the phone to the side. He turned to her opening his arms to her. She moved into them and wasn't surprised when he pulled her onto his lap and guided her head to his shoulder. He rubbed her back in long strokes, up and down her spine and the tender gesture was her undoing. The tears began slowly, but as if a floodgate opened they poured out wetting Brandon's collar.

"I'm so tired of crying." She said as she sat up wiping at her tears. "My heart is tired of this constant pain. I don't want to think about my family anymore this evening. Tomorrow is soon enough to decide what I will do about Mel."

Brandon reached over to retrieve a tissue for her.

"What do you want to do?" He said, refusing to let her up to blow her nose across the room.

"I could get some of my wedding planning books. We could go over some of the ideas. See what we like."

He gave her a dubious look, but seeing the light coming back into her eyes helped him make up his mind quickly. He nodded his head, but before he let her up he tightened his grip.

"I will be here for you no matter when or how you want to take care of your family."

She looked into his dark eyes and wanted to get lost in them. "I know and it is only one of the reasons why I love you."

He smiled and shook her slightly. "Tell me another."

She wanted to laugh at his unabashed request for another compliment. "Because you won't even complain when I bring out more wedding planning magazines than you thought I had and you will go through them with me, giving your honest opinion. Do you want another reason?" She said as she leaned back to look at him.

He was frowning. "No. That's more than enough."

She stood up to retrieve the magazines from her bedroom had the good sense not to start laughing until she was halfway across the room.

*   *   *

Paige spent most of the next day fretting about making the call to Mel. She vacillated between deciding to wait until Mel called her to discuss her parentage to just dialing the number and coming straight out with the question. The problem was Mel would likely call Paige the next day for her birthday and she did not want to talk about this on her birthday. The other was that Paige didn't think she was in the right frame of mind to discuss this with Mel at the moment. The anger and frustration she thought she'd dealt with in regards to Mel's betrayal was back in full force. It took a few hours of prayer to realize that she had forgiven Mel for the betrayal, but this was something new she would have to deal with. She decided towards the late afternoon that she would wait until she felt she could discuss it with Mel with less emotion clouding her thoughts. She needed to come to terms with the fact that she didn't know Mel as well as she thought she did. It hurt to think Mel could keep such a huge secret from her when Paige was an open book for Mel.

It should have occurred to her when Mel sent the message through Brandon that she might have been giving her a clue. No, she wouldn't go there. Nothing could make this better. She almost wished Richard had never told her then she would have been blissfully ignorant. *But for how long?*

The voice was soft, but it rang true. It was better to hear it from someone who cared than to be pierced with it like a sword from someone who didn't.

For the next couple of hours, Paige used the extra energy supplied by her roving thoughts to cleaning and dusting her apartment. It didn't matter that she'd gone over the same tiles on the kitchen and bathroom floors two days before. She needed to keep busy and she couldn't seem to concentrate long enough on her new book to get through a page, let alone a chapter. She needed to step away just long enough to get quiet.

Her phone began to ring and she sighed in relief when she saw Lady Menagerie's number show up on the display.

"Hello?"

"Pack some clothes. I need a movie night."

"Okay. What are we watching?"

"Did you call your sister today?"

"No," Paige replied automatically then wondered what one had to do with the other.

"What did you clean?" Lady Menagerie asked firmly.

"The floors," Paige said with a sigh.

"It doesn't matter what we're watching then does it."

Paige shrugged to herself. "What time should I be there?"

"After you finish packing enough clothes to stay over for two nights, take a shower – because you are not bringing the smell of your cleanser over here, get in your car and make it up the front steps."

Paige giggled at her forcefulness. She could be loveably overbearing at times, but only when she thought she would come against opposition. Paige was only too happy to surrender over the rest of her night. Brandon had asked to take her out for her birthday and she didn't want to go back on her word.

"Why two days?" She asked.

"Because I'm in the mood to kidnap you for your birthday. You need to get out of that apartment for a while and what better place to be than with me?"

Paige wasn't touching that. "Give me an hour."

"The clock is ticking." Lady Menagerie said, then there was dial tone.

Paige laughed as she pressed the off button. *Thank you.* She whispered as she made her way to her bedroom.

*   *   *

Paige sat on a mound of pillows surrounded by almost every type of junk food imaginable in Lady Menagerie's living room. When she arrived she found 8 other women lounging around the spacious room in their sleepwear. She was sent straight up to her guest room so she could change. Upon entering the living room she was given a paper tiara, a plastic wand and was sat at what she could only assume was a throne made of pillows.

"Wow, so what do I owe this honor?" she asked once bowl after bowl of chips, cookies, cupcakes, and drinks were set within her reach.

"This is 'Don't Lift a Finger, Paige' Day."

Paige looked at her watch. "But it's already eight-thirty at night. Why didn't you tell me sooner?"

"Because it just came to me a few hours ago. Do you think I would have given you a paper tiara if we'd had longer to plan?"

Lady Menagerie sat down in a chair, her arms splayed out dramatically.

It was all Paige could do to keep from laughing, but she bit her lip when Tasha Manning, a beautiful mocha colored woman, who led the singles' ministry and seemed to be on a whole other level of style than Paige, let go of a giggle and was branded with a frown from Lady Menagerie.

"Well…thank you." She said still struggling with her mirth. "I accept."

"You bet your sweet …"

"Shut yo' mouth." Pamela piped up, interrupting her. The women broke out into gales of laughter.

Lady Menagerie held her scowl for a few seconds but she gave in.

"Do I get to pick the movie? Paige asked after they'd regained some composure.

"I guess that depends on where your mind is."

Paige frowned and sucked her teeth. "First you skimp on my time, now I can't pick the movie? What kind of honor is this?"

"The kind you should be thankful for otherwise Stacey will take her little sister's crown back and Tamara will take back her wand."

Paige looked around the room, feeling a little deflated. "You mean I don't get to keep them?"

Lady Menagerie held a perfectly innocent face for 5.2 seconds then burst out laughing. The rest of the women fell out with her.

Paige looked at the women laid out in different displays of laughter feeling a bit peaked.

"You mean I don't get to keep them?" Lady Menagerie repeated in what Paige assumed was supposed to be her voice.

Paige tried to hold on to her indignation, but it was no use. Lady Menagerie's laugh was contagious.

They all collected themselves again and Lady Menagerie gave Paige the remote. "Alright, go ahead."

"Paige pressed the remote buttons until the Netflix screen appeared on the screen."

"I wonder if they have Mommy Dearest," Paige said absentmindedly. She could see the women looking at each other out of the corner of her eye.

"Paige." Lady Menagerie said with a stern look.

"What? If that's too rough for you, we can see if 'Throw Momma from the Train' is playing."

"Oooh, there is always 'The Manchurian Candidate'. The version with Angela Landsbury." Paige said as she reached for a chip. She paused for a moment looking around the room. "If you're up for it we could always watch 'Carrie'."

Lady Menagerie stood up and walked to her with her hand stretched out for the remote.

"Paige." She began, her voice going soft and placating. Paige placed the remote in her hand reluctantly then pulled it back. "Gotcha." She said laughter shining in her golden eyes.

"You need help dear." Lady Menagerie retorted as she snatched the remote out of her hand. Paige just laughed and settled back against the front of the couch on her throne of pillows.

*   *   *

Paige awoke to the sound of her phone chiming. She opened one eye to orient herself to the time but frowned as she took in the slightly familiar surroundings of her guest room in her Pastor's home. The memory of the night of movies topped off by the massacre of an ice cream cake in the early morning hours brought a smile to her lips. She glanced at the small alarm clock on the bedside table. She squinted at it to make sure she was seeing it correctly. It read 5:30 a.m. She closed her eyes groaning. *You have got to be kidding. I should have silenced my ringer.*

She reached for her phone and saw that she had three text messages. The first one had come in thirty minutes prior to Gladys' call.

Wake up. I'm on video.

The next one at 5:15 read, *Happy Birthday Mati!-video.* This one was from Vivian.

Happy Birthday, Sweetheart. I'm glad you're in my life. She smiled wide knowing she probably looked like a besotted school girl, but she didn't care. He made her happy.

She threw back the covers and rolled to the side of the bed so she could retrieve her iPad. She couldn't thank Mason enough for his thoughtfulness. She and the girls had grown close. They had to have shared at least a hundred hours on Skype and ooVoo doing everything from praying to showing off wardrobe choices.

Even though their hairstyles had remained relatively similar, their personalities and taste in clothing were vastly different. Paige loved watching them grow.

She went into the bathroom to take care of business and brush her teeth. She put a colorful scarf around her satin wrapping scarf and signed on. Twenty years ago she never thought she would have to look presentable for a phone call.

She could see that they were both logged on already and connected to their avatars. She split the screen for conferencing and let out a laugh at their identical caps that read 'It's Mati's Birthday'.

She was so overwhelmed by the gesture she covered her mouth briefly in order to get her emotions in check. "You two are adorable. I love the caps." She said through her laughter.

"Open your door," Vivian said.

"What?" she asked not comprehending.

"Just open your door Mati," Gladys said, then as an after-thought added, "Please."

Paige got back out of bed and traipsed the carpeted floor in her fuzzy blue slippers.

She opened the door as quietly as possible so as not to disturb the household. She glanced down spying a copper and rose-colored gift bag. She quickly picked it up and closed her door. When she got back to her bed she eyed her girls over the monitor. "Which one of you devised this plan?" When both girls raised their hands all she could do was chuckle to herself.

It was already a great birthday. She had laughed more in the last twelve hours than she had in the last twelve weeks.

She sifted through the matching tissue paper, uncovering a white cap with "It's my Birthday' embroidered in red.

"Wow, where did you get this? It is gorgeous." Paige said staring at her cap. The silence caught her attention and she looked up. Vivian looked a little uncomfortable, but Gladys spoke up. "Mom..uh…Aunty Mel…made them." Paige felt the words to her core. It was no longer the stabbing pain, but it hurt nonetheless. She toyed with the cap in her hands, reluctant to place it on her head.

"Mati?"

Paige looked up into Vivian's clear gray, all-too-observant, eyes. "Yes, Honey?"

"Love is the healer. It doesn't matter what package it comes in."

Paige looked between Gladys and Vivian on the split screen to see if they could tell what was going on in her mind. It was uncanny to have such watchful children.

"Why?"

Vivian looked puzzled. "Why what?

"Why'd you say that?"

"Because it's true." She said perplexed.

"Why did you say it to me?"

"Oh, because you looked sad, like you'd lost something."

She stared at her beautiful girls and thought of the sacrifices made so they could be in her life. She quirked a smile. "Thank you for the reminding me." She said as she placed the cap on her head.

Vivian smiled brightly. "You're welcome."

"So, what do you have planned today?" Gladys asked.

"I'm not sure. Lady Menagerie kidnapped me for the day, but tonight Brandon is taking me out."

"Oooh, and where is Elder Tatum taking you?"

"He says it's a surprise." She said sighing.

"What's the matter? Don't you like surprises?"

"Not particularly, no," Paige said shaking her head slightly.

"But I was a surprise," Vivian said.

"No Vivian, you are a present. Each time you smile it's a gift.."

"Awww, Mati, do you mean it?"

"More than you know."

"What about me?" Gladys asked. Her eyes alight with interest.

"You, my love have a gift of letting go and the wonderful ability to handle life-altering situations better than most adults I know." *Including me.* She said to herself.

"Both of you have such a huge capacity for love. I don't ever want you to lose that. It is to be treasured."

Both girls nodded and she saw their eyes growing wet. "Don't do it. Sniff them back or we will be crying half the morning." She warned. They giggled, but dutifully sniff and wiped until their faces were dry.

"That's better."

"Mati, I know it's your birthday and all, but I was wondering about something."

Paige adjusted the tight cap around her scarf as she answered. "What's up Gladys?"

"Are you angry with mommy?"

Paige shouldn't have been surprised, but she was. She'd steered around conversations regarding Mel for the previous few weeks and schooled her expressions so the hurt at the mention of Mel's name didn't show. Maybe Mel had said something.

"Why do you ask?"

"Well... I asked Mommy if she wanted to come on the call to wish you a 'Happy Birthday' but she said she would talk to you later."

"What's so odd about that?"

Gladys shrugged her shoulders. "It was just the way she said it. She looked like you and she hasn't been sleeping. Marc is getting concerned."

A pang of regret rang in her heart. She really hadn't handled this well, but she needed to work through a few things before she could hold a productive and healing conversation with Mel.

"Tell your mother that I said everything will be alright."

Gladys seemed to slump in her chair. "Okay."

"My daddy said he wishes you a very Happy Birthday." Paige lifted an eyebrow. "Tell your daddy I said 'Thank you.'"

"Mati have you picked your colors for your wedding yet?" Vivian asked excitedly. "I mean I know you are waiting to set the date, but you still can plan some things."

"Yes I know and we are considering mint green and cranberry."

"Really?" Gladys' lips were pursed in thought. Paige looked at Vivian who was tapping her lips in consideration. Both girls nodded their heads in agreement at the same time.

"I think that will work," Gladys said, her eyes reminding Paige of unpolished silver.

"Would you girls like to wear the same color or the same cut of dress?"

Vivian cocked her head to the side. "I don't get it."

"I was thinking that I would give you the chance to pick whether you wore the same color, but different style of dress or same style of dress, but in separate colors."

"Gladys what do you think?" Vivian asked her sister.

"We can go with separate colors. It will make it easier for people to tell us apart, but we need to make sure the cut will cover my big thighs."

"Please, you don't have to worry nearly as much about your thighs as I do about my flabby arms. Mati do you think I'll be ready if I do a few pushups every morning?"

"Eew, don't do pushups then your chest will look like a boy's. Do dips if you really think you need to, but I think your arms are fine." Gladys said with a look of dismay.

Paige looked back and forth between her girls and was content to watch them interact with one another as if they lived together. Her lips quirked at the corner as her heart gave a small lurch. She missed her sister...mother...and she was back to hurt.

"Okay, so who's wearing the green and who's wearing the cranberry?"

"I'm wearing green." Gladys almost shouted, raising her hand as if she were in class.

Vivian copied the gesture, simultaneously yelling, "I'm wearing cranberry."

"Well that was easy," Paige said laughing."

After her call with her girls, Paige decided to get up and get dressed. Besides, she could smell coffee from downstairs and it was making her mouth water.

She showered, dressed in jeans and a t-shirt that read 'It's my birthday and I'll pray for you if I want to' that she'd bought on her last book tour. She touched up her now straight as a bone hairstyle with her flat iron and walked downstairs. She heard voices as she approached the kitchen, but they didn't prepare her for the scene she came upon when she pushed to door open.

Brandon stood at the open door of the refrigerator, slightly obstructing the view of Lady Menagerie and Pastor Lawrence sharing a stolen, but heated kiss. Paige may have blushed if she didn't wish the very same love for herself and Brandon after 22 years of marriage. She cleared her throat pulling Brandon's attention away from the fridge. The smile that lit his eyes made her feel like the only woman in the world.

He came forward and hugged her tightly. "Happy Birthday, Baby." He whispered in her ear, his warm breath tickling her. She shivered and pulled back to smile up at him. She was about to ask him why he was there so early when she heard a slap and looked over to see Lady Menagerie smiling as she walked away from Pastor Lawrence rubbing her rear.

Paige shook her head in amusement and a little revulsion. They were like her parents and he was her pastor. She shook her head again to dislodge the thought, hoping it would dissipate without returning at some inopportune time, like while she was in church.

"Wipe that look off your face Birthday Girl or I will send Brandon home and you will get cereal for breakfast." Lady Menagerie said as she came forward and removed Brandon's arm from around her so she could give her a hug. Paige laughed at her high handedness accepting her hug.

Pastor Lawrence walked up and enveloped her in a rib-cracking hug that reminded her of the ones her father gave her when she was really little. She was obviously feeling a bit nostalgic.

"Happy Birthday, Little one." Pastor Lawrence said for her ears only. He only used the endearment when she was visiting at their house. He wasn't into flaunting his favoritism towards her and she appreciated it.

"You're up early Lady Menagerie." Paige said glancing at the clock on the microwave which read 7:15 a.m.

"Yes, well you need to teach your girls the meaning of different time zones. They called me at 5:15 to make sure I'd placed your present at the door. Fortunately, I'm one of those who can go back to sleep after being awakened." She said as she strolled to the fridge to retrieve eggs, bacon, flour, and a bowl of what looked like mixed fruit. She held out the eggs to her husband who handed them to Brandon and they began an assembly line from the refrigerator to the counter next to the stove. Paige watched them in for a while then went to sit down at the kitchen table after being ignored by them when she held out her hands to help.

The three of them moved around the kitchen as if they'd done it many times before.

At one point she got up to get herself a cup of coffee, but before she could reach the carafe she was gently, but firmly turned around by her shoulders and pushed back to the table.

"But I was only..." she started to say but shut her mouth as Brandon walked back to her with a cup of coffee. Without a word he placed it in front of her and moved the sugar and cream service within her reach. She smiled up at him warmly, wishing she could kiss him for his thoughtfulness. She glanced over at Lady Menagerie as she worked over the stove and spotted the smile she was trying to hide. She sighed and settled for grabbing and squeezing his hand. He surprised her by leaning down and rubbing his lips along her cheek until he reached the corner of her mouth. The movement was so quick she didn't have time to move towards him.

He smiled down at her and went back to his makeshift prep-table at the island counter.

Paige breathed deeply wishing she could slow time at that moment so she could capture and memorize everything she was feeling.

The peace and love, and wellbeing that enveloped her, warmed her more than the forgotten coffee mug between her hands.

She couldn't have asked for a better way to start her birthday. She decided this would be one of the happiest days of her life.

*   *   *

Paige sat in the passenger seat of Brandon's car watching the familiar landscape turn into streets she had vague knowledge of. The 'Welcome to Marina Del Rey' sign they'd just passed had her looking over at Brandon with a furrow between her brows.

"Please?" She said using her eyes to her advantage. They'd worked when she tried wrestling answers or candy from her father.

Brandon glanced at her briefly then did a double take. "Wow. You're pulling out all the stops. I didn't think you would stoop as low as to try and con me with your eyes." He returned his full attention to the road. "Good try though."

She shrugged good-naturedly. "It was worth a try."

"I was the youngest son of seven children. I too learned how to wrap people around my finger. Maybe one day I'll show you how the puppy dog eyes are really done." He took one hand off the wheel and searched blindly for her hand. She moved it out of reach and he laughed at her attempt to evade him.

She wanted to be irritated, but found his laughter contagious and joined in with him. "I'm going to hold you to it. Then I'm going to call your mom and commiserate with her."

He shrugged. "Who do you think I learned it from? To this day I don't believe there is much he can say 'No' to her for."

She thought about that for a moment. During the times she saw them together Ava seemed to refer to Elias on most things. Though she was nowhere near timid, you could tell she was fully submitted to him.

"How?" Paige asked.

"Because she knows what to ask for."

"Hmm," was her only reply. She thought about that for the length of their ride. She adored his family. She knew they weren't perfect, but the welcome she'd received when they visited and watching how they interacted with one another made her heart ache a little. She wanted that. She wanted to belong to a family that loved without fear of that love being used against them. They could tease each other without malice and continue to feel secure in each other's adoration. Oh how she wanted that and Brandon was giving it to her. He probably didn't know it, but Brandon was already giving her the single most important gift she'd ever receive.

A few minutes later they were pulling into a parking lot and she saw the sign for The Hornblower. She knew she'd heard the name before, but it took a moment for recognition to take hold. When it did she gasped. "Are we? Did you? You didn't." She said, excitement causing her mind to go a hundred different places at once.

Brandon put the car in park and looked over at her a smile teasing the corners of his mouth. "Yes we are. Yes I did. And..." He paused. "Yes I did. Well, that is if you're referring to the dinner cruise."

She giggled and hugged him. "You are my sweet and sour man."

He pulled back from her. "You and Lady Menagerie used that when I first met you. What does that mean?"

"Most women have a pallet that enjoys sweet and salty or slightly sour food together. It's the best of both worlds where food is concerned. You,

Brandon are also the best of both worlds. You are sweet, sensitive, and attentive, but you are not a pushover. You are a secure black man who loves God and isn't ashamed to proclaim it."

A sly grin replaced the smile. "And you knew all of this then?"

"I knew enough." She caught her bottom lip between her teeth.

He shook his head at her. "I am so incredibly blessed." She thought he would kiss her, but instead he unclasped her seatbelt and said. "I don't want to be late." He got out of the car and walked around to open her door. He gently pulled her from the car taking care not to snag his watch on her bell sleeve. The dress she wore was the only one she'd bought with Brandon in mind. The bodice was black and formfitting reaching to mid-calf. The sleeves were diaphanous white and black silk that flared out from the shoulder but cupped at the wrist. A pair of black slingback three inch heels completed the look. It reminded her of something Jackie O' would wear, but when she tried it on in the store she had to have it.

He guided her with a hand at the small of her back. He leaned in as they walked to the ship. "You look gorgeous tonight."

She couldn't help the smile that broke out on her face. "Thank you."

They boarded the ship and Paige became busy looking at the sights around her. They were seated at a semi-private candlelit table for two near a window and the waitress was taking their drink order before she brought her attention back to Brandon. She was definitely going to put this in one of her books.

"I want to talk to you about setting a date for the wedding." Brandon said pinning her with his eyes.

Paige's attention was completely riveted on him. "But I thought we'd agreed we would wait until after your…"

He silenced her by taking her hand and placing it at her lips and kissing it himself. "This is backwards. We aren't moving in faith. We are waiting for a report from man to make a decision that has nothing to do with him. Let's set a date and no matter what the reports say we live life to the fullest."

Paige thought about what he'd said. He was right they had placed themselves in some kind of limbo over the last few weeks.

She thought about what still needed to be done and tried to think of a date that would allow her to keep with those plans and not run herself ragged.

"Two months?"

"Do you think that's enough time?"

"If I can enlist your mother and sisters in a couple more areas I should be fine. It's not like we have a huge wedding party. Your brothers and sisters, my daughters and sis…" Her voice faded.

"When are you going to talk to Mel?"

She removed her hand from his. "Soon, but I don't want to talk about her now. I want to talk about you and me and wedded bliss."

"Well you make sure it is bliss and not a nightmare. I need you to be sure."

"I'm sure. She pulled out her phone and scrolled to the calendar. Two months from today is June 17th so it will have to be on June 21st if we want it to be on a Saturday."

He watched her but she didn't blink or squirm. She was sure of one thing. She wanted to marry Brandon and the sooner the better. She may have to forgo a bell or whistle, but she was getting what really mattered.

"Do you think we can get the church with such short notice?"

Paige smiled. "I have an 'in' with the Pastor, but I'll call Pamela to make sure it's free. If not, we can work around that date." This was right, she thought to herself. They were moving forward. A feeling of rightness settled in her soul and she almost glowed with it. She was getting married to the most wonderful man of God and short of God, himself, intervening she would become Mrs. Brandon Tatum in two months' time.

"All right, June 21st it is." He leaned over the table and kissed her soundly. "Now we eat."

She laughed at the lightheartedness of the moment. God, love and food. She couldn't have asked for a more perfect birthday.

*   *   *

"Who are you listening to?"

Paige was pulled from her thoughts at the sound of Lady Menagerie's voice.

She looked over at the woman who had been a friend, mother and closest confident for the past six years, aware that she'd missed her mentor's latest lecture in regards to Paige's procrastination in calling Mel.

"What do you mean?" She asked as she drew her knees up to her chest on the overstuffed loveseat in Lady Menagerie's sunroom.

"It's been obvious that you haven't been listening to God because with every day that goes by where you refuse to listen or find a means of reconciliation between you and Mel you are not only hurting her, you are hurting yourself more.

I know you miss her and though the thought of your initial conversation with her is cause for distress, you are adding to it with the anxiety of not knowing.

One thing you can do is make up your mind to forgive her. No matter why she didn't tell you, she was your mother. You release yourself from the anger and place her and your relationship with her in God's hands."

"God, in His sovereignty, omniscience, and supreme authority has one main goal; to reconcile man unto Himself and move heaven and earth so that each soul can be redeemed. His priority is loving man back into His embrace so that we can spend eternity with Him."

"What's your main objective Paige?"

Paige didn't have an answer she wanted to share. She listened quietly, giving Lady Menagerie the respect she deserved. She had come to the conclusion the day before that she was being stubborn. The constant bombardment from Brandon and Lady Menagerie finally penetrated the hurt and allowed her to make an attempt to open her mind to the possibility that Melanie had a good reason to keep her in the dark, but she wasn't ready to take any type of action towards reconciliation. She missed her sister and their closeness, but wondered if it were possible to mend what had been severed with the acquisition of such knowledge.

Mel was her mother and to be perfectly honest Paige had always treated her as such even though she didn't hold the title. Mel had been the one to sit with her when she was sick. Mel was the one she could remember reading to her at night when their parents were out or sleep, but the fear that gripped her at the thought of Mel being a marionette whose strings were being manipulated by Grace paralyzed Paige.

She could intercede in prayer for the sick and afflicted. She wasn't shaken by physical or mental illness. The few demonic deliverances she had the opportunity to participate in didn't do anything to shake her resolve in God's and the blood of Jesus' ability to protect her.

Grace though… Grace was a force she couldn't seem to rise above. After twelve years, all it took was one phone call to prove to herself that she had not built up the resistance needed not to be affected by Grace. The woman seemed to have a point to prove, but Paige couldn't begin to tell what it was.

"Paige?"

Caught wondering again, Paige gave her an apologetic smile. When Lady Menagerie didn't respond Paige took a deep breath.

"I've been listening to myself. It's been pretty loud in here." She added dispassionately.

"Well then you need to quiet down in there because this is a very serious matter." The fact that Lady Menagerie's hands landed on her hips and didn't bode well.

Paige rearranged herself on the couch, sitting up straight. She might as well admit the truth. Lady Menagerie would get it out of her eventually and from the impatience emanating from her stance she wouldn't be happy if she had to pry the rest from Paige.

"I'm afraid." She said quietly looking down at her hands avoiding the look of disappointment she knew would be in Lady Menagerie's eyes.

She felt the sofa dip next to her and still she refused to look up.

Lady Menagerie's hand came into view and she watched as she took one of her hands, holding it in her own.

"Being afraid is nothing to be ashamed of, but it is not an emotion you want to play with either. It can be a strong weapon of the enemy because he only needs to make sure the seed takes hold then you will do the rest of the work for him." She began to rub Paige's hand between her own.

"Initial fright gets your attention. It's part of your fight or flight response warning you to danger. It can also be a symptom of insecurity which comes from lack of experience in a situation which should cause you to draw closer to the one who can help you overcome it. But if left too long it will germinate and root you to the ground where you are standing and keep you from moving forward."

The hands shifted and Lady Menagerie placed a finger under Paige's chin to force her to meet her eyes. "So what aren't you trusting God to help you through, because He is not a God of fear, but of power, love and a sound mind? And, if you believe it to be so, which I believe you do, He who is in you is greater than He who is in the world."

"Grace. Grace is who I'm afraid of. More specifically, I am afraid of who I become when I'm around her."

"Who do you think you become?" Lady Menagerie asked not allowing Paige to turn away.

"Someone I really don't like." She shook her head briefly. "I become someone with angry thoughts and a biting sarcastic tongue. Someone who can't stand the sound of her name being mentioned near me, let alone talking to or seeing."

"And, as long as she is on this earth you will keep tabs on where she is so that you can stay as far away from her as possible." Lady Menagerie finished for her.

Paige nodded with conviction.

"Then she controls you." Lady Menagerie said solemnly.

Paige's eyes began to water. "Don't do it." Menagerie warned. "This is not something to be pitied nor shared with pity, you are stronger and wiser than that." Lady Menagerie said sternly releasing her chin. "You are going to learn that people only have the control over you that you give them. I thought you'd already learned this lesson last year when you went to your cousin's funeral and confessed to Gladys and Vivian about being their mother. That took a great deal of courage. What's the difference between that and dealing with Grace?"

Paige wanted to shrug, but knew Menagerie wouldn't let it go at that.

"She makes me feel like a failure." Paige said through clenched teeth. The admission rolled through her, making her queasy.

"Why?" Lady Menagerie asked, but continued before Paige could answer.

"Why, when you have overcome so much. At 14 you gave birth to twins, you accepted the gift of salvation and instead of squandering it or taking it for granted you have dedicated your life to evangelizing, learning, sharing and empowering others to grasp that same gift for themselves and seek an intimate relationship with Him. You are a prayer warrior, new mother to two beautifully spirited girls that are blessed to have a woman such as you to mentor and guide them. You are a mentor to countless other women, an author, speaker... Shall I go on?"

"I could love all of these people, but not her. I couldn't love her; my own family." Paige felt the burn in her throat and swallowed convulsively until it passed. She was tempted to let anger wash the feeling away, but she had long since passed that time in her life. "I wanted to. I really did, but every time I thought I saw any softness in her eyes she would say or do something cruel to squash any affection towards her I might be cultivating."

"Have you ever tried to see things from her perspective? Maybe she feels she had a good reason for what she was doing."

"Yeah, I used to think that love from me hurt her." Lady Menagerie leaned away from Paige.

"Really, why?"

"Because she was the devil's little sister and if she received love she would lose pieces of herself. You know like a toe or finger then eventually an arm or leg."

The fact that she delivered it without a hint of a smile had Lady Menagerie covering her mouth.

"Well." She said after a few moments. "I have to say that I've never seen you exhibit such venom towards a person. If she has so expressly rejected your love, what makes you think you have failed?"

"I pride myself on my ability to love people. I love the fact that I can see through what people clothe themselves with when they've dealt with tragic, hurtful or abusive situations. I cherish the gift of being able to love them in spite of masks, but not her and believe me I have tried. I just can't find one redeeming factor about her."

"What if it's you? What if you are her redeeming factor?" Paige considered it then realized that she'd fought against the thought because she didn't want to see Grace redeemed. She wanted to see her get her punishment.

"She took me to kill my children." She said it as a way of justifying her feelings.

"But you didn't. God intervened and now you have two very beautiful and healthy girls and due to another unfortunate situation last year, you now have a wonderful relationship with both."

Paige was quiet for a moment, neither affirming nor denying Menagerie's statement.

"What does speaking to your sister have to do with Grace? You have always had such a strong relationship with her despite Grace."

"She called Grace when I confronted her. She knows how I feel about Grace and she just invited her into the situation. I'm afraid that letting Mel back in will give Grace just cause to interfere with my life and I don't trust Mel to be the buffer she used to be."

"So you're going to throw away a lifelong relationship because you're afraid of your reflection?"

Paige closed her eyes briefly. She hated Lady Menagerie's ability to sum up a problem with such blatant truth. She wondered what Lady Menagerie would say if she said 'Yes'? She would probably kick her out of her house.

"Look, it is obvious you are struggling with the hold that Grace has on Mel so instead of chucking the whole relationship, put a couple of boundaries in place until you feel more comfortable. It's like training wheels. It gives you a sense of protection while you forge through the rougher parts of your relationship." She held up a hand. "For a while."

"And these training wheels should consist of what?"

Menagerie shrugged. "That's up to you, but it's time you began walking in your authority again. I think I allowed you too much time to 'adjust' to all of the changes happening in your life. I've babied you instead of reminding you of your purpose and duty. So, now I need you to listen to me." She shifted and leaned closer, getting in Paige's face.

"You are a child of the Most High. You are a warrior in this time of battle and I need you back in line. You got blindsided and I gave you a moment to lick your wounds, but you need to shake it off and remember whose you are and who you're fighting.

We wrestle not against flesh and blood, but against principalities, against powers, against the rulers of the darkness of this world, against spiritual wickedness in high places.

Grace is not your problem. You are. If being around her brings out things in you that don't glorify God, purge them from your being. She only speaks of things that are in you and God allowed you to see them so you can work them out. Don't look away from them in shame, combat them, and ask God what you need to do to purify yourself just as you did when you were first saved."

"I thought I was further along."

"What? Perfect?" Lady Menagerie said with a haughty tone.

"No...just less angry."

"We have many layers and facets Paige. Cleansing is a process. You know this. It's not a onetime cleanse or a single cycle of refining. There are obvious faults and vices and less pronounced iniquities that can still be used to kill, steal and destroy you just the same. Dormancy may look like deliverance for a while, but it will always wake up given the right trigger.

Get free for life Paige and get back in line. There are so many who are waiting for you to remember the authority you have been given and show them what it's like to walk in the anointing. Pray your way out, war your way out, love your way out." Lady Menagerie went silent, but the point had finally hit home.

It wasn't until the last few words that Paige realized that she wasn't just affecting herself, but those that were looking for a way from under their own oppressing spirits.

Paige sat there for a good 10 minutes going over everything in her head before Lady Menagerie spoke again.

"So, are you going to take back your family and call your sister?"

Paige's stomach roiled but she knew she'd procrastinated long enough. She glanced at her phone for the time and calculated the three-hour difference. Mel would have gotten home an hour ago. She took a deep breath and dialed the full number instead of pressing the speed dial in an effort to buy herself a few more seconds.

Mel answered after the second ring. "Paige?"

Paige's heart squeezed at the sound of Mel's voice

"Yes."

The silence was palpable. Paige's attention was averted by Lady Menagerie who had gotten up to leave the room.

At the door she turned and gave Paige an encouraging smile. Paige nodded her head.

"Hello Mel."

"How are you doing?"

"Good."

There was a painful pause, but Paige couldn't seem to fill it.

"How's Brandon?"

Paige let out a relieved breath. Could they talk as though nothing had happened? But even as the thought came she shook it aside. There were too many things already unsaid.

"He is doing well. We set a date."

"Really, when?"

"June 21st. Just over two months."

"Is that long enough?"

"I think so. We answered the questions we could without a date, you know like our colors, how big we wanted it to be, if we wanted to go with a theme, I've even gotten it down to 5 dresses. Besides Brandon's mother and sisters said they would help any way they could."

The line went quiet.

"Do you think you can forgive me?" Mel's voice was so thick Paige could barely understand the words.

"I already have Mel. I just need to know if you will be truthful with me from now going forward."

Another long pause took over the line. "I will always do what I think is best for you Paige." Mel said with a halting tone and Paige knew with utter clarity at that moment what she'd been trying to deny even in the recesses of her mind.

"So you are my mother then." Paige said with resignation.

The short gasp on the other side of the line only cemented her thought.

"Who told you that?"

"Does it really matter?"

"Yes."

Paige took a deep weary breath. "Mel, I'm really trying to keep you in my life. I miss you, but my trust in you is growing more fragile by the moment."

The other line was so quiet Paige took her phone away from her ear to make sure they were still connected.

Finally Paige heard an exasperated sigh come from the other line. "What do you want Paige?"

"I want my Mel back, without being exposed to Grace. You made it clear the last time we were together that you are still looking to Grace for answers. I can't be a part of that."

"But you are. You were born into it."

"Not anymore Mel. Going forward I need you to promise me that what goes on between the two of us is not shared with Grace."

There was a short pause.

"Then I need a similar promise from you to stop digging into her past. Either she is in your life or out."

"What about you Mel? Will you tell me about your past? Will you tell me who my father is?"

"No, but not for the reasons you might assume. I have done nothing but love and protect you your whole life. I am not doing anything now that I haven't done since you came into my life. Every move I've made since you were born has been with the intent to keep you healthy and safe."

"Am I in danger?"

"No, but I would feel a lot more comfortable if I could have your promise."

Paige considered it for a moment. She wasn't actually the one doing the digging. She could easily promise to stop something she wasn't doing, but she thought about the pain Mel's secrets had caused her and knew she could keep it from her.

"I can't promise you that. I'm not the one doing the digging, but I think it might have been a fluke so I don't believe there is any need for concern."

Mel let out a long-suffering breath. "I'm sorry Paige for all of the secrets, but I really only had your best interest at heart."

Paige heard the sincerity in her voice and allowed herself to soften to the words. She didn't want to throw away their relationship, but for at least a little while she would have to hold her at arms-length. "Do you think you will ever tell me the story of how you got pregnant so young?"

"Maybe one day."

Paige nodded to herself. It was something. "Okay."

"Yes?"

"Yes. I am either going to have to take what I can get and be all right with it, as long as you keep with my condition, or say goodbye and I'm just not ready to let go of our relationship."

"Thank you Paige. You won't regret it. I love you."

"I love you too." She felt a little awkward. What did she call her now that they both acknowledged the truth?

"Paige, one more thing."

"Yes."

"May I help with your wedding?"

Paige felt a twinge of joy lighten her heart. "You better." She said through a small laugh. I'll call you in a couple of days to discuss some of the details. It's getting late and I'm at Lady Menagerie's house.

"I will continue to keep both of you in my prayers."

"Thank you."

"No need to thank me Paige. I love you. I want you to be happy and Brandon makes you even more so."

Paige felt the familiar feeling of wellbeing when she and Mel were together. Big sister or mother she was always there for her.

"Well, goodnight. I will call you in a couple of days."

"Okay. Good night."

Paige hung up and went in search for First Lady to share her news.

By the time she was home and in her own bed she had a firm grip on her new declaration to move more in her authority and less in what she saw going on around her. She hugged her pillow to her with joy suffusing her heart. For the first time since Brandon's earlier report she felt the peace of God in regards to their future. Now that her relationship with Mel was back on the mend.

CHAPTER 34

"Just one more time and I will let it rest. I promise." His mom, Ava, said as she turned to the front of the wedding binder that housed all the details of the wedding.

Brandon wanted to groan. He was so tired. He knew it made him a little cranky, but going over arrangements again and again was not what he had in mind when he invited Paige over for some 'down time'. He just wanted to sit on his couch with his arm around her. Just feeling her warmth made him feel better.

The last cycle of chemo had been harder on him than any of his previous treatments. He felt like he'd dragged himself through the last few weeks, only to wake up to the reality of their wedding looming in front of him like a huge door he wasn't sure he had the right key to unlock. He looked over at Paige as she leaned over some particularly intriguing color or fabric of which he'd forgotten the name for just as soon as it had been spoken. Her hair was fashioned in a shiny ponytail that swept back and forth between her shoulder blades. She was wearing it straight this week and though it did nothing to take away from her beauty, he found her curls the most arresting. They always framed her face like jewels that women use to enhance their beauty. She was more than he could have imagined asking for, and soon she would be his wife.

He watched as a thin, French-tipped finger pointed at something she was trying to bring his mother's attention to, and he found himself daydreaming once again of the day she practically dragged him behind her at church so she could show Lady Menagerie her ring. She didn't fawn over the size, cut, or clarity. She didn't talk about the precious metal used for the setting. She only showed Lady Menagerie the ring on her finger with a silent, huge smile and it made him feel more like a man of wealth than anyone he knew because the most precious woman he'd had the honor to know agreed to wear his ring and state to the world that she was his. His heart thumped hard in his chest and he started slow, deep breathing in order to get it under control.

Paige looked up from the book, concern clouding her eyes, but before she could speak he took her hand and smiled at what he could only imagine was one of serene satisfaction. She stared at him for a moment before he saw the look mirrored in her eyes and felt the slight pressure of her squeeze. This was good. This was what he'd waited for. This was the intimacy he knew God talked about when he spoke of a love without words or touches. Everything that could have been said between them was expressed in that one look. If he hadn't known it before, he was sure of it now. He was home. He saw it in her eyes. No matter how long they had together they already had more than most people he knew, and he whispered a small prayer that none of the people he knew would go through life without experiencing what he knew to be true at this moment. He was full of love for this beautiful woman who couldn't be more perfect for him if God referred to him as He fashioned her line by line, bone by bone, word by word. He had it all. A peace stole over him at that moment that nearly took his breath away at its sweetness. He felt cocooned in it.

He closed his eyes to allow all of his senses to bask in the feeling, and only then realized how quiet it had gotten. He opened them languidly and saw his mother staring at him with tears in her eyes. He may have been alarmed had she not been smiling the same smile of serene contentedness. A lump formed in his throat that he was hard-pressed to swallow. This was a perfect moment and he wished it would stay; stay like this long enough for him to find the words to immortalize it so anyone who came across those words would know that it was possible to be sublimely happy with ones' life just as it was – disease, fatigue, pain-ridden and all. It was right.

*   *   *

"You make me want to be in love."

Brandon looked up from his laptop where he'd been pounding out some of the work his boss had let him take home. He was going to have to give her something really nice. He was sure he should have been fired by now he'd missed so much work, but when he would bring up the subject of resigning or going part-time she would raise her hand to silence him. "Your experience and knowledge are invaluable. It's the reason why I worked so hard to get you out here. Your numbers were great in the field and now we can use that to continue to stay ahead of the game with our new recruits. You continue to give me all you have and I will continue to keep you on my full-time schedule." She said the last in a way that brooked no room for argument. He simply nodded and exited her office as quietly as he'd come in.

"Why?" he asked his sister, Makayla, who'd arrived the day before pleading the need for 'some time off'. *How did one take time off from looking for a job?*

"You wear it so well."

Okay, slightly vague, but promising in its direction.

"How is that?"

"It seems to emanate from you like a light shining from your innermost being. It doesn't come off in waves, though. It just seeps through your pores like a sated glow." She looked at him slightly perplexed. "Do you know what I mean?"

"Uh…" He let the word lengthen on his tongue.

"You glow with it, but it isn't ostentatious or glaring," she said quickly. "It's soft and inviting. I just want to hug you in hopes that some of your happiness will rub off on me."

He didn't know what to say to this so he just nodded and looked back at his screen.

He knew he shouldn't have been surprised that his feelings showed in his appearance. It was going on three days now that he had been enveloped in this veil of peace, and he was no longer waiting for it to leave. Actually, every night he prayed to wake up with it and in the morning thanked God for the gift of it tarrying.

"Being in love is a wonderful thing, Makayla, and I'm happy I've been able to exemplify it in such a way that would make you, 'Miss Bachelorette for Life', consider it, but this is something more."

Makayla tipped her head to the side. "How?"

It was his turn to search for the words that even to this moment eluded him. Then he stopped searching for the perfect word and just described what he felt. "It's right."

"What, your relationship with Paige?" Makayla asked, trying to get clarity.

"Everything. It's all right. My life, my relationship with God, my Paige, my family, my home, my work. All of it is right. I've never felt such a wholeness, a satisfaction so deep it resonates through me."

He'd looked away as he searched for the right words, but at the end of his sentence he returned his gaze to see if she was following him. He caught the slight tremble of her lips before they turned up into a tremulous smile. She didn't say anything, but nodded her head slowly in understanding. "It's well."

Brandon expelled a relieved sigh, appreciative of her sensitivity and intuitiveness. She truly understood.

"It is well."

She nodded again and quickly swiped at the lone tear that escaped her smiling eyes.

"The wonderful part is that it affects everything I see as well. Last week I was ready to call dad to come and get mom because she was hovering so much," he admitted sheepishly.

"And now?"

"I don't even mind her questions about what type of filling we want for the third tier of our wedding cake."

Makayla laughed. "Dear brother, you need to find a way to bottle that. You could make millions."

He shook his head. "Naw, it's too wonderful to depreciate with a monetary figure. How could anyone figure the value to something they can't even find the perfect words for?" He stared at Makayla from across the table and saw the wistful expression settle upon her features.

"Yep," he said as he nodded. "It's just like that."

He watched her eyes clear and knew she'd caught a glimpse of what he was feeling. The heaviness of God's presence resting on them at that moment was priceless.

He returned his attention to the figures on his screen, but could continue to feel her eyes stray to him from time to time. He knew she'd formed some questions since their talk. He looked up a couple of times to see the contemplative expression on her face. He raised an eyebrow once in invitation but she waved it away, obviously content to mull it over in her mind first. Makayla never shied away from asking questions if propriety was the only thing standing between her and clarity. He would let her wrestle with them for as long as she wished.

"You make me feel like I did something right just being in the same family with you."

Brandon pulled his eyes away from the screen again, not at all perturbed by the thoughts that skittered away at her admission. He was floored by the profoundness of her statement. He couldn't have come up with a response if someone paid him for one. He stood up from his chair and walked around the table to pull her up from hers.

He drew her to him and wrapped his arms around her in a sound hug that became a very long loving hold. They remained like that until his mother came back from running one of her never-ending list of errands. He caught sight of her as she let herself in. She paused in the doorway for a few seconds before she continued on to the hallway leading to the bedrooms.

Later that evening, he was getting dressed for his date with Paige when his mother knocked on his door. After thirty-one years, her knock was still the same. He called out for her to enter and looked up from buttoning his shirt. She walked into the room without saying a word and came to stand close enough to reach up and finish the last two.

Here he was, a good foot taller than her, but her mere presence along with the act made him feel like a five-year-old again. Her strength would never cease to amaze him.

He let his hands rest at his sides and just watched her complete the task of making him presentable while he waited for her to share what was on her mind.

She smoothed his collar as if she were pained to let go of their connection. She finally looked up into his eyes and he saw the question even before she opened her mouth.

"Are you ready to go?"

Brandon thought about purposely misunderstanding her question, but the look of vulnerability that came into her eyes wouldn't allow him to skirt the subject for the sake of keeping things light.

He placed his hand over hers where it stopped above his heart, and staring into her eyes he delivered a firm, "No."

She looked into his eyes for a moment searching for the truth in them, and when she found it she pinched her lips to quell the slight tremble. "The other day and today with Makayla it felt like..." She stopped momentarily after her voice broke. She took a deep breath to regain her composure. "It felt like you were saying goodbye."

He bent down to hug her and breathed in her familiar scent of cocoa butter and almonds. He squeezed her slightly before releasing her. "Does that feel like goodbye?"

She stood stock still for a few seconds, assessing his face and posture then shook her head. Her countenance brightened considerably. "You are truly this happy?"

He nodded at her.

She smiled at him, her eyes roaming over his face as if to capture his expression and take it with her. "What about tomorrow?"

"Tomorrow will take care of itself. Tonight, I have a date with a gorgeous woman that makes me excited to be me."

She just smiled at him.

"Do you think this is how dad feels?" he asked, a mischievous gleam in his eyes.

"He better," she replied with the confidence of a woman secure in her husband's love. "You'll see. It isn't a love that fades, but reveals different facets of itself as you grow with one another. Some are as clear as a cloudless day and show themselves without struggle. Other facets are uncovered through trials and challenges in your relationship, but they don't shine any less bright."

As he looked down at his mother he understood the scripture that described a virtuous woman's worth as being far above rubies. He had always equated that with a man's wife, but it was true for a mother as well. There was nothing he would trade for his mother, and just being able to acknowledge that let him know he was a very blessed man.

"How many facets of dad's love do you think you have uncovered?"

"Thankfully, too many to count," she replied without hesitation.

Heart full to bursting, he leaned down and kissed his mother's cheek. He stepped back and finally noticed the tiny lines at the edges of her mouth. She looked tired, but it was no doubt with all the work she seemed to be doing lately.

"Just Paige and me tomorrow at Dr. Connor's office," he said gently but firmly.

She looked as though she was going to argue, but slowly nodded. "Either way, we are all in this together."

"There is no way I am going to spend my honeymoon with all of you," he teased her, trying to ease the pain he saw clouding her eyes.

The upturning of her lips on the sides was a sad excuse for a smile.

"Come on, Mom. It'll be all right. No need to add anxiety to the already heavy workload you're toting. Give me a real smile or I will have to stand Paige up until you do and believe me, between you, Makayla and Lady Menagerie, I have had barely a moment alone with her. I'm dying to get her to myself." He delivered the last sentence with a sly wiggle of his eyebrows that made his mother's face break into a rueful smile even as she hauled off and smacked him on the arm.

He pulled back, covering the place with his hand in feigned hurt. "Ouch. No hitting the soon-to-be-married man. You might jog something loose."

"Or knock it back in place, because there is definitely something loose in there," she said, pointing at his head.

He placed his arm across her shoulders as he turned her towards his door. "Just don't hit too hard. I'm pretty sure Paige doesn't want an addled man for a husband, above everything else."

His mother stopped him, midstride. "What else?"

"Well, there's my large, overprotective family for one. How much longer do you think she will hold out with all of you hovering about like a bunch of nosey hens?" He teased to cover his previous failure at a joke.

"What makes you think she's marrying you just for you? Maybe she's marrying you to get us?" His mother replied, her rapier wit finally making an appearance.

He squeezed her to him, kissing her temple. "I'm willing to share...a little." He added after a lengthy pause.

*   *   *

Brandon sat on Paige's couch with her stretched out across his legs and her back to the armrest. They'd adopted this position months before, but she wouldn't sit like this at his house with his mother in residence, declaring that she didn't want his mom to think she was anything less than an upstanding woman of God.

He hoped with time she would come to feel secure in his mother's admiration and love for her. Her relationship with Grace made her skittish and wary when it came to accepting love from a mother figure. He knew it wouldn't be easy, but he prayed she would come to the realization that though Grace may have paid for the food, shelter, and clothes she wore, she was never a mother to her. He wanted her to be free from the chains she'd used to shackle herself to Grace. He prayed she could forgive the woman who, in his eyes, had less than the woman in the Bible who gave her last two coins. At least that woman had faith that could be sown to reap a harvest of love, peace, security and the opportunity to spend eternity with God – not to mention the favor of Jesus, which took care of her earthly needs.

"Seek ye first the kingdom of God..." he breathed out on a sigh.

"What?" Paige asked as she stretched her legs and flexed her toes. She looked more relaxed than he'd seen her in the past two weeks, but the telltale dark smudges under her eyes let him know that she'd been lighting the candle at both ends.

He felt responsible for her stretching herself so thin. He'd tried to get his mother to recruit his sister, Marjorie, so Paige wouldn't have so much on her hands, but he soon learned that his stubborn bride-to-be was also a bit of a micromanager.

He'd thought his mother had been calling and bombarding Paige with questions and schedules, but his mother admitted that though Paige would give over tasks to her and some of his sisters, she would also continue to work on each project and call them with suggestions. She decided to just wait for Paige's 'suggestions' then work to finish the task as quick as possible. When he wanted to intercede, his mother waved him off, explaining that it was an opportunity for all of the women of the family to get to know each other better, and suggested with a devilish grin that he just let Paige sleep and recover on their honeymoon. All the responses he wanted to make to that quip were either too disrespectful or too inappropriate, so he stuffed his hands in his pockets and left the room. His mom's giggles could be heard through the walls.

"Mmm, I was just thinking that you have so much because you put God first in your life. I was just wondering why, with all that you have, do you continue to seek those things that will do nothing to add to your value?"

A tiny line formed between her brows, but before she could speak he placed a finger on her lips. "Please, I need you to listen to me just for the next few minutes and just consider what I'm saying with an open heart. Can you do that?"

The seriousness of his voice seemed to register with her and she nodded. He removed his finger from her lip and skimmed it under her right eye.

"I think you are wearing yourself thin, baby." He gave her a stern look when she would have opened her mouth.

"You told me you wouldn't take on too much, that you would share this burden with my mom, Lady Menagerie, and my sisters when I wasn't available, but I'm getting the sneaky suspicion that you are trying to do this all yourself.

Don't get me wrong. I love that you are so passionate about our day and you are putting so much care and detail into everything, but honey, if you keep this up I will be standing at the altar alone because you will have worked yourself into exhaustion. I want to enjoy the planning as well as the day *with* you, not be so worried that we have missed something or someone that we can't live in the moment."

He watched her eyes soften at his last sentence. "What's really going on? You don't usually take back assignments you've given people nor do you micromanage. What's really worrying you?"

He watched as she looked beyond his shoulder for a moment as she thought about her answer. When her eyes came back to rest on his face he was puzzled by the myriad of emotions he saw race through them, but it was the look of defeat that remained.

She shrugged her shoulder as she began. "I want it to be perfect, but not for me... For you and your family. I see your mother and all she has accomplished, and I watch Lady Menagerie and how she is able to juggle so much. I want to be a wife you can be proud of. Your mother and I get along great, and I don't want to disappoint her."

"First of all," he began pulling her legs across his lap so that her torso came closer, and he could wrap his arms around her. She gave a small squeal, but didn't resist him. "I was proud of you as the woman of God that you are. I was proud to have you as a friend when we first started spending time together. I was proud that I knew a woman who would sacrifice her life as she knew it for someone she didn't know. I was proud to have you on my arm as my girl, and I am even more proud to know you're wearing my ring. I don't believe it would change because one day out of the many we are going to spend together isn't absolutely perfect."

He tipped her chin up with his thumb as he palmed the side of her neck gently. "My mother adores you," he said as he looked in her eyes. "My sisters, brothers, and father are thrilled to have you as a new addition to our family, but most of all, I feel inordinately blessed to know that in less than a month, you will be Mrs. Brandon Tatum. I fell in love with you, Paige. I am not looking for the perfect wedding planner or wife, but I am overjoyed to have found the perfect friend and woman for me.

You are going to have to let go just a little bit, Paige, otherwise you will miss all of the fun. The fun of getting to know my sisters and family as we all work together to make this one of the best celebrations ever in the Tatum family. Take their advice, sit back and listen, and observe." He ran his fingertips through the small curls at her temples. "Enjoy the process because it's true purpose is to bring us all together so that we can stand as a unit on our wedding day. If it isn't perfect, so what? We can have a ceremony every year if you want, just like Pastor and First Lady, until you think you've mastered it. Just make sure you savor each moment because they don't come back."

He didn't know what he expected her to say, but he was thoroughly surprised by what came out of her mouth.

"Do you think we could double?"

"I'm being serious, Paige."

"So am I. I hear you, Brandon, and I will push less and enjoy more. Besides, Lady Menagerie said much the same thing earlier today," she smiled ruefully, and it did him in. He pulled her closer and breathed slowly as he memorized the feel of her again. He would never get enough of being around her. He wanted to hold her for the next week, which he knew would be full of questions surrounding his health. He just hoped for his family's and Paige's sake they could deal with the answers.

*   *   *

Paige's hand squeezed his for what had to be the hundredth time in the eight minutes they'd been waiting in Dr. Connor's office. He looked over at her and the comforting smile pulled him in. He searched her face again, gauging her emotion, and found her resolute. She was amazing to behold in that moment. He'd wondered what would prevail in her as she sat next to him – all too close to the person receiving news of reports surpassed or lost. He was neither disappointed nor surprised to see her reliance, composure, and most of all hope in bright eyes devoid of fear. She was truly a sight to behold, and she was *his*. She was his home.

He turned as the doctor entered the room. "I'm sorry for my tardiness. It has been a hectic morning," Doctor Connor said, not looking up from the folder he carried. When he finally glanced up he was momentarily arrested, his surprise giving way to delight. "And who is this lovely creature?" He asked as he came towards them.

"This is my fiancée, Elder Paige Morganson." Brandon found the statement made him want to puff up. He liked introducing her as his fiancé and wondered how much more he would like introducing her as his wife. Could he really feel happier than he already did? If he didn't think it would cause both the doctor and Paige to panic, he would give in to the burning at the back of his eyes.

Dr. Connor took Paige's hand, shaking it with enthusiasm. "I've heard some wonderful things about you, my dear. You make this man light up whenever he talks about you."

Brandon watched as Paige thanked the man, the tips of her ears coloring slightly.

"So," Dr. Connor began as he sat down behind his desk. "How have you been feeling, Brandon?"

Brandon lifted his hand, palm down, and rocked it back and forth.

"That good, eh? Did the new nausea medicine help?"

Brandon saw Paige shift in his periphery and worked on making his face blank. He hadn't wanted her to know the extent of his stomach troubles, but he figured it wouldn't be hidden too much longer with all of the weight he was losing. It wasn't as if he had much leeway to begin with. He'd caught his reflection in the mirror next to the door to his bedroom a few weeks before and noticed that his once sturdy and broad frame was beginning to look wiry. Though he didn't consider himself too vain, he removed the mirror and set it in the guest bedroom.

The hand he felt on his arm brought him back to the present.

Brandon looked over at Paige and gave her a waning smile, then focused back on the doctor.

"I have to say that I thought we would have made more progress, but I guess that would be the bad news in all of this. The good news is that the cancer seems to be arrested. This could be seen as a good sign. There has been no more spreading of the carcinoma cells that we can see. Now that it has stalled, we can work on eradicating what is there." He shuffled through the short stack of paperwork, pulling out the sheet he was looking for. "Your white cell count took a hit as we expected, but it is already starting to rally. Your liver and kidneys are doing very well and I believe we have a chance if we are slightly more aggressive with the next session."

Brandon couldn't quench the disappointment that seemed to have just laid on his shoulders like an anvil. He was hoping to have a reprieve from the weakness so he could practice some of what he preached to Paige the night before. He didn't want to go through another week under the haze of pain and nausea medicine. And what did the doctor mean by 'we'? Brandon hadn't noticed him retching next to him at the commode or lying in bed with the shakes. He wondered if he did, would he continue to force feed him copious amounts of poison? He took a deep breath, knowing he was headed towards a wallow session. He straightened his shoulders and schooled his features once again.

"Could I wait a few weeks before I begin the next session I have to go through? I would rather stand at the altar instead of sit." He knew stressing each 'I' was out of character for him, but the thought of feeling weak and helpless during his wedding, let alone wedding night, was in no way a welcoming thought. Paige was already doing so much, he needed more time to be able to feel like he was pulling his own weight."

"We could postpone…" He heard her start to whisper from his side.

"No," he said just a little too firmly then smiled sheepishly to soften his response. He took her hand in his as he let his eyes skim over her face. "We live each moment to its fullest remember?"

He watched her bite her lip as if she were trying to keep from arguing with him. Finally, she nodded and squeezed his hand back. "To its fullest." She smiled then turned back to the doctor.

"We need just a little more good news, but if you're unable to give it to us we'll just get it from God."

Brandon didn't immediately return his gaze to the doctor, but continued to gaze at Paige. She was truly a sight to behold. When he finally looked back at Dr. Connors, he caught the glint of admiration in his brown eyes as he too looked at Paige.

On the drive back to her apartment, Brandon looked over at her during the red lights, fascinated by the smile continuously playing at her lips. When he couldn't help it any longer, he asked her what she was thinking.

She looked away from the street full of brake lights in front of them, smiling even brighter. "I got my peace."

He was even more puzzled, but could only spare her a glance before the traffic began moving again. "Okaaay…"

"I was taught, like you, that when I pray and ask for answers to questions, I should expect an answer. I also know the difference between a prayer coming from me or me being led to pray by the prompting of the Holy Spirit." She took a breath.

"I've been… concerned." She seemed to be picking her words very carefully.

"Each time I go before God to pray for you, I can't help but feel that when it comes to the subject of your health, it's me praying, not the leading of the Holy Spirit. It has been a source of unease for me because I couldn't understand why I wouldn't be led by the Spirit to pray for your healing. At first I thought maybe it was because I was so close to you I couldn't hear around my wants, but I thought back to when Vivian was in the hospital. I prayed and warred in the Spirit on her behalf as though I, myself, had entered the enemy's camp and stolen back her promise of an abundant life.

When I pray for you, I am led to speak peace over you. Even this morning I was led to pray for restoration, boldness, a new level of faith, and joy unspeakable. I wanted…still want, a miracle of healing for you, but when we were in the oncologist's office I was sieged with such a strong need to protect you from the doctor's guesses, I finally listened to the voice in me I'd begun quieting whenever I didn't hear what I wanted when I prayed for you. The cancer wasn't the issue. My fear was.

It occurred to me that I've been trying to war and battle on your behalf, but that was never my purpose. My purpose is to love you, comfort you, encourage you, love you some more, marry you and pray knowing that fear in any form is the true disease. If I'm led to pray for a new level of faith for you, it means He's already preparing you with the weapons to win the next round. Where faith is there is trust, and where trust is there can be no fear. I will trust Him to heal you.

I've been trying to pray for your healing when all along you've been helping me strengthen my faith by witnessing your walk. You, Brandon Tatum, are my hero."

He listened intently to her, wanting to absorb every word and when driving became a distraction he pulled onto a side street. He now sat slack-jawed, misty-eyed, and incredibly humbled by the words of this precious woman of God. She had just given him everything he needed to succeed: her trust in him.

CHAPTER 35

If she had known the proposal came with marriage counseling, she may have reconsidered her answer. Victoria sat in front of the slightly balding, pudgy looking man seated on the other side of the desk. He did little more than ask a question or two and repeat what they'd said over the last two sessions. Victoria was tired of it. She wanted to go home... She could do her taxes for next year, clean out the stalls or the hen house...get a root canal without Novocain.

"Victoria?" She pulled herself away from her sarcastic thoughts and redirected her focus on the counselor.

"You said towards the end of the last session that the first time you were really aware of the chasm between you and Richard was during your daughter's illness, but Richard just admitted that, for him, it began many years before that."

She looked over at Richard, whose eyes pierced hers, and she was instantly contrite for allowing her thoughts to wander.

"Do you want to ask him when he began to notice it?"

She just barely checked the impulse to sucking her teeth and roll her eyes. Of course she wanted to know when he started feeling the distance. The small smirk that came to her husband's lips told her she hadn't been successful in hiding her disdain.

"When did you first notice a difference, Richard?"

The smile faded and his eyes grew solemn. "I think it was when Rachael was four. I was taking some night courses in architecture because I was sick of all of the long days at the firm away from the two of you. We had been talking about having another child."

Victoria's heart started to pound at the direction of his story. She remembered that summer. *Oh God, he couldn't have known all this time and not said anything, could he?*

She swallowed thickly, hoping she was jumping to conclusions.

"It was so hot this particular Wednesday night, class ended early because the fans were just blowing hot air and air conditioning wasn't available in that room. I was invited by a few classmates to go to dinner and get in some extra studying for Friday's test. Since I wasn't due home for another couple of hours, I thought I would spend one hour with them and come home an hour early. I only ordered dessert because I knew you'd cooked," he added, sheepishly.

Why he thought she would take exception to that now, she didn't know, but it was endearing nonetheless. Her hands began to tremble slightly so she clasped them together.

"I had just come from the restroom when I thought I saw you walking down the street. I was curious and kept watching because I could tell it was you from your stride. When I was sure it was you, I told my colleagues that I would be right back and followed you. I called your name, but you didn't hear me."

She hadn't. She was so caught up in her thoughts. All she wanted to do was get to her follow-up appointment at the clinic and get home to Rachael, who was being watched by Martha.

"I continued to follow you and watched you go into the clinic. I was going to run to catch up to you to see if anything was wrong, but by the time I made it through the doors and noticed that it was full of women, I'd lost you. I looked to see if there was anything on the walls or signs that would give me a clue as to why you would come to this clinic instead of the hospital on the other side of town.

I went to the receptionist and asked for you. I told her I was your husband, but she wouldn't admit or deny that you were there. I stood around for a moment, hoping that whatever business you had there would be quick. I think I waited fifteen minutes before I had to get back to the diner.

There were so many scenarios that ran through my head on the way home. Maybe you were pregnant and wanted to surprise me. Maybe you weren't there as a patient, but visiting one of the doctors to help get information on the needs of the women that went to that clinic. My thoughts continued to seesaw like that until I pulled into the drive and Rachael came running out to greet me. I saw that your car was there and was prepared to ask you, but Rachael told me you were upstairs in bed with a hurt head. She saw his lips lift slightly with the memory.

On my way through the house, I ran into Martha who seemed relieved to see me but only said you were in bed with a bad headache.

I went up to see that you were indeed in bed and asleep, so I went back down and joined Rachael and Martha. I asked Martha if you'd gone out earlier and she froze for a moment before nodding her head in confirmation. I asked her if she knew what for and she shook her head, but I knew she had an idea. I let it go, figuring you would tell me in the morning, so I spent the remainder of Rachael's awake time playing with her then went up to bed.

The next morning I asked you point blank if you'd been to the clinic for the headache Martha said you went to bed for, but you looked at me, blinked those pretty wide eyes and instead of answering me truthfully, you asked me, 'Why would I go to the clinic when there is a perfectly good hospital down the way?' I pressed and told you I saw you from the diner window, but you still denied it and had the nerve to get upset with me for pushing the issue so I relented, but I didn't stop trying to figure out what was going on. I couldn't understand what the big secret was."

Victoria felt like she was having an out-of-body experience. He had held onto this for over 26 years and he recalled it as if it were yesterday. Why didn't she just tell him what was going on? Oh yeah, because the first time it happened she didn't think he would survive it, he took it so hard. She just couldn't see him hurting that way – not when it was something that was wrong with her. Not when she could spare him from the continual heartache.

"I went through the bathroom cabinets and your purses in the closet for loose pieces of paper," Richard continued. "I even came home early a couple of times to intercept the mailman. All because you wouldn't tell me that you'd had another miscarriage."

Victoria closed her eyes against the pain in his gaze.

She remembered the fear and anger well. It accompanied her with each failed pregnancy. After a while, she just didn't want to try anymore. She didn't want to subject another life into her obviously hostile womb, so she'd secretly began taking birth control.

"I'm sorry," she whispered. "I was trying to spare you more pain."

"But instead you brought lies and secrets into our marriage," he finished for her.

She flinched at the harshness of his words, but reluctantly conceded to the fact that she had indeed done more harm than good in that case. She nodded almost imperceptibly. "I'm sorry. You're right, I should have told you."

He stared at her, the lines in his face relaxing, making him look younger. She was about to take a breath when his features changed and a look of vulnerability passed through his eyes. She knew what he was going to ask before he opened his mouth and heaven help her, she would tell him the truth.

"Was that the only one?" he asked quietly.

She didn't take her eyes from his as she shook her head.

She heard him gasp even though his lips barely moved, and it sent a frisson of pain through her.

"How many?" His voice was barely a croaked whisper, and his eyes were already growing wet.

"Five."

"Oh God." He tore his gaze from hers. The hoarse cry seemed loud in the deathly quiet room. He bent forward in his chair, hugging his arms around his waist. She watched as his shoulders began to shake, but was galvanized into motion when she heard the first sobs.

She was up and to him, wrapping her arms around any part she could embrace before she could think about it. She crooned and made little noises as she tried to soothe him. She rubbed his back and shoulders as she tried to stifle the crippling pain each one of his sobs lanced through her. She would lick her wounds later.

They sat like that long enough for her to lose track of the minutes. She had forgotten about the counselor until he cleared his throat and a tissue box came into her line of sight.

She extracted a few and placed them in Richard's hand, then looked up at the counselor. "I think we are done for the day." He looked as though he might want to argue, but he must have seen the set in her jaw because he remained silent.

She heard Richard's raspy "no" just before he started to shrug her off.

The motion left her feeling bereft. She needed to comfort him in this even if it was as close as she could come to getting the comfort she obviously didn't deserve from him.

He sat back and away from her, peeling her arms from around his shoulders. His rejection was so painful she wanted to cry out, but reminded herself that she had done this.

"Why?" His voice had gone cold, and she almost wished to go back a few minutes because even the hurt in his voice was easier to take than this distant, icy tone.

She reached for him again and he shifted away. She let her hand fall to her lap, but remained kneeling next to his chair. "I wanted to save you from the pain. The first time I miscarried, you took it so hard. You were almost inconsolable. You seemed to blame yourself, which was ridiculous, and it took months before you would touch me again. You were almost despondent and I couldn't stand to see you that way, especially since it was really my fault." She looked away at the end of the sentence so she missed the coolness thaw quickly, giving way to heat.

"So you decided to keep them from me? You took the option and opportunity for me to react better out of my hands. You took from me the chance to mourn with you and comfort you each time you kept it from me. You did this." He motioned his hand back and forth between the two of them. "You built this Grand Canyon between us with the lies, deception, and secrets you've kept over the years."

She shook her head, trying to stop this runaway train before it disseminated what was left of their fragile marriage.

"Please, I did it for you."

"No Victoria, you did it for yourself. You went at it like the independently blind fool you are. I knew you had some serious control issues, but this is too much. You weren't supposed to go through it alone.

We were married." The use of the past tense gave her pause, and panic shot to her heart.

"I was only trying to save you pain. I was wrong. I see that now. I…"

He silenced her with a hand. "You were trying to save me pain? You were trying to save me pain," he repeated snidely as he stood up, moving even further away from her. "Well, you've done one hell of a job. Good try, but I think you failed." His caustic reply stopped her cold. The sarcasm dripping from his words found their mark and she began to withdraw to protect herself. She used his chair to help her stand, but when she turned to go back to her chair she felt his hand grasp her arm.

"Oh no you don't. You don't get a reprieve from this. I want you right front and center. I want you to see what you've caused."

The counselor stepped forward and Richard raised his other hand towards him. "Don't worry, Doc, I won't physically harm her." He released his grip on her as if to appease him then turned back to Victoria. "But you will stand right there and you will hear what I have to say. You will not utter another word in defense or compilation. You are going to hear me beyond all of those upside down thoughts in that addled brain of yours. Understood?"

She nodded.

"For 33 years, you and I have been volleying for a role that was inherently mine as the husband. You, with your ideas about what it means to survive; what you believed you still needed to protect your heart from because of what that boy and your parents did to you in college. You took what they did to you out on me and our marriage."

She wanted to deny it, but was too afraid he would keep the promise radiating from his eyes. He would walk out on her. She was sure of it.

"As close as we got, there was still that place in your heart you never let me into. At first I thought you just needed time and I convinced myself that what I had of you was enough, but as the years came and went, that space only grew wider. It was my fault. I should have forced you to see what you were doing to us – to our marriage – but I wanted you to love me enough to do it on your own. Well, it's time for you to make a decision."

"Richard, ultimatums are never a good idea…" The counselor began.

"Thanks Doc, but I've got this," Richard interrupted, not taking his eyes off of Victoria.

Victoria looked quickly between Richard and the counselor to see if he would object further, but the man simply shut his mouth and folded his hands. She didn't know what she thought of that.

"You didn't trust that I could comfort you, protect you, or help make the pain go away. You thought me too weak because I feel so deeply? No, Victoria, it's you who's lost touch with their emotions."

He stopped and pointed to his chair. "I sat there doubled over in pain and though you came to comfort me, you shed not one tear. Not one. What, did you shed them all when you were getting rid of the evidence of our children?" The last sentence hit her like a blow to her solar plexus. She reeled with the impact, shaking her head vehemently. "Or are only the dead worthy of your tears?"

That slapped her as if he'd raised his own hand to her and she wanted to unsheathe her claws and gouge out his tongue. She only stopped herself when she took a moment to see the wild hurt in his eyes, and she knew she would take it. If it would give him what he needed, she would take the stripes of his words.

He stopped his tirade and looked at her for one long moment, then looked away in disgust.

He stepped away as if to leave, and her heart seized. She opened her mouth to plead with him not to leave her, but the counselor spoke first.

"Richard." He held up imploring hands.

"She's right this time. This session is over. I'll call you if I want to schedule another."

"I think you have made a great deal of progress today. It would be a shame to lose it..." The counselor began.

"I will call you," Richard said with finality.

He was at the door when he spoke again. Without turning he said, "We are leaving, Victoria."

The rush of relief that overtook her had her knees weak. She quickly picked up her purse and followed him to the door, sparing the counselor a cursory nod.

They were in the car heading away from the office before he spoke. "Where are the bodies, Victoria?" He didn't look away from the road, but she saw his hands tighten on the wheel.

She swallowed, her throat going dry. "They were cremated."

She watched as his knuckles went pale on the wheel.

"Then?" he asked.

"I buried them."

He took a deep breath.

"Where?"

She turned to look out of the passenger window. Maybe she should have stayed with the counselor.

"Where, Victoria?" His voice took her to a frightening place.

"The garden."

The car swerved slightly and she looked back towards the front, startled by the movement. He quickly regained control and after a few moments, sped up.

When they were exiting the car, he stopped Victoria from going into the house with one word. "Come."

She bristled at the command, but followed him obediently around the back to the garden.

They reached the divide between the walkway and the path leading into the garden when he stopped. "Show me," he said.

"You could say 'please'," she mumbled almost inaudibly.

"Don't push me, Victoria."

Victoria led him through the maze of flowers to the far corner where two angel statues stood about three feet high. There was a bench along the low wall that allowed one to sit and look over the garden as a whole. There was a mix of flowers surrounding the statues. Blue rhododendrons were held back from their climb by loose ties, white and pink hydrangeas were slightly raised from the middle of the area, and pale, yellow daylilies were dispersed in and around the other flowers. Persian Carpet Zinnias surrounded the bed of flowers like a bright red and yellow border.

"Where?" Richard croaked.

"Scattered around the flowerbed. There are three here. Two boys and one girl."

"Did–" He took a deep breath clearing his throat. "Did you name them?"

"She shook her head, unable to form words around the lump in her throat. Finally, when she thought she could speak, she added breath to her thoughts.

"I gave them flowers. It didn't seem right to name them without you."

He looked over at her, but she was unable to make out his expression. After a minute, he nodded.

She watched him as he looked down at the flower bed trying to find any sign of what caused this part of the garden to flourish. Perhaps it was the fact that it flourished that was the very sign, but she could do one better.

"I have something that may bring some clarity. May I go and get it?"

Richard looked at her, his eyes softening slightly before he nodded.

Victoria beat a hasty retreat. If they were going to discuss the babies, she might as well tell him everything. She walked as quickly to her office as possible. She went to the safe and retrieved her journals covering the six years she lost child after child. The five books were a heavy load, but with longer, slower strides, she made it back to the garden fairly quickly.

When she approached, he looked up and watched her, seemingly transfixed, as she sat down on the bench. She shuffled through the books then opened one, turning the pages until she'd reached the area she'd been looking for. She handed the book, splayed open, to him.

He took it hesitantly, not taking his eyes off of her for a long moment.

When he looked down and began reading, she knew the exact moment realization struck him. His shoulders went taunt as if to stave off an onslaught of emotion, but when he began reading out loud his voice was strong and clear.

My sweet girl, I would have loved to have met you. It seems it was not to be, so I will remember you in daylilies because while you were growing inside of me my days were filled with sunshine. When I think of your brother, Shane, who your father and I had to say goodbye to last year, I wonder if he's shown you the ropes. I wish I could give you a name, but it wouldn't be fair to Richard so instead I will make you part of the other thing that gives me so much joy and when I nurture your daylilies, I will think of nurturing you, my sweet girl. Tell your big brother I said, "Hello and mommy loves you both."

Neither one of their eyes were dry when he finished.

"How far along were you?" he asked, now looking at the daylilies.

"Eighteen weeks, four and a half months. It was different than the first time. I didn't have as much bleeding, but the cramping was awful. I spent the morning right after you left for work in the hospital. Martha picked me up on the way to get Rachael from pre-school. The day you saw me in town I was going to my follow-up appointment. Your friend, Paul, was on call and I couldn't chance him seeing me."

She watched his shoulders slump slightly at her words. The deception was very clear.

He was quiet for a long time before he looked up at her, tears streaking his cheeks and seemed to be surprised to see her cheeks just as wet. But then, why wouldn't he be surprised? Hadn't he only a few hours ago accused her of being emotionless?

"Let's name her Lilly. She feels like a 'Lilly'. Just like her flower."

She nodded feeling as though she'd been given a reprieve. "Lilly is the perfect name," she replied with a shy smile.

They were silent for at least ten minutes when he came over to sit next to her on the bench. He handed her the book and she went to the page of their next child. She inclined her head towards the rhododendrons. When he still looked puzzled she said, "The blue flowers." He nodded his understanding and took the book back from her.

My darling baby boy. My heart is heavier than it should be because I know if I don't let you go, I won't be able to move forward. I could tell you were special right from the start. The doctor said you were three months, which makes you my birthday baby. Your father and I conceived you during a surprise getaway trip to a beautiful Bed and Breakfast in Tulsa. There were rhododendrons growing outside our window and I thought they were one of the most beautiful flowers. Just like you. I wanted you so badly I could taste it. We would have been great friends because I could already feel myself bonding with you. And though you may never know what kisses and hugs are, you know my love. It will always be yours.

When he was done reading, he just shook his head. "What do you think of Justin for a name?" Her smile was tremulous and she nodded. Her heart felt lighter than it had in decades.

"You shouldn't have gone through this by yourself. You should have come to me. We could have at least comforted each other."

He looked up at her. His face drawn, his eyes wet.

"We can't go on like this. We can't work with you treating this like some type of business collaboration where everything you believe doesn't have anything to do with me gets set on your side of the shelf. I want it all, Victoria, and if you aren't willing to give it to me, we should call it quits now."

"Yes," she said without hesitation.

"Yes what?" He eyed her skeptically.

"Yes, I will give you everything. I will share everything. No more secrets. Just ask me, and I will tell you."

Richard watched her for a few moments, then with all solemnity asked her the one thing she'd forgotten she didn't want to share.

"Did you have pictures taken of Mason with a woman?"

She went silent. *Damn.* She didn't see that coming. What was he playing at? If she lied, he would leave her. If she said yes, he could also leave her. She stared at him, trying to read him, but was thwarted when he looked down at the book, shielding him from her.

It was then that she came to the realization that he already knew. She didn't know how he knew for sure, but he knew. He already knew and he had stayed.

"Yes," she said as she folded her hands together.

She watched him take one breath, then two. "I want you to stop."

Victoria's breath caught. She didn't usually ask questions she didn't want to know the answer to, but she had no more cards on this table to turn over.

"Is that an ultimatum?" she asked slowly, over-enunciating.

He looked up at her with surprise in his eyes. "No." He shook his head. "It's a desire of mine that I am sharing with you. One I hope you will consider doing for me."

Victoria began to heat up. She had worked too hard to make sure that her granddaughter had a safe and privileged place to grow up. Mason deserved to lose her if he picked the bottle over her.

She pressed her lips together, knowing Richard was waiting for an answer. "I will think about it."

She saw the disappointment cloud his eyes for a moment, then he squared his shoulders and handed her back the book.

"Can we go through them all?"

She offered him a ghost of a smile, and turned to the child she'd grown the zinnias for.

They spent the rest of the day moving throughout the garden. She would point out the flowers and go to the passage in her journal for that particular child, and he would read it out loud as if they were giving a memorial to each one. They would name them, and then spend a few moments in silence; she in remembrance, and him in recognition of the life they'd lost.

The sun was setting when he finished reading the last passage. "I want to have stones set for each one of them. I want them to be known. They don't have to be huge, just something that recognizes them for who they were. Can we do that?" His eyes were imploring and she couldn't have denied him anything at the moment. No matter how it might look to guests, her children deserved to be recognized. He was right.

"Yes."

He reached out, skimming his hand along her cheek. "Thank you. Thank you for sharing them. Thank you for the journals and the flowers, and waiting for me to name them."

She ignored the tears running down her cheeks and concentrated on his touch – the gratitude in his eyes, and the love in his words. Her heart felt like it would pound out of her chest and she didn't mind. It was now light enough to fly.

"I think I understand why you did it. That doesn't mean that I don't feel cheated or angry, because this wound is still way too fresh. I can't say I would have handled all the losses as well as you seemed to, but from now on, we do this together and where one of us is weak the other one will add strength. I need you to trust that when you are feeling weak, you can come to me for the comfort and strength you need."

"I do." And she realized as she said the words that she really did. Today had been a turning point in their marriage, and their lives as husband and wife.

"Can we renew our vows out here?"

He never looked away from her eyes. "Yes, Vickie. We can renew our vows here."

She smiled then because she couldn't help herself. The joy she felt was incomparable to nothing else she'd known, and it seemed only right when he slowly wrapped his arms around her and pulled her closer. She watched as his lips came closer and sighed in that instance where joy met comfort, and she felt secure in his love. The kiss that was meant to seal their agreement deepened and grew into a profession of love, a concession to a new beginning, and the happy realization that they had time to make it right.

*   *   *

Richard and Victoria renewed their vows on a slightly overcast day, deep in the middle of May. Mary was Victoria's attendant and her husband, Paul, was Richard's best man.

Victoria had picked a long, buttercup yellow, satin sheath gown with an overlay of lace that skimmed her curves. She wore her hair carefully coiffed into a French roll with wisps of hair left out around her temples and nape to soften the look. She held a bouquet of flowers representing each of their children from the garden and when she walked down the path to Richard standing in the center of their garden, she couldn't help the smile that took over her features. He was riveting in a charcoal grey tuxedo with a silver blue tie. His toffee colored skin shown in beautiful contrast to the white shirt and the small lines at the edges of his warm, chocolate eyes enhanced the smile he returned to her.

Over the month since the counseling session that took them to a new place in their relationship, they talked about some of their insecurities and asked questions that they'd been afraid to ask. They would take rides to nowhere in particular and talk as they had when they were newly married. Instead of reading individually or watching television in bed at night, they would talk into the wee hours or read to one another. They went back to a lot of the things they did for one another before the pain and hurt set in.

Richard even confessed to being reluctant to pursue the subject of her keeping her second miscarriage a secret because he was just too relieved that she wasn't having an affair. He told her that the changes in her mood and passion towards him had changed dramatically and though he'd tried to bring up the subject, she just chalked it up to being too tired or just not in the mood, and dismissed it as quickly as possible.

On the Saturday of the third week after their time of revelation in the garden, Richard surprised Victoria with a trip into Oklahoma City. They had lunch at one of her favorite restaurants nestled in the corner of a hotel she would stay in sometimes when visiting Richard during the week, since he didn't always have the time to commute.

He drove them to North Park Mall where she used to shop when she waited for him. She thought he was just feeling nostalgic, but when they entered the jewelry store her mind started racing.

Richard shook hands with the manager and introduced the short and swarthy man to Victoria. She barely remembered her manners before she was placed in a chair facing Richard.

"So I figured," he began, as he took her hands in his. "That since we are essentially starting over, I would give you something to represent our new beginning. When I first proposed to you some 33 years ago, I bought your engagement ring from this store. I thought it would be fitting I give you a new one from the same store."

Victoria took her left hand away from his. Her heart beat hard and fast in fear. She never considered herself a superstitious person, but she didn't know if she could part with her ring. "But I love this one."

Richard smiled at her before he pulled her hand away from her chest. "I'm not replacing it, honey, I'm adding to it."

There was a blue velvet ring box set in front of them on the glass counter. Richard thanked the manager and picked up the box.

"Before I give it to you, though, I have to say something."

Victoria sat still in her seat. She wasn't usually caught off guard like this, but Richard always seemed to be one step ahead of her. How had she forgotten that over the years?

He took a deep breath then looked her square in the eye. "I need to ask your forgiveness for not being more persistent regarding our communication and relationship as a whole over the years. I let my own insecurities and complacency in our marriage cause gaps that were almost insurmountable. I even considered just ending everything a few times because the thought of all we had to overcome was daunting."

Victoria looked away briefly to see how many of the store's staff were witnessing this. She was feeling uncomfortable with the venue in which Richard chose to make this supplication. When she saw they had all retreated to a respectable distance and many of them weren't even paying them any attention, she was relieved.

The pressure of Richard's finger on her chin brought her eyes back to him.

"Will you forgive me?" he asked, his heart in his eyes.

"I already have," she stated firmly, then bit her lip and took the plunge. "Will you forgive me for the secrets I kept about our children, Rachael, and Vivian? Will you forgive me for not giving you the chance to mourn with me or be the husband you were meant to be to me?" She looked earnestly into chocolate eyes that had become a little wet with her request, and held her breath until she heard the answer that helped wash hundreds of days of pain away.

"Yes. I already have." He kissed her. "I do." He kissed her again. "And I will." He gave her one more, quick peck on the lips then with an expression akin to a little boy opening gifts on Christmas day, he opened the box and her eyes went wide with the beauty of the ring.

Richard lifted the stunning ring with its platinum encased row of diamonds shaped into a soft arrow from the box and slid it onto her finger. It sat snugly against her other ring in perfect alignment as if they were made as a pair.

"How did you do this?"

Richard shrugged. "I have my ways. Do you like it?"

She tore her eyes away from the set and took his face in her hands. "I love it, almost as much as I love you."

"Now that, Mrs. Branchett, is the perfect answer."

The next morning, she decided to surprise him and was up and dressed for church before he was ready to leave.

He seemed startled when she came out of the library with her purse in hand.

"Where are you going?"

"With you, if it's okay."

She watched him misstep as he walked towards her, his eyes wide.

"I'm going to church."

"Yes, I know."

His face broke into a wide grin. "Well then." He lent her his elbow and she placed her hand in its crook. "I think you'll have a good time. The pastor is pretty funny sometimes, but you can tell how much he loves God. He doesn't preach as much as teach, and he is truly anointed and humble. I really think you'll like him."

Victoria slowed her steps enough to get his attention. He'd become so animated and caught up with sharing the things that made his church and pastor special, he was a few steps ahead of her before he noticed their separation.

"I," she floundered and tried to clear her throat. "I just wanted to visit – to see what you and Mary were talking about. I don't know if I'm ready for anything more. I... I don't know."

She saw the contrition take over his features and he walked back to her. "I'm sorry. I'm just so excited to share this with you. No one is going to ask more of you than you can give, especially me, and I promise I won't be disappointed if you aren't ready to commit. It's great just being able to have you join me." When she continued to hesitate, he reaffirmed his statement. "I promise, no more than what you wish to give. I'll be happy just to have you sitting next to me."

Victoria finally nodded and allowed him to lead her from the house.

On the way to church, Victoria started reminiscing about the day before and one particular question took hold and nipped at her conscience until she voiced it. She looked over at Richard, pursing her lips before she spoke up. "Why did you stay? Why did you stay all of this time?"

He looked at her. His brows furrowed in confusion, but it only took a couple of seconds for the realization to hit him.

"Why did I stay married to you?"

She nodded.

"I chose to," he said, matter-of-factly.

"Yes, but why?"

"No. I chose to love you," he said, smiling slowly. That same smile that he used to charm her into submission with when they were first married.

"You're mine. I don't give up what's mine that easily."

She felt giddy at his words.

"You don't say?"

"Yeah, I say." He grinned at her. Then his lips slowly flattened out and the next look he gave her was full of the love he'd just spoken of. "I love you because I choose to continue to love you. I chose to stay because I love you."

Victoria smiled brightly, secure in his answer. She snuggled into the seat and let his confession embrace her like a warm blanket.

*   *   *

And now she was standing in front of the man she was about to pledge the rest of her life to, again, but this time she knew where some of the pitfalls lay and she was equipped with some mighty weapons. His enthusiasm in sharing his days and passions with her was contagious, and they talked to catch up as much as they did just to continue to be around each other.

She reached out and touched one of the lapels on his jacket. "Nice," she said, grinning mischievously.

"Behave yourself," he said, mirroring her look then leaned forward and whispered close to her ear. "I'm trying to make an honest woman of you."

She screwed up her face, causing him to laugh out loud.

"Life with you definitely isn't boring."

She shrugged her shoulders. "Yeah, but you knew that the first time you married me."

"Yes I did, but this time I'm hoping to season it with God."

She nodded, neither in agreement or denial of his statement.

"One day, honey. You will know the peace I've come to cherish. Until then, I will share what I can, but don't settle because He has a measure stored up just for you."

She felt the pull of his words and wanted to give in, but feeling self-conscious, she only smiled. Still, the word 'soon' kept resounding in her heart like a whisper and she knew it was only a matter of time before she let go of those last seeds of doubt.

CHAPTER 36

Mason had taken up jogging. Well, not the overall exercise with the labored breathing and constant conversation volleying between cheering himself on and trying to convince himself to take one more stride across the street to his car. He just gave the appearance of moving up and down the street, keeping the front of the brownstone his therapist worked out of, in sight. This was the third evening in a row that he'd taken to "exercising" in this area.

He had tried waiting for T. Anderson to return his email for a week, but that soon became a hazard because though he had allowed Vivian to finally sync his personal email to his phone, he couldn't allow more than five minutes to go by without checking it and it took 10 minutes to get to work every day. Vivian would be highly disappointed to know that he was placing other motorists' lives in danger because he was anxiously waiting for a woman who seemed familiar though he'd never seen her before, to communicate with him while claiming her card case.

If nothing else, he would be in shape enough to do an eight-minute mile if he kept this up. He reached the end of the street and had turned around when he spotted her getting out of her car across the street. He took a deep breath and hoped his appearance would match his story of being in the middle of a jog. He timed his strides so that they would intersect and frowned to himself as a thought crossed his mind. He hoped she wouldn't think he was stalking her because he wasn't at all the type. He had a daughter, for goodness sakes. He considered his actions from the previous week, and almost stopped halfway to her. He had been stalking her in a way, but couldn't this just be considered an act from a Good Samaritan? After all, it was a very expensive looking case and she was new in the area. She could use her cards. He picked up his pace once again having convinced himself of his good deed and thus given his confidence a needed boost. He looked away from her so she wouldn't see him watching her and guessed that he'd planned this. At the last moment, he looked up and narrowly stopped himself from running into her again. The fright in her eyes morphed into surprise, and then into open amusement.

He worked at a surprised expression himself, but was sure he had it down since he'd practiced it in the mirror a couple of times. He jogged in place a couple of seconds then stopped. "Woman with the beautiful green eyes." He watched as the color entered her cheeks. Her smile brightened and she pointed her hand at him.

"The architect that gives walking tours around Chicago."

"Mason Jenson," he added, when seeming to be at a loss for his name.

421

"Mason Jenson," she repeated, nodding her head. She took in his attire, and he watched her as her eyes scanned him from head to toe and back.

"You live around here?" Her expression became guarded.

He decided to be honest just in case she took him up on his offer to give her that tour and things progressed.

"Not really, but this is a great street to run on because the road and sidewalks are so wide."

She looked at the sidewalk from whence he came as though to assess it for herself, then she shrugged and looked back at him. "Well," she breathed then looked toward the brownstone after gazing at her watch. "I don't want to interrupt your exercise. See you around, Mason Jenson." She moved to take a step, and he raised his hand to get her to stay.

"Um, did you notice losing a card holder?"

She stopped and looked at him with an expression he couldn't decipher. He decided to go on.

"After you went into the building last week, I found a silver case with cards in it that had your picture, or what I think is your picture, on them. It had an initial and a last name." He looked skyward as if to try and search his memory. "I think it said 'T. Anderson'?" He ended as if asking a question and saw the light of recognition come into her eyes.

"Oh wow. I've been looking for that. I thought I wouldn't see it again. Do you have it with you?"

He looked down at himself as if to note his lack of pockets. She grinned sheepishly, realizing he wouldn't be running with her card case even if he did have pockets.

"Sorry," he said, trying not to crack a smile so he didn't embarrass her. "I tried emailing the address on the card, but I didn't get a response."

She frowned up at him. "Really? When?"

"I think it was the night after I ran into you right here," he said, wondering why this was news to her. He just knew she had just decided not to email him back, but on the off chance that he was wrong, at least he'd lost almost five pounds over the last three days.

"Your email must have gone to my spam. I have a very sensitive and highly protected provider. I can't tell you how many times I've been hacked and I moved to a provider that is known for its high security. Usually I have to contact someone first in order for their email to get into my inbox."

Spam. It went into her Spam box and here he was racking his brain, trying to figure out why she wouldn't want to retrieve her case and wondering if he'd made such a bad first impression, she would rather call it a lost cause instead of seeing him again. He felt foolish and just a little bit desperate.

He thought this T. Anderson would be a welcomed distraction from is thoughts of Paige. He hoped this would grow into a healthy relationship, whether it was a friendship or more, but if he was acting this way after only seeing her once, it didn't bode well. Maybe he should just make arrangements to mail the case to her.

He looked at her for a moment then failing to come up with something clever he began to retreat from his plan to get to know her. He opened his mouth, but she spoke before he could.

"May I email the address on your card so that we can schedule a time and place where I can get the case back from you?"

The deep breath he took in surprise kept him from spewing forth his first thought. *"You kept my card?" Thank goodness for that.* At that point he probably would have just given up and walked away. He shook himself.

"My number is on the card. You could call me," he finally said in return.

Her cheeks grew redder with his statement.

"Yes, I could do that," she said, with a little embarrassment.

"What's the matter?" He asked, wanting to know the source of her discomfort.

"I'm so used to texting or emailing, I rarely use my phone for what it was originally made for. Yes, I can call you."

"Boy, if calling seems like a social challenge then I wonder what you will think of my next idea."

"I didn't say that making a call was a social challenge, it is just usually my last choice because the people I normally communicate with want as much information as quick as possible. Talking is used as a last resort or reserved for those times you introduce yourself, do a presentation, or need more clarity."

"Do you talk to your sister, other family members, or friends?" Mason asked, wanting to get a better understanding of where this standoffishness ended.

"Sure, but you're none of those."

Well, she couldn't have made it any more plain. "Are you always so ambiguous with your statements?" He joked as a way to smooth the sting of her bluntness.

She seemed to catch on to the tone of her statement, and looked down. "Sorry," she shrugged again. "Maybe I have a little practicing to do." She emphasized her statement by lifting her thumb and forefinger, and bringing them within an inch of each other.

"You can practice on me," Mason said, then wanted to kick himself.

"Kinda persistent, aren't you?" she said, giving him an assessing look.

It was his turn to shrug. "I figure since I was the one that found your case, fate was on my side. Who am I to look a gift horse in the mouth?"

"Fate?" She inquired, and the way she said it puzzled him.

"Yes. Do you believe in fate?"

"Not really. I believe I'm in charge of my own destiny," she said, shifting her purse on her shoulder, and he knew his time was running short.

"Well, does your destiny have room for a walking tour of the best parts of the city or a cup of coffee at the diner on the corner of 34th and Myra St. tomorrow at 5:30 p.m.?"

She laughed, and it transformed her somewhat stiff demeanor into a woman he now needed to be around more, even if it was just to be the one that brought about this transformation.

The laugh wasn't given into with abandonment as Paige did, but there was a softening from her shoulders to her hairline. He found it alluring.

She stopped slowly, watching him watch her. "What is it? You have a funny look on your face."

"You have a fascinating laugh to watch."

"Well, that's odd. Usually when I laugh, everyone around me is laughing as well instead of watching me laugh."

He thought about her reply, and noted that this was the second time she said something he could have taken offense to. He wondered if it was a sign of nervousness or if she was just this blunt. He didn't even consider asking her.

"Sorry. I didn't mean to stare or be weird about it. I just found it nice." He figured at this point he had either done enough damage where she would just email him and ask him to send her the case, or she was one of three women in the world that thought his eccentricities were charming.

She cocked her head to the side, studying him intently then seemed to remember herself. "I'm going to be late if I don't get going. Mason Jenson, I will email you." She took a step, and he stopped her one more time.

"Since I saw fit to try to return your case to you, do you think you could tell me what the 'T' stands for?"

She pursed her lips as if she were giving it some deep thought and finally huffed. "Okay. It's Tabitha."

He smiled, feeling as though he'd accomplished a great feat. "Thank you very much, Tabitha Anderson. I look forward to getting your email."

Her laugh came again. "You don't talk like you do a lot of emailing."

"Of course I do. I even have my email synced to my phone."

She grinned at his attempt at sounding high tech. "Yeah...wow." She nodded her head slowly. "You are really on the cutting edge of technology."

"I wouldn't go that far. You know things change second by second. By now, I was cutting edge two years ago."

She smirked at him then moved away.

"Mason Jenson. It was nice almost running into you again. I really have to go."

He nodded and let her pass. He watched her walk up the steps to the door of the brownstone. Her shiny, light-brown, hair swinging across her shoulders caught the light of the waning day perfectly and he stood transfixed as she turned and waved 'goodbye'. He pulled himself out of his stupor just in time to wave back before she disappeared behind the door.

He stood on the sidewalk chuckling to himself, then looked around to make sure no one was watching him. He set off on a jog towards his car around the corner then stopped, remembering that he didn't like jogging, and walked the rest of the way to his vehicle.

When he walked in his front door, he was met with the sight of his daughter twirling in front of the entry hall mirror in her junior bride's dress. Reality came rolling back on him, but for once it didn't bring with it the gut-punching pain.

Tabitha may just be the answer to many of his daughter's prayers. He just hoped she didn't take too long to email him and then agree to see him.

"Daddy. What do you think?" Vivian twirled again and he had to admit that the dress fit her long frame perfectly. From what Vivian said, its color was cranberry with a mint green sash. She also shared that Gladys would wear an identical dress in style, but her dress would be mint green with a cranberry sash at the waist.

It was a boat neck, sleeveless dress with faux buttons running down the back. The girls opted for a hidden zipper under the right arm because it could be fitted to their narrow bodies easily. The dress flared out at the waist with the help of a tea-length petticoat.

Mason had been lectured on every detail as soon as Vivian had been told what she was to wear. Vivian had begged him to take her to the bridal store Paige had told them about the next day. He had only relented when he'd learned that Gladys too was going to the bridal shop in Atlanta to try hers' on, and they needed to be able to compare and give their approval. After that first torturous visit, it was fitting after fitting until Monday when Vivian brought her dress home.

"Aren't you afraid you will get something on it before you get it to Los Angeles? This is the second night in a row that I've come home to find you twirling around in that dress."

"It's just so beautiful, and I look beautiful in it." Though he was glad Vivian loved what she saw, he could already see her freaking out if she got anything on it.

"It won't be so beautiful if you continue to wear it and mess it up before you can take the gorgeous pictures I know you will with the rest of the bridal party." The words were like bile in his mouth and as quickly as they came into his head he couldn't wait to get them out, but the same words were like acid to his ears, which were now bleeding – *thank you very much.* He tried hard to put on a happy face for Vivian who was beside herself with excitement. He wouldn't be surprised if he ended up seeing four of Vivian and Gladys in the wedding photos, their energy causing them to move back and forth so fast they multiplied right there in front of everyone.

"Okay." The small voice pulled him out of his musings.

He turned to see his daughter's sulking form move towards his bedroom and he felt a small pang of guilt for being the cause.

"Hun."

She turned slowly.

"You are right, you know. You are absolutely beautiful, but it isn't just the dress."

The corners of her lips only lifted enough to bring her mouth to a straight line.

"Just do me a favor, will you?"

She shrugged at him, and he had to work to keep the smile off of his face. She was adorable when she pouted.

"Don't grow up too fast. Your poor dad wouldn't know what to do if you left him so soon."

Her mouth quirked. She knew his game, but he was hoping for a little mercy.

She came back and lifted up on her toes so she could kiss him on the cheek. He moved to put his arms around her and she squealed.

"No, Daddy, you're sweaty and you'll ruin my dress."

"But I want a hug. Just a small one," he said, slowly lumbering towards her with his arms outstretched. She screamed in mock horror and ran to her room to escape his sweaty arms and shirt.

He chuckled to himself as he walked to his bedroom to take a shower and rinse off the two hours of sweat build up he'd gained waiting for Tabitha Anderson. *Tabitha Anderson,* how he hoped she would email or call him soon.

*   *   *

Mason was sitting in front of his computer at work, trying to find the prints showing the bearing wall of a room he was helping to renovate. It was an easy project and didn't require all of his attention, so he went through the motions while he considered just dropping off Tabitha's case at one of the receptionist's offices in the brownstone when he went in for his appointment with Dr. Seagret. He'd also considered speaking to Dr. Seagret about Tabitha, but didn't think the good doctor would give his approval since Mason's motivation for seeking her out wasn't completely innocent.

He couldn't deny the fact that she intrigued him, and her ability to evade his advances without outright rejecting him kept him on his toes. He wasn't absolutely certain how far he wanted to take things, or if he was even ready. All he knew was that the past few weeks had been a welcomed reprieve from the constant ache caused by wanting someone he had no rights to.

After another week without a call or email, and resigned to the now glaring fact that Tabitha would not contact him, Mason stopped checking his phone with the same fervency as the weeks before, but relegated himself to perusing his account once during lunch and again right before he left the office.

So it was with no little surprise that when he scanned his mail and saw the subject title, 'WILL TRADE YOU MY CASE FOR COFFEE', he froze, not wanting to hope for too much.

He slowly touched his hand to the display and selected the email. Once it opened, he let out a breath he felt he'd been holding for almost a month.

Hello Mason Jenson,

I was wondering if you still had my card case.

If so, how about a trade? Coffee for my case? Let me know?

She signed it *T. Anderson* with her phone number underneath. He smiled, enjoying her playful note. If nothing else, this would definitely be interesting. The ball was now in his court and he wondered how far things could progress before he had to accompany his daughter to Paige's wedding.

He looked at his surroundings quickly and noted that most of his coworkers were either busy packing up their things or moving towards the

427

door. Many nights he would be right beside them, but since his computer was in the living room, he couldn't guarantee the privacy needed to pen his response. True, he could email her from his phone, but the keys were too small for his hands and the last thing he wanted to do was write an embarrassing typo that would cause her to change her mind.

He hit the 'reply' key and glanced at the desks closest to him one more time before penning his response.

Dear Tabitha Anderson,

No trade needed. The coffee is on me because I offered. I'm hoping it will be accompanied by some very pleasant conversation.

I will call you later this evening with a time and place.

M. Jenson

He read over his email a couple more times to make sure the grammar and spelling were correct. It was a simple message with no room for misunderstanding. He nodded his head briefly before clicking 'send' then began to pack up his things to get ready to leave.

He was in his car turning the ignition when he heard the chime of his phone informing of him of an email. Could she be responding that quickly? If it was her, she must have been in front of her computer.

Unable to fight the temptation, he turned his car back off and opened his email. His finger froze over the subject previewed on his phone's window and he considered the intelligence of his next move.

It read, 'My personal invite'. He hoped beyond hope that it was from one of his acquaintances inviting him to a party or even a small business opportunity that would give him the option of becoming financially independent by inviting his small contact list of friends to join as well. He breathed in, letting his exhale blow through his lips in a whistle and pressed down on the subject title.

Another window opened and he could read the sender's name. 'EldPMor...' He closed his eyes. He knew who it was. He'd received emails from her before, even memorized her address. He placed his phone face down on the passenger's seat. He was not going to tempt fate. He would read it after he got home, changed, and was in a quiet place where he would allow the emotions to slay him if need be.

Most of his drive was done on autopilot; he was so deep in thought. He didn't know why the email surprised him. His child was turning around like the ballerina on the end of a stick in her jewelry box every time he got home this week. She was wearing the dress as an attendant in Paige's wedding. He had been okay…well not okay but was dealing, he thought, admirably with it. There were twinges here or there, but for the most part he was coping well. No drunken binges or days called off from work. He was even in the middle of making plans to see someone new, so why did that email feel like a dagger slowly sliding between his ribs? It made no sense. He had tried everything he could think of to stay away, to distance his heart and respect her wishes. Brandon and he would never be friends, but they could have a cordial conversation if needed. What was it about that woman that crawled under his skin and took residence? If he thought He would have helped, he would have asked God for help to get her out of his system.

By the time he'd reached his place and unfolded himself from the car, he was resolved to place even more room between them. He would read the email after he called Tabitha. He had put his life on hold for too long.

"Hello, Ms. T, Anderson," Mason greeted once he heard Tabitha answer the call.

"Hello, Mr. Mason Jenson," she replied. He could hear the smile on her lips and enjoyed it almost as much as the familiarity with which they greeted one another.

"How are you doing this evening?" He asked, keeping his voice light.

"Good. I've had a very productive day," she responded.

He listened for any noise in the background that would give away what she was doing, but it was silent.

"Did I interrupt you? You weren't in the middle of anything were you?"

"No, I was just sitting here trying to decide what I was going to have for dinner. Have you eaten?"

Surprised by the question and wondering if there were something behind it, he paused before speaking. "No. Not yet. Why?"

"Calm down. I wasn't hinting at anything. I was just trying to see if your choice would give me any ideas."

He didn't know whether to play it off or confess that she'd hit the mark. He decided to ignore it all together. "You don't have any idea what you want to eat?"

"Nope. It's rare that I get a craving. Usually I just look in the refrigerator until something piques my interest."

"What if it doesn't?"

"I will just fall back on my snack of choice. It's usually peanut butter and crackers or cheese and crackers, or both."

He could almost see her nod.

"Can you cook?"

"Yes, but I'm not going to cook something I'm not going to want to eat by the time it's done. Can you cook?"

"Does cereal count? I can do a mean Cocoa Pebbles. I can even turn the milk chocolate if I'm patient."

She started laughing, but it sobered almost as fast.

"Do you have children?"

Darn. He was trying to avoid this topic for as long as possible, but he forgot about the cereal being a dead giveaway. Oh well. She would find out eventually.

"Yes, a daughter."

The line was quiet.

"Her mother?"

He closed his eyes briefly.

"Deceased."

"I'm sorry."

After almost three years, he still didn't know what to say when people apologized. So he went with what he felt.

"No apology needed. You asked and I answered."

More silence.

"How old is your daughter?"

"Twelve going on 62. She acts more like my mother sometimes."

"That is just our way."

Wanting to get off the subject of his daughter with a virtual stranger, he took a breath and got to the point of his call.

"So, I was calling to see if you were interested in meeting me for coffee at Mr. Belgian's on 34th and Meister St.? It is relatively close to the offices where we, um, met."

She didn't hesitate with his change of topic.

"Sure. Things are picking up and I'm going to need my card case."

At first he didn't know how to take her response, but her slow almost quiet laughter caught his ear and his breath came easily as he realized she was teasing him.

"Well, maybe I should hold out for dinner," he replied.

"I have a 'no tolerance rule' regarding extortion, Mr. Jenson."

Her voice was so serious, he thought maybe his joke had gone bad. He went quiet for a moment, hoping to hear more laughter. When it didn't come, he stumbled over his words to correct the misunderstanding. He was going for his second pass when she began laughing again.

"I'm sorry, Mason, I was only kidding. I didn't think you were trying to hold my cards hostage. I tend to joke when I get nervous – and not well."

His curiosity picked up as his heart slowed. He could work with that if they stayed relatively harmless. Maybe he would try a little of his own.

"You should call me Mr. Jenson and I think I will just mail your cards to you. I try to teach my daughter that jokes hold no respect for the other person's feelings," he stopped breathing to hear her reaction. She was quiet. Obviously waiting to see if he was playing with her.

"Once again, I am sorry. I really didn't mean any disrespect by it," she said, trying to placate him.

"Well, I say you should be."

She was quiet for a couple more moments before she sighed and began.

"Yes, I think you should just mail them to me. I will give you my P.O. Box, if you'd like."

"Sure, let me just get a pen." He paused the amount of time he thought it would take for a person to retrieve a pen. "Okay. I have one. So, how does Friday afternoon sound?"

The other line was so quiet he thought she might have hung up at first. He quickly took the phone away from his face to make sure they were still connected.

"What?" Came her pensive voice.

"Coffee, Ms. T. Anderson. Will Friday at noon be good at Mr. Belgian's?"

"But you…" she began before he cut her off.

"…were joking, Ms. Anderson."

The line was quiet for a few moments before a light chuckle came over the phone. "Touché, Mr. Jenson."

"Aww, call me 'Mason'."

"I see I'm going to have to watch myself around you, Mason."

He shrugged, knowing she couldn't see him. "I'm pretty harmless."

"Yeah. I'll be the judge of that."

"So Friday, noon?" He asked again, trying to solidify their plans before they went any further.

"Friday at noon will work. Could you give me the address?"

"Sure, do you have a pen?"

She giggled. "Just a second." When she came back, she asked him, "Did you really go get a pen before?"

"Nope."

"You're good."

"Yep."

After another half an hour of easy conversation with Tabitha, Mason ended the call, stating he needed to try and fix something for dinner. It was mostly the truth, but he also knew he had another email waiting and the subject was not going to be anything to laugh at.

He went to Vivian's door and knocked even though it was ajar.

"Yes?" She said by way of welcome.

"Hey, Hun, are you hungry? I could microwave something."

She lay on her stomach, staring at something on her laptop, her socked feet hitting the pillows behind her in an offhanded rhythm.

She stopped all movement as she considered his question.

"No, that's okay. I'm not all that hungry. I had a pretty heavy lunch. We won this competition in History and got pizza."

"Are you sure? I think I could put together something light."

"That's okay, really."

"All right."

He was turning from the door when he heard her. "Dad?"

"Yes?"

He turned and looked at her.

She watched him for a moment, then shook her head. "Never mind."

"Are you sure?"

"Yes. I'm good." She shifted her attention back to the screen and he felt a little snubbed by her dismissal. Hoping to keep their still fragile truth he relented and turned and walked to the kitchen to fix himself something to eat.

Later that evening, with nothing else to use as procrastination, he opened the email he'd been avoiding.

Dear Mason,

I hope this email finds you well.

I figure you can tell from the subject what this email is about, but I hope you keep reading.

I didn't know if I should send this to you in light of our relationship and how you may feel about me marrying Brandon, but you are family and you deserve to be invited, not given a cursory invite because our daughter is in my bridal party.

He tried not to enjoy the way she continued to refer to Vivian as their daughter. He knew it was courtesy and nurturing more than anything else.

I know this will bring about some level of awkwardness on both our sides, but it is not enough that I wouldn't want to share this day with you or allow you to see our beautiful daughter walk down the aisle in her dress (which I know for a fact she has tried on at least 10 times. Please try to keep it somewhat fresh for the next two weeks LOL).

He caught himself smiling and pinched his lips together before he continued reading.

Seriously, Mason. I am personally asking you, yes by way of email, to come to my wedding. You are my family and though I have gained quite a bit over the last year, I would miss it if you weren't there and so will your daughter. I am pulling out all of the stops. Will you please come? For me?

Paige

The last line was the proverbial brick that sank the ship in his resolve. Vivian had asked, cajoled, begged, pouted and finally tried to bribe him into accompanying her and he had held off, but one simple, pleading email from Paige and he was considering the time so he could call Richard and tell him they had one more leaving out on the flight in a little over two weeks. He shook his head, sighing heavily. How he wanted to resist her, but being able to see her again at her own request and not as the barely tolerable father of her biological daughter was looking brighter by the minute. He had nowhere to go with that, but to Los Angeles.

Well, at least he had a coffee date with a woman that possessed a good sense of humor to look forward to before then. He shook his head at himself, hoping more than anything that it wasn't as hopeless as it felt at that moment.

Mason sat at the table, his knee bobbing under the table a mile a minute. He checked his watch for what had to be the fifteenth time in the last five minutes. He knew he arrived at the restaurant early. He wanted to make sure he got a table with a modicum of privacy in the usually busy establishment, but now that his watch showed that they were two minutes on the other side of their meeting time, his nervousness had ratcheted up a few levels. Was she going to stand him up? Had she changed her mind? He couldn't think of anything he may have said during their last call that would have turned her off.

His waitress came around again asking him if he wanted his coffee warmed up, but finally noticing the nervous bounce of his knee, he declined. He unfolded the menu, trying to find anything to take his mind off of the slow changing numbers on his watch.

As he perused the oversized pages, he wondered if choosing a restaurant that served primarily breakfast foods at lunch was a good idea. Maybe she didn't want breakfast. Why didn't he give her an option?

"Mr. Mason Jenson?"

The sound of his name had his head snapping up and there standing before him was Tabitha, looking professional in a light blue, slightly diaphanous blouse with a camisole and a navy blue lightweight pencil skirt. Her shiny hair looked as though it were secured at the nape of her neck in a bun.

It took him a moment to stop staring and stand to welcome her. He raised his hand to shake hers, then came around to seat her. He caught a light scent of gardenias as she moved in front of him. He felt as though time and the energy in the room had sped up with her presence. He had to work hard to appear relaxed as he sat across from her and attempted to make small talk.

"I'm sorry I'm late. Have you been waiting long?" He shook his head to the negative. "I was afraid you'd think I wasn't coming. You didn't answer your phone." He reached into his jacket pocket and pulled out his phone, only to discover that it was dead. He'd forgotten to charge it the night before, which was almost a miracle in itself.

"I had a meeting run over and there was some kind of traffic jam on Mission Street." She looked a little winded, so he kept quiet while she vented. It was actually comforting to know he wasn't the only one feeling a little discombobulated.

After a full minute, their waitress came back around. "I see she didn't stand you up. Good for you," the woman said with such sincerity he couldn't be upset with her giving away his true level of anxiety.

Tabitha looked up from the menu she was scanning, pausing mid-rant to stare at him. "I thought you said you just got here?"

"No, you asked me if I'd been here long and I said 'No'," he clarified.

"Did you think I was standing you up?"

His only response was a shrug. "Are you ready to order?" She nodded and gave her order to the waitress and he followed suit.

When they were alone, again he opened his mouth to ask her about her week, but she beat him.

"Well, I wasn't," she said, in what could have been a pout as she looked down while spreading her napkin in her lap.

He thought the comment, though he was sure she didn't mean to say out loud, was adorable. It made him feel a little more comfortable with her. If that was any hint at her inability to filter her thoughts, it would make it easier for him to know where he stood with her.

"Do you need to be back soon?" she asked.

"No, I went into the office early so I could take an extended lunch. I'm good for a couple of hours. Besides, I just turned in a project and with it being Friday, I would be hesitant to start on a new one."

She nodded her head in understanding. She looked as if she was going to apologize again, but he trumped her with the question he'd been holding on to since she accepted his invitation.

"Why did you say 'Yes' to meeting me here today?"

He seemed to have caught her off guard because she just stared at him for a moment. "Um," she stalled then cocked her head to the side. "Do you want the filtered or unfiltered version?"

"Whichever is the most honest," he responded without hesitation.

"The filtered answer is I thought you were interesting and your persistence was flattering. I could use a friend to show me around Chicago, and you don't feel like you have stalker tendencies." She took a deep breath. "The unfiltered version is that I wanted my cards as soon as possible. It was cute, if not just a little disturbing, that you would jog in the area so you could run into me again and after doing a surface background check on you, I thought you were pretty harmless."

Mason was speechless. She did a background check on him? *What is the world coming to?* He asked himself, growing slightly indignant before he remembered he'd basically done the same thing when he looked her up. Still, he didn't really know how he felt so he took another sip of his now lukewarm coffee.

"Too honest?" she asked, a small quirk of her lips causing him to wonder if she would apologize if he said 'yes'. He didn't know what to think of her. The conversation left him feeling off kilter.

"No, but if you keep this up I might need a compass to read you."

Her shoulder's drooped slightly. "Too honest," she said, on an exhaled breath.

He smiled at the insight he gained from the one gesture. He retrieved her case from his jacket pocket and slid it across the table to her. She looked up at him with an unreadable expression.

"It wouldn't do for me to forget to give it back to you when it was one of the things I promised you to get you to meet with me," he offered. "And this way, I'll know that when I ask to see you again, if you say 'yes' it'll be because you want to get to know me and not just because you are trying to get something from me." He grinned at her to make it plain he was teasing her, and he saw relief cross her features right before a smile lit up her green eyes, reminding him of sun-kissed emeralds. He vowed right then that if she allowed it, he would work on making her smile more often.

After that, he stuck to questions about her work until they were served their meal, hoping this would get her to relax even more. He'd just finished his last bite when she asked about Vivian.

"So, you have a twelve-year-old. What's her name?"

He hesitated for a moment then shrugged off his reluctance to even mention her. "Vivian," he answered, not offering any more.

She pressed her lips together momentarily and he saw the questions forming. "I bet she's beautiful."

He nodded. "Absolutely, and I'm not just saying that because I'm her father."

"I believe you. If she has any of your features or humor, she's not only good looking, she's a ham."

He shrugged his shoulders again. "Her humor is just a tad dryer than mine, and a lot more intellectual. She got that from her mother."

She smiled and fiddled with her cup and spoon. He knew he was withdrawing from the conversation, but he couldn't help feeling overprotective where Vivian was concerned.

Tabitha watched him for a minute and he made it easy for her. He was in no hurry to leave her. They'd had a nice time, especially for a lunch date with time restraints. It could have been awkward and much quicker. He wanted to see her again.

"So, how about taking me up on my offer to show you the town?"

She inclined her head slowly. "I would like that."

"Tomorrow?"

A look of regret crossed her face. "I have a previous engagement for tomorrow and next weekend. How about the following weekend?"

He winced. "I'll be out of town. My daughter's in a wedding." He didn't know what caused him to add that last part, but it was out of his mouth before he could censor it.

"Oh, how nice for her. Is she excited?"

"Is she? I've been trying to keep her out of her dress because I know if she gets something on it, her mom will kill me."

It was her reaction that made him rethink his comment. He watched her eyes cloud over and her lips thin before she asked him with evident coolness. "You told me her mother was deceased."

He heaved a sigh. "My wife and I adopted Vivian when she was a baby. Last year, I met her biological mother when Vivian needed a life-saving surgery. They have grown close and she will be in her mother's wedding that weekend."

He watched Tabitha gauging him for the truth. He shrugged one more time, allowing her to come to her own conclusion.

He reached into his back pocket after glancing at the check. Out of the corner of his eye he saw Tabitha reaching for her purse, and he stopped to glare at her. When she caught his eye, she slowly removed her hand from inside her purse and had the good sense to look sheepish.

He figured her response to his next question would let him know whether she believed him or not.

"The following weekend should be fine though. I could give you a call when we get back on Tuesday." He watched and waited for her response and though it was slow to come, he was pleasantly surprised at her answer.

"The weekend after you get back should be fine, but you could call me before you go out of town." He felt the smile take over the lower half of his face, but she seemed to rethink her request before he could reply. "If you have time..." her sentence faded as she took in his expression.

"I think I can find some time," he said with a grin.

She smiled back at him.

Yeah. He would find the time to call her before he left. He just hoped he would want to call her when he came back. He wanted it to be his choice. He wanted it to be up to him. He no longer wanted to be ruled by the emotions *she* provoked. He had something more to look forward to. *Something more.* All his life, he seemed to be reaching for it. If Tabitha could be it, then he would go for it.

*   *   *

Mason sat in front of his home computer. He had taken care of his flight arrangements, put his tux in the cleaners, and had even sought advice from a now ecstatic Vivian on a present. All that was left was to respond was to Paige's email.

More than a dozen comments had run through his head since he'd decided to accept her invitation, but what stared back at him were three words. *I'll be there.*

Simple, direct, and impartial.

Three words that could suffocate his future or set him free.

He took a deep breath, then pressed the 'send' key.

EPILOGUE

June 21st came in overcast, but Paige wasn't concerned. Overcast, gray, misting, or raining; she was getting married today. She stood at the window of her fifth-floor hotel room and looked over the grounds. This particular hotel had beautifully sculpted lawns, but their rose garden was the true beauty and in June it made her feel as though life, though it could be fragile at times, was also resilient. She glanced back at the clock on the entertainment center in her suite area and sighed in both impatience at the early hour and excitement of this being the last morning that she would wake up single.

She went back to looking over the grounds, and when her gaze shifted over to the tented area where she would be having her reception later, she felt giddiness take over. She would be Mrs. Brandon Tatum by the time she entered that tent this evening. It was funny how her thoughts over the past week were positioned around that phrase, 'By the time I see this day again, month again, time, place or person...I will be Mrs. Brandon Tatum'. She, of course, had tried it in different variations: Mrs. Paige Tatum, Elder Paige Tatum, and before she had made the decision to fully change her name, she placed with Mrs. Paige Morganson-Tatum. She didn't have to worry about losing her identification with her books because she had made the decision to brand her name and make it the name of her company. Even though she was changing her immediate name she would not have to change the name of her company since she was, in essence, its employee.

Her attention was taken away from the window when she heard a knock at the door. Tightening her robe around her waist a little more, she walked to the door and was surprised after looking through the peephole, then opened the door to a man with a room service cart. The smell of coffee wafted up to her nose, slowing her response.

"I didn't order anything."

The server picked up a tab and said, "For the soon to be Mrs. Tatum on her wedding morning. You have to start your day out right. Do I still have to do everything?" Even through the server's stilted reading she could tell who the note was from.

"Mel," she said through a smile before giving the server permission to enter her room.

She ate her breakfast of fruit, cottage cheese, and toast at the small table near her window. The coffee, she drank all around the room as she continued to take in the serene moments she knew would be her last until maybe the next morning.

She glanced at the clock again and decided to take a long bath before Mel and Lady Menagerie arrived to start the 'pre-party' as they called it the day before when she shooed them from her room, requesting a little more time to herself.

She had ended the night as she had for the last two months: on the phone with Brandon.

The wedding was scheduled for three o'clock, still a good eight hours away, but from the breakfast surprise she knew she had no more than two more hours to herself before her peaceful morning reprieve ended.

An hour and a half later, her phone began to chime the ringtone that always brought a smile to her face. Freshly soaked, moisturized, and now dressed in a robe provided by the hotel, she strode to the cell lying on the coffee table in the common area.

"Good morning."

"And a beautiful morning to you. I'm happy to hear I didn't wake you."

"You could have called a couple of hours ago, and you still wouldn't have awakened me," she breathed, happy to hear his voice.

"Are you all right?"

"Yes. Just excited."

She heard the breath he let go of, but 'yes' was all he said.

She grew quiet. "Are you all right?"

"Yes, absolutely. I am just happy your early rising was due to excitement and not dread."

She stifled a laugh, but knew she failed at keeping all of the humor out of her voice with her next statement. "Mr. Tatum, are you nervous?"

"Maybe a little," he replied without hesitating.

"Why?" She sat on the couch.

"Aren't you?"

"That's not an answer, Brandon."

The line was quiet for a moment then he spoke. "It's you. It's you Paige. I'm about to make a covenant to God and a commitment to you, the woman I could never have dreamed I'd have for myself. I know we have been working towards this, but now that we are here it seems a little surreal."

"I know what you mean. I'm trying to hold on to every moment so I don't forget one second of this day. I'm actually happy I woke up early because it gives me time with myself and God to help keep this all in perspective. I'm looking forward to seeing you at the end of that aisle when they open the doors, but I'm also excited by the potential of every conversation I can have today. All of our family and friends will be with us today and we have the opportunity to touch each one of them with the love and happiness we will share with them today."

Brandon started chuckling over the line. "And here I thought you were excited by the prospect of becoming Mrs. Brandon Tatum."

"Well, that did cross my mind," she replied with more than a little sass.

"Sweetie, every word, every vow, every look I give you today in that church and on that altar comes from every dream, every hope, and every breath that has led me to you."

Paige felt his words to her very soul, and she couldn't hold back the emotion in her voice even as she tried to lighten the moment. "It's good you called early because if you make me cry after Mel does my makeup, she will kill you."

She heard his low chuckle from the other line. "I consider myself warned. How is it going with the two of you?"

Paige hugged her free arm around herself. "It is getting better, you know, more comfortable. Instead of trying to move her into the place of mother in my life; one, you know I can barely grasp anyway. I just decided to continue to move forward with our relationship as is. I still have a lot of questions and she hasn't been forthcoming with most of the answers to them, but I came to the realization that she was always more than just a sister. I can't ignore the pain her betrayal brought, but I can't deny the love either."

"I think you allowing her to share in this day with you will go a long way to helping the both of you heal." Brandon said, sounding more hopeful than certain, so she answered in kind.

"That is one of my prayers for today." Her mind began to wander through the different, possible scenarios before he pulled her back with his next question.

"May I call you later?"

"I guess it depends on what you're going to say. I wasn't kidding about Mel."

"Tell her to keep reinforcements on hand."

She laughed. "I'll tell her you said so."

"I'm not afraid of her," Brandon said, his voice lowering an octave.

"Yeah, I'll tell her that too," Paige deadpanned.

"Exactly how long would you like to be married to me?" he asked, his voice rising.

Paige laughed outright, but sobered before she spoke. "Forever, baby, forever."

"Just the answer I was looking for."

She couldn't keep from smiling into the phone.

The knock on the door distracted her from her witty remark.

"Baby, I have to go. There's someone at the door and considering the time, I think it is either Lady Menagerie or Mel."

"Okay sweetie. I love you and I will see you soon."

"I love you too," she responded as she got up from the couch to answer the door.

"Paige?" His tone caused her to slow.

"Yes?"

"You don't have to tell Mel what I said."

Paige couldn't help the laugh that escaped her lips. "Consider it one of my wedding presents to you, my sweet."

"One of?"

"Yes. I'll give you the other one tonight. I got to go now," she said, peeping through the hole. It was Lady Menagerie.

"Wait, Paige–"

She cut him off, whispering in the phone, "I'll see you later, baby," then hung up with a sly smile.

She schooled her features before she opened the door, knowing she would get teased if the woman caught wind of her thoughts, but it was in vain as proven by Lady Menagerie's first words.

"Just as long as you know you have a good seven hours before you can give him anything more than a phone call. This may be your wedding day, but we will be keeping an eye on you until well into your reception. No skipping out for some..."

"Lady Menagerie!" Paige almost yelled to keep the woman from finishing her sentence.

"What? You are an almost married mother of two. Surely you can't be squeamish."

"You are still my First Lady and my mother in a lot of ways. I just can't imagine you finishing that sentence," Paige said, walking back to the couch.

"Besides, it's not like I'm some randy teenager whose main purpose for getting married is because I can't wait to get in the sack with my boyfriend."

Lady Menagerie stared at Paige so hard she felt like one of those unfortunate butterflies pinned on a corkboard, sitting under a high powered microscope. She refused to squirm and instead lifted her chin just enough to appear defiant.

The only shift in Lady Menagerie's expression was the lift of her left eyebrow, but it spoke volumes. Paige gradually lowered her chin and then her eyes.

"Wow. Really?" Lady Menagerie moved over to the other side of the couch.

"What?" Paige asked, being careful to keep any challenge from her tone.

"How is it that I didn't realize this before today?"

Paige wondered what she may have given away in her comment. Could Lady Menagerie see through her bravado? True, she wasn't a virgin, but she couldn't help getting nervous just thinking about her wedding night. Though she and Brandon had agreed that hugging and some heavy kissing would be the extent of their physical intimacy before they were married, she was aware of the deep attraction they shared that sat like over warm embers in a continually banked fire. There was also the possibility of either of their past relationships having a slight influence.

"You are a seventy-five year-old in a twenty-seven-year-old's body."

Paige's wandering thoughts took a U-turn at her comment. "What?"

"The last generation that used the words 'randy' and 'sack' also wore bloomers and dungarees. You are not old enough to wear dungarees, and if you ever wear bloomers you better be in someone's play."

Paige opened and closed her mouth, trying to shift gears. "What?"

Lady Menagerie lightly sucked her teeth. "I don't care that you're a bestselling author. In real life, you are a young female Elder of a predominantly black church in Southern California after the millennium."

Paige shook her head trying to hide her smile, but it was no use. Lady Menagerie was beginning the morning in rare form.

Paige pulled her knees in close to her chest, crossing her legs at the ankles. She took a deep breath and let the silence fill the air again. She seemed to be working harder and harder to keep the quiet she woke with as the hour grew later.

"What's on your mind, Paige?" Lady Menagerie asked, her voice sobering.

Paige rocked herself as she got her thoughts in line. She looked up into Lady Menagerie's warm brown eyes. "I'm afraid."

"Yes."

That's all she said. "Yes." *How is a girl supposed to work with that?*

She looked over Lady Menagerie's features and noticed the softening of her mouth and the growing wetness in her eyes. Paige was caught by the unexpected show of emotion. She started blinking rapidly in response as she tried to staunch her reaction. She knew if she didn't hold tight, she would be crying all day.

She glanced down at Lady Menagerie's hands folded loosely in her lap but smothered the impulse to crawl up under her arm, thus forcing herself into the woman's embrace. As welcome as she knew she would be, she needed the reassurance that she wasn't taking advantage of the day or the moment.

When she looked back up she saw a moment of sadness cross through Lady Menagerie's eyes, but it was gone quickly.

"It's been quite a few years since I've been with anyone."

"Are you afraid you've forgotten?" The woman across from her had the nerve to frown a little.

"No." She shook her head. "I'm afraid I'll remember."

"Paige."

Paige looked up from the hands she stared at as she made the last admission.

"You saw a psychiatrist about that."

Paige nodded.

"Did you bring up any of these thoughts to Brandon or my husband during your premarital counseling?"

"In a general type of way."

"How general?" Lady Menagerie's eyes narrowed slightly.

"Pastor asked me if what happened with my cousin still colored my perceptions of physical intimacy. I told him 'No'."

Lady Menagerie's lips came together in a thin line then pursed in annoyance. "Ugh, men. I told him couples needed to counsel with him and then a woman. Men tend to get too focused on things." She stopped her murmuring and shot Paige a small look of impatience. "Why did you allow it to stop at that? The counseling was for you. You were only going to get out of it what you were willing to be honest about." She shook her head. "Children."

"Is there any more coffee or tea?"

Paige pointed to the table next to the window. "Both. The carafe of coffee is in silver and the hot water is in black. Would you like me to make it for you?"

"No. I will make my own while you talk." She got up and had only taken three steps when she asked the question.

"What are you afraid you are going to remember before, during, or after you are being physically intimate with your husband tonight?"

Paige smiled to herself. Lady Menagerie was trying to be as detailed as possible.

"I'm afraid I'm going to remember other men. I'm afraid things will change afterward. Though I know there is a big difference between my relationship with Brandon and the men I slept with when I was younger, I can't help but be a little concerned that I might pull back. It's what I did to protect myself before and though I know I don't have any reason to protect myself against Brandon, I'm wondering why it's been on my mind so much lately."

Lady Menagerie finished fixing her tea then came back to the couch before she responded.

"This is usually the time your mind goes wild with hopes and fears. You are about to change your life in a few hours. Why wouldn't you be more contemplative about those things you've once struggled with?" Paige watched her stir the liquid in the pretty china cup, then glanced at the clock on the blue-ray.

"I asked Mel to give us some time alone together. She wasn't crazy about it, but relented after a moment. She'll be here in about 45 minutes."

Surprised, Paige asked the first question that came to mind. "How did you get her to agree?"

Lady Menagerie took a sip then blinked at Paige. "I asked her very prettily," she said with a crook of her lips, the action nearly screaming that she wasn't sharing what was discussed.

Paige felt a little guilty at her relief in having more time to talk to Lady Menagerie and more time before she became the center of so much attention.

"All right, back to you, Paige." Lady Menagerie turned her body to face Paige on the couch. "Does this have anything to do with Brandon's test results from Wednesday?"

Paige couldn't hide the surprise she knew shown on her face. They'd discussed keeping the news to themselves or at least from their families until after their honeymoon. After a month and a half of extremely aggressive sessions of chemo and radiation, the CAT scan results Dr. Connor went over with them the previous Wednesday were disappointing. Not only had there been no change in the size of the lesion, a cluster of abnormal cells were found on his pancreas. Brandon went in for a biopsy Thursday after the doctor pulled some strings, but they decided to wait until after they got back from their cruise to the US Virgin Islands.

"He told you."

Lady Menagerie shook her head. "He told your pastor, but gave him permission to share it with me. I believe he wanted to make sure you had someone you could talk to. He's extremely thoughtful."

Paige nodded, wondering why he hadn't told her.

"So, do you want to talk about it?" Lady Menagerie asked, reaching her hand towards Paige's now resting on the back of the couch, but Paige moved it out of reach. She didn't know if she could keep composed enough to express her fear if she allowed even that small bit of comfort.

"How do I cross this level of intimacy with him and still protect myself? In the past, I found ways of distancing myself when I was physically intimate with men. Even without knowing it at the time, I held a lot of myself closed off. Even more so once we'd had sex."

"I know it's easier said than done, but you told me you and Brandon discussed this when you decided to get married. No one is promised tomorrow and even with this latest report, you aren't guaranteed more or less time. Ultimately, it is God's decision so that is where your ultimate trust has to go. It's not some concept that works for certain situations. It must be part of your reality and interlaced with every situation, thought, and decision you make. Besides," Lady Menagerie said with a small shrug, "physical intimacy isn't the deepest level of intimacy. You surpassed that when you entrusted him with your emotions, thoughts and will, as well as your spirit. Don't get me wrong, physical intimacy is also important, as I'm sure you learned in counseling, because it helps to solidify the physical bond. The recreational aspect of it is also a plus. Have fun with him. Love him. Hold him. Cherish each other no matter what report you get from man. That's what you're doing today. Don't do it in half measures, otherwise you will regret not being able to answer your questions."

"What questions?"

"Did you love on him as much as you could have? Did you treasure every moment you had together? Did you do and say everything God placed on your heart to do to assure him that you happily embraced God's will in regards to the two of you? What you are saying today, with the covenant you are making with God and one another, is that you believe without a doubt that Brandon is the man God has for your and he is saying the same about you. If God has placed the two of you together, then trust in that. You already know to let your relationship with God lead your relationship with Brandon, but don't forget to keep God in the middle of it all and you don't have to worry about being blindsided or crippled by anything that happens. And don't put up obstacles where they don't need to be by using your past as an excuse to cheat yourself out of what God wants for you, Paige."

This time she leaned forward and took Paige's hand. "And the next time you want to be held or hugged or comforted by me, don't hesitate like a stepchild standing on the sidelines. I love you like my own daughter. I don't know what else to do to prove that to you." She squeezed Paige's hand almost painfully.

Paige gave in to her earlier yearning and all but crawled into Lady Menagerie's lap. Her heart stuttered then calmed as Lady Menagerie's hands rubbed her arms and rocked her.

"I want my happy ending," Paige whispered.

"Who says you won't get it?" Lady Menagerie replied.

Paige fell silent.

"I, for one, believe today is one huge happy ending to your life as a single woman, but more than that, it's part of the happy ending you embraced when you accepted God's gift of eternity and dedicated yourself to Him.

I know you are looking for decades with Brandon and everything that that encompasses in your dreams, but baby, each minute, hour, and day you end with happiness is also your happy ending."

Paige thought about that. She knew what Lady Menagerie was saying and tried not to feel as though she was getting a consolation prize instead of the time she wanted, but it was hard not to want more at the moment.

"That report didn't say you weren't going to get more time, Paige. Pray what God has been prompting you to pray and you will get what you need." Lady Menagerie said as though she could read her thoughts, then hugged her tighter.

"I want to stay here where it's safe." Paige asked, just short of begging.

"You have five minutes," Lady Menagerie whispered back. "Your sister will be here soon."

Paige heaved a sigh, but didn't move.

"It's a beautiful day for a wedding."

Paige nodded her head in agreement then stiffened abruptly with her next thought.

"I spoke to Mason Wednesday."

Lady Menagerie's hands stilled for a moment then resumed their rubbing. "And?" she prompted. "Haven't you been communicating with him this whole time, especially with your growing relationship with Vivian?"

"I personally invited him to the wedding. He wasn't going to come otherwise, and Vivian really wanted him here."

"Just Vivian?" Lady Menagerie said, moving back so she could look into Paige's eyes.

Paige's gaze skittered to the right as she tried to make sense of her emotions. She didn't even know why she brought it up now. It had no real bearing on this day. Before she finished the thought, she knew she was lying.

"I needed to know he was going to be all right."

"But that's not your job."

"It is, indirectly. He's taking care of my daughter. We will always be bound in that way. I just didn't want him to feel like he wasn't welcome, like he isn't a part of our family." Paige couldn't keep the pleading out of her voice. She needed help in understanding this inexplicable need to keep Mason as a friend. Maybe it was simply her yearning to become as close to Vivian as possible – and knowing that he could make that nearly impossible if he wanted – but there was a niggling in the back of her head that made things just a little hazy.

"It can't be easy for him to be here, watching all of this; watching you getting married to someone else. I don't think this was one of your brighter moments."

"That's just it. As much as I want him here today, I wouldn't have reached out to him personally if Brandon hadn't suggested it."

Lady Menagerie's head jerked in surprise. Then her eyes narrowed on Paige. "Why?"

"I'm not entirely sure. We don't usually talk about Mason outside of his relation to Vivian. I was a little surprised myself and said as much. I'm not interested in a drama-filled wedding, but he assured me that it would be best if we could celebrate together."

"How did Mason sound?"

"Wary, reluctant, ingratiating and a little obnoxious. He asked if his attendance would count as his present," she said, still feeling slighted by his reaction.

Lady Menagerie's lips twitched at the edges before she pinched them together. "Be careful, Paige."

"Of what? I'm getting married today to Brandon, the man I love." Paige replied hastily, hating the defensiveness in her voice.

"Have you considered how hard this might be on him?"

Paige nodded. She had thought about it constantly. Truth be told, she was surprised he accepted. She hoped it meant he was moving on with his life. She really wanted him to be happy.

"You told me he, at best, had an aversion to God even though his wife had a healthy relationship with Him. I just don't want you to represent Jesus in any other way except one that will draw Mason closer to him. Even if that means you stepping away from him for a while."

Paige's heart fell a little at the thought, but she nodded her agreement. She knew Lady Menagerie was just far enough to be objective.

Lady Menagerie patted her on the lap. "Well, let's get moving. We are getting you married in..." She paused to look at her watch. "Five hours, two minutes and 26...25...24"

"I get it," Paige giggled as she held up her hand to stop the countdown. The knock at the door bid the end of their mother-daughter time. Paige gave Lady Menagerie a quick hug and 'thank you', then went to answer the door. She was halfway to her destination when Lady Menagerie warned her. "I mean it Paige. We'll be watching during the reception to make sure you don't sneak away for a little sex preview." Paige turned around, horrified by what she'd just said even though she knew deep down Lady Menagerie was trying to desensitize her in the fastest way she knew how. "I wouldn't..." she tried to get out through her sputtering and shocked laughter.

Lady Menagerie gave a shooing motion with her hand. "Answer the door, child. We have work to do." Paige turned back from the door but not so soon that she didn't catch the small smile that formed on Lady Menagerie's lips.

Right before she opened the door she turned back, pointing her finger at her spiritual mom. "I saw that smile." Lady Menagerie shrugged, unrepentant.

Two and a half hours later, Paige was sitting in front of the vanity mirror in the master bedroom watching as her hairdresser, Copper, whose real name was Gwendolyn, but had been nicknamed for her fascinating hair color when she was young, finished testing the last roller.

"Alright. Your curls are set, but I'm going to let you stay in the rollers as long as possible so you don't have to worry about the style falling anytime today." Paige had opted to wear her hair half up and half down with fat, rhinestone-decorated ringlets framing her face. It was more than she would usually go for, but she knew Brandon liked her hair down and she'd seen a style in a bridal magazine that she thought was tasteful. "I can start on the base of your makeup or we can just do the whole thing after you get some lunch."

Paige's stomach answered for her with a loud grumble. Copper frowned. "Didn't you eat breakfast?"

"Yes, about five hundred hours ago. Mel had breakfast sent up to my room around 7:30 a.m. I tried getting something from one of the trays outside, but Mel has me bound to some invisible schedule that would rival any military timetable. If she balks, will you create a diversion?"

"I got ya back," Copper said, raising her chin in defiance, her freckle-covered cheeks warring with her hardened expression as she tried to imitate Queen Latifah's character in 'Set It Off'.

Paige shook her head. "You scare me when you do that. You should be in films."

Copper shrugged a shoulder. "My mom would beat me. I grew up in Sherman Oaks and went to a predominately white private school. She doesn't know that I learned most of my slang and cuss words from the girls who smoked in the bathroom during lunch."

Paige looked at Copper's toasted cream complexion in the mirror and smiled. The woman was 5'9" and thin, but far from skinny with her rounded curves. She could have been a model for skincare because her face was flawless. Paige had met Copper at church soon after she'd joined Skylight Temple. Copper commented on how beautiful she thought Paige's hair was and that she did hair at a nearby salon. If Paige didn't already have a hairdresser, she was willing to do her hair at the discounted rate she charged for church members.

Paige took her up on her offer a few weeks later when she had a special work event to go to, and after the amazing job Copper did with her tresses, she made a standing appointment for every second and fourth Saturday. Over the last five years, Paige had followed her from beauty shop to salon, each one a step up from the last until

Copper opened her own Spa and Salon on the north end of San Fernando Valley a little more than a year ago. Paige didn't mind the trek. Copper was gifted with hair and cosmetics, but more than that, she was beautiful inside and out. Though they didn't get to hang out much, if at all, they would make the most of their time together every other Saturday if Paige wasn't traveling. Sometimes, Paige would get just a quick wash and set so they could sit back and talk since Copper would block out two hours for them no matter what.

"How's your mother doing?"

"She's doing better since I brought her home. We go walking before I open the Spa, and I try to get home in time to have dinner with her. The doctors say she's well on her way to a full recovery. They were able to start rehabilitation quick enough for her to regain most of the movement on her right arm. She was fortunate the stroke wasn't stronger."

"Will you be coming back to Skylight when she makes her full recovery?"

Copper shrugged as she finished packing up her hair dryer. "I'm taking it one day at a time."

Copper attended a sister church due to her inability to get to Skylight Temple for Sunday service because the caregiver didn't work on Sundays.

Paige made a mental note to ask Lady Menagerie about a way to support members who couldn't make it to church every Sunday because they were taking care of a sick relative. They had a number of nurses and caregivers in the church. They could possibly offer their services on a rotational basis. One or two Sundays a month was better than none.

"Mati, you have a visitor," Vivian said with a bright smile on her face as she entered the bedroom in the shell pink, ankle-length brushed cotton robe Paige had gotten for her and Gladys. "I also brought you lunch. Auntie Mel said you need to eat, no matter who is here to see you." Her hair was pinned up at the crown of her head with her curls springing free like water from a fountain. They came to rest a few inches past the makeshift ponytail. There were also wisps of ringlets at her neck and temples. She looked like one of the fairies in a fairytale coloring book Paige had as a child.

"She also said you have 30 minutes before we give you your gifts to go with your dress." Paige's stomach knotted but she smiled at the look of excitement in Vivian's eyes.

"Tell Auntie Mel, 'Yes Sir'." Vivian giggled and set what looked to be a Chicken Caesar salad on the side table. "Would you like me to have your guest come in now?" Paige tried to smile, but simply nodded. She was beginning to feel a little smothered. The common area was nearly packed with family. She loved having them there, but the village of women in the other room was nearly ten deep, and now she had a visitor.

Copper, feeling her tension, told everyone she wasn't to be interrupted for at least an hour and then it could be only one person at a time. Paige thanked her profusely, to which Copper replied, "You think I do your hair just because you pay me? I have to get in some counseling time." She smiled wide and Paige laughed.

"Who is it?" she asked as Vivian walked back to the door.

"Gran."

Paige stiffened then took a deep breath. She shouldn't be alarmed. Victoria, from their last talk, was just getting back from her honeymoon with Richard. She'd sounded happier than Paige had ever heard her, and that was the only reason Paige asked Copper to give them some privacy when Victoria stepped through the door.

"There's no real future for the two of you."

No sooner were these words said than Paige regretted agreeing to see her before the wedding.

"Yes there is," Paige said, moving restlessly around the room, her half-eaten salad forgotten. "We have tomorrow and the next day. Those are all in the future."

"You know what I mean," Victoria said as she sat on the bed, turning every now and then to follow Paige around the room with her eyes.

"Yes, and you need to know what I mean, otherwise there will be a lot more moments slipping by you unnoticed and uncherished.

Each moment with Brandon is a gift and whether we get five months or five decades together, I will not spend a moment regretting the decision I make today," Paige said, finally choosing to sit back on the chair to the vanity, but this time she turned it so that she was facing Victoria.

"I believe God brought us together, and I'm not going to squander that because it looks like we have less time than others."

"Don't you want someone you can grow old with?" Victoria asked.

Paige took a breath, hoping her patience didn't run out before Victoria understood she couldn't convince her not to go through with the wedding.

How Victoria found out about Brandon's latest diagnosis she wasn't saying, but it made Paige even more wary about their relationship.

"I know plenty of people who grow old and hate each other.
I'm looking for quality in my time with Brandon, not just quantity."

"You think you have all the answers. I just don't want to see you hurt."

"Everyone gets hurt, Victoria. The difference is who you go to for comfort. I'm not admitting or giving credence to any type of time limit in regards to my relationship with Brandon. I am only stating that the time I do have with him will be lived to the fullest because tomorrow is promised to no one." Paige listened to herself as she spoke with conviction to Victoria, and she believed every word she said. She had the gift of love for herself, from God and from a wonderful man she would be meeting at the altar in a little over two hours. She was about to tell Victoria that she was going to have to resume getting ready, when Victoria spoke up.

"How are you so sure?"

"Sure of what?"

"Sure of God? After everything you've been through; why are you so sure He has your best interest in mind?" The look of vulnerability that Paige caught before Victoria was able to mask it had her rethinking her haste. She answered as honestly as she knew how.

"One, because I'm still here when I did just about everything I could to destroy myself. He showed me – then taught me – how to love myself. He has proven Himself to me over and over. His Word teaches me and guides me to another level of consciousness. My perception of situations and people add to my life, not take away from it because God's word tells me that He is the creator of every great and wonderful thing. He means things only for my good. It's a knowing right here." She pressed at her abdomen under her solar plexus.

"I know it is Him speaking to me, giving me counsel that keeps me at peace and safe from physical and spiritual harm." She paused for a moment and when Victoria didn't speak, she went on. "How do you know Richard loves you?"

"I can see it and feel it," she answered quietly. "He has proven it time and time again with his patience, the way he looks at me as if I am the most valuable thing in his life; the way he speaks to me, provides for me, and shows by the things he does that he has my best interest at heart."

Paige shrugged slightly. "It sounds like God had been showing you Himself through Richard. It always helps to have a parallel, no matter how finite it is. I'm sorry about those that misrepresented God to you, but now you know *that* wasn't God. He's not interested in humiliating you, bringing you shame, or condemnation. His characteristics are more along the line of showing you His love in different facets, making you feel cherished, and restoring you to wholeness no matter what that means for you.

You say Richard loves, cherishes and protects you, and so does God – except God takes it further. The love He has for you is everlasting and unconditional. His forgiveness, when you ask, is not numbered and once it is given, it is forgotten. There is nothing you can do and nowhere you can go to separate yourself from Him. If He has to step into your own private little hell to get you, He will."

"What do I have to do?"

Paige stared at Victoria for a moment then hoped the disbelief that ran through her mind briefly didn't cross her features. "You believe. You believe that because all of the things I just said are true that God sent His son Jesus to earth and He died on the cross, taking on our sins so that God could have a personal relationship with us and we could have eternal life with Him. Then you repeat after me the words that say the same."

Paige waited patiently, hoping no one would interrupt before Victoria truly made up her mind.

She watched the woman as she took a deep breath. "Alright. I'm ready."

Paige couldn't hold back the smile that pulled at her lips. Her heart was suddenly a hundred pounds lighter.

She got up and walked over to Victoria, took her hands and began. "We pray, and you repeat after me in asking Jesus Christ to come into your heart."

Victoria nodded.

"Dear Lord," Paige began, with Victoria repeating right after her. "I come before You, humbly asking You to come into my heart. I believe that Your Son, Jesus Christ, died on the cross for me and You raised Him from the dead so that I could have eternal life with You. I believe Him to be my Lord and Savior and I give my heart to You. In Jesus' name, Amen."

By the time they stopped praying, Paige was in tears. One, very precious soul had been saved and claimed for the Lord.

Mel knocked and walked in a couple of minutes later to find the two women still hugging and crying.

"See, I knew it wasn't a good idea to start on your make up early." Paige pulled back, looking at Victoria, and they burst out laughing. Even Victoria couldn't help but notice that Mel was in rare form.

Victoria wiped her eyes on a handkerchief she took from her sleeve, then patted Paige lightly on the cheek. "I'm going to let you finish getting ready for your wedding before Sargent Sister goes into overdrive." She stopped to look in Paige's eyes, the small smile causing Paige to mist up all over again. "Thank you, Paige, for everything."

Not feeling comfortable taking any gratitude for what she knew God orchestrated, she just inclined her head.

*   *   *

Brandon paced the small conference room just off of the lobby. He looked at his watch again. He had three hours before he met his bride at the altar. His dad and his groomsmen were due to arrive in his room in an hour and he was feeling caged in this small room, hoping the person he asked to meet him wouldn't stand him up. He calculated the time and told himself he would give them five more minutes, then he would have to forego this for another time.

The door opened and he whipped around to stare at the man that just entered.

"Hello, Mr. Jenson."

"Hello, Elder Tatum," Mason replied as he closed the door behind him.

Brandon couldn't help quirking his lips. "You can call me Brandon." Mason shrugged as though it didn't make any difference to him. Brandon could see there may be a few layers of distrust he had to get through in order to even get the point he wanted to make, across.

"Okay, well, let me just get to the point," Brandon said on a breath as he walked over to the table to take a seat. Mason took his lead and sat in a chair opposite Brandon on the other side of the small table.

Brandon laced his hand together, undecided on what else to do with them. "First, I'd like to say 'thank you' for accompanying your daughter to our wedding. I know it means a lot to Paige to have you here." He could see the effort Mason was making to keep his face expressionless and tried to make what he was about to say as direct as possible.

"I wish we could have met under different circumstances because I think we could have been friends."

He watched the smirk appear and disappear just as quickly from Mason's face, and resisted the temptation to ask him what he was thinking. He was sure if it was him sitting on the other side of the table, he would have a few comments held back by a thick thread of common decency himself.

He leaned back in his chair. "You know, Paige doesn't have a lot of friends – well, she didn't before my family carved their own spots in her life. You and your friendship became very important to her in a pivotal point in her life. That, plus the fact that you are the decision maker when it comes to her spending time with Vivian."

"I wouldn't do anything to try and keep them apart."

"You've already proven that. You have had so many chances to exert your superiority in this situation, but you have been nothing but gracious," Brandon quickly replied.

"I wouldn't only be hurting Paige; I would be hurting Vivian," Mason said, his voice never raising an octave.

"That's one of the reasons why I wanted to talk to you." Brandon adjusted himself in his chair, trying to buy some time while he went over his words for maybe the 50th time since finding out that Mason would be attending the wedding.

"What I'm about to say to you will be overstepping my bounds as Paige's fiancé and it will probably make me extremely vulnerable, but the other option is unbearable."

"I'm pretty sure you know that I have been battling with cancer for a while now." He waited for Mason's nod before he continued.

"Well the latest report was not favorable, but Paige and I made a promise to each other that whatever news we received before the wedding would not keep us from moving forward with our life."

His heart sped up at the thought of what he was about to say, but he couldn't go back now. "The decision Paige made in November wasn't between you and me." He took a deep breath, rubbing his palms against one another. "The Sunday morning you visited Skylight Temple and I saw the two of you sitting next to one another, I noticed something I have been trying to ignore ever since. When the two of you are in the same room, there is an undercurrent that flows between you." He saw the astonishment on Mason's face, but when he opened his mouth to talk, Brandon held up a hand.

"I'm not accusing you or her of anything. I am merely stating a fact. I can do this because I know without a shadow of a doubt that she loves me and I am the one standing at that altar with her today, only because God told her and myself that it was to be so." He paused. "Well that; and I hounded her something fierce once I knew she was the one for me." He finished with a self-deprecating laugh.

"The reason I bring this up is, if things should continue on this path, I'm not going to be with her for the decades I hoped and maybe not even for the years or months, either."

He watched Mason's face grow pale then begin to redden, and he knew he was coming to the wrong conclusion. As he himself may have, if the shoe was on the other foot.

"Paige is going to need all of her friends, especially the ones she feels she doesn't have the right to have; the ones whose opinions matter. The ones that are close enough to see through the masks she's going to put up.

I know today is going to be rough for you and in all of this I would say you are the better man because I don't care how hard she begged, I wouldn't have come, but because you did it shows me I was right about you."

Brandon took one last, deep breath before he brought his point home. "I need you to make sure you keep your hands off of Paige when I pass."

He saw Mason's hazel eyes widen then darken. Yep. He'd made his point clear.

"I think I've heard enough," Mason said, starting to rise.

"If you leave now, you will make things harder for Paige."

Mason didn't sit back down, but he didn't move towards the door either. "Harder for Paige, or for you?"

Brandon sat back a little, belying the restlessness he felt. "Paige picked God in November. She told me if God had told her that neither one of us were the man He had for her, she would have dealt with it but she still would have had the same type of relationship she has with you now because of Vivian. You will be in her life for as long as Vivian is alive and probably longer than that, and there is no severing that bond unless you do it yourself.

One surefire way to do that is to push her into a relationship at a time in her life where she would constantly question whether she made the right decision. That would destroy not only what you have, it would cause her to question her ability to hear God, and that's the last thing I want for her."

"Are you telling me to wait on the sidelines and continue to pine for her while you slowly die?"

Brandon took a few deep breaths while he tried to remember how this must look to Mason. He prayed for strength not to reach across the table and beat some sense into the man who brought out every possessive bone in his body.

When he thought he had his temper back under control, he opened his mouth but Mason spoke first. "Not that it's any of your business, but I'm seeing someone."

He stared at Brandon like it was supposed to make a difference in what he was asking, but it didn't. "I'm happy to hear that. Really I am because regardless of what you think, I wouldn't begrudge you your happiness."

Brandon rubbed his forehead, slightly weary. "Look Mason, all I really want is for you to be open to continuing your friendship with Paige."

"She stopped calling me, Brandon," Mason said, pointing at his own chest. "Not the other way around. Yet you request this meeting so you can ask that I not close the door to Paige's and my friendship."

"She's afraid you're angry with her."

"No Brandon, she's uncomfortable around me because I make her feel things she would like to pretend she doesn't." Mason said, leaning towards Brandon across the table. "And she's right to do so."

"And now that you are seeing someone else?"

Mason shrugged. "I am still my own man."

Brandon waited for him to continue and when he didn't, he reluctantly asked. "Which means?"

Mason replied without hesitation. "I won't let you play the knight in shining armor so that even after death she will think you above reproach, Brandon. You're crossing the line, even as an overprotective, overbearing yet loving fiancé. If you asked me, if you were so concerned about how she would fair without you, you should have decided to end it before it began."

"Yes. It was selfish of me, but I fell in love with her and when I wanted to give up and break it off for her sake, she wouldn't let me. So yes, I am here now imploring you to help take care of a woman I cherish if I don't get healed in this life."

Mason sat down but continued to regard Brandon, skeptically. "Why is that?"

"What?" Brandon asked warily.

"Why haven't you been healed? I know my daughter has been praying for you. I hear her. I'm absolutely sure Paige has been praying and with no doubt, so has your church. Why is there even a need for this conversation if you believe in a God of miracles and answered prayers?"

"Sounds like you know a little more than what you let on, Mason." Brandon couldn't help the defensive tone in his voice.

Mason shrugged, seeming nonplused by the comment.

Brandon let out a breath. "God answers prayers all the time, Mason. Sometimes the answer is 'yes', sometimes the answer is 'no', and other times it is 'wait'."

Mason's eyebrows drew together. "So why would it be 'no' when it is between life and death, and everything you want starts with staying alive?"

"You and I see life and death differently. You see the end of life as the result of what happens after the last breath leaves these bodies. That is only a transition for me; a movement of my spirit and soul from this earthly body to my heavenly body. From the moment I accepted Jesus into my heart and life, I became something more – well, my consciousness did. I came into an awareness that there was more than what I could see or feel with this body. I was given the gift of eternal life with the Creator of everything we see, don't see, love, and innately strive for. I have the blessed honor to be able to and desire to acknowledge the only being that could bring me peace in my life."

"Alright, so let's get off the merry-go-round and you tell me why, the Being you pray to for healing for yourself and others isn't healing your body. Why aren't you getting the same 'miracle healing' your people would say my daughter got?"

And there it was. The question he knew Mason would eventually come to if they stayed on this line of questioning, and all he could think of was what he was told. He hoped it would be enough. If not he would have to truly wipe his shoes of this undertaking and cut his losses.

"This isn't my first bout with cancer." The widening of Mason's eyes told him that Paige hadn't discussed this with him.

"If He healed you the first time, what makes you think He won't heal you this time?"

Brandon thought over his answer a couple of seconds before he spoke. "He will always heal me. He will either heal me in this body or give me complete healing and I will reside with Him in heaven, but I know how you mean it so I will answer that question as well. When I prayed and asked him about healing me from cancer the first time, He said my illness would not be unto death. I held onto that through everything the doctors said I needed to do to get better and I praised God for His healing hand in it all.

This time God told me to continue to do His work and that the cancer was not my enemy – fear was. So I have once again followed my doctor's instructions and I will praise God for His healing hand in it all, and I will do it with more years added to this life or with my last breath because either way His perfect will, will be done in my life.

Mason was silent for a moment, and Brandon let his words sink in.

"What about Paige?"

"I love her. She is the gift I didn't expect to have, but as much as I want to live decades with her and have children with her, and see them have children, I love God more."

"Why would a God who loves you as much as you say he does allow you to find a woman such as Paige, marry her, and not give you the opportunity to make a life with her?"

"We can't meet in this conversation, Mason, because we are coming at it from two different directions. Mine is from the knowledge of a God that loves, cherishes, and protects me and that is the perspective of where my explanation begins. It colors everything I see Him as. Your perspective seems to be steeped in distrust and skepticism, even though those closest to you share a relationship with Him. You see me leaving this life as a loss, a sacrifice…a forfeiture of earthly desires, but all I can see is what I will gain.

It's my honor to protect, provide for, and be the one to please my wife to be. I am only asking that in the event that I can't do that anymore, that you would be the friend she needs you to be and not hold what you believe to be her choice against her."

* * *

"Where've you been man?" Dominy greeted when Brandon walked back into his room.

"I had some loose ends to tie up," Brandon replied as nonchalantly as he could. Dominy was like a bloodhound and he wasn't about to share his meeting with Mason with anyone.

"Were you trying to get a peek at the bride-to-be? You'll be seeing her in two hours."

Brandon smiled at the ribbing, neither admitting nor denying it.

He walked over to sit next to his father, who was lounging on the couch in his tuxedo pants and shirt with all but the top three buttons in place.

He looked over at him, staring at him for a moment then patted him hard on the knee. "You ready?"

Brandon nodded, feeling the truth of it resound in him.

Elias Sr. nodded in return, and returned his gaze to the television. "Then you better start getting ready, you don't want to be late and have her thinking you changed your mind."

Brandon, preparing to obey his father's order, was halfway between sitting and standing when his father finished. "Again."

He looked behind him to see a small smirk riding his father's lips. "Et Tu, father?"

Elias shrugged. "I figure if I remind you every now and then of what you almost lost, you may work harder to hang on to it."

Brandon straightened to his full height and turned around to look at his father. Did he dare ask? He shrugged to himself. "Which is?"

Elias looked up from the television to him and stated matter-of-factly. "Love, son. Always love," then went back to watching the game.

* * *

"You don't seem nervous at all," Dominy said as they sat in the back of the limo, as it made its way to the church. Brandon looked over at his brothers and father before he answered. "Nope."

"Why?"

"Why what?"

"Why aren't you nervous?"

Brandon shrugged. "Maybe to a certain degree I am. I want to make sure everything Paige wants this day to be, is achieved. I hope it is a day she wants to reminisce upon over and over because it reminds her of how happy it made her."

"What about you?"

"I know it's a big step, but I'm more excited about becoming her husband than nervous. I'm looking forward to seeing her when I wake in the morning and watching her sleep before I close my eyes at night. Getting ready with her in the morning, finding room for my clothes in any of her closets."

"Good luck with that," Theodore barked.

Brandon snickered, not in the least fazed by his brother's remark.

"Leave him alone, Theodore. It's all new to him. I remember you on your wedding day. I won't tell everyone where we found the rings that morning."

Theodore gave his dad a belligerent look. "I told you, I wanted to make sure they were in a safe place," he grumbled.

Dominy started laughing. "Where did you find them?"

Theodore looked at his dad, and Elias, Sr. smirked then looked out the window.

"Nowhere," Theodore mumbled.

"In the freezer, frozen in a glass of water," Samuel said, throwing up a shoulder to Theodore's threat to hit him. "Hey, he said he wouldn't tell everyone."

"I never said anything like that."

"Really?" Dominy guffawed. Brandon chuckled then stopped.

"Samuel, weren't you Theodore's best man? Why didn't you have the rings?"

"He was afraid I would misplace them because I was concerned about Sara. She was close to her due date with Marily at the time."

"Concerned?" E.J. scoffed. "You were a basket case. I don't blame Theodore for taking matters into his own hands."

"Speaking of rings…"

"No need to even bring it up," Dominy said, patting his left jacket pocket. His eyes went wide momentarily then he patted his right, and sighed in relief." Brandon couldn't think of anything over trying to get his heart to start again. The rest of the men in the car just shook their heads and chuckled.

As they pulled up to the church, Brandon looked out the window before turning back to his father. "Well dad, I don't think we will find a quieter moment on these grounds. Do you want to do the honors?"

His father reached across the space between their legs and clasped his hand and the rest of the men followed suit and bowed their heads.

*   *   *

Brandon stood at the front of the church, Dominy to his left, once again on display, but this time he was more than happy to share every emotion with their family and friends in attendance. He began to whisper to Dominy from the side of his mouth. "Did I tell you how much I appreciate you coming even though Robin is as big as a..."

"Finish that sentence and I'm telling her every word."

"I just want you and Robin to know how much I appreciate the sacrifice. I know she's extremely close to her due date and you want to be with her." He shrugged his shoulders. "I feel the love, man."

"Oh, don't start getting choked up now. You still have the appearance of your bride-to-be and your vows to get through. Besides it's only forty-eight hours. I will be back by her side by tomorrow afternoon, but she did say if she delivers while I'm here, she won't be naming him after you."

Brandon looked over at Dominy. "You're naming your first child after me?"

Dominy smirked. "Not the first name, but it's a tossup between your name and my cousin, Herbert, for the middle name."

Brandon stared at him with a disbelieving expression on his face. "Really?"

"Yes, really." Dominy said, flicking an invisible piece of lint from his shoulder.

"You would name your kid after a cousin that used to set your pet's tails on fire instead of your best friend, who you admire?"

"Getting a little big headed, aren't you?"

Brandon sucked his teeth at Dominy, but he just continued to look towards the back of the church.

Brandon opened his mouth to say something but the music began, wrenching his attention from his former friend.

He watched as the door leading to the center aisle opened and watched as his sister, Marjorie, made her way forward in the timed steps they'd practiced at the rehearsal the night before. She was met at the bottom of the stairs leading to the pulpit by her husband, who kissed her hand and led her the place she would stand for the remainder of the ceremony before returning to his place at the far end of Brandon.

Marjorie was followed by Everzie then Makayla, who were also met by their partners, and then Dana who was attended to by Dominy. When he looked forward again, it was to see Gladys and Vivian walking side by side looking like slightly smaller versions of the bridesmaids that preceded them. Brandon searched the audience, catching a glimpse of a smile on Mason's lips before he was blocked from view by a woman in a particularly large, green hat. Knowing Mel was probably helping Paige with her dress, he threw both girls encouraging smiles.

Next came Reina, Everzie and Theodore's little girl, who began to sprinkle deep red rose petals along the white roll of cotton that had been rolled out just prior to her decent. She was so meticulous that Everzie had to motion for her to quicken her pace. Seeing her mother signing she sped up her pace and noticing that she still had petals in her basket when she reached the end of the aisle, she dumped them unceremoniously before climbing the stairs to stand in front of Vivian and Gladys.

The music changed, and Brandon's heart sped up. The doors that had closed behind Reina began to open and everyone began to stand. Brandon stood up straighter and took a deep breath, but he needn't have because the moment he caught sight of Paige, all of the air left his lungs. He may have made a sound, he didn't know, but Dominy whispered to him, "Breathe man or you won't make it till she gets to you."

Brandon struggled to remember which movement would bring air back into his body and blinked when the heat in his chest made the vision in white coming towards him blur. He took in the much-needed breath, and Paige came back into focus. The closer she got, the harder his heart beat until she was halfway down the aisle on Mark's arm and Dominy was poking him in the side so he could go down and meet her.

He worked hard to place one foot in front of the other until he reached her side. The white lace dress with crystal beading at the edges of her scalloped neckline accented her collarbone and delicate shoulders. The white sleeves, beginning just past her shoulders, contrasted beautifully against her caramel colored skin. Her dress, fitted at the bodice, showed off her small waist and ended at a V in front of a skirt that came away from her body slightly and flowed into a train that he was sure followed her a good six feet.

Brandon shook Mark's hand as they practiced the night before, just before he lifted Paige's veil and kissed her on the cheek. He placed her hand in Brandon's and all he could do was stare at her. She was more beautiful than he could have imagined. Her hair was collected high behind her tiara and masses of curls incrusted with crystals came down like a waterfall around her face, making her cheeks glow, but the smile she gave him made her all the more dazzling.

Her makeup represented the wedding colors with a light gold, green eyeshadow that made her eyes sparkle. The cranberry-colored lipstick highlighted the color in her cheeks and went perfectly with her bouquet.

"I think you're supposed to walk me up to Pastor now," Paige whispered, conspiratorially.

Brandon blinked and smiled embarrassed. "You are so beautiful, you bewitch me and I forget myself." Her smile widened and she kissed his cheek. "I love you," she whispered softly. He stared at her feeling as though the whole moment just dropped into time.

A loud cough drew their attention from the pulpit. "You want to bring your bride-to-be up here? It's too late to elope." The statement elicited a laugh from the bridal party and audience alike.

Brandon, seeming unfazed, brought Paige's hand to his lips and kissed her knuckles slowly. "Ready?"

"Since the day you kissed me." The words and sincerity in her gaze humbled him to speechlessness, so he quietly led her to the vine decorated arch where their pastor waited.

Brandon watched Paige carefully, working hard to commit her every word and expression to memory so he could replay this moment over and over in his mind. He wouldn't let his mind wander during the prayer or the explanation of the covenant they were coming into agreement with. He recited his vows, staring into Paige's eyes, wanting to portray the earnestness in his heart. He would do anything for this woman who came into his life a mere year ago and turned his stony heart to flesh.

When she spoke her vows her voice was strong, but the wetness in her eyes threatened to spill over and he prayed she would win the fight against the tears, otherwise he was afraid his hard-fought reserve would be lost.

She'd reached her second to last line before the first tear escaped and began its journey down her cheek. "Till death do us part," she repeated as she placed the ring on his finger and his heart filled, but it was the smile that broke it wide open and destroyed the rest of his resolve.

He heard his pastor say, "You may kiss your bride." And instead of wiping her tears, he cupped her jaws in his hands and brought her lips to his. He didn't know if it was her tears or his that he tasted as he claimed her mouth in a searing kiss, but he wouldn't let go until he was sure he'd communicated his love and adoration for her.

He let go of her lips slowly and feeling her rock slightly, he slipped an arm around her waist to steady her. He touched his forehead to hers and watched her smile softly.

"You take my breath away," she sighed dreamily.

"It's only fair. You did it to me just walking down the aisle."

She laughed and hugged him tightly. When she released him she lifted small fingers to wipe his cheeks and he returned the gesture.

"May I present to you Mr. and Mrs. Brandon Tatum." Pastor Lawrence stated loudly and they broke apart, and turned to the audience.

They made their way down the aisle hugging and shaking hands with a few people then racing the rest of the way to the doors and into the coordinator's hands. They walked into a room off the side of the sanctuary that would afford them a moment of privacy before they would be called for pictures once everyone had left for the reception.

Brandon hugged Paige to him tight enough to absorb her feeling. She was his wife. His wife. The words kept flowing through his mind. This beautiful, intelligent, God-fearing and loving woman was now his wife. His' to protect, love, honor, cherish and kiss at will. He laughed at the joy it brought to his heart.

She pulled away just enough to see his face. "What?"

He looked at her face, grazing his knuckles over her temple and was simply at a loss for words. There was nothing that could describe the rightness of this moment. His beautiful Paige in his arms, her eyes drawing him in, and a slow smile on her lips tempting him to taste her. So he gave into it and kissed her deeply, slowly, and thoroughly.

"I love you very much Mrs. Tatum," he said when he caught his breath.

He watched as she looked up into his eyes. "And I love you, Mr. Brandon Tatum. You have made every one of my dreams and desires come true."

"Really?" He asked, genuinely shaken.

"You gave me your heart and it is so gorgeous, I'm overwhelmed by it. I'm moved to tears with the knowledge that God would gift me with such a wonderful man as you. Beyond my vows, I promise to be the best wife you could ever imagine."

"Awww, baby. You already are."

Two hours later, deep in the celebration of the reception, Paige took advantage of a short reprieve from kissing, hugging, dancing or thanking a guest, and laid her head on her husband's shoulder and watched the people interacting with one another around the room.

After a moment, her eyes came to rest on Mason's. She smiled, serenely and he returned it fleetingly. Feeling a deep peace settle over her heart, she couldn't help but smile wider then mouthed 'thank you' across the room. She watched as he placed his right hand over his heart and inclined his head then mouthed, "You're welcome." She stared at him for a moment then sighed and shifted her gaze. Who she saw next wiped the smile from her face.

A woman walked over, taking the vacant seat next to Richard. She placed her hand on his shoulder, drawing both he and his wife's attention. "Good afternoon, Richard. Aren't you looking healthy? It's been a while." Victoria glanced at Richard, but only saw confusion marring his handsome features. The woman reached around him, offering her hand to Victoria. "Hello, I don't think we've formally met."

Victoria replaced her expression with that of a statue – surprise was the only thing that woman would get from her. She nodded her acknowledgment then took the offered hand the woman still presented before her.

"Victoria Branchett," she stated as she shook her hand quickly.

"I'm Grace Morganson-Dillard." Neither one of them caught on to the fact that she didn't give her association. They were still reeling from the fact that Grace knew Richard.

Grace looked at Richard, impaling him with her gaze. "Did you tell your wife that you've been in my affairs?" She followed Richard's darting gaze to his wife, and looked over to Victoria in time to see the confusion cross her features.

"Mmmm. I take that as a 'no'." She returned her gaze to Richard. "I suggest you tell your men to withdraw their search. You won't like what you discover." Her voice dropped low and the small smirk thinned out. Her eyes becoming hard as glass, she continued. "You have a beautiful family, Richard. I suggest you focus your energies on keeping what's left of them safe and sound." She slowly stood up, her black, shimmering, floor-length gown unfolding provocatively and she rose. "Enjoy this…" Her eyes swept across the room and her mouth pursed in distaste. "This party. I often wonder why certain religions believe in celebrating their dead." The icy stupor melted at her last remark and Richard moved to stand, but Victoria placed a hand on his shoulder.

Grace looked between the two of them then gave them a beautifully wicked smile. "Until we meet again." She stood, turning around and going back the way she came.

This is the end of this book, but the story continues

My Garment of Praise For Your Spirit of Heaviness, the third book in the Promises to Zion Series, is available on Amazon.

Dear Reader,

This book was definitely heavier than the My Beauty For Your Ashes which was more of an introduction to this world. I cried through more parts in this one, but I came away with a feeling of calm as if I were purged of the heavier emotions.

It's hard to express the gratitude I feel for you choosing to spend your time in my world so I will just say thank you and ask that you would take a moment and leave a review. I am curious to see what you thought. How did the emotional highs and lows of the characters affect you?

Please send your questions or thoughts to me at tawcarlisle@gmail.com

You can also visit my website at www.tawcarlisle.com and follow me at www.twitter.com/traciwcarlisle and www.facebook.com/traciwoodencarlisle

I am working on my next book because my characters just won't leave me alone and my crew-of-a-few are diligently combing the pages to make sure I didn't leave out any important details…

Until next time,

Keep reading and expand your dreams

Traci Wooden-Carlisle

About the Author

Traci Wooden-Carlisle lives in San Diego with her husband. She designs jewelry, writes as much as she can and freelances as a graphic artist. She loves her coffee in the morning and fuzzy slippers at night. She loves to read anything romantic – the more inspirational the better. For fun she dances and teaches the occasional fitness class.

My Books

Promises of Zion series

My Beauty for Your Ashes
My Oil of Joy for Your Mourning
My Garment of Praise for Your Spirit of Heaviness

Next in the series:
Promises Fulfilled

Chandler County Series
Missing Destiny
Missing Us

Coming in December
Missing the Gift

Chances Are...Series
Chances Are

Made in the USA
Las Vegas, NV
24 January 2024

84837136R00262